本成果受到中国人民大学
“建设世界一流大学（学科）和特色发展引导专项资金”
专项经费的支持。

19世纪『三国演义』英译文献研究

王燕／著

中国社会科学出版社

图书在版编目（CIP）数据

19 世纪《三国演义》英译文献研究/王燕著．—北京：
中国社会科学出版社，2018．4
ISBN 978－7－5203－2425－0

Ⅰ．①1…　Ⅱ．①王…　Ⅲ．①《三国演义》—英语—
文学翻译—研究—19 世纪　Ⅳ．①I207．413②H315．9

中国版本图书馆 CIP 数据核字（2018）第 078360 号

出 版 人　赵剑英
责任编辑　郭晓鸿
特约编辑　席建海
责任校对　闫　萃
责任印制　戴　宽

出　　版　中国社会科学出版社
社　　址　北京鼓楼西大街甲 158 号
邮　　编　100720
网　　址　http://www.csspw.cn
发 行 部　010－84083685
门 市 部　010－84029450
经　　销　新华书店及其他书店

印　　刷　北京明恒达印务有限公司
装　　订　廊坊市广阳区广增装订厂
版　　次　2018 年 4 月第 1 版
印　　次　2018 年 4 月第 1 次印刷

开　　本　710×1000　1/16
印　　张　33.25
插　　页　2
字　　数　448 千字
定　　价　138.00 元

目　录

第二部分　人物译介文献研究

第三部分　章节选译文献研究

第四部分　汉语教材文献研究

绪 论

一 研究背景

在中国文学史上，19 世纪既是中西文化碰撞期，也是古典步入现代的文化转型期。学界在研究这一时期的文学时，关注较多的是“西学东渐”，却相对忽略了“中学西传”，尤其是中国古典小说的早期海外传播。当时的译者主要是清代来华传教士与外交官，这个特殊的群体以及他们之于中国古典小说的贡献，是一个长期以来被各方忽略的话题。研究“外交史”与“宗教史”的学者，不会深入探究清代来华西士之于“中国文学”的贡献；而研究“中国文学”的学者，也很少有人注意清代来华西士这个特殊的群体。另外，他们的著述不仅用英文撰写，而且散布于欧美各大图书馆。资料搜寻的困难和语言的障碍，更使这批英译资料的整理与研究举步维艰。

虽然在文学史的研究中长期阙如，但清代来华西士对于中国小说的译介，起步之早、贡献之大，绝不亚于梁启超发动的“小说界革命”。“小说界革命”兴起之前，清朝来华西士就曾大力提倡过小说。如英国著名汉学目录学家伟烈亚力（Alexander Wylie，1815—1887）1867 年出版的《汉籍解题》（*Notes on Chinese Literature*）曾云："最优秀的小说作品并没被中国人纳入国家文献。在这个问题上，某些接受了欧洲思想的人却感到小说和传奇故事（novels and romances）这类内容非常重要。尽管文人对小说存有偏见，但小说给予该国各时期风俗习惯以敏锐的洞察，小说提供了一种日新月异的语言的典范，事实上，小说还是绝大多数中国人借以获得历史知识的唯一渠道，此外，小说对（中国人）性格的形成也定然产生了影响，这些因素都不容人不考虑其重要性。"① 或许正是基于这种认识，伟烈亚力在其作品中，毫不犹豫地开列了 137 种禁毁小说、14 种欧译小说、85 种笔记小说和 14 种通俗小说，这对于研究中国禁毁小说的面貌，对于了解中国古代小说的海外传播，乃至深入探讨清代来华西士的"中国小说观"，都有不可估量的学术价值。

事实上，像伟烈亚力这样重视中国小说的早期来华西士比比皆是，第一位来华新教传教士马礼逊（Robert Morrison，1782—1834）就是一个很好的例子。1807 年，马礼逊来到澳门，为学习汉语和了解中国文化，逐步认识到通俗文学的重要性。1812 年，马礼逊就翻译了《红楼梦》第四回，其手稿目前保存在"伦敦布道会"（London Missionary Society）档案中。1816 年，马礼逊编写的汉语教材——《中文对话与单句》（*Dialogues and Detached Sentences in the Chinese Language*）引用《红楼梦》中的语句为语料学习汉语，并建议学生如果读不懂《大学》（*The Da Xue*），可以先读《红楼梦》。1815 年，东印度公司出资出版了他编写的《华英字典》（*A Dictionary of the Chinese Language*），其中所列"孔明"（kung – ming）词条就采用了"桃园结义"（*The Oath Took in the Peach Garden*）等《三国演义》中的情节，还第一次用"历史小说"（a historical novel）来定义《三国演义》的文体属性。1817 年，马礼逊撰写的《中国一览》（*A View of China*）再次倡导：

① A. Wylie，*Notes on Chinese Literature*，Shanghai，China，1867，p. 161.

"对一个欧洲人来说，没有中国人帮助，要学好中文几乎是不可能的。掌握中文最好的途径是从阅读一本小说（fiction）开始，小说即'琐言'（Seaou Shwŏ，Small talk）。它们并非全用白话（colloquial）创作。《好逑传》（*Happy Courtship*）英文译作 *The Pleasing History*，是白话的。《红楼梦》（*Dreams of the Red Chamber*）采用北京方言，也是白话的。"① 正是受这种观念的影响，中国古典小说开启了大规模的西行之旅。

19 世纪以马礼逊、伟烈亚力、米怜（William Milne，1785—1822）、德庇时（John Francis Davis，1795—1890）、郭实腊（Karl Friedrich August Gützlaff，1803—1851）、卫三畏（Samuel Wells Williams，1812—1884）等传教士和外交官为代表的西方人译介的小说多达 40 种。其中既有《三国演义》《红楼梦》《水浒传》《西游记》等章回体小说，也有《今古奇观》《聊斋志异》等中短篇小说。

这批西译文献弥足珍贵，有着重要的学术价值。然而，有趣的是：第一，当代中西学者在研究古典小说，尤其是《三国演义》《红楼梦》等经典作品时，明清时期的文献几乎搜罗殆尽，哪怕一文一诗，均从文人笔记、稗官野史，乃至家谱、方志中钩稽出来，如获至宝，甚至辑成各类资料全编、大辞典等皇皇巨著。但嘉庆以降，出自传教士、外交官之手的相关文献却罕有关注；第二，虽然当代中西学者很少提及这批清代来华西士撰写的英文文献，但马礼逊、郭实腊等人创造和使用的某些文体概念却不胫而走，沿用至今。"历史小说"这一文体概念的使用就颇具代表性。

1902 年，梁启超创办的小说期刊《新小说》第一次使用"历史小说"这一概念，但在他之前，马礼逊、郭实腊已用 historical novel 来概括《三国演义》的文体属性。在当时，这种用西方文体概念替换中国古典小说传统

---

① Rev. R. Morrison, *A View of China*, Macao: Printed at the Honorable East India Company's Press, By P. P. Thoms, 1817, p. 120.

称谓的做法，实现了中西小说文体类型的初步对接。可是，使用“历史小说”这一概念毕竟是马礼逊、郭实腊译介《三国演义》时的权宜之计，带有明显的实验性特点，不幸的是这类牵强附会的文体概念不胫而走，从此成为流行术语。时至今日，尚未有人利用早期来华西士的翻译材料深入探究这些常用文体术语的文化生成，更没有人认真省思这种文体之间的强行联袂给中国小说的传播与研究带来的诸多误读、误判。浦安迪教授（Andrew H. Plaks）在《中国叙事学》（*Chinese Narrative*）“导言”中明确指出：“严格地说，中国明清章回体长篇小说（Ming Qing Full - length Xiao - shuo）并不是一种与西方的 novel 完全等同的文类，二者既有各自不同的家谱，也有各自不同的文化功能。”① 但他担忧的只是严复、林纾把 novel 译成了“小说”，却没有提及马礼逊、郭实腊等人把“演义”转换成了“历史小说”。

近百年来，涉及上述议题的最引人瞩目的成果是 1988 年王丽娜女士撰写的《中国古典小说戏曲名著在国外》，涉及语种之众，胪陈资料之多，令人叹服。此后，相关专著、论文不断出现。最近几年，已有学者开始将主要精力投入这一研究领域，但整体看来依然存在两方面不足。其一，学者们或探讨某一传教士的文学贡献，或结合某一翻译理论分析一部译作的翻译策略，尚未能全面系统地整理相关书目、整合相关文献，甚至《三国演义》《红楼梦》等经典小说的翻译史还在草创阶段。其二，多数研究都是孤立地分析问题，且眼光多局限于著名传教士或经典小说，来华西士译介中国小说的相互影响，以及译文出现的共同特色均被忽略，这不利于全面反思域外中国古典小说译作的文学意义和文化功能。

围绕这批材料，值得深思的问题很多。比如，马礼逊、郭实腊等来华西士的中国古典小说翻译与研究是在怎样的文化背景下展开的？他们主要采用了哪些翻译方式？他们的译作在经过必要的文化改写、文化阐释后，

---

① ［美］浦安迪：《中国叙事学》，北京大学出版社 1996 年版，第 25 页。

再现了怎样的中国小说？这批 19 世纪的汉学家形成了怎样的“中国小说观”？他们的文学翻译塑造了怎样的“中国历史”和“中国形象”？在“他者审视”下的传统小说是否因为这个特殊群体的关注而有所改变？他们的译介对于当今的中国小说海外传播又提供了哪些可资借鉴的经验？在汉学勃兴的今天，我们对于这些话题的追问显然并非多余。

二　资料搜集

1807 年，随着第一位英国新教传教士马礼逊的来华，中国古典小说开始大规模踏上西行之旅。在“四大名著”中，19 世纪英语世界对于《三国演义》的译介最为重视。它不仅被第一位英国来华新教传教士马礼逊看作翻译《圣经》的文体范本，而且被郭实腊、德庇时、卫三畏、艾约瑟（Joseph Edkins，1823—1905）、谢卫楼（Davello Zelotos Sheffield，1841—1913）等著名传教士或外交官多次译介，这些业余汉学家对于《三国演义》的关注与评论，达到了前所未有的高度。

近十余年，学界开始关注这批《三国演义》英译资料，只是由于它们或者曾刊载于《亚洲杂志》（*The Asiatic Journal*）、《中国丛报》（*The Chinese Repository*）、《中国评论》（*The China Review*）、《教务杂志》（*The Chinese Recorder and Missionary Journal*）等罕见英文报刊，或者发表在《拾级大成》（*Easy Lessons in Chinese*）、《汉语会话》（*Chinese Conversation*）等早期汉语教材，这些杂志或教材虽然部分可以借助谷歌图书（Google Books）、互联网档案馆（Internet Archive）等公共学术网站查阅，但实体书分散收藏在哈佛大学图书馆、伦敦大学亚非学院图书馆等欧美各地，搜集起来有一定难度，相关研究错漏百出、蜗步难移也就在所难免。

笔者自 2001 年博士毕业以来任教于中国人民大学文学院，主要从事明清文学与中国古典小说的教学与研究。近十余年来有幸得到美国弗里曼基金会（Freeman Foundation）、中国国家留学基金委（CSC）、日本学术振兴会（JSPS）等机构的资助，先后到香港中文大学（CUHK）、美国伊利诺伊大学（UIUC）、英国伦敦大学亚非学院（SOAS）、日本关西大学（Kansai University）等中外大学访学，陆续搜集到 20 余种 19 世纪《三国演义》英译资料，为进一步的研究奠定了基础。

在 19 世纪中国小说英译史上，许多问题悬而未决、疑窦丛生，主要受资料所限，以致以讹传讹。

比如，英国汉学家德庇时翻译《三国演义》的情形长期以来颇为扑朔迷离。学界较早关注这一话题的学者是王丽娜女士，1988 年，她在《中国古典小说戏曲名著在国外》一书中说："1834 年由中国澳门东印度公司出版的德庇时（J. F. Davis，1795—1890）译注的《汉文诗解》（*Poeseos Sinensis Commentarii*），还收有《三国演义》中的咏史诗若干首，这些诗的原文是从《皇家亚洲学报》转录的，原书未见。"① 次年，在《英国汉学家德庇时之中国古典文学译著与北图藏本》一文中，王丽娜女士再次指出："德庇时也往往引《三国演义》《好逑传》《红楼梦》等中国通俗小说中的诗歌韵语与《老生儿》《汉宫秋》《长生殿》等中国戏曲中的唱词，用以说明中国诗歌与中国小说戏曲的密切关系。"② 这两段文字使学界得出了一个错误判断：《汉文诗解》在论说中国诗歌时引用了《三国演义》中的咏史诗。

实际上，据笔者调查，1870 年出版的《汉文诗解》增订版共引用中国诗歌 100 首，这些诗歌有的是完整地翻译了全诗，有的只是摘译了其中的一两句，其中确有引自小说、戏曲的诗词韵文 16 首：包括《好逑传》11 首、

① 王丽娜：《中国古典小说戏曲名著在国外》，学林出版社 1988 年版，第 15 页。

② 王丽娜：《英国汉学家德庇时之中国古典文学译著与北图藏本》，《文献》1989 年第 1 期，第 273—274 页。

《红楼梦》1首、《清平山堂话本熊龙峰四种小说》2首、《长生殿》1首、《老生儿》1首。经过仔细查找，在《汉文诗解》的正文部分并没有发现引自《三国演义》的咏史诗。甚至涉及三国故事的诗行，也仅有“魏蜀吴，争汉鼎。号三国，迄两晋”这两句，但这两句出自《三字经》。

值得注意的是，虽然王丽娜女士的观点不够准确，但在学界影响深远，此后不少学者提及《三国演义》都会想到《汉文诗解》。如国学网（www. guoxue. com）发表的陈友冰教授的文章《英国汉学的阶段性特征及成因探析——以中国古典文学研究为中心》一文云：“德庇士也是英国汉学家中最早注意到中国古典戏曲、小说的，他编译过《好逑传》（1829）等明清小说，他翻译的《中国小说选》（1822）是英国最早的中国小说英译本。鉴于汉学家在翻译《三国演义》时大都回避了其中的诗词，他译注的《汉文诗解》专门收有《三国演义》的一些咏史诗。”在此，《三国演义》中的咏史诗甚至成了德庇时特意保留诗词韵文、尊重原著文体风貌的典范。

有趣的是，虽然在《汉文诗解》的正文中找不到《三国演义》的只言片语，但德庇时确实为《三国演义》的英译做出了巨大贡献，而且他翻译的《三国志节译文》（*Extracts from the History of the Three States*）也确实刊载在《汉文诗解》中，只是其译文并非咏史诗，也并非出现在《汉文诗解》正文中，而是作为“附录”刊载于1834年澳门出版的《汉文诗解》中。只是这个版本印量有限，极为罕见，故此德庇时对于《三国演义》的译介长期以来信息错乱也就在所难免了。

要找到德庇时翻译的《三国志节译文》英文文本，首先需要全面调查《汉文诗解》的前后三个版本。该作最早并非以单行本刊行，而是作为文章发表于1829年《英国皇家亚洲学会会刊》（*Transactions of the Royal Asiatic Society of Great Britain and Ireland*）第二卷（第393—461页）。同年在伦敦出版了单行本，这里不妨称之为“首刊本”。书名同时使用了三种文字：页面顶端由右而左是四个行楷“汉文诗解”，下面是拉丁文书名“POESEOS

SINENSIS COMMENTARII”，英文名“On the Poetry of the Chinese”紧随其后。

1834 年，澳门东印度公司出版社（The East India Company's Press）再次出版了此书，在此不妨称之为“澳门本”，该版本书名未加改动，同样出之以三种文字示人。值得注意的是，这个版本在封面上直接标明文后附有几篇译作和文章（Translations & Detached Pieces）。通过目录可以查知附录的四篇作品分别为：《出使北京》（*Embassy to Peking*）、《三国志节译文》《论中国的自杀》（*Note on Homicides in China*）和一首用拉丁文创作的诗歌（*Cave of Camoens*，*Macao*）。德庇时在 2 月 20 日写于澳门的简短序言中称这几篇附录的文章“皆与中国相关”。

1870 年，伦敦阿谢尔出版公司（Asher and Co.）再次出版了“增订本”《汉文诗解》，该版本保留了前两个版本的中文名和拉丁文名，英文名改为 The Poetry of the Chinese。与此前两个版本相比，“增订本”《汉文诗解》扩充了引述诗篇，增加了萧纲的《江南弄》、王涯的《送春词》及 30 首《春园采茶词》，部分评价性文字也有所改动。同时，删除了“澳门本”《汉文诗解》正文后的所有附录文章，包括《三国志节译文》。

由此可见，刊载《三国志节译文》的《汉文诗解》仅有 1834 年出版的“澳门本”，1829 年出版的“首刊本”和 1870 年出版的“增订本”均未提及《三国演义》，如果对《汉文诗解》的三个版本调查得不够全面，就很难注意到作为“附录”出现的《三国志节译文》。

此外，德庇时在“澳门本”序言中说：Several applications for the Treatise on Poetry，which could not be supplied in this country，led to the reprint（without publication）of a limited number of copies。由此可知，1829 年伦敦出版的“首刊本”《汉文诗解》在中国难以买到，而 1834 年出版的“澳门本”也只是为了满足少数人的需求而重印的限量版，这个版本不但数量有限，而且没有公开发行。故此，德庇时之于《三国演义》的翻译长期以来少为人知也就不难理解了。

搜集资料需要四处奔波，有的需要集腋成裘，历经数年之久方有所获，但也确实乐在其中，不乏惊喜。比如，19 世纪英国著名传教士兼汉学家艾约瑟对于《三国演义》的译介，学界长期无人关注，究其原因，主要是他的译文出现在《汉语会话》（*Chinese Conversation*）中，该书在国内未见藏本。2013 年笔者在伦敦大学访学时，曾在大英图书馆（The British Library）和伦敦大学亚非学院图书馆（SOAS Library）检索到该书。笔者当时虽在调查《三国演义》英译资料，但根据题名，误以为《汉语会话》不过是本普通的汉语教材，故未加翻阅。

2015 年笔者在指导中国人民大学本科生李勤撰写毕业论文“《借靴》的海外传播”时，发现《借靴》最早以 *The Borrowed Boots* 之名发表于 1852 年出版的《汉语会话》。除了《借靴》，《汉语会话》中还有《琵琶记》和《三国演义》的英译文，于是立即请伦敦大学的卢荻教授帮助拍摄了部分图片，一时颇为兴奋，如获至宝，只是当时未能细读全书，故不敢贸然撰文。

2016 年，笔者受日本学术振兴会（JSPS）资助，赴日本关西大学短期访学，该校图书馆馆长内田庆市教授是研究明清时期欧美汉学家的著名学者。在一次交谈中，他透露自己 1998 年在哈佛大学访学时，曾在波士顿校本部最大的图书馆 Widener Library 复印了全本《汉语会话》。两天后，内田教授在家中为我找到了 18 年前复印的《汉语会话》，我连忙请当时在关西大学做博士后的胡珍子老师帮助扫描了全书，由此得以一窥全貌，为相关问题的研究创造了条件。

由于本书涉及的多数资料极为罕见，故笔者将相关英文文献整理后附于正文后。以便海内外《三国演义》爱好者与研究者“奇文共欣赏，疑义相与析”。

首先，英文原文全部进行输入、校勘，除了直接更正某些明显的标点错误外，与现代英语拼读方式不同的某些 19 世纪单词拼读方式，如 behaviour、endeavouring、honour、neighbours、marvellous、monopolise 等，均予以保留。其他错误则以“编者按”的方式进行标示、更正。其次，为了方便不谙英文的广大读者的阅读和研究，相关译文全部回译为中文。再次，对于以中英文合璧形式刊印的“汉语教材类”资料，以“文献图片”的方式影印再现其原始风貌，以便国内外《三国演义》研究者或语言学家考察其版本价值、研究其语音特点。

三　综合评价文献

本著作主要研究八位欧美汉学家的 20 多种英文文献，中英文合计 20 余万字。根据翻译目的和译作内容，整体分为四个部分：一是综合评价文献；二是人物译介文献；三是章节选译文献；四是汉语教材文献。在研究方面，特点有三：一是注意结合历史语境介绍译者情况、汉学成就；二是强调结合译文文本分析翻译策略和主要成就；三是从接受史的角度，考察译作产生的学术影响及文化意义。以下分而述之。

本著作第一部分“综合评价文献研究”精选了两位著名汉学家的评论：一是第一位英国来华新教传教士马礼逊对于《三国演义》的相关介绍，作为英译《三国演义》的首位积极倡导者，他的相关论说有着开启先河的重要价值；二是第一位德国来华新教传教士郭实腊对于《三国演义》的相关评论，他是第一位撰写独立论文推介《三国演义》的评论者。

学界追溯《三国演义》在英语世界的最早译介时，通常会提及汤姆斯（Peter Perring Thoms，1790—1855）翻译的《著名丞相董卓之死》（*The Death of the Celebrated Minister Tung - cho*）。其实，在汤姆斯之前，马礼逊对于《三国演义》已有所论及。他的译介集中出现在两个文献中。

一是他本人编辑的《华英字典》（*A Dictionary of the Chinese Language*），这是第一部中英对照双语字典，也是中国境内第一部用西方活字印刷术排印的书籍，共三部六卷。第一部 1815 年在澳门出版，根据《康熙字典》214 部部首编排文字，收录汉字词条 4 万多个。在第 39 部“子”部下，列有“孔明”一条，与“三国”故事密切相关。通过分析这一词条的编辑体例，笔者发现由于马礼逊过分倚重正典和讲究资料的多元，相对淡化了《三国演义》对于塑造孔明形象的重要性。但该词条是最早用“历史小说”来定义《三国演义》文体属性的文献资料，并由此展开了欧美世界的三国人物画廊。

二是 1820 年在马六甲出版的《新教在华传教前十年回顾》（*A Retrospect of the First Ten Years of the Protestant Mission to China*），作者是第二位来华英国新教传教士米怜。书中记载：1811 年前后，马礼逊在中译《圣经》的过程中，比较了中文的三种文体——文言（a high）、白话（a low）和折中体（a middle style）。“文不甚深，言不甚俗”的《三国演义》是“折中体”写作的典范，马礼逊提议用这种文体来中译《圣经》。《圣经》是经典中的“圣典”，而《三国演义》则是“通俗演义”，这种匪夷所思的联袂，为《三国演义》的西行之路打开了方便之门，使这部在中国遭受禁毁的小说，意外地踏上了西行之旅。

马礼逊对于《三国演义》的论述虽篇幅有限，但对于这部中国“演义”的早期海外传播却产生了深远影响，几乎开启了清朝中后期《三国演义》走向欧美的种种可能。

1838 年 9 月，近代著名英文报刊《中国丛报》第 7 卷发表了一篇题为《三国志评论》（*Notice of the San Kwŏ Che*）的论文。作者署作“某通讯员”，经过考察，实乃第一位德国来华新教传教士郭实腊，德文名为 Karl Friedrich August Gützlaff，又作郭实猎、郭士立等。

郭实腊既是恪尽职守四处传播福音的传教士，又是面目狰狞狂妄地叫器武力侵华的侵略者。此外，他还是语言的天才、多产的汉学家。英国汉学家伟烈亚力的《来华新教传教士回忆录》（*Memorials of Protestant Missionaries to the Chinese*）辑录了他的 85 种著作。同时，他还为报刊撰写了大量文章。据统计，仅在《中国丛报》上刊载的文章就多达 51 篇，除了《三国演义》，他还在该刊向西方读者介绍了《红楼梦》《聊斋志异》《苏东坡全集》《海国图志》等经典名著。

《三国志评论》近四分之三的篇幅是对于原著内容的概述，评论文字只有开头和结尾的几段。在情节译介方面，主要介绍了灵帝登基、黄巾起义、桃园结义、废立汉帝、诛灭董卓等故事。其显著特点有二：一是译者对于《三国演义》的战争描写颇为厌倦，故此较少涉及赤壁之战等相关内容；二是对于具有宗教色彩的玄幻情节颇为好奇，竭力保留了“小霸王怒斩于吉”“左慈掷杯戏曹操”等故事。

在人物译介方面，《三国演义》原著涉及一千余人，著名人物亦不下数十人。由于篇幅所限，郭实腊择其精要，大量删减，明确译出姓名的人物共计 12 人，集中笔墨介绍的仅有曹操和孔明二人。在人物评价上，基本把握了罗贯中“尊刘贬曹”的思想倾向，对蜀汉人物多有肯定，对曹魏集团则褒贬各半。上述情节和人物，成了 19 世纪西方汉学家特别关注的内容。

郭实腊是西方汉学史上系统评论《三国演义》的第一人，其评论具有以下特点：第一，尽管存在某些译介错误和文化误读，但他对于《三国演义》的整体把握和概括大致准确；第二，对《三国演义》的文学性给予高度评价，将之推许为中国文学的典范之作；第三，作为一个跨语际、跨文化的阅读者，郭实腊天然地具有一种西方的视角和比较的眼光，这使他的评论别具特色。比如，把曹操比作丹东、把关羽比作法兰西国王法拉蒙德等。

郭实腊是鸦片战争前译介中国历史小说最多的传教士汉学家，仅在《中国丛报》上发表的相关评论就有 4 篇，除了《三国演义》，还论及《平南后传》《正德皇游江南》和《南宋志传》三种。经过他的大力推介，《三国演义》等中国历史小说在清代来华西士中获得了广泛认可，在当时几乎造就了一枝独秀的文体神话，这对于推动中国小说的海外译介意义重大。

四 人物译介文献

在所有三国人物中，晚清来华西士介绍得最为详尽的是孔明和曹操。1843 年，《中国丛报》发表了美魏茶（William Charles Milne，1815—1863）撰写的《孔明评论》（*Notice of Kungming*），简单介绍了孔明的一生。1885 年《教务杂志》第 16 卷分两次连载了《曹操生平及时代概况》，作者是美国传教士谢卫楼。该文是英语世界对于曹操形象的首次译介，也是曹操形象在西方世界的首次系统建构。

美魏茶是英国第二位来华新教传教士米怜的儿子，亦称“小米怜”，广州出生英国长大，后子承父业，加入伦敦布道会，成了一名来华新教传教士。美魏茶不仅是基督教福音的传播者，也是 19 世纪中国历史的见证人和记录者，他撰写的《生活在中国》（*Life in China*）忠实记录了他在中国 14 年的所见所闻，是近代宁波、上海等东南地区社会发展的历史见证。

作为一名传教士，美魏茶在中西文化交流史上的地位主要得益于他对《圣经》的翻译，译介《三国演义》在其文化生活中只是一个很小的插曲。1841 年 2 月，19 世纪著名英文报刊《中国丛报》第 10 卷第 2 期发表了美魏茶译介的《黄巾起义》（*The Rebellion of the Yellow Caps*）；1843 年 3 月，同刊第 12 卷第 3 期发表了他撰写的《孔明评论》。

美魏茶之所以译介《黄巾起义》主要是受了德国新教传教士郭实腊的影响，两人都认为“黄巾起义”揭开了汉末动乱的序幕，是帝国分裂的肇端，故此，起义本身也就有了特殊的意义和译介的必要。美魏茶在文中提到拟介绍“黄巾军的兴起和发展，直至其首领的死亡”。实际译介内容主要出自《三国演义》前两章，其中对于“黄巾起义”发动者张氏三兄弟的介绍文字数量有限，文章所叙核心人物是刘备、关羽和张飞。比之原著，美魏茶对于起义领袖的态度发生了根本改变，由否定而肯定，由贬斥而褒扬。比如他将张角译介为 liberator mundi，这在西方文化传统中含有“救世主”之意。

《孔明评论》是英语世界对于“孔明”形象的第一次系统介绍，比之马礼逊的“孔明”词条更为详尽，因此具有一定的开创性。在人物译介方面，美魏茶为了突出孔明，最大限度地精简了三国人物。在故事情节译介方面，简要介绍了“三顾茅庐”和“刘备托孤”，重点介绍了“六出祁山”，其中对于第六次北伐的译介尤为详尽。文中不但直接引用了孔明的言辞，还详细介绍了木牛流马及孔明之死。《孔明评论》对孔明这一人物形象进行了全面肯定，同时也为孔明故事的译介留下了较大空间。

整体看来，《黄巾起义》和《孔明评论》这两篇文章对于介绍三国故事的历史背景，以及孔明形象的早期海外传播都产生了一定影响，是《三国演义》海外传播史上不可或缺的一环。

明清以降，随着《三国演义》的深入人心和三国戏曲的广泛传播，曹操形象由历史人物而成为文学典型，资料来源的差异、评论立场的不同虽然为曹操形象的多元解读提供了可能，但大致没有突破“治世之能臣，乱世之奸雄”的传统论调，曹操形象的反思与重建，显然需要一个全新的文化体系与历史坐标。

19 世纪初期，《三国演义》开始走向英语世界，曹操形象随之开启了西行之旅，这为曹操在世界历史版图的重构创造了条件。就目前所知，最早提及曹操的英国人是第一位来华新教传教士马礼逊，他在 1815 年出版的《华英字典》中将曹操之名拼读为 Tsaou – tsaou，字典中还出现了“篡位者曹操”“曹操倚仗军威决不肯和”等提及曹操的短语或句子。此后半个世纪，英语世界关于曹操的介绍均为节译的片段，曹操形象始终处于一种支离破碎的状态。

直到1885年才出现了第一篇系统讨论曹操的文章——《曹操生平及时代概况》（*A Sketch of the Life and Times of Ts' ao Ts' ao*）。该文刊载于《教务杂志》1885年第16卷，分两次连载于11月发行的第10期和12月发行的第11期。该刊是1868—1941年间在华传教士创办的英文刊物，前后出刊72年，是中国近现代史上连续性最好、延续时间最长的英文期刊，以其丰富的内容和大量图片、自身的公信力和权威性，成为来华西士最忠诚的“在华日志”，也是目前研究近现代中西文化交流的珍贵文献之一。

作者谢卫楼在当时名震一时，被同时期来华的明恩溥（Arthur Henderson Smith，1845—1932）称为“最著名、最有能力的教育家之一”。1841年8月，谢卫楼出生于纽约州的怀俄明县。1866年入神学院，后加入美国海外传教差会“美部会”，28岁来华传教，在华生涯长达44年之久。1913年7月病逝于北戴河。他建立的潞河书院即华北协和大学的前身，后并入燕京大学，最终成为北京大学的重要渊源和组成部分。他不仅编著有《万国通鉴》等多种汉学著作，而且对于中国教育及中西文化交流都做出过重要贡献。

作为英语世界系统评价曹操形象的长篇大论，《曹操生平及时代概况》一文在《三国演义》海外传播史上具有一定价值。在谢卫楼的笔下，曹操生活的三国时代被比作“希腊的伯罗奔尼撒战争时代”，该文将三国时代置于世界版图的历史框架，从而为曹操形象的建构提供了一个全新的场域。文章内容虽然主要取材于《三国演义》，但没有照搬中国小说的叙事模式，在人物评价方面则主动摆脱了明清以降的正统观念和忠奸立场。曹操由此不再是《三国演义》中的一代奸雄，更不是民间舞台上的白脸奸相，他甚至走出了中国语言的文学传统，被用英文符码打造成一个拿破仑式的军事奇才。由此，经过谢卫楼改写与重构的曹操形象焕然一新，开启了三国人物西行之旅的多彩篇章。

五 章节翻译文献

在章节翻译方面，汤姆斯与德庇时的英译资料尤为难得，在《三国演义》英译史上举足轻重。如果说马礼逊是第一个把《三国演义》介绍到英语世界的西方人，汤姆斯则是第一个英译《三国演义》文本的西方人，他翻译的《著名丞相董卓之死》分三次连载于《亚洲杂志》1820 年第 10 卷、1821 年第 11 卷，是《三国演义》第一篇英译文。第二任香港总督德庇时的《三国志节译文》作为附录，刊载于 1834 年版《汉文诗解》正文之后，虽然长期湮没不闻，却是《三国演义》英译史上的重要一环。汤姆斯和德庇时的译作，由于资料罕见而备受瞩目。

在中英文化交流史上，汤姆斯原本是一位名不见经传的小人物，但自从他踏上中国的土地，就开始了自己的传奇。就职业身份而言，汤姆斯是一位英国印刷工，1814 年 9 月为了印刷马礼逊的《华英字典》而来到澳门印刷所，半年内研制出适合中英文合刊的活字。有学者认为汤姆斯研制的这批活字，是中国最早的一批中文铅合金活字，汤姆斯的名字因此而被载入中国活字印刷史。

在与中国文字日复一日的密切接触中，汤姆斯由一名职业技师，逐渐变成了一位中国文学爱好者和翻译者。从 1814 年至 1825 年，汤姆斯在中国工作长达十年之久，其间翻译了《三国演义》《今古奇观》《花笺记》等中国文学作品，成为鸦片战争前最有成就的业余汉学家之一。德国文坛巨擘歌德读到《花笺记》时，称赞该作是“一部伟大的诗篇”，并据此创作了闻名遐迩的《中德四季晨昏吟咏》。歌德对于《花笺记》的赞誉，与1824年汤姆斯对于该作的英译密切相关。

尽管对于汉学界来说，英译《花笺记》是汤姆斯的成名之作，但对于他本人来说，英译《三国演义》似乎才是他努力的方向。在英译《花笺记》的封底，有则“出书广告”（Ready for the press），提及汤姆斯要把《三国演义》全本翻译为英文。现在虽难以考证这个宏大的计划最终是否完成了，但一位来自异邦的工匠对于《三国演义》的持久兴趣和翻译魄力，是当时其他汉学家难以比拟的。

《著名丞相董卓之死》所译内容包括两部分：一是汤姆斯在第一个注释中相对完整地翻译了“金人瑞”所作的《三国志序》；二是围绕董卓生平，翻译了《三国演义》第八回和第九回中的相关内容。具体而言，始于“却说董卓在长安，闻孙坚已死”，止于“众贼杀了王允，一面又差人将王允宗族老幼，尽行杀害。士民无不下泪”。概而言之，主要是王允利用美人计，联合吕布，杀了董卓。这是《三国演义》中最著名的桥段之一，屡屡被改编为戏曲“连环计”或“凤仪亭”。自汤姆斯译本问世后，该故事成为19世纪英语世界反复译介的三国故事之一。

汤姆斯译作的学术贡献主要体现在两个方面：首先，在对“演义”这一特殊文体的认定上，汤姆斯在马礼逊的“历史小说”之外，提出了“历史”说，他是西方汉学史上《三国演义》“历史”说的始作俑者。其次，《著名丞相董卓之死》的英译不仅使西方读者了解了“连环计”这个故事，还使他们意识到“才子书”或“十才子”系列作品的存在，由此而推动了包括《三国演义》在内的中国小说的整体英译。

第二任香港总督德庇时是19世纪第一位向英语世界系统介绍中国小说、戏曲和诗词的英国汉学家。在中国小说英译方面，他是李渔小说的最早英译者，1822年出版的《中国小说》（*Chinese Novels*）翻译了李渔短篇小说集《十二楼》中的三个故事。1829年，根据嘉庆丙寅年镌刻的“福文堂藏板”

重译了《好逑传》(*The Fortunate Union*)。在中国戏曲英译方面，翻译了元代杂剧作家武汉臣的《老生儿》和马致远的《汉宫秋》，打破了《赵氏孤儿》在欧洲汉学界一枝独秀的局面。在中国诗歌英译方面，他的《汉文诗解》为中国诗歌的英译树立了第一座丰碑，该作是第一部尝试着全面、系统地介绍中国诗歌的专著，在欧洲流传甚广，影响颇大，堪称西方中国诗学研究的奠基之作。

德庇时的《三国志节译文》主要涉及三方面内容：一是"导言"部分介绍了译者对《三国演义》的基本认识；二是从《三国演义》第二回中摘译了《造反的张氏三兄弟的命运》(*Fate of the Three Rebel Brothers Chang*)；三是从《三国演义》第三回中摘译了《何进的历史与命运》(*History and Fate of Ho – tsin*)。译者认为全译这部卷帙浩繁的中国小说在当时是个"亟待实现的梦"，由此只能借这两篇节译文来展示《三国演义》的冰山一角。

《三国志节译文》虽长期湮没不闻，但其学术价值却不容低估，它为《三国演义》的海外译介提供了新的起点。在"导言"中，德庇时说："该作已被寓居中国多年、而今担任卢卡尼亚大主教的塞吉神父（Padre Segui）全部或部分地译成了西班牙文。此外，皇家亚洲学会还有一个以前的拉丁文译本。"目前学界对于德庇时提及的两个译本尚无研究，如果他的记载无误，西班牙译本当是 19 世纪初的译作，而拉丁文译本也许时间更早，或为《三国演义》西行之旅的真正起点。

《三国志节译文》第一次以中英文合璧的方式翻译并排印了《三国演义》，对于学习汉语的西方读者应该具有一定的参考价值，同时，中文的在场也使西方读者得以目睹了《三国演义》的文字特点和历史风貌。经过对比，不难发现，德庇时采用的中文底本是毛评本《三国演义》，只是译者在排印时删除了所有注释和评论性文字，仅保留了原著的正文部分。表面看来，这部分中文字迹清晰，排列整齐，细加考订不难发现，其中鲁鱼亥豕、错漏屡现。这在一定程度上体现了当时汉学家的中文功底和校勘水平。

从接受史的角度来看，《三国志节译文》影响有限。但在研究开埠之前的英国对于中国文化的理解与接受方面，仍然是一个难得的个案。它以自身独特的存在言说着中国文学西行之旅的步履维艰。

六　汉语教材文献

将中国小说作为汉语学习的工具，是 19 世纪汉学家接受中国小说的重要方式。美国“汉学之父”卫三畏的《拾级大成》和英国汉学家艾约瑟的《汉语会话》，是以《三国演义》为汉语教材的典范。两人对《三国演义》的了解，在某种程度上可以说超过了此前的评论家及翻译者，这是他们选择《三国演义》作为汉语语料的重要原因。

卫三畏被称为“美国汉学第一人”，集传教士、外交官和汉学家于一身，在中美外交史上举足轻重。他 1833 年来华，1876 年返美，在华 40 余年，从一名普通的印刷工，做到美国驻华使团的秘书和翻译。1878 年受聘耶鲁大学，成为美国历史上第一位汉学教授。

在《三国演义》英译史上，卫三畏功不可没。他是第一位将《三国演义》翻译到英语世界的美国人。他的译介主要出现在三部作品中：《拾级大成》《中国总论》和《中国丛报》。其中，以汉语教材《拾级大成》的引用最为频繁，故此，卫三畏成为 19 世纪以《三国演义》教授汉语的典范。

1842 年，卫三畏编撰的《拾级大成》出版，该作是为英语世界的读者编写的汉语学习材料，尤其适合于粤语方言的学习。《拾级大成》八分之一的篇幅引用了《三国演义》的文字，集中分布在五个章节：第一次出现在第三章，卫三畏在介绍中国标点符号时，引用了《三国演义》中的一句话。第二次出现在第四章，该章共从《三国演义》《玉娇梨》《聊斋志异》中引用了 91 个句子，其中有 68 个句子出自《三国演义》。第三次出现在第八章，该章从《三国演义》中选用了两个故事："孔融之智"和"王允设计诱吕布"。最后两次出现在第九章和第十章，两章重复引用了 73 个《三国演义》中的句子，前一章提供英文，后一章提供汉语，两相对照，可以练习英汉互译。

1848 年，卫三畏出版了《中国总论》(*The Middle Kingdom*)，这是美国汉学史上第一部系统介绍中国知识的百科全书。《中国总论》大约有四页篇幅涉及《三国演义》，主体内容是将《拾级大成》第八章引用的第二个故事——"王允设计诱吕布"完整地翻译成了英文，这无异于为《拾级大成》的读者提供了一份汉译英的标准答案。卫三畏前后两次引用"连环计"，对于这一故事的西传产生了重要影响。只是在《中国总论》中，卫三畏犯了一个极其低级的错误，他将《三国志》与《三国演义》混为一谈，由此受到梅辉立（William Frederick Mayers，1831—1878）等汉学家的严肃批评。

1849 年 6 月，卫三畏在其担任编辑的《中国丛报》上刊载了一篇文章，题名《三合会会员的誓言及其来源》(*Oath Taken by Members of the Triad Society, and Notices of its Origin*)。作者认为"三合会"誓言受到了"桃园结义"的启发，故此，在注释中翻译了《三国演义》第一回"宴桃园豪杰三结义"中的相关文字。作为一个注释，"桃园结义"几乎可以独立成文，在篇幅上远远超过了一般的注释，由此可见卫三畏对于《三国演义》的熟稔和喜爱。

整体看来，卫三畏对于《三国演义》的译介主要有以下四个特点：第一，根据在中国的生活阅历与社会观察，卫三畏认为《三国演义》是"一部真正天才的作品，在普及历史知识方面发挥了重要作用"，这是他反复译介该作的根本原因。第二，卫三畏的译介文刊发于综合性中国学读物，从而为《三国演义》的海外传播拓展了道路。第三，卫三畏对于《三国演义》的译介始终抱持着一种实用主义观念。这种实用主义观念使《三国演义》

从古代而至近代，由中文而入英文，径直走进了19世纪来华西士的语言学习与日常沟通，以一种极具亲和力的方式步入了他们的中国认知与学术视野，由此而为这部历史演义的美国之旅开辟了一条独特的路径。

艾约瑟在中国居留57年之久，集传教士、语言学家、翻译家于一身。作为一名传教士，宗教翻译与研究是艾约瑟终生的兴趣，他面向中英文读者，用两种文字双向介绍彼此的宗教知识，在中西宗教交流史上扮演了重要角色。在西学东渐方面，艾约瑟的成就尤其显著。无论是就职于墨海书馆还是大清帝国海关，艾约瑟都致力于西学的翻译与出版。其代表作《西学启蒙十六种》由李鸿章、曾纪泽作序。

在中国语言研究方面，艾约瑟可谓建树颇丰。他编纂的《汉语官话口语语法》（*A Grammar of the Chinese Colloquial Language*，*Commonly Called the Mandarin Dialect*，1857）等语言学著作，近年来陆续被回译成中文，这些著作涉及汉语的方言与官话、汉字与音韵、语法及结构、来源及生成等各个方面，在语言学界备受瞩目。除了专著，他还是《六合丛谈》《中西闻见录》《万国公报》《北华捷报》等报刊的创办者或撰稿人，为这些刊物撰写了数百篇文章，是19世纪传教士中屈指可数的高产作家，也是中西方公认的“中国通”。

在文学翻译方面，艾约瑟最显著的成就，就是1852年上海墨海书馆出版的《汉语会话》，该作受马礼逊《中文对话与单句》、马若瑟（Joseph de Prémare，1666—1736）《汉语札记》（*The Notitia Linguae Sinicae*）的启发，在汉语学习选材上使用了两人都很重视的小说和戏曲，实际上是《借靴》《琵琶记》和《三国演义》三种作品的英译合集，除此之外再没掺杂任何其他中文语料。

《汉语会话》分为两个部分，第一部分为“对话”（Dialogue），主要内容取自《借靴》和《琵琶记》两部戏曲，是中英文合璧的本子。总体来看，在戏曲翻译方面，艾约瑟不仅是《借靴》的最早英译者，也是第一个大量英译《琵琶记》折子戏的来华西士。他对中国戏曲，尤其是《琵琶记》的高度评价，在某种程度上推动了这部“南曲之首”的海外传播。

《汉语会话》的第二部分内容取自《三国演义》第二十九回，题名“神仙于吉之死”（*The Death of Yu Keih, the Magician*）。艾约瑟的翻译以“直译”为主，兼有“意译”，最大限度地保留了原著的文化信息。除了正文，艾约瑟还直接翻译了 20 条毛宗岗父子的评语，用以说明“中国批评的精神和方式”。

在《三国演义》中，于吉被刻画成一个普救万民、受人爱戴、呼风唤雨、精魂不死的活神仙；孙策虽称霸江南、为人至孝，却性情暴躁、固执己见，因此在怒杀于吉后，被其阴魂索命、伤重而亡。毛氏父子对孙策大加赞扬，对于吉却充满狐疑。叱责异教、反对鬼神是艾约瑟等西方传教士一贯的立场，毛氏父子的评论恰恰契合了他的这一宗教立场，这或许是艾约瑟翻译 20 条评语的根本原因。

《汉语会话》对于中国戏曲、小说的重视，是艾约瑟译介中国文化的一大特点。1857 年，他在《汉语官话口语语法》一书中说：“无论是小说，还是戏剧，都不见于皇家目录。这些作品在中国人看来仅仅是娱乐型的，不值得学者去研究。但是对于外国人来说，它们却饶有趣味，体现了东方人的想象力，就像我们的戏剧和小说体现了西方人的想象力一样。同时，这些作品也能让外国人快捷地了解这个国家的历史、习俗和语言。”① 艾约瑟对于中国戏曲、小说的正面评论，显然有利于这类通俗文学作品的早期海外传播。

① Joseph Edkins, *A Grammar of the Chinese Colloquial Language, Commonly called the Mandarin Dialect*, Shanghai: Presbyterian Mission Press, 1864, pp. 270 – 271.

第一部分

综合评论文献研究

一　马礼逊对于《三国演义》的首倡之功*

学者们追溯《三国演义》在英语世界的最早译介时，通常会提及汤姆斯翻译的《著名丞相董卓之死》，该文分三次连载于1820年和1821年出版的《亚洲杂志》。[①]其实，在汤姆斯之前，已有西方人论及《三国演义》，这就是第一位来华新教传教士、英国汉学家马礼逊。

据笔者调查，与马礼逊相关的著述中，至少有四次提及《三国演义》：第一次记载于他编辑的《华英字典》第一部，1815年出版。第二次记载于他写作的《中国一览》，1817年出版，仅一句话："《三国志》是有关三国时期的事件的一部历史小说，因其文体和写作才华而备受推崇。"[②]第三次记载于英国新教传教士米怜写作的《新教在华传教前十年回顾》，1820年出版。第四次没有正式出版，出现在马礼逊为他自己带回英国的一万卷中文书籍编写的书目上，目前这份Morrison's Manuscript Catelogue完好地保存在伦敦大学亚非学院图书馆。其中提到："《三国志》（第一才子），

---

*相关研究以"马礼逊与《三国演义》的早期海外传播"为题，发表于《中国文化研究》2011年第4期。

① *The Asiatic Journal*. Vol. Ⅹ. December 1820, pp. 525 – 532; Vol. Ⅺ. February 1821, pp. 109 – 114; March 1821, pp. 233 – 242. London.

② Rev. R. Morrison, *A View of China*, Macao: Printed at the Honorable the East India Company's Press, By P. P. Thoms, 1817, p. 120.

Historical novel, good style.” 以上四次记载虽篇幅有限，但对于《三国演义》的早期海外传播却产生了深远影响，几乎开启了清朝中后期《三国演义》走向欧美的种种可能。

汤姆斯是应东印度公司之聘，从英国来到澳门的印刷工（Printer），上述三种正式出版的文献的印制均出自汤姆斯之手。其中有关《三国演义》的文字，他定然是知晓的，因此，或许正是受了马礼逊的影响，汤姆斯才围绕董卓这一人物，节译了《三国演义》的部分内容。但人们讨论《三国演义》在英语世界的早期译介时，却常常忽略马礼逊，直接把这顶桂冠错误地戴在汤姆斯的头上。

《马礼逊回忆录》所刊马礼逊图片

（一）《华英字典》中的“孔明”词条

《华英字典》由马礼逊独立编著，它不仅是第一部中英对照双语字典，也是中国境内第一部用西方活字印刷术排印的书籍，共分三部六卷：第一部三卷，第二部两卷，第三部一卷。自1815年出版第一卷至1823年出版最后一卷，前后耗时近十年。其中，第一部依《康熙字典》中的214部部首排列，每个汉字部首下复设多音节词和成语，收录汉字词条4万多个。

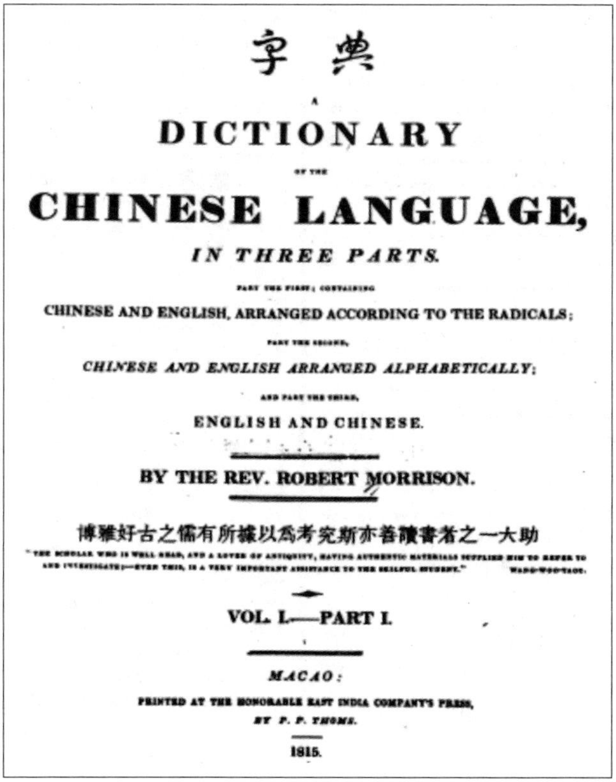
字典

A

DICTIONARY

OF THE

CHINESE LANGUAGE,

IN THREE PARTS.

PART THE FIRST; CONTAINING

CHINESE AND ENGLISH, ARRANGED ACCORDING TO THE RADICALS;

PART THE SECOND,

CHINESE AND ENGLISH ARRANGED ALPHABETICALLY;

AND PART THE THIRD,

ENGLISH AND CHINESE.

BY THE REV. ROBERT MORRISON.

博雅好古之儒有所據以為考究斯亦善讀書者之一大助

"THE SCHOLAR WHO IS WELL READ, AND A LOVER OF ANTIQUITY, HAVING AUTHENTIC MATERIALS SUPPLIED HIM TO REFER TO AND INVESTIGATE;—EVEN THIS, IS A VERY IMPORTANT ASSISTANCE TO THE SKILFUL STUDENT."

VOL. I.—PART I.

MACAO:

PRINTED AT THE HONORABLE EAST INDIA COMPANY'S PRESS,

BY P. P. THOMS.

1815.

《华英字典》第一部第一卷

在第 39 个部首——“子”部下，列有“孔明”一条，与“三国”故事密切相关，并且明确指出“《三国志》是那时的一部历史小说”。这一词条出现在嘉庆二十年（1815）出版的《华英字典》第一部第一卷第 714 页至第 716 页，或为英语世界最早提及《三国演义》的文字记录。

子 Tsze. I. 39th Radical. 714

special commission to instruct the world. When an attempt was made on his life, he said, Tëen săng tih yu yu, hwan tuy ke joo yu ho 天生德于予桓魋其如予何 as Heaven has produced such a degree of virtue in me, what can Hwan-tuy do to me? On conceiving himself a successor to Wăn-wang, as a preacher of righteousness in the world, he said in time of danger 天之未喪斯文也匡人其如予何 if Heaven means not to obliterate this doctrine from the earth, the men of Kwang can do nothing to me.

The disciples of Confucius suspected his private character on two occasions; once when he paid his respects to a woman of doubtful character, on which occurrence he imprecated the vengeance of heaven, if any guilt attached to him. The other was, when in a vicious neighbourhood, where the men would not listen to his teaching 童子見門人惑 he admitted a boy to see him, which made his pupils suspect him of that vice, which was so common amongst the poets and sages of Greece and Rome.

The books referred to on this brief memoir say nothing of the colour of Confucius, but the effigies of him, seen by the writer of this in the northern parts of China, represent him as of a dark swarthy colour.

Kung-ming 丨明 or Choo-kŏ-leang 諸葛亮 lived in the close of the reign of Hëen-te 獻帝 (A. D. 220), the last Emperor of the Han dynasty; and he took a conspicuous part in the civil wars of the San-kwŏ 三國 which succeeded the overthrow of that family, after swaying the sceptre of China 400 years. Kung-ming was a native of the Lang-yay 琊琊 mountains, on the sea coast of Shan-tung province. The 綱目發明 Kang-mŭh fă ming asserts, that, from the period of the original three dynasties called San tae 三代 Wei han tih tëen hea wei ching 惟漢得天下為正 the Han dynasty alone obtained the empire in a correct manner, and held it 踰四百年 more than four hundred years. Chih te yih min, mŏ fei Han yew 尺地一民莫非漢有 not a cubit of ground, nor a single plebeian but was possessed by the Han family.

The Emperor Hwan 桓 and Ling 靈 first 不君 failed in the duties, and maintaining the authority of, great monarchs, by which conduct they brought on the ruin of their family. A person named Tung-chŏ 董卓 who possessed 才武膂力少比 military talents and personal strength seldom equalled, and 少好俠 rather fond of knight errantry, was one of the first who 煽火英雄羣起 fanned the flame and raised in a flock all the heroes of the day. The eunuchs obtained and trifled with the imperial authority; and it is said, that about this time 9 eclipses of the sun are recorded; 7 overthrows or rending of mountains; 11 earthquakes; 4 extensive inundations, 2 famines in which the people ate each other; and 20 disturbances or wars on the frontier; the court remained dissipated, and taxes were increased. (Leih-tae-tung-ke-peaou, 3 vol. § 4, page 53.)

Tung-chŏ attained a high office in which he abused his authority most cruelly, and at an early period of the then commotions, lost his life. Of his conduct, this is a specimen. Having 飲誘降 by a feast inveigled a few hundred insurgents to surrender, he had them overpowered whilst seated at the table, and of some 斷其舌 he cut out their tongues,—of some 斬手足 he cut off the hands and feet—of others he 鑿眼 chiselled out their eyes; and some 鑊煮之 he boiled in chaldrons; and the poor victims 未死 half dead 偃轉杯案閒 lay or rolled about amongst the dishes on the table. The affrighted guests dropt the spoons and chopsticks from their hands; but 卓飲食自若 Mr Chŏ drank and ate with perfect self composure. The poor wretch met his fate in an early stage of the business. Leu-poo 呂布 murdered him in a gate-way of the palace, and, as was the horrid custom of the times 夷三族 exterminated all his kindred within three degrees of consanguinity. (Tih-shih-yih She, 38 vol. 三國六 5 page.)

About this time 黃巾賊張角等起 the yellow capped rebels, Chang-keŏ and his associates arose. This man pretended to cure diseases by 呪符水 imprecations and water charms; and under this pretext, associated with himself several hundred thousands of followers, whom he organised, and placed generals over them. The troubles of this period brought forward Tsaou-tsaou 曹操 whom, a Spanish priest, who had read his exploits in the original, has called the Buonaparte of China.

《华英字典》“孔明”词条

“孔明”词条篇幅占大八开印本两页有余，旁征博引，资料来源相当丰富。如，论及汉朝时，引证《纲目发明》云：“自三代以降，惟汉得天下为正，踰四百年，尺地一民莫非汉有。”讲到桓灵不君、宠信佞臣、宦官弄权、灾异四起时，从《历代统纪表》中引述了系列数字：“据称有9次日月失色，7次山崩地裂，11次地震，4次洪水，2次饥荒易子而食，20次骚乱殃及边疆。朝廷奢靡，横征暴敛。”为证明“董卓位居显职而为人残忍”，引证《二十一史·三国》曰：“有一事颇能显其行止。卓以宴饮诱降反者数百人，于坐中先断其舌，或斩手足，或凿眼，或镬煮之，未死，偃转杯案间，会者皆战栗亡失匕箸，而卓饮食自若。但此可鄙之徒旋即步入穷途末路。吕布杀之于掖门，并依彼时骇人习俗夷其三族。”这些文字与原文虽有出入，但因明确开列文献名称、卷次、页码，言之凿凿，以史为证，俨然以正典示人。作为孔明生平介绍的前叙，这种展开方式一开始就将人物置于信实的语境。

有关孔明的正文，依然引用颇丰，类书、传说纷至沓来，来源出处大致了然。介绍孔明的战略战术时，马礼逊曰：“孔明是一位占星家，精通伏羲八卦，并据此发明了用一种作战队形来安营扎寨的阵列图示——八阵图（《三才图会》第97卷）。八阵图初以五人为一伍，十伍为一队；八队为一阵，440人；八阵为一部，3520人；此谓小成；每八部28160人设一将；八成为一军，225280人，此谓大成。”马礼逊不仅在括号内注明这段文字出自类书《三才图会》，为方便西人查阅，还不忘指出：“详情参考《中国百科全书》（*The Chinese Encyclopedia*）。”① “刘备托孤”一段源自《三国演义》，或因最后附会了民间传说，马礼逊认为没必要另注出处。所谓“刘备之子被托付给孔明照顾，后来他继承了后汉王位。当他年幼时，赵子龙将军曾

① 《三才图会》是关于“三才”，即天、地、人的图谱式类书，被欧洲汉学家称为《中国百科全书》（*The Chinese Encyclopedia*）。见《华英字典》*A Dictionary of the Chinese Language: Chinese and English Arranged according to the Radicals*, by Robert Morrison, Printed at the Honorable East India Company's Press, by P. P. Thoms, 1822, p. 140.

在百万军中藏阿斗，阿斗总是酣睡于一片嘈杂的战火之中，由此而形成了一句俗语：阿斗一生原是睡不醒。事实证明他是个愚蠢的浪子，阿斗这个名字被用来打趣或训诫男孩，起到现在还相当于骂他是个傻瓜”“阿斗一生原是睡不醒”这句俗语在当时的流行程度，恐怕不亚于“乐不思蜀”“扶不起的阿斗”，否则就不会进入马礼逊的字典了。这也说明，马礼逊在介绍孔明时，无论正典、俗谚，都收入笔端，格外重视资料的多元。

值得注意的是，马礼逊虽然给不少文献列明出处，但涉及《三国演义》的内容反而被忽略，他显然没意识到这部小说对于塑造孔明形象的举足轻重，因此，“孔明”词条虽然详备，却很难区分何谓正史中的孔明，何谓稗官野史中的孔明。如“王朝的一方乃皇室的一位后裔——刘备，沦落为卖席贩履的。还有一位关羽，以卖豆腐起家，在当时名扬天下，后被尊奉为中国的战神（the Mars of China），号称关夫子。第三位是张飞，原本是个卖肉的小贩或屠夫。此三人结义，庄严宣誓，匡扶汉室。由他们而引出了文章开头提到的孔明。孔明是指挥军队的谋士或军师将军（secretary）”。这段“桃园结义”显系出自《三国演义》，但马礼逊没有注明出处。

有些出自小说的情节，还被归之于正史。最典型的一段是：“有关孔明的严肃记载，写到他所尽忠的国家及其命运时，有几处描绘得相当生动，乃至催人泪下。孔明临终前，曾因对手司马懿拒不出战而恼怒。为诱其出战，他送了一套女装给他，要求他或者耻辱地接下女装，或者像个男人那样出来迎战。然而司马懿却坚守不出。54 岁那年，因为身体微恙和天象征兆，他预感到死之将至。可为了汉室，他还想活下去；有人劝他用祈禳之法挽回其命。于是，他在帐内按一定的次序点起一定数量的灯，对着上天和星宿，跪下祷告曰：亮生于乱世，甘老林泉，承昭烈皇帝三顾之恩，托孤之重，不敢不竭犬马之劳。不意阳寿将终。谨书尺素，上告穹苍：伏望天慈，俯垂鉴听，曲延臣算，使得上报君恩，下救民命，永延汉祀。非敢妄祈，实由情切。祝毕，俯伏待旦；吐血不止，终年 54 岁。尽管祈禳之法缓解了孔明的疾病，但中国人普遍认为死为定数。此后，效仿孔明，根据天上的星宿布灯、祈祷念咒的做法，一直流传至今。”这段文字的最后介绍了中国的民俗，但主要情节应出自“五丈原诸葛禳星”，而马礼逊却把它看作“严肃记载”。

由以上分析可以看出，在材料的使用上，“孔明”词条一是过分倚重于正典，二是过分讲究资料的多元。权威的正典和驳杂的资料，本来就使身为稗官野史的《三国演义》难以立足，更何况马礼逊又不曾为其使用的小说情节注明出处，他对《三国演义》的介绍，自然难以给人留下深刻印象。有一点，虽然马礼逊只提到一句，却着实令人警醒。他说：“《三国志》是那时的一部历史小说，它赋予孔明一种取得神助的能力，他作战时总是一手执扇，一手执巾（an hankerchief）。严肃的史学家并不如是说。”这句话是“孔明”词条中唯一点题介绍《三国演义》的文字。在此，马礼逊曲解了“羽扇纶巾”；但是，他把《三国演义》的书名音译为 San - kwŏ - che，在当时看来倒无大碍。最早的《三国演义》版本题名《三国志通俗演义》，明清之际流行的多数本子也名之以《三国志》，如《绣像古本李卓吾原评三国志》《绣像三国志演义第一才子书》等，所以，马礼逊把我们今天通称为《三国演义》的这部小说直呼为《三国志》，在当时实属自然。有趣的是，他指出这是一部“历史小说”（an historical novel），是有别于“严肃的史学家”之说的另类著述，这或许是欧美学界用这一概念来定义《三国演义》的文体属性的最早尝试；在 1817 年出版的《中国一览》中，马礼逊又重申了这一文体定义。此后，晚清来华西士逐步接纳了这一概念，开始用“历史小说”来译介“通俗演义”类作品。例如，卫三畏 1880 年翻译《列国志》时，直接用“历史小说”（*A Chinese Historical Novel*）指称《列国志》。[①] 遗憾的是，人们在追溯“历史小说”的创作缘起时，尚未有人引证这一资料。

---

① S. Wells Williams, “A Chinese Historical Novel”, *The New Englander*, Vol. 39, 1880, New Haven: W. L. Kingsley, Proprietor and Publisher, p. 30.

尽管《华英字典》的“孔明”词条并没有凸显《三国演义》的重要，但它却以有限的文字展开了三国人物画廊，孔明、董卓、张角、曹操、刘备、关羽、张飞、孙权、司马懿等接踵而至，他们充满谋略和智慧，历尽征战与兴废，这些熠熠生辉的人物从此开启了他们的西行之旅。

首先对这些人物产生兴趣的是汤姆斯。他之所以来中国，很大程度上就是为了在东印度公司的资助下印制马礼逊的作品，尤其是六卷本的《华英字典》。米怜对此曾有所介绍，他说：“1814 年 9 月 2 日，汤姆斯抵达澳门，他努力制作金属活字；在克服重重困难后，取得了意想不到的巨大成功。浇铸和雕刻中文活字上的某些障碍，使第一年的印刷工作进展缓慢。1816 年 1 月，第一批《字典》印刷完毕并送回英国，他继续印刷第二批《字典》和《中英对话》一书。”① 既然《华英字典》由汤姆斯印制，很难想象他会忽略“孔明”词条。与此同时也不难设想，汤姆斯这时还在努力学习汉语，并着手翻译《著名丞相董卓之死》，这篇译作在 1820 年与他印制的第二部第二卷《华英字典》同时面世。作为马礼逊作品的印制者，汤姆斯对三国人物的重视或许正是受了马礼逊的影响。

在所有三国人物中，清代来华西士介绍得最为详尽的还是孔明。1843 年，颇负盛誉的英文杂志《中国丛报》发表了美魏茶撰写的《孔明评论》，简单介绍了孔明的一生，认为《三国志》是“有史以来最优秀的中国故事之一”。从 1877 年至 1879 年，晚清另一闻名遐迩的英文杂志《中国评论》分 12 次连载了司登得（G. C. Stent）撰写的《孔明生平简介》（*Brief Sketches from the Life of Kung Ming*）。该文开篇即称：“从古至今，没哪位政治家或军事家像本文的主人公孔明那样，因其智慧、忠诚、勇敢等真正伟人所具有的诸般特点，而得到如此多的尊崇，受到如此高的仰慕。他的名字成为美

① William Milne, *A Retrospect of the First Ten Years of the Protestant Mission to China*, Malacca: printed at the Anglo – Chinese Press, 1820, p. 130.

德的同义词；他本人则成为现代社会初出茅庐的政治家效仿的典范；那些想青史留名的人紧紧追随着他的军事智慧；他的谋略被行诸诗文；他的行为亦展露于数不胜数的戏曲，在舞台上，他就是太阳，散发着中国骑士精神的光芒，尽管微弱，却是三国时代的显著特点。”① 该文从三顾茅庐、火烧博望坡，到真假孔明、毒书赚司马，围绕孔明生平，选译了《三国演义》中的 39 个故事片段，这是晚清时期英语世界篇幅最长的一篇介绍孔明的文字。值得注意的是，美魏茶是马礼逊最亲密的挚友米怜的儿子；而司登得也是步马礼逊后尘来到中国的英国人，由他编纂的《汉英合璧相连字典》（*A Chinese and English Vocabulary in the Pekinese Dialect*）“序言”的开篇就说：“尽管威妥玛（Mr. Wade）、马礼逊和麦都思（Mr. Medhurst）的著作大大有助于本字典的编纂，但本书的创作缘起还应主要归功于小说阅读。”② 显然，司登得对于马礼逊的字典并不陌生。他们之于孔明的关注，或许正是源于《华英字典》的“孔明”词条。

此外，在“孔明”词条中，马礼逊说有位西班牙牧师（a Spanish priest）读过《三国演义》原著，并称曹操为“中国的波拿巴”（the Bonaparte of China）。这位西班牙牧师究系何人？他为《三国演义》做出了怎样的贡献？这些问题至今还是小说史上的未解之谜。同时，19 世纪有多位论者将曹操与拿破仑相提并论，马礼逊是这一观点的始作俑者。

除了“孔明”词条，《华英字典》其他地方也有涉及《三国演义》的句子。比如，1822 年出版的第三部第 20 页有“玄德大惊滚下马”；第 29 页有“起兵讨曹操”；第 47 页有“吕布勇而无谋”；等等。相比于“孔明”词条，这些句子虽然比较零散，但也可以看出马礼逊对于这部小说的熟稔和青睐。

---

① G. C. S. , “Brief Sketches from the Life of K’ung - Ming”, *The China Review*, Vol. 5, No. 5, 1877, p. 311.

② George Carter Stent, *A Chinese and English Vocabulary in the Pekinese Dialect*, Shanghai, 1871, preface.

（二）《圣经》中译与《三国》文体

《新教在华传教前十年回顾》一书于 1820 年在马六甲出版，作者米怜说："掌握汉语并将《圣经》译成中文，是在华传教工作的首要目标。"1811 年前后，在将《圣经》译成中文的过程中，马礼逊对译文的文体风格颇感困惑。他将中文文体划分为三类：文言（a high）、白话（a low）和折中体（a middle style）。四书五经语体简洁，极为经典，乃"文言"文体的典范之作；大多数用口语撰写的小说是"白话"文体的代表；《三国演义》则是"折中体"的代表。后来，马礼逊发现，在上述三种文体之外，还有一种比白话小说更为口语化的作品——《圣谕》。马礼逊最初想仿效《圣谕》翻译《圣经》。然而，在谨慎考虑后，他还是决定采用折中体。因这种语体从各方面看都最适宜于翻译《圣经》这样一本旨在广泛传播的书。"一方面，这种语体具有一种古代经书的庄严和尊贵，又没有因过于凝练而晦涩难懂。另一方面，对于那些阅读能力尚可的读者来说，这种文体明白晓畅，又不会陷入口语粗糙的泥沼。这种文体既不会让那些目不识丁的人感到高不可攀，也不会让那些受过良好教育的人感到粗鄙难耐。"马礼逊注意到："每当中国人进行严肃的谈话时，都假装鄙视口语化的小说作品，但同时，他们又不得不承认古代经书的风格没有普遍的适用性。他们对《三国》体例欣喜若狂。"如此，《三国》文体自然得到马礼逊的格外青睐，他说："将经书的注疏（*commentaries*）与《三国》结合在一起的文体，更适合中文版《圣经》（*Sacred Scriptures*）以及一般的神学理论著作。这些注疏中所涉及的通常是一些严肃的主题，需要全神贯注地反复研读，因此其文体风格可能也更适合于神圣事物的尊贵性；而以《三国》为范本所造就的风格，会使语言的表达更为平实和流畅。”①

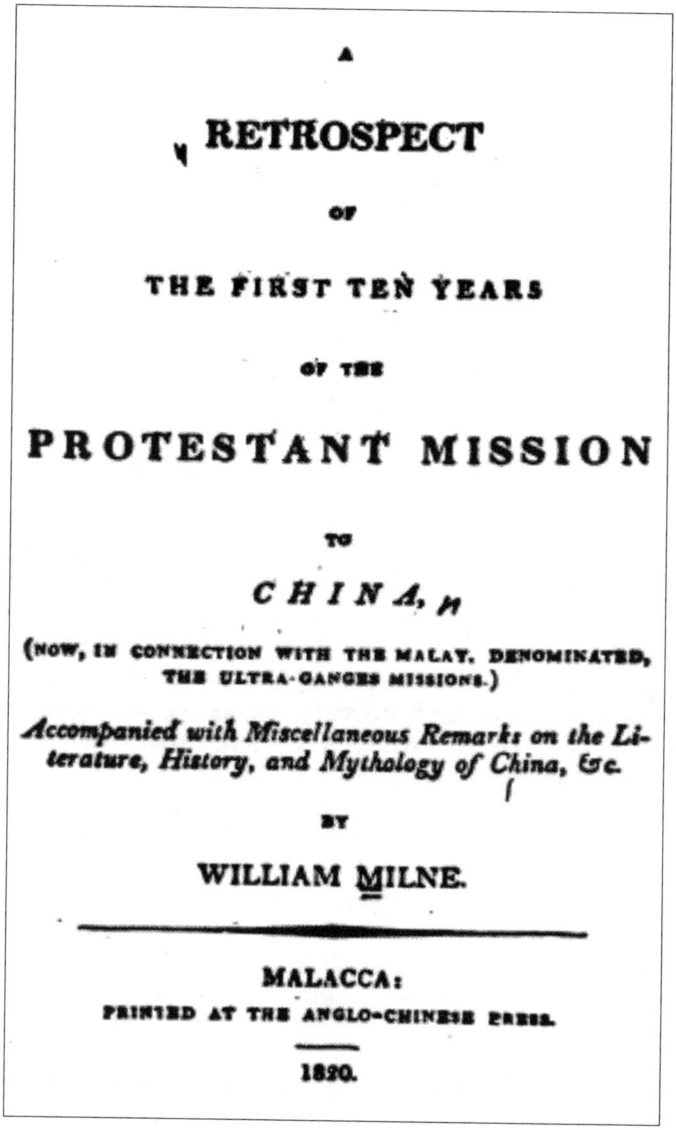
A

RETROSPECT

OF

THE FIRST TEN YEARS

OF THE

PROTESTANT MISSION

TO

CHINA,

(NOW, IN CONNECTION WITH THE MALAY, DENOMINATED, THE ULTRA-GANGES MISSIONS.)

Accompanied with Miscellaneous Remarks on the Literature, History, and Mythology of China, &c.

BY

WILLIAM MILNE.

MALACCA:

PRINTED AT THE ANGLO-CHINESE PRESS.

1820.

《新教在华传教前十年回顾》

① William Milne, *A Retrospect of the First Ten Years of the Protestant Mission to China*, Malacca: Printed at the Anglo－Chinese Press, 1820, pp. 89－90.

83

SECTION IX.

The Acts of the Apostles printed—Chinese Grammar finished—Family Affliction—Tract and Catechism composed—Human beings much influenced by circumstances—The Epistles translated and printed. Donation from the B. and F. Bible Society. Style proper for a version of the Scriptures into Chinese. The ancient classical books not fit to be imitated, and why.

IN 1810, Mr. Morriſon, having acquired ſufficient acquaintance with the Chineſe language, to ſatisfy himſelf that the tranſlation of the ACTS OF THE APOSTLES which he brought out with him, would, if amended and reviſed, be uſeful, he accordingly made ſuch corrections as he deemed neceſſary, and tried (what yet remained doubtful,) the practicability of printing the Holy Scriptures. The attempt ſucceeded; and he felt not a little encouraged in aſcertaining that ſuch works could be accompliſhed with conſiderable facility: he thought an important point was now gained; and having proved that it was practicable for perſons in the ſervice of the Miſſionary Society, to print the ſacred writings in China, he felt as if he could die more willingly than before. He had effected enough to encourage the Society to ſend a ſucceſſor. The charge for printing the Acts of the Apoſtles, was exorbitantly high. It amounted to more than half a dollar per copy;—the price at which the whole New Teſtament has ſince been

《圣经》中译的恰当风格

笔者不避繁冗地引述以上文字，主要是因为其中涉及的三个问题格外值得深思，这段文字在讨论《三国》文体的同时，几乎昭示了19世纪来华西士介入《三国演义》话题的种种可能。

第一，根据马礼逊的分析不难得出以下结论：为了有效地训导百姓，中国官员竟然可以用比“白话小说”更为粗浅的口语来直解《圣谕》，以代皇帝立言；对于传教士来说，为了宣教布道，在翻译中文《圣经》时，为什么不能选择《三国演义》这一最具亲和力的文体来代神立言呢？或许正是基于这种考虑，马礼逊把《三国演义》文体作为中译《圣经》的首选风格，这显示了自利玛窦（Matteo Ricci，1552—1610）以来走“文化适应”策略的传教士一贯奉守的实用理性精神。尽管用《三国演义》的杯来装《圣经》的酒在今天看来似乎有些不伦不类，但在当时，两者的联袂却颇有些难兄难弟的况味。一方面，嘉庆以来，凡稗官小说，连同其流通渠道“小说坊肆”一概遭到严禁，“《三国志》上慢忠义，《水浒传》下诱强梁。实起祸之端倪，招邪之领袖，”① 自然在查禁之列。另一方面，马礼逊在1814年3月12日的日记中写道：“澳门的中国官员公布谕令：禁止中国人接受外国人宗教。”② 传教及出版宗教读物都在禁止之列，翻译和出版《圣经》自不待言。用一种被禁毁的小说的文体风格来译介一种被禁毁的宗教读物，可见在马礼逊酝酿这一翻译策略之始，两者在官方不受欢迎的程度似乎旗鼓相当，都身处危难之境。但站在中西文化交流的角度，我们又着实为之庆幸。尽管马礼逊译介的《圣经》，其成败得失至今难有定论，这种文体上的斟酌究竟如何成全了《圣经》的中国之旅很难探究；但《圣经》毕竟是经典中的“圣典”，是至高无上的文本，《三国演义》则是通俗演义，是被禁毁的小说，这种匪夷所思的拼接，为《三国演义》的西行之路打开

① （清）悟梦子：《灵台小补》之《梨园粗论》，清道光十二年（1832），中国国家图书馆藏本。

② Eilza Morrison, *Memoirs of the Life and Labours of Robert Morrison*, Vol. I., London: Longman, Orme, Brown, Green, and Longmans, 1839, p. 402.

了方便之门，使这部在中国遭受禁毁的小说，意外地踏上了西行之途。

第二，在《华英字典》中，马礼逊初识《三国演义》，既已指出这是一部“历史小说”。但此处，马礼逊把《三国演义》与“口语化的小说作品”截然分开，甚至将它们分别看作“折中体”和“白话体”的代表作，这极易给人造成一种错觉：即作为“历史小说”的《三国演义》在文体上有别于一般的小说，尤其是白话小说。汤姆斯在《著名丞相董卓之死》的按语中，干脆把《三国志》说成史书，是一部文学性很强的史书。他说：“本文故事摘译自《三国志》（*San-kwo-che*），这是一部有关中国内战的最著名的史书。这部史书得到中国人的大力推崇，不仅是因为它的文学价值，还因为它对于（中国人如此认为）其所涉及的那段时期的战争与灾难的丰富而准确的叙述。”这种文体定位的模糊至少持续了 20 年之久。1840 年，《伊索寓言》的译者罗伯聃（Robert Thom，1807—1846）在《意拾喻言》（*Esop's Fables*）的“序言”中，把中文“书面语”分为“古文”和“时文”两类，后者又细分为六种：文章（时文之首）、诗赋、谕契、书札、传志、杂录（时文之末）。其中，“传志”包括“所有史书、传记和一流的历史小说，例如《三国志》《列国传》等”；“杂录”作为“时文之末”，乃“文中糟粕，是最简单、最卑微的文体。这类作品包括所有的荒唐小说和垃圾故事（silly novels and trash of stories）”。[①] 尽管罗伯聃把《三国志》定位于“历史小说”（historical novel），但在分类上还是强调其“传志”性，并把这类作品和涵盖着一般小说的“杂录”区分开来，其分类模式依然没有摆脱马礼逊的格局。

这种文体上的混淆与错位显然会影响西方人对于《三国演义》的正确认识和总体评价。1838 年，德国传教士郭实腊在《三国志评论》一文中说：

① Mun Mooy Seen - Shang, *Esop's Fables Written in Chinese*, Printed at the Canton Press Office, 1840, Preface Ⅶ.

这部作品可以被看作历史著述文体风格的典范，但绝不能把它当成一切作品的榜样。书中几乎找不到集中描写自然的段落，它是对生活在那个时代的、具有各种情感及恶习的人的记录。同样的措辞经常反复出现，这本书与其说是以辞采华茂名扬天下，不如说是因简洁精练而著称于世。”① 1848年，卫三畏在《中国总论》（*The Middle Kingdom*）中误把陈寿当成了《三国演义》的作者，还说：“这部作品具有双重属性，时间跨度很长，必然缺少一部小说所应有的整体性。”② 直到1867年，英国外交官梅辉立才在《中日释疑》（*Notes and Queries*）上发表文章，指出郭实腊与卫三畏的错误。③ 19世纪后期，随着《三国演义》节译本和评论文的大量涌现，多数来华西士方能洞悉《三国演义》的文体属性，突出的标志是他们对《三国志》书名的意译，由早期较为单一的“History of the Three States”复增了“Three Kingdom Novel”“the Romance of the Three kingdoms”等称谓。

第三，马礼逊把《三国演义》比作“中国的《旁观者》（*Spectator*）”，后者是18世纪初英国的畅销杂志之一。英国著名作家、评论家约翰逊博士（Dr. Johnson，1709—1784）说过：“那些想要写出完美英文作品的作家，应该夜以继日地潜心学习爱迪生（Addison，1672—1719）的文章。”爱迪生是英国诗文作家、剧作家，他不仅是《旁观者》的创办者之一，也是该杂志的主要撰稿人之一。马礼逊认为，“同样的说法也适用于《三国》。学习中文的人，无论是在交谈中，还是在书写时，若想轻松、流畅地表达自己的想法，都应该仔细研读和模仿《三国》。”这种表述为《三国演义》在英语世界的传播指明了一种途径：它可以充当来华西士的汉语学习教材。

---

① “Notes of the San Kwo Che, or History of the Three Kingdom”, *The Chinese Repository*, Vol. Ⅶ, No. 5. September, 1838, p. 249.

② S. Wells Williams, *The Middle Kingdom*, New York and London, Wiley and Putnum, 1848, Vol. 1, p. 545.

③ W. F. Mayers, “Chinese Works of Fiction”, *Notes and Queries*, Oct. 31. 1867, p. 137.

事实上，晚清西士之译介《三国演义》，不少情况即出于汉语学习的需要。1842 年，澳门出版了卫三畏编写的《拾级大成》，这是一部汉语工具书，“是为刚刚开始学习汉语的人编写的，读者对象不仅包括已经来华的外国人，也包括还在本国或正在来华途中的外国人。”① 全书共 10 个章节，其中 5 个章节采用了《三国演义》中的段落或句子。如第四章“阅读练习”，作者共译介了 91 个句子，每个句子依次给出中文、拼音、逐字英译和符合英语表达习惯的完整翻译。其中半数以上的句子出自《三国演义》，首句即“吕布无义之人不可信也”。另外，施约翰（John Steele）翻译的《舌战群儒》（*The Logomachy*）以《第一才子三国志演义》为底本翻译了第 43 回“诸葛亮舌战群儒　鲁子敬力排众议”。中国国家图书馆收藏的 1905 年版本共 62 页，包括地图、序言、导论、朝代、原文、英文注释、人名索引、词汇表、部首表等。而加利福尼亚大学图书馆收藏的 1907 年版本仅 20 页英文，包括序言、导论、回评译文、原文译文和夹批译文。译者在写于 1905 年 3 月 15 日的“序言”中说：“本书面向刚开始学习中文书面语的学生，争取满足他们对于一本简易教材的要求。”写于 1907 年 5 月 21 日的“序言”则说：“学生们明确提出要求，希望有一个译文；这也为修正此前的错误提供了一个机会。”可见，无论是前一个版本的详尽注释，还是后一个版本的全文译介，都是为了满足学生的汉语学习需求。有趣的是，在梳理《三国演义》的早期海外传播时，人们通常不会绕过《拾级大成》和《舌战群儒》，但却从未有人提及其编辑理念——把《三国演义》作为汉语教材——最初的倡导者是马礼逊。

---

① S. Wells Williams，拾级大成，*Easy Lessons in Chinese*: *or Progressive Exercises to Facilitate the Study of that Language*，Macao：Printed at the Office of the Chinese Repository，1842.，Preface，p. i.

（三）汉语学习与小说英译

在中国古典小说的早期海外传播方面，除了《三国演义》，马礼逊还是《红楼梦》的最早推介者。他至少四次提及《红楼梦》，鉴于这些资料极为罕见，笔者著录如下。第一，1812 年，为了学习汉语，马礼逊翻译了《红楼梦》第四回，译文没有正式出版，手稿目前保存在伦敦大学亚非学院图书馆（SOAS Library），这篇手译稿是目前所知欧美汉学界对于《红楼梦》的最早译介。第二，1816 年马礼逊在其编写的《中文对话与单句》中，拟想了一段师生之间的对话。学生问："初学（中文）看甚么书为好?"先生回答说："先学《大学》要紧。"学生说："恐怕《大学》难明白。"先生说："其次念《红楼梦》甚好。"学生又问："《红楼梦》书，有多少本?"先生回答："共二十本书。此书说的全是京话。"① 这是笔者在哈佛大学韩南教授（Patrick Hanan）的亲自引导下于哈佛燕京图书馆看到的汉语学习教材，其中保存了一段中英文合璧的《红楼梦》英译片断。第三，1817 年马礼逊在其撰写的《中国一览》的"结语"（conclusion）中说："对一个欧洲人来说，没有中国人帮助，要学好中文几乎是不可能的。掌握中文最好的途径是从阅读一本小说（fiction）开始，小说即'琐言'（Seaou Shwǒ，Small talk）。它们并非全用白话（colloquial）创作。《好逑传》（*Happy Courtship*）英文译作 *The Pleasing History*，是白话的。《红楼梦》（*Dreams*

① Robert Morrison, *Dialogues and Detached Sentences in the Chinese Language*, Macao: Printed at the Honorable East India Company's press, by P. P. Thoms, 1816., pp. 64 – 66.

of the Red Chamber）采用北京方言，也是白话的。”① 第四，1822 年出版的《华英字典》第三部所列的词汇与句子，尤其是长句，不少出自《红楼梦》。如“不可因我之不肖，自护己短，一并使其泯灭”“黛玉同姊妹们至王夫人处”，贾母、鸳鸯、李纨、袭人等人名亦赫然在列。

通览以上资料，不难发现一个有趣的现象：马礼逊推崇《红楼梦》的方式与倡导《三国演义》的方式如出一辙，都把它们视为汉语学习的敲门砖，甚至是“最好的途径”。他虽然强调阅读中国小说的重要性，但这不过是他为翻译《圣经》所做的语言准备。如何解释这一现象呢?

1814 年 3 月 28 日马礼逊在日记中说：“帝国的叛乱引起了人心浮动。一人向皇帝上书严禁小说类的娱乐读物。中国人称这类书为小说（small talk）。小说里经常有反抗政府压迫之类的故事，因此被看作是有害的。小说还常有破坏道德的倾向，严格正派的父母有时完全禁止其子女阅读小说。”② 由此可见，马礼逊对于中国古典小说在中国的处境早有耳闻，他对这类作品并非全无顾忌，在这样的背景下，我们很难指望他对《三国演义》投入太大的热情。

1827 年 10 月 30 日的日记又说：“为了帮助异教徒了解真理，我最好做些什么呢？当我思考这个问题时就想到了写作。如果我继续学习中国的典雅文学（the polite literature），可能得学到死的那刻；但我能够写浅近的中文，所以我想我最好打消学习异教徒学问（lore）的念头，用简单的中文句子教授基督教教义。根据我的感觉，异教徒中国人的作品同希腊、罗马以及现代欧洲的放荡诗人的作品一样令人反感（但仅此而已）。贺拉斯（Horace）最典雅最受欢迎的作品中充满了可恶的东西，比拜伦勋爵（*mi* lord Bi-

① Rev. R. Morrison, *A View of China*, Macao: Printed at the Honorable East India Company's Press, By P. P. Thoms, 1817, p. 120.

② Eilza Morrison, *Memoirs of the Life and Labours of Robert Morrison*, Vol. Ⅰ, London: Longman, Orme, Brown, Green, and Longmans, 1839, p. 402.

ron）的作品还要糟。但是除了这些所谓‘优秀作家’的不道德，我对他们无知的呕心沥血之作的乏味无用没有兴趣，浅尝辄止；完全没必要为了风格或任何这样的目标而研究它们。”① 这段话显示了一个虔诚的传教士对于世俗文学的偏见，他对贺拉斯、拜伦的作品尚且如此排斥，遑论中国文学，更不必说《三国演义》《红楼梦》这样的禁毁小说了。

尽管如此，马礼逊对于这两部作品的首倡之功依然是不容抹杀的，他至少让西方人很早就注意到了这类作品的存在，由此而使两部最为经典的中国章回体小说很早就站到了通往西方的路口上，从而对中国古典小说的早期海外传播发挥了引导作用。

① Eilza Morrison, *Memoirs of the Life and Labours of Robert Morrison*, Vol. Ⅱ, London: Longman, Orme, Brown, Green, and Longmans, 1839, p. 381.

附：英文原文

材料一

A Dictionary of the Chinese Language①

KUNG-MING 丨明 or Choo-kŏ-leang 諸葛亮 lived in the close of the reign of Hëen-te 獻帝（A. D. 226）, the last Emperor of the Han dynasty; and he took a conspicuous part in the civil wars of the San-kwŏ 三國 which succeeded the overthrow of that family, after swaying the sceptre of China 400 years. Kung-ming was a native of the Lang-yay 瑯琊 mountains, on the sea coast of Shan-tung province. The 綱目發明 Kang-mŭh fă ming asserts, that, from the period of the original three dynasties called San tae 三代 Wei han tĭh tëen hea wei ching 惟漢得天下爲正 the Han dynasty alone obtained the empire in a correct manner, and held it 踰四百年 more than four hundred years. Chĭh te yĭh min, mŏ fei Han yew 尺地一民莫非漢有 not a cubit of ground, nor a single plebeian but was possessed by the Han family.

① Robert Morrison, *A Dictionary of the Chinese Language*, Macao: Printed at the Honorable East India Company's Press, by P. P. Thoms, 1815 – 23, pp. 714 – 716.

The Emperor Hwan 桓 and Ling 靈 first 不君 failed in the duties, and maintaining the authority of, great monarchs, by which conduct they brought on the ruin of their family. A person named Tung-chŏ 董卓 who possessed 才武膂力少比 military talents and personal strength seldom equalled, and 少好俠 rather fond of knight errantry, was one of the first who 煽火英雄羣起 fanned the flame and raised in a flock all the heroes of the day. The eunuchs obtained and trifled with the imperial authority; and it is said, that about this time 9 eclipses of the sun are recorded; 7 overthrows or rending of mountains; 11 earthquakes; 4 extensive inundations, 2 famines in which the people ate each other; and 20 disturbances or wars on the frontier; the court remained dissipated, and taxes were increased. (Leĭh-tae-tung-ke-peaou, 3 vol. & 4, page 55.)

Tung-chŏ attained a high office in which he abused his authority most cruelly, and at an early period of the then commotions, lost his life. Of his conduct, this is a specimen. Having 飲誘降 by a feast inveigled a few hundred insurgents to surrender, he had them overpowered whilst seated at the table, and of some 斷其舌 he cut out their tongues, —of some 斬手足 he cut off the hands and feet—of others he 鑿眼 chiselled out their eyes; and some 鑊煮之 he boiled in chaldrons; and the poor victims 未死 half dead 偃轉杯案間 lay or rolled about amongst the dishes on the table. The affrighted guests dropt the spoons and chopsticks from their hands; but 卓飲食自若 Mr Chŏ drank and ate with perfect self composure. The poor wretch met his fate in an early stage of the business. Leu-poo 呂布 murdered him in a gate-way of the palace, and, as was the horrid custom of the times 夷三族 exterminated all his kindred within three degrees of consanguinity. (Urh-shĭh-yĭh She, 38 vol. 三國六 5 page.)

About this time 黃巾賊張角等起 the yellow capped rebels, Chang-keŏ and his associates arose. This man pretended to cure diseases by 咒符水 imprecations and water charms; and under this pretext, associated with himself several hundred thousands of followers, whom he organised, and placed generals over them. The troubles of this period brought forward Tsaou-tsaou 曹操 whom, a Spanish priest, who had read his exploits in the original, has called the Bonaparte of China.

On the side of the Imperial family, were, 1st Lew-pe 劉備 descended from royal ancestors, but reduced to be 賣蓆 a seller of mats or of straw sandals. 2nd, Kwan-yu 關羽 who rose from being 賣荳腐 a seller of sowins, to such eminence at that time, as to be now worshipped as the Mars of China, under the name of Kwan-foo-tsze. 3rd, Chang-fei 張飛 who was originally 賣肉 a seller of flesh, or a butcher.

These *three* men united themselves by a solemn oath to retrieve the fortunes of Han; and they had attached to them, the person whose name is at the head of this article. Kung-ming 丨 明 the 謀士 or 軍師將軍 secretary at war, who accompanied the armies. They had also Yuen-shaou 袁紹 Leu poo 呂布 and others. This party finally formed 蜀國 the kingdom Shŭh.

Tsaou tsaou 曹操 headed the party who established 魏國 the kingdom Wei; and Sun-keuen 孫權 was he who raised himself to the throne of 吴國 the kingdom Woo. The secretary, Kung-ming, was eight cubits in stature; and deemed very highly of himself; always comparing himself to Kwang-chung 管仲 and 樂毅 Yŏ-e, persons famous in their day.

Kung-ming was sincerely devoted to 劉備 *Lew-pe*, who became the Chaou lëĕ te 昭烈帝 of the 後漢 latter Han. He excelled greatly in what was much valued at that time, and has been much admired in China ever since, stratagems in war. He was an astrologer and versed in the doctrines of the 八卦 *eight* diagrams of *Fŭh-he*; to correspond to these, he invented a form of encamping an army in a sort of battle array, called Pa chin too 八陣圖 the eight regiment figure. (San-tsae Too-hwuy, 97th vol.) He began with *five* men whom he called 伍 Woo, he formed ten woo into a company, which he called 隊 Tuy; *eight* tuy he formed in a 陣 Chin, or regiment, consisting of 440 men. *Eight* Chin 陣 constituted a Poo 部 consisting of 3, 520 men. These he called a 小成 small division; *eight* of these Poo, or 28, 160 men had a Tseang 將 or general; *eight* of these divisions formed a Keun 軍 or army 225, 280 men, which he called 大成 a large division. (For a full detail accompanied by a print, see the above reference to the Chinese Encyclopedia.)

In allusion to the far-famed *Pa-chin-too* of Kung-ming, some medical writers in China, arrange their remedies by the same phraseology, when they profess to attack disease.

The San-kwŏ-che, an historical novel of that period, attributes to Kung-ming an ability to procure the aid of spiritual beings, and always sends him into battle with a fan in one hand, and an handkerchief in the other. The grave histories do not notice this circumstance. Some of his letters, essays, on different subjects; orders to the army, and so forth, are preserved; and are thought to add greatly to his reputation; they are in twenty-four pieces of composition, containing 140, 112 characters.

The serious accounts of Kung-ming, several times represent him as deeply affected, even to tears, with the state of the country and the fortunes of that party which he espoused.

A little before his death, he was much irritated that his opponent Sze-ma-e 司馬懿 would not bring his army out of their strong holds to fight; and, with a view of provoking him to do it, he sent a suit of woman's apparel to him as a present, and desired him either to accept the woman's attire with shame, or to come forth like a man. Sze-ma-e however, persisted in acting on the defensive. In his

54th year he anticipated, from existing indisposition, and an astrological prognostic, that he was about to die. But for the sake of Han's house, he still wished to live; and he was induced to 用祈禳之法挽回其命 employ forms of prayer and supplication, to bring back his life, —that is, to have the term of his life protracted. His prayer was addressed to Heaven, and the stars; to correspond to which, he lit up lamps in a certain number, and order, within his tent; and prostrating himself, prayed thus, 亮生於亂世甘老林泉 (I) Leung, being born into the world in times of anarchy would glady have remained till old age, secluded amongst forests and fountains of water; but having been called forth by the reiterated visits of the Emperor; having been entrusted with the care of his son, 不敢不竭犬馬之勞 I dared not to decline my utmost exertions, and to labour as a dog or horse in his service—I now apprehend my life is drawing to a close, and therefore 謹書尺素 I have reverently written a short prayer 上告穹蒼 to announce these things to heaven's azure canopy; and prostrate hope that Heaven will graciously bow down, look and listen 天慈俯垂鑒聽 and 曲延臣算 bend circumstances to lengthen the number of my days; that I may recompense my sovereign, and rescue his people, and render the house of Han perpetual; 非敢妄祈實由情切 I presume not to offer irreverent unreasonable prayers—I am impelled by the most acute and sincere feelings.

Having finished his prayer 祝畢 he remained prostrate on the earth till morning; when 吐血不止 a constant spitting of blood came on, of which he died in the 54th year of his age. Notwithstanding Kung-ming's ill success in praying to have his days protracted; and its being the popular belief of Chinese, that 死為定數 the number of days which shall precede death, is *a fixed number*; the arrangement of lamps corresponding to the stars of heaven, and spells, and incantations, in imitation of Kung-ming, are still practiced in China.

Kung-ming is famous for having invented 木牛流馬 wooden bullocks and go-horses which were a sort of vehicle 轉運糧草 for transporting provisions, and forage; with these two advantages 人不大勞牛馬不食 that the men were not much fatigued; and such bullocks and horses did not eat.

The son of *Lew-pe* who was committed to Kung-ming's care, and who succeeded his father on the throne of the *How han*, which ended with his life was, as a child, called 阿斗 O-tow the general 趙子龍 Chaou-tsze-lung, 百萬軍中藏阿斗 when millions of men were fighting, still carried in his bosom the boy *O-tow*, who often slept amidst the crash of arms, and all the din of battle; hence the saying 阿斗一生原是睡不醒 it was O-tow's fate never to awake all his life; he proved a besotted debauchee; and the name *O-tow* applied in raillery or anger to any boy, is still equivalent, to "stupid blockhead."

材料二

A Retrospect of the First Ten Years of the Protestant Mission to China①

Style proper for a version of the Scriptures into Chinese. The ancient classical books not fit to be imitated, and why.

In rendering the Sacred Scriptures into Chinese, Mr. Morrison felt at a loss for some time, as to the *kind of style* most proper to be adopted. In Chinese books, as in those of most other nations, there are three kinds of style: —a high, a low, and a middle style. The style which prevails in the 五經 Woo-king and 四書 Sze-shoo, is remarkably concise, and considered highly *classical*. Most works of fiction

① 编者按: William Milne, *A Retrospect of the First Ten Years of the Protestant Mission to China*, Malacca: Printed at the Anglo-Chinese Press, 1820, pp. 89 – 93.

of the lighter sort are written in a style perfectly *coloquial.* The 三國 San-kwŏ,[1] a work much admired in China, holds in point of style, a *middle place* between these two. He at first inclined to the middle style; but afterwards, on seeing an Imperial work, called 聖諭 Shing-yu, designed to be read twice a month, in the Public Halls of the different provinces, for the instruction of the people in relative, and political duties, and which is paraphrased in a perfectly colloquial style, he resolved to imitate this work.

1st. Because it is more easily understood by the bulk of the people.

2d. Because it is intelligible when read in an audience, which the high classical style is not at all. The middle style is also intelligible when read in public, but not so easily understood as the lower style.

3d. Because it can be quoted verbatim when preaching, and understood by the people without any paraphrastic explanation. However, on reconsidering the subject, he decided on a middle style as in all respects best adapted for a book intended for general circulation. On the one hand, it possesses something of the gravity and dignity of the ancient classical books, without that extreme conciseness which renders them so hard to be understood. On the other hand, it is intelligible to all who can read to any tolerable extent, without sinking into colloquial coarseness. It is not above the illiterate, nor below the better educated. The Chinese whenever they speak seriously, affect to despise the colloquial works of fiction, while at the same time, they are obliged to acknowledge that the style of the ancient classical books is not adapted for general usefulness. Of the style of the 三國 San-kwŏ, they speak in raptures. It may indeed, in as far as style is concerned, be considered the Spectator of China. Dr. Johnson said, that "He who

① The San-kwo fills twenty closely printed thin duodecimo volumes.

would make himself perfect in a good English style, should give his days and nights to Addison." The same may be said of the San-kwo. The student of Chinese, who would express himself with ease and general acceptance, either in conversation or in writing, ought carefully to read and imitate the San-kwŏ. A style formed from a union of the *commentaries* on the classical books, with the San-kwŏ, is well suited to a version of the Sacred Scriptures, and to theological writings in general. The subjects treated of in these commentaries are often of a grave cast; hence the style which a frequent and attentive perusal of them, would form, is likely to be much adapted to the dignity of divine things; while that formed on the model of the San-kwŏ, will produce a smooth and easy flow of expression.

It has been, and probably still is the opinion of some, that a version of the Holy Scriptures into Chinese, should be made in imitation of the style of the text of the classical books, e. g. of the 五經 Woo-king, the 四書 Sze-shoo; and particularly the writings of 孟子 Măng-tsze, have been mentioned as holding a first place in those books which the translator should copy after. But, with all due deference to those who hold this opinion, the writer cannot help thinking differently. In a critique, or apology to the public, the names of Chinese philosophers, sound well, and may produce an effect on those who have not the means of looking more narrowly into the subject.

If we consider what is *probable* and what the *actual fact* is, with regard to these writings, it will not perhaps appear perfectly evident, that they ought to be imitated. For, the Chinese classical books, if they be, what no one doubts, a faithful collection of the maxims and productions of those eminent men to whom they are ascribed, then the style is more than *two thousand years old*. Taking into the account the frequent changes and fluctuations to which all languages are subject, is it *probable* that a style of language which prevailed twenty centuries ago, should be suited to modern times? Is there any such example on record? If any one object: "that though the language and style of other countries have changed, yet those of China have not;" —It is answered that the great difficulty which all learned Chinese find in understanding their ancient books, bears much against the objection; especially when we consider that the difficulty does not arise merely from the reference to customs, and usuages long since obsolete, and the relations of things of which we, in the latter end of the world, know almost nothing; but also from the *style* and *structure* of *the language* itself. Again, if we attend to the *actual fact*, we shall find that the Chinese classical books are not even supposed to be intelligible without a *commentary*. The naked text is never read, except by children for the sake of learning the *sound*, and under the explanation of a schoolmaster; or by persons who have previously read it with the commentary; and it is not understood by one fifth of those who have spent several years in reading it, notwithstanding their having enjoyed the advantages of both a commentary and a teacher. If it be objected that the difficulty arises not from the *style*, but from the *subject*—it is answered that, with the exception of the 易經 *Yeb-king*, and the 中庸 *Chung-yung*, which treat of abstruse astrological and metaphysical topics, the others have no great difficulties in their respective *subjects*, but what arises occasionally from allusions to ancient usuages, the definitions of which have not been clearly handed down in history.

A very considerable part of the most esteemed classical books, namely the Sze-shoo, is filled with *maxims* and *aphorisms*, which require a style of a peculiar character, and which is but ill suited to historical narration, or to subjects where a certain train of thought is preserved throughout a paragraph of five, ten, or twenty sentences.

With respect to Măng-tsze, his style is generally masculine and animated;

but partakes of a certain levity to which his mind was sometimes subject; and the same difficulties attend his writings which attend the other classical books, though perhaps not always to the same extent.

China, it is true, has scarcely any *modern* writers of note; but Choo-tsze and his contemporaries who wrote in the 12th century, were eminent authors; and is it not more reasonable to suppose that the style of language which prevailed six hundred years ago, is better adapted to modern use than that which prevailed two thousand years ago? Choo-tsze paraphrased most of the *King*, or classical books; and confesses himself often at a loss for the genuine sense of the text, from its extreme age and brevity. The writer has therefore no hesitation in giving it as his decided opinion, that the style of the books commonly called *King*, is by no means fit to be imitated in general, either in a version of the sacred volume, or in theological writings—or indeed, in any work intended for extensive perusal and usefulness among all classes. For, admitting that a version of the Scriptures formed on the style of the classical books, would be understood by the learned, and perhaps admired by them, yet the generality of the people would be able to understand, but very little of it. A deal of hard work would be left to the preacher and commentator, which the translator, by imitating models of more modern date, might prevent.

中文回译

材料一

《华英字典》[1]

孔明，又称诸葛亮，大约生活在汉朝最后一位皇帝——汉献帝统治末期（公元226年），他在三国内战中发挥了显著作用，这场战争推翻了汉家对于中国长达400年的统治。孔明是瑯琊山人，瑯琊山位于山东省沿海。《纲目发明》云：“自三代以降，惟汉得天下为正，踰四百年，尺地一民莫非汉有。”

“桓灵不君”，在他们掌握政权时，汉家走向灭亡。一个名叫董卓的人，“才武膂力少比”，“少好侠”，乃当日“煽火英雄群起”中之一员。其时宦官弄权，据称有9次日月失色，7次山崩地裂，11次地震，4次洪水，2次饥荒易子而食，20次骚乱殃及边疆。朝廷奢靡，横征暴敛（《历代统纪表》，第3卷，第4册，第55页）。

董卓位居显职而为人残忍，骚乱之初就丧了命。有一事颇能显其行止。

---

① 编者按：［英］马礼逊：《华英字典》第1部分第1卷，（澳门）东印度公司汤姆斯印，1815年，第714—716页。

董卓以“饮诱降”反者数百人，于坐中先“断其舌”，或“斩手足”，或“凿眼”，或“镬煮之”，“未死”，“偃转杯案间”，会者皆战栗亡失匕箸，而“卓饮食自若”。但此可鄙之徒旋即步入穷途末路。吕布杀之于掖门，并依彼时骇人习俗“夷三族”（《二十一史·三国·六》，第三十八卷，第5页）。

其时“黄巾贼张角等起”，此人假装能用“咒”和“符水”治病，以此为借口，招徕数十万信徒，他将这些人组织起来，又安排将领统率他们。这时的暴乱引出了曹操，一位西班牙牧师通过阅读原著了解到他的功绩，将他称为“中国的波拿巴”。

王朝的一方乃皇室的一位后裔——刘备，沦落为“卖席”贩履的。还有一位关羽，以“卖豆腐”起家，在当时名扬天下，后被尊奉为中国的战神，号称关夫子。第三位是张飞，原本是个“卖肉”的小贩或屠夫。

此三人结义，庄严宣誓，匡扶汉室。由他们而引出了文章开头提到的孔明。孔明是指挥军队的“谋士”或“军师将军”。这帮人联手袁绍、吕布等人，最终建立了“蜀国”。

曹操领导的一派建立了“魏国”，孙权成了“吴国”国君。谋士孔明，身高八尺，自视甚高，常常自比为他们那个时代著名的“管仲”和“乐毅”。

孔明对刘备忠心耿耿，刘备后来成了“后汉昭烈帝”。孔明被时人所推崇，在中国一直因其战争谋略而受到颂扬。他是一位占星家，精通伏羲“八卦”，并据此发明了用一种作战队形来安营扎寨的阵列图示——八阵图（《三才图会》第97卷）。八阵图初以五人为一“伍”，十伍为一“队”；八队为一“阵”，440人；八“阵”为一“部”，3520人；此谓“小成”；每八部28160人设一“将”；八成为一“军”，225280人，此谓“大成”（详情参考《中国百科全书》）。

提及孔明闻名遐迩的八阵图，某些中国的医药书作者声称他们在对付疾病时，也会用同样的方法来开处方。

《三国志》是那时的一部历史小说，它赋予孔明一种取得神助的能力，他作战时总是一手执扇，一手执巾。严肃的史学家并不如是说。孔明不同内容的书信、文章，还有军令等，都被保存了下来，人们认为这对他的声望影响很大。这些作品一共有 24 篇，共 140112 字。

有关孔明的严肃记载，写到他所尽忠的国家及其命运时，有几处描绘得相当生动，乃至催人泪下。

孔明临终前，曾因对手司马懿拒不出战而恼怒。为诱其出战，他送了一套女装给他，要求他或者耻辱地接下女装，或者像个男人那样出来迎战。然而司马懿却坚守不出。54 岁那年，因为身体微恙和天象征兆，他预感到死之将至。可为了汉室，他还想活下去；有人劝他“用祈禳之法挽回其命”。于是，他在帐内按一定的次序点起一定数量的灯，对着上天和星宿，跪下祷告曰：“亮生于乱世，甘老林泉”，承昭烈皇帝三顾之恩，托孤之重，“不敢不竭犬马之劳”。不意阳寿将终。“谨书尺素，上告穹苍”：伏望“天慈”，“俯垂鉴听，曲延臣算”，使得上报君恩，下救民命，永延汉祀。“非敢妄祈，实由情切”。

“祝毕”，俯伏待旦；“吐血不止”，终年 54 岁。尽管祈禳之法缓解了孔明的疾病，但中国人普遍认为“死为定数”。此后，效仿孔明，根据天上的星宿布灯、祈祷念咒的做法，一直流传至今。

孔明因发明了能够“转运粮草”的“木牛流马”而著称，它们有两个优点——“人不大劳，牛马不食”。

刘备之子被托付给孔明照顾，后来他继承了后汉王位。当他年幼时，赵子龙将军曾在“百万军中藏阿斗”，阿斗总是酣睡于一片嘈杂的战火之中，由此而形成了一句俗语：“阿斗一生原是睡不醒”。事实证明他是个愚蠢的浪子，“阿斗”这个名字被用来打趣或训诫男孩，直到现在还相当于骂他是个“傻瓜”。

材料二

《新教在华传教前十年回顾》[①]

《圣经》中译的恰当风格。不适合模仿古代典籍，原因何在。

在将《圣经》翻译成中文的过程中，马礼逊先生一度对选用哪种文体最为恰当感到茫然无措。正如其他大多数国家一样，中文书籍也有三种文风：文言、白话和折中体。“四书”和“五经”的文体非常简洁，被视若经典。通俗类作品中的大部分小说，均以十分口语化的文体写就。《三国》[②]在中国备受推崇，就其文风而言，介乎二者之间。马礼逊先生起初倾向于采用折中体，但是后来看到了一本名叫《圣谕》的书，其文体是纯粹的口语，每月在各省公署宣读两次，旨在训诫相关人员，指导其政治职责，马礼逊先生决心仿效这本《圣谕》。

第一，因为广大百姓更易理解。

第二，向观众宣读时浅显易懂，经典文言体则全然不同。折中体在公众场合宣读时同样浅显易懂，但不如白话体更易理解。

第三，在布道时白话体可以逐字引述，不用任何解释百姓就能明白。

但是，经过再三考虑，他决定采用折中体；因为这种文体从各方面来看都最适合于一本旨在广泛流通的书。一方面，这种文体具有一种古代经书的庄严和尊贵，又没有因过于凝练而晦涩难懂。另一方面，对于那些阅读能力尚可的读者来说，这种文体明白晓畅，又不会陷入口语粗糙的泥沼。这种文体既不会让那些目不识丁的人感到高不可攀，也不会让那些受过良好教育的人感到粗鄙难耐。每当中国人进行严肃的谈话时，都假装鄙视口语化的小说

---

① 编者按：［英］米怜：《新教在华传教前十年回顾》，马六甲英华书院，1820 年，第 89—93 页。

② 《三国》二十卷，约小十二开本。

作品，但同时，他们又不得不承认古代经书的风格没有普遍的适用性。他们对《三国》体例欣喜若狂。就文风而论，这本书确实可以被看作中国的《旁观者》（*The Spectator*）。约翰逊博士（Dr. Johnson）说："那些想要写出完美英文作品的作家，应该夜以继日地潜心学习爱迪生（Addison）的文章。"[①] 同样的说法也适用于《三国》。学习中文的人，无论是在交谈中，还是在书写时，若想轻松、流畅地表述自己的想法，都应该仔细研读和模仿《三国》。将经书的注疏与《三国》结合在一起的文体，更适合中文版《圣经》以及一般的神学理论著作。这些注疏中所涉及的通常是一些严肃的主题，需要全神贯注地反复研读，因此其文体风格可能也更适合于神圣事物的尊贵性；而以《三国》为范本所造就的风格，会使语言的表达更为平实和流畅。

时至今日，或许依然有人认为中译本《圣经》应该模仿经书的文风，比如"四书"和"五经"的文风；尤其是被视为经书之首的《孟子》，被认为是《圣经》译者最应仿效的一部经书。但是，尽管持此观点的人值得尊重，本书作者却禁不住产生不同的想法。在一篇公开发表的评论文或辩论文中，引用中国哲学家的大名，也许会对那些不想对此问题做深入探究的人产生影响。

对于这些经书来说，如果我们考虑一下什么是可能的，什么又是事实，它们应该被模仿看上去或许就不那么理所当然了。因为如果中国的经书真的是圣贤箴言的忠实记录，那么其文风已超过两千年之久。再考虑一下所有语言都会经历的改动和变化，那么两千年前盛行的文体依然可能适合现代吗？历史上有过这种先例吗？如果有人反对说："尽管其他国家的语言和文风都已经改变了，但是中国的还没有。"答案是所有中国读书人在理解他们的古书时出现的巨大困难，就很好地反驳了这种反对意见；尤其是当我们考虑到这些困难不仅来自对风俗的解说、久已过时的用法，以及处于世界另一端的我们几乎一无所知的复杂关联，而且来自汉语本身的风格和结

① 编者按：爱迪生（Addison）是《旁观者》杂志的创办人之一。

构。还有，如果我们再考虑一下这一事实，我们会发现如果没有注疏，中国的经书并不那么浅显易懂。除了在学校老师的解说下学习诵读的孩子，没有人只读经书的单一文本；或者以前已经借着注疏读过这部经书的人才会只读文本。而且，即使有注疏和老师的帮助，在读了数年经书的人中，仍有五分之一的人不能理解其意。如果又有人反对说，困难不仅来自其文体，而且来自其主题。答案是，除了涉及深奥的星象及玄学主题的《易经》和《中庸》，其他经书的主题并不太难领会，只有某些偶尔出现的古代用法的典故，其本义在历史上没有被清楚地流传下来。

在经书最受推崇的“四书”中，有相当一部分内容是格言和警句，这就需要一种特殊的文风，但这种文风并不适合历史性的叙事，也不适合表达某些主题，这些主题保存在一连串的思想中，由 5 句、10 句或 20 句语句组成的段落构成。

至于《孟子》，其文风通常来说阳刚又活泼，但有时在表达思想时又带有几分轻率，书中存在其他经书中同样出现的困难，虽然这些困难并不总是相同的。

确实，现代中国几乎没有著名作家。但是，十二世纪的朱子（Choo-tsze）及他同时代的人却都是著名作家；600 年前流行的语言风格，比起 2000 多年前流行的语言风格，不是更适合于现代拿来用吗？这种推测不是更合理吗？朱子注解了大部分的“经”或经书，他自己也承认，由于年代久远和过于简洁，他经常对文本的真正含义感到茫然。因此，本书作者毫不犹豫地给出自己的明确观点；这些通常被称为“经”的文风，一般来说绝不适合用来仿效，这种文风既不能用在翻译《圣经》中，也不能用在翻译神学著作中，甚至不能用在任何想要在社会各阶层中被广泛阅读和使用的书中。因为即使中国的有识之士理解甚至赞赏以经书风格写就的中译本《圣经》，大多数普通民众也只能理解其中的少部分内容。因为这将会给传教士和评注者带来大量艰苦的工作；但是如果译者模仿更为现代的文风，或许就能防止这一情况的发生。

二　郭实腊与《三国志评论》*

1838年9月，中国近代史上影响最大的英文杂志——《中国丛报》发表了一篇题为《三国志评论》的长篇大论，其中的《三国志》，实际指的是《三国志演义》，即我们现在所称的《三国演义》。这篇书评是《三国演义》在英语世界出现的第一篇系统评论。它出自何人之手？作者是如何看待《三国演义》这部中国小说的？文章发表后在英语世界引起了怎样的回响？厘清上述问题，对于研究19世纪西方人视野中的《三国演义》具有重要意义。遗憾的是，至今学界对这篇书评罕有研究。本部分内容在考订《三国志评论》作者的基础上，分析了这篇书评四方面的情况：情节译介、人物重构，以及作者对于《三国演义》的总体评价和译介缘由，并结合当时的历史语境探索了该作对于《三国演义》等历史小说的海外译介产生的深远影响。

---

* 相关研究以“19世纪西方人视野中的《三国演义》——以郭实腊的《三国志评论》为中心”为题，发表于《中国文化研究》2016年第4期。

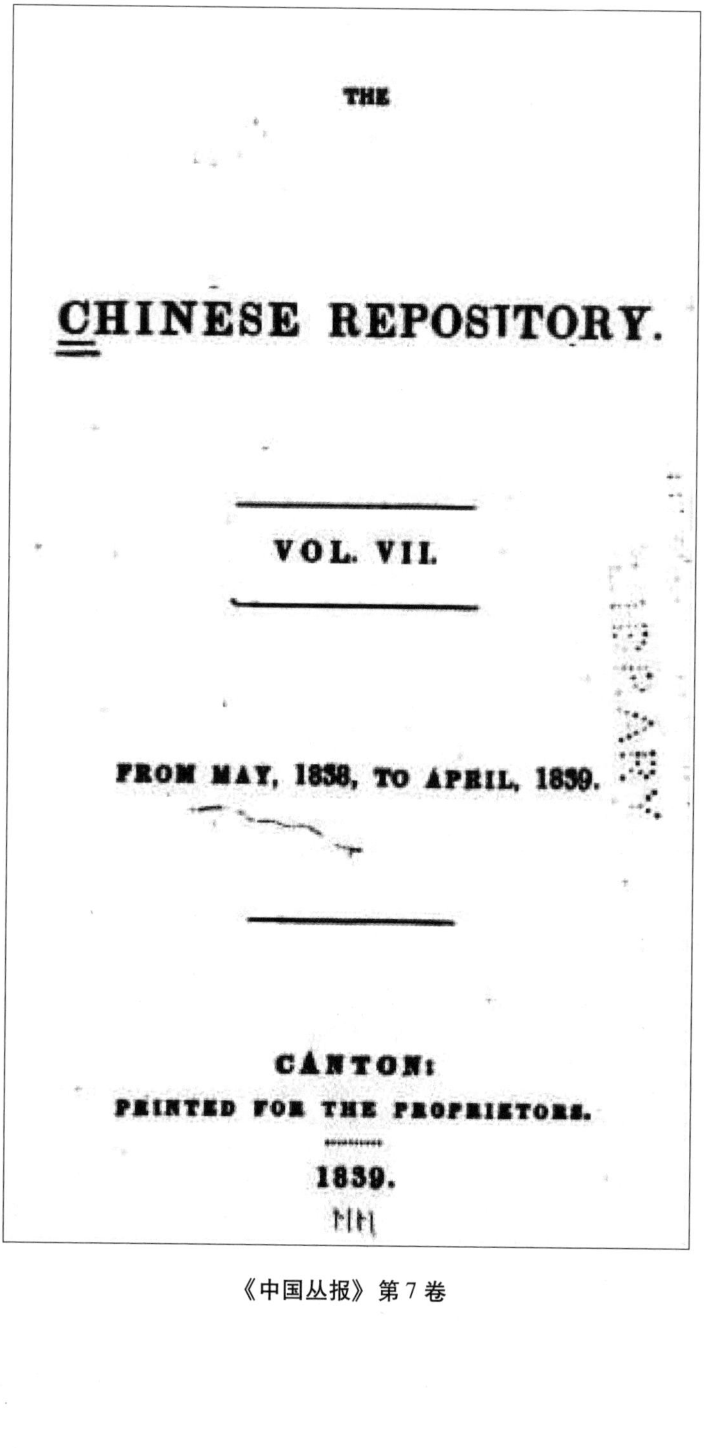

THE

CHINESE REPOSITORY.

VOL. VII.

FROM MAY, 1838, TO APRIL, 1839.

CANTON:

PRINTED FOR THE PROPRIETORS.

1839.

《中国丛报》第7卷

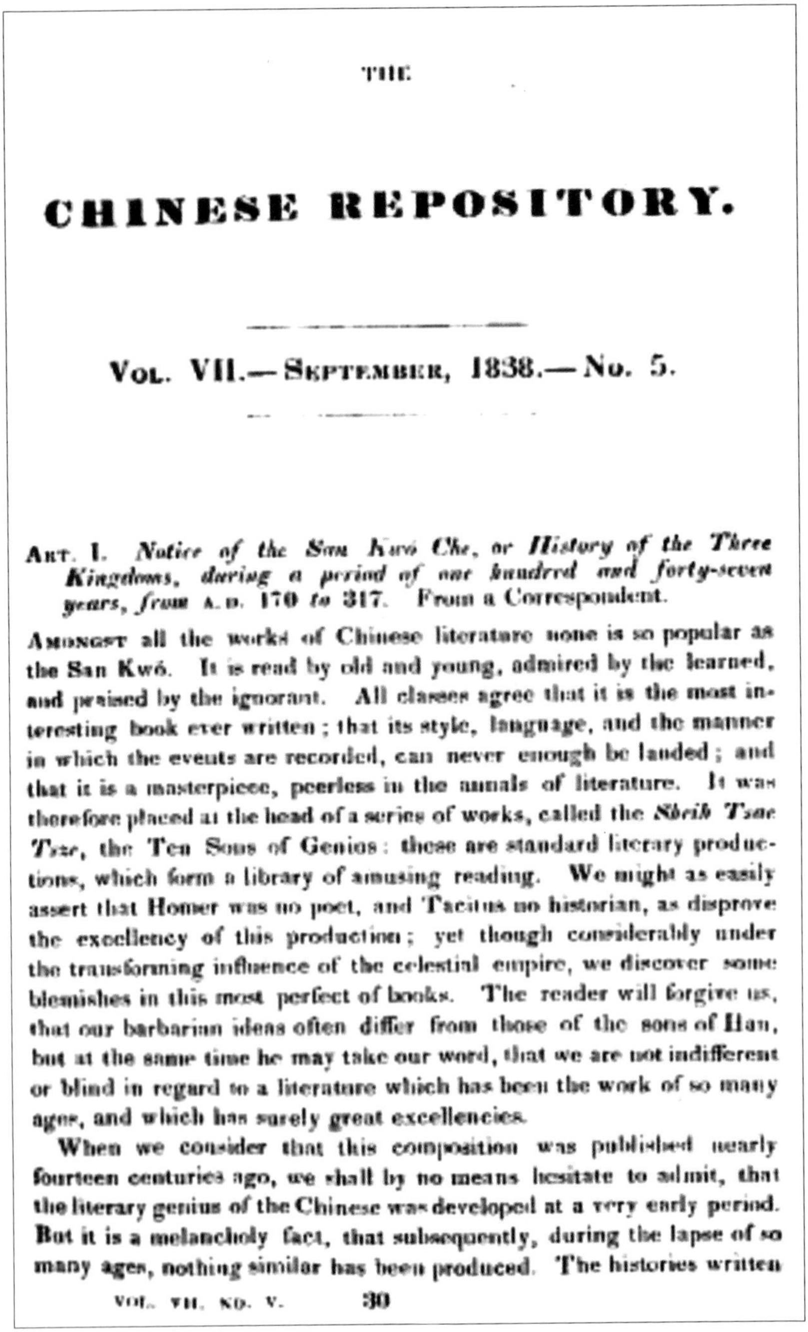

THE

CHINESE REPOSITORY.

VOL. VII.—SEPTEMBER, 1838.—No. 5.

ART. I. *Notice of the San Kwŏ Che, or History of the Three Kingdoms, during a period of one hundred and forty-seven years, from* A. D. *170 to 317.* From a Correspondent.

AMONGST all the works of Chinese literature none is so popular as the San Kwŏ. It is read by old and young, admired by the learned, and praised by the ignorant. All classes agree that it is the most interesting book ever written; that its style, language, and the manner in which the events are recorded, can never enough be lauded; and that it is a masterpiece, peerless in the annals of literature. It was therefore placed at the head of a series of works, called the *Sheih Tsae Tsze*, the Ten Sons of Genius: these are standard literary productions, which form a library of amusing reading. We might as easily assert that Homer was no poet, and Tacitus no historian, as disprove the excellency of this production; yet though considerably under the transforming influence of the celestial empire, we discover some blemishes in this most perfect of books. The reader will forgive us, that our barbarian ideas often differ from those of the sons of Han, but at the same time he may take our word, that we are not indifferent or blind in regard to a literature which has been the work of so many ages, and which has surely great excellencies.

When we consider that this composition was published nearly fourteen centuries ago, we shall by no means hesitate to admit, that the literary genius of the Chinese was developed at a very early period. But it is a melancholy fact, that subsequently, during the lapse of so many ages, nothing similar has been produced. The histories written

VOL. VII. NO. V. 30

郭实腊的《三国志评论》

（一）语言的天才与多产的汉学家

《三国志评论》发表于《中国丛报》，该刊是西方第一份主要以中国为研究对象的刊物，也是鸦片战争前后在中国影响最大的英文期刊。1832 年 5 月由美国传教士裨治文（Elijah Coleman Bridgman，1801—1861）创刊于广州，编者主要是道光年间来华的西方人，尤以传教士和外交官为多，1851 年 12 月停刊，存续 20 年，共发行 20 卷 232 期，内容涉及道光年间中国的政治、军事、社会、宗教、文学、艺术等方方面面，是研究 19 世纪中西文化交流的重要资料。

《三国志评论》一文没有明确开列作者姓名，只道稿件来自某"通讯员"（Correspondent），这为考订作者带来一定难度。所幸 1851 年 12 月《中国丛报》停刊时出版的一册"总索引"（*General Index of Subjects Contained in the Twenty Volumes of the Chinese Repository*：*With an Arranged List of the Articles*），为这一问题的解决提供了线索。"总索引"将《中国丛报》刊载的文章分为地理、政治、军事、历史等 30 类，并在每一类下列出了相关文章。分类前，编者裨治文和卫三畏指出，有五位作者的文章以姓名首字母标示出来，其中 C. G. 指的是 Charles Gutzlaff，即第一位来华德国新教传教士郭实腊的英文名，德文名为 Karl Friedrich August Gützlaff，中文又译作郭实猎、郭士立、郭甲利、德忌笠、居茨拉夫等。《三国志评论》被"总索引"编者归入第五类"中国历史"（Chinese History），题名 Notice of the *San Kwoh Chi*，or History of the Three States，and its little value as a history. C. G. Vol Ⅶ. 233，题后署名 C. G.，由此分析，这篇文章当出自郭实腊之手。

1803 年 7 月 8 日，郭实腊出生于普鲁士的普立兹镇（Pyritz），1827 年开始到东南亚传教，一生往来于中国内地、香港、澳门、马来、新加坡、泰国等地。他的名声鹊起源于 1831 年、1832 年、1833 年三次沿中国海岸的考察及其《中国沿海三次航行记》（*Journals of Three Voyages along the Coast of China in 1831, 1832 and 1833*），他的冒险精神以及他所提供的大清帝国的末世图景在西方引起了巨大轰动。1840 年第一次鸦片战争期间，郭实腊以翻译、向导及间谍的身份参与了战争及《中英南京条约》签订的全过程。在英军占领定海、宁波、镇海后，还曾先后被委任为三地“民政长官”，成为英帝国侵华的“帮凶”。此后郭实腊长期担任港英政府的中文秘书，直至 1851 年 8 月 9 日病逝并安葬于香港，结束了其富有传奇色彩的一生。纵观郭实腊一生，他既是恪尽职守四处传播福音的传教士，又是面目狰狞狂妄地叫嚣武力侵华的侵略者。

郭实腊是语言的天才、多产的汉学家。除母语德文外，他还懂英文、日文等多国语言，甚至除了中国官话，还通晓广东话、福建话等中国方言。伟烈亚力的《来华新教传教士回忆录》辑录了郭实腊的 85 种著述，其中包括中文著述 61 种、英文著述 9 种、德文著述 7 种、荷兰文著述 5 种、日文著述 2 种、暹罗文著述 1 种。他的著述不仅语种多样，而且内容庞杂，广泛涉及宗教、文化、政治、外交、经济、贸易、历史、地理等各个方面，在许多领域都有骄人的成绩和卓越的贡献。目前学界研究较多的主要有两种：一是 1833 年 8 月郭实腊以“爱汉者”名义在广州一手创办的《东西洋考每月统记传》，该杂志不仅是中国境内出版的最早的中文期刊，而且是中国境内发行的第一种介绍西方文明的刊物，其版式和内容，对此后创办的中文期刊产生了深远影响；二是成书于 1840 年的《贸易通志》，该著既是第一部传入中国介绍西方经济学思想的作品，也是鸦片战争时期中国知识分子了解世界的重要参考资料。

除了上述 85 种作品，伟烈亚力指出：“郭实腊还用英文及别的欧洲语言，为《中国丛报》及其他刊物撰写了许多文章，在他身后还有为编写一部英汉字典而留下的大量手稿。”① 实际上，郭实腊不仅是《中国丛报》的主要撰稿人之一，而且这份期刊的创办甚至也与他密切相关。顾钧、杨慧玲在2008年整理出版的《〈中国丛报〉篇名目录及分类索引》总索引“前言”中说：“促使裨治文办刊的一个更为直接的原因是德国传教士郭实腊的日记。1831年郭实腊不顾清政府的禁令乘船沿中国海岸航行，从曼谷出发直到天津，历时半年（6月至12月），他的日记详细记录了沿途的所见所闻。1832年1月裨治文结识了郭实腊，当时郭实腊刚刚结束了第一次冒险，又在准备第二次冒险（后来又有第三次）。郭实腊的日记引起了裨治文的兴趣，在当时外国人的活动范围只能局限在广州、澳门的情况下，此日记无疑具有很高的资料价值，裨治文希望为这份难得的目击实录尽快提供一个发表的场所。《中国丛报》创刊后，郭实腊的日记以连载的形式与读者见面，成为最初几期的主要文章。”②

据统计，郭实腊在《中国丛报》刊载的文章总计51篇，在类别上，以“中国历史”和“语言文学”两类最多。除了《三国志评论》，“中国历史”门类中明确标注由郭实腊撰写的文章还有6篇，分别是《中国历史著作及作家的特点》（*Character of Chinese Historical Works and Writers*）、《中国历代年表笺注》（*Chronology and Notices of Dynasties in China*）、《南宋志传》（*History of the Southern Sung Dynasty*）、《明史》（*History of the Ming Dynasty*）、《正德皇游江南》（*Rambles of the Emperor Chingtih*）、《平南后传》（*Latter Pacification of the South*）。在第九类“语言文学”（Language，Literature，& c.）中，署名郭实腊的文章共有6篇，分别是《中国经典的特征及概貌》（*Character and Syn-*

---

① Alexander Wylie，*Memorials of Protestant Missionaries to the Chinese*，Shanghae：American Presbyterian Mission Press，1867，p. 66.

② 张西平主编，顾钧、杨慧玲整理：《〈中国丛报〉篇名目录及分类索引》（*List of Articles and Subject Index of Chinese Repository*），广西师范大学出版社2008年版，前言。

opsis of the Chinese Classics)、《书经评论》(*Review of the Shú King, or Book of Records*)、《海国图志》(*Hái-kwoh Tú-chí, or Lin's Geography, called Statistical Notices of the Ocean Kingdoms, with Maps*)、《红楼梦》(*Dreams of the Red Chamber*)、《智囊补》(*Sack of Wisdom, a Story Book*)、《苏东坡作品评论》(*Review of the Works of the Poet Sú Tungpo*)。由以上篇目可以看出，郭实腊对中国历史、中国小说格外青睐，对历史类题材的中国小说更是情有独钟。事实上，除了《三国演义》，上文提到的多数作品，如《红楼梦》《海国图志》等，都是由郭实腊最早或较早介绍给西方读者的。

郭实腊画像

（二）情节取舍与人物重构

郭实腊的《三国志评论》发表之前，英语世界对于《三国演义》的译介屈指可数，仅有马礼逊的简介、汤姆斯翻译的《著名丞相董卓之死》和德庇时翻译的《三国志节译文》。在完整的英译本阙如的情况下，郭实腊首先必须对《三国》故事做一个整体概述，然后再做深入评论。但值得注意的是，《三国志评论》虽然冠之以 Notice 之名，除了开头和结尾的几段“评论”，全文近四分之三的篇幅是对原著内容的整体概述，由此，复述故事喧宾夺主，成为《三国志评论》的主要内容。

《三国演义》人物繁多，情节复杂，郭实腊若想在有限的篇幅内浓缩整部作品殊为不易，因此，大幅度删减情节是《三国志评论》的首要特色。总体看来，郭实腊的介绍基本涵盖了三国历史兴衰始末，只是在前后内容上明显有所侧重，突出的特点是对于“前十回”的概述较为详尽，主要介绍了以下几个情节：灵帝登基、黄巾起义、桃园结义、废立汉帝、诛灭董卓。对于上述情节，郭实腊大致介绍了主要人物与故事脉络，具体细节则殊少涉猎。如“诛灭董卓”一事，十八年前，汤姆斯就已将原著第八回与第九回英译为《著名丞相董卓之死》，发表于《亚洲杂志》，郭实腊却将这两回内容浓缩为以下一段：“经过一番深思熟虑，该派首领很快意识到，董卓是不能被武力征服的。由此，他们选了一个美人让他垮台。美人曲意逢迎，甚得宠幸，同时引起了另一个人的嫉妒，那人是他手下的能吏，也是他收养的义子，这位暴君受诏登基，以证明皇帝遵照他的旨意让位于他。在董卓赶赴皇宫的路上，出现了许多凶兆，但董卓急于得到唾手可得的帝位，继续前行。这时，他的义子，一心想占有义父的宠妾，暗中埋下了伏兵。当朝臣们汇集朝堂之上，董卓正要登上通向宝座的台阶时，伏兵趁其不备进行突袭，他的义子首先给了他致命的一剑。”① 在此，郭实腊只勾勒了美人计的大致轮廓，甚至没有译出王允、貂蝉、吕布之名。“前十回”内容介绍尚且如此简略，此后的情节则更是粗陈梗概。

在中国古代小说中，《三国演义》以擅写战争而著称于世，涉及大小战事 40 余次，官渡之战、赤壁之战等著名战役更是家喻户晓，备受推崇。郭实腊对于《三国》战事却颇不以为然，这突出地表现在他对于相关文字的负面评论上。他说：“接着又开始了一场旷日持久的战争，讲述得索然无味。”又说：“随后的战争细节非常无聊，而且千篇一律；我们可以将它们浓缩成几句话。大约有四到十万大军突然出现，进入战场。如何让士兵们在短短几天之内武装起来，得到训练，并连续数月提供补给，在我们看来是不可能解决的问题。根据天朝现在计算‘无可计数’的方法，我们或许应该把‘数万’读成‘数百’。战争的胜利与否常常取决于几员猛士的威力，他们骑马在前，冲锋陷阵，在经过一番骂阵后，向最勇猛的战将提出单挑，大队人马则全部留在后方踮足观战，看谁取胜。一旦决出胜负，胜者骑马冲进战栗的人群，砍杀和驱逐他们，如同对付一群绵羊。”这些文字，不仅显示了郭实腊对于《三国演义》战争文字的百般厌倦，而且透露了他对当时中国军队虚报人数的嘲讽，以及对古代战将骂阵之风的戏谑。本着这种认识，他大量删去了《三国演义》有关战争的叙述，对于官渡之战就只字未提，赤壁之战也简单概括为以下一段：“战争一场接着一场，曹操想方设法打败玄德，却处处碰壁。孔明的决策使曹操的所有计划均以失败告终。急于打败对手的曹操组建了一支水军，自以为是地认为将来可以借此前后夹击敌人。与此同时，孔明建造了一些火船，里面装满了硫黄、

---

① Charles Gutzlaff, “Notice of the San Kwŏ Che, or History of the Three Kingdoms”, *The Chinese Repository*, Vol. Ⅶ., No. 5 (September 1838), p. 238. 本部分所引《三国志评论》均出自《中国丛报》第 7 卷第 233—249 页，此后不再一一注释。

硝石和其他可燃物，让船顺流而下，直达曹操的船队。曹操所有的船都被点着了，他惊慌失措，几乎丧命。这是一场决定性的胜利，使曹操在很长一段时间里一蹶不振，丧失斗志，与此同时，汉的拥护者却变得越来越强大。"《三国演义》用八回文字描写的战争，在此却只是曹操、诸葛亮角逐的一个片段。

郭实腊在大量删减《三国演义》战争文字的同时，却竭力保留了具有玄幻色彩的情节内容。在概述"小霸王怒斩于吉"时，他以"将军"指称孙策，没有翻译孙策之名，也没有论及其雄才大略。对于道士于吉的呼风唤雨等超凡异能，反而做了详细描述，并进一步评论道："这个细节显示了道教在那时是多么的流行。"在概述"左慈掷杯戏曹操"时，郭实腊对于道士左慈的神奇法术也多有介绍。他说："饮宴时来了一位衣衫褴褛的道士，他扮作术士，表演了许多离奇的法术。桌上神奇地摆满了帝国各处弄来的美味佳肴，曹操被术士非同寻常的道术吓得目瞪口呆。他疑窦顿生，于是下令抓住道士，但哪里也找不到他。很快，又出现了一群装扮相同的人。曹操抓住并杀了他们，但他们又复活过来，猛烈攻击这个十恶不赦的人，打得他无处藏身。丞相被折磨得身染重疾。"在概述"治风疾神医身死"时，其中的个别情节，连中国读者也未必熟悉，郭实腊却不避琐碎，娓娓道来。他说："大约就在这时，曹操决定修建一个新的宫殿。为了得到合适的木材，必须砍伐一棵名贵的树木。尽管有人告诫他这样做过于鲁莽，但他依然坚持己见。当他的命令最终被执行时，这棵树的灵魂——一个淘气的精灵，在他睡觉时使他身负重伤，以报复他的亵渎神灵。"郭实腊对于《三国演义》玄幻情节的敏感，一方面固然是因为这些情节本身的神奇怪异、引人入胜；另一方面则是他身为传教士，对于中国本土宗教充满好奇，对于体现道家法术的道士的言行举止，自然多一分关注与思考。

《三国演义》原著涉及一千余人，著名人物亦不下数十人。郭文篇幅有限，在人物介绍上必然择其精要、有所取舍。考察全文，郭实腊明确译出姓名的三国人物共计 12 人，按出场先后顺序依次为：灵帝、献帝、曹操、孙权、刘备、张角、关羽、张飞、董卓、赵云、孔明、曹丕。对于这些人物，郭实腊并非平均用力，而是集中笔墨介绍了曹操和孔明二人。对于曹操，郭实腊重点译介了他行刺董卓、招募义兵、移驾许都、割发代首、许田打围，以及杀死祢正平、吉太医、董贵妃的故事。对于孔明，则主要介绍了三顾茅庐、赤壁之战、草船借箭、白帝城托孤、七擒孟获、病逝五丈原、真假孔明等情节。中间还穿插了“美髯公千里走单骑”“小霸王怒斩于吉”“刘皇叔洞房续佳偶”等故事。郭实腊以曹操、孔明为焦点，通过介绍二人生平经历的重大事件，不仅塑造了两人各自的形象，而且串联起了魏、蜀、吴三国的兴衰存亡，这两个人物遂成为译者复述《三国》故事的两大支柱。

在对三国人物的评价上，郭实腊基本把握了罗贯中“尊刘贬曹”的思想倾向，对蜀汉人物多有肯定，对曹魏集团则褒贬各半。如，对于孔明，译者极尽赞美之能事，甫一出场，就强调其重要性。文中写道，刘备三顾茅庐后，“孔明就成了《三国》中的主要人物；他的正直、才智、耐心、毅力，以及作为政治家和军事家的天资禀赋，都使他声名远播”。在复述“七擒孟获”前，又云：“这场复杂的战役被描绘得惟妙惟肖，孔明的丰功伟绩体现的智勇双全被叙述得那么完美，以致我们在别的中国史中再难找到可以与之相提并论的篇章。”对于曹操则塑造了其“治世之能臣，乱世之奸雄”的双重个性。如，郭实腊一方面说：“曹操再三宣誓尽忠后，成为皇帝的贴身侍卫，他秉持正义，严以执法，成为摇摇欲坠的皇权的支柱。”另一方面又说：“曹操的功绩以胆量魄力著称于世，为达目的，他会无所顾忌地采用任何卑劣的手段。打仗是他与生俱来的一部分，任何失败都不能抑制他对战争的狂热，其对手能给他的最大惩罚，就是让他平静地生活。”与孔明相比，郭实腊笔下的曹操形象更立体，也更丰满，他是郭文复述《三国》故事的真正主线。

作为中国第一部长篇章回体小说，《三国演义》本身就是一部平面化的小说，书中的人物往往具有一种脸谱化的色彩。郭实腊对此颇有领悟，所以，他笔下的人物，尤其是曹操、孔明之外的人物，大多性格单薄，形象单一。如，对于灵帝，突出了他的孱弱昏聩，不理朝政，以致宦官掌权，卖官鬻爵，造成了国家政治腐败，战乱频仍；对于刘、关、张三人，主要强调其身材之高大，兵器之精良，作战之勇敢，彼此之忠诚；对于董卓，则刻画了他的飞扬跋扈和残忍暴虐，他毒死皇帝、勒死皇后，杀人如麻，嗜血如命，使国家受难、百姓恐慌。

除了以上 12 人，其余的三国人物均没有译出姓氏名号，大多以人物身份或与主角的关系来指称。前者如“皇帝”“将军”“道士”“医生”等；后者如将吕布称为董卓的“义子”，将董承称为皇帝的“亲戚”等。如此，一个个人物被概括成各自的身份，成为推动故事情节发展的棋子。各个角色在一个个身份定位或人事关系中，按部就班，各从其类，自然而然地融为整部巨著的一个组成部分或因果节点。

郭实腊如此省略人物名号，自有其客观原因。一是译者在文中提到：“由于许多人名与地名存在避讳，所以有时令人相当困惑。”由此可见，正确地翻译人名，对于译者来讲显然存在一定难度。二是用人物身份或与主角的关系来取代具体人名，对于一部译作来说也有其自身的合理性。且不说英译的中文人名对于西方读者来说难免拗口，容易影响文章的可读性与流畅性；次要人物过多，枝蔓横生，也容易使故事碎片化，从而破坏故事的整体感与连贯性。这种介绍方式不仅避免了逐一介绍人物的琐碎，也有利于展现故事的整体逻辑。对于概括《三国演义》这样一部线索繁杂的作品来说，删减人物是必要的；对于并不熟悉中国历史的西方读者来说，用身份指代各色人物亦是明智之举。

当然，这样的人物删减和人称指代也为译文带来一些问题，突出地表现在两个方面：一是不少关键人物被严重忽略，如吕布、周瑜、孙策、司马懿等，虽然分别简介了与之相关的美人计、草船借箭、怒杀于吉、三国归晋等情节，但郭实腊不仅没有译出四人姓名，与之相关的更多信息也被完全忽略。二是人物删减过于严重之处，文脉断裂，个别地方难以理解，甚至出现明显误读。如郭文在复述“斩蔡阳兄弟释疑”时说：The reconciliation being thus cemented by blood, the chivalric knight entered the camp of Shaou Yuen。此处 the chivalric knight 显然指的是关羽，但 Shaou Yuen 就难以判断究竟为谁。根据读音，似为“袁绍”，但在郭实腊此前编写的《中国历史概览》（*A Sketch of Chinese History*）中，“袁绍”被拼读为 Yuen Chaou。[①] 根据文意，回译为“赵云”更为妥当。因郭文下一段指出：Shaou Yuen 力图恢复汉家天下，占据四川，故此处唯有理解为“赵云”，才能与后文相符。类似问题虽然数量有限，不至于影响到读者对全文的理解，但郭文三国人物删减严重，不少人物都是一笔带过，由此而使多数人物形象模糊或过于单薄，却是不争的事实。

（三）译者评价与译介缘由

郭实腊是西方文化史上系统评价《三国演义》的第一人，也是给予该作充分肯定的欧洲人。《三国志评论》主要内容是复述原著，对于该作的评论，主要集中在郭文的开头三段和结尾四段，此外，文中还穿插着大量即兴评论。整体看来，郭实腊对于《三国演义》的评论具有以下几个特点。

第一，郭实腊对于《三国演义》的创作年代存在很大误会，但对其核

---

① Charles Gutzlaff, *A Sketch of Chinese History, Ancient and Modern*, London: Smith, Elder and Co., Cornhill, Booksellers to their majesties, 1834, p. 265.

心内容的整体把握和概括却大致准确。他认为《三国》出版于1400年前的汉代，这一时期，文学复兴，学者受到前所未有的尊重，大批民族史家应运而生，写作的狂热随之而起。“在这个奥古斯都时代（Augustan epoch），三国成为一个奇谈；天才的著述者似乎获得了神力，他尽力把虚构与史实巧妙地糅合在一起，以彻底吸引读者的注意力。《三国》展现了公元170年至317年间最真实的画卷，这一时期三国（San Kwŏ）兴起。为取悦读者，全文穿插了各种各样的奇闻逸事，夸大其词，迷惑其说。它讲述了汉朝最后两位皇帝——灵帝和献帝（Ling te and Heën te），是怎样因为他们的软弱无能和荒淫无度而使国家陷入一片混乱；结果其中的一员大将曹操（Tsaou Tsaou），如何名义上为天子作战实际上却为魏国打造基础，与此同时孙权（Sun Keuen）建立了吴国，最后是汉朝的一位后裔刘备（Lew Pei）建立了蜀国，又称后汉，直到一位新的野心勃勃的统治者以晋朝（Tsin Dynasty）的名义统一了三国（公元279）。”《三国演义》叙事始于建宁二年（169），终于孙皓降晋（280），郭实腊的时间定位虽有错乱，但对三国的建立与主要人物的概述却简洁而精确。

第二，郭实腊对《三国演义》的文学性给予高度评价，将之推许为中国文学的典范之作。他说“在所有的中国文学作品中，没有哪部作品像《三国》那样风靡天下。人们不分年龄老幼、学识高下，无不对之交口称赞。社会各阶层都认为这是有史以来最有趣的一部书；其风格、语言、叙述方式都无可挑剔。作为一部杰作，它在文学史上无与伦比。”又说：“本书描写占领京城、胜者凯旋，以及军队出发前普遍的恐惧、作战策略、统治者的怯懦的段落，值得仔细精读，而且确实是中国才子的典范之作。作者越是涉及大灾大难，语言就越是有力，情感也更为悲怆。没有谁在仔细阅读过这部作品之后不对书中的事件留下深刻的印象，它们在眼前一闪而过，最后形成一个宏伟的结局，即一个统一的君主政体。”文章的结尾处，郭实腊进一步肯定说：“我们确信，没有哪个读过中国作品的人，会否认这个已被普遍接受的观点，即《三国志》是中国最优秀的作品之一。”整体看来，郭实腊对于《三国演义》的推崇可谓史无前例、空前绝后。

第三，郭实腊对于《三国演义》并非一味褒扬，而是有所批评和否定，这是他评论《三国》之初就自觉树立的观念。他说：“我们若想轻易否定这部作品的卓越，就如同断言荷马（Homer）不是诗人，而塔西佗（Tacitus）也不是历史学家；但是尽管受到天朝大国的很大影响，我们还是发现了这部完美之作的某些瑕疵。”在他看来，“瑕疵”集中在两个方面，一是对于该作战争文字的否定。他说：“其中有些章节非常枯燥乏味，经常重复，而另一些章节除了编号、军队的行进和撤退外就别无内容。但是每当作者描写国内的场景，或者离开战场而把读者带入皇宫和朝廷时，他的痛快爽利似乎就成了他最大的优势，我们越是跟着他深入细节，就越能发现其措辞的优美。”二是对于《三国》文体风格之局限性的认识。他说：“这部作品可以被看作历史著述文体风格的典范，但绝不能把它当成一切作品的榜样。书中几乎找不到集中描写自然的段落，它是对生活在那个时代的、具有各种情感及恶习的人的记录。同样的措辞经常反复出现，这本书与其说是以辞采华茂名扬天下，不如说是因简洁精练而著称于世。”

第四，在复述三国故事时，郭实腊大部分时间是个冷静的讲述者，但某些时候，他也主动充当了一个不太安分的评论者，对《三国》的艺术成就、叙述风格等，时常加以评点。如论及董卓废帝时，他不由地发出感叹，说：“所有这一切讲述得都很精彩，一些段落确实令人赞叹。”论及锦囊计时，郭实腊又禁不住发出评论：“《三国》中的上述内容叙述简洁，措辞优美，超过了本书的其他部分。”讲到孔明之死时，又说：“作者以一种无比悲惨的语言讲述了他临终前的场景，十分值得认真细读（公元223年）。”这些评点，一方面源于阅读的冲动，另一方面或许是受了所读《三国》版本的启发。细读郭文，不难发现他所阅读的版本是评注本《三国演义》，他说：“学习汉语的人会发现在每章的开头有对前一章内容所作的评注，文中也穿插了大量评论，通过这种方式来吸引读者，同时引导着读者去仔细思考叙述的精美。”在中国评论者的启发下，为了有效地吸引西方读者，郭实腊对《三国演义》的评点，几乎贯穿了故事复述的始末。

第五，作为一个跨语际、跨文化的阅读者，郭实腊对于三国人物天然地具有一种西方的视角和比较的眼光，这使他的人物评论别具特色。比如，他把曹操比作丹东，说：“曹操像法国恐怖时期的丹东（Danton）那样受到爱戴，只是他所依仗的更多的不是民心，而是士兵们手里的刀剑。”丹东作为法国大革命时雅各宾派的领袖人物，受启蒙思想家孟德斯鸠、卢梭等人影响，尊重民权，崇尚自由，力主废黜国王，实行共和。但雅各宾派专政后，他支持恐怖政策，开始大肆屠杀政敌，这与曹操确有相似之处。这种比较，也使郭实腊摆脱了中国传统的正朔观念和忠奸之论，为世人理解曹操提供了一种新的可能。在复述“美髯公千里走单骑”时，他把关羽比作法兰西国王法拉蒙德（Pharamond），说关羽“像个真正的游侠骑士那样，不顾一切，奋勇向前；谁挡了他的路，都注定会死；甚至他的名字都让人不寒而栗，最勇猛的军队听了也会闻风丧胆。这些丰功伟绩，被讲述得像法拉蒙德的罗曼史那样有趣”。这种比较，一方面凸显了关羽骁勇善战、所向披靡，同时也强调了三国故事的虚构性和趣味性。此外，第一个尝试着全译《三国演义》的英国人邓罗（C. H. Brewitt-Taylor，1857—1938）将书名译作 *Romance of the Three Kingdoms*，不知是否受了文中所提之“法拉蒙德的罗曼史”（the romance of Pharamond）的启发。

郭实腊之所以撰写《三国志评论》，与他对中国历史和中国小说的研究密切相关。

第一，从史学的角度来看，郭实腊对于中国历史情有独钟，1838 年撰写《三国志评论》之前，郭实腊已对中国历史有了全面系统的研究。1834 年，他撰写的《中国历史概览》在伦敦出版。在这本英文专著中，郭实腊把中国历史划分为四个阶段：“三皇五帝”构成的“神话时期”（mythological era）、夏商周秦汉构成的“古代时期”（ancient history，B. C. 2207 to A. D. 263）、魏晋唐宋元构成的“中世纪”（history of the middle ages，A. D. 264 to 1367），以及明清以来的“现代时期”（modern history，A. D. 1368 to 1833）。在述及汉代后期历史时，郭实腊明显受《三国演义》影响，先后提及灵帝、张角、张让、袁绍、李儒、董卓、献帝、蔡邕、曹操等人。在简单介绍董卓之死、曹丕代汉、刘备建蜀后，具体情节没再展开，接着隆重推出了《三国演义》，说：“中国最流行的一部作品，是一部历史小说，名叫《三国》，即三个国家，该著为无情的怒火引发的战争提供了一幅真实画卷。尽管其细节格外枯燥，并且还掺杂着虚构，但中国人却把这部作品看作是那个英雄时代的礼仪的真实画卷。其后诞生了‘三国’之名，意谓三个国家；因为汉、魏、吴这三个国家争夺王权，互相不承认对方的主公凌驾在自家之上。”[①] 由此可见，撰写《三国志评论》之前，郭实腊对于《三国演义》已有所涉猎，甚至将之作为正史加以引用。

第二，从文学的角度来看，郭实腊对于中国小说，尤其是历史小说和英雄传奇格外看重，1838 出版的《中国开门》（*China Opened*）充分显示了他的这一阅读嗜好。在这部英文专著中，有一节标题为“中国小说”（Works of Fiction），但实际内容却主要是介绍《三国演义》及其他历史小说和英雄传奇。郭实腊说：“历史写作方式的枯燥乏味，阅读人名时的兴趣索然，以及大量的时代纪年，很早就促使中国作家，具有了用历史小说来讲述事件的观念。《三国志》，或曰三个国家的历史，似乎给这类作品提供了第一次动力。尽管它描述的是一小段历史，即三国争霸时，但其内容却为我们提供了当时的一幅生动画卷。我们与英雄们生活在一起，我们对这些人变得熟悉起来，我们了解到那么早的时期中国人就完成了什么；我们被

① Charles Gutzlaff，*A Sketch of Chinese History*，*Ancient and Modern*，London：Smith，Elder and Co.，Cornhill，Booksellers to their majesties，1834，pp. 269 – 270.

带入宫廷，进入各个家族内部。凡虚构之作，无论怎样夸大其词，人们还是能够轻而易举地把叙事和故事区分开来。每个朝代都有类似的作品；每个伟人都能找到他的传记，每次灾难也都有其虚构者。尽管其间有许多垃圾，但也有许多优秀之作，每个外国人，若想写一部优秀的中国史，都应去阅读它们。”① 郭实腊指出，这类作品若列举起来，可以提供一个长达几页的书目。于是，他择其要者列出四种，包括两种历史小说：《平南传》（*The Ping-nan-chuen*）和《周传》（*The Chow chuĕn*）；两种英雄传奇：《群英杰传》（*The Keun-ying-keĕ-chuen*）和《萃忠传》（*The Tsuy-chung-chuen*）。

除了历史小说与英雄传奇，郭实腊将其他小说一并归为“普通小说”（common novels）之列，他说：“普通小说人手一册。许多作品粗俗不堪，其中，《十才子》（Shih-tsae-tsze）（十个才子的呕心沥血之作）是一套精选的小说合集，其中有一部作品让人读了不寒而栗。如果这个民族的道德情况真的堕落到百姓贩卖人肉的地步，恶心至此而不战栗，那么他们就远远落在食人族的后面了。但我们相信，这只是某个荒谬作家杜撰的一部小说。这些放肆的作品遭到政府的禁绝；但是由于它们的内容刺激着人们堕落的胃口，反而使阅读变得更加贪婪。”② 此处郭实腊将《十才子》解释为“十个才子的呕心沥血之作”（the lucubrations of the ten talented men），这种理解大致是准确的，但在同年发表的《三国志评论》中，他又把《十才子》错误地解释为“十个天才的儿子”（The Ten Sons of Genius），由此可见他对于中国小说的整体认识实际上还比较肤浅。从郭实腊对于“中国小说”的介绍顺序、分类模式及褒贬态度来看，他对历史小说和英雄传奇的重视要远远高于“普通小说”。职是之故，作为历史小说的翘楚之作，他在《中国丛

---

① Charles Gutzlaff, *China Opened*; *or*, *A Display of the Topography*, *History*, *Customs*, *Manners*, *Arts*, *Manufactures*, *Commerce*, *Literature*, *Religion*, *Jurisprudence*, *etc. of the Chinese Empire*, Vol. Ⅰ., London: Smith, Elder and Co. 65, Cornhill, 1838, pp. 467 – 468.

② Ibid., p. 468.

报》上首先译介《三国演义》也就不难理解了。

第三，除了《三国演义》，郭实腊还是第一个向英语世界的读者系统推介《红楼梦》和《聊斋志异》的早期汉学家，能够同时成为这三部经典小说的推介者，除了卓越的文学洞察力，应该与他对中国民间阅读倾向的观察与调研密切相关。比如，1842 年 4 月《中国丛报》第 11 卷第 4 期发表了郭实腊撰写的《聊斋志异》译介文，概述了《祝翁》《张诚》《曾友于》《续黄粱》等 9 篇聊斋故事，虽然译者把《聊斋志异》看作一部“道教传奇”（Extraordinary Legends of the Táuist），或者说是一部宣讲“道家信条”（the doctrines of the Táu sect）的异教读物，对其中的佛道思想不以为然，却注意到这部小说在民间备受欢迎。他说：“由中国人手上的许多副本推断，我们认为《聊斋志异》是一部相当流行的作品。中国人在闲暇时喜欢翻阅此类作品，并开怀大笑，尽管他们最初装作并不相信它们。”[①] 郭实腊在同年 5 月第 5 期《中国丛报》上发表的《红楼梦》译介文中表达了类似的看法。虽然他认为《红楼梦》除了闺阁琐谈几乎空洞无物，就艺术性而言更是乏善可陈，但发现：“在中国小说中，这部力作享有很高声誉。”[②] 由此可见，在郭实腊看来，推荐中国人喜欢的作品，正视他们真实的阅读趣味，似乎比衡量和裁定这些作品自身的思想性和艺术性更为重要。所以，尽管他认为《聊斋志异》和《红楼梦》不足称道，但既然其在民间广受欢迎，也就有了向西方读者推介的必要。《三国演义》不仅具有历史价值和文学价值，而且像《聊斋志异》和《红楼梦》那样在民间老少咸宜、风靡天下，自然更有推介的必要，这或许是郭实腊在众多的中国文学作品中首推《三国演义》的重要原因。

---

① Charles Gutzlaff, “Liáu Chái Í Chí, or Extraordinary Legends from Liáu Chái”, *The Chinese Repository*, Vol. XI, No. 4, 1842, p. 202.

② Charles. Gutzlaff, “Dreams in the Red Chamber”, *The Chinese Repository*, Vol. XI., No. 5, 1842, p. 266.

（四）《三国志评论》的影响与价值

作为英语世界第一篇全面评论《三国演义》的文章，郭实腊的《三国志评论》对于《三国演义》乃至中国小说的早期海外传播产生了重要影响。

首先，郭实腊译介的三国情节和人物，成为19世纪西方汉学家阅读和翻译《三国演义》的首选内容。比如，“小霸王怒斩于吉”出自《三国演义》第29回，自郭实腊提及后，遂成为19世纪英语世界反复译介的桥段。1852年，艾约瑟编译的《汉语会话》共翻译了三部中文作品：一是清代戏曲选集《缀白裘》中的“高腔”《借靴》；二是《琵琶记》中的《吃糠》《描容》《别坟》《寺中遗像》《两贤相遘》《书馆》；三是《三国演义》第29回，即“小霸王怒斩于吉”。此外，邓罗1925年出版英译《三国志演义》（*San kuo, or Romance of the Three Kingdoms*）全译本之前，曾尝试着翻译过几个章节片段，其中之一即《孙策之死》（*The Death of Sun Tse*），刊于《中国评论》1889年第18卷第3期。艾约瑟和邓罗这两位19世纪著名汉学家关注“于吉”这样一位三国时代的“小人物”，与此前郭实腊对于《三国演义》的褒扬以及对第29回内容的早期译介应该有着直接的关系。

其次，郭实腊是第一次鸦片战争前译介中国历史小说最多的传教士汉学家，仅在《中国丛报》上发表的相关评论文就有4篇，除了《三国演义》，另有《平南后传》《正德皇游江南》和《南宋志传》三种。《平南后传》的译介，显然受了《三国演义》的影响，郭实腊开篇即云：“《三国志》（*The San Kwŏ Che*）如此广受推崇，作者之名在中国人中如此备受追捧，致使这种写作模式很快有了众多的模仿者。眼下的这部作品即属此类，虽然它远不及《三国志》这一典范之作，但也不失为一部值得外国人关注的中国才子的不朽之作（*a monument of Chinese genius*）。"①《平南后传》这部"平庸之作"因模仿《三国演义》，竟被郭实腊推许为"不朽之作"。这种对于历史小说的溢美之词在他译介的《南宋志传》中有增无减。他说："我们发现这本书的一个缺点是它并没有像其标题所显示的那样涵盖南宋王朝的历史。但它却是我们读过的最有趣的一本中国书。其文体不仅简洁明晰，而且显示了无与伦比的美，或许可以被看作优秀创作的一个典范之作。"② 由此可见，郭实腊对于历史小说的偏爱，使这类题材自身获得了某种评价功能，是不是一部历史小说或者一部"名副其实"的历史小说，成了衡量一部小说优劣的前提和标准。像《南宋志传》这样一部略微"名不副实"的历史小说，但凡进入历史小说的行列，就不难让郭实腊发现其文体的诸多优点。

再者，郭实腊对于《三国演义》等中国历史小说的褒扬，明显影响了其他来华西士对这类题材的认识，从而推动了某些历史小说的海外传播。如《正德皇游江南》序于"道光壬辰季秋"，即 1832 年秋天，1840 年 6 月，郭实腊就在《中国丛报》上对这部"最新出版"（the newest book）的中国小说做了内容简介，标题为 *Chingtih hwang Yew Keängnan*：*The Rambles of the emperor Chingtih in Keängnan*。他说："这部小说囊括了正德统治时期最初六年的历史，与史实高度吻合，但又比枯燥的史料更为有趣。"③ 郭实腊的这篇书评显然引起了来华西士的广泛关注，其中最著名的就是以英译"四书五经"著称于世的英国汉学家理雅各（James Legge，1815—1897）。1842 年 1 月，为了让马六甲英华书院（Anglo-Chinese College）的学生何进善（Tkin

① Charles Gutzlaff，"Ping Nan How Chuen，or an account of the Latter Pacification of the South"，*The Chinese Repository*，Vol. Ⅻ.，No. 10，1838，p. 281.

② Charles Gutzlaff，"History of the Southern Sung Dynasty"，*The Chinese Repository*，Vol. Ⅺ.，No. 10，1842，p. 540.

③ Charles Gutzlaff，"Chingtih hwang Yew Keängnan：The Rambles of the emperor Chingtih in Keängnan"，*The Chinese Repository*，Vol. Ⅸ.，No. 6，1842，p. 73.

Shen，1817—1871）提高英语，进而翻译深奥的《书经》（Shoo King），理雅各先让他尝试着翻译《正德皇游江南》这部中国小说。何进善的翻译工作进展相当顺利，一年后，理雅各作序的英文全译本《正德皇游江南》（*The Rambles of the Emperor Ching Tĭh in Këang Nan*）就在英国伦敦出版了。其译名与郭实腊的译法如出一辙。在“序言”中，理雅各也像郭实腊那样强调了这部作品的历史价值。他说：“我们发现这个故事像欧洲的大多数历史小说那样于史有据。宦官的阴谋、他们对于幼主的引诱以及反叛者的暴乱，这些与当前的中国历史全部一致。所以，相比于从其他自诩为更加优秀的作品中可能获得的信息，这部作品将有助于传达一个有关中国朝廷和皇帝地位的更加准确的观念。”① 正是因为有了郭实腊的译介，《正德皇游江南》这种平庸的历史小说，才在问世后十年就顺利完成了英译文全译本，很快出现在西方读者面前。

整体看来，尽管郭实腊的《三国志评论》一文存在某些细节上的错误和文化上的误读，对于《三国演义》艺术成就的某些评价也不够恰当，但他对于该作内容的整体概括和把握却是比较准确的，字里行间也渗透着对这部作品的肯定与赞赏。关注和研究《三国演义》这样的历史小说，对于郭实腊这些来华西士而言是一种语言能力的体现和文化品格的提升，正如他自己所言，对《三国演义》的阅读，可以显示当时的来华西士“对于这样一部产生久远，又确实非常优秀的文学作品，我们既非漠不关心，也非视而不见”。另外，经过郭实腊的大力推介，《三国演义》等历史小说在清代来华西士中获得了广泛认同，在当时几乎造就了历史小说一枝独秀的文体神话，这对于中国小说的早期海外传播意义重大。

---

① *The Rambles of the Emperor Ching Tĭh in Këang Nan*, translated by Tkin Shen, Student of the Anglo-Chinese College, Malacca, with a preface by James Legge, D. D. President of the College, London: Longman and Co. A. K. Newman & Co. , Leadenhall Street, 1843, Vol. Ⅰ. , Preface Ⅶ.

附：英文原文

ART. I. *Notice of the San Kwŏ Che, or History of the Three Kingdoms, during a period of one hundred and forty-seven years, from A. D. 170 to 317.* From a Correspondent. ①

Amongst all the works of Chinese literature none is so popular as the San Kwŏ. It is read by old and young, admired by the learned, and praised by the ignorant. All classes agree that it is the most interesting book ever written; that its style, language, and the manner in which the events are recorded, can never enough be lauded; and that it is a masterpiece, peerless in the annals of literature. It was therefore placed at the head of a series of works, called the *Sheih Tsae Tsze*, the Ten Sons of Genius; these are standard literary productions, which form a library of amusing reading. We might as easily assert that Homer was no poet, and Tacitus no historian, as disprove the excellency of this production; yet though considerably under the transforming influence of the celestial empire, we discover some blemishes in this most perfect of books. The reader will forgive us, that our barbari-

① "*Notice of the San Kwŏ Che*", *The Chinese Repository*, Vol. Ⅶ., From May, 1838 to April, 1839, Canton: Printed for the Proprietors, pp. 233–249.

an ideas often differ from those of the sons of Han, but at the same time he may take our word, that we are not indifferent or blind in regard to a literature which has been the work of so many ages, and which has surely great excellencies.

When we consider that this composition was published nearly fourteen centuries ago, we shall by no means hesitate to admit, that the literary genius of the Chinese was developed at a very early period. But it is a melancholy fact, that subsequently, during the lapse of so many ages, nothing similar has been produced. The histories written by the most learned scholars of the empire, are generally dry and often uninteresting, so that they moulder on the shelves, whilst the San Kwŏ is perused by every one who knows just a sufficient number of characters to read a common book. Though the work consists of no less than 24 volumes, there are few people who do not read it more than once. It is a disgrace, even amongst the illiterate classes, not to be conversant with the facts related in it. We have often been in company with Chinese who dwelt with delight, perhaps for the tenth time, upon the exploits of the heroes in times of yore. Their poetry, and even their serious writings, are enlivened by allusions to the San Kwŏ, and both temples as well as private houses are adorned with pictures which represent the famous actions of the principal generals, or the battles whereby the fate of empires was decided. Some of the worthies of those times have been deified, and constitute objects of adoration to this very day.

The editor in his introduction endeavors to give a just idea of the work, by praising its excellencies, and dwelling upon the extraordinary personages whose history fills the pages of this book. China having enjoyed the advantages of a fixed system of government since Confucius, was just emerging from barbarism, when Che hwangte made an end of the feudal system, by uniting in the third century before Christ, all the states under his sceptre. At once a warrior and legislator, he wished to excel his predecessors, and being aware that the Confucian system would deaden the naturally free spirit of the people, he annihilated with an unsparing hand the literature of his country. It may however be supposed, that his most strenuous endeavors could only partially succeed in such an extensive empire, where so many thousands of copies were dispersed; but he appears to have for a time directed the attention of the nation to more important pursuits than the mere perusal of ancient books. Scarcely, however, had the Han princes (B. C. 202) taken possession of the throne, when they became the most munificent patrons of classical lore. Literature soon revived, and scholars were never more highly esteemed than during their reign. It was then that the first national historians flourished, and the mania for writing became as general as it is in our times in the west. To this Augustan epoch, the San Kwŏ forms the episode; genius had then obtained its greatest strength and seemed to exhaust itself in this one effort of blending fiction and historical truth so artfully as to take entire possession of the reader's mind. The San Kwŏ gives a most faithful picture of the period A. D. 170 – 317 during which time three kingdoms (San Kwŏ) flourished, and for the sake of amusing the reader intersperses sundry anecdotes, and exaggerates or mystifies the incidents. It recounts, how the two last reigning Han princes, Ling te and Heën te, threw the empire into anarchy by their weakness and dissolute habits; how subsequently one of the generals, Tsaou Tsaou, whilst nominally fighting for the emperor, laid the foundation of the Wei state, whilst Sun Keuen gave rise to the kingdom of Woo, and finally Lew Pei, a scion of the Han dynasty, obtained the sway of Shuh, sometimes called the How Han empire, until a new enterprising chief united all three (A. D. 279,) under the name of the Tsin dynasty. Such are in short the contents of the wonderful book. We now enter into details.

When Ling te ascended the throne (A. D. 168), he thought it far more easy to spend the greater part of his days amongst the eunuchs and women of his harem than to take the reins of government in his own hands. His confidants were the most degraded of the country, and amongst them the eunuchs held all the lucrative offices of government. From this voluptuous stupor, the monarch was roused by the appearance of a green serpent, which was gliding down the rafters, just when he was in the act of giving audience. The monster disappeared, but immediately afterwards the capital suffered by an earthquake, and the sea made large inroads into the maritime provinces. These and many other portentous signs struck the weak prince with terror; he inquired about the causes, but received from his ministers evasive answers. Misrule brought the people to despair, a leader only was wanting to head the revolt, and he was soon found.

There lived at that time three brothers who possessed considerable literary talents. Infectious diseases had just spread amongst the people, and they went out to gather herbs in order to render medical assistance. Whilst thus engaged, they met a genius, who holding to the eldest three books, said, 'Great is the science these volumes contain, go renovate the empire and extensively administer relief to the people. Yet if you harbor a wayward heart, your reward will be evil.' Satisfied with these enigmatical words, Chang Keŏ① the elder brother busily studied the scrolls, and from hence learned to raise the wind and call forth rain. During the prevalence of the plague he restored the sufferers by administering some water over which he pronounced a spell. Being very successful in his practice, his followers grew rapidly in numbers, and conceived the idea of gaining possession of the empire by erecting a yellow standard. The emperor having received timely notice of their treasonable purpose seized some of their adherents, and either decapitated

① 编者按：此处人名后缺一逗号。

them or put them into prison. This roused the spirit of the leaders, they organized their armies, and, as they wore yellow caps, or rather handkerchiefs, to be distinguished from the imperialists, they were known as a distinct party, under the name of the Yellow Caps. Thus opens the great drama, and from this moment the sword was never sheathed.

Whilst the imperial mind was still wavering what measures to adopt, three heroes, Lew Pei, more generally known under the name of Heuen-tih (a relation of the Han dynasty), Kwan Yu, and Chang Fei, came forth as by magic, swore, in a peach-garden after having sacrificed a black cow and a white horse, eternal fidelity to each other, and invoked heaven and earth to witness their engagement. They were giants of their race, of an uncommon stature, and endowed with all the qualities for becoming great heroes. Having procured for themselves some horses, and manufactured immense swords, which Goliath would hardly have been able to wield, they met 30, 000 Yellow Caps, with about a thousand only of their own followers. Now it was very evident to them, that this would be a very unequal combat, and Heuentih therefore rode forward to abuse these outlaws, a business in which Chinese heroes greatly excel. Thus the affair might have ended, but happily their long swords served them this time; he cut down the leader, and the rest immediately dispersed. Their subsequent career was a series of brilliant victories, the Yellow Caps were routed in every engagement, and though they availed themselves occasionally of their power to raise the wind and envelop the hostile armies in impenetrable darkness, they were beaten in every battle.

The court was in the meanwhile occupied with the most frivolous pursuits. Those brave men who had bled for their country, after having announced the signal victories they obtained over the rebels, were sent back to spend their lives in obscurity, or denounced as dangerous plotters. The eunuchs resumed the full power, sold the most important offices to the highest bidder, and surrounded the emperor so completely, that nobody could obtain access to him. Scarcely therefore was the rebellion of the Yellow Caps quelled, when new swarms of robbers disturbed the peace of the country. The emperor whilst sitting amongst his eunuchs enjoying himself, was informed of these disasters. Being deeply touched with the recital, he died apparently of grief (189).

Some of the most celebrated generals scarcely noticing the death of their sovereign, determined immediately upon the entire extirpation of this brood of vipers; yet only one had sufficient courage to face these formidable courtiers. To punish him for his audacity, they cut off his head and hung it from the window of the palace. This atrocity so much incensed the partisans of the general, that they set fire to the imperial residence, and with drawn swords rushing into the flames, exterminated the whole race of parasites. The sight exhibited to the spectators was dreadful; some were thrown out of the windows and smashed to pieces on the pavement, whilst others pierced with murderous weapons sunk shrieking into the flames. All was horror and consternation, and the young emperor scarcely escaped with his life.

The sword being once drawn was not so soon to be sheathed. Violent means once employed, if proving successful, render a similar course henceforth necessary. The sacredness of the court was violated, and the grandeur surrounding the throne profaned, and the young monarch was no longer secure in his harem. Whilst the palace was all in flames, he fled with his brother, not knowing whither he went. The night coming on, he lost himself in a thicket, and deeply bewailing his lot, threw himself down on the ground. When lo! what should happen, a swarm of fire flies darted forth and lighted the way to a farm. Here he was well entertained, and on the following morning was met by some courtiers who conducted him back to the palace. Intrigue was here immediately set on foot to dethrone him, and one of the generals, an unprincipled violent man, whose aid had been invoked for the destruction of the eunuchs, declared that such a young popinjay ought not to reign. Having overcome the party opposed to his views, either by the sword or by bribes, he deposed the emperor in an open assembly, after an ephemeral reign of five months, and raised his brother, afterwards named Heën te, to the throne. The imperial captive deeply bewailed his lot, and in the anguish of his heart composed some stanzas, in which he envied the freedom of the twittering swallow, and called for an avenger of his wrongs. This was considered high treason by the general; he sent therefore a cup of poisoned wine to the emperor, which he forced him to swallow, whilst his minion threw the empress dowager from the upper story of the palace, and afterwards commanded the soldiers to strangle her. All this is related with great spirit, and some of the passages are really sublime.

Tung Chŏ having raised his protcge to the throne, now gave entire vent to his cruelties. The capital Loyang was depopulated, in order to remove the court to Changngan, and the monster strung up 2000 heads as a trophy, to strike terror into the nation. The nobles wept at the misfortunes of their country, and none dared to murmur, because it was a reign of terror, and to fall under the suspicion of the tyrant was certain death.

There lived at that time a man of the name of Tsaou Tsaou, who had signalized himself in the war against the Yellow Caps, and being equally brave and intriguing laughed at the useless whining of his fellow-officers. He possessed all the requisites for becoming a tyrant, and conscious of his high qualities he resolved upon the ruin of Tung Chŏ. Having first insinuated himself into his favor, and failed in an attempt to assassinate him, he returned on a swift charger, the present of the general, to his native country, and in a short time raised a considerable army, by inviting all the worthies of those times to his banners. The very commencement of his career was marked with blood, he killed a whole family who had hospitably received him when he was a fugitive, and in the first battle satiated his desire for carnage. But his objects being decidedly patriotic, he was as much caressed as Danton during the reign of terror in France, yet he relied more on the sword of his soldiers than upon popularity. His first efforts to overthrow Tung Chŏ proved ineffectual, he was routed and the generals of the patriotic host begun to quarrel with each other. Upon mature reflection the leaders of this faction easily perceived, that Tung Chŏ could not be subdued by force of arms. A beautiful woman was therefore chosen to effect his ruin. Having ingratiated herself in his good graces, and roused the jealousy of one of his most able officers, his own adopted son, the overbearing tyrant was summoned to the presence of his sovereign, in order to witness the act of abdication in his favor. On his way to the palace, many sinister omens happened, but Tung Chŏ pressed forward eager to obtain the crown which was in his grasp. Here his own son, anxious to possess the concubine of his adopted father, had stationed soldiers in ambush. Whilst the courtiers were assembled in the hall of audience, and Tung Chŏ just on the point of ascending the stairs, they pounced upon their unwary victim, his son aiming the first death blow.

The partisans of this monster however came to revenge their leader. They did not at first succeed in their efforts, but all on a sudden they routed their antagonists and approached the capital. Here the weak emperor was obliged to dissemble and ennoble the rebel leaders. A new struggle soon ensued, and it was very doubtful who would obtain the mastery. At this juncture, Tsaou Tsaou again entered the arena of military fame. He waited until the contending parties had weakened one another by hard fought battles, and, improving upon those troublesome times, led a host of desperadoes into the field in order to take possession of the empire. Being informed of the miserable situation of his sovereign, he immediately offered his assistance. The capital had become a scene of desolation, the courtiers had been dispersed, the grass grew in the very courts of the palace, and the few remaining followers of the monarch had not sufficient money to buy horses in order to meet Tsaou Tsaou, who was on his way to proffer his promised aid. Having made a great many professions of loyalty, he secured the person of the emperor, executed rigid justice, and became the prop of a tottering throne. Stern and unrelenting, his words were commands, and the leaders of the various factions trembled, whenever he threatened to avenge the wrongs of his sovereign. As however there were many who were actuated by similar motives of usurpation, and had gained military renown in hard fought battles, Tsaou's wishes for aggrandizement met only with partial success. Equally impetuous in all his actions, he had once nearly lost his life by spending his time with a dissolute woman, and neglecting the cares of his camp. Aroused by the imminent danger that surrounded him, he again launched forward like a lion, and beat his enemies wherever he met them. His discipline was very severe. On one occasion he had prohibited his soldiers to trample upon the fields of wheat, which were then ripe for harvest, under pain of decapitation. He was the first who unwittingly transgressed this ordinance, and being reminded by his officers of his blunder, he drew his sword in order to stab himself to atone for the misdemeanor. Being however withheld from committing suicide, he cut off his hair and strewing it upon the ground remarked, this may serve instead of my head. By this act he obtained a greater sway over the soldiery than by the most splendid victory. A protracted campaign shortly ensued, which is very uninterestingly told. Tsaou remaining master of the field, returned in triumph to the capital. He had been nominated prime minister and commander-in-chief with the title of duke, and in fact ruled the empire. Having once gone out with the emperor hunting, he offended the courtiers by arrogating to himself the honor of having shot a stag, and a conspiracy was entered into against him. The monarch himself, loath to be any longer under the tutelage of such a man wrote an order with his own blood, commanding his faithful servants to execute vengeance upon Tsaou Tsaou. This paper he concealed in a girdle, and made a present of it to one of his relations. The plot against his life was in consequence soon arranged, but the execution deferred until a convenient opportunity should occur.

One very naturally asks, where were the heroes all this while who quelled the rebellion of the Yellow Caps? After their victories they were undecided what party to choose, and seeing their former companion in arms, Tsaou Tsaou, at the head of the administration, they gradually joined his fortunes. Heuentih was at court, when one of his relations requested him to enter into the conspiracy against the magnate. Being unwilling to refuse such a request, but overcautious to commit himself, he accepted, with Chang Fei, another of the heroes, the command of an army against the remaining rebels. Having defeated them, he thought it very dangerous to throw himself upon the mercy of Tsaou Tsaou, and therefore joined one of his antagonists, to resist his aggressions, and if possible to free the country from the usurper. —The prime minister lay sick on his bed when this fatal news reached his ears. Excited by such an unforeseen misfortune, he recovered as if by magic, but instead of crushing the insurgents by a bold stroke, he set down for the first time in his life to philosophize with a sage about the maxims of good government. To free himself from the importunities of his politician, he sent him with a message to a rough warrior. Here he commenced as customary to discourse upon the principles of wisdom, but offended this gruff son of war so much, that he had him decapitated.

The leader of the conspiracy had in the meanwhile fallen dangerously ill. A physician, summoned to administer medical aid, heard in the incoherent ravings of his patient the outline of the plot. He immediately promised his aid in the execution of his design, by giving Tsaou Tsaou a dose of poison, and in token of the sincerity of his professions he bit off his finger. Unfortunately the conversation was overheard by some slaves. Their master, suspicious of their having gotten the wind of this secret, wished first to kill them, but was dissuaded from committing this cruel act by his wife. He therefore put them into chains. One of them however broke loose during the night, and went directly to the minister to inform him what he had heard. Tsaou Tsaou, therefore, feigned sickness and requested that physician to attend him. When the prescription was prepared, he wanted to force the doctor to drink first of it, but he smashed the phial on the ground. He was tortured in the most excruciating manner, yet betrayed nobody. The statesman sent immediately a general invitation to the principal courtiers, and amongst them were all the conspirators except one; the leech having been led into their presence and anew put on the rack, remained immoveable, and finally threw himself down the stairs and was crushed to death. In the meanwhile the papers relative to the plot were seized, the accomplices executed, and even the palace profaned. Tsaou Tsaou himself entered its precints① and demanded the death of the empress. His sovereign pleaded for mercy, and as this was granted, he asked for respite, because his wife was pregnant, that her life might be spared until she had given birth to the child. Tsaou asked with a sneer: will not her wicked brood take revenge? and immediately dispatched her.

Having thus cut off root and branch of the conspirators, he marched immedi-

① 编者按：precints 应为 precincts。

ately with a formidable army in order to quell the rebellion. Whilst success was attending his arms, the third① member of the trio, Kwan Yu, who had performed great feats of valor in the service of the generalissimo, went over to the opposite party. His path, whilst executing this design, was beset with dangers. He had taken two female relations of Heuentih under his protection, and had to fight his way single handed, through thousands of opposing enemies. Like a true knight-errant he braved them all; whosoever obstructed his passage was certain of death; his very name spread terror and disheartened the bravest garrison. After all these exploits, which are as amusingly told as the romance of Pharamond, he finally met with his sworn brother Chang Fei. Instead of heartily greeting him after so long an absence, be upbraided Kwan Yu for his perfidy in having served Tsaou Tsaou, and tried to kill him in single combat. But Kwan Yu protested his innocence, and, as a sure proof, showed the head of one of Tsaou's best generals, which he had struck off. The reconciliation being thus cemented by blood, the chivalric knight entered the camp of Shaou Yuen.

The latter was then at the head of the party which aimed at the reëstablishment of the house of Han in all its pristine glory. The territory in possession of this faction comprised the western part of China, at present known under the name of Szechuen province. Tsaou Tsaou swayed the country to the north of the Yangtsze keäng; whilst another of the famous generals, who had put down the Yellow Caps, usurped the southern provinces. This latter possessed considerable tact to keep the equilibrium between the two factions; he was alternately the ally of one or the other, and thus remained in safety. It happened once that he was wounded by some assassins, and during the time of his recovery a Taou priest presented

① 编者按：third 应为 second。

himself in the capital, and attracted so much notice, that he began to be afraid of a rebellion amongst his soldiers. The troubles occasioned by the Yellow Caps were partly fomented by the Taou sect, and the general considered this man as an emissary to cause insubordination in his army. Having given orders for his execution, nobody dared to strike the man, who pretended to be one of the genii, and had by his prayers caused rain to fall upon the parched ground. One bold fellow however severed his head with one stroke from the body, and the spirit of the priest immediately ascended in a halo of azure ether to heaven. From this moment the general was hunted by his acquaintance, and died in consequence of the terrible dread he experienced on seeing the spectre. The minute detail of the facts show how popular Taouism was at that time. Sun Keuen, his brother, succeeded him, and laid the foundation of the Woo state.

The partisans of the Han dynasty endeavored in vain to stop the victorious career of the usurper. They were either defeated by force of arms or overcome by stratagem. The leader finally gave up his cause in hopeless despair and died shortly afterwards. Heuentih, or Lew Pei as he is also called, became now the chieftain. Disheartened and without any resources, he engaged a sage to become his counsellor, and from that time his affairs took a favorable turn. Tsaou Tsaou however enticed his adviser away, and thus defeated all the plans of Lew Pei. In this emergency, the commander went in search of another worthy, who lived in rural retirement, but whose fame was notwithstanding very great. His name was Kung Ming (Kŏ Leäng, as he is also called). He at first postponed an interview and repeatedly left his cottage, whenever Heuentih approached; but finally he was prevailed upon to accept of the invidious office of director. From henceforth he is a leading character of the San Kwŏ; his integrity, wisdom, patience, perseverance, and the highest talents of a statesman and general, have given just celebrity to his name.

When Tsaou Tsaou heard of him, he treated him at first as a visionary, who would very soon lead his master into irreparable mistakes. But he was in a short time undeceived. Battle followed upon battle, whatever human ingenuity could devise was employed to defeat Heuentih, but Tsaou Tsaou was overpowered on all sides. There was in the counsels of Kung Ming something which made all his plans prove abortive. Anxious however to baffle his enemies, he had constructed a river navy, and gloried in the prospect of being thus enabled to attack the hostile army in front and rear. Kung Ming in the meanwhile built some fire boats, which he filled with sulphur, saltpetre, and other combustibles, and let them run down with the tide upon the armament. All the vessels being set on fire, consternation was general, and scarcely did the general escape with his life. This proved a decisive victory, Tsaou Tsaou was for a long time paralyzed and unable daily to follow his ambitious designs, whilst the partisans of Han grew stronger.

Yet in the midst of signal success, Kung Ming had his enemies, who envied his good fortune and tried to assassinate him. The minister was however too shrewd, and either eluded these machinations or turned them to his advantage. On a certain day, a general who was his inveterate enemy had made him promise to procure 40, 000 arrows for the army within a few days, and if he did not realize the number he was to be condemned by a court martial. Kung Ming immediately fitted up a number of boats, into which he put straw men, and thus advanced during a thick fog to the enemy's lines which were along the banks of the river. Scarcely was he opposite to them, when a shower of arrows issued from the camp, they all stuck in the straw soldiers, and having thus collected a sufficient number, he returned triumphantly to his friends, and amply satisfied the demands of his enemies.

Gifted with great foresight, Kung Ming anticipated dangers and whilst arranging his measures, he always reckoned upon the probable chances. Thus it happened that he was seldom outwitted by Tsaou Tsaou. By his address Sun Keuen had been prevailed upon to join in attacking the usurper. This alliance however being based upon sordid self-interest proved rather injurious to the cause. To cement the bonds of friendship still stronger, Heuentih was induced to marry a relation of the prince of Woo. This unprincipled politician wished to draw him into a snare, and either to take the hero prisoner or to slay him. The descendant of Han was not fully aware of this plot, and hastened to the capital in order to fetch his bride. After much delay he was finally admitted into the chamber of the princess, whose waiting women received him with drawn swords but did not dare to attack him. Having bought them over, and conciliated the affections of his new wife, the hero gave himself up to pleasure, forgetful of his dignity and the struggle in which he was engaged. From this lethargy he was finally roused by admonitions from Kung Ming, who, when he departed, had enclosed directions for his conduct in three different bags, which were successively to be opened wherever the danger was most imminent. Heuentih escaped with his bride and had to fight his way back to the camp, being repeatedly surrounded by assassins and parties of soldiers. To revenge this perfidy, Sun's army was attacked with the utmost fury, and nearly annihilated. The above facts are related in the San Kwŏ with inimitable simplicity and a beauty of expression not exceeded in any other part of the book.

The succeeding details of battles are very tiresome, and abound in tautology; we may condense them in a few words. Armies amounting from 40, 000 to 100, 000 men were raised in an instant and led into the field. How the soldiers could be armed and drilled within a few days, and provisioned for months together, is to us a problem which we have never been able to solve. Perhaps for so many ten thousands, we ought to read so many hundreds, according to the present mode of counting the inumerable① hosts of the celestial empire. Victory was generally decided by the prowess of a few brave individuals, who rode in front of the lines, and, after having sufficiently abused them, challenged the bravest to single combat, whilst the great mass of the army remained all on tiptoe to see who would be the conquerors. As soon as the contest was decided, the victors rode amongst the trembling multitudes, slaughtering and driving them before them like sheep. From henceforth the brave champions were no more to be found, until a captain of great renown summoned them to appear again under his standards.

Tsaou Tsaou's exploits were marked by boldness, whilst he never scrupled to avail himself of the most disreputable means to gain his end. War was his element, no reverses could damp his ardor, and the greatest punishment which his opponents could have inflicted upon him, would have been to let him live in peace. Puffed up with his great victories he returned A. D. 218 to the capital. All this while the emperor had passed his days like a voluptuary, in the recesses of the palace, and never intermeddled with public affairs. But the insolence of Tsaou Tsaou roused him from this stupor, and upon the suggestion of his favorite wife he issued a proclamation, calling upon Heuentih and Sun Keuen to free him from the tyranny of his prime minister. This paper, a courtier dexterously wrapped up in his hair. Unfortunately the wind blew off his cap, just when he had left the palace, and the plot was once more discovered. Two hundred relations of the emperor were publicly executed. The monarch embraced his beloved spouse in order to screen her from the fury of Tsaou Tsaou, but in vain; she was butchered in cold blood. In order to achieve the triumph, and mock the shadow of an emperor, the general gave him his own daughter in marriage, and thus considering his fortune to be estab-

① 编者按：inumerable 应为 innumerable。

lished on a firm basis, he listened to his flatterers, and received the appointment of king of Wei. On the day of his instalment, he prepared a splendid banquet for his illustrious guests. In the midst of their revelry, there appeared a Taou① priest in mean apparel, who acting the juggler, performed most extraordinary tricks. The table was supplied with the choicest delicacies from every part of the empire by magic, and Tsaou Tsaou stood petrified at the uncommon skill of the sorcerer. On a sudden he had some misgivings, he gave orders that the priest should be seized, but he was nowhere to be found. Soon, however, there appeared a number of men clad in the same garb. The minister seized and executed them, but they became again alive, and buffeted the author of so much evil, who could find no place to hide himself. Such sufferings occasioned a dangerous disease. The warrior was obliged to submit himself to the treatment of a physician, who was a sage and could also read the stars. He foretold a conflagration of the capital in which the life of the hero would be endangered. This calamity ensued by the joint machinations of powerful conspirators, who had determined upon the tyrant's death and held an army in readiness to extirpate the whole family of Tsaou. But their measures were ill concerted, and though the city was burnt to ashes, the object of their hatred escaped, to become once more the terror of all loyal Chinese.

As soon as Kung Ming heard of the news of Tsaou's exaltation, he prevailed upon Heuentih, by entreaties and threats, to assume the royal diadem and call himself king of Han. In the same degree as Tsaou by his cruelties had alienated the hearts of the people, the descendant of the reigning family had gained their love. This event therefore caused general rejoicing, and the congratulation of the multitude was sincere. Yet the joy was soon damped. A rupture with the Woo state

① 编者按：Taou 应为 Tsaou。

had unavoidably taken place, and the prince of that country being particularly incensed against one of the sworn brothers who conquered the Yellow Caps, took him prisoner, and sent his head to Tsaou Tsaou. This misfortune so much affected the new king, that he almost lost his reason. His wounded mind however was quieted by an apparition of the departed hero. About this time, Tsaou Tsaou determined upon the building of a new palace. In order to obtain proper timber, a very venerable tree had to be cut down. Though warned against such a rash act, the king insisted upon it. When finally his commands had been executed, the spirit of this tree, a mischievous elf, wounded the hero severely in his sleep, to avenge the sacrilege. There lived at that period a surgeon, who with admirable skill scraped the very bones of his patients which were diseased, and even opened the abdomen in order to remove the cause of disease. He was therefore called to perform a similar operation upon the king; yet the latter, fearing that he was a hired assassin, had him thrown into prison. Here the famous leech died, and his posthumous works, which contained prescriptions for the cure of all complaints were burnt by an inconsiderate woman; thus the world has lost the most extraordinary discoveries. Tsaou's disease grew in the meanwhile worse, he was advised to deprecate the wrath of the idols by instituting sacrifices, but thought with Confucius that these would be of no avail. Finally, seeing his end approaching, after having lived sixty-six years, and for more than thirty laid the empire waste, he called his counsellors and sons, and appointed Tsaou Pei the most intelligent amongst the latter his successor. Advising his numerous concubines to gain a livelihood by making silken shoes, and like Alaric strictly commanding to hide his burial place, the man, who for such a long time had disturbed the world, was laid low in the dust in common with all ordinary mortals. His last moments of existence were passed in anguish, for he beheld the spectres of the murdered empresses all sprinkled with blood standing before his bed. He died as he lived, hardened and unrelenting.

His son, still more ambitious than his father, drove the weak emperor Heën te from the throne, and sat himself upon the dragon's seat. Yet, though this measure was suggested by his creatures, the majority of the people were highly displeased, and heaven and earth combined to execrate this usurpation (A. D. 220). In the same year Kung Ming forced the king of Han to declare himself emperor. Though he ascended with great reluctance the throne, yet, once in possession of unlimited power, the yielding and docile prince became obstinate and domineering. Notwithstanding the most urgent remonstrances①, he declared war against the king of Woo, and suffered defeat upon defeat. At the very commencement of this campaign, Chang Fei, the second②of the trio who were the leading characters under Ling te, was assassinated by some ruffians. This as well as the utter discomfiture of his troops preyed so much upon his spirits, that he became dangerously ill. He freely confessed his errors, and asked forgiveness from his ministers. His mind was full of evil forebodings of futurity. He therefore appointed Kung Ming regent during the minority of his son, and in fact put upon this faithful servant the whole heavy burthen of the empire. The deathbed scenes are told in the most pathetic language, and are worthy of the most attentive perusal. (A. D. 223.)

This is the period during which Kung Ming shone with a lustre not eclipsed by any other statesman who held the helm of the empire. Our author passes the highest eulogiums upon this wonderful man, but does not ascribe all the praise to his sagacity which was naturally very great. Kung Ming was a stargazer, and read

① 编者按：remonstrances 应为 remonstrance。
② 编者按：second 应为 third。

the coming events in the firmament of heaven. Quite certain of futurity, and knowing the course of things by intuition, he stood always prepared against every emergency.

The news of the emperor's death, on reaching Tsaou Pei, spread the most lively joy throughout the court. A council of state was immediately summoned, and the annihilation of the new Han dynasty, which in history bears the name of the How Han (After Han) —resolved upon. A most comprehensive plan to this end was immediately arranged. The armies of Wei were to penetrate the northern frontiers, whilst the king of Woo attacked the east; the Sefan (a Tibetan tribe) from the west, and the Burmans or Laos (we are uncertain which nation) from the south. This measure was most faithfully executed, and within less than two months more than a million of hostile warriors crossed the frontiers of Han.

Messenger after messenger arrived to bring the most dismal news; the whole nation was in a state of consternation and expected its inevitable ruin to be near at hand. There was only one man who seemed not to care for the approaching downfall of the kingdom, he lived in ease and comfort whilst all were trembling and gathering their last strength for a desperate resistance; this was Kung Ming. He would not even admit the military officers to an audience in order to concert measures for the defense of the country, but appeared to have fallen into a state of lethargy from which nothing could recall him. It was no doubt his wish to rouse the spirit of the nation by the sight of fearful danger, and to let every man fight for his own life and property, which made him so long defer the execution of his mature plans. Within less than twenty-four hours the armies for the defense of the country were already in full march; the vain glorious king of Woo was to be gained by an embassy; against the prince of Wei the best generals were dispatched; and the regent himself faced the barbarians. This complicated campaign is described in a masterly manner, and the extraordinary feats of prowess and wisdom displayed by Kung Ming are so well related, that we have never yet found aught in any other Chinese history which could be compared to this. In overcoming the Burmans, Kung Ming used less force than art to convince them of the impossibility of resistance. Seven times he took the king prisoner, and seven times he released him. Such conduct gained the heart of the barbarians, and they became firmly attached to the great general. When the troubles in the west and south were stilled, Kung Ming bent all his strength upon defeating the armies of Wei. In this enterprize he was only partially successful, and he had to accuse himself before his master and ask his dismissal on account of the blunders he had committed. Such magnanimous conduct touched the emperor of Han to the very quick, and he reinstated his skillful general in all his former dignities. The emperor of Wei perceived very soon, that as long as Kung Ming remained at the head of the army, he could never conquer Han. He therefore prevailed upon the weak prince his master, by means of artful insinuations, to recall his faithful servant. Twice this happened, and the emperor was again forced to give him back his commission, and beg him to protect the country. Having roused the jealousy of the king of Woo to engage in a new war against the usurper, he amused the enemy with sundry maneuvres, but could not induce them to engage in battle. Unforeseen misfortunes weighed very heavily upon his mind. Under these circumstances he read in the stars, that his end was approaching and prepared himself for death. Full of the important charge he had hitherto held, he gave his dying commands, and departed this life in the very eve of battle. The hostile army only rejoiced, whilst all the country wept as if a father had died. Of this enthusiasm the commander-in-chief availed himself, and, having dressed up the corpse of Kung Ming in his customary grotesque garb, he put the same on a chariot at the head of the troops. The enemies were dismayed and fled in the utmost consternation, whilst the soldiers of Han braved all dangers and obtained a most complete victory over the army of Wei.

With the decease of this great man, another period commences. The downfall of the Han state was from this moment sealed. Scarcely had the regent closed his eyes, when the generals of his army rose upon each other, whilst the prince, unconcerned about the dreadful events which daily happened, spent his life in security amongst his women. The rulers of Wei, instead of taking advantage of this state of things, fell into the same vices as the emperor of Han, and designing military leaders treated them just in the same manner as their grandsire Tsaou Tsaou had treated Heën te. In the meanwhile the arms of Wei proved victorious; the pusillanimous emperor of Han hemmed in on every side was obliged to abdicate the throne in favor of his rival, and the state of Woo could no longer stop the irresistible torrent. There was only one man who rejoiced at the prostrate state in which the empire was thrown, and this was the prince of Tsin, the commander-in-chief of the Wei forces. He no longer conquered for his master, whom he despised in his heart, and whom finally he deposed, but he strove for his own aggrandizement. In this endeavor he proved very successful, so that he saw himself, A. D. 264, sole master and maintained the sway for himself and his posterity during a period of four generations.

The passages which describe the capture of capitals, the triumphs of the victors, the general terror which preceded their march, their stratagems, the cowardice of the rulers, are worthy of the most attentive perusal, and are really fine specimens of Chinese genius. The nearer the author approaches the great catastrophe, the more powerful the language and the greater the pathos. Nobody can rise from the perusal without retaining a lasting impression of the events, which have rapidly passed before his eyes and are wound up in the grand result—universal monarchy.

The further we have proceeded in the perusal of the work, the more pleasure we have found in knowing the details. There is something forbidding in the many names both of men and places, so that the mind becomes quite bewildered. Several chapters are very barren of interest and abound in repetitions, whilst others contain nothing but numberings, and marches, and countermarches of armies. But whenever the author relates domestic scenes, or leaves the field of battle to introduce his readers into the palace and council of the princes, his raciness appears to the greatest advantage, and the more we enter with him into particulars, the greater the beauties of diction we discover.

The work may pass as a model of style for historical writings, but can by no means serve as a pattern for all kinds of composition. Highly descriptive passages of nature are scarcely anywhere to be found, it is a record of men as they were in those times with all their passions and vices. The same phrases often occur again and again, and the book is more remarkable for terseness than copiousness. The sentences are neatly turned, euphony is nowhere neglected, but the writer is far more intent upon giving original thoughts than smooth and well turned phraseology, and in this particular he differs from his countrymen in general.

The Chinese student will find at the head of each chapter explanatory notes of the foregoing one, and moreover many remarks inserted between the text, whereby his attention is arrested and his mind is led to ponder upon the exquisite beauties of the tale. When he has attentively perused the work, let him decide, whether the editor was too profuse of his praises, or whether he has kept within proper bounds. We are certain that nobody who has any taste in Chinese composition, will dissent from the generally received opinion, that the San Kwŏ Che is one of the best productions of the Chinese.

中文回译

《三国志》（*San Kwŏ Che*），或曰《三国史》（*History of the Three Kingdoms*）评论，自公元 170 年至 317 年，共 147 年。来自某通讯员（Correspondent）。[①]

在所有的中国文学作品中，没有哪部作品像《三国》那样风靡天下。人们不分年龄老幼、学识高下，无不对之交口称赞。社会各阶层都认为这是有史以来最有趣的一部书；其风格、语言、叙述方式都无可挑剔。作为一部杰作，它在文学史上无与伦比。职是之故，人们才把它置于《十才子》（*Sheih Tsae Tsze*）系列丛书之首，《十才子》取天才的十个儿子之意（the Ten Sons of Genius）；[②] 这是一套公认的优秀文学作品，读之兴味盎然。我们若想轻易否定这部作品的卓越，就如同断言荷马（Homer）不是诗人，而塔西佗（Tacitus）也不是历史学家；但是尽管受到天朝大国的很大影响，我们还是发现了这部完美之作的某些瑕疵。读者会原谅我们的，因为我们这些野蛮人的想法常常有别于大汉子民（the sons of Han），但是与此同时，他们或许也会相信我们的话，这就是对于这样一部产生久远，又确实非常优秀的文学作品，我们既非漠不关心，也非视而不见。

---

① 编者按：《三国志评论》，刊于《中国丛报》第 7 卷，1838 年 5 月至 1839 年 4 月合刊本，第 233—249 页。

② 编者按：此处对于“十才子”理解有误。

当我们意识到这部作品已经出版了近 1400 年时，我们会毫不犹豫地承认，中国的文学天才在很久之前就诞生了。但是一个令人沮丧的事实是，在随后的很长一段时间里，却再没有产生过类似的作品。帝国的饱学之士写就的历史，通常枯燥乏味、兴趣索然，以致朽烂于书架之上，而《三国》却被每个认识几个大字、足以读懂普通读物的人，拿来细细品味。尽管该书不下 24 卷，却很少有人只读过一次。哪怕是目不识丁的人，若不熟悉书里讲述的事情，也是一件丢脸的事。我们经常看到中国人兴致勃勃地讲述昔日英雄的丰功伟绩，在他或许已经是第十次了。他们的诗歌，乃至他们的严肃之作，都因提及三国而妙趣横生，甚至无论是寺庙还是私宅，都装饰着那些代表主要将领的著名行动或决定王朝命运的战役的图画。那时某些杰出人物就已被神化，直到今天他们依然是被崇拜的偶像。

作者本人在介绍该著时，会努力给它一个公正的评价，赞美其优点，详细介绍其非凡人物，这些人物的经历充斥于全书。自孔子以来，中国就享有一个稳定的政治体系，刚刚摆脱野蛮，始皇帝（Che hwangte）就于公元前 3 世纪，通过大一统，结束了封建制度（feudal system）[①]，使所有诸侯国统辖在他的王权之下。很快，这位渴望超越前人的战将和立法者，意识到儒家思想会削弱人们天生的自由精神，他就以严厉的手段，毁掉了国内的文献。然而，可想而知，帝国如此广大，副本成千上万，四处散播，无论他怎么努力，也只能取得部分胜利；但他似乎一度把国民的注意力引导到更重要的事情上去了，而不是一味只盯着古书。可是，汉天子（公元前 202 年）甫一掌权，就成了古典知识最慷慨的支持者。文学很快复兴，学者们也比任何时期都受尊重。正是在那个时期，第一批民族史家大量涌现，写作的狂热堪比当今的西方。在这个奥古斯都时代（Augustan epoch），三国成为一个奇谈；天才的著述者似乎获得了神力，他尽力把虚构与史实巧妙

① 编者按：此处所言“封建制度”指的是诸侯林立、各自为国。

地糅合在一起，以彻底吸引读者的注意力。《三国》展现了公元170年至317年间最真实的画卷，这一时期三国（San Kwŏ）兴起。为取悦读者，全文穿插了各种各样的奇闻逸事，夸大其词，迷惑其说。它讲述了汉朝最后两位皇帝——灵帝和献帝（Ling te and Heën te），是怎样因为他们的软弱无能和荒淫无度而使国家陷入一片混乱；结果其中的一员大将曹操（Tsaou Tsaou），如何名义上为天子作战实际上却为魏国打造基础，与此同时孙权（Sun Keuen）建立了吴国，最后是汉朝的一位后裔刘备（Lew Pei）建立了蜀国，又称后汉，直到一位新的野心勃勃的统治者以晋朝（Tsin Dynasty）的名义统一了三国（公元279年）。以上就是这部杰作的内容简介。我们现在详细讲述。

灵帝登基时（公元168年），他认为在太监和后宫嫔妃们间聊度光阴，要比亲理朝政容易得多。他的心腹全是国家最腐败堕落的人，太监把持了一切有利可图的职位。一日听政时，灵帝在酒色迷离中被一条从房梁上滑落的青蛇吓了一跳。怪物虽然消失了，可是紧接着京城遭受了地震，海水泛滥淹没了沿海诸省。这些灾难，还有许多其他的不祥之兆使这个懦弱的皇帝惊恐不安；他诏问缘由，但从大臣们那里得到的只是敷衍之辞。种种暴政使人民陷入绝望，只差一人揭竿而起，带头反抗，这人很快就出现了。

那时有兄弟三人才华出众。瘟疫在百姓中肆意蔓延，他们就出去采药以助人疗疾。一天采药时，遇见一位智者，交给老大三本书，说："此中学问博大，去革新国家，普救世人吧。若萌异心，必获恶报。"大哥张角（Chang Keŏ）听到这些不可思议的话很是高兴，急忙攻习，从此学会了呼风唤雨的本领。在瘟疫肆虐期间，他通过施撒念过咒语的符水来治病救人。由于疗效显著，他的追随者数量剧增，还谋划着竖起黄旗，改朝换代。皇帝很快得知了他们的叛乱，抓住他们的一些信众，或斩首，或下狱。此举震撼了义军领袖，他们组建起自己的军队，头戴黄帽或黄巾，以区别于朝廷军队，他们被视为异类，号称"黄巾军"（the Yellow Caps）。这部伟大的戏剧就此拉开序幕，从此干戈不断。

正当皇帝的内心还在犹豫不定之时，三位英雄——刘备（Lew Pei）、关羽（Kwan Yu）和张飞（Chang Fei）奇迹般地出现了，其中刘备之名玄德（Heuen-tih）（汉室后裔）更为人熟知。这三人在牲祭了一头黑牛和一匹白马后，在桃园盟誓，表示对彼此永远忠诚，并祭告天地以见证他们的誓言。他们都是自己族裔的伟人，体格魁梧，具有成为英雄豪杰的所有品质。在获得了一些马匹，又铸造了巨人歌利亚（Goliath）[①] 也难以挥动的上好刀剑后，遭遇了三万黄巾军，虽然这时他们仅有千余人。显然，这是一场力量悬殊的战斗，于是玄德出马上前骂阵——中国的英雄格外擅长此道。战事本该就此结束，幸亏他们的长剑这时派上了用场；他砍下了敌军主帅的首级，余众瞬间溃散。此后他们所向披靡，战绩辉煌，黄巾军则节节败退，溃不成军，尽管有时黄巾军也利用法术使风雷大作，把敌军包裹在密不透风的黑雾里，但他们还是每战必败。

与此同时朝廷却沉浸于荒淫腐化。那些为国流血的勇士，在表奏完他们在反击叛乱时取得的战绩后，即被遣退回来，在黯淡中聊度余生，还有的被告发为危险的阴谋家。宦官们重新把持了朝政，把最重要的爵位卖给出价最高的人，他们完全封锁了皇帝的视听，不让任何人有机会接近他。因此，黄巾军的叛乱还没被镇压下去，新的盗贼再度蜂起，天下大乱。皇帝还在与宦官们纵情享乐时，得知了这些灾难。他百感交集，明显因悲痛而丧生（公元 189 年）。

那些著名将领几乎不曾注意到君主的死，他们决定立刻彻底根除奸臣同党；然而只有一人胆识过人，敢于面对这些可怕的朝臣。为了惩罚他的胆大妄为，奸臣们砍下了他的头，挂在宫墙之外。这种暴行激怒了将军的追随者，他们放火焚烧了皇宫，提刀携剑冲进大火，杀死了奸臣的全家。

---

① 编者按：歌利亚，《旧约》中的著名巨人，骁勇善战，后被大卫所杀。

展现在读者面前的是一片恐怖：一些人被扔出窗外，在地上摔得七零八落，另一些则被凶器刺得遍体鳞伤，尖叫着坠入火海。到处都是恐怖与惊惶，年幼的皇帝几乎难以逃生。

兵戈之乱一旦爆发，就不会很快结束。暴力手段一旦被采用，事实证明行之有效，类似的暴行就会接踵而至。朝廷的神圣受到侵犯，皇权的庄严遭到亵渎，幼帝也不能再安居后宫。皇宫陷入一片火海，幼帝带着弟弟一起逃亡，却不知去往何处。夜幕降临时，他们在灌木丛中迷失了方向，深深哀叹自己的命运，跌坐在地。唉，该当如何是好？一群流萤飞过，照亮了一条通往农庄的路。在农庄他受到款待，第二天上午见到一群大臣，把他送回了皇宫。废帝的阴谋很快在此酝酿，有一员残暴的大将，在歼灭阉党时曾出力援助，宣称不应该让这样一位年轻的花花公子治理国家。他或用武力，或行贿赂，说服了与他意见相左的派系，在众臣朝会时，宣布废黜执政仅短短五个月的皇帝，然后将皇帝的弟弟，也就是后来的献帝，推上皇位。被囚禁的皇帝哀怨命运之不幸，由于内心无比悲痛，写了些诗歌，表达了他对呢喃燕雀来去自由的羡慕，并想为自己遭受的不公报仇雪恨。这被那员大将视为大逆不道；于是他给皇帝送去了一杯毒酒，强迫他喝了下去；同时，他的手下把皇后从皇宫的楼上推下，然后又命令士兵将她扼死。所有这一切都讲述得格外精彩，一些段落确实令人赞叹。

董卓（Tung Chǒ）扶植自己的人登上皇位，而今可以彻底施其暴虐了。为迁都长安（Changngan），首都洛阳（Loyang）人口损失大半，这个恶魔还绞死了2000人作为战利品，使国家笼罩在一片恐怖中。贵族们为国家的不幸痛哭流涕，却不敢抱怨，因为这是一个恐怖的时期，受到暴君的猜忌则必死无疑。

那时有个叫曹操（Tsaou Tsaou）的人，在对抗黄巾军的战斗中崭露头角，他智勇双全，由此而嘲笑同僚无用的牢骚。他具有成为一名暴君的所有条件，认识到自己的天资后，决心推翻董卓。他首先巧妙地赢得了董卓的欢心，在刺杀他的企图失败后，快马加鞭，返回故乡，出任统帅，邀请当时的名人义士聚其麾下，很快招募起一支可观的队伍。他的事业一开始就充满了血腥，当他还是个逃犯时就杀光了热情接纳他的一家人，在第一场战斗中也是为所欲为，大肆屠杀。但是他的追求毫无疑问是出于爱国的目的，他像法国恐怖时期的丹东（Danton）那样受到爱戴，只是他所依仗的更多的不是民心，而是士兵们手里的刀剑。第一次推翻董卓的努力没能成功，他被打败了，爱国将士们也开始相互争吵。经过一番深思熟虑，该派首领很快意识到，董卓是不能被武力征服的。由此，他们选了一个美人让他垮台。美人曲意逢迎，甚得宠幸，同时引起了另一个人的嫉妒，那人是他手下的能吏，也是他收养的义子，这位暴君受诏登基，以证明皇帝遵照他的旨意让位于他。在董卓赶赴皇宫的路上，出现了许多凶兆，但董卓急于得到唾手可得的帝位，继续前行。这时，他的义子，一心想占有义父的宠妾，暗中埋下了伏兵。当朝臣们汇集朝堂之上，董卓正要登上通向宝座的台阶时，伏兵趁其不备进行突袭，他的义子首先给了他致命的一剑。

然而，这位暴君的支持者却来替他们的首领报仇。起初，他们并没成功，但后来却突然打败对手，攻入京城。懦弱的皇帝被迫掩饰情感，并给叛贼的首领晋封。一场新的斗争接踵而至，很难确定谁会掌权。在这个关键时刻，曹操再次登上军事舞台。等战斗的双方经过血战彼此削弱后，他才伺机而动，带领一群暴徒为攫取政权而加入战斗。在得知皇帝的惨况后，他立即前去救援。国都已沦为废墟，朝臣四散，皇宫内荆棘遍布，皇帝所剩不多的侍臣甚至没有足够的钱购买马匹，以迎接答应前来救援的曹操。曹操再三宣誓尽忠后，成为皇帝的贴身侍卫，他秉持正义，严以执法，成为摇摇欲坠的皇权的支柱。他说的话就是命令，严厉而无情，每当他威胁要替皇帝遭受的不义而报仇时，各方人士都吓得战战兢兢。然而，由于还有很多人想要篡夺皇位，他们同样在艰难的战斗中获得了很高的军威，曹操图谋壮大的愿望只能获得局部成功。曹操行事一向鲁莽冲动，有一次寻花问柳，差点丢了性命，还忘记了料理军务。他从迫在眉睫的危难中醒来，像头狮子那样突出重围，一路所向披靡。他的纪律严明。一次他严禁士兵践踏麦地，因为麦子很快就要成熟收割了，如有违抗，即被斩首。他是第一个不小心违反了这一禁令的人，当部将提醒他时，他拔出剑来刺向自己以弥补过错。他没有自杀，而是割下了自己的头发，扔在地上，权且代替首级。他的这些举措对士兵们产生的影响，比他最为辉煌的战绩还要大。接着又开始了一场旷日持久的战争，讲述得索然无味。曹操依然是战场的主宰，凯旋回京。他被任命为丞相（prime minister）兼主帅（commander-in-chief），还被赐予公爵的头衔，事实上统治着国家。一次随皇帝出猎，曹操因僭越领受猎鹿的荣誉而触怒了朝臣，他们达成一纸密谋，共讨曹操。皇帝自己，因不愿继续被这样一个人颐指气使，用自己的鲜血书写了一纸诏令，命令忠于他的人处决曹操，实施报复。他把这纸诏令藏在腰带中，作为礼物赐给了他的一位亲戚。讨伐曹操的密谋由此很快得以部署，只是为了等待一个适当的时机而被推迟。

自然会有人问，那些镇压了黄巾军反叛的英雄都到哪里去了？在取得胜利之后，他们没有决定投入某个阵营，看到以前的战斗伙伴曹操做了首领，他们逐渐加入了他的阵营。玄德也在朝廷，这时他的一个亲友邀请他加入反对曹操的密谋集团。虽然他不想拒绝这一请求，但做得非常谨慎，他与另一位英雄张飞，领受军命抗击残余的叛军。打败他们后，玄德觉得让自己任由曹操摆布是非常危险的，所以加入了曹操的一位对手的军队，来抵抗他的进攻，这或许还有可能把国家从篡贼手中解救出来，当这个致命的消息传到丞相的耳朵时，他正卧病在床。这个意想不到的灾祸刺激了他，他奇迹般康复了，但他没有急于采取果断行动来粉碎叛乱，而是生平第一次安排时间与一位圣哲探讨仁政的准则。为了让自己摆脱幕僚的纠缠，他让一位赳赳武夫给他送了个信。由此，圣哲开始像以前那样探讨智慧的准则，却大大冒犯了这个穷兵黩武的人，以致惨遭斩首。

此期间密谋者的首领身患重病。一位被传唤进去给他治病的医生，通过病人的呓语断断续续听说了密谋的梗概。他当即承诺给曹操一剂毒药，以帮助他实施计划，为了证明自己的忠诚，他咬掉了一根手指。不幸的是他们的对话被一些家奴听到了。主人怀疑他们会泄露机密，想杀了他们，但被妻子劝阻了这一残忍的行动。于是，主人把他们锁了起来。其中一人晚上逃了出去，径直跑到丞相那里告诉了他自己听说的一切。曹操于是假装生病，叫医生来照料他。药准备好后，他逼迫医生先喝，但医生却在地上打碎了药罐。医生受到极刑逼供，却没出卖任何人。曹操立即下令邀请诸位大臣，除了一人，别的同谋者都在其中；医生被带到现场，再次遭受了严刑拷打，但毫不动摇，最后撞阶而死。与此同时，密谋文书被搜出，同谋者被处决，甚至连皇宫也遭到亵渎。曹操来到后宫，下令杀了皇后。皇帝为她求情，因皇后身怀有孕，请求缓期执行，可待其分娩后再行处决，此乃常情。曹操冷笑道：难道其逆子不会报仇雪恨吗？接着立即处死了她。

就这样将合谋者斩草除根后，他立即带领一支强大的军队前去平息叛乱。军队即将得胜时，结义兄弟中排行老三①，并在其麾下立下赫赫战功的关羽转投了对手。在实施这一计划时，一路上困难重重。他保护着玄德的两位女眷，孤军奋战，对抗数千敌军。像个真正的游侠骑士那样，不顾一切，奋勇向前；谁挡了他的路，都注定会死；甚至他的名字都让人不寒而栗，最勇猛的军队听了也会闻风丧胆。这些丰功伟绩，被讲述得像法拉蒙（Pharamond）的罗曼史那样有趣。这之后，他终于见到了结义兄弟张飞。久别重逢，张飞不但没有热情迎接，反而指责关羽背信弃义，出侍曹操，遂向其挑战，想杀了他。但关羽证明了自己的清白，拿出了一个可靠的证据，那就是他砍下的曹操最好的一员大将的头颅。在用鲜血达成和解后，

① 编者按：“老三”应为“老二”。

义士来到赵云（Shaou Yuen）[①] 的营寨。

那时后者正带领一帮人，力图恢复汉家昔日的荣耀。他们占据的领地位于中国的西部，即目前被称为四川省（Szechuen province）的地方。曹操拥有扬子江以北的地方；与此同时，镇压黄巾军的另一位著名将领，侵占了南方诸省。他相当老谋深算，在两股势力之间保持平衡；通过轮流与两派结盟，以维护自身安全。有一次他被刺客所伤，在身体恢复期间，一位道士来到京城，引起轰动，使他开始担心士兵叛乱。黄巾军引发的动乱在一定程度上就是由道教煽动的，该将军认为，这个人就是到他的军队里来引发叛乱的间谍。处决道士的命令下达后，却没人敢动手，因为道士曾扮成鬼神，通过祈祷，求来雨水，降临在这片干涸的土地上。一个鲁莽的家伙一刀砍下了他的头，道士的灵魂立即化作一道蓝光升入天堂。从此以后，将军就被其熟人追赶，最终因看到鬼魂，惊惧而死。这个细节显示了道教在那时是多么的流行。他的弟弟孙权（Sun Keuen）继承了他的事业，随后为吴国的建立奠定了基础。

汉朝的余党没能挡住篡位者的成功。他们不是被武力打败了，就是被阴谋降服了。他们的首领最终在绝望中放弃了自己的事业，没过多久就死了。玄德，也称刘备，而今成了领袖。在他心灰意懒又一无所有的时候，任用了一位贤士做谋臣，从那以后，他的事业峰回路转。然而，曹操却怂恿刘备的谋臣离开他，由此毁掉他所有的计划。在这紧急时刻，刘备开始寻觅另一位贤士，他隐居山野，却名声显赫。这人名叫孔明（Kung Ming），又称葛亮（Kŏ Leäng）[②]。玄德造访时，他先是推辞不见，屡屡离开草舍；但最终还是被说服，答应出任令人嫉妒的丞相（Director）一职。此后，孔

① 编者按：此处不确定是不是“赵云”，因“赵云”二字在马礼逊《华英字典》中分别被注音为“Chaou”和“Yun”，而非“Shaou”和“Yuen”。分别见《华英字典》第一部第 28、1051、1047、726 页，大象出版社 2008 年版。

② 编者按：此处对“诸葛亮”之名翻译有误。

明就成了《三国》中的主要人物；他的正直、才智、耐心、毅力，以及作为政治家和军事家的天资禀赋，都使他声名远播。

曹操听说孔明的时候，最初只是把他看作一个空想家，以为他会很快带领其主犯下不可挽救的错误。但很快他就醒悟过来。战争一场接着一场，曹操想方设法打败玄德，却处处碰壁。孔明的决策使曹操的所有计划均以失败告终。急于打败对手的曹操组建了一支水军，自以为是地认为将来可以借此前后夹击敌人。与此同时，孔明建造了一些火船，里面装满了硫黄、硝石和其他可燃物，让船顺流而下，直达曹操的船队。曹操所有的船都被点着了，他惊慌失措，几乎丧命。这是一场决定性的胜利，使曹操在很长一段时间里一蹶不振，丧失斗志，与此同时，汉的拥护者却变得越来越强大。

然而，就在取得显著胜利的时候，孔明不断树敌，对手嫉恨孔明的好运，并想杀了他。只是军师（The minister）非常精明，他要么避开了暗算，要么化险为夷、转危为安。一日，一位对孔明忌恨已久的将军，让他承诺几天内为军队提供四万支箭，如果不能如数兑现，就要接受军法处置。孔明立即装备了一些船，船上摆放了些稻草人，浓雾弥漫时驶往河流对岸敌军的阵线。两军尚未对垒，漫天箭矢像下雨般从对方军营射来，全都射在了稻草人身上，由此凑够了数量，胜利回到友人身边，同时也充分满足了对手的要求。

孔明天赋奇才，未卜先知，能预测危险并准备对策，他总是能够把握先机。一旦碰上这种情况，他就很少让曹操以智取胜。他游说孙权联手一起抗击篡权者。然而，事实证明，这种建立在肮脏的各自利益基础上的联盟对其事业而言有害无益。为巩固联盟，增进友谊，玄德被诱导与吴王联姻。这个不讲原则的政客想让他落入圈套，或囚禁他，或杀了他。这位汉朝后裔没有充分意识到这是个阴谋，他很快赶赴吴都去迎娶他的新娘。几经周折，他才被恩准进入公主的闺房，侍女们拔剑相迎，只是不敢攻击他。他取得了她们的信任，又赢得了新婚妻子的好感，这位英雄由此开始耽于享乐，忘记了自己的尊严和战斗。最终，孔明的警告将他从沉睡中唤醒。在他启程时，孔明把行动指示放进了三个不同的袋子，大难临头时就逐一打开。玄德带上新娘逃跑，打回营寨，一路上屡屡被杀手和追兵围剿。为报复吴国的背信弃义，孙权的军队遭到猛烈攻击，几乎全军覆没。《三国》中的上述内容叙述简洁，措辞优美，超过了本书的其他部分。

随后的战争细节非常无聊，而且千篇一律；我们可以将它们浓缩成几句话。大约有四到十万大军突然出现，进入战场。如何让士兵们在短短几天之内武装起来，得到训练，并连续数月提供补给，在我们看来是不可能解决的问题。根据天朝现在计算“无可计数”的方法，我们或许应该把“数万”读成“数百”。战争的胜利与否常常取决于几员猛士的威力，他们骑马在前，冲锋陷阵，在经过一番骂阵后，向最勇猛的战将提出单挑，大队人马则全部留在后方踮足观战，看谁取胜。一旦决出胜负，胜者骑马冲进战栗的人群，砍杀和驱逐他们，如同对付一群绵羊。从此以后，就再也找不到英勇的战将了，直到一位名将把他们召集起来，以他的名义重现于世。

曹操的功绩以胆量魄力著称于世，为达目的，他会无所顾忌地采用任何卑劣的手段。打仗是他与生俱来的一部分，任何失败都不能抑制他对战争的狂热，其对手能给他的最大惩罚，就是让他平静地生活。辉煌的战绩使他飞扬跋扈，公元 218 年，曹操回到都城。而这时，皇帝却像个酒色之徒那样聊度时日，深居内宫，从不理政。但是曹操的傲慢使其从麻木中醒来，在他最得宠的妻子的建议下，发布了一纸诏书，诏令玄德和孙权把他从丞相的暴政中解救出来。这封密诏被一位朝臣巧妙地藏在头发里。不幸的是他刚一离开皇宫，一阵风就刮掉了他的帽子，密谋再次暴露。皇帝的两百位亲眷被斩于市。皇帝抱住爱妻，想让她躲过曹操的暴虐，却无济于事；

她被残忍地杀害了。为赢得胜利并挟持皇帝，曹操把自己的女儿嫁给了皇帝，借以巩固事业，他还听从谗言，接受了魏王的封位。受封的那天，曹操备下燕飨，大宴宾客。饮宴时来了一位衣衫褴褛的道士，他扮作术士，表演了许多离奇的法术。桌上神奇地摆满了帝国各处弄来的美味佳肴，曹操被术士非同寻常的道术吓得目瞪口呆。他疑窦顿生，于是下令抓住道士，但哪里也找不到他。很快，又出现了一群装扮相同的人。曹操抓住并杀了他们，但他们又复活过来，猛烈攻击这个十恶不赦的人，打得他无处藏身。丞相被折磨得身染重疾。这位英雄不得不被送去就医，医生是位圣哲，也懂得星相。他预言说都城的一场灾难会危及曹操的性命。这场灾难是由强大的反叛者联手策划的阴谋，他们发誓要处死曹操，还有一支军队要剿灭整个曹氏家族。但是他们的计划却不够协调，尽管城池被烧成了灰烬，他们的仇人却逃脱了，再次使所有的忠士身陷恐惧。

当孔明听说曹操封王的消息后，他或恳求，或威胁，劝玄德继承皇权，自封汉王。曹操在多大程度上因残暴而失去民心，汉室后裔就在多大程度上赢得了百姓的爱戴。此事令群情激越，民众致以诚挚的祝贺。然而，欢乐很快消失了。与吴国的决裂不可避免地发生了，那位战胜了黄巾军的结义兄弟尤其令吴王愤怒，他把他囚禁起来，又将其首级献给了曹操。这个噩耗使新王悲痛欲绝，他几乎丧失了理智。但他受伤的心灵得到了已逝英魂的安抚。大约就在这时，曹操决定修建一个新的宫殿。为了得到合适的木材，必须砍伐一棵名贵的树木。尽管有人告诫他这样做过于鲁莽，但他依然坚持己见。当他的命令最终被执行时，这棵树的灵魂——一个淘气的精灵，在他睡觉时使他身负重伤，以报复他的亵渎神灵。那时有一位医术高明的医生，能为病人刮骨疗毒，甚至能打开腹部以切除病根。因此他被传唤来给曹操做一个类似的手术。然而，曹操却担心他是个被人利用的刺客，把他关进了大牢。神医就此身亡，他的遗著，其中记载着治疗各种疾病的药方，也被一个鲁莽的女人烧了；从此，世人失去了这些最非凡的发现。与此同时，曹操的病情日益恶化，有人建议他通过献祭[①]来平息神怒，但想到孔子（Confucius）说过的话，他就觉得无济于事。最后，眼看大限将至，在活了六十六年，横行天下三十多年后，曹操叫来大臣和儿子，指定诸子中最聪明的曹丕（Tsaou Pei）做他的继承人。建议其妻妾编织丝履以谋生，还像阿拉里克（Alaric）那样，下令将其坟墓隐藏起来，这个长时间扰乱天下的人，像所有凡夫俗子一样埋入尘土。他的弥留之际是在痛苦中度过的，因为他看到被他杀害的皇后们的幽灵浑身是血地站在他的床前。他的死就像活着时一样——坚毅而又冷酷。

他的儿子曹丕，比父亲还要野心勃勃，他把软弱的献帝赶下宝座，自己坐上了龙椅。然而，尽管此举是臣僚们的主意，却引起了大多数人的强烈不满，他的篡位遭到了天地的诅咒（公元220年）。同年，孔明迫使汉王称帝。尽管汉王登基时很不情愿，但一旦掌握了大权，这位柔顺、温良的君主就变得顽固、专横起来。尽管大臣急切劝谏，他还是对吴宣战，连遭战败。在这场战争刚刚开始时，曾在灵帝手下担任大将的三兄弟中的老二[②]，就被一些恶棍害死了。张飞之死，以及军队的彻底战败，使他精神饱受折磨，以致身染重病。他坦然承认了自己的错误，并祈求大臣们的原谅。他内心充满了对于继承人的不祥预感。所以，任命孔明摄政，辅佐幼主，实际是把整个国家的重担都交给了这位忠实的仆人。作者以一种无比悲惨的语言讲述了他临终前的场景，十分值得认真细读（公元223年）。

这段时期，孔明大放异彩，其他执掌国家大权的政治家相比之下无不黯然失色。我们的作者给予这位优秀人物以最高的礼赞，但并没有把所有的赞美都归因于他的天生睿智。孔明是个星相家，能通过天相来预测未来之事。他对未来了如指掌，而且能凭借直觉知道事情的进程，面对危机，

---

① 编者按：对于“设醮修禳”的误解。

② 编者按：“老二”应为“老三”。

他总能做好准备。

皇帝的死讯传到曹丕那里，欢乐的气氛传布朝廷上下。大臣们立即被召来，决定歼灭史称后汉（After Han）的这个新的汉朝。为此，一个极其周密的计划被立即制订出来。魏军攻入北方边境，与此同时，吴王攻打南边；西番（Sefan）（一个藏族部落）攻打西部，缅甸或老挝（Burmans or Laos）（我们不确定是哪个国家）攻打东边。这个计划得到切实执行，不到两个月，一百多万敌军越过了汉的边境。

一个个信使不断送来无比悲惨的消息；整个国家陷入一片恐慌，人们都担心不可避免的亡国之灾行将到来；这时只有一人似乎对即将倾覆的国家漠不关心，当所有的人心惊胆战，为殊死抵抗而积攒最后一点力量时，他却过着安逸、舒适的生活；这人就是孔明。他甚至不接见为了保卫国家而协调对策的军事将领，表面看来，他似乎陷入了一种萎靡不振的状态，什么都叫不醒他。毫无疑问，他是希望通过这种可怕的危险来激发国人的斗志，让每一个人为自己的生命和财产而战斗，这使他迟迟没能将自己成熟的计划付诸实践。不到二十四小时，卫国部队就全部出发了；一位使臣去对付自负的吴王；最勇猛的战将被派去抗击魏王；丞相（the regent）自己则亲自出征，讨伐蛮夷。这场复杂的战役被描绘得惟妙惟肖，孔明的丰功伟绩体现的智勇双全被叙述得那么完美，以致我们在别的中国史中再难找到可以与之相提并论的篇章。在征服缅甸（Burmans）[①] 时，孔明更多地使用技巧而非武力来使他们相信抵抗是不可能的。他七次俘获了蛮王，又七次释放了他。这种举动赢得了蛮夷之心，他们由此坚决地归顺了这位伟大的将领。在西部和南部的战乱平息后，孔明调集全部兵力，攻打魏军。但这次出征他只取得了部分胜利，还被迫在君主面前自责，引咎自辞。这种高尚之举很快感动了汉帝，他恢复了这位高明的将领昔日所有的荣衔。

① 编者按："缅甸"应为"南蛮"。

魏王很快意识到，只要孔明继续担任军队统帅，他就不可能征服后汉。所以，魏王通过巧妙的暗讽，诱使那位软弱的汉王，也就是孔明的后主，召回他忠实的仆人。反复召回了两次，但后主还是被迫让他回去赴任，并请求他保卫国家。在激起吴王的嫉妒，使其投入一场新的讨伐篡位者的战争后，孔明利用各种策略来戏弄敌人，却没能诱其出战。无法预见的厄运沉重地压在心头。在这种情况下，孔明夜观天象，发现死期将至，于是准备后事。由此，他满负重任，发布遗命，就在战争开始的前夕，孔明去世了。敌军一片欢欣鼓舞，而整个蜀国却无比悲痛，如丧考妣。主帅（the commander-in-chief）利用这种群情激越，给孔明的尸首穿上他平时所穿的奇装异服，接着在军前战车上摆放了一个同样的木偶。敌军见此大惊，四处逃窜，而汉军奋勇前进，彻底战胜了魏军。

随着这个伟人的去世，另一个时代开始了。蜀汉的衰亡就此开始。丞相未及瞑目，军队里的将领们就开始了相互争斗，而后主却对每天发生的可怕事情毫不关心，只是在女人们中间安度光阴。魏国的统治者，不但没有利用这种局面，反而像汉王那样身染恶习，狡猾的军事领袖用他们的祖父曹操当初对待献帝的方式来对待他们。与此同时，魏国的军队取得了胜利；怯懦的汉王被四面包围，被迫放弃了皇权，让位于对手，而吴国也不能阻止这股不可抗拒的洪流。只有一个人对蜀国的降服感到欣喜，他就是魏军的主帅晋（Tsin）王。他不再为内心鄙视、最终又被他废黜的主人继续征战了，而是为他自己的壮大而奋斗。他的努力非常成功，于是在公元264年，使自己成了唯一的统治者，他和他的后代把持政权四代之久。

本书描写占领京城、胜者凯旋，以及军队出发前普遍的恐惧、作战策略、统治者的怯懦的段落，值得仔细精读，而且确实是中国才子的典范之作。作者越是涉及大灾大难，语言就越是有力，情感也更为悲怆。没有谁在仔细阅读过这部作品之后不对书中的事件留下深刻的印象，它们在眼前一闪而过，最后形成一个宏伟的结局，即一个统一的君主政体。

我们越是深入品味这部作品，就越为其中发现的细节而高兴。由于许多人名与地名存在避讳，所以有时令人相当困惑。其中有些章节非常枯燥乏味，经常重复，而另一些章节除了编号、军队的行进和撤退外就别无内容。但是每当作者描写国内的场景，或者离开战场而把读者带入皇宫和朝廷时，他的痛快爽利似乎就成了他最大的优势，我们越是跟着他深入细节，就越能发现其措辞的优美。

这部作品可以被看作历史著述文体风格的典范，但绝不能把它当成一切作品的榜样。书中几乎找不到集中描写自然的段落，它是对生活在那个时代的、具有各种情感及恶习的人的记录。同样的措辞经常反复出现，这本书与其说是以辞采华茂名扬天下，不如说是因简洁精练而著称于世。它的句子灵活多变，处处和谐悦耳，但作者更想追求的是提供独特的思想，而非语言上的文从字顺、灵活多变，在这点上，他有别于中国的普通作家。

学习汉语的人会发现在每章的开头有对前一章内容所做的评注，文中也穿插了大量评论，通过这种方式来吸引读者，同时引导着读者去仔细思考叙述的精美。当您仔细阅读完这部作品后，再来自己决定本人的赞美是过于慷慨，还是保持在了适当的范围之内。我们确信，没有哪个读过中国作品的人，会否认这个已被普遍接受的观点，即《三国志》是中国最优秀的作品之一。

第二部分

人物译介文献研究

一 美魏茶的三国人物画廊

美魏茶又名“小米怜”，是英国第二位来华新教传教士米怜的儿子，广州出生，英国长大，后子承父业，加入伦敦布道会，成了一名来华新教传教士。美魏茶不仅是基督教福音的传播者，也是19世纪中国历史的亲历者和记录者，他撰写的《生活在中国》(*Life in China*) 忠实地记录了自己14年间在中国的所见所闻，是19世纪中国宁波、上海等东南地区社会发展的历史见证。美魏茶一生的努力与功业，正如他在《生活在中国》一书中所说的那样，主要致力于两个方面：“第一，向英国人传播更加真实可靠的关于中国人的知识，帮助英国人摆脱长期以来固守的关于中国及其社会状况等各个方面的错误而又荒谬的印象；第二，这种努力或许也有助于提高或唤醒现代真正的慈善家的善心，以推动中国的基督教文明以及纯粹的基督教事业的发展。”①

① William C. Milne, *Life in China*, London: G. Routledge & Co. Farringdon Street; New York: 18, Beekman Street, 1857, Preface, V.

MR. AND MRS. MILNE.

美魏茶的父母（Mr. and Mrs. Milne）

作为一名传教士，美魏茶在中西文化交流史上的地位主要得益于他对《圣经》的翻译，译介《三国演义》在其文化生活中只是一个很小的插曲。1841 年 2 月，19 世纪著名英文报刊《中国丛报》第 10 卷第 2 期发表了美魏茶译介的《黄巾起义》（*The Rebellion of the Yellow Caps*）；1843 年 3 月，同刊第 12 卷第 3 期发表了美魏茶撰写的《孔明评论》（*Notices of Kungming*）。这两篇文章对于介绍三国故事出现的历史背景，以及塑造英语世界中的孔明形象，都发挥了一定作用，是《三国演义》海外传播史上不可或缺的一环。

本部分内容在搜集译者资讯、细读第一手英文资料的基础上，探讨了美魏茶对于《三国演义》的译介之功。对于《黄巾起义》，主要考察了译介缘由、版本来源、译介方式和主要内容；对于《孔明评论》，则重点分析了其人物塑造、情节翻译两方面的特点，以及文章发表后在西方汉学界产生的影响。

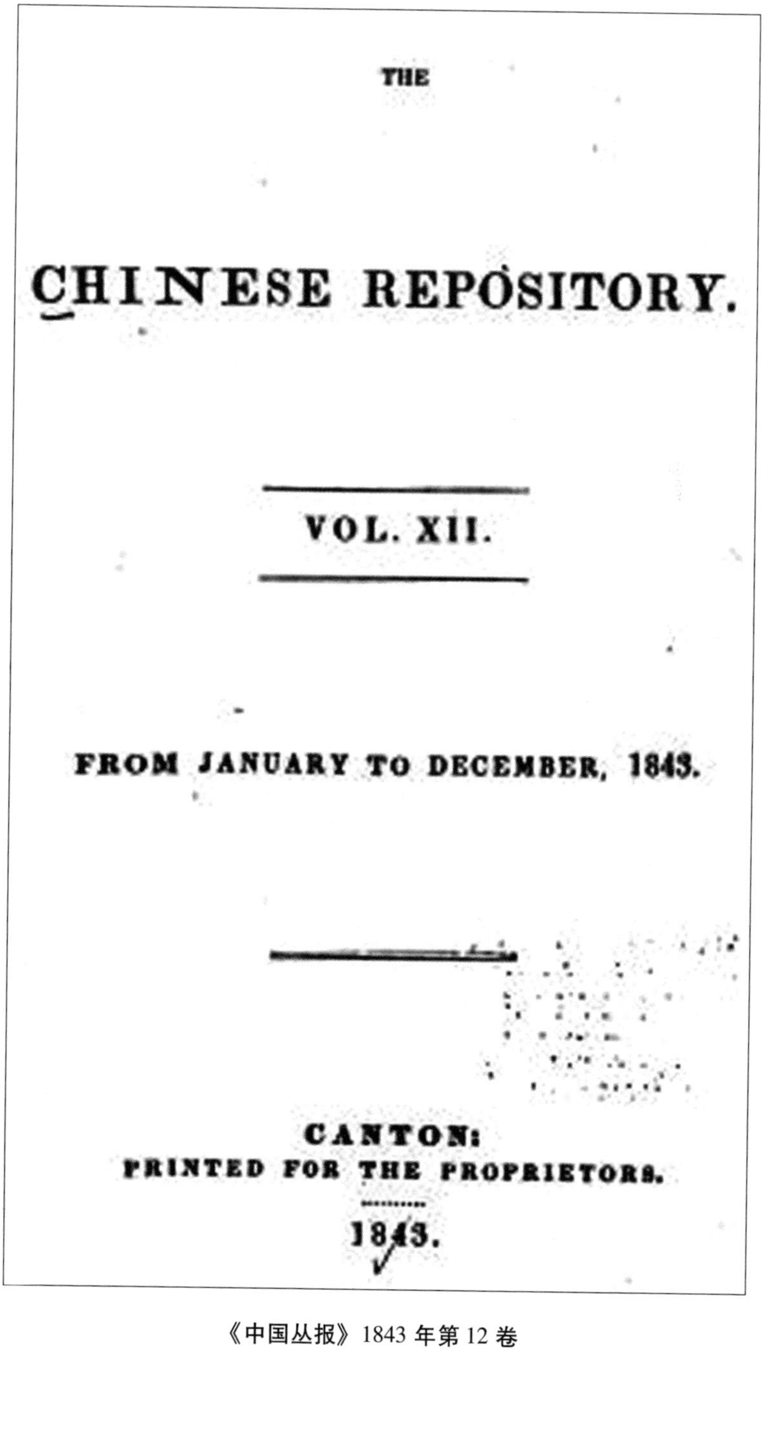
THE

CHINESE REPOSITORY.

VOL. XII.

FROM JANUARY TO DECEMBER, 1843.

CANTON:
PRINTED FOR THE PROPRIETORS.

1843.

《中国丛报》1843 年第 12 卷

known,) with his own hand destroyed two of the rebels who were attempting to climb over the palace walls. This bold act caused the other rebels to fall back with terror, and thus the sacred abode was preserved in quiet. Judging from the protrait which we have seen, his majesty is tall, thin, and of a dark complexion. He is now sixty years of age, and apparently strong and robust. He is reputed to be "of a generous disposition, diligent, attentive to government, and economical in his expenditure." He is greatly revered by his subjects, and apparently much swayed by the counsels of his ministers, of whom some are very able men,—though we much fear as he says, "they know not what truth is." Of the emperor's present line of policy much remains to be said. It will be questioned and scanned as that of his predecessors never was. The old order of things is passing away, and now—

Magnus ab integro sæclorum nascitur ordo.

Art. V. *The Rebellion of the Yellow Caps, compiled from the History of the Three States.**

As the insurrection, that ended in that dismemberment of the Chinese empire which became the foundation of the popular *San Kwŏ Che*, or "History of the Three States," forms the subject of an interesting passage in the records of former times, we take the liberty of inserting, in the pages of the Repository, a short digest of the account of the rise and progress of the Yellow Caps to the death of their first leaders, as given in the first and second sections of that work.

The history of the Three States—Shŭh, Wei, and Woo—opens by dating the origin of those causes, which led to the division of the empire into three kingdoms, at the reigns of Hwan (A. D. 147) and Ling (A. D. 168), the immediate predecessors of Heuen, the last emperor of the Han dynasty. The historian finds occasion for the civil wars, that caused the downfall of that house and disjointed the whole empire, in the corrupt state of the government, which had shut up the avenues to preferment against the good and the wise, and admitted

* See volume seventh, number fifth, pp. 232-249, for a brief account of this work.

美魏茶所译《黄巾起义》

126　*Notices of Kungming, a Chinese Hero.*　March,

mentioned above. Harber Rock may be steered for directly it bears to the southward of east.

N. B. This channel requires further examination.

On Kúláng sú are five batteries; two on the south end mounting fifteen and nine guns, two on the south side having seven and three guns, and one on the northwest side mounting eight guns. On Tsipan point were two batteries, and on the points further to the westward three other, one of six and two of five guns.

The rise and fall of the tide from one day's observation on the full moon in September, was fourteen feet and a half; at this period, however, the night tides exceed the day by two feet. The change in the depth, in all probability, three days after full and change would exceed sixteen feet. This would be of great importance to vessels requiring repair, particularly as sites for docks, and ample materials for making them, are to be found upon the island of Kúláng sú, as well as in other parts of the harbor.

Kúláng sú.—This island is well adapted for a settlement; it is 2·85 miles in circumference. The channel between it and Amoy is 675 yards wide. The ridge of hills on this island is higher than those opposite. There are two distinct ridges upon the island, which might be separately defended, the highest part being 280 feet above the sea. The geological features of the island are principally granite, the soil being formed of it in a decomposed state. Large boulders of it also occur in many places, both upon the shores and the highest part of the island. Fresh water from wells was plentiful, and the cultivation and artificial channels for leading it to boats, lead me to suppose that there is always a good supply of this article. There are many houses upon the island, and the population may be estimated at between 3000 and 4000.

Art. III. *Notices of Kungming, one of the heroes of the San Kwoh Chí.*

This celebrated personage is the greatest hero recorded in the San Kwoh Chí, or History of the Three States, which is one of the best written Chinese tales that has been written; and taking into consideration that it is now 600 years since it was written, we may

美魏茶所译《孔明评论》

（一）从米怜到小米怜

1839 年，美魏茶与理雅各、合信（Benjamin Hobson，1816—1873）一起乘坐“斯图尔特号”（Eliza Stewart）轮船来到中国。由此，伟烈亚力在 1867 年所著的《新教在华传教士回忆录》中，将三人的传记资料排在一起、前后相承，理雅各居首，美魏茶次之，合信最后，三人分别是该著介绍的第 15、16、17 位新教传教士，而伟烈亚力在这部人物传记中介绍的第三位传教士，就是美魏茶的父亲米怜。

根据伟烈亚力的记载，美魏茶是米怜双胞胎儿子中的一个，1815 年 4 月 22 日出生，当时米怜为了传教，在广州与马六甲之间辗转奔波，美魏茶就出生在父母由广州赴马六甲的路上。1817 年 9 月 3 日，美魏茶 2 岁时第一次随父母回到中国，翌年 2 月 17 日返回马六甲。由于当时中国实行严厉的禁教政策，米怜面对恶劣的传教条件，生活劳顿。美魏茶四岁丧母，七岁丧父。1822 年，被送回英国，此后在亚伯丁的马修神学院（Marischal College，Aberdeen）接受神学训练，获得学位。1839 年 7 月 19 日，美魏茶被伦敦布道会委派到中国传教，与理雅各、合信乘坐同一条船，经过百余日航行，于 12 月 18 日抵达澳门。

此后，美魏茶开始了在中国长达 14 年的生命历程。抵达澳门后，他很快加入马礼逊教育协会（The Morrison Education Society），协助马礼逊宣教、办学。1841 年，美魏茶和其他传教士到香港考察建立传教中心事宜。同年 4 月至 9 月，全面代理马礼逊教育协会的学校、图书馆工作。1842 年 2 月，前往舟山、宁波考察，此后长期居留在两地。1843 年 7 月 7 日至 8 月 12 日，行程 1300 英里，穿越浙江、江苏和广东三个省，抵达香港，出席伦敦布道会在那里召开的系列会议。在 8 月 25 日的会上，美魏茶与麦都思（Walter Henry Medhurst，1796—1857）、马儒翰（J. R. Morrison，1814—1843）组成《圣经》翻译委员会。1844 年 7 月 26 日至 1846 年 8 月 25 日，离开香港返回英国，与弗朗西丝（Frances Williamina）结婚。回到中国后，继续从事《圣经》翻译工作，并出任上海《圣经》翻译委员会宁波代表。1850 年 7 月，在完成《新约》翻译后，继续出任同一职务翻译《旧约》，1852 年底，完成《旧约》的翻译。1854 年年初，因健康问题返回英国。1856 年，不再为传教工作服务。1858 年返回中国后，改任福州领事馆的译员，直到 1861 年英国政府成立英国公使馆（British Legation），到北京出任公使馆译员的指导教师。1863 年 5 月 15 日，美魏茶死于中风，葬在北京安定门外的俄国公墓。①

美魏茶的父亲米怜年仅 37 岁英年早逝，他在中国生活 10 年，以虔敬的态度和勤勉的精神留下诸多著述，在《新教在华传教士回忆录》中，伟烈亚力著录了米怜的中文著作 21 种，英文著作 3 种，其中有《求世者言行真史记》（*Life of Christ*）、《进小门走窄路解论》（*Tract on the Strait Gate*）、《张远两友相论》（*Dialogues between Chang and Yuen*）、《乡训五十二则》（*Twelve Village Sermons*）等对新教传播产生了深远影响的宗教宣传书册，有号称中国历史上第一份中文近代报刊的《察世俗每月统记传》（*Chinese Monthly Magazine*），有记录新教早期传教事业的《新教在华传教前十年回顾》，这些作品不仅渗透着米怜个人的宗教使命和生命体验，也是新教在华宣教事业的拓荒性作品。

美魏茶享年 52 岁，在中国生活 14 年，但在著述方面却不及其父，伟烈亚力著录了他的中文译作六种，英文著作 1 种。总体看来，这些著述可以分

---

① Alexander Wylie，*Memorials of Protestant Missionaries to the Chinese*，Shanghae：American Presbyterian Mission Press，1867，pp. 122 - 124.

为两类。

一是宗教读物。伟烈亚力著录的六种中文译作中，除了用上海方言翻译的《马太传福音书》(*Matthew's Gospel*)，其余五种均是他人译作的修订本或改编本。其中，三种是米怜译作的修订本：《福音广训》(*Village Sermons*)、《真道入门》(*Introduction to the True Doctrine*) 和《张远两友相论》；一种是马礼逊译作的修订本《路加传福音书》(*The Gospel of St. Luke*)；一种是纽曼·豪尔 (Rev. Newman Hall) 作品的改编本《警恶箴言》(*The Sinner's Friend*)。此外，还有与麦都思合译的《新约全书》(*New Testament*) 和《旧约全书》(*Old Testament*)，以及《中国丛报》上发表的与其他传教士讨论"deity"中译的一篇文章。这些作品显示了美魏茶的传教士职业特色，只是与同时期的理雅各、麦都思等人相比，这部分宗教读物整体看来成就有限。

二是中国纪行。1843 年 6 月，美魏茶在《中国丛报》第 12 卷发表了《中国的亚洲霍乱》(*Notices of the Asiatic Cholera in China*)，文章标明"宁波来稿"。此后，他以《宁波居住七个月》(*Notices of a seven months' residence in the city of Ningpo*) 为题，在《中国丛报》1844 年第 13 卷和 1847 年第 16 卷连载了自己的宁波见闻，记录了他 1842 年 12 月 7 日至 1843 年 7 月 7 日的宁波生活。1854 年，他将自己的中国纪行结集出版，形成专著《生活在中国》。在"序言"中，美魏茶首先论证了自己书写中国的合法性和可信度。他说自 1839 年来到中国，至 1854 年撰写本作，除了返回英国的两年，他在中国居住了 14 年。走访过澳门、香港、广州、舟山、宁波、上海等许多城市，还穿越了浙江、江苏和广东 3 个省。《生活在中国》记录的就是这些个人经历。全书共分为四个部分：第一部分讨论了英美流行的中国观念，在他看来某些观念非常离谱，对于中华帝国的居民来说极不公正。另外三个部分则分别记录了自己在宁波与上海的生活经历，以及行程 1300 英里穿越中国国内的沿途见闻，提供了涉及中国人生活及习俗的正面信息。相比于美魏茶的宗教读物，这部分个人纪行的作品更有特色，对于研究 19 世纪中期的宁波和上海，以及东南诸省，都是难得的史料。

除了以上两类作品，美魏茶涉及中国文化的论述，就是《中国丛报》刊载的两篇《三国演义》译介文——《黄巾起义》和《孔明评论》，这是美魏茶译介中国文学作品的重要学术贡献。《黄巾起义》有作者署名，《孔明评论》没有署名，参考 1851 年 12 月《中国丛报》停刊时出版的“总索引”，在《中国历史》（Chinese History）一栏中，《孔明评论》改名 *Sketch of Kungming*, *from the San Kwoh Chí*，作者署名 W. C. Milne，由此得知该文作者为美魏茶。

（二）从“张氏三兄弟”到“结义三兄弟”

美魏茶对于“黄巾起义”的翻译，显然受了德国来华传教士郭实腊的影响。1838 年 9 月，郭实腊在《中国丛报》第 7 卷第 5 期发表了《三国志评论》一文，这是英语世界对《三国演义》所做的首次系统评论。美魏茶在《黄巾起义》的标题后注明该文“编译自《三国志》”，接着，为《三国志》添加了一个注释：“参考第 7 卷第 5 期第 232 页至 249 页有关该作的简介”。这篇“简介”指的正是郭实腊的《三国志评论》。

在《三国志评论》中，郭实腊虽多次提及“黄巾起义”，但介绍文字仅有一段。他说：“那时有兄弟三人才华出众。瘟疫在百姓中肆意蔓延，他们就出去采药以助人疗疾。一天采药时，遇见一位智者（a genius），交给老大三本书，说：‘此中学问博大，去革新国家，普救世人吧。若萌异心，必获恶报。’大哥张角（Chang Keŏ）听到这些不可思议的话很是高兴，急忙攻习，从此学会了呼风唤雨的本领。在瘟疫肆虐期间，他通过施撒念过咒语的符水来治病救人。由于疗效显著，他的追随者数量剧增，还谋划着竖起黄旗，改朝换代。皇帝很快得知了他们的叛乱，抓住他们的一些信众，或斩首，或下狱。此举震撼了义军领袖，他们组建起自己的军队，头戴黄帽或黄巾，以区别于朝廷军队，他们被视为异类，号称‘黄巾军’（the Yellow Caps）。这部伟大的戏剧就此拉开序幕，从此干戈不断。”①

郭实腊认为“黄巾起义”揭开了汉末动乱的序幕，这种表述显然强调了“黄巾起义”的重要性。故此，美魏茶开篇即云：“黄巾起义（The Rebellion of the Yellow Caps）使中华帝国分崩离析，从而为风靡一时的《三国志》（*San Kwo Che*，*or History of the Three States*）的写作奠定了基础，并形成了一段历史佳话。”② 由此可见，两人都把“黄巾起义”看作开启“三国”历史的起点，这次起义也就有了特别的意义和译介的必要。

考察底本是评论译介文的基础，美魏茶所用《三国演义》底本当是清朝最流行的毛评本，明显的证据是在他的译介文中有这样两句话：

> This Tsaou Tsaou displayed early in life a roving and wily disposition, which it was impossible for his father or his uncle to curb. However, men perceived that he was qualified for the times, and foresaw his future eminence, at the prediction of which Tsaou Tsaou was not a little delighted.

回译为中文，可以表述为：“曹操早年就表现出了狡猾机变的个性，他的父亲和叔叔几乎管不了他。然而，人们却认为他生逢其时，并预言他将会显达，曹操听说了这些却毫不惊喜。”结合毛评本《三国演义》，这段话应该是对以下情节的概述。原文曰：

---

① “Notice of the San Kwŏ Che”, *The Chinese Repository*, Vol. Ⅶ., From May, 1838 to April, 1839, Canton: Printed for the Proprietors, p. 235.

② 本文所引美魏茶的《黄巾起义》，均出自《中国丛报》1841 年第 10 卷，第 98—103 页，此后不再一一注释。“The Rebellion of the Yellow Caps”, *The Chinese Repository*, Vol. Ⅹ., From January to December, 1841, Canton: Printed for the Proprietors, pp. 98 – 103.

> 操幼时，好游猎，喜歌舞；有权谋，多机变。操有叔父，见操游荡无度，尝怒之，玄德之叔父奇其侄，曹操之叔父怒其侄，都是好叔父。言于曹嵩，嵩责操。操忽心生一计，见叔父来，诈倒于地，作中风之状。叔父惊告嵩，嵩急视之。操故无恙。嵩曰："叔言汝中风，今已愈乎？"操曰："儿自来无此病；因失爱于叔父，故见罔耳。"欺其父、欺其叔，他日安得不欺其君乎？玄德孝其母，曹瞒欺其父、叔，邪正便判。嵩信其言。后叔父但言操过，嵩并不听。因此操得恣意放荡。时人有桥玄者，谓操曰："天下将乱，非命世之才不能济。能安之者，其在君乎？"南阳何颙见操，言："汉室将亡，安天下者必此人也。"二人皆不识曹操，曹操闻之亦不喜。①

以上引文中，中间插入的小字是毛纶、毛宗岗父子所写的"夹批"。美魏茶文中所言"曹操听说了这些却毫不惊喜"，显然是毛氏父子的夹批"曹操闻之亦不喜"。只是他混淆了原著中的"正文"与"夹批"，所以才在译文中直接引入了"夹批"，但这一"夹批"的出现，却为我们推测他采用的底本提供了便利。

就译介方式而言，美魏茶在文章标题中注明"黄巾起义"的内容"编译"（compile）自《三国志》，这就意味着，他的译介不是严格遵照原著进行"翻译"，而是有选择地进行"编译"。译者拟根据《三国演义》前两章，简述"黄巾军的兴起和发展，直至其首领的死亡"。按照这一规划，文章涉及的主要人物当是与"黄巾起义"密切相关的张氏三兄弟。实际上，他对张角、张宝的介绍比较详尽，对于张梁，仅有两三句话。

文章对于张角、张宝的译介各有侧重，开头主要写张角，重点介绍了其个人经历及对于"黄巾军"的组建发挥的作用。美魏茶说："就在国家面临剧局之际，巨鹿郡（the principality of Keuluh）一家出现了一位领袖

---

① （明）罗贯中著，（清）毛宗岗批注：《第一才子书三国演义》，线装书局2007年版，第7页。

人物。这户人家姓张，有兄弟三人。老大叫张角（Chang Keŏ），是义军首领，曾经遇到一位自称是山神的奇士的指点。这位南华圣人（sage of Nan-hwa）把张角叫到一边，送他一本书，同时宣称他会成为'救世主'（liberator mundi），又威胁他说如果拒绝他的任命，就会遭到厄运。说完，奇士就消失了。张角得到此书，用心攻习，直至最后获得了超人的力量，能够呼风唤雨。灵帝在位第十八年的元月发生了一场瘟疫，疫情肆虐。在这场瘟疫中，张角成功利用神奇的纸张和有魔力的水（magical papers and charm-waters）治愈病人，由此而使自己名声大振，他还通过四处差遣徒众来扩大自己的影响，这些人被他点化，能用超自然的异能征服瘟疫。这样他获得了众人拥戴，并在各地分立渠师，只等时机一到揭竿而起。"

这段文字介绍了张角得到天书，习得异能，广收门徒，准备起义，整体看来基本符合原著内容。特点有二：一是某些地方修正了郭实腊的说法。比如，郭实腊把"以天书三卷授之"，译作"交给老大三本书"，很容易使人误以为张角得到的《太平要术》是三种不同的书，而美魏茶结合文本实际，恰当地译作"送他一本书"。二是某些文化专有项的翻译有些突兀，两种语言的对接与转换显得艰涩。比如，将"代天宣化，普救世人"理解成"救世主"；将"咒书和符水"译作"神奇的纸张和有魔力的水"。语言转换的艰难，凸显了道教影响下兴起的"黄巾起义"自身的宗教色彩。

对于张宝的介绍主要出现在文章的末尾，笔墨集中在其妖术上。美魏茶说："一场会战接踵而至，张宝作起妖术（magical art）（风雷大作，一股黑气从天而降，黑气中出现了无数勇士），使对手惊慌失措，仓皇撤退。但是，再次交战时，张宝的妖术（juggle）就不那么灵验了，因为朱儁以其超人的智谋化解了他的妖术。他事先准备了大量猪、羊、狗血，搬运到附近高坡上，等前次的妖术再次出现时，立即从高处泼下。两军交战时，'张宝作法，风雷大作，飞沙走石，黑气漫天，滚滚人马，自天而下'。玄德调转马头，慌忙撤退，张宝驱兵赶来，等他追到高处时，污血从上泼下，但见‘空中纸人草马，纷纷坠地。风雷顿息，砂石不飞’。张宝见法术已破，被迫逃命，艰难地抵达一处要塞，遂与军队坚守不出。”

郭实腊在介绍“黄巾起义”时，并没提及张宝，对于其“妖术”，更是完全省略。相比之下，美魏茶对于这部分内容却格外关注。尤其是在整篇译介文中，魏美茶只有两次遵照原著进行翻译：一是在首次提及张宝“妖术”（magical art）时，美魏茶在括号里所做的注释，实际是对原著中出现的以下文字的翻译：“只见风雷大作，一股黑气从天而降，黑气中似有无限人马杀来”；二是两军交战时，“张宝作法，风雷大作，飞沙走石，黑气漫天，滚滚人马，自天而下”，当对手从高处泼下污血后，但见“空中纸人草马，纷纷坠地。风雷顿息，砂石不飞”。美魏茶用“引号”标注的两句，不仅紧扣原著，而且译得也比较生动，比如他将后一句译作：in the air, paper-men and grass-horses, falling in confusion to the ground. The wind and thunder ceased, nor did the sand and stones continue to fly about。由此说明涉及“妖术”的文字定然是对美魏茶带来很大震撼，这应是他回到原著翻译细节的根本原因。此后西方人多次译介张宝妖术，或许正是源于同样的阅读体验。

张角、张宝只是美魏茶在文章开头和结尾分别论及的人物，实际上，文章主体部分大量叙写的核心人物是刘备及其结义兄弟关羽、张飞。这三人命运的何去何从，才是文章遵循的真正主线。在“黄巾起义”发动后，美魏茶笔锋一转，立即推出了结义三兄弟。他说：“就起义者一方而言，他们首先进攻之地为幽州（Yew），该地校尉（lieutenant）随即出榜招募义兵。这纸榜文引出了著名的刘备玄德（Lew Pe Heuentĭh），他是汉室后裔，亲友都曾预言日后他必显贵。与此同时，这纸榜文还使玄德结交了英雄张飞（Chang Fei）和关羽（Kwan Yu），三人相识后，就相互约定，同心同德，共扶汉室。”虽然没有详细介绍“桃园结义”，但美魏茶此后的叙述却没有直接追随张氏三兄弟的足迹，而是转到了结义三兄弟的身上，并相继介绍了三人的以下行踪：一是三人首先投奔刘焉，跟着其手下将领邹靖出战，首战告捷，在邹靖被困时用计解救。二是离开刘焉后，赶去救援卢植，卢植却命令他们转战颍地，前去救援皇甫嵩和朱儁。当刘备赶到颍地时，战争已结束，唯剩论功行赏，三人只得返回卢植处，却发现卢植被人陷害，正被押往京城。三是在关羽的建议下，三人返回故地，在北归途中，遇到黄巾军，将张角大军打得四处溃逃，同时救了董卓，却遭到冷遇。四是张飞不满于董卓的傲慢，于是三人转投朱儁，受到礼遇，在朱儁的指挥下，破了张宝的妖术，张氏三兄弟相继败亡。由此结束了译者对于“黄巾起义”的整体介绍。

美魏茶遵循的主线由“张氏三兄弟”转到“结义三兄弟”身上，这种视角的转换恰恰体现了他对原著内容的理解基本准确。整体看来，美魏茶对于“黄巾起义”的译介主要取材于《三国演义》前两回，尤其是第一回，因为第二回开篇不久就迎来了黄巾军的全面败亡。第一回回目为“宴桃园豪杰三结义　斩黄巾英雄首立功”，由此不难看出，作者提及“黄巾”不过是为英雄们“立功”而树立的靶场，这里的“英雄”，显然指的是桃园结义的三兄弟。毛氏父子早已点出这一立意，两人在“时巨鹿郡有兄弟三人”后面的夹批中说：“以此兄弟三人，引出桃园兄弟三人来。”由此可见，在原著中，作者论及“黄巾起义”这一历史事件，不过是为了凸显结义三兄弟的乱世豪杰身世而铺展的历史背景，黄巾起义本身并非作者用心之所在，更不是作者叙事之关键。美魏茶既想交代这一事件，又想遵循《三国演义》叙事主线，就很难避开这三个人物。与结义三兄弟相比，张氏三兄弟虽然是“黄巾起义”的领袖人物，也只能屈居其次。

同样的情况还出现在美魏茶对于“曹操”这一人物的介绍上。毛氏父子在第一回“回评”中说：“百忙中忽入刘、曹二小传：一则自幼便大，一则自幼便奸；一则中山靖王之后，一则中常侍之养孙：低昂已判矣。”由此可见，毛氏父子认为，在写作手法上，《三国演义》作者让曹操出现在第一回，是为了让他与刘备形成一种鲜明的对照。美魏茶在概述第一回时，自然不能对曹操等闲视之，于是文中出现了一段文字介绍曹操。译者曰：“这时，另一位时代英雄人物曹操（Tsaou Tsaou）（一位西班牙著者称他是‘中国的波拿巴’）出现了，前来分享这天的荣誉和战利品。曹操早年就表现出了狡猾机变的个性，他的父亲和叔叔几乎管不了他。然而，人们却发现他生逢其时，并预言他将会显达，曹操听说了这些却毫不惊喜。二十岁时，他步入官场，为人严正，以致成了恶人畏惧的人物。几次升迁后，拜为骑都尉（an officer of cavalry），由此组建了一支军队捍卫朝廷。”这段文字与“黄巾起义”及其领袖关系不大，突然插入，不免突兀，但《三国演义》原著就是如此，美魏茶的译介既然完全脱胎于《三国演义》前两回，自然难以忽略原著中对于曹操的大段介绍。此外，括号内注释提到的“西班牙著者”或许是寓居中国多年、后来担任卢卡尼亚大主教（Archbishop of Luconia）的塞吉神父（Padre Segui），德庇时在1834年澳门出版的《汉文诗解》中曾对他有所提及，他说《三国演义》曾被塞吉神父全部或部分地译成西班牙文。[①] 由此推测，美魏茶读到的或许正是塞吉神父翻译的这一西班牙译本，倘这一推测无误，那么，美魏茶的这一注释不仅为西班牙译本的存在提供了一个佐证，也为曹操形象的海外建构提供了一种对比的可能，即塞吉神父很早就将曹操与波拿巴联系在了一起。

整体看来，相比于原著，美魏茶笔下的“黄巾起义”的显著不同是对于起义者的态度发生了根本改变：由否定而肯定，由贬斥而褒扬。比如，美魏茶用 sage of Nanhwa，即“南华圣人”来翻译“南华老仙”，由此消解了“老仙”这一称谓中具有的宗教色彩，而“南华圣人”又称张角为liber-

① John Francis Davis，汉文诗解，*Poeseos Sinensis Commentarii*，*On the Poetry of the Chinese*，Macao，China：Printed at the Honorable East India Company's Press，By G. J. Steyn and Brother，1834，pp. 156 – 157.

ator mundi，这在西方文化传统中被理解为“救世主”，显然是一美誉。对于美魏茶这样的基督教传教士来说，liberator 一词甚至具有一种神圣性，耶稣就常被称为 liberator 或 pre-liberator。对照原著，liberator mundi 理应是对于“太平道人”的译解，倘若直译“太平道人”，将“道人”译作 taoist，其异教色彩很容易引起英语读者的反感。美魏茶没有直译“太平道人”，而是巧妙地将其转化为“救世主”，其中自然隐含着一种态度的转变，他显然有意将黄巾军的起义领袖树立为正面形象。又如，在原著中，黄巾军被定义为“反国逆贼”，无论是朝廷命官还是民间义士，提及黄巾军，一概称之为“贼”或“贼众”。如：“四方百姓，裹黄巾从张角反者四五十万。贼势浩大，官军望风而靡。”美魏茶在提到黄巾军时，常用 insurrection 或 rebel，即“叛军”或“反叛者”这类中性词；而从不使用 thief 或 traitor，即“盗贼”或“叛徒”这类贬义词。对于 18 世纪末期经历过法国大革命、美国独立战争的西方读者来说，被定义为“叛军”或“反叛者”的黄巾军是一种反抗政府的武装力量，他们非但未必象征着乾坤颠倒、天下大乱，甚至被看作改革和激变的伟大动力，具有代表先进力量的革命者反对旧制度、追求新秩序的意味。

（三）“孔明”形象的全面解读

“黄巾起义”发表两年后，1843 年 3 月，美魏茶在《中国丛报》第 12 卷第 3 期发表了《孔明评论》。这是英语世界对于“孔明”形象的第一次全面解读，具有一定的开创性。

美魏茶对于孔明的解读，在人物和情节方面，具有以下两方面特点。

第一，在人物译介方面，为突出孔明，美魏茶最大限度地精简了三国人物。《孔明评论》中翻译的人名仅有五位，按出场顺序依次为：玄德（Hiuente）、孔明（Kungming）、曹睿（Tsáujui）、司马懿（Sz' má I'）、孙权（Sunkiuen）。五人中，除了孔明，另外三人分别是蜀、魏、吴三国的君王，而司马懿是孔明去世前最强有力的劲敌，在文中不可或缺，由此可见，在人物删减方面，美魏茶可谓不遗余力。除了以上五人，其他人物均被略去姓名，他们主要以两种方式出场：一是作为上述五个主要人物的从属人员。如，刘备带着关羽、张飞"三顾茅庐"，请孔明出山，文中省略了关羽、张飞的姓名，只道是玄德的"几位心腹"（a few intimate followers）。二是以人物在故事情节中扮演的角色或身份出场，主要涉及以下诸人：后主刘禅（emperor）、使臣邓芝（embassy）、将军陆逊（general）、老臣李福（old minister），以及以官员（officer）身份出场的马谡、李严、夏侯霸和魏延。三国故事繁杂、人物众多，对于初涉汉语的外国人来讲，理清其中脉络颇为不易，在核心人物之外精简次要人物显然很有必要。对于作者而言，这样做有利于集中笔墨介绍主要人物；对于读者而言，精简人物也有利于降低阅读难度，减轻阅读疲劳。

同时，需要注意的是：精简人物不可避免地给《孔明评论》带来了两方面问题。

首先，三国人物形象原本就具有明显的脸谱化特征，大量人物的删减，使孔明形象变得更加单薄。如三顾茅庐时，刘备带领关羽、张飞三次前往隆中拜访孔明：第一次没见到孔明，但听到了田间农夫传唱的孔明所作的歌谣，遇到孔明的朋友崔州平；第二次也没见到孔明，却遇到了他的两位友人——石广元和孟公威，以及孔明之弟诸葛均和孔明之岳父黄承彦；第三次造访才得以目睹孔明风采，正面描绘了这一山中高士的智慧与谋略。这些人物大多从侧面烘托了孔明形象，哪怕是出场的一个童子，也能彰显孔明的不同凡俗。刘备第一次登门造访，唯恐孔明不加重视，特意自报家门道："汉左将军、宜城亭侯、豫州牧、皇叔刘备特来拜见先生。"然而，孔明的童子根本不吃这套，只淡淡地回应了一句：“我记不得许多名字。”刘备听罢，自觉无趣，只得主动拿掉了头上的光环，交代一句道：“你只说刘备来访。”童子尚且不慕权贵，主人自然淡泊明志，这里明写童子，实际是在暗褒孔明。在美魏茶的笔下，这些陪衬人物及其个性化的语言均被删除，孔明形象也就难以立体呈现。

其次，精简人物带来的更大问题，是对于人物和事件的误解与错解。比如，孔明临终前，将平生所学诉诸笔端，交付姜维，文中省略了姜维之名，只道是孔明“最特殊的友人”，即 his most particular friends，但这里的“友人”用的是复数形式，很容易让人误以为孔明所托之人并非一人。又如，在曹魏方面，美魏茶主要提及了曹睿和司马懿两个人物，相关情节的叙述也大致围绕二人展开，但在概括重要战事时却出现了明显差误。美魏茶说：“听说蜀汉来犯，魏王曹睿调集兵力，任命司马懿为统帅，他是一位勇猛老练的将军，在前次战斗中刚与孔明交过手，曹睿派他出兵，命其占据要塞和山中关隘，加强防御，但绝不应战；据他推测，蜀军的粮草很快就会消耗殆尽，在他们主动撤退时再行进攻会更加有利。”① 对比原著，不难看出，在这次蜀汉交战中，司马懿发现蜀军行粮不足，故主张坚守不出，等蜀军被迫撤退时，再乘虚追击。于是上奏曹睿，曹睿欣然同意，欲派司马懿亲自上阵，但司马懿担心东吴称帝，陆逊来犯，故举荐曹真出战。曹真接旨，以为坚守不出乃是曹睿的战术，却被其手下大将郭淮一语道破此乃司马懿之战术，对于曹魏集团来说，这一战术颇合时宜，故郭淮夸赞司马懿“深识诸葛亮用兵之法”，进而预言日后能御蜀兵者，非司马懿莫属。与原著相比，美魏茶在概述这一事件时，显然张冠李戴，把司马懿的战术错置在了曹睿身上，这与曹真、郭淮等人物的省略有着直接的关系。

---

① 本文所引美魏茶的《孔明评论》，均出自《中国丛报》1843 年第 12 卷，第 126—135 页，此后不再一一注释。“Notices of Kungming”, *The Chinese Repository*, Vol. Ⅻ, From January to December, 1843, Canton: Printed for the Proprietors, pp. 126 - 135.

第二，在情节译介方面，《孔明评论》在“三顾茅庐”之后，立即转入“刘备托孤”，这两个情节都是一笔带过，美魏茶着力叙述的是刘备死后孔明辅佐幼主、独掌大权期间发生的故事。首先介绍了《三国演义》第85回的内容“刘先主遗诏托孤儿　诸葛亮安居平五路”。接着，跳过“七擒孟获”，直奔“六出祁山”，即孔明带兵进行的北伐战争。美魏茶概述的内容，大致对应着《三国演义》第91回“祭泸水汉相班师　伐中原武侯上表”至第105回“武侯预伏锦囊计　魏主拆取承露盘”。这部分内容占据了《孔明评论》百分之七十的篇幅，是美魏茶译介文的重心所在。

在《三国演义》中，“六出祁山”是孔明一生中亲自指挥的最重要的军事行动，也是最能体现其军事智慧的情节单元。第一次，蜀汉军队斩了曹魏五将，生擒魏国驸马夏侯楙，孔明智取三城，降伏姜维，骂死王朗，打败曹真，大破西羌兵，屡屡得胜。只是后来因马谡违令、误失街亭而被迫撤退。孔明临危不惧，用“空城计”智退司马懿，此后退兵，自贬其职。第二次，孔明出兵包围陈仓，被魏将郝昭所阻，又有王双前来救援，孔明令魏延对抗王双，自引大军攻打祁山，大破魏兵。后因粮草不济被迫撤兵。第三次孔明在祁山，命姜维、王平分取武都、阴平，连败魏军都督司马懿，后因孔明生病，遂将大军屯于汉中，自回成都养病。第四次，曹魏以曹真、司马懿为正副都督，进攻汉中，却遭连日阴雨。孔明气死曹真，打败司马懿，后司马懿坚守不出，又令蜀汉降将苟安散布谣言，诬蔑孔明自恃功大，图谋篡国。后主听后，诏回孔明。孔明被迫退兵。第五次，孔明复出祁山，用“缩地之法”牵制魏军，趁机割了陇上小麦以充军粮。后来都护李严因粮草不济，谎称吴国攻蜀，向孔明告急，孔明连忙撤兵，撤退途中杀了魏将张郃。第六次，孔明兵分五路，再出祁山，魏将郑文前来诈降，孔明识破其策，将计就计，大败魏军，火烧上方谷，夺取渭南。司马懿坚守不出，孔明屯兵五丈原，不久病死。“六出祁山”占据了《三国演义》15回的内容，在篇幅上超过“赤壁大战”和“七擒孟获”，是刘、关、张去世之后，孔明独自维持蜀汉局面的重头戏。

对比原著，不难发现，美魏茶对于“六出祁山”的介绍整体看来比较完整，只是内容详略严重失当。在“六出祁山”中，他对于前五次战事叙述都相当简略。在叙述“一出祁山”时，甚至与此前的“安居平五路”混在一起，其中还一语带过了“七擒孟获”。对于这三次重大战事，美魏茶的全部叙述仅有一段，他说：

> 吴、魏得知玄德已故，而他的儿子又是一个愚笨的君主，遂认为这是一个彻底摧毁摇摇欲坠的汉室的绝好机会；为确保成功，他们召集了一些蛮族部落前来援助，以帮助他们从各个方向同时发动进攻。在安排好战事、下达完命令后，他们立刻穿过边境，开始了一场歼灭战；孔明在稍作延迟后，集中起所有兵力，分成几队人马各自执行任务，他自己则亲自带领一支队伍进军蛮族；不仅降服了他们，还通过慷慨、仁慈的实际行动，使他们站到了自己这边。针对反复无常的吴王，他派了一名一直以来战无不胜的使者前去游说，让他站到了对自己有利的一方，现在就只剩下与魏国对抗了，他此时全力以赴，甚至攻入了魏的地盘。但是，由于委以重任的某些官员的错误之举，他没能像往常那样好运，他几乎被敌军包围，连后路也被掐断了；即便身陷险境，他也没有失去一贯的沉着冷静，尽管敌人知道如何围剿，但孔明却破坏了他们的所有方案，并且最终安全地撤回蜀汉，没失一兵一卒。之后，因处理失当，被迫撤退，孔明向君主请罪，获得恩准后，他被降级。

在“六出祁山”中，《三国演义》对“一出祁山”敷演最多，作者用了 6 回篇幅加以陈述，内容涉及第 91 回“祭泸水汉相班师　伐中原武侯上表”至第 96 回“孔明挥泪斩马谡　周鲂断发赚曹休”。其中不仅有着《出师表》这一千古奇文，还有“空城计”这一亘古奇策，这些有趣的故事在美魏茶的讲述中均被省略；“安居平五路”“七擒孟获”这两出重头戏，更是掺杂其间、粗陈梗概。对于第二、三、四、五次北伐，美魏茶同样轻描淡写。除了简述出征始末，其中的细节一概省略。比如，对于第五次北伐战争，美魏茶只是简单地概括为以下几句："在证明了指控全属捏造后，孔明重获荣誉，再次率兵远征。可是尚未出发，就又接到情报，说吴国非但没站在蜀汉这边，反而投靠了魏国，正带着无数兵力打来。由于担心遭到围攻，而且考虑到所有兵力仅足以保住国土，他再次撤回蜀汉。此时，孔明发现这是一个陷害自己的骗局，由此倍感屈辱。原来这是运送补给的官员延误了他的部署，于是利用上述诡计召回了军队。当诡计被揭穿时，这位官员的不忠不义之举遭到了严厉惩罚，原因是他只顾一己之私而不顾国家利益。"

美魏茶对于前五次北伐的叙述可谓简约至极，相比之下，他对于第六次北伐的叙述不但不惜笔墨，甚至略显铺张，在"六出祁山"中，第六次占了近四分之三的篇幅。美魏茶不仅交代了第六次北伐的来龙去脉，对其中的个别细节还进行了详细转述，他对于孔明言辞的直接引用，对于"木牛流马"的仔细解说，以及对于"孔明之死"的详细陈述都值得称道。

其一，对于孔明言辞的直接引用。一篇旨在简要概括人物生平的文章通常很难容纳人物语言，但在转述第六次北伐时，美魏茶却两次直接引用了孔明的言辞。一是在描写出征前的孔明时，美魏茶说："孔明一刻也没有忘记他对先帝许下的诺言，而今又开始精神抖擞地为下一场战役做准备，尽管后主要求他稍事休息，也让国家有一段太平日子，他却拒绝了。他说：'我受先王知遇之恩，发誓竭力尽忠，使贼人服从汉室统治，大业未成，我不会稍事休息。我已经多次出兵讨伐叛军了，至今也还只是取得了部分胜利；所以现在我向圣主发誓，不把他们彻底消灭，誓不再见，大业不成，誓不再还。'"对比原著，孔明行前入朝对后主所奏之辞，以及在昭烈庙中对先帝所祭之辞，与美魏茶翻译的这段话均有差异。尽管没有直译原文，但他却融合其意，化用其语，以孔明的自陈之辞巧妙地显示了他对于蜀汉政权的忠心。二是在祈禳时看到代表自己命运的主灯不幸被扑灭时，美魏茶再次直接引用了孔明的言辞，他说：“如此一来，他所有的希望都破灭了，只得努力安抚自己面对现实，他叹口气说：‘我们的生死有定，我们的命运不可改变。’”（Our life and death are destined, and we can do nothing to avert our fate.）这句话显然直接译自原文。原著有云：“孔明弃剑而叹曰：‘死生有命，不可得而禳也！’”这一语言细节生动地表现了孔明大业未成身先死的悲痛与无奈。

其二，对于“木牛流马”的仔细解说。美魏茶说：“因为我们的英雄拥有魔力，经常施出奇招，有时使其对手无计可施，几乎把他们吓个半死。有一次，驮畜的所有饲料，以及士兵的所有供给，都需要从数里之外运来，途经一处山地，靠近魏营。其艰难险阻几乎阻断了军用物资的运输，殃及几十万人，由此孔明决定制造木牛木马，这些木牛木马利用特殊的机关便可发动起来，这样它们就像真正的牛马那样能走能跑。孔明发现这些木制动物非常方便，因为它们很好地满足了制造它们的目的，这不但使孔明因此而获得了常规物资，而且更有利的是，他的这些运输工具还不会消耗它们所运送的物资。在诱敌深入时它们也很有用，一直在窥探孔明的人获悉了他的新发明，也想拥有这些如此有用的牲畜。因为他们没有一个样品，自己又制造不出来，于是决定埋伏起来，等它们经过时截获一些。探子将此事报与孔明，这并没有超出他的预料，他已为此做好了充分准备，还埋下了伏兵，使敌人损失惨重。然而，在讲求实际的时代，我们认为故事的这部分内容会让人觉得太过离奇，不足为信。我们在一个地方得知，机器的核心部分在舌头上。一次，当一群木牛木马被魏兵紧追猛赶时，随军士兵扭动了它们嘴里的机关，这时木牛木马就停了下来，寸步不行，对捕获者而言毫无用处。”这段对于“木牛流马”的转述异常详尽，既交代了这一特殊战备装置的制造材质、核心机关，也介绍了其主要用途与功能优势。

其三，对于“孔明之死”的详细解说。首先，美魏茶分析了孔明之死的两个原因：第一，在第六次北伐中，孔明千方百计诱使司马懿出战，但司马懿坚守不出，这时又传来吴军战败、随即撤军的消息，孔明得知后昏厥过去，此后百病缠身，自知死期将至。这是孔明之死的直接原因。第二，长期以来，上至国家政务，下至军士需求，孔明无不亲力亲为。长此以往，积劳成疾，这是孔明之死的深层原因。其次，美魏茶讲述了孔明为了避免早亡所做的努力，概括介绍了“五丈原诸葛禳星”。“禳星”即攘除灾星，这是一种颇具道家文化色彩的活动，美魏茶用基督教文化的“祷告”（prayer）对之做了解释。对“祈禳之法”的过程与目的也做了简要译介，他说：“孔明在做了一番祈祷后，点起若干灯，其中一盏代表着他的命数；如果这盏灯能够持续燃烧七天不灭，就预示着他的生命会延长，但是如果中间灭了，就预示着他会死去。”最后，“禳星”失败后，孔明开始安排后事，美魏茶对这一过程也做了详细译介。孔明首先召集将领，发布遗令，部署后续战事。接着上奏后主，劝他以先帝为榜样，举贤任能，摒弃奸邪。后主接到表奏，无比震惊，立即派老臣前去问讯此后国事如何处理。孔明在道出两人姓名后，咽气身亡，享年 54 岁。在其身后，美魏茶还补记了二事：一是孔明以“木像”吓退司马懿，所谓“死诸葛能走生仲达”。二是蜀军安全撤回国内后，方才为孔明举丧，朝廷上下，为之哀痛，众皆落泪，如丧考妣。

整体看来，美魏茶对于第六次北伐的译介结构完整、脉络清楚、内容充实、细节醒目。对照原著，也有个别地方的概括、理解存在明显错误。比如，在原著中，孔明禳星时扑灭主灯的是魏延，文中提到：“忽听得寨外呐喊，方欲令人出问，魏延飞步入告曰：魏兵至矣！延脚步急，竟将主灯扑灭。”而在《孔明评论》中却是孔明自己踏灭了主灯，即：“孔明正在帐中祈祷，而今他已持续祈祷了六日：他的灯仍然明亮如故，他开始振作起来，以为能躲过这场劫难，这时只听营外一片嘈杂，一名官员匆匆入帐禀报被袭之事。孔明匆忙转身回座，没有注意到地上摆放的东西，一脚踏上了那盏致命的灯，灯光瞬间熄灭。”又如，李福奉后主之命，在孔明临终前赶到军营询问他身后谁可继任，原著写作：“福奉天子命，问丞相百年后，谁可任大事者。”这里的“丞相百年后”是“孔明过世后”的委婉表达，然而，美魏茶却将此译作后主“派遣了一名老臣前去询问孔明今后百年将会发生的事情”（what appearance matters would wear a hundred years hence）。类似的错误在《孔明评论》中屈指可数，不会影响读者对孔明形象的整体接受。

《孔明评论》翻译特色及其对于后世产生的影响，主要体现在以下三个方面。

第一，美魏茶对于孔明这一人物形象进行了全面肯定。比如，开卷伊始，美魏茶就称孔明是“最伟大的英雄”；“三顾茅庐”之后，评论道“既然得到了先王的信任，他就下定决心要鞠躬尽瘁、履行职责，他的胆略、才智和能力，很快得到了考验”；在“七擒孟获”时，他“不仅降服了他们，还通过慷慨、仁慈的实际行动，使他们站到了自己这边”；在“六出祁山”时，“尽管身陷险境，他也没有失去一贯的沉着冷静”。孔明去世后，美魏茶不无痛惜地说：“这位政治家就此结束了他的一生，享年 54 岁。他一生勤于政事，言行磊落，自从担负起保卫国家的重任，就立下誓言，国不太平，绝不休息，他忠实地信守了这一诺言。”这些肯定性评论对于孔明形象在英语世界的传播势必发挥了正面影响。

第二，在“六出祁山”中，不少情节凸显了孔明神机妙算、多智近妖的特点，但美魏茶本着客观求实的态度，几乎全部删除了类似情节。最典型的莫若第 101 回“出陇上诸葛妆神　奔剑阁张郃中计”。第五次北伐中，孔明为了让蜀兵割陇上之麦，所以自己装神弄鬼，引诱魏军前来追赶。文中写道：“孔明见魏兵赶来，便教回车，遥望蜀营缓缓而行。魏兵皆骤马追赶，但见阴风习习，冷雾漫漫。尽力赶了一程，追之不上。各人大惊，都勒住马言曰：‘奇怪！我等急急赶了三十里，只见在前，追之不上，如之奈何?’孔明见兵不来，又令推车过来，朝着魏兵歇下。魏兵犹豫良久，又放马赶来。孔明复回车慢慢而行。魏兵又赶了二十里，只见在前，不曾赶上，尽皆痴呆。孔明教回过车，朝着魏军，推车倒行。魏兵又欲追赶。后来司马懿自引一军到，传令曰：‘孔明善会八门遁甲，能驱六丁六甲之神。此乃六甲天书内缩地之法也。众军不可追之。’”类似的手段在第六次北伐中也曾用到，文中写道：“三更以后，天复清朗。孔明在山头上鸣金收军。原来二更时阴云暗黑，乃孔明用遁甲之法；后收兵已了，天复清朗，乃孔明驱六丁六甲扫荡浮云也。”这种神出鬼没的军事手段，在正常的军事战争中匪夷所思。鲁迅在《中国小说史略》中评论《三国演义》：“至于写人，亦颇有失，以致欲显刘备之长厚而似伪，状诸葛之多智而近妖。”① 鲁迅对于孔明形象的批评，或许正是因为道术手段的频繁运用。但在美魏茶的文章中，作者对类似情节却不为所动，他所论及的故事大多符合现实逻辑，对于涉及巫蛊、神异的内容，几乎全部予以删除。哪怕对于“木牛流马”这一神奇装置，也禁不住对其合理性提出质疑，美魏茶评论道：However, we suppose that in these matter-of-fact days, this part of the tale will be regarded as rather too farfetched, and unworthy of credit. 即：“在讲求实际的时代，我们认为故事的这部分内容会让人觉得太过离奇，不足为信。”由此，美魏茶所构建的孔明形象，是祛除了“妖道”色彩的符合理性精神的人物形象。

第三，大量传统经典孔明故事的删减，使得美魏茶笔下的孔明形象不免单薄，但也为孔明故事的译介留下了较大空间。《三国演义》问世后，广为人知的孔明故事多达几十则：刘备托孤之前，除了“三顾茅庐”，关于孔明的著名桥段还有火烧新野、舌战群儒、草船借箭、借东风、三气周瑜、智取汉中、八阵图等；刘备托孤之后，最重要的情节是“七擒孟获”和“六出祁山”，美魏茶集中笔墨介绍了后者，对于前者只是一笔带过。这些精彩故事的缺失，必然会影响孔明形象的丰富性和生动性。然而，值得注意的是，尽管美魏茶

---

① 鲁迅：《中国小说史略》，上海古籍出版社 2011 年版，第 87 页。

笔下的孔明只是北伐中的孔明，但这个孔明形象却得到了译介者的充分肯定，因此，孔明很快成了英语世界译介三国人物的焦点所在。从 1877 年至 1879 年，前后三年间，英国人司登得在《中国评论》上分 12 次连载了《孔明生平概况》一文，讲述了 39 个孔明故事。直到 20 世纪初期，英语世界译介的孔明故事依然层出不穷。比如，1902 年，上海圣约翰大学校长卜舫济（Rev. F. L. Hawks Pott，D. D.，1864—1947）在《亚东杂志》（*The East of Asia Magazine*）上发表了《三国选》（*Selections from "The Three Kingdoms"*）一文，其中所选的三个故事中，就有“草船借箭”（The Arrows of Ts'ao Ts'ao's Troops shot into the straw figures made by Chu-ko-liang）的故事。又如，1905 年，约翰·斯蒂尔（John Steele）将《三国演义》第 43 回编成中英文合璧的英语教材，题名《舌战群儒》（*The Logomachy*），以单行本形式出版；1907 年，又出版了该章内容的英文全译本，依然是单行本发行，以配合英语教材的使用。这些孔明故事的翻译，使孔明成了 19 世纪海外中国文学形象中的璀璨之星。

附：英文原文

材料一

The Rebellion of the Yellow Caps, compiled from the History of the Three States. ①

As the insurrection, that ended in that dismemberment of the Chinese empire which became the foundation of the popular *San Kwŏ Che*, or "History of the Three States" forms the subject of an interesting passage in the records of former times, we take the liberty of inserting, in the pages of the Repository, a short digest of the account of the rise and progress of the Yellow Caps to the death of their first leaders, as given in the first and second sections of that work.

The history of the Three States—Shŭh, Wei, and Woo—opens by dating the origin of those causes, which led to the division of the empire into three kingdoms, at the reigns of Hwan (A. D. 147) and Ling (A. D. 168), the immediate

① See Volume seventh, number fifth. pp. 232 – 249, for a brief account of this work. 编者按：郭实腊的文章刊于《中国丛报》第7卷第233—249页，非232—249页。应为美魏茶记载之误。本文刊于 *The Chinese Repository*, Vol. X., From January to December, 1841, Canton: Printed for the Proprietors, pp. 98 – 103。

predecessors of Heuen, the last emperor of the Han dynasty. The historian finds occasion for the civil wars, that caused the downfall of that house and disjointed the whole empire, in the corrupt state of the government, which had shut up the avenues to preferment against the good and the wise, and admitted eunuchs, — that class of weak, low, and depraved courtiers, —into the councils of the state. It was the emperor Hwan who began this course of degeneracy, and the dire consequences of it were gradually evinced during the reign of his successor, more weak than himself. Soon after Ling had ascended the throne, signs most strange and alarming appeared in the heavens and on the earth, all portentous of some approaching calamity. The sagacious and patriotic of the princes knew full well the occasion of all this, and presumed to warn their sovereign of a crisis at hand. His own fears were to some degree excited, but they were speedily dispelled by the craft of the eunuchs, who induced their master to degrade those ministers, who had dared to remonstrate with imperial majesty. Finding that their opportunity had now come, the eunuchs formed themselves into a body of counselors, called the *shĭh chang she*, or "the ten constant attendants," and, enjoying the emperor's implicit confidence, they took the reins of government into their own hands. Having thus briefly pointed out the causes of future calamities, the historian, like a patriot, sighs over the weaknesses of his sovereign and the misfortunes of his country, "Alas, my father! The imperial government waxed worse every day, until there was universal disaffection, and marauders rose up like wasps."

At this time, when the country had become disposed for change, a leader appeared in a family of the principality of Keuluh. In this family there were three brothers, whose surname was Chang. Chang Keŏ, the eldest of them, was chief in the insurrection, to which he had been incited by an interview with a singular personage, who gave himself out to be one of the mountain genii. This sage of

Nanhwa called Chang Keŏ aside, and put a book into his hands, at the same time announcing that he was to be the "*liberator mundi*," and threatening the worst of evils, if he should decline his appointment. On this, the stranger vanished. Keŏ took the book and devoted himself to its study, till at length he gained superhuman power, and was able to control the elements of nature.

It happened, that in the eighteenth year of Ling's reign, and in the first month, a pestilence broke out, and raged furiously among the people. During that plague, Chang Keŏ rendered himself popular, in curing large numbers by the successful use of magical papers and charm-waters, and increased his own influence by sending forth, to every part of the country, men who had been inspired by him, with supernatural virtue to overcome the same distemper. In this way he gained the confidence of myriads, who were disposed by him in various districts under regular leaders, and he only waited for a fit time when to carry his projects into execution.

Very shortly after, he gave out that the time had arrived, when the reigning family should cease and give place to another line of emperors; and he assured his countrymen that heaven would favor them, as a new cycle was just opening. Thus he won an immense body of the nation over to his side. To render the plot complete, he sent one of his trusty followers to form an alliance with one of the eunuchs, and, lest they should lose the present opportunity through delay, he dispatched a second confidant to apprize the intriguing party at court of the badge adopted by their allies, and of the day when they would rise; but the messenger, who had been intrusted with the final instructions, repented and discovered the scheme to the imperial cabinet.

This disclosure led to the immediate seizure and imprisonment of Fung Seu and his party, who formed the court cabal; and the imperial troops were ordered out to crush the first symptoms of insurrection.

When the rebel generals Chang Keŏ, Chang Paou, and Chang Leäng heard that their secrets had been betrayed, they took it as a sign for an instantaneous rise, and, assuming high sounding titles, they put forth a public manifesto, calling for the aid of their countrymen. They were at once joined by 400, 000 or 500, 000 men, who all wore yellow caps, in sign of their attachment to the new cause, from which circumstance this insurrection is generally designated in history, "the rebellion of the Yellow Caps." While the rebels were scattering themselves over the country, orders were issued by the emperor that every district should be in readiness to defend itself, and that three of his chung lang tseäng (high generals) should proceed with troops to subdue the Yellow Caps.

The first act of aggression, on the part of the malcontents, was in the district of Yew, the lieutenant of which immediately issued a proclamation for a general levy of troops. —This call brought forth the famous Lew Pe Heuentĭh, a descendant in the line of the Han family, who, it had been predicted by his relatives and comrades, would some day rise to eminence. It, at the same time, brought Heuentĭh in contact with the heroes Chang Fei and Kwan Yu, the result of which interview was that these three persons entered into a solemn covenant to stand by each other in supporting the interests of the house of Han, and to keep the unity of mind and purpose inviolate.

Thus leagued, these heroes of the *San Kwŏ Che* sally forth to join the ranks of lieutenant Lew Yen, who gladly welcomed them. His excellency, hearing in a few days that a party of the enemy was coming down upon one of his districts, gave orders to his officer Tsow Tsing, to proceed against them and avail himself of the assistance of Heuentĭh, whose comrades signalized themselves in the first onset, by killing—the one a colonel, the other the general of the rebel troops. On this, a large body of the enemy seeing themselves thus early deprived of some of their leaders, joined the imperial party; and the lieutenant of Yew conferred rewards on the victors.

But, on the day following the victory, he received a dispatch from the governor of Tsing department, to the effect that he was placed in imminent danger by the siege, which had been laid against him. His request, that auxiliaries should be sent to him, was forthwith granted; and in a very little time the siege was raised, chiefly through the stratagems of the three brothers.

Immediately on the distribution of rewards by the gov. of Tsing, Heuentĭh and his comrades separated themselves from the troops of Yew, to hasten to the relief of Loo Chĭh, (Heuentĭh's former tutor, and one of the chunglang tseäng already spoken of,) who was then engaged in contest with Chang Keŏ, the leader of the rebellion. On their reaching the scene of warfare, Loo Chĭh was much pleased with this mark of attachment in his late pupil, but directed him to proceed to the assistance of his colleagues Hwangfoo Sung and Choo Sun who were, in the Ying district, waging war against Chang Keŏ's brothers. While Heuentĭh was advancing towards Ying, the imperialists had routed the Yellow Caps, —who fled in all directions before the conquerors. At that instant, another hero of those times, Tsaou Tsaou, (called by a Spanish writer 'the Buonaparte of China,') made his appearance, to share in the glory and the spoils of the day. —This Tsaou Tsaou displayed early in life a roving and wily disposition, which it was impossible for his father or his uncle to curb. However, men perceived that he was qualified for the times, and foresaw his future eminence, at the prediction of which Tsaou Tsaou was not a little delighted. At the age of twenty, he entered office, and conducted himself with strict impartiality, so that he became a terror to evil-doers. After a few minor promotions, he was made an officer of cavalry, and it was then he led forth a company to assist the imperial house.

Heuentĭh arrived only in season to congratulate the victors on the repulse of the enemy, and detailed his interview with his tutor Loo Chĭh, to whom the two chung lang tseäng directed the three brothers to return, as they felt persuaded the fugitives would immediately resort to Kwangtsung, where Chang Keŏ was besieged by Loo Chĭh. The brothers at once retraced their steps, but had proceeded only half the distance, when they met Loo Chĭh confined in a cage and guarded by a party of soldiers, who were conducting him to the capital. The captive explained that he had been maligned at court, and that, under the false representations of a crown officer, who had been sent down to extort money from him but had failed in his attempts, he had orders from the emperor to hasten to the capital for examination, and that meanwhile Tung chŏ was appointed to superintend those hostilities against the chief Chang Keŏ, which had well nigh been closed, but for this unhappy interruption. Chang Fei, when he heard this account, got furious, and was on the point of cutting down the guards with his sword, when Heuentĭh quieted him by the irresistible argument that, as it was the emperor's will, nothing could be done in opposition to it. So Loo Chĭh was allowed to pass on to meet his doom.

At the advice of Kwan Yu, the sworn brothers resolved to return without delay, to their native district. But on their progress northward, they perceive, from the din of war, that conflicting parties are at hand. It is the imperial bands routed and put to flight by Chang Keŏ's overpowering numbers. Heuentĭh and his friends take a stand and, by a vigorous attack, beat the rebels back, and saved the honor of the throne. It was Tung chŏ (Loo Chĭh's substitute,) who had been thus rescued by an unknown branch of the imperial house, but this general treated his deliverers only with disrespect, which the ever ardent Chang Fei could not brook, and he swore that nothing should appease him, short of the blood of the haughty and uncivil Tung chŏ.

However, his brothers Heuentĭh and Kwan Yu successfully remonstrated with him; but, as it was their united opinion, that, rather than join the corps of such an officer, they should put themselves under the banner of Choo Sun one of his colleagues, they accordingly proceeded to enter his ranks, and were treated by him with all urbanity. As that general was engaged in an attack on the rebel Paou's forces, he took the faithful three with him. In this instance, Heuentĭh also signalized himself in a close combat with one of the enemy's colonels, whom he left dead on the field. A general engagement instantly ensued, when general Paou, by some magical art (which produced a storm of wind and thunder, and drew down a black cloud from heaven, in which appeared a countless host of matchless warriors,) drove his opponents back in fear and consternation.

But, on the next assault, Paou's juggle was not so successful, as it was rendered futile by the superior stratagem of Choo Sun. He, immediately after he found Paou having recourse to his magical powers, had arranged that a quantity of the blood of pigs, sheep, and dogs, should be collected and carried up to a neighboring height, and that, on the first appearance of the same phenomena which had occurred before, this should be poured down. When the assault was made, "Chang Paou acted the magician, there was a tremendous wind and thunder, the sand flew, and the stones ran (along the ground), a black cloud overcast the sky, and an immense number of men and horses fell from heaven," Heuentĭh turned his horse and hastily retreated, while Chang Paou pursued him, with all his men, as far as the rising ground, when the mixture was thrown down from its top, and then there could be seen "in the air, paper-men and grass-horses, falling in confusion to the ground. The wind and thunder ceased, nor did the sand and stones continue to fly about." Chang Paou, finding himself baffled in this attempt, was obliged to flee for his life, and, with difficulty reached one of his fortresses, where he shut himself up and his troops.

While Choo Sun was occupied in besieging Chang Paou, he heard that his colleague Hwangfoo Sung, had been appointed to take the place of Tung chŏ, whose frequent losses had occasioned his degradation from office; that, when Hwangfoo entered upon his office, Chang Keŏ died, and was succeeded in command by his brother Chang Leäng; that Chang Leäng had been cut off by Hwang, for which achievement the emperor promoted him, and yielded to his intercessions in behalf of the defamed Loo Chĭh, whose misfortune has been noticed; and that Tsaou Tsaou also had been promoted in consideration of the services, he had lent in support of the imperial cause. Choo Sun, on hearing all this intelligence was stimulated to a simultaneous attack of the town, in which Chang Paou had taken shelter, and he brought the besieged to such a stress at length, that one of Paou's own officers beheaded his master and delivered up the city to the imperial general. Thus fell the first leaders of "the rebellion of the Yellow Caps."

W. C.

材料二

Notices of Kungming, one of the heroes of the San Kwóh Chí①

THIS celebrated personage is the greatest hero recorded in the San Kwóh Chí, or History of the Three States, which is one of the best written Chinese tales that has been written; and taking into consideration that it is now 600 years since it

① 编者按: *The Chinese Repository*, Vol. Ⅻ, From January to December, 1843, Canton: Printed for the Proprietors, pp. 126 - 135.

was written, we may also say that it is equal if not superior to any English novel of the 13th century, or a much later period. The Chinese hold it in great esteem, which they show by frequently reading it, and indeed they have good reasons for so doing, as some of its passages are really sublime; that from which we take these remarks, is in our opinion one of the most worthy of notice. Perhaps before entering at once into that part where our hero approaches his latter end, it would not be here amiss, to mention a few particulars that occurred during his celebrated career. As the story goes, the early part of his life was spent amongst woods and streams, through which he delighted to roam, and though possessed of such extraordinary talents, he preferred solitude, and the pleasures of a country life, to engaging at all in the affairs of state; but Hiuente, the then reigning sovereign of Hán, a very valiant and virtuous prince, and who just at that time was doing all in his power to collect the worthies of the land at his court, hearing of his fame, went in person to search him out. The season was then far advanced in winter, and the snow lay thick on the ground; yet notwithstanding, the monarch accompanied by a few intimate followers started in quest of Kungming; but after a long and wearisome journey, on arriving at his cottage, they had to bear the disappointment of finding him absent from home, and as none of the remaining inmates could inform where he had gone, they were obliged forthwith to return. But Hiuente was not so easily to be baffled in his attempts to gather together a number of wise councillors and instructors, and he determined again to go and visit him in his solitude; and shortly afterwards, during the same rigorous weather set out for that purpose, but was as formerly unsuccessful. He then deferred it until the next spring, when he began to make extensive arrangements for the subjugation of the two states of Wú and Wei (this being the time when the empire was divided into three parts, Wei, Wú, and Hán or Shuh, each of whom was striving for mastery over the two others), and as he was now more in need of good advice than ever, he resolved to go once more in quest of this great worthy, who had been described to him as possessing the greatest wisdom of any sage under heaven. Fortunately he found him at home, and having acquainted him with the object of his visit, he requested him to accompany him to the capital, but as Kungming preferred the peaceful quietude of his humble cottage, to the riotous pleasures that always attend a court, it took some time to obtain his consent thereto, till at last he yielded to the intreaties of his prince, and to Hiuente's unspeakable joy, accompanied him back.

Hiuente then commenced a campaign with his enemies, and with Kungming at his elbow, from whom he sought council and advice in all matters of consequence, proved victorious in all his undertakings; indeed, everything with which our hero had to do, gave success to his employers, and throughout the whole story, there is hardly a single instance recorded of its being otherwise. But Hiuente, after a series of victories, followed the way of all flesh, and as sooner or later, each one of us must do, drew near his latter end. On his death-bed, which is most affectingly and beautifully described, he appointed Kungming to be regent, and having made him promise to follow up the great work, and spend his last breath in conquering the whole of China, he intrusted him with the welfare of the empire, and then breathed his last.

Kungming had now to bear a truly heavy burden, the reins of government were put into his hands, and the happiness of the country was entirely dependant on him, but having once received the trust of the late emperor he resolved to exert himself to the utmost in fulfilling it, and his courage, wisdom, and skill were very soon put to the test. The states of Wú and Wei perceiving that Hiuente was dead, and that his son was an imbecile prince, thought this a good opportunity for totally annihilating the now tottering house of Hán; and to make it the more sure they called in the aid of some barbarian tribes, to help them in effecting a simultaneous attack on all sides. Matters being thus arranged, and the signal given, they all at once crossed the frontiers, and commenced their work of extermination; but Kungming after some short delay, collected the whole of the forces, which, having divided into several divisions and assigned to each their task, he himself with an army marched against the barbarians, whom he not only subjugated, but also by acts of generosity and benevolence, brought over to his cause. To the fickle prince of Wú, he sent an embassy in which he was so far successful as to bring him also over to his interests, and now having Wei alone to contend with, he directed all his efforts in that quarter, and even invaded his territory. But here through the mismanagement of some of his officers whom he had intrusted with important services, he did not meet with his accustomed good fortune, being nearly surrounded by the enemy, and his retreat also cut off; yet in these trying circumstances he did not lose his wonted presence of mind, for though the enemy had made certain of their prey, he disconcerted all their plans, and in the end effected a safe withdrawal to Hán, without losing a man.

He then begged the emperor to punish him for his mismanagement in being obliged to return, which was actually done, and he was degraded a few steps; but in a short time his honors were again restored, and another army was raised to attack Wei, which he was appointed to command. On hearing of the invasion, the prince of Wei, Tsáujui, collected his forces, and having appointed Sz' má I', a brave and experienced officer, who had fought in the last campaign against Kungming, to be commander-in-chief, he sent him off, with instructions to keep possession of the strongholds and mountain passes, fortifying himself strongly therein, but on no account to engage the enemy; for he conjectured, that their provisions would soon be consumed, when they would of themselves retire, and then could be attacked to great advantage. This proved in the end to be the case, for the army of Shuh having been only provided with a slender commissariat, and all Kungming's endeavors to provoke the enemy to fight proving abortive, they were forced much against their will to withdraw; but owing to the masterly style in which the retreat was managed, this was accomplished without loss, to the great chagrin of the opposing party.

But their absence was only for a short time, for as soon as Kungming had made arrangements for the regular supply of the army, and had moreover obtained the assent of Wú to invade Wei on the other side, he, ever eager to fulfill the trust imposed upon him, again set out on his mission. The enemy acted on the same plan as before, but notwithstanding their precautions, Kungming by his address, brought them to an engagement several times, which never failed to end in their being defeated with great loss; but though he also took some of their cities, still they were not sufficiently weakened to be obliged to abandon their intrenched camp. However, thinking that by degrees he would weary them out, Kungming pushed on his operations with greater vigor, but just as victory was beginning to crown his efforts, he received a summons to repair forthwith to the capital.

It came from his sovereign, and therefore it must be obeyed, so that however much against his wish, he was obliged to relinquish the prize which was almost within his grasp. Having no experienced officer who could be intrusted with the command of the army, the retreat was sounded, and all went back to their own territory. Here he found that a courtier had slandered him, giving out reports that he intended to possess himself of the country and depose the emperor; who having listened to these calumnies, had recalled him to give an account of his conduct. Having proved the charges to be all false, and being acquitted with honor, he again marched on the same expedition, but had hardly gone, before reports reached him that the state of Wú, instead of siding with Hán, had gone over to Wei, and was marching with innumerable forces to overwhelm him.

Fearing that he would be surrounded, and thinking that all the forces were but enough for the defense of his own country, he once more withdrew into Hán, where he had the mortification of perceiving that this was a trick that had been played upon him by the officer who supplied the army with stores, and who being behindhand in his arrangements, had made use of the above stratagem to bring the army back. On the deceit being found out, the officer was severely punished for his perfidy in thinking more of his own interests than those of his country. Kungming, never losing sight of his promise which he made to his former patron, now began vigorously to prepare for another campaign, and though the emperor requested him to enjoy a little relaxation, and give peace to the land for a season, he refused to comply; for, said he, "I have received the trust of his late majesty, and sworn to exert myself to the utmost, in subjecting these thievish bands to the rule of the house of Hán, and until I have fulfilled this great work, I will not give myself a moment's ease. I have already gone out many times against these rebels, but as yet have only had partial success; therefore I now swear that your majesty shall not see my face again until I have completely conquered them, nor will I again return until this be accomplished." and he faithfully kept his word. Things now wore a little better appearance, for it was proved beyond doubt that Wú had collected a large army, which had already arrived at the frontiers of Wei; Kungming with redoubled ardor again set out on his last undertaking, and once more took leave of his country, which he never beheld again.

As soon as the enemy perceived that another invasion was in contemplation, they immediately put the country into a state of defense, and intrenched themselves as strongly as ever; so that when the invaders arrived, they found that they had no despicable foe to contend with, but one which would call forth all the exertions of their noble chief to cope with. His scheme was to do all in his power by insults and other maneuvres to cause the enemy to come out and fight a pitched battle, when he felt certain that he would be enabled to put them entirely to the rout; whilst on the other hand the commander-in-chief of the army of Wei well knew by former experience the talents of his rival, and that his safety, and the only way by which he could compel the hostile army to retire, depended upon his keeping up a vigilant guard, and remaining quietly within his trenches.

Yet notwithstanding his alertness, he was often caught in the snares of Kungming, though not to such an extent as to insure the defeat of his whole force; for our hero, possessing magical arts often played most curious tricks, which sometimes put his opponents to their very wit's end, and almost terrified them out of their lives. It seems that on one occasion, all the fodder for the beasts of burden, as well as the provisions for the soldiers, had to be brought from a distance of many miles, and through a hilly country, close to the camp of Wei. These difficulties almost prevented the transport of the subsistence of an army, consisting of several hundred thousand men, and therefore he determined to construct wooden cows and horses, which were set in motion by means of extraordinary machinery, so that they could walk and run like those of nature. These kind of animals he found to be very convenient, as they admirably suited the purpose for which they were made, and not only did he thus obtain regular supplies, but what was more advantageous, his porters did not help to consume what they carried. They were also useful in enticing the enemy into ambuscades, who being always on the lookout, obtained knowledge of Kungming's new invention, and also wished to obtain possession of such profitable beasts. As they could not themselves manufacture them without a pattern, they resolved to lie in wait, and capture some as they drove past. The spies having reported this to Kungming, which indeed did not exceed his expectations, and for which he was fully prepared, he also laid men in ambush, and routed the enemy with great loss. However, we suppose that in these matter-of-fact days, this part of the tale will be regarded as rather too far fetched, and unworthy of credit. We are told in one place, that the chief part of the machinery lay in the tips of the tongue, and one occasion as the herd was being hotly chased by a party of Wei soldiers, the pursued wrenched this member out of their mouths, when the animals stopped unable to move an inch, and proving of no use to the captors.

At this time the army of Wú crossed the frontier in great numbers, and in accordance with their agreement made a descent upon the territory of Wei, the prince of which being roused by the imminent danger, determined to oppose them at once with all the force that he could muster; and having sent reinforcements to his general Sz'má I' who was opposing Kungming, and orders to continue on the defensive, and not give his opponent any opportunity for fighting, he himself set out at the head of his army to oppose the new comers. Luckily for him, he had hardly arrived in their vicinity before his scouts captured one of their messengers who was carrying a dispatch to Sunkiuen the sovereign of Wú, in which his generals informed him of the whole line of conduct they intended to pursue, with a description of their plans, &c., &c. Having obtained this information of their intended movements, he instantly adopted measures by which he could disconcert them, and attacking the force unawares, defeated it in one or two engagements, so that the expedition was obliged to return without effecting anything.

In the meantime, Kungming had been doing his utmost to provoke Sz'má I'to a battle, and though he often highly incensed him by his insolence, still he could not force him to leave his camp. Whilst he was laboring under these and other disappointments, the news of the defeat of the army of Wú, and its subsequent return arrived. On hearing it, he fainted away, and though he soon revived, disease had taken hold of him, and he expressed his fears that he was about to die. His constitution had for sometime been gradually undermining from the arduous duties he performed, for there was nothing that he did not look after in person, from the affairs of state, down to the wants of the private soldier. It is no surprise then, that after he had gone on in this way for years without remission, that his health began to give way, and only required a shock like this to crush him at once into the grave. On the day that he received the fatal intelligence he took to his bed, and having moreover perceived by the stars that his end was approaching, he signified the same to his attendants. They at first tried to laugh it off, but perceiving that he was really serious, they became concerned, and begged him to employ prayer as a means for averting such a calamity. Kungming listened to their advice, and amongst other forms of supplication he lighted a number of lamps, amongst which was placed the one of his destiny; for it was so that if this continued burning for seven days without going out, it was a sign that his life would be lengthened, but if it was extinguished during that time, it signified that he would die. All arrangements being completed, he knelt down and prayed in the most pathetic terms, that he might be spared for a short time, in order to carry out the great work that he had begun, and fulfill the promise that he had made to his late prince. It was on account of his country that he made these supplications, and therefore he trusted that heaven would graciously listen to them, in order that the lives of the people might be saved, and the house of Hán preserved. Having finished praying, he arose, and though he spit blood without cessation, and his sickness had arisen to an alarming height, he still attended to the ordinary affairs of the army throughout the day, whilst during the night he repeated the same ceremonies.

It should be observed, that Sz'má I' was also a star-gazer, and was enabled to foresee future events; and happening, just about the time when Kungming was taken sick to scan the constellations, he noticed that the star of his rival did not burn as clearly as usual, but with a dim and flickering light, by which he knew that he must be very ill, and could not remain much longer in the world. He was thereupon exceedingly glad, and to be still more sure he immediately dispatched an officer with a party of men to spy out whether it was indeed the case. Just as they arrived at the camp of Shuh, Kungming was in his tent at his devotions, which he had continued now for six days: his lamp still continuing to burn as brightly as ever, he began to cheer up, thinking that the danger had past, when a loud noise was heard outside the camp, and an officer hurriedly entered to report that they were attacked. At the same moment Kungming hastily turned round to return to his post, and not taking heed to what was spread out on the floor, he trod on the fatal lamp, and the light was instantly extinguished. Thus all his hopes were blighted, but trying to reconcile himself to his situation, he only sighed and said, "Our life and death are destined, and we can do nothing to avert our fate."

Knowing from this that it was the will of heaven that he should die, he forthwith began to prepare for that solemn hour; and having called all his principal officers together he delivered to each his dying commands, the most important of which were that they should continue to act under the old principles, and that the commander-in-chief, whom he then nominated, should employ the same old trustworthy generals that he had hitherto done, in whom he put most implicit reliance; that on his death, they should gradually retreat into their own land, and put off wailing and lamenting until their arrival there; for if done now it could only inform the enemy of his demise, and they would be instantly attacked; that if such should be the case, they should make up an image of him, in his usual dress, and put it at the head of the troops, which would strike consternation into the forces of Wei, and they would then obtain a complete victory. He also foretold some events that would soon come to pass, and left behind him in writing, the way in which affairs ought to be managed; he also gave over to those who were his most particular friends the books which he had written during his life, together with some discoveries in archery, &c.

Having done this he sat down and drew up a long memorial to the emperor, in which he acknowledged his faults in not having conquered his enemies or given peace to the empire, for which he humbly begged to be forgiven; that it had ever been his most earnest wish to have done so, but that heaven had seen fit to put obstacles in the way, which he most sincerely regretted. In conclusion he exhorted him to follow the example of his august father, and always exert himself in giving peace to the land; but that if he wished to improve the manners of his people, he should advance the worthy and ever take care to banish the wicked from his person.

When this was received, the whole court was thrown into consternation, but nobody felt it more than the emperor himself, for he well knew that Kungming was the strongest support of his throne, which otherwise would long ago have been cast down. However, as he was very anxious to know somewhat of futurity respecting the kingdom, he instantly dispatched an old minister to go and make inquiries of Kungming what appearance matters would wear a hundred years hence, but on his arrival at the camp he found him already speechless. Presently, he again opened his eyes and seeing this minister by his bedside, said to him, I already know for what purpose you have come here. The minister said that he had received commands to come and ask him who could be intrusted with the great affairs of the empire, a century hence. The man was named: and who after him was the next question: another person was again mentioned. And who then? Kungming did not answer. Surprised at his silence all the officers advanced to look at him, and found that he had already breathed his last.

Thus ended the life of this statesman, in the 54th year of his age. He had always shown himself zealous in the affairs of the ministry, never failing to express his true opinions, and when he had taken upon himself to defend his country, and had sworn not to rest until he had freed it from its misery, he faithfully kept his word.

Though it occurred after our hero's death, it would perhaps not be out of the way to mention, that agreeable to Kungming's instructions, after his decease, the army of Hán was immediately set in motion on their return home. This being perceived by Sz'má I', he forthwith pursued them, concluding that this retrograde movement was in consequence of Kungming's death, and thinking that they would be dispirited by the loss of their leader, he expected to gain an easy victory over them. What then was his astonishment on coming up with them to find out that they were drawn up in order of battle to receive him, and that at their head should be no less a personage than Kungming himself (at least so he thought). The total defeat of the army of Wei then followed, after which that of Hán quietly, returned to its own territory, where the troops buried their general, and then gave vent to their lamentations. The whole court went into mourning, and there were none, who did not weep as if they had lost a father.

中文回译

材料一

黄巾起义，编译自《三国志》[①]

黄巾起义（The Rebellion of the Yellow Caps）使中华帝国分崩离析，从而为风靡一时的《三国志》（*San Kwŏ Che*, or "*History of the Three States*"）的写作奠定了基础，并形成了一段历史佳话，在《中国丛报》中，我们冒昧地插入了这个简短的摘要，简述黄巾军的兴起和发展，直至其首领的死亡，正如该著第一、二章所介绍的那样。

魏、蜀、吴三国的历史，即《三国志》，以追叙导致帝国三分天下的根源开篇，溯及汉朝的最后一位皇帝献帝之前的两个皇帝——桓（公元147年）、灵（公元168年）统治时期。史学家发现内战导致了朝廷的垮台和整个帝国的分裂，腐朽的朝廷封锁了选才任能的大道，却任用宦官——一个懦弱、低贱而又堕落的侍臣阶层——参与政事。腐朽从桓帝开始初露端倪，至其继任者统治时期渐趋明显，愈加堕落，灵帝即位不久，异相现于天，

---

① 参考《中国丛报》相关文章，第7卷第5期第232—249页，该文对《三国志》做了简单介绍。编者按：《中国丛报》第10卷，1841年1—12月合订本，广州出版，第98—103页。

警示显于地，凶兆灾难步步逼近。贤良忠士洞悉一切，冒死进谏，告诫皇帝大难临头。皇帝自己亦有所畏惧，但这种畏惧心理很快被太监们的谗言驱散，他们诱使皇帝对胆敢进谏的大臣降级革职。太监们发现时机成熟，于是联合参政，朋比为奸，号称“十常侍”，他们利用皇帝的宠信把持朝政。简单指出未来灾难的起因后，史学家像个爱国忠士，面对帝王的懦弱和国家的不幸唏嘘嗟叹：“唉，上天呀！朝政日非，民心动荡，盗贼蜂起。”

就在国家面临剧变之际，巨鹿郡（the principality of Keuluh）一家出现了一位领袖人物。这户人家姓张，有兄弟三人。老大叫张角（Chang Keŏ），是义军首领，曾经遇到一位自称是山神的奇士的指点。这位南华圣人（sage of Nanhwa）把张角叫到一边，送他一本书，同时宣称他会成为“救世主”（liberator mundi），又威胁他说如果拒绝他的任命，就会遭到厄运。说完，奇士就消失了。张角得到此书，用心攻习，直至最后获得了超人的力量，能够呼风唤雨。

灵帝在位第十八年的元月发生了一场瘟疫，疫情肆虐。在这场瘟疫中，张角成功利用神奇的纸张和有魔力的水（magical papers and charm-waters）治愈病人，由此而使自己名声大振，他还通过四处差遣徒众来扩大自己的影响，这些人被他点化，能用超自然的异能征服瘟疫。这样他获得了众人拥戴，并在各地分立渠师，只等时机一到揭竿而起。

不久，他宣布时机成熟，到了结束当前统治、改朝换代的时候了；他向部众保证上天会庇护他们，一个新的朝代即将开始。由此他赢得了众人的支持。为确保计划成功，他派了一个心腹结交了一位宦官，并且，为防止延误时日，错失良机，再次派一个心腹给朝中宦官报信，告知举事时义军采用的标识和起义的时间；然而，这个得知最终命令的信使却临阵反悔，向朝廷告发了行动计划。

事情败露，朝中内应封谞（Fung Seu）等人立即被捕入狱；朝廷军队也奉命出发，镇压起义。

义军领袖张角、张宝（Chang Paou）、张梁（Chang Leäng）闻知事变，他们认为这是让他们立即起事的征兆，于是喊着响亮的口号，当众申言，号召乡民援助。即刻纠集起四五十万人，全部裹上黄巾，作为加入义军的标志，由此这一起义在历史上通常被称为“黄巾起义”。当义军在全国四处扩张时，皇帝诏令各地备战，三位中郎将（高级将帅）将领兵讨伐黄巾军。

就起义者一方而言，他们首先进攻之地为幽州（Yew），该地校尉（lieutenant）随即出榜招募义兵。这纸榜文引出了著名的刘备玄德（Lew Pe Heuentǐh），他是汉室后裔，亲友都曾预言日后他必显贵。与此同时，这纸榜文还使玄德结交了英雄张飞（Chang Fei）和关羽（Kwan Yu），三人相识后，就相互约定，同心同德，共扶汉室。

结义后，《三国志》里的英雄们前去投奔校尉刘焉（lieutenant Lew Yen）的队伍，刘焉非常热情地接纳了他们。不数日，一股敌军前来进犯，校尉命令手下军官邹靖（Tsow Tsing）前去破敌，并令玄德助战，玄德的结义兄弟杀了一个副将（colonel）、一个主帅（the general），初次作战即战绩显赫。大批敌军见顷刻间失去了许多将帅，纷纷倒戈加入朝廷军队；幽州校尉亦奖赏了凯旋的军士。

但取胜后的第二天，他就接到邹靖军队的急件，说濒临危险，深陷围困。需要援军前去搭救，这一请求很快得到应允；接着迅速发起了围攻，出谋划策的人主要是三兄弟。

邹靖犒劳完军队，玄德一行随即离开了刘焉的部队，赶去救援卢植（Loo Chǐh）（玄德从前的老师，上文提到的中郎将中的一个），那时他正与义军首领张角作战。当他们赶到战地时，卢植对弟子的加入甚是高兴，但命令他去援助同僚皇甫嵩（Hwangfoo Sung）和朱儁（Choo Sun），当时他们正在颍地（Ying district）与张角的兄弟对垒。玄德赶往颍地时，朝廷军队（the imperialists）已经打败了四处溃逃的黄巾军。这时，另一位时代英雄人物曹操（Tsaou Tsaou）（一位西班牙著者称他是“中国的波拿巴”）出现了，前来分享这天的荣誉和战利品。曹操早年就表现出了狡猾机变的个性，他的父亲和叔叔几乎管不了他。然而，人们却认为他生逢其时，并预言他将会显达，曹操听说了这些却毫不惊喜。二十岁时，他步入官场，为人严正，以致成了恶人畏惧的人物。几次升迁后，拜为骑都尉（an officer of cavalry），由此组建了一支军队捍卫朝廷。

玄德赶到时，敌军已退，唯剩庆功领赏，他详述了其师卢植之意，两位中郎将确信逃兵会立即投奔卢植围困张角的广宗（Kwangtsung）一地，于是指引三兄弟返回卢植处。三兄弟当即返回，但行至半路，却遇见卢植被囚在槛车内，由一簇士兵押往京城。卢植解释说他在朝中被人诽谤，一位朝廷命官索贿不成，编造谎言，皇帝命其速回京城问罪，与此同时，委派董卓（Tung chŏ）督察战况，对抗张角，如果战斗不是这样被不幸中断，本该早就结束了。张飞听罢，勃然大怒，拔剑要斩护送军人，玄德连忙阻止他说皇帝之命不可违抗。于是卢植继续前行，去迎接自己的命运。

在关羽的建议下，结义兄弟决定立即返回故地。北行途中，战声大作，他们意识到战事迫近。朝廷军队大败，被所向披靡的张角大军打得四处溃逃。玄德一行站在朝廷一边，有力打击了叛军，捍卫了朝廷尊严。这支汉室的无名军队就此救了董卓（接替卢植的人），但董卓对他们却缺乏敬意，这使一贯性情刚烈的张飞不堪忍受，他发誓说不杀了傲慢无礼的董卓，难消其气。

然而，其兄玄德和关羽成功地劝服了他；三人一致认为，与其听命于董卓，不如投至朱儁麾下，于是三人一起加入了朱儁的军队，并受到礼遇。当时朱儁正和叛军张宝作战，他带上了忠实可靠的三兄弟。玄德在与一位敌军将领短兵相接时大显身手，使之遗尸沙场。一场会战接踵而至，张宝作起妖术（magical art）（风雷大作，一股黑气从天而降，黑气中出现了无数勇士），使对手惊慌失措，仓皇撤退。

但是，再次交战时，张宝的妖术（juggle）就不那么灵验了，因为朱儁以其超人的智谋化解了他的妖术。他事先准备了大量猪、羊、狗血，搬运到附近高坡上，等前次的妖术再次出现时，立即从高处泼下。两军交战时，“张宝作法，风雷大作，飞沙走石，黑气漫天，滚滚人马，自天而下”。玄德调转马头，慌忙撤退，张宝驱兵赶来，等他追到高处时，污血从上泼下，但见“空中纸人草马，纷纷坠地。风雷顿息，砂石不飞”。张宝见法术已破，被迫逃命，艰难地抵达一处要塞，遂与军队坚守不出。

正当朱儁围攻张宝时，听说董卓因屡次战败而被降职，皇甫嵩取而代之；皇甫到时，张角已死，其弟张梁接着统领从众；皇甫斩了张梁，由此获得皇帝嘉奖，又替被人陷害的卢植说情，使皇帝发现了他的冤情；曹操也因效命汉业，按功升职。朱儁得知，备受鼓舞，立即猛攻张宝驻地，最终形成围剿，迫使张宝自己手下的一员将领斩其首级，并向朝廷命官交出了城池。“黄巾起义”的首领们就此被剿灭了。

美魏茶

材料二

孔明评论——《三国志》中的一位英雄[①]

孔明这一著名人物是《三国志》（*Sán Kwóh Chí*），或曰《三国史》（*History of the Three States*）中记载的最伟大的英雄，该著是迄今最优秀的中国故事（tale）之一；想想吧，至今它已问世六百年之久，如果不能说它比 13 世纪或后来的英国小说更加优秀，我们或许也可以说它们不相上下。中国人给予这部作品极高评价，这可以从他们对该著的反复阅读上看出来，由于某些章节确实写得很好，中国人也确实有理由去反复阅读这些章节；

① 编者按：《中国丛报》第 12 卷，1843 年 1—12 月合订本，广州出版，第 126—135 页。

下面我们对这些章节做了些评论，在我们看来，这是最值得注意的内容。在开始讲述我们的英雄的最终结局之前，或许最好不要错过介绍他辉煌一生中的几个细节。故事是这样开始的，孔明早年闲居林泉，喜欢云游四方，尽管天资超逸，却宁愿伏处僻壤，安于乡野生活也不愿参与国事；但是，后汉的统治者玄德（Hiuente），一位英勇无畏、道德高尚的君主，当时正在海内广求贤士，他听说了孔明的英名，于是亲自寻访。时值隆冬，地上积雪很厚；尽管如此，在几位心腹的陪同下，这位君王仍然前去寻访；经过长途跋涉，终于到达了孔明的庐舍，却很失望地发现他并不在家，由于留在家里的人不知道他的去向，他们被迫立刻返回。但是玄德招贤纳才的决心不会那么轻易受挫，他决定再次前往其隐居之地进行拜访；此后不久，在一个同样严寒的天气，他们再次为此出发，但像上次一样无功而返。后来，他们推迟此事，直到来年的春天，那时他正为征服吴、魏两国而做全面部署（当时帝国一分为三，魏、吴和汉，或称为蜀，每个国家都想征服另外两个），此时，玄德比任何时候都更需要妙计良策，所以他下定决心再次寻访这位大贤，因为有人说他是天下最智慧的圣人。幸运的是玄德发现孔明在家，告诉他来意后，玄德便请孔明跟他一道回京，但孔明更喜欢寒舍的闲静，而非庙堂的喧嚣，因此，蜀王花了些工夫才使孔明最终同意了他的恳求，玄德喜出望外，与孔明一同返回。

之后，玄德与他的敌人开始了一场大战，孔明从旁辅佐，所有重大事件都向他征求政见，他的神机妙算使战争大获全胜；的确，我们的英雄所做的每件事，都给他的主公带来了胜利，通观全书，几乎无一例外。但是玄德在一系列胜利后，走上了所有血肉之躯或早或晚都必然要走的那条路，他步入了人生终点。病榻之侧的这段文字最为感人，描写优美，他委任孔明摄政，并让他发誓继承伟业，直到生命的最后一息都要尽力统一帝国，他把家国大业托付给孔明后，便气绝而亡。

孔明现在被迫承担起这一真正沉重的重担，国家的政权交到了他的手里，国家的命运也全部仰仗于他，不过，既然得到了先王的信任，他就下定决心要鞠躬尽瘁、履行职责，他的胆略、才智和能力，很快得到了考验。吴、魏得知玄德已故，而他的儿子又是一个愚笨的君主[①]，遂认为这是一个彻底摧毁摇摇欲坠的汉室的绝好机会；为确保成功，他们召集了一些蛮族部落前来援助，以帮助他们从各个方向同时发动进攻。在安排好战事、下达完命令后，他们立刻穿过边境，开始了一场歼灭战；孔明在稍作延迟后，集中起所有兵力，分成几队人马各自执行任务，他自己则亲自带领一支队伍进军蛮族；不仅降服了他们，还通过慷慨、仁慈的实际行动，使他们站到了自己这边。针对反复无常的吴王，他派了一名一直以来战无不胜的使者[②]前去游说，让他站到了对自己有利的一方，现在就只剩下与魏国对抗了，他此时全力以赴，甚至攻入了魏的地盘。但是，由于委以重任的某些官员的错误之举[③]，他没能像往常那样好运，他几乎被敌军包围，连后路也被掐断了；即便身陷险境，他也没有失去一贯的沉着冷静，尽管敌人知道如何围剿，但孔明却破坏了他们的所有方案，并且最终安全地撤回蜀汉，没失一兵一卒。

之后，因处理失当，被迫撤退，孔明向君主请罪，获得恩准后，他被降级；但旋即官复原职，调集另一军队举兵伐魏，他被任命为统帅。听说蜀汉来犯，魏王曹睿（Tsáujui）调集兵力，任命司马懿（Sz’ má I’）为统帅，他是一位勇猛老练的将军，在前次战斗中刚与孔明交过手，曹睿派他出兵，命其占据要塞和山中关隘，加强防御，但绝不应战；据他推测，蜀军的粮草很快就会消耗殆尽，在他们主动撤退时再行进攻会更加有利。最终证明情况确实如此，因蜀军粮草供给不足，孔明诱敌应战的所有努力一一落空，他们不得不违心地撤退，然而，让魏军恼恨的是，由于撤退组织

① 编者按：此指刘禅。
② 编者按：此指邓芝。
③ 编者按：此指马谡。

得相当严密，蜀军毫发无损地完成了撤兵。

但是撤兵只是告一段落，孔明一旦为军队准备好了常规补给，而且在吴国同意从另一方向攻打魏国后，一直渴望去履行先主嘱托的孔明，就再次奉命出发了。敌军采取了与此前一样的战术，但是尽管他们有所防范，孔明通过搦战，还是使他们出战了几次，只是他们从来没有被打得损失惨重过；尽管孔明也占领了敌军的几个城池，但他们也还没有虚弱到被迫放弃固守的战营的地步。但是，想到这样有可能逐渐拖垮敌人，孔明就以更大的热情继续推进自己的军事行动，可是，当胜利即将来临以奖励他所付出的诸般努力的时候，他却接到一纸诏令，让他立即返回京城。

由于诏令来自君王，他必须遵从，所以无论怎样违背初衷，他都被迫放弃自己唾手可得的胜利。因为缺乏能够委托其带军的有经验的将军，撤退是明智之举，所有的人都撤回了他们自己的领地。这时，他发现一位朝臣诽谤他，说他要谋权篡位；君王听信了谗言，召他回朝解释自己的行为。在证明了指控全属捏造后，孔明重获荣誉，再次率兵远征。可是尚未出发，就又接到情报，说吴国非但没站在蜀汉这边，反而投靠了魏国，正带着无数兵力打来。

由于担心遭到围攻，而且考虑到所有兵力仅足以保住国土，他再次撤回蜀汉。此时，孔明发现这是一个陷害自己的骗局，由此倍感屈辱。原来这是运送补给的官员①延误了他的部署，于是利用上述诡计召回了军队。当诡计被揭穿时，这位官员的不忠不义之举遭到了严厉惩罚，原因是他只顾一己之私而不顾国家利益。孔明一刻也没有忘记他对先帝许下的诺言，而今又开始精神抖擞地为下一场战役做准备，尽管后主要求他稍事休息，也让国家有一段太平日子，他却拒绝了。他说："我受先王知遇之恩，发誓竭力尽忠，使贼人服从汉室统治，大业未成，我不会稍事休息。我已经多次

① 编者按：此指李严。

出兵讨伐叛军了，至今也还只是取得了部分胜利；所以现在我向圣主发誓，不把他们彻底消灭，誓不再见，大业不成，誓不再还。”他忠实地持守着自己的誓言。情势而今出现了某些好转，毫无疑问，事实证明吴国已调集大军，抵达魏国边境；孔明怀着双倍热情再次奔赴使命，也再次离乡去国，此行却再没回来。

敌军一旦发觉蜀军在酝酿又一次进攻，便立即使国家进入了战备状态，并像以前那样坚守不出；所以，等蜀军兵临城下时，他们找不到可以与之对阵的敌人，只有一人需要对付，但这人需要他们的最高将领使出浑身解数。孔明的计划是通过辱骂或别的手段千方百计诱敌出战，他确信那样能够把敌人一举歼灭；然而，在另一方面，魏军的统帅根据以往的经验很了解对手的才智，因此，保住自身的安全，并逼迫敌军撤退的唯一办法，就是保持警惕，并继续安静地留在战壕里。

尽管魏军的统帅[①]很机警，但还是经常上孔明的当，只是孔明还无法万无一失地彻底消灭对手的全部兵力；因为我们的英雄拥有魔力，经常施出奇招，有时使其对手无计可施，几乎把他们吓个半死。有一次，驮畜的所有饲料，以及士兵的所有供给，都需要从数里之外运来，途经一处山地，靠近魏营。其艰难险阻几乎阻断了军用物资的运输，殃及几十万人，由此孔明决定制造木牛木马，这些木牛木马利用特殊的机关便可发动起来，这样它们就像真正的牛马那样能走能跑。孔明发现这些木制动物非常方便，因为它们很好地满足了制造它们的目的，这不但使孔明因此而获得了常规物资，而且更有利的是，他的这些运输工具还不会消耗它们所运送的物资。在诱敌深入时它们也很有用，一直在窥探孔明的人获悉了他的新发明，也想拥有这些如此有用的牲畜。因为他们没有一个样品，自己又制造不出来，于是决定埋伏起来，等它们经过时截获一些。探子将此事报与孔明，这并

① 编者按：此指司马懿。

没有超出他的预料，他已为此做好了充分准备，还埋下了伏兵，使敌人损失惨重。然而，在讲求实际的时代，我们认为故事的这部分内容会让人觉得太过离奇，不足为信。我们在一个地方得知，机器的核心部分在舌头上。一次，当一群木牛木马被魏兵紧追猛赶时，随军士兵扭动了它们嘴里的机关，这时木牛木马就停了下来，寸步不行，对捕获者而言毫无用处。

正在这时，大批吴军越过边境，根据吴蜀双方的盟约袭击魏国，魏王被突如其来的灾难震撼，决定立即调集所有能够召集的兵力进行反击；并给他的将军司马懿派遣了增援部队，司马懿当时正与孔明作战，魏王命他继续坚守不出，不要给对手以任何交战机会，然后他御驾亲征，率军反击新来的敌军。幸运的是，魏王尚未抵达交界之处时，侦察兵就擒获了一名给吴王孙权（Sunkiuen）送信的信使，信中有将领们①提供给吴王的打算采取的所有行动方针和详细计划等。得到吴军的动向后，魏王立即采取了破坏措施，出其不意，攻其不备，一两个回合就打赢了，所以，吴国的这次远征不得不无功而返。

同时，孔明一直在想尽办法引诱司马懿出战，尽管孔明的侮辱常常激怒司马懿，却不能逼其出营。当孔明正在为搦战及其他令人沮丧的事情操劳伤神时，他又收到了吴军战败、随即撤军的消息。刚一听说这一消息，他便昏厥过去，尽管很快醒来，却已诸病缠身，他开始担心自己死期降至。孔明的身体长期以来已被繁重的公务逐步淘空，上至国家政务，下至军士需求，他无不亲力亲为。如此这般持续多年，不得缓解，孔明的身体由此开始变得衰弱也就不足为奇了，只需一次这样的打击，就可以让他立即走进坟墓。收到致命情报的那天，他倒在了床上，而且，他还通过星相观测到他的大限将至，他把这一预测告诉了侍从人员。众侍从最初想一笑置之，却发现孔明确实病情严重，由此才变得重视起来，他们恳求孔明通过祷告

---

① 编者按：此指陆逊。

(prayer) 来避免此难。孔明听从了他们的建议，在做了一番祈祷后，点起若干灯，其中一盏代表着他的命数；如果这盏灯能够持续燃烧七天不灭，就预示着他的生命会延长，但是如果中间灭了，就预示着他会死去。一切安排妥当后，孔明跪下，以极尽悲哀的语言祈祷说，为了完成自己业已开始的伟业，实现他对先帝许下的承诺，祈求上天多给他点时日。他做祈祷是为了国家，所以，为了挽救百姓的生命，保住汉室，他相信上天会仁慈地聆听他的祷告。祈祷完后，他站起来，尽管吐血不止，病入膏肓，仍然整日处理军中的日常琐务，晚上则重复同样的仪式。

需要注意的是，司马懿也是一位星相家，并能预测未来之事；正当孔明带病观测星相的时候，司马懿发现对手的星暗淡摇曳，不像往常那么明亮，据此得知孔明定然病得很重，将不久于世。由此喜出望外，为了进一步确定这一情况，即刻派遣一名官员①带上一帮人前去探听虚实。当他们到达蜀营时，孔明正在帐中祈祷，而今他已持续祈祷了六日：他的灯仍然明亮如故，他开始振作起来，以为能躲过这场劫难，这时只听营外一片嘈杂，一名官员②匆匆入帐禀报被袭之事。孔明匆忙转身回座，没有注意到地上摆放的东西，一脚踏上了那盏致命的灯，灯光瞬间熄灭。如此一来，他所有的希望都破灭了，只得努力安抚自己面对现实，他叹口气说："我们的生死有定，我们的命运不可改变。"

知道天意如此，他将不久于世，孔明即刻开始为这一庄严时刻做准备；将所有重要将领一起召集来后，他逐一交代了自己的遗命，其中最重要的是他们应该继续遵照旧制行事，他随后任命的统帅，也应该像他一直所做的那样，任用同样一批值得信赖的老将，也是孔明绝对信任的人；他死后，他们应该逐步撤回本国，含悲忍泪直至抵达国内；因为如果现在哀悼只会

① 编者按：此指夏侯霸。
② 编者按：此指魏延。

告诉敌人他的死讯，他们必会立即出击；假若果真如此，他们需要制作一尊孔明的雕像，穿上他平时所穿的衣服，置于阵前，可使魏军望而生畏，然后他们可以全身而退。他还预言了一些即将发生的事情，并在其身后写下了如何处理这些事务的方式；又将毕生所写书稿，以及他在连弩等方面的一些发明，交付给了他最特殊的友人。

这之后，他坐下来给皇帝写了一纸长文，上表皇帝，承认自己的错误在于既没能克敌制胜，也没能保国太平，为此他谦卑地乞求得到宽恕；尽管这曾是他最想完成的热望，但上天却在这条路上设置了障碍，使他感到无比遗憾。最后，他劝后主要以他威严的父亲为榜样，永远努力为社稷谋太平；但是如果他想厚民风、促教化，就应推举贤良，摒弃奸邪。

后主收到表奏后，朝廷上下一片震惊，后主尤为惊慌失措，因为他很清楚孔明是其王位的最有力的支持，否则他早被推翻了。然而，由于他急于知晓关乎国家未来的事情，于是立即派遣了一名老臣[①]前去询问孔明今后百年将会发生的事情，但当老臣赶到营帐时却发现孔明已经不能说话了。过了一会，孔明再次睁开眼，看到大臣立于身边，对他说道，我已经知道您的来意了。大臣称他奉命而来，想问孔明今后百年国家大业可交付与谁。孔明道出一人。这之后呢？大臣又问，孔明又道出另一人。再以后呢？孔明没再回答。所有官员因为他的沉默而感到惊讶，上前看时，发现他已经咽下了最后一口气。

这位政治家就此结束了他的一生，享年 54 岁。他一生勤于政事，言行磊落，自从担负起保卫国家的重任，就立下誓言，国不太平，绝不休息，他忠实地信守了这一诺言。

尽管以下这些事情发生在我们的英雄死后，但在此略作陈述或许也不会离题太远。孔明死后，遵照他的遗命，汉军即刻开始拔营撤退。这一动

---

① 编者按：此指李福。

向被司马懿察觉，他立即驱兵追赶，因断定撤军行动乃是孔明已死的结果，又想到他们因痛失统帅而意气消沉，所以他希望能够轻易取胜。然而令他震惊的是当他追上汉军时，却发现他们正严阵以待，位列阵首的不是别人，正是孔明（至少他是这么想的）。魏军随即被彻底击败，此后，汉军悄然撤回国内，安葬了他们的统帅，并且抒发了他们的哀悼之情。朝廷上下，为之哀痛，众皆落泪，如丧考妣。

二　谢卫楼与曹操形象的海外建构*

明清以降，随着《三国演义》的深入人心和三国戏曲的广泛传播，曹操形象由历史人物而成为文学典型，资料来源的差异、评论立场的不同虽然为曹操形象的多元解读提供了可能，但大致没有突破“治世之能臣，乱世之奸雄”的传统论调，曹操形象的反思与重建，显然需要一个全新的文化体系与历史坐标。

19 世纪初期，《三国演义》开始走向英语世界，曹操形象随之开启了西行之旅，这为曹操在世界历史版图的重构创造了条件。就目前所知，最早提及曹操的英国人是第一位来华新教传教士马礼逊，他在 1815 年出版的《华英字典》中，将曹操之名拼读为 Tsaou-tsaou，字典中出现了“篡位者曹操”“曹操倚仗军威决不肯和”等提及曹操的短语或句子。[①]此后半个世纪，英语世界关于曹操的介绍均为节译的片段，曹操形象始终处于一种支离破碎的状态。

直到 1885 年才出现了第一篇系统讨论曹操的文章，这就是美国传教士谢卫楼撰写的《曹操生平及时代概况》。[②]谢卫楼在当时名震一时，被同时期

* 相关研究以“谢卫楼与曹操形象的海外建构”为题，发表于《文学评论》2018 年第 1 期。

① Robert Morrison, *Dictionary of the Chinese Language*, Vol. Ⅰ., Part Ⅰ., Macao: Printed at the Honorable East India Company's Press, by P. P. Thoms, 1815.

② 后文简称此文为《曹操》。

来华的明恩溥誉为“最著名、最有能力的教育家之一”[①]。他不仅编著有《万国通鉴》等多种汉学著作，而且对于中国教育及中西文化交流都做出过重要贡献。

在谢卫楼的笔下，曹操生活的三国时代被比作“希腊的伯罗奔尼撒战争时代”，曹操本人也彻底摆脱了传统文本固化的脸谱形象，被塑造成一个拿破仑式的军事奇才。作为英语世界系统评价曹操形象的长篇大论，《曹操》一文在《三国演义》海外传播史上具有一定研究价值。只是由于该文用英文撰写，又刊登在当时较为罕见的英文杂志《教务杂志》上，故长期以来被学界忽略。

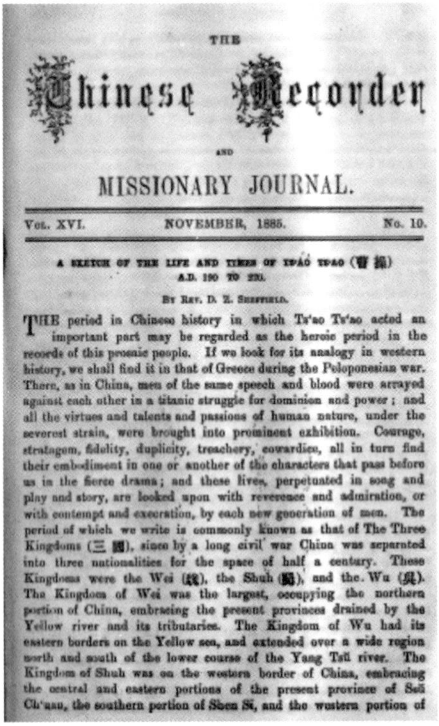

THE

Chinese Recorder

AND

MISSIONARY JOURNAL.

Vol. XVI. NOVEMBER, 1885. No. 10.

A SKETCH OF THE LIFE AND TIMES OF TS'AO TS'AO (曹操)
A.D. 190 TO 220.

By Rev. D. Z. Sheffield.

THE period in Chinese history in which Ts'ao Ts'ao acted an important part may be regarded as the heroic period in the records of this prosaic people. If we look for its analogy in western history, we shall find it in that of Greece during the Peloponesian war. There, as in China, men of the same speech and blood were arrayed against each other in a titanic struggle for dominion and power; and all the virtues and talents and passions of human nature, under the severest strain, were brought into prominent exhibition. Courage, stratagem, fidelity, duplicity, treachery, cowardice, all in turn find their embodiment in one or another of the characters that pass before us in the fierce drama; and these lives, perpetuated in song and play and story, are looked upon with reverence and admiration, or with contempt and execration, by each new generation of men. The period of which we write is commonly known as that of The Three Kingdoms (三國), since by a long civil war China was separated into three nationalities for the space of half a century. These Kingdoms were the Wei (魏), the Shuh (蜀), and the Wu (吳). The Kingdom of Wei was the largest, occupying the northern portion of China, embracing the present provinces drained by the Yellow river and its tributaries. The Kingdom of Wu had its eastern borders on the Yellow sea, and extended over a wide region north and south of the lower course of the Yang Tsü river. The Kingdom of Shuh was on the western border of China, embracing the central and eastern portions of the present province of Ssŭ Ch'uan, the southern portion of Shen Si, and the western portion of

《教务杂志》刊载之《曹操生平及时代概况》

① A. H. Smith, “In Memoriam Dr. Devello Z. Sheffield”, *The Chinese Recorder and Missionary Journal*, September, 1913, p. 565.

（一）从传教士到教育家

《曹操》一文刊载于《教务杂志》1885 年第 16 卷，分两次连载于 11 月发行的第 10 期和 12 月发行的第 11 期。该刊是 1868—1941 年间在华传教士创办的英文刊物，前后出刊 72 年，是中国近现代史上连续性最好、延续时间最长的英文期刊，以其丰富的内容和大量图片、自身的公信力和权威性，成为来华西士最忠实的“在华日志”，也是目前研究近现代中西文化交流的珍贵文献之一。

《教务杂志》的前身是基督教新教传教士于 1867 年在福州美华书局（Methodist Press in Foochow）创办的《传教士记录》（*The Missionary Recorder*），该刊刊行一年后，于翌年 5 月更名《中国记录和传教士杂志》，即通常所称的《教务杂志》，依然由福州美华书局出版，1872 年 5 月出完第 4 卷后停刊。1874 年 1 月，《教务杂志》停刊两年后在上海复刊，由上海美华书馆（American Presbyterian Mission Press）出版，双月刊，此后连续出版 67 年。1932 年改由中国人经营的基督教印刷机构 Thomas Chu & Sons 出版。1941 年 12 月终刊。晚清时期负责该刊编辑工作的传教士有裴来尔（L. N. Wheeler，1839—1893）、保灵（S. L. Baldwin，1835—1902）、卢公明（Justus Doolittle，1824—1880）、伟烈亚力、哈巴安德（A. Patton Happer，1818—1894）、古立克（L. H. Gulick，1828—1891）、费启鸿（G. F. Fitch，1845—1923）等，其中，伟烈亚力、卢公明等都是这一时期的著名汉学家，对中西文化交流做出过巨大贡献。

1885 年《曹操》发表时，《教务杂志》已有了十多年的办刊历史，这一时期该刊最大的变化是自 3 月起，杂志由双月刊恢复为月刊，所需稿件明显增加，尽管如此，当时的稿源却似乎并不短缺。1885 年 4 月，《教务杂志》“编者记”（Editorials Notes and Missionary News）一栏，不但没有像往常那样呼吁读者投稿，反而声称稿件太多，篇幅太长。编者说：“我们需要的是短小、辛辣、凝练、易读的文章，通常不要超过 8 到 10 页，如果能限制在 8 页以内则更好。”“我们呼吁朋友们的作品字数少一点，思考深入一点。”[①] 这一时期稿源的相对充足得益于来华传教士人数的增多。根据 1886 年 1 月《教务杂志》的统计，1885 年在华传教士总计有 914 人，比 1884 年增加了 60 人。[②]《曹操》一文在稿源相对充足的情况下能够作为开卷第一篇文章连载两期，每期篇幅 8 页，达到了《教务杂志》规定的最大限量，这一切都显示了编者对该文的重视。更何况《教务杂志》具有同人杂志性质，以刊载在华传教士的文章为主，作为一篇与传教事业并不直接相关的文章，《曹操》一文得以连载，更见出了该文自身的价值与意义。

《曹操》作者署名 D. Z. Sheffield，即美国传教士谢卫楼，全名 Davello Zelotos Sheffield。1841 年 8 月 31 日，谢卫楼出生于纽约州的怀俄明县（Wyoming County），南北战争期间曾服役两年，战后返乡任教三年。1866 年入奥本神学院（Auburn Theological Seminary）学习，在此期间，他开始向往海外传教，毕业前加入美国海外传教差会“美部会”（The American Board of Commissioners for Foreign Missions），并被派遣到中国华北传道团。1869 年 5 月毕业，被授以圣职，11 月 28 日，28 岁的谢卫楼携新婚妻子抵达北京城东

① “Editorials Notes and Missionary News”, *The Chinese Recorder and Missionary Journal*, April, 1885, p. 155.

② “Editorials Notes and Missionary News”, *The Chinese Recorder and Missionary Journal*, January, 1886, p. 49.

的直隶通州，由此开始了长达44年的在华生涯。[①] 1913年7月1日，72岁的谢卫楼在北戴河因病去世。

谢卫楼去世一个月后，《教务杂志》发表了美以美教会中国教区主教贝施福（Bishop Bashford，1849—1919）的《悼念谢卫楼》（*In Memoriam Dr. D. Z. Sheffield*）一文，文中说："美部会向中国派遣过一些很有能力的人，谢卫楼位居前列。他的天资禀赋，以及作为一名中国研究者的卓越才能，他在高等教育领域的长期工作，还有对中国人的真挚感情，都使他在来华传教士中脱颖而出、卓尔不群。"[②] 9月1日，明恩溥再次撰写《悼念谢卫楼》（*In memoriam Dr. Devello Z. Sheffield*）一文，详细介绍谢卫楼生平，文中回忆说：谢卫楼抵达通州时，那里的传教工作尚处于起步阶段（an embryonic stage）。他刻苦学习汉语，很快取得了显著成效。来到中国五年，就成了"华北地区最有前途的传教士之一"（one of the coming men in North China）。[③]

终其一生，谢卫楼既是一位恪尽职守的传教士，也是一位孜孜以求的教育家，他在教育方面的成就，甚至超过了其传教事业。作为一名传教士，在传教与教育的关系问题上，谢卫楼的态度前后有所变化。他最初对于教会办学心存芥蒂，担心发展教育会影响传教，后来在传教的过程中却越来越倚重于教育，乃至由一名传教士变成了一位教育家。态度转变的标志是他1890年6月在《教务杂志》上发表的文章——《教会教育与其他传教工作分支之间的关系》（*The Relation of Christian Education to Other*

---

① Roberto Paterno，"Devello Z. Sheffield and the Founding of the North China College"，*American Missionaries in China*，Edited by Kwang-ching Liu，Published by the East Asian Research Center，Harvard University，1970，p. 84.

② Bishop Bashford，"In Memoriam Dr. D. Z. Sheffield"，*The Chinese Recorder*，August 1，1913，p. 503.

③ A. H. Smith，"In Memoriam Dr. Devello Z. Sheffield"，*The Chinese Recorde*，September 1，1913，p. 567.

Branches of Mission Work）。文章的最后，谢卫楼说："本文的目的是敦促人们重视教育在传教机构中的重要性，同时告诫那些空有布道热情的传教士不要忘记教育在造就传教人员方面的作用，如果没有教育，传教士的努力不但有失偏颇，结果也常常令人失望。"① 这篇文章明确显示谢卫楼对于教会办学的态度，由此前的保守变得激进。罗伯特·帕特诺（Roberto Paterno）在《谢卫楼与华北协和大学的建立》（*Devello Z. Sheffield and the Founding of the North China College*）一文中说：这篇文章的发表，说明"谢卫楼现在也变成了一个教育事业的倡导者，一个热情地拥护高等教育工作的人"②。

谢卫楼来华后不久就投入了教育实践，兴办学堂是他在华期间的主要工作，突出的贡献是将一所蒙学逐步发展成一所大学。1868 年，美国公理会传教士江戴德（Lyman Dwight Chapin，1836—1894）在通州建立了一所蒙学——潞河男塾，谢卫楼到来后立即投入教学，并将之发展成潞河中学，1893 年升级为大学——潞河书院，1904 年改名华北协和大学（The North China College）。随着学校规模的不断扩大，谢卫楼由一名中学校长变为大学校长，主持大学工作长达 20 年之久，直到 1909 年卸任回国短暂休假，校长之职改由另一位美国公理会传教士高厚德（Howard S. Galt，1872—1948）接任，翌年返回通州后，谢卫楼依然回到华北协和大学任教，两年后死于任上。1919 年，华北协和大学与北京汇文大学等合并为燕京大学，由司徒雷登（John Leighton Stuart，1876—1962）担任校长。1952 年，燕京大学的文科、理科并入北京大学。由此，谢卫楼倾注一生心血创办的学校，成了北京大学的重要渊源和组成部分。

---

① "The Relation of Christian Education to Other Branches of Mission Work", *The Chinese Recorder and Missionary Journal*, June, 1890, p. 257.

② Roberto Paterno, "Devello Z. Sheffield and the Founding of the North China College", *American Missionaries in China*, Edited and with An Introduction by Kwang-ching Liu, Published by the East Asian Research Center, Harvard University, 1970, p. 72.

谢卫楼（D. Z. Sheffield，1841—1913）

（二）《万国通鉴》中的“中国事略”

投身教学、从事教育使既当校长又当老师的谢卫楼有了更多学习和了解中国历史的机会，这为他撰写《曹操》一文奠定了基础。1885 年《曹操》一文发表时，谢卫楼对于中国历史已经有了较为系统的把握，这从潞河中学开设的课程以及谢卫楼本人的著作中即可看出。

在课程方面，根据吴义雄先生提供的《潞河书院名册》，1893 年之前潞河中学开设的课程大致包括三个方面：一是中国的四书五经、历史、古文、时文、诗文等；二是《圣经》研读等神学课程；三是“西国纲鉴、算法与格致”。[①] 既然《书册》中有“历史”“西国纲鉴”等科目，谢卫楼对于中西历史均应有所了解。在著作方面，《曹操》发表之前谢卫楼出版有一部世界通史——《万国通鉴》，该书以《万国史论》等书名多次再版。目前所见最早版本出版于光绪八年（1882），比较常见的是2012年台湾影印的戊戌年（1898）杭州石印的《万国史论》。

《万国通鉴》是当时罕见的用中文撰写的“世界通史”，这部书在晚清受到了中西学者的关注。明恩溥说：“1881年，谢卫楼出版了一部世界史，用中文书写，附有地图和索引，共6卷。在当时很少有这类著作行世，也没有哪部作品涉及范围如此之广。它被广泛地用作教科书，有一些特殊装帧的副本还在官员们中间流传。通过这种渠道，许多中国人第一次获得了他们关于世界各国的知识。”[②] 光绪二十二年（1896），梁启超在《时务报》上刊登的《西学书目表》中推荐的“史志”类书籍总计25种，大部分为编译的外国史书。通史类作品仅有2种：一是日本冈本监辅的《万国史记》；二是谢卫楼著、赵如光译的《万国通鉴》。由此可见，《万国通鉴》在晚清颇受时人认可。

《万国通鉴》在中国史书编纂史上具有重要意义。复旦大学教授邹振环认为：首先，该书是晚清首次采取卷、章、段三位一体结构的世界史，这是此前出现的《古今万国通鉴》和《万国史记》都不曾采用过的编辑体例。其次，《万国通鉴》首次采用了与中国传统史书完全不同的历史分期法，将西方历史划分为古世代、中世代和近世代。尽管《万国通鉴》没有用这种历史分期法对中国历史进行分期，但它还是为东西方历史的横向比较提供了时间坐标。再者，《万国通鉴》首次将中国、蒙古国、日本与印度的历史，编纂成“东方国度”第一卷，由此而将东方国家的历史置于整个世界

① 吴义雄：《谢卫楼与晚清西学输入》，《中山大学学报》2007年第5期，第46页。

② A. H. Smith, “In Memoriam Dr. Devello Z. Sheffield”, *The Chinese Recorder and Missionary Journal*, September, 1913, p. 566.

历史的认识框架。该书采取了统一的纪年法，在中国历史部分标注了耶稣纪年，并附录了英文人名、地名索引，由此显示了作者对于一种统一的世界史编写模式的追求。这一方法此后逐步被中国学者接受，成了中国学界编写“万国史”的通行模式。①

《万国通鉴》版本较多，但内容大致相同，通常分为四卷：第一卷为“东方国度”；第二卷为“西方古世代”；第三卷为“西方中世代”；第四卷为“西方近世代”。第一卷“东方国度”又分为四章：第一章论中国事略、第二章论蒙古国事略、第三章论日本国事略、第四章论印度国事略。在四国事略中，“中国事略”最为详尽，总计大约二万五千字，篇幅比其他三国事略的总和还多出一倍。但作为一部中国史，其内容难免粗疏。此外，这部书使用的是浅近的文言，语言表达比较流畅。光绪八年，赵如光为《万国通鉴》所写的“序”中明确表示“是书乃美国牧师谢公卫楼所著”，自己则担任“笔述”，由此推测，文字的流畅与赵如光的润色密切相关，只是这位中文“笔述”是否参与了具体内容的写作难以推测。如果没有赵如光的帮助，仅凭谢卫楼一己之力撰写这样一部中国简史，在当时看来绝非易事。

翻阅“中国事略”不难发现，谢卫楼对中国历史有着较为系统的了解。他将“中国事略”分为 25 段，自三皇五帝讲至 1875 年光绪即位。其中，“第九段论东汉事略”和“第十段论后汉三国事略”与罗贯中创作的《三国演义》所述内容密切相关。比如，涉及后汉始末的全部文字如下：“后汉刘备建都于西蜀，是为昭烈帝，曾与关羽、张飞结为兄弟，同心协力扶助汉室。羽、飞大有忠义勇敢，又有诸葛亮运筹帷幄，韬略越众，多出奇计良谋，遂有荆襄巴蜀之地。后因孙权袭取荆州，杀关羽，帝率师讨之，为吴将陆逊所败，遂因忿得疾而崩。子禅嗣位，是为后帝，封丞相诸葛亮为武乡侯。时有苗蛮背叛，亮带兵南征，生擒苗长孟获，凡七擒七纵，此后苗

① 邹振环：《晚清史书编纂体例从传统到近代的转变》，《河北学刊》2010 年第 2 期，第 3—4 页。

党畏服，永不敢叛。帝又命亮伐魏，多立战功。亮薨，遗表举用蒋琬、姜维，人心咸服。因后主宠用宦官黄皓，旧日典型[①]渐渐废弛，至后帝四十一年，魏大臣司马昭遣邓艾等袭蜀，帝降魏，废为安乐公，后汉遂灭。”[②] 刘关张三结义之事，于史无据，但在《三国演义》中却被演绎得格外生动，这里的后汉历史，显然受到了《三国演义》的影响。

《万国通鉴》表明谢卫楼对于曹操这一人物颇为熟稔。赵如光在开篇序言中就提到了曹操，即“桀纣为君，昏庸无道；操莽为相，跋扈不臣”。在“第九段论东汉事略”中，也有一段文字论及曹操：“杨奉、韩暹彼此争功，扰乱国政，大将军董承忧之，乃诏曹操入都。操带本部兵马至洛阳，从此将赏罚之大权尽归于操。操即逼帝迁都于许昌（今河南开封府许州），操自封为魏王。董承即与刘备等同谋杀操，其事败露，即杀灭董承，战败刘备。时董承女在宫为贵人，亦被操所杀。伏皇后大惧，密诏伊父灭操，事亦败露。操即带剑入宫，弑皇后，并皇子二人，其不臣之心于斯为极矣。操死后，其子丕废献帝为山阳公，篡汉践天子位，改国号曰魏，是为文帝（按《史记》献帝在位三十一年曹丕篡位）。当曹操自封为魏王之时，有孙权据江东（今江苏江宁府）为吴国；刘备据西蜀（今四川成都府）为蜀国，时称为魏、蜀、吴三国。此时曹丕虽篡，而后世之论史者，多以西蜀为正统，因刘备系汉朝宗室，仍可兴朝立政，汉室不灭，所以称西蜀为后汉焉。”[③] 这段文字蕴含的“拥刘反曹”的政治立场有悖于《三国志》，其中所记曹操事迹与《三国演义》所述曹操始末颇为吻合，由此推测，谢卫楼的三国知识当主要来自《三国演义》等稗官野史，他对三国历史与人物的熟悉，为他三年后创作《曹操》一文奠定了基础。

---

① 编者按：原文误，“典型”当为“典刑”。

② 林庆彰等主编：《晚清四部丛刊》第七编《万国史论》，文听阁图书有限公司 2012 年版，第 33—34 页。

③ 同上书，第 32—33 页。

（三）比较的眼光与世界的视野

《曹操生平及时代概况》一题包含两方面内容：一是对于曹操生平的译介；二是对于曹操生活时代的译介。在篇幅比例上，前者为主，后者为辅。相比于晚清史家的相关论述，《曹操》一文另起炉灶、别具特色。作为一个具有世界史眼光的教育家，谢卫楼笔下的《曹操》开篇就具有宏大的历史视野，将曹操及其生活的三国时代置于世界版图的认识框架。

首先，从时代特点来看，谢卫楼称曹操生活的时代是“英雄时代”，在西方历史上堪比“希腊的伯罗奔尼撒战争时期”。他说：“那时的希腊和中国一样，操着同种语言、流着同样鲜血的人们，为了领土和权力相互残杀，进行着一场规模空前的战争；在严峻的考验下，人类的一切美德、智慧和情感被清楚地显现出来。在这场激烈的演剧中，勇气、计谋、忠诚、欺骗、背叛、怯懦，所有这一切，在经过我们面前的一个个人物身上显露无遗。他们的人生，被永久保存在歌曲、戏曲和故事中，也被一代代人观摩，或尊敬崇拜，或轻蔑憎恶。”①

希腊的伯罗奔尼撒战争是以雅典为首的提洛同盟与以斯巴达为首的伯罗奔尼撒联盟之间的一场战争。古希腊历史学家修昔底德所著的《伯罗奔尼撒战争史》将这场战争称为“雅典人与斯巴达人之间的战争”，谢卫楼沿用了这一说法，在《万国通鉴》第二卷第七章“论希利尼国事略”中，以

---

① Rev. D. Z. Sheffield, “A Sketch of the Life and Times of Ts‘ao Ts‘ao（曹操）”, *The Chinese Recorder and Missionary Journal*, Shanghai: American Presbyterian Mission Press, Volume XVI. November 1885, No. 10., pp. 401-407; December 1885, No., 11, pp. 441-449. 本部分引自《曹操》一文的内容，一律同此，后文不再一一注释。

第十二段“雅典人与斯怕他人二十七年战争”为题，介绍了伯罗奔尼撒战争的缘由及始末。由此可见，谢卫楼对这场战争颇为熟悉，在他看来，三国之战与伯罗奔尼撒战争之间的相同之处主要体现在三个方面：一是二者都是为了争夺领土与权力而展开的规模空前的大战；二是在参战人员身上体现出了某些人类德行、智慧与情感的共性；三是两场战争都以多种艺术形式流传下来，垂鉴后世。

这种比较的眼光和世界的视野不但为《曹操》一文铺垫了一个雄浑深厚、波澜壮阔的时代背景，而且将三国时代纳入世界历史。由此，三国战事不再是一时一地的征战，而是人类历史上的大战；其中的人物也不再是为了个人野心而出生入死的乱臣贼子，而是有着权力欲望等人类共性的典型个体。这种评论突破了中国与西方，消弭了群体与个人。后者尤为重要，它有利于引导人们从普遍人性的角度重新认识曹操。无论对于中国读者还是西方读者，这一角度折射出的曹操都是一个全新的形象。

其次，从时间阶段来看，谢卫楼发现，在曹操生活的汉献帝执政的三十年间，中国深陷三国之乱，而当时的罗马帝国同样战事频仍，皇权更迭频繁。他在《曹操》一文中说：

> 如果回到同一时期的西方史，我们发现中国的这段战乱时期，与罗马帝国屠杀与革命的野蛮情景完全相同。高尚的马库斯·奥利利悟（Marcus Aurelius）有个堕落的儿子堪莫度（Commodus），在无耻的引诱下，成了一个荒淫、残忍的暴君，乃至沦落为一名马戏团的演员和角斗士，他下令处死所有自己憎恨或惧怕的人，直到公元 192 年，曾经受他迫害的人将他勒死在自己的寝宫里。接任的是正直而在位短暂的培提纳斯（Pertinax），执政不到数月，便被禁卫军武力流放了，罗马帝国的王位以一千五百万美元的价格拍卖给了一位富有的元老院议员——底底悟·如利阿努（Didius Julianus）。此后，大将阿勒拜努（Albi-

nus）、色伟入（Severus）和奈革耳（Niger）为争夺权力展开大战，结果色伟入获胜，敌手溃败。色伟入严酷统治十八年后，由其子喀拉喀拉（Caracalla）和基他（Geta）接任。两兄弟殊死相争，最终基他被杀，两万名被认为是其同党者，亦被屠杀。喀拉喀拉肆虐统治了五年，接着是玛盔努（Macrinus）统治的两年。他的美德遭到腐败军人的忌恨，被迫让位于恶魔伊拉嘎巴鲁（Elagabalus），他四年的统治充斥着残酷的压迫和无耻的放纵。

以上关于罗马帝王人名的回译，没有采用现在通行的译法，而是一律采用了谢卫楼在《万国通鉴》中的译法。谢卫楼之所以能够进行这种横向历史比较，源于他对中西历史的熟稔。他在《万国通鉴》第二卷“西方古世代”之第八章“论罗马国事略”中，对于上述罗马帝王均有介绍，其中不乏详尽的叙述。比如，“第十九段罗马国事自堪莫度至代欧盔西安”开篇所述“堪莫度”事略，全文如下：

奥利利悟之子堪莫度承接父位，三年遵用父之贤臣，行施善政。惜其性质柔懦。后为嬖臣诱惑，怠于国事，多行虐政。时有人暗谋，遣人行刺。刺客至堪莫度之前，拔刀语曰：“议院遣我将此刀与汝。”堪莫度急避之，刺客之言乃深入其心，令其疑忌议院官，不忘报仇也。常有恶人诬控官员，堪莫度不辨虚实，即行妄杀。为人最好射箭掷枪，其技出众。或于戏场，令人放出百狮，四面奔驰咆哮，数万百姓，周围聚看，帝射百箭，百发百中。或在戏场与人耍斗，多次将与斗者杀之。其先时宠爱之妃玛西亚，偶闻其将欲杀己，即暗使人将帝毒害。时在耶稣后一百九十三年。①

① 林庆彰等主编：《晚清四部丛刊》第七编《万国史论》，文听阁图书有限公司2012年版，第308—309页。

这段“堪莫度”小史为读者勾画出的人物形象，与《曹操》一文中所谓的“荒淫、残忍的暴君”不谋而合。谢卫楼对于世界历史和人物的了解，使他在译介曹操形象时得以宕开笔墨、从容比较。

同时，三国时代与罗马帝国战乱时期的对比，也为曹操这一人物提供了一个全新的阐释场。那时从西方到东方，从朝廷到民间，不断上演着宫廷阴谋和民间暴乱，人性的欲望——尤其是对权力的渴望纵横肆虐。正如爱德华·吉本（Edward Gibbon，1737—1794）在《罗马帝国衰亡史》中所说的那样：“在人类的欲望当中，对于权力的热爱，是最强烈而又不容共享，那是由于人类尊荣的极致来自天下万众的臣服。过去因内战动乱，社会法律失去力量，取而代之者更难满足人道的要求，争夺的激情、胜利的荣耀、成就的绝望、对过去伤害的记忆以及对未来危险的恐惧，在在都造成神智的激愤与怜悯之声的沉寂。每一页的历史记录，都因这种争夺权力的动机，而沾满内战的鲜血。”[①] 这是“堪莫度”（现译康茂德）统治时期的罗马状况，与三国时期的一片乱象何其相像。

再者，在人物分析上，谢卫楼将曹操比作拿破仑，在具体介绍曹操生平事迹之前，让西方读者对曹操的个性特点有了一个基本认识。他说：“曹操的性格和经历令西方学者想到拿破仑一世。曹操像拿破仑那样明智地选贤任能，委以重任。其军事行动同样以计划谨慎、精明以及执行大胆、迅速为特点。他也像拿破仑那样既宽宏大量又奸诈残忍，抓住一切机会进行自我扩张。”《万国通鉴》将拿破仑译为“那袁利安”，谢卫楼在该著第四卷“西方近世代”之“论法国民变事略”中，对其做了详尽介绍。他说：“论那袁利安权巍势赫，为大国皇帝，有多国归其辖制，其他大国

① ［英］爱德华·吉本：《罗马帝国衰亡史Ⅰ》，席代岳译，吉林出版集团有限责任公司2016年版，第97页。

亦无不畏服，惜其为人狂傲，不合中道，其权虽荣，故不能长久。”① 又说：“论那哀利安之为人，其行军列阵，世人无与匹俦，但其所行之事，多为己之荣名，少思他人之益，所以上主终废其尊贵荣耀也。”② 由此可见，谢卫楼之所以介绍曹操时联系拿破仑，一方面源于他对世界历史与人物的熟稔；另一方面曹操与拿破仑在政治智慧、军事才华及个人野心方面确有相通之处。

经过“时代特点”“时间阶段”“人物分析”三方面的对比，谢卫楼总结说：“由此，在世界历史的同一时期，尽管东、西方两大文明的中心彼此分开、相去甚远，甚至不知道对方的存在，却在同样剧烈的人欲横流中震荡，追求享乐与奢华、荣誉与权力。”这些对比虽然只是三言两语，却成了全文的点睛之笔，受到西方读者的好评。1886 年，《中国评论》刊载了德国传教士欧德理（Ernest John Eitel，1838—1908）撰写的系列新书短评（Notices of New Books and Literary Intelligence），其中第三篇介绍了《教务杂志》刊载的内容。开篇伊始，欧德理就说：“在我们面前的这四期《教务杂志》中，涉及纯粹汉学主题（on purely sinology subjects）的文章相对而言少之又少。其中，居首的是 1885 年第 10 期刊载的谢卫楼撰写的《曹操生平及时代概况》，文章偶尔进行的历史对比（historical parallels）活泼生动，例如，作者将曹操比作拿破仑。”③ 由此可见，世界版图中的曹操形象与三国时代，确实令西方读者耳目一新、印象深刻。

---

① 林庆彰等主编：《晚清四部丛刊》第七编《万国史论》，文听阁图书有限公司 2012 年版，第 602 页。

② 同上书，第 605 页。

③ E. J. E.，“Notices of New Books and Literary Intelligence”，*The China Review*，*or notes & queries on the Far East*，Vol. XIV，No. 5，1886，p. 209.

（四）资料来源与人物重构

查找《曹操》一文的资料来源是研究这篇人物评论的基本前提。《曹操》一文的主要内容是对曹操生平的简述和评论，但在主角出场之前，谢卫楼以大段文字介绍了黄巾起义和董卓之死。

谢卫楼说：三国时期的政治混乱，主要源于连续几任皇帝的懦弱无能，高官显爵落入无耻宦官和朝廷弄臣之手。"就在这个动荡不安的时代，中国历史上一个被称为'黄巾贼'（the Yellow Turbaned Rebels）的秘密军事组织，在如今的山东地区兴起，很快发展到邻近地区，规模急剧扩张，使全国满目疮痍、人心惶惶。"其后围绕"董卓之死"叙及何进、董卓、王允、吕布、李傕、郭汜等人物，此后才引入曹操这一人物形象，他说："在简述这一时期的历史之前，让我们回看几年，追溯曹操从仕途崛起，直至手握强权的过程。其父曹嵩（Ts'ao Sung）乃著名宦官曹腾（Ts'ao T'eng）的养子，从曹腾开始采用曹姓。曹操生于浙江北部的徐州（Hsü Chou）。自幼机敏过人，果断而有智谋。"上述历史背景及叙事顺序，与《三国演义》第一回"宴桃园豪杰三结义　斩黄巾英雄首立功"大致吻合；与《三国志》开篇文字却截然不同。

《三国志·魏志》以魏武帝曹操开篇，作者陈寿首先介绍曹操的家世背景和个性特点，其后才论及黄巾起义。原文如下："太祖武皇帝，沛国谯人也，姓曹，讳操，字孟德，汉相国参之后。桓帝世，曹腾为中常侍、大长秋，封费亭侯。养子嵩嗣，官至太尉，莫能审其生出本末。嵩生太祖。太祖少机警，有权数，而任侠放荡，不治行业，故世人未之奇也，惟梁国桥玄、南阳何颙异焉。玄谓太祖曰：'天下将乱，非命世之才不能济也，能安之者，其在君乎！’年二十，举孝廉为郎，除洛阳北部尉，迁顿丘令，征拜议郎。光和末，黄巾起。拜骑都尉，讨颍川贼。”① 显然，这一逻辑起点及叙事顺序与《曹操》一文恰好倒置。由此推测，《曹操》一文主要取材于《三国演义》，而非《三国志》。

尽管如此，谢卫楼并没有完全弃正史而循小说，某些情节明显来自正史。比如，译文中提到曹操在山东驱散黑山贼，因而被袁绍表为太守。小说中无此情节，但《三国志》中却明确写道："黑山贼于毒、白绕、眭固等，十余万众略魏郡、东郡，王肱不能御，太祖引兵入东郡，击白绕于濮阳，破之。袁绍因表太祖为东郡太守，治东武阳。"② 只是相比小说，这些直接采自正史的内容少之又少。由此可见，晚清时期，《三国演义》的影响大大超过了正史，以致在西方人评论汉末人物时，出现了真伪杂糅、难以分辨的现象。

虽然主要取材于《三国演义》，谢卫楼笔下的曹操与小说中的曹操却迥然有别。从具体内容来看，《三国演义》涉及一千多个人物、四十多场战争，性格鲜明的人物形象举不胜举，惊心动魄的大小战役此起彼落。作为章回体小说，人物的典型化和情节的曲折化是这一文体的重要特征，作品可以通过外貌描写、心理活动、语言对话等细节对人物做全方位刻画，由此而使罗贯中笔下的曹操立体生动、呼之欲出。而《曹操》一文则主要译介曹操一人、战事三场，主题集中，笔墨简约。作为一篇人物评述类文章，以记叙为主、议论为辅，全文平铺直叙、粗陈梗概，不但没有任何细节描写和情景渲染，叙事笔法还带有一种史家的简洁与平实。

《曹操》一文围绕曹操生平，主要介绍了四方面情况。一是曹操在剿灭黄巾军、镇压黑山贼的过程中屡建军功，不断升迁。后来又与袁绍、王匡

① （晋）陈寿：《裴松之注三国志》，天津古籍出版社 2009 年版，第 1—3 页。
② 同上书，第 5 页。

联手抗击董卓，此期间不断收编队伍，壮大实力，很快建立起自己的队伍，并跻身强将之列。二是曹操应朝臣董承之约，赴京城洛阳勤王。他力压群雄，出任统帅，但个人野心也很快暴露。在将皇帝迁至许都后，彻底控制了皇权，挟天子以令诸侯。谢卫楼对于上述两方面情况的介绍整体看来比较简略，他用力更勤的是对于后两方面情况的介绍：一是在国家分裂、豪强混战中，曹操先后战胜了张绣、袁术和吕布，继而打败了盘踞北方的最强有力的对手袁绍，接着利用袁氏兄弟内讧，剿灭袁氏家族，这部分内容主要围绕官渡之战展开。二是在占领中国的中部、东部和北部后，曹操利用手中的权力，与刘备、孙权作战，进一步攻占南部和西部，恢复中国大一统的局面，这部分内容主要围绕赤壁之战和荆州之战展开。整体来看，谢卫楼介绍的后两方面内容，前者奠定了曹操统一北方的基础，后者形成了三足鼎立的局面，这正是《三国演义》前 78 回，也就是曹操在世期间演绎的重点。

由于近半笔墨都在讲述战事，所以谢卫楼笔下的曹操主要是作为军事家的曹操。谢卫楼对“官渡之战”的叙述尤为详细。在曹操与袁绍的对决中，谢卫楼通过袁绍的刚愎自用、不纳良言，来反衬曹操的刚毅果断、从善如流。他在文中写道：袁绍攻打许都时，田丰建议他不可轻敌、谨慎出兵，但袁绍不听规劝，执意进兵。在白马之战中，身在曹营的关羽杀了颜良、文丑两员大将，令袁军元气大伤、军心涣散。值此之际，袁绍又不听沮授之谏，再次向曹操发起挑战。曹军虽一度被迫撤军，但曹操采纳了许攸的计谋，果断决策，迅速出兵，攻入乌巢，烧了袁军辎重。紧急关头，袁绍却听了郭图的建议，偷袭曹营，惨遭失败。郭图将失败的罪责转嫁到张郃、高贤[①]二将身上，致使两员战将一怒之下投奔曹营，袁军由此陷入混乱，人心惶惶。袁绍在撤退时尽失心腹，仓皇逃窜，内心伤悲，殃及身体，

① 编者按：谢卫楼英译文中，误把“高览”写作“高贤”。

很快亡故。此后，曹操又采纳荀彧、郭嘉的建议，乘胜追击袁氏三兄弟，利用袁谭、袁尚之间的矛盾，彻底剿灭了袁氏家族。谢卫楼的上述介绍，使袁绍的鲁莽草率和曹操的审时度势、袁绍的愚顽自负与曹操的善于纳谏跃然纸上。虽然每至紧要关头都是谋士献计转败为胜，但曹操能够虚心纳谏、择善从之，这正是一个杰出的军事家所应具备的胸怀与远见。

为了突出作为军事家的曹操的勇进与谋略，在战事叙述的详略与篇幅上，谢卫楼也做了明显调整，这主要体现在他对赤壁之战的简化和对荆州之战的强调上。赤壁之战，正史与小说的文字笔墨相去甚远。《三国志》对于赤壁之战的记载分散而又零碎，《武帝纪》中仅用三两句话简单交代了战争经过与结果，所谓："公至赤壁，与备战，不利。于是大疫，吏士多死者，乃引军还。备遂有荆州江南诸郡。"① 在《三国演义》中，赤壁之战所占篇幅之多在所有战事中首屈一指，可以说从战争的初期，即第四十一回"刘玄德携民渡江"算起，直至第五十回"关云长义释曹操"为止，前后十回，总计五万余字。舌战群儒、智激孙权、智激周瑜、群英会、草船借箭、苦肉计、连环计、借东风等情节张弛有度、妙趣横生，整个过程彰显了诸葛亮之智。曹操虽兵力强大、主动出击，却节节败退、仓皇逃窜。谢卫楼对于赤壁之战的介绍明显采自《三国演义》，但其叙述却大大缩减。他简要介绍了曹操夺得荆州、继续东进，以百万大军攻打吴国之事。诸葛亮提议孙刘联盟，对付曹军，于是有了赤壁之战。在对赤壁之战的叙述过程中，谢卫楼只提到诸葛亮一次，火攻与诈降之法也几乎全部归功于周瑜和黄盖。虽然埋没了诸葛亮，但曹操的表现在这时确实乏善可陈，除了开头的声势浩大、主动出战，就是最后的仓皇撤退、痛失荆州。

为了弥补赤壁之战中曹操的恃强自负、毫无作为，荆州之战被谢卫楼充分重视起来，在篇幅上毫不逊色于他对赤壁之战的叙述。《三国志》对于

① （晋）陈寿：《裴松之注三国志》，天津古籍出版社 2009 年版，第 26 页。

荆州之战和关羽之死的记载都极其简略。陈寿说："冬十月，军还洛阳。孙权遣使上书，以讨关羽自效。王自洛阳南征羽，未至，晃攻羽，破之，羽走，仁围解。王军摩陂。二十五年春正月，至洛阳。权击斩羽，传其首。"① 相比之下，谢卫楼的介绍明显取自小说，较之正史更为详尽。他说：赤壁之战的直接后果是荆州落入孙权之手。孙权将荆州转借刘备，刘备命关羽防守荆州，自己则攻取汉中。孙权见刘备势力壮大，心生嫉妒，于是多次索要荆州，刘备却屡屡借故不还。与此同时，关羽从荆州北进，战胜了于禁和庞德，从曹操手中夺下樊城，接着派兵攻打襄阳，甚至逼得曹操考虑迁都。谋士司马懿建议曹操与孙权联手，共同对付关羽。曹操、孙权为了各自夺回樊城和荆州，两相联手。孙权手下大将吕蒙建议攻打樊城，以引诱关羽前去救援，借机夺取荆州。为此，陆逊取代吕蒙据守陆口，他的谦卑之态使关羽误以为孙权无意攻取荆州，于是将全部兵力集结到樊城，而孙权却派吕蒙带领精兵偷袭荆州。曹操早就得知了这一计划，本该保守秘密的他，却告知了关羽以及自己的樊城驻军，此举不但激励了曹军士气，还使关羽明知中计又进退两难。这时，曹操大将徐晃前来攻打樊城，吕蒙又占领了荆州，关羽灰心丧气、仓皇奔逃，路上被孙权将领潘璋斩杀。

如果说赤壁之战的主角是诸葛亮，荆州之战的主角则是关羽，谢卫楼在介绍赤壁之战时几乎完全忽略了诸葛亮之智，相比之下，他在介绍荆州之战时还是重视了关羽的忠勇与自负。只是在这两场战争中，曹操都是个缺乏亮色的背景性人物，所以谢卫楼也只能重点简述战争始末。可是字里行间不难看出，他一直在努力回到曹操，注意展现曹操的作为与才干。比如，荆州之战中，曹操得知孙权欲偷袭荆州，本应秘而不宣，曹操却反其道而行之，这一做法确实高明，毛氏父子在回评中说："孙权之策荆州，与

① （晋）陈寿在：《裴松之注三国志》，天津古籍出版社2009年版，第44—45页。

曹操之策樊城，各一机谋也。吴致魏书，而嘱魏勿泄，恐关公知之而回救，则荆州之袭未稳矣。魏得吴书，而故令公知。使荆兵知之而欲归，则樊城之围自解矣。”① 只是这一主动泄密之计原本是谋士董昭提供，而谢卫楼不但不提，还直接放在了曹操身上，倘若是有意为之，自然是为了弥补曹操在赤壁之战和荆州之战上的黯然失色、碌碌无为。

综上所述，就译介内容来看，谢卫楼从《三国演义》中提取素材，围绕曹操生平，以平实的笔法简单介绍了他四方面的情况，突出了曹操的军事智慧与才干。

（五）忠奸立场与正统观念

就评论立场而言，相比于罗贯中、毛宗岗等中国论家，谢卫楼主动摆脱了正统观念与忠奸立场，他对曹操的认识与评价带有一种朴素的历史辩证思想，因而整体看来显得置身局外、客观公允。

三国故事“帝魏寇蜀”或“拥刘反曹”的正统观念由来已久，至《三国演义》写作时达到顶峰。陈寿撰写《三国志》时以曹魏为正统，故在为曹操作“本纪”时，虽然以史家立场写人叙事，但还是因这一正统观念而对曹操多有回护，所以他笔下的曹操乃一“非常之人，超世之杰”。北宋时期，司马光编修《资治通鉴》时试图摆脱正统与僭伪套路，他说：“止叙国家之兴衰，著生民之休戚，使观者自择其善恶得失，以为劝诫，非若《春秋》之褒贬之法，拨乱世反诸正也。”② 但其《魏纪》采用曹魏国号纪年，

① （明）罗贯中著，（清）毛宗岗批注：《第一才子书三国演义》，线装书局 2007 年版，第 677 页。

② （宋）司马光：《资治通鉴》，中华书局 2007 年版，第 536 页。

事实也就承认了曹魏的正统地位。南宋时期，朝廷偏安一隅，处境颇类蜀汉，朱熹作《通鉴纲目》，为了明正统、斥篡贼、立纲常、扶名教，改蜀汉为正统。这正是三国故事被编成戏曲、搬上舞台的时候。元末明初，民族矛盾加剧，带有纲常伦理色彩的正统观念深入人心，有着浓郁“帝王师”思想的罗贯中在撰写《三国演义》时继承了“拥刘贬曹”的叙事立场，从而把曹操塑造成了一个“乱世奸雄”的形象。

谢卫楼来华的晚清时期，正值《三国演义》毛评本广为传播之际，毛纶、毛宗岗父子对于正统观念和忠奸立场推波助澜、推崇备至。二人在评点《三国演义》时，开篇定调，指出：“读《三国志》者，当知有正统、闰运、僭国之别。正统者何？蜀汉是也。僭国者何？吴、魏是也。闰运者何？晋是也。”① 二人对于正统观的拥护体现了那个时代的民心所向。在人物塑造方面，这一正统观念最显著的后果是所谓忠奸立场的确立，即将曹操与刘备对立起来，塑造成一正一反、泾渭分明的两个形象，刘备是汉室后裔，为人长厚，宽政爱民，乃一正统明君；曹操则是乱臣贼子，为人奸诈，残暴凶狠，乃一千古奸雄。正如毛氏父子在《三国演义》第一回的评语中所说：“百忙中忽入刘、曹二小传，一则自幼便大，一则自幼便奸；一则中山靖王之后，一则中常侍之养孙，低昂已判矣。后人犹有以魏为正统，而书蜀兵入寇者，何哉？”② 这一评点，完全从正统观念衡量曹、刘高下。

《曹操》一文对于正统观念和忠奸立场提出质疑，突出表现在谢卫楼在叙及刘备这一曹操的对立面人物时，不但没有采用《三国演义》处处呵护、一味褒扬的态度，反而通过他反衬了曹操的慷慨大度和顾全大局。比如，刘备在《曹操》一文中初次登场，谢卫楼是这样介绍的：“就在此时，中国历史上有名的忠勇之士刘备一度加入了曹军。此前他曾与吕布联合，但他

---

① （明）罗贯中著，（清）毛宗岗批注：《第一才子书三国演义》，线装书局 2007 年版，第 140 页。

② 同上书，第 1 页。

奸诈的盟友嫉妒其声望和军事才能，遂反目成仇，吕布在战争中打败了刘备，刘备遂逃至曹营。曹操的一些官员了解刘备的个性特点，劝曹操就此灭掉刘备，但曹操听从了更有雅量的劝言，他令刘备在其军队中担任指挥，希望他对这位宿敌的慷慨之举，能够吸引更多的人前来投靠自己，以帮助他最终战胜更多的敌手。”此处的曹操不计前嫌、招贤纳士，表现得宽容大度、深明大义。又如，当刘备参与董承谋约，设计除掉曹操时，谢卫楼表示：“在中国的伦理道德中，刘备接受邀请，私下背叛一个曾在危难之际有恩于他的人被看作正当，大概是因为他是为了皇帝的利益而反对一个野心勃勃、肆无忌惮的人。是时，曹操已任命刘备为独立指挥，命他去迎战袁绍，给他最后的一击。然而刘备非但没有执行曹操的命令，反而占领了徐州，并加入了袁绍的联盟。”可见，在谢卫楼看来刘备背信弃义、恩将仇报之举令人费解，此后攻占徐州、转投袁绍之举更是出尔反尔、自毁形象。

文章最后，谢卫楼通过多个角度正面剖析曹操这一人物形象。在与关羽、刘备的对比中，显示了历史的眼光与辩证的思想。他说：

> 曹操的性格特点，正如我们从中国历史中总结的那样，具有多个方面。他在个人生活习惯方面节俭而朴素，对友慷慨，对敌残暴。你可以指责他虚伪、背叛，但是这些缺点却似乎已经司空见惯，他唯一超过前人的是他对于人的本性及动机的深刻体察。他最残忍的行动是对那些暗算过他的人的报复。包括皇后及其二子就因此被杀。如果我们以道义与正直的正确标准来衡量这种残忍的行为，我们必然会加以谴责，但是我们必须多多少少用那个时代的标准来公正地衡量他。如果我们将曹操与他的两个最为著名的对手——关羽和刘备作个对比，我们肯定同意他具有同样的勇气与决心，作为一个军事家与政治家，他还拥有更大的能力。毋庸置疑，曹操的行动目的，从中国人最终的分析结果来看，在很大程度上是自私的，但他的自私并不是那种小气、

> 卑鄙的自私，曹操个人扩张的谋略是与国家未来的繁荣发展联系在一起的。站在中国人的立场来看，他最大的罪恶便是篡夺帝王之权，就因为此，他的名字遭到一代又一代人的痛骂；而关羽和刘备，却因为他们保护汉室的勇气和忠义，被提升到神灵的行列。

谢卫楼在回溯历史的基础上直面曹操的多重性格，面对这一复杂人物，他表示人们应该回到三国时代，用历史的标准来衡量他。尤其是当把曹操与关羽、刘备进行对比时，作为一个军事家和政治家的曹操不但勇敢、刚毅，而且更有才干。同时，曹操的军事行动虽然是为了个人私利，但他的自私不是那种小气、卑鄙的自私，因为其政治谋略与国家未来的繁荣发展密切相关。只是在中国人看来，曹操与关羽、刘备两相对立：一方阴谋篡权，一方忠实捍卫。不同的政治立场使他们双方在中国遭遇了截然不同的命运：一方遭受唾骂，一方被奉若神灵。在这种貌似平静的论述中，隐含着谢卫楼对于正统观念和忠奸立场的不以为然。这种呼吁回到历史语境、自觉摆脱固有观念的评论，赋予《曹操》一文一种客观的立场和超然的态度，从而为曹操形象的海外建构开启了一个新的起点。

19 世纪翻译、介绍、评论、改编《三国演义》的来华西士约有二十余人，其中不乏著名传教士与外交官。第一位英国来华新教传教士马礼逊在其编纂的《华英字典》中就提及了《三国志》（San-kwŏ-che）；第一位德国来华新教传教士郭实腊在《三国志评论》中给予《三国演义》高度评价；第一位以英文撰写《中国文学史》（*A History of Chinese Literature*）的英国外交官翟理斯（Herbert Allen Giles，1845—1935）翻译过不少《三国演义》的片段；号称“美国汉学第一人”的卫三畏在其汉语教材《拾级大成》中大量引用《三国演义》的语句。这些来华西士对于《三国演义》的海外传播发挥了举足轻重的作用。需要指出的是：在当时所有英译资料中，《曹操》一文是唯一以曹操这一人物形象为主题的作品，这使它成为研究《三国演义》西行之旅的不可或缺的一环。

作为一名著名传教士，谢卫楼的文字一般情况下都浸染着一种浓郁的宗教情怀。赵如光在为《万国通鉴》所写的“序”中说：“夫西士东来，宣播真道，每于圣书而外，多所著作，非徒炫奇，实为传道之一助耳。”谢卫楼在《万国通鉴》中将中国上古史与《圣经》故事无缝接驳。他说：“按《圣经》挪亚以后，众人建造巴别台之时，上主淆乱其口音，使各族人民散居四方。主之意旨，盖欲其生育繁多，充满宇宙也。越数百年，有人居伊及，居印度，又有附近伯辣河两边之平原创立国度者，亦有东徙于黄河之西东建国者。当时未有文字简编，故确实事迹至今无传，乃有后人凭空结撰，造出许多荒渺无稽之谈、虚诞不经之事，故孔子删书断自唐虞。”① 这种以教义羽翼史传的做法，使《万国通鉴》交织着浓郁的宗教思想。与之相比，《曹操》一文却始终保持着一种历史的叙事和客观的立场，完全看不出著者的传教士身份和宗教热情。尤其有趣的是，此前来华传教士因职业敏感而热衷于译介的离奇情节，典型的如“左慈掷杯戏曹操”和“洛阳城曹操感神”，在专门介绍曹操的谢卫楼的文章中却只字未提，这更加凸显了他对于历史叙事的坚守和对于客观评论的执着。

《曹操》一文的素材主要取自《三国演义》，但谢卫楼却没有照搬小说的叙事模式，他主动摆脱了《三国演义》的正统观念和忠奸立场，努力以一种朴素的历史辩证思想还原历史本相。由此，谢卫楼所扮演的角色既不是一个忠实的译者，也不是一个故事转述人（story-teller），而是一个历史事件的叙述者和历史人物的评论者。本着这种立场，他对《三国演义》的内容做了大量删减与改写，通过材料的剪辑实现了某种程度的“再创作”。谢卫楼对于曹操形象的全新建构在于将其置身于世界历史的舞台，从而为评

① 林庆彰等主编：《晚清四部丛刊》第七编《万国史论》，文听阁图书有限公司 2012 年版，第 11 页。

判这一人物提供了一个全新的场域。曹操由此不再是《三国演义》中的一代奸雄，更不是民间舞台上的白脸奸贼，他甚至走出了中国语言的文学传统，被用英文符码打造成一个拿破仑式的人物。法国作家雨果在《悲惨世界》中说拿破仑是战争中的米开朗琪罗，是重建废墟的宗师巨匠。“他当然有污点，有疏失，甚至有罪恶，就是说，他是一个人；但是他在疏失中仍是庄严的，在污点中仍是卓越的，在罪恶中也还是有雄才大略的。”① 曹操与拿破仑的类比，注定了谢卫楼要从普遍人性的角度理解这一历史人物。由此，经过谢卫楼改写与重构的曹操形象焕然一新，开启了三国人物西行之旅的多彩篇章。

① ［法］雨果：《悲惨世界》，李丹、方于译，人民文学出版社 1984 年版，第 777 页。

附：英文原文

材料一

A SKETCH OF THE LIFE AND TIMES OF TS' AO TS' AO (曹操)[1]

A. D. 190 TO 220.

By Rev. D. Z. SHEFFIELD.

THE period in Chinese history in which Ts' ao Ts' ao acted an important part may be regarded as the heroic period in the records of this prosaic people. If we look for its analogy in western history, we shall find it in that of Greece during the Peloponesian war. There, as in China, men of the same speech and blood were arrayed against each other in a titanic struggle for dominion and power; and all the virtues and talents and passions of human nature, under the severest strain, were brought into prominent exhibition. Courage, stratagem, fidelity, duplicity, treachery, cowardice, all in turn find their embodiment in one or another of the characters that pass before us in the fierce drama; and these lives, perpetuated in song and play and story, are looked upon with reverence and admiration, or with

---

① 编者按：*The Chinese Recorder and Missionary Journal* (1868 - 1912), Shanghai: American Presbytrian Mission Press. Vol. XVI, No. 1, 1885, pp. 401 - 407.

contempt and execration, by each new generation of men. The period of which we write is commonly known as that of The Three Kingdoms (三國), since by a long civil war China was separated into three nationalities for the space of half a century. These Kingdoms were the Wei (魏), the Shuh (蜀), and the Wu (吳). The Kingdom of Wei was the largest, occupying the northern portion of China, embracing the present provinces drained by the Yellow river and its tributaries. The Kingdom of Wu had its eastern borders on the Yellow sea, and extended over a wide region north and south of the lower course of the Yang Tsŭ river. The Kingdom of Shuh was on the western border of China, embracing the central and eastern portions of the present province of Ssŭ Ch'uan, the southern portion of Shen Si, and the western portion of Hu Pei. The whole line of southern provinces, as they now appear on the map of China, was then the home of barbarian tribes, yielding only a semi-obedience to their stronger neighbors, and regarded by them with indifference or contempt.

The emperor whom Ts'ao Ts'ao nominally served, but really ruled, for a term of years, was Hsien Ti (獻帝), whose reign embraced a period of thirty years, from A. D. 190 to 220. If we turn to contemporaneous western history throughout this period, we find that the anarchy in China was fully paralleled by the wild scenes of carnage and revolution in the Roman Empire. Commodus, the degenerate son of the virtuous Marcus Aurelius, under the seductions of unscrupulous favorites, became a cruel, licentious tyrant, descending to become a circus performer and gladiator, issuing his warrants of death against all he hated or feared, until in A. D. 192 he was strangled in his bedroom by those whose destruction he had decreed. The brief reign of the upright Pertinax succeeded, but he was dispatched in a few months by the swords of the Prætorian guard, and the imperial crown of Rome was sold at auction to a rich senator, Didius Julianus, for fifteen millions of dollars. Following this there was a struggle for power between the great military leaders Albinus, Severus, and Niger, resulting in the triumph of Severus, and the destruction of his enemies. The stern reign of Severus for eighteen years was succeeded by that of his sons, Caracalla and Geta. A deadly quarrel between the brothers ended in the murder of Geta, and the slaughter of twenty thousand persons who were supposed to be his friends. The abandoned and oppressive reign of Caracalla for five years was succeeded by the two years' reign of Macrinus. His very virtues made him hateful to the corrupt soldiery, and he was sacrificed to give place to the monster Elagabalus, whose four years' reign was filled with cruel oppression and infamous debauchery.

Thus at the same period in the world's history, the two great centres of civilization, the eastern and the western, though separated so far that they hardly knew of each other's existence, were convulsed by the same fierce passions of unbridled human nature, in their thirst for pleasure and luxury, for glory and dominion.

If we seek for the causes of the derangement of government throughout China during this period, we shall find it in the effeminacy of the monarchs of the few preceding reigns, allowing the highest position of honor and power and emolument to be struggled for by unscrupulous eunuchs and court parasites. This corruption at the head of government begot its legitimate fruits in disaffection and lawlessness throughout the empire. A secret military organization, known in Chinese history as the Yellow Turbaned Rebels (黄巾贼), took its rise in the region of the present province of Shan Tung during those troublous times, and soon propagated itself in contiguous regions, swelling to enormous proportions, and filling the country with desolation and alarm. Armies were organized and sent against them, succeeding at length in breaking their power, and scattering their numbers; but military leaders learned in the school of war to appreciate their own capacities and strength, and the government was destined to be overturned by the very power that it had evoked for its protection. The Emperor Ling（靈帝）dying during these disturbed times, his son Pien（辯）, who had not yet arrived at manhood, succeeded to the throne. The supreme power rested in the hands of two empresses who intrusted the affairs of government to their favorite eunuchs. At length Hê Chin（何進）, brother to one of the empresses, resolved to break the power of the eunuchs, but instead of acting promptly, in the use of means within easy reach, he procrastinated, and through evil counsel called an army to his aid, to do the work which could have been accomplished by the palace guard, and a few executioners. The general invited to give this assistance was Tung Cho（董卓）, a man of courage and ability, but of unscrupulous ambition. He had already achieved celebrity in the war against the Yellow Turbaned Rebels, and now recognized his opportunity for a higher step in his promotion to place and power. He promptly obeyed the summons, and destroyed many of the eunuchs, deposing, and at length killing, the young Emperor, and setting up in his stead a younger brother, the Emperor Hsien（獻帝）of the present narrative. It was soon perceived by the officers of government that the ultimate plan of Tung Cho was to set aside the new boy Emperor, as soon as his own plans of action were consummated, and to place himself upon the throne. The generals engaged in war against the Yellow Turbaned Rebels now turned against the prospective usurper. Tung Cho, desiring to secure a stronger place of defense remote from his enemies, compelled the Emperor with his court to remove from Lê Yang（洛陽）, in the province of Hê Nan, to Ch'ang An（長安）, the present Hsi An（西安）, in the province of Shen Si. Tung Cho lingered behind the imperial escort with a portion of his army, to plunder and destroy the palace and ancestral temple, and to rifle the tombs of preceding emperors of their treasures. He followed on to the new capital, and built for himself, at a convenient distance from the city, a strong citadel, storing it with provisions, and filling it with his ill-gotten wealth, purposing that if he met with reverses in his schemes for power, to retire within the walls of his citadel where he could defend himself from his enemies for a long term of years. But his greed and cruelty were multiplying his secret as well as his open enemies. At length Wang Yün (王允), a high civil officer, persuaded Lü Pu (吕布), an officer under Tung Cho, to join with him in a stratagem to accomplish the destruction of the hated tyrant. A visit of the high officials upon the young Emperor was arranged, to congratulate him on his recovery from a slight sickness. An ambush of soldiers awaited the entrance of Tung Cho with his escort through the gate into the Forbidden City. Lü Pu at the proper moment led the attack, and dispatched his master with his own hands. The fact of the death of the tyrant was no sooner published abroad, than the people of the entire city gave themselves up to feasting and rejoicing. The mutilated body was left for days unburied, and a taper was contemptuously thrust into it to give light by night. Wang Yün had destroyed his great enemy, but two generals of Tung Cho, Li Ch'üeh (李傕), and Kuo Ssŭ (郭汜), marched their armies against Ch'ang An, captured the city, and put Wang Yün to death. Lü Pu escaped to Shan Tung, where we shall hear from him again. The two generals soon quarrelled and fought with each other for the prize of power which had fallen into their hands. While they were thus wasting their strength in mutual destruction, other officers removed the Emperor from this scene of anarchy to the old capital at Lê Yang; but in turn their jealousies and rivalries continued to fill the seat of empire with bloodshed and confusion.

At this point in the sketch of the history of the times, let us turn back for a few years, to trace the steps of Ts'ao Ts'ao in his rising career, until he grasps the reigns of government in his powerful hand. The father of Ts'ao Ts'ao, Ts'ao Sung (曹嵩), was the adopted son of a distinguished eunuch Ts'ao T'eng (曹

騰), from whom the name of Ts‘ao is derived. Ts‘ao Ts‘ao was born in the city of Hsü Chou (徐州), in the northern portion of the province of Chê Chiang. From youth he was distinguished for acuteness of perception, promptness of decision and facility of resource. The character and career of Ts‘ao Ts‘ao has much in it that reminds the western scholar of the first Napoleon. Like Napoleon he chose wisely those to whom he entrusted the execution of his undertakings. His military evolutions were characterized by the same carefulness and sagacity in planning, and boldness and rapidity in execution. Like Napoleon he could make a display of generosity and magnanimity and could also be treacherous and cruel, seizing upon every opportunity to promote his own aggrandizement. It is said of Ts‘ao Ts‘ao that if he had lived in a period of good government he would have been an officer of ability, but living in a period of anarchy he was an unprincipled leader. 治世之能臣亂世之奸雄. His military talent found its first opportunity for display in the war against the Yellow Turhaned Rebels, where he soon achieved distinction, and was promoted to the magistracy of Chi Nan (濟南), the present capital of the province of Shan Tung. At this juncture Tung Cho had already grasped the reins of government. Ts‘ao Ts‘ao now leagued with two powerful generals Yuan Shao (袁紹), and Wang K‘uang (王匡), to overthrow the power of the tyrant. Their armies rendezvoused at Suan Tsao (酸棗), the present K‘ai T‘eng T‘u, capital of the province of Hê Nan. Ts‘ao Ts‘ao urged to an immediate forward movement, but his confederates feared to match strength at once with their resolute enemy. Ts‘ao Ts‘ao, impatient of delay, marched forth with his single command, but was defeated by Tung Cho in a battle at Jung Yang (榮陽), and fell back to his old position. He now proposed a plan of united attack, but it being rejected he withdrew from his confederates to Whai Ch‘ing (懷慶), a point north of the Yellow river, but still within the vicinity of the enemy. Not daring to attack Tung Cho again with his small command, his restless energy found exercise in dispersing a body of Black Mountain Rebels (黑山賊), in the region of the present Tuan Ch'ang in Shan Tung, For this service Yuan Shao promoted him to the governorship of the region. At this time the Yellow Turbaned Rebels, numbering many hundred thousands, were plundering and desolating the region of Yen Chou, to the south east of Tung Ch'ang. The surviving officers and subordinates fled to Ts'ao Ts'ao, and begged his help to deliver them from their scourge. The rebels were too strong for him to venture a direct attack, but by a series of adroit movements he out-generalled his lawless enemies, and defeated them in detail. Over three hundred thousand men at length laid down their arms, and submitted to his authority. He selected from this multitude the strongest and most active men, and incorporated them with his own army. From this time he took rank among the most powerful generals and his movements assumed a national importance. A little later the father of Ts'ao Ts'ao, while coming to join his son, was murdered by an officer of the governor of Hsü Chou. In revenge for this, Ts'ao Ts'ao visited a fierce retribution upon the cities of that region, giving rein to his soldiers to destroy and murder at pleasure.

At this point the sketch of the career of Ts'ao Ts'ao unites with that of the young Emperor Hsien already given. We left the Emperor at Lê Yang under the guardianship of officers who were contending with one another for leadership. Tung Ch'eng (董承), a faithful officer of government, desiring to put an end to these factions, and bring order out of anarchy, sent a messenger to Ts'ao Ts'ao, inviting him to come with his army to the assistance of the Emperor.① The officers

① The Chinese have a saying with reference to the overthrow of Tung Cho and the calling in of Ts'ao Ts'ao: "You expel a wolf from the front gate and allow a tiger to enter at the back one." 前門去狼後门進虎。

were divided in counsel as to his wisest course of action; some urging that he should first restore order throughout the region of Shan Tung; but Ts'ao Ts'ao recognized in the crisis an opportunity which he must not lose. He marched his army to Lê Yang, and easily overawed any who might have wished to oppose his power. He was appointed President of the Board of War, and exercised his authority with promptness and discrimination. The personal ambition of Ts'ao Ts'ao soon made itself manifest in his removing the Emperor from Lê Yang to Hsü（許都）, a city some days' journey across the mountains to the south-east. By this act he obtained entire control of the Emperor, and could administer the government as he pleased under the cover of Imperial direction.

To return to the former confederates of Ts'ao Ts'ao, whom we left idly encamped at Suan Tsao, fearing the power of Tung Cho. At length their provisions gave out, and they were compelled to separate. The jealousies and ambitions of the leaders soon brought them into conflict one with another, and each grasped such a portion of the country as he was able to hold against his enemies. Yuan Shao, the most powerful general, controlled the region north of the Yellow river, with Chi Chou（冀州）in southern Chih Li, as his centre of military action. Yuan Shu（袁紹）① held Shou Ch'un（壽春）, the present Shou Chou in An Hui, assuming to himself the name of Emperor. Sun Ch'i（孫策）held Chiang Tung（江東）, the present Su Chou in Chiang Su. Liu Piao（劉表）held Ching Chou（荆州）, in Hu Pei, an important military centre on the north bank of the Yang Tsŭ river, a little east of I Ch'ang. Lü Pu, the murderer of Tung Cho, held Hsü Chou in northern Chiang Su, the birth-place of Ts'ao Ts'ao. Chang Hsin（張繡）held Wan Cheng（晼城）, the present An Ch'ing in south-western An

① 编者按："袁绍"当为"袁术"，英文拼读正确，中文注释错误。

Hui. Chang Lu（張魯）held Han Chung（漢中），in southern Shen Si. Liu Yen（劉焉）held I Chou（益州），the present Ch'eng Tu of Ssŭ Ch'uan. Thus, as the result of the past misgovernment, China was broken into a number of rival and contending states. The subsequent history of Ts'ao Ts'ao consists of a record of his efforts to reduce the government to its original unity, with the supreme power centred in his own hands. His first movements were against his enemies to the east and southeast, and Chang Hsin and Yuan Shu were subjugated in order. Ts'ao Ts'ao now turned his arms against Lü Pu in Hsü Chou. It was at this time that Liu Pei, whose name is highly honored in Chinese history for his courage and integrity, joined his fortune to that of Ts'ao Ts'ao for a period. He had previously been confederated with Lü Pu, but his treacherous ally, jealous of his reputation and military talent, turned upon him, and defeated him in battle, at which Liu Pei fled, to the camp of Ts'ao Ts'ao. Some of the officers of Ts'ao Ts'ao, knowing the character of Liu Pei, recommended his destruction, but Ts'ao Ts'ao followed more generous counsels, and gave him a command in his own army, hoping that this act of magnanimity to a former enemy would induce yet others to come to his support, and thus facilitate his ultimate triumph over his many adversaries. Ts'ao Ts'ao inflicted several defeats upon Lü Pu in open battle, compelling him at length to take shelter behind the walls of Hsia Fou（下邳），a small city to the east of Hsü Chou. Ts'ao Ts'ao caused the waters of the neighboring river to be turned from their channel, and conducted into the city, making the position of Lü Pu untenable. At this extremity his under officers purchased clemency of Ts'ao Ts'ao by delivering their master into his hands, and the death order ended his courageous but unscrupulous career.

(To be continued.)

材料二

A SKETCH OF THE LIFE AND TIMES OF TS‘AO TS‘AO（曹操）①

A. D. 190 TO 220.

By Rev. D. Z. SHEFFIELD.

(Continued from page 407.)

Ts‘AO TS‘AO was now free to measure strength with his great enemy Yuan Shao, who with a powerful army controlled the northern portion of China. Ts‘ao Ts‘ao placed a low estimate upon the military ability of Yuan Shao, counting as much for success upon his indiscretion in plans of action, and suspicion of his subordinate officers, together with his self-confidence, as upon his own superior military stratagem. The army of Ts‘ao Ts‘ao had already occupied Li Yang（黎陽）, in southern Chih Li, to resist the anticipated attack of Yuan Shao, when a conspiracy against the life of Ts‘ao Ts‘ao was disclosed, that altered his plans of action for the present. The Emperor, anxious to rid himself from the yoke which Ts‘ao Ts‘ao imposed upon him, had secretly communicated with Tung Ch‘eng, the officer who had formerly called Ts‘ao Ts‘ao to the Emperor's assistance, intimating his desire that Ts‘ao Ts‘ao should in some way be disposed of. Liu Pei was invited to take part in the conspiracy. He has been justified in Chinese ethics for accepting the invitation to secretly turn against the man who had befriended him in the time of his extremity, by the uncertain logic, that he was acting in behalf of the Emperor against an ambitious and unscrupulous subject. Meanwhile Liu Pei had

① 编者按：*The Chinese Recorder and Missionary Journal* (*1868 – 1912*), Shanghai: American Presbytrian Mission Press, Vol. XVI., Dec. 1, 1885, pp. 441-449.

been entrusted by Ts'ao Ts'ao with an independent command, and sent against Yuan Shao, to give the finishing blow to his overthrow.

Instead of carrying out the instructions of Ts'ao Ts'ao, Liu Pei occupied Hsü Chou, and joined in league with Yuan Shao. The conspiracy of Tung Ch'eng was brought to light, and his own deaths, including that of his entire family, paid the penalty of its disclosure. Ts'ao Ts'ao, thirsting for revenge upon Liu Pei, resolved to defer his meditated attack upon Yuan Shao, and strike a quick blow against his new and bold enemy. Officers of Ts'ao Ts'ao warned him of danger of attack from the rear by the stronger force of Yuan Shao; but he counted correctly upon the tardy action of his antagonist, and Liu Pei was hopelessly routed, and Kuan Yü, (關羽) —ubsequently① canonized as the God of War—was taken prisoner, while the army of Yuan Shao was lying idly in camp, with the subordinate officers chafing at the indecision of their leader. Ts'ao Ts'ao was already returning with his victorious army, when Yuan Shao announced to his officers his purpose to march upon the capital at Hsü. His more sagacious counselor T'ien Feng (田豐), who had previously urged him to follow upon Ts'ao Ts'ao's rear, now warned him that the capital was well defended, and that Ts'ao Ts'ao would follow him with an army that was not to be despised. He urged to a more cautious line of action, selecting strong positions for his army, and improving advantageous opportunities to inflict loss upon his enemy, thus weakening him in detail, until at length he could be easily overwhelmed. This wise counsel was rejected, and Yuan Shao advanced his army to Li Yang—Ts'ao Ts'ao's old position—sending Yen Liang (顏良) in command of a division of the army, to attack Po Ma (白馬), an important military position, held by a detachment of Ts'ao Ts'ao's ar-

---

① 编者按：应为 subsequently。

my. Ts' ao Ts' ao marched to its support, and Kuan Yü, mounted upon his fleet and powerful war-horse, dashed into the midst of the enemy's ranks, severing the head of Yen Liang from the body, and escaping before his guard could comprehend what had happened. In like manner he afterwards cut off the head of Wên Ch' ou (文醜), thus weakening Yuan Shao by the loss of two distinguished officers. The attack upon Po Ma was a failure, and the army of Yuan Shao began to be depressed with fear. Against the counsel of his aid Ten Shou (沮授), Yuan Shao advanced towards the lines of Ts' ao Ts' ao, offering battle. Ts' ao Ts' ao accepted the challenge, but was driven back to his intrenchments by the superior numbers of the enemy. At this juncture Hsü Yin, a general in the army of Yuan Shao, angry at his master for imprisoning a member of his family, deserted to Ts' ao Ts' ao, and informed him that Yuan Shao had a large supply of provisions for his army at Wu Ch' ao (烏巢), a little south of the Yellow river, which could be easily destroyed, and the army reduced to extremity. Ts' ao Ts' ao, always prompt in decision, took with him five thousand soldiers, foot and cavalry, disguising them as he travelled through the country, by carrying flags made in imitation of those of the army of Yuan Shao, and by forced marches soon reached Wu Ch' ao, setting fire to the provisions, and defeating a force sent by Yuan Shao to protect them.

Yuan Shao, following the unwise counsels of Kuo T' u(郭圖), had attacked the defenses of Ts' ao Ts' ao's camp during his absence, and suffered a severe repulse. Kuo T'u chagrined with the miscarriage of his plans, charged the fault of the defeat upon Chang Hê (張郃), Kao Lan (高賢)①, and others who had opposed the attack. Chang Hê and Kao Lan, disgusted at the general mismanage-

① 编者按：根据原著，"高贤" 应为 "高览"，英文拼读正确，中文注释错误。

ment, and enraged at this false accusation, burned their weapons of war, and fled to the camp of Ts' ao Ts' ao. At this the camp of Yuan Shao became a scene of anarchy and confusion. Losing all heart at his reverses, he escaped across the river with his son T' an(袁譚), protected by a small body of cavalry. His distress of mind preyed upon his body, and soon death terminated his career.

Ts' ao Ts' ao now turned his attention to Liu Pei, who was investing the city of Ju Nan (汝南), —the present Ju Ning T' u in southern Hê Nan. Liu Pei was defeated and fled to Ching Chou, where he joined himself to Liu Piao. Ts' ao Ts' ao was at first disposed to move against Liu Piao, but was advised by his counselor Hsün Yü (荀彧), to follow up his victory over Yuan Shao, and put out the last fire-brands of rebellion, lest they should again kindle into flames.

At the death of Yuan Shao, his third son, Yuan Shang (袁尚), ambitious for power, usurped the rights of the oldest son, Yuan T' an, and drawing after him a strong following of the army, assumed the rank and authority of his father. Yuan T' an was preparing to attack his brother, to recover his position, when the approach of the army of Ts' ao Ts' ao compelled him to take up a defensive position at Li Yang. Ts' ao Ts' ao inflicted a defeat upon him, at which Yuan Shang, knowing that the overthrow of his brother would open the way for an attack upon himself, hastened to his assistance. Ts' ao Ts' ao defeated the united forces of the two brothers, and compelled them to retreat upon Chi Chou. The officers of Ts' ao Ts' ao were eager to attack the city, but his counsellor Kuo Chia (郭嘉), urged him to leave the brothers to themselves for a time, confident that when relieved from the fear of attack from without, their old jealousies would revive and drive them apart, when they could be defeated with little effort. Ts' ao Ts' ao therefore withdrew his army, and moved southward to carry out his plan of attack upon Liu Piao. The prophesy of Kuo Chia was soon fulfilled. The two brothers separated and marshalled their respective forces in battle against each other. Yuan T'an was defeated and driven to take refuge behind the walls of Ping Yuan（平原）— the present Tê Chou in the northern border of Shan Tung. In his extremity he sent to Ts'ao Ts'ao for help. Ts'ao Ts 'ao moved rapidly upon Chi Chou, flooding the city from the neighboring river. Yuan Shang came to the rescue of his capital, but was utterly overthrown in a severe battle, and fled to Yu Chou（幽州）, in the present region of Peking. Chi Chou was surrendered to Ts'ao Ts'ao. The officers of Yin Chou, military and civil, perceiving that the cause of Yuan Shang was a hopeless one, threw off his authority and acknowledged allegiance to Ts'ao Ts'ao. Yuan Shang, with his brother Yuan Hsi（袁熙）, fled from Yu Chou to the Kingdom of Wu Huan（烏桓）, the name of a border tribe living in the region west of the Liao river. Yuan T'an, who asked assistance from Ts'ao Ts'ao when in extremity, soon rebelled against his authority, but was defeated and beheaded. The brothers, Yuan Shang and Yuan Hsi, persuaded T'a Tun（蹋頓）, a powerful chief among the Wu Huan, to espouse their cause; and organizing an army out of the Chinese refugees that they found in the country, they began to make inroads upon the north-eastern borders of China. The counselors of Ts'ao Ts'ao were divided as to the wisdom of marching against this remote enemy, while there was a more powerful enemy in the southern borders of China. It was pointed out that Liu Piao and Liu Pei might improve the opportunity of his absence from the capital to attack and possibly capture it. To this Kuo Chia made answer that Liu Piao was only a fine talker, that he was jealous of the superior military ability of Liu Pei, and would entrust to him no important enterprise. Ts'ao Ts'ao decided to follow the counsel of Kuo Chia, and marched northward to I Chou（易州）, southwest of Peking. From this point he moved with light baggage to Wu Chung（無终）, the present Yü T'ien. The army was delayed by heavy rains and almost impassable roads. The mountain passes beyond were strongly defended by the enemy. Ts'ao Ts'ao made the bold resolve to cross the mountains to the northward, then moving eastward to attack the enemy from the rear. The undertaking was full of difficulty, but it was successfully accomplished. The Yuan brothers, with their confederates, when they discovered the movement of Ts'ao Ts'ao, fell back from their defensive position, and marched against him with a powerful force of cavalry. Ts'ao Ts'ao accepted battle, and again his courage and skill were crowned with success. T'a Tun was captured and beheaded, and multitudes of his followers submitted to the authority of Ts'ao Ts'ao. The brothers, Shang and Hsi, fled to Liao Tung, but the terror of Ts'ao Ts'ao's name had travelled before them, and the governor of that region soon sent their heads to him as a proof of friendship. Winter had now set in, and the army of Ts'ao Ts'ao nearly perished among the mountains for lack of food and water, but the soldiers sunk deep wells for water, and fed upon their horses, and thus at length extricated themselves from their difficulties.

The authority of Ts'ao Ts'ao was now established in the central, eastern, and northern portions of China, but in the south and west there were still powerful enemies to dispute his rule. He now addressed himself to the work of conquering them. Liu Piao died during Ts'ao Ts'ao's absence in the north, and his son Liu Tsung（劉琮）, succeeded to the government of Ching Chow. He had no courage to contend against such an enemy as Ts'ao Ts'ao, and on learning that his army was approaching, sent messengers acknowledging his authority. Liu Pei, thus suddenly deprived of the support of his former ally, was compelled to retreat to the south. Ts'ao Ts'ao occupied Ching Chou, and prepared for a movement towards the east. Sun Ch'uen（孫權）, at the death of his brother Sun Ch'ê, had succeeded to the governorship of Chiang Tung, —known in the history of the times as the Kingdom of Wu. Ts‘ao Ts‘ao now sent a pompous letter to Sun Ch‘uen, informing him that Liu Tsung had already, with bound hands, surrendered to the Emperor, and that he was on the way with a million of soldiers, by land and water, to have a grand hunt in the Kingdom of Wu, inviting him to participate in the sport, —under this figure challenging him to a measure of strength in battle. Sun Ch‘uen consulted with his officers as to the course to pursue. Many of them urged him to acknowledge the authority of Ts‘ao Ts‘ao. Others advised him to try the hazard of battle. At this juncture Chu Kê Liang（諸葛亮）, the trusted counselor of Liu Pei, crossed the river and proposed a plan of united action between Sun Ch‘uen and Liu Pei. The plan was accepted, and Chou Yü（周瑜）, was placed in command of thirty thousand soldiers, who with Liu Pei fitted out a fleet of vessels, and moved against the fleet of Ts‘ao Ts‘ao, lying in the Yang Tsŭ river at the foot of mount Ch‘ih Pi（赤壁山）, south east of the present city of Wu Ch‘ang. The engagement was to the advantage of the confederates, and Ts‘ao Ts‘ao withdrew his fleet to the northern bank of the river. At this juncture an officer of Chou Yü, Hwang Kai（黄蓋）, proposed to his superior a plan by which the fleet of Ts‘ao Ts‘ao might be destroyed. Ts‘ao Ts‘ao, without experience in naval warfare, had adopted the curious expedient of fastening the ships together by iron chains, that the soldiers might pass from one vessel to the other, and give support in time of battle. The proposal of Huan Kai was to make ready ten vessels, each loaded with light combustible material, saturated with oil, and hidden from sight by cloth screens. Each vessel was to have in tow a small boat, upon which the sailors at the proper moment could make their escape. The vessels were to be sent against the fleet of Ts‘ao Ts‘ao, and when within a short distance, to be set on fire. The plan was carried out, and Huan Kai headed the expedition. A strong south-east wind favored the undertaking. He had previously sent a false communication to

Ts'ao Ts'ao, intimating the intention to desert to him on the first favoring opportunity. The army of Ts'ao Ts'ao lay encamped along the northern bank of the river behind the fleet, and watched with eager curiosity the approach of the little squadron of vessels. When they had reached the center of the river, the sails were set, and they moved rapidly forward. Soon the mystery was solved when the vessels were suddenly wrapped in flames, and bore down upon the fleet of Ts'ao Ts'ao. The fire leaped upon the masts and rigging of the doomed ships, and rolled forward in its resistless course of desolation. Soon the fleet was one vast sea of fire, and the flames swept onward in their devouring course among the adjoining camps and burning and stifling men and horses. Chou Yü and Liu Pie①, moved forward with their armies at the sound of the drum, and completed the overthrow of the vast army of Ts'ao Ts'ao. Out of his boasted million of soldiers with which he proposed to hunt in the Kingdom of Wu, scarcely a body guard was left to follow him in his retreat.

As the result of this defeat, Ching Chou fell into the hands of Sun Ch'uen, and the enemies of Ts'ao Ts'ao strengthened themselves against him in the south and west. Subsequently Chang Lu, governor of Han Chung, in southern Shen Si, rebelled against Ts'ao Ts'ao, but was easily defeated, and the defense of this important military position was entrusted to two officers of ability, Hsia Hou Yuan (夏侯渊)② and Chang Hê. Meanwhile Sun Ch'uen had temporarily given Ching Chou to Liu Pei as a base of operations. Liu Pei committed the defense of Ching Chou to his sworn brother, Kuan Yü, and by successful operations in Pa and Shuh, the present Ssŭ Ch'uan, had made himself governor of the region. He now

---

① 编者按：英译文原文中为 Liu Pie，应为 Liu Pei。

② 编者按：英译文原文中少一半括号，多一逗号，此处根据上下文，做了修订。

resolved to add Han Chung to his possessions, and moved against that city from the south-west. Hsia Hou Yuan marched forth and accepted battle, but was utterly routed, and falling into the hands of the enemy, paid the penalty of defeat by the forfeiture of his life. Ts'ao Ts'ao hastened to the defense of Han Chung. Liu Pei declined battle on terms of equality, and holding an advantageous position, resolved to exhaust the army of Ts'ao Ts'ao by hunger and sickness. At length disease making havoc in the ranks of Ts'ao Ts'ao, he was compelled to withdraw, and Han Chung passed from his control into the hands of Liu Pei. Sun Ch 'uen, jealous of the increasing power of Liu Pei, had repeatedly demanded that Ching Chou should be given back to him, but Liu Pei found excuses for delaying to comply with the demand. Following Liu Pei's successful movement upon Han Chung, Kuan Yü moved north-ward from Ching Chou to invest Fan Ch'eng（樊城）, a city in northern Hu Pei near Hsiang Yang on the Han river. It was an important southern military position under Ts'ao Ts'ao, and was defended by a strong garrison. Ts'ao Ts'ao also sent two divisions of soldiers under Yü Chin（于禁）and P 'ang Tê（龐德）, to encamp north of the city for its further protection. Protracted rains caused the Han river to rise and flood the adjacent country. Kuan Yü improved the occasion to attack the weak position of Yü Chin and P 'ang Tê with a strong fleet of boats. Yü Chin, despairing of successful resistance, capitulated to Kuan Yü. P'ang Tê was captured and beheaded. The investment of Fan Ch'eng was now pressed with the utmost vigor. A division of the army was also dispatched to attack Hsiang Yang. The fame of Kuan Yü's virtue and prowess was widely proclaimed among the people, and Ts'ao Ts'ao began to consider the question of removing his capital to a more secure position. His resources were not however exhausted. His counselor Ssŭ Ma I（司馬懿）, reminded him of the jealousy of Sun Chu'en towards Liu Pei, and proposed that a secret league should be entered into with Sun Ch‘uen, promising to recognize his right to the governorship of Chiang Tung on the condition that he would attack Kuan Yü from the rear, and thus compel his withdrawal from Fan Ch‘eng. Sun Ch‘uen, desirous to recover Ching Chou from the hands of his rival, readily acceded to the proposal. Lü Meng,（吕蒙）, an officer in command of a division of the army of Sun Ch‘uen, stationed at Lu K‘ou（陸口）, near the present Wu Ch‘ang, proposed to his superior a stratagem by which Kuan Yü could be induced to concentrate his troops about Fan Ch‘en and leave Ching Chou unprotected. The proposal of Lü Meng was, that he should withdraw his army from Lu K‘ou, and that Lu Hsün（陸遜）, an obscure officer, but a man of courage and ability, should be sent to occupy the place. The plan was adopted, and Lu Hsün addressed a letter to Kuan Yü, extolling his military achievements, couched in language of modest self-depreciation. Kuan Yü, judging from the withdrawal of Lü Meng from his advanced position, that Sun Ch‘uen had no intention of attacking Ching Chou, gradually concentrated his entire army about Fan Ch‘eng. Sun Ch‘uen appointed Lü Meng to the command of a small division of picked soldiers, secreting them in a fleet of vessels disguised as vessels of merchandise. The fleet set sail from Hsün Yang（潯陽）, —the present Chin Chiang in Chiang Hsi, —and moved rapidly up the river towards Ching Chou. Ts‘ao Ts‘ao was early informed of this movement that he might properly cooperate. Though charged with secrecy, he resolved to inform Kuan Yü of the stratagem, and also his own garrison in Fan Ch‘eng. His motive was to alarm Kuan Yü for the safety of Ching Chou, and thus induce him to raise the siege of Fan Ch‘eng. The news communicated to his own garrison would of course stimulate them to a more resolute defense. Ts‘ao Ts‘ao marched to the relief of the besieged city, causing arrows to which letters were fastened to be shot into the city, and also into the camp of Kuan Yü, announcing the movement of Lü Meng against Ching

Chou. The result was as he had anticipated. Kuan Yü perceived the trap into which he had fallen, and was irresolute as to the means of escape. A division of Ts'ao Ts'ao's army under Hsü Huang (徐晃), made a successful attack upon his lines. At this he broke up camp and began a retreat. He soon learned that Ching Chou had fallen into the hands of Lü Meng, and now beset in front and rear, with officers and men rapidly deserting him, he lost heart, and with a few faithful followers attempted to make his escape, but was overtaken and killed by P'an Ch'ang (潘璋), an officer of Sun Ch'uen.

Ts'ao Ts'ao now conciliated the good will of Sun Ch 'uen by conferring upon him various honorary titles, and in turn Sun Ch'uen acknowledged allegiance to Ts'ao Ts'ao, and further urged him to set aside Hsien Ti, who was but a name, and assume to himself the title of Emperor. Ts'ao Ts'ao, who cared more for the substance of power than for its outward display, replied that if it was the will of Heaven that he should act the part of King Wên, of the dynasty of Chou, he was contented, —signifying by this answer that as King Wên was the actual founder of the Chou dynasty, while his son Wu was the first sovereign in name, so he would be content to found a new dynasty over which his son should be the first to bear the imperial name. But the restless and eventful career of Ts'ao Ts'ao was drawing to its close. Returning from his successful expedition against Kuan Yü, he reached Lê Yang, where after a brief sickness he died at the age of sixty six (A. D. 220). His oldest son Ts'ao P'ei assumed his father's power, and at once degraded Hsien Ti from his empty rank, and took to himself the title of Emperor, with the dynastic name of Wei.

The character of Ts'ao Ts'ao, as we gather it from Chinese history, was a many-sided one. He was frugal and unostentatious in his habits of private life, was generous in his friendship, but cruel in his hatreds. He can be charged with falsehood and treachery, but these vices seem to have been almost universal, and he only surpassed his teachers by his superior knowledge of men's character and motives. His worst acts of cruelty were in visiting vengeance upon those who plotted against his life. The Empress for this cause was destroyed, together with her two sons. While we must condemn such acts of cruelty as measured by the true standand of honor and integrity, we must in justice measure him somewhat by the standard of the times. If we compare Ts'ao Ts'ao with his two most celebrated antagonists, Kuan Ti and Liu Pei, we must accord to him a like high order of courage and resolution, together with much higher ability as a general and a statesman. Doubtless his motives of conduct in their ultimate analysis were largely selfish, but his selfishness was not of a petty or sordid type, and his schemes for personal aggrandizement were blended with plans for the future prosperity of the kingdom. His great crime, as measured from the Chinese stand-point, was his usurpation of inperial power, for which crime his name has been execrated from generation to generation, while Kuan Ti and Liu Pei have been promoted to the rank of gods, for their courage and fidelity in defense of the House of Han.

中文回译

材料一

曹操生平及时代概况[①]

公元190—220年

谢卫楼

在一般人的记载中，曹操扮演了重要角色的中国历史时期堪称英雄时代。如果我们想在西方历史中找到一个类似的时代，或许会发现它相当于希腊的伯罗奔尼撒战争时期。那时的希腊和中国一样，操着同种语言、流着同样鲜血的人们，为了领土和权力相互残杀，进行着一场规模空前的战争；在严峻的考验下，人类的一切美德、智慧和情感被清楚地显现出来。在这场激烈的演剧中，勇气、计谋、忠诚、欺骗、背叛、怯懦，所有这一切，在经过我们面前的一个个人物身上显露无遗。他们的人生，被永久保存在歌曲、戏曲和故事中，也被一代代人观摩，或尊敬崇拜，或轻蔑憎恶。我们所写的这个时期，通常被称为“三国”（The Three Kingdoms），一场旷

① 编者按：《教务杂志》第16卷，1885年11月，上海，第401—407页。

日持久的内战后，中国分裂成了三个国家，时间长达半个世纪。这三国便是魏（Wei）、蜀（Shuh）、吴（Wu）。魏国最大，据有中国北方，占据了当今黄河及其支流流经的各省。吴国东至黄海，跨越长江下游南北两岸的广袤地域。蜀国居于中国西部，包括如今四川（Ssŭ Ch‘uan）中东部、陕西（Shen Si）南部，以及湖北（Hu Pei）西部。当今中国地图上的整个南部地区，那时还是未开化的部落，只是勉强屈从于他们的强邻，并被他们怠慢着、蔑视着。

曹操名义上尊奉、实际上却挟持多年的皇帝，乃汉献帝（Hsien Ti），在位三十年（公元 190—220 年）。如果回到同一时期的西方史，我们发现中国的这段战乱时期，与罗马帝国屠杀与革命的野蛮情景完全相同。高尚的马库斯·奥利利悟（Marcus Aurelius）① 有个堕落的儿子堪莫度（Commodus），在无耻的引诱下，成了一个荒淫、残忍的暴君，乃至沦落为一名马戏团的演员和角斗士，他下令处死所有自己憎恨或惧怕的人，直到公元 192 年，曾经受他迫害的人将他勒死在自己的寝宫里。接任的是正直而在位短暂的培提纳斯（Pertinax），执政不到数月，便被禁卫军武力流放了，罗马帝国的王位以一千五百万美元的价格拍卖给了一位富有的元老院议员——底底悟·如利阿努（Didius Julianus）。此后，大将阿勒拜努（Albinus）、色伟入（Severus）和奈革耳（Niger）为争夺权力展开大战，结果色伟入获胜，敌手溃败。色伟入严酷统治十八年后，由其子喀拉喀拉（Caracalla）和基他（Geta）接任。两兄弟殊死相争，最终基他被杀，两万名被认为是其同党者，亦被屠杀。喀拉喀拉肆虐统治了五年，接着是玛盔努（Macrinus）统治的两年。他的美德遭到腐败军人的忌恨，被迫让位于恶魔伊拉嘎巴鲁（Elagabalus），他四年的统治充斥着残酷的压迫和无耻的放纵。

由此，在世界历史的同一时期，尽管东西方两大文明的中心彼此分开、

① 编者按：本段出现的罗马帝王名字，一律采用谢卫楼所著《万国通鉴》中的中译名回译。

相去甚远，甚至不知道对方的存在，却在同样剧烈的人欲横流中震荡，追求享乐与奢华、荣誉与权力。

究其原因，我们发现，这段时期的中国政府混乱，乃是源于连续几任统治者的软弱，这使得高爵显贵之位，被无耻宦官及朝廷弄臣竞相瓜分。上层官僚的腐败带来了相应的恶果——政治背叛与违法乱纪遍及帝国。就在这个动荡不安的时代，中国历史上一个被称为“黄巾贼”（the Yellow Turbaned Rebels）的秘密军事组织，在如今的山东地区兴起，很快发展到邻近地区，规模急剧扩张，使全国满目疮痍、人心惶惶。被组织起来前去镇压他们的军队，最终成功地粉碎了黄巾军的势力，驱散其兵力；然而军事领袖们却在战争中各自学会了如何提高自身的能力及兵力，而朝廷注定会被这股原本招募来保护它的力量所颠覆。灵帝（The Emperor Ling）卒于这一战乱时期，其子辩（Pien）尚未成年，便继承了皇位。大权掌握在两位皇后的手中，她们将朝廷事务交给了得宠的宦官。最终，其中一位皇后的哥哥何进（Hê Chin）决心打破宦官的政权，但没能迅速行动，在一切唾手可得时，他却因迟缓而耽搁了，他让奸人召来援军，把本该由皇宫侍卫或几个刽子手完成的事，交由援军来做。请来援助的大将乃董卓（Tung Cho），他有胆有识却野心勃勃。董卓在抗击“黄巾贼”的战斗中已声名显赫，这时意识到这是博取更高地位和权力的时机。他立即应诏，诛杀宦官，废黜乃至弑杀了少帝，拥立其弟，即对他有利的更为年幼的献帝（the Emperor Hsien）为主，这就是现在所讲的三国故事中的皇帝。朝廷官员很快察觉，董卓的最终目的，是把幼帝置于一边，一旦自己的行动计划圆满实现，就自立为帝。对抗“黄巾贼”的将领，现在转而对抗这个未来的篡位者。而董卓，为了远离对手、确保其位，胁迫献帝将朝廷从河南（Hê Nan）洛阳（Lê Yang）迁至长安（Ch‘ang An），即现在的陕西（Shen Si）西安（Hsi An）。董卓与一部分军队逗留在皇家护卫军之后，洗劫皇宫，捣毁太庙，抢走先皇陵墓中的珍宝。随后跟随皇帝来到新都，在距离都城较为方便的地方，为自己建了一座坚固的城池，储备粮食，堆满不义之财，目的是倘若篡权不成，退回城内，亦可御敌数年。然而他的贪婪与残暴不仅暴露了他的秘密，也使他成为众矢之的。最终，文官王允（Wang Yün）说服董卓手下的一名将领吕布（Lü Pu），一同设计除掉这个令人憎恶的暴君。幼帝微恙初愈，群臣准备探望。伏兵等着董卓及其军队跨进禁城的大门。吕布及时出击，亲手斩了他的主人。暴君之死的消息刚一传播开来，举城百姓立即设宴庆祝。董卓被肢解，曝尸数日，一个捻子被塞进尸体，彻夜点起天灯。王允虽杀了劲敌，但董卓的两员大将——李傕（Li Ch'üeh）、郭汜（Kuo Ssŭ）却进兵长安，占领城池，杀了王允。吕布逃至山东，后面我们还会提到他。李、郭二人很快内讧，为争夺到手的权力而自相残杀。正当他们在相互毁灭中消耗力量时，其他官员却将皇帝移至旧都洛阳，离开了这一乱局；但是，他们的猜忌和争斗却使帝王之座继续充斥着杀戮与混乱。

在简述这一时期的历史之前，让我们回看几年，追溯曹操从仕途崛起，直至手握强权的过程。其父曹嵩（Ts'ao Sung）乃著名宦官曹腾（Ts'ao T'eng）的养子，从曹腾开始采用曹姓。曹操生于浙江北部的徐州（Hsü Chou）。自幼机敏过人，果断而有智谋。曹操的性格和经历令西方学者想到拿破仑一世。曹操像拿破仑那样明智地选贤任能，委以重任。其军事行动同样以计划谨慎、精明以及执行大胆、迅速为特点。他也像拿破仑那样既宽宏大量又奸诈残忍，抓住一切机会进行自我扩张。据说曹操乃“治世之能臣，乱世之奸雄”。抗击“黄巾贼”第一次给了他展示军事才能的机会，随之获得军功，迁济南（Chi Nan）相，济南乃现在的山东（Shan Tung）省府。此时董卓已执掌大权。曹操联合袁绍（Yuan Shao）、王匡（Wang K'uang）两员大将推翻董卓。他们的军队集结于酸枣（Suan Tsao），即现在的河南省开封府（K'ai T'eng T'u）。曹操想即刻出兵，但其盟军却害怕立即与敌军交战。曹操容不得迟疑，遂孤军出击，却在荥阳（Jung Yang）一战中被董卓打败，退回故地。而后他设计联合出击，却遭到反对，遂退出联盟，来到怀庆（Whai Ch‘ing），这是黄河以北的一个据点，却仍邻近敌军。因兵力悬殊，曹操未敢再攻董卓，他旺盛的精力在当今山东东昌（Tuan Ch‘ang）[①] 一带驱散黑山贼（Black Mountain Rebels）时找到了用武之地，因此而被袁绍表为太守。是时数十万“黄巾贼”劫掠兖州（Yen Chou），兖州位于东昌（Tung Ch‘ang）东南。幸存下来的官员及其部下投奔曹操，请求他帮助摆脱灾难。叛军太强，曹军不敢贸然直攻，但通过系列灵活调遣，他以优越的战术打败了叛军，并将之逐个击破。最终三十万人放下武器，向曹操投降。他从众人中精选最强壮有力者，并入曹军。从此以后，曹操跻身强将之列，一举一动举国重视。不久以后，曹父来投曹操，路上被徐州太守所杀。为报父仇，曹操杀来，凶狠地报复徐州各地，令士兵恣意破坏杀戮。

至此曹操的生涯与上述所提的年轻的皇帝献帝联系了起来。之前我们说到献帝在洛阳，护驾大臣正为夺权而彼此争斗。忠臣董承（Tung Ch‘eng）欲结束内讧，在混乱中恢复秩序，于是给曹操送信，邀他带兵前来勤王。[②] 官员们讨论时对此明智之举怀有分歧；一些人敦促他应该首先恢复山东的秩序；但曹操却认为这是紧要时刻绝对不能错失的机会。于是他进军洛阳，轻而易举地吓住了那些图谋反对他的人。他被任命为军事统帅，行使权力敏锐而有法度。曹操的个人野心很快在把皇帝从洛阳迁至许都（Hsü）时表现了出来，去往许都需翻山越岭，向东南行进数日方可抵达。迁至许都后，曹操彻底控制了皇帝，并且喜欢打着圣旨的名义随心所欲地管理朝政。

且说曹操的盟军因怕董卓势大，扎营酸枣。最终粮草耗尽，被迫离散。诸将相互猜忌、野心勃勃，很快彼此争斗，各据一方，聊以御敌。势力最

---

① 编者按：Tuan Ch‘ang 或为 Tung Ch‘ang 之误，故译为东昌。

② 中国人在提到推翻董卓后召来曹操时常说：前门去狼，后门进虎。

强的是袁绍，他据有黄河以北，并把直隶（Chih Li）南部的冀州（Chi Chou），作为其军事中心。袁绍（Yuan Shu）①据有寿春（Shou Ch‘un），乃今日之安徽（An Hui）寿州（Shou Chou），自立为王。孙策（Sun Ch‘i）据有江东（Chiang Tung），乃今日之江苏（Chiang Su）苏州（Su Chou）。刘表（Liu Piao）据有湖北荆州（Ching Chou），乃扬子江（the Yang Tsŭ river）北岸的重要军事中心，位于宜昌（I Ch‘ang）以东。杀了董卓的吕布，据有江苏北部的徐州，乃曹操出生地。张绣（Chang Hsin）据有皖城（Wan Cheng），乃今日安徽西南之安庆（An Ch‘ing）。张鲁（Chang Lu）据有陕西（Shen Si）南部之汉中（Han Chung）。刘焉（Liu Yen）据有益州（I Chou），乃今日之四川（Ssŭ Ch‘uan）成都（Ch‘eng Tu）。就这样，过去的恶政使中国分裂成了多个相互敌对、倾轧的邦国。曹操后来的历史就是讲他集大权于手中，努力恢复大一统的局面。他首战东部和东南部敌人，依次征服了张绣和袁术。转而引兵攻打徐州的吕布。就在此时，中国历史上有名的忠勇之士刘备（Liu Pei）一度加入了曹军。此前他曾与吕布联合，但他奸诈的盟友嫉妒其声望和军事才能，遂反目成仇，吕布在战争中打败了刘备，刘备遂逃至曹营。曹操的一些官员了解刘备的个性特点，劝曹操就此灭掉刘备，但曹操听从了更有雅量的劝言，他令刘备在其军队中担任指挥，希望他对这位宿敌的慷慨之举，能够吸引更多的人前来投靠自己，以帮助他最终战胜更多的敌手。曹操在面对面的战斗中几次打败了吕布，迫使他避居下邳（Hsia Fou）城下，下邳乃徐州东部的一个小城。曹操将邻近的河水从水渠里改道过来，引进城里，使吕布据点被淹，难以为继。在此危难之际，吕布手下的官员为换取曹操的仁慈，把他交到了曹操手里，吕布被斩，结束了他英勇无畏但肆无忌惮的一生。

（未完待续）

① 编者按："袁绍"当为"袁术"，英文拼读正确，中文注释错误。

材料二

曹操生平及时代概况[①]

公元 190—220 年

谢卫楼

（上接第 407 页）

曹操而今可以与他最大的敌人袁绍决一雌雄了，袁绍占据着中国北方，有一支强大的军队。曹操并不看重袁绍的军事力量，认为自己的胜算在于袁绍行动计划的轻率、对手下官员的怀疑，还有他的自负，而他自己则具有卓越的军事谋略。曹军占领了直隶南部的黎阳（Li Yang），以防袁绍来攻，这时一个谋害曹操性命的阴谋被戳穿，暂时改变了曹操的行动计划。急于摆脱曹操控制的献帝，已经与先前召曹操前来勤王的官员董承私下沟通，暗示想用计除掉曹操。刘备也被请来参与密谋。在中国的伦理道德中，刘备接受邀请，私下背叛一个曾在危难之际有恩于他的人被看作正当，大概是因为他是为了皇帝的利益而反对一个野心勃勃、肆无忌惮的人。是时，曹操已任命刘备为独立指挥，命他去迎战袁绍，给他最后的一击。

然而刘备非但没有执行曹操的命令，反而占领了徐州，并加入了袁绍的联盟。董承阴谋败露，他和全家被满门抄斩，这是他为此付出的代价。渴望报复刘备的曹操，决定暂不攻打袁绍，而是突袭刘备这个后来的大胆敌人。曹操手下官员提醒他攻击比自己强大的袁绍支持的队伍是危险的；但曹操认为袁绍行动迟缓，大战之后刘备溃不成军，关羽（Kuan

① 编者按：《教务杂志》第 16 卷，1885 年 12 月，上海，第 441—449 页。

Yü）——后来被奉为战神——被俘，袁绍大军正无所事事地待在营里，手下将士正气恼于他的优柔寡断。当袁绍向将士们宣称欲进兵许都时，曹操已凯旋。袁绍颇有远见的谋士田丰（T'ien Feng）曾建议他袭击曹操后方，而今又提醒他许都防御坚固，曹操又有军队随从，不可轻敌。他建议袁绍谨慎行动，为军队选一有利位置，寻找时机让敌人蒙受损失，以逐个削弱曹军，直至最终一举制胜。然而袁绍拒绝了这一良策，转而进军黎阳——曹操以前的一个据点——派颜良（Yen Liang）带领一队人马，前去攻打白马（Po Ma），白马乃一军事重地，掌握在曹军手中。曹操前来支援，关羽战马迅疾强壮，他纵身上马，冲入敌阵，砍了颜良首级，不等卫兵反应过来，就已逃走了。接着，关羽又以同样方式砍下文丑（Wên Ch'ou）的头，袁绍就此损失两员大将，元气大伤。白马之战的失败使袁军开始惊惧、沮丧。袁绍不顾谋士沮授（Ten Shou）① 之谏，执意向曹军进军，进行挑战。曹操接战，却被人数众多的袁军打回战壕。当此之际，袁军将领许攸（Hsü Yin）因怨恨袁绍收捕其家人而投奔曹操，告诉曹操，袁绍在黄河以南的乌巢（Wu Ch'ao）存有大批军粮辎重，极易烧毁，以陷袁军于绝境。曹操一向决策迅速，他立即引五千步兵、骑兵，伪装起来通过其境，打着袁军旗号，急行军很快抵达乌巢，点燃粮草，并击败了袁绍派来保护粮草的军队。

袁绍听从了愚蠢的谋士郭图（Kuo Túu）的建议，趁曹操不在时攻打曹营，却遭到惨败。郭图因计划失败而深感懊恼，他将战败的错误归咎于张郃（Chang Hê）和高贤（Kao Lan）② 等反对攻营的人。张郃、高贤对此错误处置心存不满，对此诬告也格外愤怒，于是烧了武器，投奔曹营。此时，袁营陷入混乱、人心惶惶。袁绍撤退时尽失心腹，在一小队骑兵的保护下，

① 编者按："沮"字注音错误。

② 编者按：根据原著，"高贤"应为"高览"。英文拼读正确，中文注释错误。

与其子袁谭（T‘an）渡河而逃。他内心悲痛，殃及身体，很快亡故，终其生涯。

曹操接着将矛头转向刘备，刘备此时正屯兵于汝南（Ju Nan），即如今河南南部之汝宁府（Ju Ning T‘u）。刘备大败，逃至荆州投奔刘表。曹操本想前去攻打刘表，但谋士荀彧（Hsün Yü）劝他乘胜追击袁绍，扑灭袁氏叛军的最后一息余烬，以免他们再次复燃。

袁绍死后，三子袁尚（Yuan Shang）野心勃勃，篡夺了长子袁谭之位，率领大军，摆出一副父亲的权望。袁谭正准备攻打袁尚，夺回权位，这时曹军的到来迫使他不得不先防守黎阳。曹操大败袁谭，袁尚知道袁谭覆亡，将为曹操攻打自己开辟道路，遂速去救援。曹操打败了兄弟二人的联军，迫使他们退回冀州。曹军将领急于攻城，但谋士郭嘉（Kuo Chia）却建议暂时不必理会袁氏兄弟，相信他们在不担心外部攻击时，以前的妒火就会复燃，兄弟之间分崩离析，那时只要一点力气就能打败他们。于是曹操撤回军队，向南进发，以实现攻打刘表的计划。郭嘉的预言很快应验。袁氏二兄弟分道扬镳，各自领兵，相互攻打。袁谭战败，逃至平原（Ping Yuan）城下避难，平原乃如今山东北部边境之德州（Tê Chou）。在此危难之际，他修书一封向曹操求助。曹操迅速出兵冀州，从临近的河里引水淹没城池。袁尚前来救援，但经过一场激战后，彻底溃败，逃至幽州（Yu Chou），即如今之北京（Peking）地区。冀州归降曹操。幽州（Yin Chou）[①] 文武官员，见袁尚霸业无望，遂抛下官位，公开效忠曹操。袁尚与其兄袁熙（Yuan Hsi），自幽州（Yu Chou）逃至乌桓国（the Kingdom of Wu Huan），乌桓是辽河（the Liao river）西岸的一个边境部落。危难时刻向曹操求援的袁谭，很快背信弃义，但被曹操打败并斩首。袁尚和袁熙二兄弟，说服了乌桓强

---

① 编者按：“Yin Chou”或为“Yu Chou”（幽州）之误，因译者拼读“许攸”（Hsü Yin）之“攸”时也音译为“Yin”。

大的首领蹋顿（T‘a Tun）支持他们的大业；用他们在乌桓找到的中国难民组织了一支队伍，开始侵犯中国的东北边境。前去攻打这个远方的敌人是否明智，曹操的谋士们对此持有歧见，因为此时在中国的南部边境，还有一支更为强大的敌人。需要指出的是，刘表和刘备很有可能会利用曹操离开都城的时机打来，并占领都城。对此，郭嘉认为，刘表只会纸上谈兵，他嫉妒刘备杰出的军事才能，只会让刘备去做无关紧要的事。曹操决定听从郭嘉的建议，向北进军北京西南的易州（I Chou）。由此，曹操轻装上阵，移兵无终（Wu Chung），即如今之玉田（Yü T‘ien）。军队被大雨和几乎难以通行的道路耽搁。远处的山路被敌军坚守着。曹操毅然决定翻山越岭，向北挺进，然后东进，以从后方攻击敌人。这项任务充满困难，却被顺利完成了。当袁氏兄弟与其盟军发现了曹操的行动时，他们从防守处退却，带领一支强大的骑兵向曹操攻来。曹操应战，再次凭借勇气和计谋取得胜利。蹋顿被俘斩首，许多部下归降曹操。袁尚、袁熙兄弟逃至辽东（Liao Tung），然曹操威名早已远扬，辽东太守很快将二袁首级献上，以示友好。冬天来了，曹军因山中食物和水短缺而几近灭亡，但士兵们挖掘深井取水，吃了马匹，由此最终渡过了难关。

如今曹操的权威已在中国的中部、东部和北部建立起来，但是南部和西部依然有强大的敌人反抗他的统治。曹操而今要着手征服他们。曹操离开北方期间刘表死去，其子刘琮（Liu Tsung）继任荆州太守。刘琮没有勇气与曹操这样的敌人抗衡，闻知曹军逼近，派人送信表示投降。刘备突然失去了盟军的支持，被迫退居南方。曹操夺得荆州，准备东进。孙权（Sun Ch‘uen）在其兄孙策死后，继任江东之主，在历史上号称吴国。曹操给孙权下一战书，告诉他刘琮已束手投降，他正带百万大军，从陆路和水路向吴国进发，请他应战。这个兵力迫使孙权估计一下自己的战斗实力。孙权与将领们商议对策，许多人怂恿他投降曹操，其他人则建议他冒险一战。当此之际，刘备忠实的谋士诸葛亮（Chu Kê Liang）渡江而来，提出了一个孙权、刘备联合行动的计划。孙权听从了他的计策，周瑜（Chou Yü）受命指挥三万大军，与刘备一同装备了一队战船，前去攻击曹操的舰队，当时曹军舰队正在赤壁山（Ch'ih Pi）下，即当今武昌城（Wu Ch'ang）东南的扬子江上。这次交战联军处于有利地势，曹操将舰队撤至长江北岸。在这关键时刻，周瑜手下的一员将领黄盖（Hwang Kai）向他提出了一个计划，或许可以用来摧毁曹操的舰队。由于缺乏水上作战经验，曹操采用了一种奇怪的应急手段，将战船用铁链拴在一起，这样士兵们就可以从这条船走到另一条船，打仗时便可相互支援。而黄盖的建议则是准备十条战船，各船全都装满柴草，灌满膏油，蒙上布帐，以防发现。每条战船均拖着一艘小船，以备士兵在适当的时候逃走。战船被派去攻打曹操的舰队，在离曹军近处点火。周瑜实施了这一计划，黄盖领军出征。一股强劲的东南风帮了大忙。黄盖此前已给曹操发去一封假信，暗示他自己一有机会就向他投降。曹军在战船后面的沿河北岸一带安营扎寨，急切地注视着是否有一小队船只驶来。当这小队船只抵达河中心时，扬起帆，快速前进。帆船突然遍体着火，冲向曹操的舰队，秘密很快被揭晓了。大火烧至在劫难逃的舰队的桅杆和绳索上，滚滚向前，势不可挡。很快舰队就变成了一个巨大的火海，火焰横扫一切，扑向连营，士兵和战马被烧着，窒息而亡。周瑜和刘备在战鼓声中领兵前进，大举歼灭曹军。曹操夸口用来攻打吴国的百万大军，几乎没有一个卫兵得以幸存下来跟着他撤退。

战败的结果是荆州落入孙权之手，南部和西部反抗曹操的敌军势力更加强大。其后，陕西南部的汉中太守张鲁反曹，但轻易就被曹操打败了，这一重要军事据点的防守被交给了夏侯渊（Hsia Hou Yuan）和张郃两员能将。此时孙权将荆州暂时送给了刘备，作为作战基地。刘备命结义兄弟关羽防守荆州，并通过对巴蜀，即当今之四川的成功治理，成了该地的太守。而今刘备决定再把汉中据为已有，从西南挺进该城。夏侯渊引兵迎战，但最终却溃不成军，落入敌手，并为战败付出了生命的代价。曹操速来支援汉中。刘备见势均力敌，拒绝出战，他占据有利地势，设法用饥饿和疾病消耗曹军兵力。最终，疾病在曹军中肆虐，曹操被迫撤退，汉中从曹操之手转由刘备控制。孙权嫉妒刘备不断增长的势力，数次要求归还荆州，但刘备却寻找借口，推迟归还。随着刘备胜利挺进汉中，关羽从荆州向北前进，夺取樊城（Fan Ch'eng），此城位于湖北北部，在汉水（Han river）边靠近襄阳（Hsiang Yang）的地方。这是曹操在南部的一个军事重镇，被强大的驻军防守着。曹操同样派出两支军队，由于禁（Yü Chin）、庞德（P'ang Tê）带领，在城北扎营，以作防守。持续降雨使汉水猛涨，淹没了邻近地区。关羽抓住机会，率一支精壮船队袭击了于禁和庞德的薄弱之处。于禁料想反抗无望，遂投降关羽。庞德被生擒后斩首。樊城之役使士气高涨。另有一支小分队被派去攻打襄阳。关羽的忠勇在民众中广泛传播，曹操开始考虑将都城迁至更安全的地方。好在他的物资尚未耗尽。谋士司马懿（Ssŭ Ma I）提醒他孙权对于刘备的嫉妒，提议与孙权建立一个秘密联盟，承诺只要孙权从后面袭击关羽，迫使他退出樊城，就承认他对江东的统辖之权。孙权想从刘备手中夺回荆州，欣然接受了这一提议。孙权的一位将领吕蒙（Lü Meng）驻扎于陆口（Lu K'ou），接近现在的武昌，他向孙权献上一计，可引诱关羽将军队集结于樊城，令荆州失守。吕蒙之计是自己从陆口撤军，派陆逊（Lu Hsün）前来据守陆口。陆逊虽不出名，却有勇有能。这一计划被采纳，陆逊致信关羽，赞颂其军事成就，姿态卑微，言辞谦逊。关羽考虑到吕蒙已从前沿阵地撤退，孙权无意攻取荆州，于是逐渐将全部军队集中到了樊城。孙权派吕蒙带领一小拨精兵，隐匿于船队，装扮成商船。船队从浔阳（Hsün Yang）——而今之江西（Chiang Hsi）九江（Chin Chiang）——起航，迅速沿江上行至荆州。曹操早就得知了这一他需要适当配合的行动。尽管被告以保守秘密，但他却决定让关羽以及自己在樊城的驻军知道这一计谋。其目的是警告关羽注意荆州的安危，以此帮助他速解樊城之围。这一消息传到驻守在樊城的曹军那里，当然也会激励战士们坚决防守。曹操带兵前去救援被围困的城池，将信绑在箭上射进城里，同时也射进关羽的营寨，告诉他吕蒙攻打荆州的行动。结果如其所料。关羽意识到自己中了计，对于如何逃走举棋不定。徐晃（Hsü Huang）带领的一支曹军成功地突破了防线。关羽见此，拔寨撤营，开始撤退。他很快得知荆州已经落入了吕蒙之手，而今自己被前后夹攻，官兵旋即弃他而去，他灰心丧气，试图与几个忠实的随从逃走，但被孙权的将领潘璋（P‘an Ch‘ang）追上并斩杀了。

曹操为赢得孙权的友好，授予他各种荣誉称号，孙权也表示效忠于曹操，并劝曹操取代徒有虚名的献帝，自立为帝。相比于表面的煊赫，曹操更看重实权，对此他回答道，如果这是上天的旨意，那么他愿成为周朝（Chou）的文王（King Wên），那样他就心满意足了。这一回答意味着，虽然文王是周朝的实际建立者，但他的儿子武王（Wu）却是第一位名义上的君主，所以他愿意建立一个新的王朝，让他的儿子做第一位君主。但曹操那不得安宁、屡遭变故的一生就要走向结束了。远征关羽凯旋后，曹操来到洛阳，在生了一场病之后，很快薨于六十六岁（公元 220 年）。他的长子曹丕（Ts‘ao P‘ei）继承父权，立即废黜了空有名头的献帝，自立为帝，改国号魏。

曹操的性格特点，正如我们从中国历史中总结的那样，具有多个方面。他在个人生活习惯方面节俭而朴素，对友慷慨，对敌残暴。你可以指责他虚伪、背叛，但是这些缺点却似乎已经司空见惯，他唯一超过前人的是他对于人的本性及动机的深刻体察。他最残忍的行动是对那些暗算过他的人的报复。包括皇后及其二子就因此被杀。如果我们以道义与正直的正确标准来衡量这种残忍的行为，我们必然会加以谴责，但是我们必须多多少少用那个时代的标准来公正地衡量他。如果我们将曹操与他的两个最为著名的对手——关羽和刘备作个对比，我们肯定同意他具有同样的勇气与决心，作为一个军事家与政治家，他还拥有更大的能力。毋庸置疑，曹操的行动目的，从中国人最终的分析结果来看，在很大程度上是自私的，但他的自私并不是那种小气、卑鄙的自私，曹操个人扩张的谋略是与国家未来的繁荣发展联系在一起的。站在中国人的立场来看，他最大的罪恶便是篡夺帝王之权，就因为此，他的名字遭到一代又一代人的痛骂；而关羽和刘备，却因为他们保护汉室的勇气和忠义，被提升到神灵的行列。

第三部分

章节选译文献研究

一　汤姆斯与《著名丞相董卓之死》*

《三国演义》何时开始传入英语世界的？最早的译介者是如何翻译和看待这部作品的？该译文在西方产生了怎样的影响？《三国演义》的首次英译是这部经典之作西传的逻辑起点，起点的确切定位与深入分析，对于探讨《三国演义》的西行之旅至关重要，但偏偏是在这个问题上，学界至今存在诸多差误。从文本的角度节译《三国演义》，并在英语世界公开发表的是汤姆斯。最早提供这一信息的是王丽娜女士，1982 年，她在《〈三国演义〉在国外》一文中指出："汤姆斯（P. P. Thoms）译《著名丞相董卓之死》（*The Death of the Celebrated Minister Tung-cho*），载 1820 年版《亚洲杂志》（AJ）第一辑卷 10 及 1821 年版《亚洲杂志》第一辑卷 11，内容是《三国演义》第一至第九回的节译。"[①]1988 年，这段文字被载入她本人的专著《中国古典小说戏曲名著在国外》。这一观点在学界产生了深远影响，此后国内学者论及《三国演义》的早期英译，大多采用此说。

2012 年，郑锦怀所撰《〈三国演义〉早期英译百年（1820—1921）》一

* 相关研究以"汤姆斯与《三国演义》的首次英译"为题，发表于《文学遗产》2017 年第 3 期。

① 王丽娜：《〈三国演义〉在国外》，《文献》1982 年第 2 期，第 48 页。

文，对王丽娜的观点有所订正，指出："汤姆斯所译《三国演义》第一回至第九回的标题为 'The Death of the Celebrated Minister Tung-cho'（中译为《著名丞相董卓之死》），在 1920—1921 年间分三次连载于 *Asiatic Journal*（《亚洲杂志》），其刊载期次与页码分别为第 1 辑第 10 卷（1820 年 12 月；The Asiatic Journal for December，1820）第 525—532 页、第 1 辑第 11 卷（1821 年 2 月；The Asiatic Journal for February，1821）第 109—114 页与第 1 辑第 12 卷（1821 年 3 月；The Asiatic Journal for March，1821）第 233—242 页。"[①] 这段文字虽然提供了更详细的信息，但依然存在三个错误：一是把"1820—1821"误作"1920—1921"；二是《亚洲杂志》确实分三次连载了汤姆斯的译文，但第三次连载于"第 11 卷"，而非"第 12 卷"；三是汤姆斯翻译的内容实际出自《三国演义》第八回与第九回，并非王、郑二人所言的前九回。2015 年，郑锦怀在《国际汉学》发表《彼得·佩林·汤姆斯：由印刷工而汉学家》一文，纠正了第一点笔误，后面的两个错误依然如故。

由以上分析不难看出，目前学界对于《三国演义》首次英译的基本资料著录尚且有误，深入的研究自是难以企及。这与几百年来《三国演义》的家喻户晓，以及三国研究的备受瞩目颇不相侔，也与当下日趋密集的中西文化交流气象有异。有鉴于此，本部分内容在介绍汤姆斯其人其作的基础上，结合《三国》原著，深入分析了汤译《三国》的翻译策略和文化影响。这不仅有利于发掘汤译的学术价值，对于探索《三国演义》的早期英译、拓展《三国演义》的研究格局，也有一定意义。

---

① 郑锦怀：《〈三国演义〉早期英译百年（1820—1921）》，《明清小说研究》2012 年第 3 期，第 89 页。

FOR

DECEMBER, 1820.

ORIGINAL COMMUNICATIONS,

&c. &c. &c.

THE DEATH

OF THE

CELEBRATED MINISTER TUNG-CHO.*

TRANSLATED FROM THE CHINESE BY MR. P. P. THOMS.

(Originally communicated to the Editor of the Asiatic Journal.)

At the death of Tsze-këen, Tung-cho was residing at Chang-gan. When he heard of the late Emperor's decease, he said within himself, "Now will I turn a deaf ear to my conscience, and listen only to my ambition." The youth and inexperience of Tsze-këen's son and successor, who was only in his seventeenth year, embolden-

* The narrative in the text is extracted and translated into English from the San-kwo-che, a Chinese history of the most celebrated of their civil wars. This history is much esteemed by the Chinese, not only for its literary merit, but because it contains (as they imagine) a copious and accurate narrative of the wars and calamities of the period to which it relates. The following extracts from the preface to the work are laid before the reader in order that he may judge of the estimation in which the work itself is held by the Chinese literati. This preface is from the pen, or rather pencil, of Kin-jin-say, who flourished in the reign of Shun-che, about one hundred and fifty years ago.

EXTRACTS FROM THE PREFACE TO THE SAN-KWO-CHE.

When I published my comments on the six literary works which bear the respective titles of Chwang, Saou, Ma-che-she-ke, Too-che-leuh, Shway-fo and Se-hang, the learned of the empire applauded my labours, and were pleased to assure me that I had shewn myself not badly versed in the authors whom I had presumed to expound. Encouraged by their approbation, I now venture to submit to them the observations which I have made in perusing the History of the San-kwo. The first of these observations is, that it is not, like some pretended histories, a mere work of imagination, but accurately accords with what is elsewhere related of antiquity, and may be as safely relied on as the Standard History of China itself. But if we consider the History of the San-kwo in the light of an authentic narrative of facts, we shall find that all other histories, however admirable, fall far beneath it both in interest and in literary merit. But since all history, from Tsin and Chow upward and from Han and Tang downward, is bottomed in the Standard History of China, why, it may be asked, is the History of the San-kwo entitled to peculiar admiration? To this I answer, that the wars of the San-kwo, when compared with all

Asiatic Journ.—No. 60.　　Vol. X.　　3 Y

《亚洲杂志》所载《著名丞相董卓之死》

（一）“印刷工”汉学家

在中英文化交流史上，汤姆斯是一位名不见经传的小人物，但在中国文学的英译方面，他却堪称鸦片战争前最有成就的业余汉学家之一。

就职业身份而言，汤姆斯是19世纪英国的一名印刷工（printer），但自从踏上中国的领土，这位默默无闻的印刷工就开始了他的传奇。1814年，东印度公司（The East India Company）为推动中英贸易、博取文化声名，董事会经过慎重考虑，决定赞助第一位英国来华新教传教士马礼逊印制他编纂的《华英字典》，于是出资雇了英国专业技师汤姆斯。4月9日，汤姆斯带着先进的印刷设备，搭乘东印度公司货轮“托马斯·格林威尔号”（Thomas Grenville），经过五个月的海上漂泊，9月2日由朴茨茅斯（Portsmouth）抵达澳门（Macao），随即创办英国东印度公司澳门印刷所，半年即研制出适合中英文合刊的活字。有学者认为汤姆斯研制的这批活字，是“中国最早的也是世界最早的第一批中文铅合金活字”[①]。汤姆斯的名字，因此而被载入中国活字印刷史。[②]

作为一名印刷工，汤姆斯的工作，尤其是他印刷的《华英字典》，受到了时人的普遍赞赏。马礼逊对于汤姆斯的工作给予了充分肯定。《华英字典》封面除了印着编者的名字，还赫然印着“印刷者”汤姆斯的名字。马礼逊在《华英字典》第一卷的“致辞”（Advertisement）中说：“公允地说，字典印刷期间，作者远在印刷所九十英里之外。印刷者（汤姆斯）独自一

① 叶再生：《出版史研究》第一辑，中国书籍出版社1993年版，第25页。
② 张秀民、韩琦：《中国活字印刷史》，中国书籍出版社1998年版，第167页。

人包揽了所有工作，既充当排字工、印刷工，也充当读者和校勘者，帮助他的唯有一些不懂英文的当地人。”① 继马礼逊之后来华的第二位英国传教士米怜在《新教在华传教前十年回顾》一书中说：“汤姆斯努力制作金属活字，在克服巨大困难后，取得了意想不到的成功。因为在铸造和雕刻汉字时遇到了许多障碍，第一年的印刷工作进展格外缓慢。1816 年 1 月，《华英字典》的第一部分印刷完毕并送回国内。”②

在与中国人及中国文字日复一日的密切接触中，汤姆斯逐渐由一名职业技师，变成了一位中国文学的爱好者和翻译者。从 1814 年至 1825 年，汤姆斯在中国工作长达十年之久。十年间，他不但顺利印制了六大卷《华英字典》，而且排印了大量与中国语言、文学相关的书籍，由此对中国文学与文化产生了浓厚兴趣，并逐步着手翻译中文作品。1818 年 12 月，汤姆斯在澳门将拟话本小说集《今古奇观》中的《宋金郎团圆破毡笠》（*The Affectionate Pair*）译成英文，1820 年在伦敦发行了单行本。接着翻译了《三国演义》的第八回与第九回，同年分三次连载于《亚洲杂志》。这两篇译作虽然只是汤姆斯初试译笔，但对《今古奇观》及《三国演义》的西传却意义非凡。

汤姆斯译作篇幅最长、影响最大的作品是《花笺记》（*Chinese Courtship*）。这是一部被称为“木鱼”的广东说唱文学作品，内容是演绎才子佳人的爱情故事，文体乃韵文创作的长篇叙事诗，汤姆斯将之比作中国的史诗（epic），用诗行（in verse）译成英文，1824 年在澳门印刷所排印成书，整部译作长达 247 页。书后除了附录有大量与中英贸易相关的中国税务信息，还翻译了 32 位中国女性的小传及其诗作，其中包括苏蕙的《璿玑图回文诗》及《百美图咏》（*Pĭh-mei-she-yung* or *The Songs of a Hundred Beautiful*

---

① Robert Morrison, *A Dictionary of the Chinese Language*, Vol. Ⅰ., Part Ⅰ., Macao: Printed at the Honorable East India Company's Press, By P. P. Thoms, 1815.

② William Milne, *A Retrospect of the First Ten Years of the Protestant Mission to China*, Malacca: Printed at the Anglo-Chinese Press, 1820, p. 130.

Women）中的部分内容。三年后，德国文坛巨擘歌德读到《花笺记》，称赞该作是“一部伟大的诗篇”，并据此创作了闻名遐迩的《中德四季晨昏吟咏》。西方对汤姆斯译作的评论，至此臻于顶点。①《花笺记》的翻译以及该作文体的特殊，使汤姆斯在中国文学英译史上开创了诸多先例，他成了英语世界“第一个翻译中国叙事歌谣的人、第一个翻译中国方言作品的人、第一个翻译中国用韵文创作的爱情故事的人、第一个翻译中国女性诗作的人”②。

尽管对于汉学界来说，《花笺记》被看作汤译中国文学的最高成就；但对他本人来说，翻译《三国演义》似乎才是他努力的方向。在汤译《花笺记》的封底，有则从未被人提及的“出书广告”（Ready for the press），这则广告显示了汤姆斯在《三国》翻译上的勃勃雄心。广告全文如下：“这是一部有关三个国家的史书，译自《三国志》，并参以该时期之三国正史。作品详细描述了致使中国分裂的种种灾祸，由灵帝登基，至三国归晋；提供了大量有关中国人风俗习惯的有趣资讯；其中包括官方公文、战争始末、政治阴谋等。两卷，八开本，汤姆斯译。读者若想先睹为快，可参考 1820 年 12 月《亚洲杂志》第一页刊载的样文。”③ 由此可见，1820 年翻译完《三国演义》第八回、第九回后，汤姆斯对翻译《三国》的热情并未就此消歇。这则“出书广告”的刊登，虽不足以说明汤译《三国》业已完工，但至少表示那时的汤姆斯依然心系《三国》。遗憾的是，第二年 3 月，马礼逊字典印刷完后，汤姆斯就结束了澳门工作而返回英国，《三国》之译遂不知所终。

---

① 王燕：《〈花笺记〉：第一部中国“史诗”的西行之旅》，《文学评论》2014 年第 5 期。

② Patricia Sieber，“Universal Brotherhood Revisited：Peter Perring Thoms（1790 – 1855），Artisan Practices and the Genesis of a Chinacentric Sinology”，*Representation* 130，Spring 2015，p. 30.

③ Peter Perring Thoms，*Chinese Courtship*，London：Published by Parbury，Allen，and Kingsbury，Leadenhall-street，Sold by John Murray，Albemale-street；and by Thomas Blanshard，14，City-road；Macao，China：Printed at the Honorable East India Company's Press，1824.

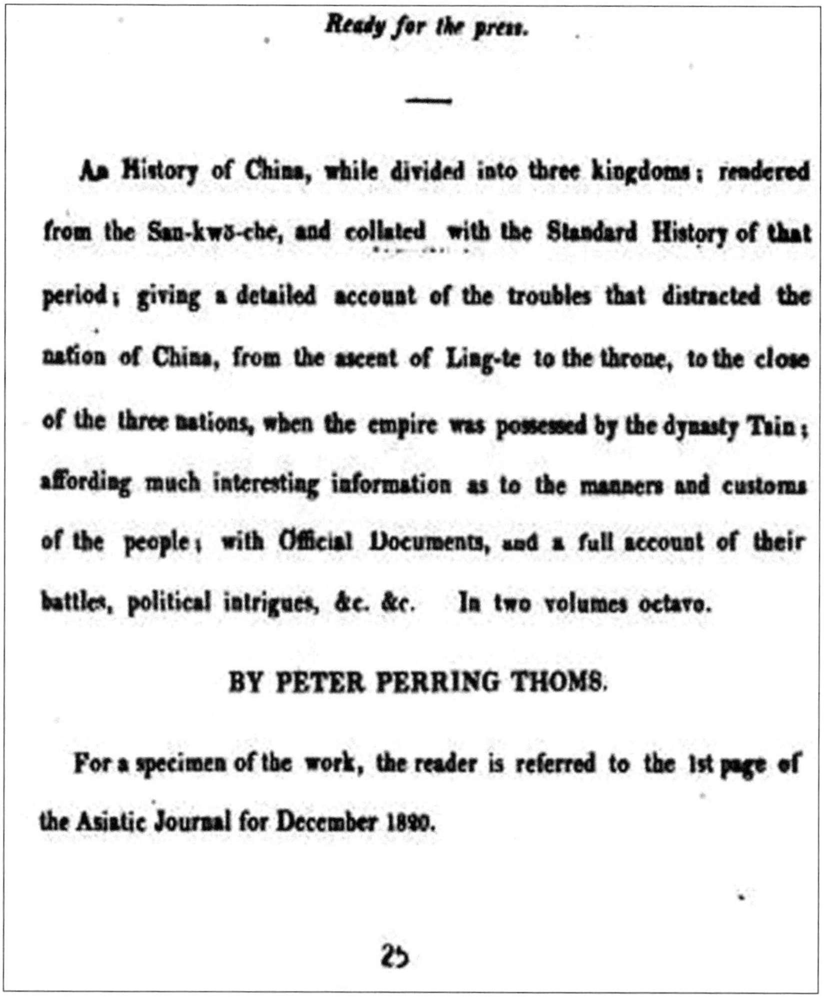

Ready for the press.

An History of China, while divided into three kingdoms; rendered from the San-kwŏ-che, and collated with the Standard History of that period; giving a detailed account of the troubles that distracted the nation of China, from the ascent of Ling-te to the throne, to the close of the three nations, when the empire was possessed by the dynasty Tsin; affording much interesting information as to the manners and customs of the people; with Official Documents, and a full account of their battles, political intrigues, &c. &c. In two volumes octavo.

BY PETER PERRING THOMS.

For a specimen of the work, the reader is referred to the 1st page of the Asiatic Journal for December 1820.

25

《花笺记》封底所刊《三国演义》广告

但这个宏大的出版计划所透露的信息，是一位来自异邦的职业工匠对于《三国演义》的持久兴趣和翻译魄力，仅此而言，他就是当时任何一个汉学家所无可比拟的。汤姆斯之前的英译中国通俗文学作品数量有限，目前查知的仅有威尔金森（James Wilkinson）翻译、帕西（James Percy）整理出版的《好逑传》（*Hau Kiou Choaan* or *The Pleasing History*）、德庇时翻译的《三与楼》（*Three Dedicated Rooms*）等屈指可数的几篇，均属于中、短篇小说；《三国演义》《红楼梦》等长篇小说的节译尚未出现。从汤姆斯英译《三国》开始，中国的长篇小说才以较为本真的面貌出现在英语读者面前。

（二）文本解读与文化阐释

汤姆斯为何选译《三国》？他采用的是哪个底本？究竟翻译了哪些内容？在翻译方法和文字表达上具有怎样的特点？唯有结合当时的文化语境细读译作，方能解答这些问题。

汤姆斯之所以选译《三国》，与马礼逊密切相关。最早将《三国演义》介绍到英语世界的西方人是马礼逊。他曾多次提及《三国》，对该作的海外传播产生了深远影响。1815 年，马礼逊编辑的《华英字典》“孔明”（Kung-ming）词条，不但从文体的角度界定《三国演义》是一部“历史小说”，而且介绍了“桃园结义”等个别情节。[①] 1817 年，马礼逊编辑的《中国一览》在罗列三国时期的重要事件时，首先介绍了《三国演义》。他说：“《三国志》是

① Robert Morrison, A *Dictionary of the Chinese Language*, Vol. Ⅰ., Part. Ⅰ., Macao: Printed at the Honorable East India Company's Press, by P. P. Thoms, 1815, p. 715.

记录三国事件的一部历史小说，因其文体和写作才华而备受推崇，并被看作是叙事类作品的典范。"① 这两部作品均由汤姆斯印制，对于自己亲手印制的作品，汤姆斯理应格外熟稔，从这两部作品中，他不难得知《三国演义》。

事实上，马礼逊对于《三国演义》的讨论，在当时更为热烈，他甚至将这部小说与《圣经》的中译联系在一起。1820 年，汤译《三国》出版的同年，米怜在《新教在华传教前十年回顾》一书中记载：马礼逊在翻译《圣经》时主张采用《三国演义》文白参半、雅俗共赏的语体风格，他认为唯有这种介于文白之间的折中体（a middle style），才适合翻译《圣经》这样一部旨在广泛传播的书。除此之外，马礼逊还认为，"学习中文的人，无论是在交谈中，还是在书写时，若想轻松、流畅地表达自己的想法，都应该仔细研读和模仿《三国》"②。汤姆斯虽然不是《新教在华传教前十年回顾》的印刷者，但他与马礼逊、米怜交往密切，二人对《三国演义》的重视定然对汤姆斯有所启发：既然《圣经》翻译和汉语学习都离不开《三国演义》，阅读与翻译这部作品也就成了当务之急。

经笔者考订，汤译《三国》采用的底本是毛纶、毛宗岗评本。原因有二：一是马礼逊、汤姆斯在提及《三国》书名时，中文写作《三国志》，英文音译为 *San-kwŏ-che* 或 *San-kwo-che*。根据刘世德先生对《三国演义》版本的研究，"书名叫《三国志》的都是所谓'批评'本。一共有四种：李卓吾评本、钟伯敬评本、李笠翁评本、毛宗岗评本"③。在这四种评本中，毛评本是清代流布最广的版本，对于汤姆斯而言不难购得。二是证明汤姆斯采用毛评本最直接的证据，是他几乎全文翻译了金圣叹为《三国演义》撰写

---

① Robert Morrison, *A View of China*, Macao: Printed at the Honorable East India Company's Press, By P. P. Thoms, 1817, p. 45.

② William Milne, *A Retrospect of the First Ten Years of the Protestant Mission to China*, Malacca: Printed at the Anglo-Chinese Press, 1820, pp. 90 – 91.

③ 刘世德：《刘世德话三国》，中华书局 2007 年版，第 25 页。

的《三国志序》。这篇英译序言出现在英译文题目的注释中，序前汤姆斯介绍说：“序言出自金人瑞（Kin-jin-suy）之手，他活跃于大约 150 年前的顺治（Shun-che）统治时期。”毛评本显著的特点，即卷首附有一篇托名金圣叹所作的序言，署作“顺治岁次甲申嘉平朔日金人瑞圣叹氏题”。由此推测，汤姆斯所用底本当是清代最流行的毛评本。

除了注释中所译金圣叹序言，汤译文正文所译内容，主要是毛评本第八回“王司徒巧使连环计　董太师大闹凤仪亭”和第九回“除暴凶吕布助司徒　犯长安李傕听贾诩”，并非学界普遍认为的第一回至第九回。具体而言，始于“却说董卓在长安，闻孙坚已死”，至“众贼杀了王允，一面又差人将王允宗族老幼，尽行杀害。士民无不下泪”。这两回的内容，概而言之，主要是王允利用美人计，联合吕布，杀了董卓，最后吕布转投袁术，王允被董卓余党杀害。这是《三国演义》中最著名的桥段之一，屡屡被改编为戏曲“连环计”或“凤仪亭”。何以选译这两回内容，汤姆斯并没有给出明确说明，但开卷即选择了这部小说中最引人入胜的情节，正显示了译者个人的洞察与识见。

在翻译方法上，汤译《三国》最显著的特点是“忠于原著”。《三国演义》第八回、第九回涉及人物众多，除了董卓、王允、貂蝉、吕布四个主要角色，还有李儒、李肃、李傕、郭汜、张济、樊稠等次要人物，以及李蒙、王方等一闪即逝的人物。汤译《三国》不但没有省略任何人物，而且细心捕捉他们的一言一行。最典型的莫过于“董卓掷戟刺布”一幕。自吕布“执戟”随董卓入朝开始，原著先后出现了十个“戟”，有提戟、掷戟、打戟、拾戟等，毛氏父子在相应位置也点出了“戟”的在场。汤姆斯显然注意到了“戟”的重要性，为了再现这一场景，他也让吕布一出场就手握画戟（with his javelin in his hand），接着陆续翻译了十个与“戟”相关的动作，如 took his javelin，threw the javelin，struck the javelin，seized the javelin。为了避免句子冗长，有两次文中不便直接翻译“提戟”的动作时，汤姆斯不惜在括号里注明吕布“依然手握画戟”（still holding his javelin in his hand）。这种亦步亦趋、紧随原著的精神似乎有点过于较真，但对于传达原著风貌，却有积极意义。

实际上，“忠于原著”是汤姆斯译作的一贯风格。1818 年翻译《宋金郎》时，他就严格遵循原著，以致个别字句译得相当生硬，如将“三分骨气”译作 three parts of their breath and bone；还有些句子因拘泥于原著反被误译，如将“宋金无面目见江东父老”，译作 Sung-kin had not resolution to look at his father of the eastern river。为了保持原著风貌，汤姆斯甚至尝试着翻译出了文章中的大部分诗词韵文，如将“姑苏城外寒山寺，夜半钟声到客船”译作：On the cold hill，without the city Koo-soo，stands the lonely temple；Half the night o'er，the sound of its bell visits each stranger's boat。这种恪守原著的风格遭到了时人的批评。1822 年，《亚洲杂志》第 13 卷的相关《书评》完整转述了汤译《宋金郎》的主要情节，并称其转述没有篡改基本情节，却赋予故事一种“风趣幽默”的风格。作者认为这种风格更符合原著者的意图，因为“每个国家的普通百姓都喜欢风趣幽默，正是通过这种方式，作家才能屡屡顺利地将美好的道德灌输给愚昧的民众”①。由此而委婉地批评汤姆斯的翻译所采用的“严肃风格”（grave style）过于严正矜持，不够活泼灵动。但这种批评显然没能改变汤姆斯忠于原著的精神，1824 年翻译《花笺记》时，他恪守原著的决心似乎更加坚定，在序言中就声称要保留“原著的精神”（the spirit of the original）。《花笺记》不但附录有中文，甚至在翻译的格式上也与中文诗句一一对应，从而保留了木鱼特有的韵文形式。

虽然同样是“忠于原著”，汤译《三国》在诗歌、韵文的处理上，与此前的《宋金郎》和此后的《花笺记》都有着显著差异。汤姆斯几乎删除了《三国》中出现的所有诗词韵文，著名的如“司徒妙算托红裙，不用干戈不

① “Review of Books,” *The Asiatic Journal and Monthly Miscellany*, Vol. XIII, 1822, p. 565.

用兵。三战虎牢徒费力，凯歌却奏凤仪亭”。另外还有貂蝉、董卓、王允的赞诗，以及回目、回末附诗和悬念句。如第八回回末，李儒闯入花园寻找董卓并将其撞倒，原文附诗两句“冲天怒气高千丈，仆地肥躯做一堆”，后有悬念句“未知此人是谁，且听下文分解”，这些诗词韵文均被汤姆斯省略。但与情节发展密切相关的那首童谣——“千里草，何青青。十日卜，不得生”，汤姆斯不但精心译出，而且为这首拆字诗添加了注释。由此可见，在“删”与“留”之间，汤姆斯做了仔细考量，这或许与他对《三国》文体属性的认知密切有关。

汤姆斯认为，《三国演义》是一部史书，而《宋金郎》和《花笺记》却是爱情故事，他将前者的题目译作 The *Affectionate Pair*（《深情的一对》），后者译作 *Chinese Courtship*（《中国式求爱》），两个译名都不免香艳，具有浓郁的文学色彩。在《三国演义》中，“连环计”或“凤仪亭”原本是这部作品中最软媚的文字，毛氏父子回前评论即云：“前卷方叙龙争虎斗，此卷忽写燕语莺声、温柔旖旎，真如铙吹之后忽听玉箫，疾雷之余忽见好月，令读者应接不暇。”① 但汤姆斯却赋予这段故事一个颇具历史意味的译名《著名丞相董卓之死》。作为一部史书，其中自然不宜出现大量抒情诗作，这或许是一向忠于原著的汤姆斯精心删除其中的诗词韵文的重要原因。

尽管忠于原著，但在具体的文字表达上，为了将原著简洁雅训的文言转化成通俗流畅的现代英语，汤姆斯在翻译时做了某些细节改动。不妨摘取一段译文，对比原著，以显示汤译《三国》的文字风貌。比如，一向被用来表现董卓暴虐的这段文字：

> 一日，卓出横门。百官皆送，卓留宴，适北地招安降卒数百人到。卓即命于座前，或断其手足，或凿其眼睛，或割其舌，或以大锅煮之。

① （明）罗贯中著，（清）毛宗岗批注：《第一才子书三国演义》，线装书局 2007 年版，第 58 页。

哀号之声震天，百官战栗失箸，卓饮食谈笑自若。

汤姆斯翻译如下：

On one of these occasions, and whilst he and his guests were in the midst of their carouse, some hundreds of deserters, relying upon a proclamation in which he had promised a general pardon, came in from the northern provinces and yielded themselves up to the clemency of Tung-cho. Instantly he commanded them into his presence. Regardless of his word, he sentenced them upon the spot, some to have their hands and feet lopped off, others to have their eyes torn out, and others, still more miserable, to becast alive into boiling cauldrons; and whilst the cries and groans of the wretched sufferers rent the very heavens, and the ministers, aghast with horror, dropped the chopsticks from their nerveless hands, Tung-cho reclined himself at his ease, drinking, jesting and laughing, as though nothing in the world had happened to mar the festivity of the assembly.

对比原著，这段译文在三个地方略有出入。首先，为了解释“招安”二字，汤译文添加了董卓先下令赦免降卒，降卒到来后，却自食其言、立即处决的含义，虽然内容上有所增益，却通过董卓的出尔反尔、变化无常，生动刻画了这个暴君的阴险、丑恶。其次，在原文列举的四大施虐行为中，汤姆斯没有翻译“或割其舌”，却把原文的并列句改为递进句，译作：“逃兵有的被砍断手足，有的被挖去眼睛，还有更残忍的是被活活扔进滚烫的大锅。”随着语义的递进，场面的恐怖似乎也在层层升级。再者，面对惨不忍睹的血腥，百官与董卓的表现截然不同，对此，汤姆斯略有展开，解释得格外贴切，他说：“百官惊惧，以致颤抖的双手拿不住筷子。董卓却镇定自若，依旧饮酒谈笑，仿佛世间什么都不曾发生过，以致糟蹋了欢宴。”百官的惊惧与董卓的从容，形成鲜明对比，董卓的残忍与暴虐被表现得淋漓尽致。在此，汤姆斯为“筷子”添加注释说“中国人用筷子把食物夹进嘴里”，文字虽浅显，但对于不熟悉中国饮食习惯的西方人来说，却并不多余。细读译文，不难发现：汤姆斯在翻译《三国演义》时，虽然没有像《花笺记》那样逐字对译（literally translation），但在主题的表达上却常有异曲同工之妙。由此，他为《三国演义》提供了一个通俗流畅的英译选段，这为该著的海外传播开启了一个良好的发端。

作为自学成才的业余汉学家，汤姆斯的翻译不可避免地存在着诸多问题。首先，文中有个别文字识别错误，尤其表现在人名的音译上。比如，他将“郭汜”译作 Ko-fan，又将“董旻”译作“Tung-yan”。何以如此？考之《华英字典》，其中有“氾”字而无“汜”字；“旻”字虽有，但另有“晏”字与之形近，由此推测，汤姆斯错将“汜”字认作“氾”，又将“晏”字当成了“旻”。[1] 其次，有些含有中国成语的句子，虽保持了中国语言的特殊表达，却令英语读者不知所云。如“布一时错见，来日自当负荆”，译作：Leu-poo sees his error, and tomorrow will bring a bundle of brambles and dopenance for his fault。对于不知道“负荆请罪”这一典故的西方读者来说，读到吕布背着“一捆荆棘”（a bundle of brambles）到王允家去“忏悔”（dopenance），一定会觉得莫名其妙。又如“貂蝉亦以秋波送情”，“秋波”原指眼睛明眸善睐、以目传情，而汤姆斯却将此译作“吕布心中如秋波荡漾”（his bosom hove like the autumnal wave）。再者，相比于《宋金郎》与《花笺记》，汤姆斯给《三国》添加的注释较少。许多专有名词，尤其是表示人物身份与职衔的专有名词，如司徒（Tsze-too）、元帅（Yun-kew-en）等，大部分只做音译而未加注解，难免令人费解。

---

① ［英］马礼逊：《华英字典》，大象出版社 2008 年版，“氾”“旻”“晏”字分别出自第 4 卷第 150、586、1004 页。

（三）“历史说”与“才子书”

首先，“演义”是一种特殊的文体，19世纪西方人关于这一文体的认识，主要分成两种观点，一是马礼逊提出的“历史小说”，二是汤姆斯提出的“历史”。此后19世纪的汉学著作，无论是介绍中国文学还是言及中国历史，大都著录《三国》，这与马礼逊与汤姆斯对该著的文体界定密切相关。

马礼逊认为《三国演义》是一部历史小说，而汤姆斯则认为它是一部史书，只不过，与一般史书相比，《三国演义》不但对当时的战乱有着真切的描写，而且具有很高的文学价值，因此受到中国人的大力推崇。在小说翻译上，汤姆斯深受马礼逊的影响，他在《宋金郎》翻译的序言中，就曾专门向马礼逊致谢；但在《三国演义》的文体属性上，却没有照搬马礼逊的观点，而是在研究与对比的基础上，形成自己的认识，由此显示了汤姆斯学者般的认真与审慎。

“演义”是介于“历史”与“小说”之间的一种文体，在两者之间，史实居多而虚构较少，清代章学诚即云“七分史实、三分虚构”。胡适甚至因此而批评它“拘守历史的故事太严，而想象力太少，创造力太薄弱”。认为《三国演义》实际是“一部绝好的通俗历史”①。汤姆斯未必知道比自己早半个世纪的章学诚的观点，也不可能了解比自己晚一个世纪的胡适的观点，他对《三国演义》文体的认识首先来自金圣叹序。毛评本金圣叹序中明确指出：《三国演义》“据实指陈，非属臆造，堪与经史相表里。由是观之，奇又莫奇于《三国志演义》矣！”汤姆斯将此译作：“首先，这部作品

① 胡适：《中国章回小说考证》，北京师范大学出版社2013年版，第272—273页。

不像某些伪史那样纯属臆造，而是与别的古代记录高度吻合，完全可以将之看作一部中国正史（the Standard History of China）。但是，如果我们把它看作一部记录史实的信史，我们发现，其他的史书，无论怎么好，在阅读趣味与文学性方面，都远不及《三国志》。”他之所以翻译金圣叹序，就是为了让西方人了解中国知识分子对于《三国演义》的认识。在对《三国演义》文体属性的界定上，他没有妄自揣测，而是直接采纳了中国评论家金圣叹的看法，既强调其历史性，也关注其文学性。

译文的最后，汤姆斯进一步结合“正史”重构了“董卓之死”，对译文所述主要人物的命运进行了历史还原。他所引“正史”严格依照历史纪年，其叙事体例显然不是出自“纪传体”的《三国志》或《后汉书》，而是“编年体”的《资治通鉴》。根据《资治通鉴》所载，孝灵皇帝中平六年，七月，“何进召卓使将兵诣京师”；八月，“董卓至显阳苑，远见火起，知有变，引兵急进”；九月，“卓复会群僚于崇德前殿，遂胁太后策废少帝”，废帝为弘农王，立陈留王为帝。接着，“董卓自为太尉，领前将军事，加节传、斧钺、虎贲，更封郿侯”；十一月，“以董卓为相国”。孝献皇帝初平元年，“正月，关东州郡皆起兵以讨董卓”。初平二年，“二月，丁丑，以董卓为太师，位在诸侯王上”。初平三年，“夏，四月，丁巳，帝有疾新愈，大会未央殿”，王允联合吕布刺杀董卓，“暴卓尸于市”；六月，李傕杀王允，“吕布自武关奔南阳”；“九月，以李傕为车骑将军、领司隶校尉、假节；郭汜为后将军，樊稠为右将军，张济为骠骑将军，皆封侯。”[①] 这些记载与汤姆斯所述均相吻合。其意义不仅在于显示了译者对中国历史典籍的熟稔，更重要的是，他以“正史”的在场，强化了《三国演义》的历史性，从而为确定《三国演义》的最终属性做了最后的论证。

汤姆斯在翻译金圣叹序和引证《资治通鉴》的基础上，提出了《三国

① （宋）司马光：《资治通鉴》，中华书局 2007 年版，第 459—471 页。

演义》"历史论"，与马礼逊的《三国演义》"小说论"形成鲜明对比。此后，无论是西方人论及中国文学著作还是中国史学著作，在叙述三国这一时期时，多提及《三国演义》，这为《三国演义》的海外传播拓宽了道路。只是在讨论这两种观点的具体形成时，后来的汉学家未必直接提及马礼逊或汤姆斯的名字。比如，1844 年托马斯·桑顿（Thomas Thornton）在其所著的《中国史》（*A History of China*）一书中说："《三国志》声称对于献帝退位之后的内战提供了一个详细的记录。由此而进入了董卓执政的前期阶段。许多人认为，这种绝对建基于历史的、对于内战丰富而详细的叙述，是完全真实的；而另一些人则把它看作是一部由真实的历史材料加工而成的虚构之作。它的流行或许可以归因于文体的讨人欢喜、事件的丰富多彩，以及间或点缀的戏剧性对话，这使该作看起来很像我们所说的历史小说，这在中国是一种常见的文体形式。它原本是一部三国史，由生逢其后的陈寿（Chin-show）写成；在此基础上创作的小说，则出自元代罗贯中（Lo-kwan-chung）之手，他使该作与真实的历史更趋吻合。"① 由此可见，鸦片战争前后确有不少西方人把《三国演义》看作一部信史。无论他们是否上溯至汤姆斯，一个不容否认的事实是：他是这一观点的开创者。

其次，《著名丞相董卓之死》的翻译，不仅让西方读者了解了《三国演义》的一个故事，还使他们意识到"才子书"或"十才子"系列作品的存在，由此而推动了包括《三国演义》在内的中国小说的英译。

根据《三国演义》第八、九回改编的中国戏曲，大都取名《连环计》或《凤仪亭》，题名"董卓之死"则是文化移植中的一个新创。汤姆斯之后，这个故事不断被改换题名，反复译介，成为西方人最熟悉的《三国》故事之一。比如，亚历山大（G. G. Alexander，1821—1897）翻译的《中国

① Thomas Thornton，*A History of China*，London：Wm. H. Allen and Co.，7，Leadenhall Street，1844，Vol. Ⅰ.，p. 401.

史之一章：大臣的计谋》（*A Chapter of Chinese History*：*The Minister's Stratagem*），发表于 1861 年 5 月 25 日的《每周一报》（*Once A Week*）。像汤姆斯一样，亚历山大也把《三国》看作一部史书。1867 年，亚历山大又将这一故事改编为一个五幕剧，取名《貂蝉》（*Teaou-shin*），《连环计》或《凤仪亭》从此有了英国人独创的戏剧版本。这种由中国小说到英国戏剧的文体转型与文化移植，不啻为文化史上的一个创举。又如，1925 年，邓罗（C. H. Brewitt-Taylor，1857—1938）翻译的《三国演义》（*San Kuo*，*or*，*Romance of the Three Kingdoms*）由上海别发洋行（Shanghai：Kelly & Walsh）出版，这是《三国演义》的第一个英文全译本，邓罗因此闻名于世，只是学界很少有人提及，他在全译《三国》之前曾节译过若干片段，其中就有“董卓之死”这一桥段，该文 1892 年发表于《中国评论》第 20 卷，题名《阴谋与爱情》（*A Deep-laid Plot and A Love Scene*）。

除了英国汉学界，汤姆斯的译文还传至法国汉学界。《著名丞相董卓之死》刊载于《亚洲杂志》，该刊创刊于 1816 年，至 1845 年停刊，前后三十年，发行 73 卷，兼有英文版及法文版，在欧洲影响深远。汤姆斯的译文也随着《亚洲杂志》传至欧洲。1834 年法国著名汉学家儒莲（Stanislas Julien，1797—1873）翻译的《赵氏孤儿》（*Tchao-Chi-Kou-Eul*：*Ou L'Orphelin de La Chine*）文后附有一篇《三国》译文，题名《董卓之死》（*La Mort de Tongtcho*），这篇译文被看作法译《三国》的开端。英法首译《三国》，均从“董卓之死”开始，这显然不能仅仅看作一个巧合。

就目前调查所知，汤姆斯是第一个向西方读者介绍“才子书”的英国人。汤姆斯所采用的《三国演义》底本是毛评本。毛评本在清代被称为“第一才子书”，原因是金圣叹序中有这么一句话：“而今而后，知第一才子书之目又果在《三国志演义》也。”汤姆斯将此译作：This emboldens me to declare，both to my contemporaries and to posterity，that the Te-yeh-tsae-tsze（the work which evinces the highest literary talent）is “The History of the Civil

Wars of China”。在此，他把《三国志演义》译作《中国内战史》，该作被称为“第一才子”书，汤姆斯将之音译为 Te-yeh-tsae-tsze，意译为“最具文采的书”。显然，汤姆斯在译介《三国演义》的同时，也强调了“才子书”这一评价体系的存在。既然有所谓“第一才子书”，被推许为“第八才子书”的《花笺记》自然也值得关注，这或许是他四年后翻译《花笺记》的重要原因，因为在《花笺记》“序言”中，汤姆斯特意指出这部地方说唱文学在中国位列第八，所谓“The Eighth's Chinese Literary Work”。

随着中国小说的不断译介，汤姆斯引入的“才子书”这一概念在西方世界不胫而走、广泛传播。1838 年，德国传教士郭实腊在《中国开门》（*China Opened*）中将“十才子”（Shih-tsae-tsze）理解为“十个才子的呕心沥血之作”（the lucubrations of the ten talented men）。[①] 但在同年发表的《三国志评论》中，又把《十才子》错误地理解为“十个天才的儿子”（The Ten Sons of Genius）。[②] 1867 年，英国外交官梅辉立在《中日释疑》（*Notes and Queries*）上发表系列书评介绍中国小说，在评论“传奇小说”（romantic novels）时指出：“‘才子书’（Work of a Ts'ai-tz'）这一称谓来自著名编辑兼评论家金圣叹的图书分类。”又说：“‘才子’不仅被金圣叹用来指称传奇小说作家，而且被发展成了一个特定称谓，用来指称十部著名作品，通常称之为‘十才子’（Ten Ts'ai-tz），其中的四部由金圣叹编辑成书。”[③] 1897 年，美国传教士丁义华（E. W. Thwing）在《中国小说》（*Chinese Fiction*）一文中将中国小说一分为二：历史小说和传奇小说，位列后者之首的就是“十才子”（Shap ta‘oi tsz'）。有趣的是，他沿袭了郭实腊的错误，也把“十才子”解释为“十个天才的儿子”

---

① Charles Gutzlaff, *China Opened; or, A Display of the Topography, History, Customs, Manners, Arts, Manufactures, Commerce, Literature, Religion, Jurisprudence, etc. of the Chinese Empire*, Vol. Ⅰ., London: Smith, Elder and Co. 65, Cornhill, 1838, p. 468.

② “*Notice of the San Kwŏ Che*”, *The Chinese Repository*, Vol. Ⅻ., From May, 1838 to April, 1839, Canton: Printed for the Proprietors, pp. 233.

③ W. F. Mayers, “Bibliograoical”, *Notes and Queries*, Dec. 31, 1867.

(Ten Sons of Talent)。[①] 直到 1936 年，陈铨写作《中德文学研究》时，他还慨叹："其实这十部书里面，真正够得上称才子书的，也不过《三国志演义》《水浒传》《西厢记》《琵琶记》，其余比较相差太远。"但是，这个观念却被根深蒂固地沿用下来，以致"最近德国人孔（Franz Kuhn）在他《好逑传》译本跋语里边，仍然把十才子书的标准来审定《好逑传》在中国文学上的地位"[②]。"才子书"这一概念影响如此深远，或许是汤姆斯始料未及的。

上述各国来华西士对于"才子书"或"十才子"的音译或理解，与汤姆斯相比不尽相同，说明他们很有可能是从中文语境中直接习得了这两个概念。丁义华就曾指出：几乎当时的每个书店都能见到"十才子"。但汤姆斯的影响并未被彻底遮蔽。比如，郭实腊对于"才子"二字的拼读与汤姆斯完全相同，均为 tsae tsze；梅辉立在介绍"十才子"时像汤姆斯那样联系着金圣叹，他对"三国"的拼读也与汤姆斯完全相同，均为 San Kwo；丁义华开列的第八才子《花笺》书名直接采用了汤姆斯翻译的 *Chinese Courtship*。事实上，在当时，丁义华并非没有别的选择。1867 年，J. Chalmers 将《花笺记》书名译作 *The History of the Flowery Billet*；1868 年，香港总督包令（John Bowring，1792—1872）又将书名译作 *The Flowery Scroll*。恰恰是这些细节的提示，令人很难相信这些学者全然不了解汤姆斯的译作。毕竟，他在 19 世纪 20 年代就在英语世界播撒了"才子书"的种子，不仅如此，他还翻译了"十才子"中的两部，二者在早期中国文学英译史上全都创造了辉煌业绩：《三国演义》的不少片段和语句被广泛用作汉语学习语料，相关的翻译、评论、改编之作多达数十篇，这部历史演义几乎成了三国时代的象征；而《花笺记》这部罕为人知的木鱼书，在汤译本后又出现了五种语言的五个译本。这些中国文学英译史上的神话，不能不从汤姆斯说起。

---

① E. W. Thwing, "Chinese Fiction", *The China Review, or notes & queries on the Far East*, Vol. 22, No. 6. 1897, pp. 760 - 761.

② 陈铨：《中德文学研究》，商务印书馆 1936 年版，第 19 至 20 页。

附：英文原文

材料一

THE DEATH OF THE CELEBRATED MINISTER TUNG-CHO. ①

TRANSLATED FROM THE CHINESE BY MR. P. P. THOMS.

(*Originally communicated to the Editor of the Asiatic Journal.*)

At the death of Tsze-këen, Tung-cho was residing at Chang-gan. When he heard of the late Emperor's decease, he said within himself, "Now will I turn a

① 编者按：*The Asiatic Journal and Monthly Register for British India and its Depencies.* Vol. X., July to December. 1820. London, pp. 525 – 532. 以下英文是汤姆斯为题目添加的注释。

The narrative in the text is extracted and translated into English from the San-kwo-che, a Chinese history of the most celebrated of their civil wars. This history is much esteemed by the Chinese, not only for its literary merit, but because it contains (as they imagine) a copious and accurate narrative of the wars and calamities of the period to which it relates. The following extracts from the preface to the work are laid before the reader in order that he may judge of the estimation in which the work itself is held by the Chinese literati. This preface is from the pen, or rather pencil, of Kin-jin-suy, who flourished in the reign of Shun-che, about one hundred and fifty years ago.

EXTRACTS FROM THE PREFACE TO THE SAN-KWO-CHE

When I published my comments on the six literary works which bear the respective titles of Chwang, Saou, Ma-che-she-ke, Too-che-leuh, Shwuy-fo and Se-leang, the learned of the empire applauded my labours, and were pleased to assure me that I had shewn myself not badly versed in the authors whom I had presumed to expound. Encouraged by their approbation, I now venture to submit to them the observations which I have made in perusing the History of the San-kwo. The first of these observations is, that it is not,

deaf ear to my conscience, and listen only to my ambition." The youth and inexperience of Tsze-këen's son and successor, who was only in his seventeenth year,

---

like some pretended histories, a mere work of imagination, but accurately accords with what is elsewhere related of antiquity, and may be as safely relied on as the Standard History of China itself. But if we consider the History of the San-kwo in the light of an authentic narrative of facts, we shall find that all other histories, however admirable, fall far beneath it both in interest and in literary merit. But since all history, from Tsin and Chow upward and from Han and Tang downward, is bottomed in the Standard History of China, why, it may be asked, is the History of the San-kwo entitled to peculiar admiration? To this I answer, that the wars of the San-kwo, when compared with all other wars, whether ancient or modern, are wars of the most interesting nature; and that the historian of those wars, when compared with all other historians, whether ancient or modern, is an author of unrivalled merit. What is there in the affairs, whether civil or military, of any other age that can compare in interest with those of the San-kwo? And as to all other historical productions, are they not, when contrasted with the History of the San-kwo, the productions of ordinary pens?

As often as I reflect upon the power and resources which were possessed by each of the three parties engaged in these mighty struggles, so dark and incomprehensible do I find the ways of heaven that I almost lose my confidence in its wisdom and its justice. When on the death of Hëen-te (Hëen-te, who was the last Emperor of the Eastern Han Dynasty, died about A. D. 226. On his death the civil wars began.), of the dynasty Han, the government of the empire was usurped by the minister Tung-cho, a host of veteran soldiers started up in arms and the nation was thrown into confusion. If Heaven had earlier blest Lew-pe with the sage counsels of Kung-ming, he would in the first instance have made himself sure of the country of King-Leang; and then proceeding to Ho-pih, would have thence dispatched advices to Wae-nan, Keaug-tung, Tsin and Yung; the affairs of the distracted empire would have been peaceably adjusted, and in power and reputation he would have rivalled Kwang-woo, the illustrious restorer of the family of Han. Had Heaven given this turn to the affairs of the empire, I should not have ventured to question either the wisdom or the justice of its decrees. But in the events which actually happened we see nothing but a scene of confusion: we behold Tung-cho seduced by his ambition to usurp the throne, but losing his life in the attempt, and Tsaou-tsaou dictating to the nobles under the guise of imperial authority. For though in the first month of each year, and on the first day of each month, that ambitious minister ostensibly held council on the affairs of the nation in the name of the Emperor, the substantial powers of Government were exercised by himself. Unable to restore tranquillity to the state, what was Lew-pe to do? The northern and southern portions of the empire were seized upon by usurpers, who formed out of those districts the kingdoms of Woo and Wae. The only portion of the empire which still obeyed Lew-pe was the country of Se-nan, where he established his government. If, indeed, he had not been aided by the wisdom and valour of Kung-ming in the wars which he waged on the eastern and western sides of this remnant of his dominions, Leang-yeh with many other places would have been subdued by Tsaou-tsaou; the kingdom of Woo, unable to subsist as an independent power, would also have fallen under his yoke; Tsaou-tsaou, like another Wang-mang, would have held the whole patrimony of Han in subjection to his usurped authority; and in the absolute triumph of that atrocious tyrant posterity might well have questioned the wisdom and the justice of the Heavens. Adverting as I pass to the arrival of Tsaou-tsaou at Tung-ying, when in consequence of his repeated defeats the three independent states which

emboldened the minister in his wickedness; for he concluded that his designs would meet with no serious obstacle in any opposition that the young prince could

---

had arisen out of these contests were firmly and equally established, I now proceed to draw a hasty sketch of the history of his life: of the life of the tyrant, whose whole existence was a tissue of enormous crimes, and who was no less abhorred by the gods than he was dreaded and detested by men. And here I can only relate, in the most general terms, that there was a period in his eventful career in which libels were put forth against him in every town of the empire; in which he was insulted and reviled to his face; and in which his life was openly sought with the javelin, and covertly aimed at with poison and the dagger. But though assailed by these and a thousand dangers beside; though compelled to cut off his beard that he might escape his enemies in disguise; though so close upon the brink of destruction as on one occasion to have his teeth knocked out, and on another to be thrown from his horse and dragged along the ground; though pursued by that relentless hatred which was justly due to his atrocious crimes; still did he escape the untimely end to which his destiny seemed to lead him, still did the multitude of his enemies hardly outnumber the host of his adherents. Whether the escape of the tyrant from an ignominious end accorded or not with the will of heaven, it is not for me to determine. This is certain: had his life been other than it was, the three hostile dynasties which arose out of the civil wars would have never existed. Here I shall dismiss Tsaou-tsaou, the formidable foe of the dynasty of Han, and who, like some corroding insect, gnawed his way to the very heart of their empire.

But not content with one successful rebel, the Heavens raised up another in the person of Chow-yu—the founder of the kingdom of Woo, and in wisdom, valour and fortune the worthy and equal rival of the loyal Kung-ming. In addition to Tsaou-tsaou and Chow-yu, the Heavens gave birth to Szë-ma-e—the successor of Tsaou-tsaou in the kingdom of Wae, and his successor also in crime and in infamy. In its fears that some one of the three states which it had just established might be oppressed by one or both of the other two, Heaven placed on the thrones of all of them sovereigns of equal ability.

From the most remote antiquity downward, usurpers have from time to time arisen, and of these usurpers many have succeeded in establishing themselves as kings. Thus, during one period, there were subsisting at one and the same time twelve independent states; during another period, seven independent states; during another period, sixteen independent states. Thus, the northern and the southern dynasties reigned through the same period. Thus, the eastern and western Wae dynasties existed together. Thus, the former Leang dynasty was superseded by the later Leang dynasty. But it is remarkable that in these instances the contentions for power were speedily determined. What distinguishes the wars of the San-kwo is this, that they were continued through sixty years; and that as the three independent states which were parties to the contest were established at one and the same period, so were they at once annihilated.

Of the literary merit of this admirable work, I may observe, that they are equally felt by all classes of readers. The scholar is delighted with it; the mere man of business is interested by it; the soldier warms with pleasure at the perusal of it; the very vulgar are moved by it.

Having one day called on a friend, I saw upon his table the rough draft of a commentary which Maou-tsze had composed on the History of the San-kwo. On the very first inspection of it, I found that the sentiments of Maou-tsze accorded with my own. This emboldens me to declare, both to my contemporaries and to posterity, that the Te-yeh-tsae-tsze (the work which evinces the highest literary talent) is "The History of the Civil Wars of China." These few words, by way of preface, I therefore send to Maou-tsze, in order that he may prefix them to the next edition of the History of the San-Kwo, and that posterity may thence be informed of the conformity of our opinions with regard to its literary merits.

offer to them. Accordingly, he assumed the title of Shang-foo (guardian or protector of the prince). Whenever he went abroad, or returned to his palace, he surrounded himself with imperial state. His brother, Tung-yan, be raised to the rank of duke and to the station of lieutenant-general in the imperial army. His nephew, Tung-hwang, be appointed to the offices of attendant at the imperial palace and commander of the Emperor's body-guard. Every member of his family, young as well as old, assumed the title of duke.

At the distance of two hundred and fifty le from Chang-gan he founded a new city, to which he gave the name of Me-too. In the building of this celebrated city he employed two hundred and fifty thousand workmen. He enclosed it with a wall, which, in height and breadth, rivalled the solid and lofty wall of the imperial city Chang-gan. Within the city he erected a palace, a treasury, and also store-houses large enough to hold twenty years' provisions for a numerous army. He chose from among the women of the empire eight hundred comely damsels, and sent them to his new city to aid in the peopling of it. To this city he removed the whole of his family, and also deposited there his treasure; which last consisted of an immense quantity of gold, diamonds, pearls and rich silks.

In the course of his administration, Tung-cho was often obliged to visit, and sometimes to reside for a month or fortnight at a time at the imperial city Chang-gan. On his return from any of these visits, the ministers of state would accompany him to the outside of the eastern gate of the imperial city, there to take their leave of him; but before they took their leave, would drink wine in company with Tung-cho, in a tent which he ordered to be pitched for that purpose just without the city gate.

On one of these occasions, and whilst he and his guests were in the midst of their carouse, some hundreds of deserters, relying upon a proclamation in which he had promised a general pardon, came in from the northern provinces and yielded themselves up to the clemency of Tung-cho. Instantly he commanded them into his presence. Regardless of his word, he sentenced them upon the spot, some to have their hands and feet lopped off, others to have their eyes torn out, and others, still more miserable, to be cast alive into boiling cauldrons; and whilst the cries and groans of the wretched sufferers rent the very heavens, and the ministers, aghast with horror, dropped the chopsticks① from their nerveless hands, Tung-cho reclined himself at his ease, drinking, jesting and laughing, as though nothing in the world had happened to mar the festivity of the assembly.

On another occasion, whilst he was feasting at a great entertainment in the city, with the ministers of state about him, and had drunk plentifully of wine, Leu-poo entered the banqueting room, and walking up to Tung-cho, whispered a few words in his ear. The ministers turned pale with terror, when Tung-cho answered with a smile: "It is thus, is it? Seize Tsze-kung (the Chang-wan) and drag him from the apartment." The order was obeyed; and in a few minutes an inferior officer of the guards entered the room, and presented Tung-cho with the head of the Chang-wan lying in a blood-coloured trencher. At this woeful spectacle, the very souls of the ministers fainted within them; but Tung-cho, with a smiling aspect, exhorted them to take courage, informing them "that the Chang-wan had conspired with Wae-shŭh to destroy him; that a letter addressed by the Chang-wan to his fellow-conspirator, and containing intimations of their treason, had been delivered by mistake into the hands of Tung-cho's adopted son, Fung-sëen②; and that on this discovery of the Chang-wan's guilt, Tung-cho had ordered his head to

① With these the Chinese lift their food to their months.

② A name borne by Leu-poo.

be struck off: that they, the ministers, were not implicated in his guilt, and ought not therefore to take alarm at his punishment." To this exhortation, the ministers only answered, "True, true;" and then took their leave of Tung-cho with all possible expedition.

Wang-yun, the Tsze-too, who had been one of the guests, returned to his home sorrowfully pondering on what had happened at the banquet. Unable to rest, he took his staff, walked out by moonlight into the garden behind the house, and leaning against a rail which supported some rose-bushes, gazed at the passing clouds and wept. Whilst thus engaged, he was surprised at hearing the sighs and lamentations of some unknown person, who was concealed in an adjoining arbour. Gently drawing nigh, that he might find out who it was, he was astonished at discovering Teaou-shin, a girl whom in her early childhood he had adopted into his family, and carefully instructed in the arts of dancing and singing, whom he had ever treated with the tenderness of a father, and who having grown up to the age of sixteen under his fostering care, was now a beautiful and attractive young woman. Hearing her sighs, he asked her, in a tone of rebuke, why she grieved, and of what offence she had been guilty? "Offence!" answered the girl, falling at the same time on her knees, "how can I, who am supported by your bounty, and who am ever thinking on your kindness, how can I have ventured to offend?" — "If you have not offended," replied her master, "why are you here at this late hour of the night sighing and grieving?" — "Do you wish me," said Teaou-shin, "to open my whole heart to you?" — "Do so," answered Wang-yun, "and remember that you cannot hide the truth from me." — "Let me begin, then," replied Teaou-Shin, "by thanking you from the bottom of my heart for your goodness in bringing me up, and more especially for the instructions which you have given me in the arts of dancing and singing. Such, and so unvarying has been your kindness to me, that though I died in your service, though, to serve you, I gave up my flesh to be stripped bit by bit from my bones; and my bones to be ground to powder, never, never could I requite you one ten-thousandth part of the manifold benefits which I have received at your hauds. I have marked of late that the brows of my honoured master have been knit together by some inward grief; I have not presumed to pry into the cause of your unhappiness, but I cannot but feel convinced that it is some public care which thus presses upon your spirits. When I beheld you this evening restless and uneasy, I was grieved at your unhappiness; and, little suspecting that you would follow me into the garden, I stole to this sequestered spot that I might indulge my grief in secret. If I can assuage your sorrows, if aught that I can do will avail my generous benefactor, command me: you shall find that I will not shrink from ten thousand deaths."

"Who could have thought it!" exclaimed Wang-yun, striking the ground with his staff, "who could have thought that the tottering dynasty of Han was destined to find support from this orphan damsel! Follow me to the painted chamber."

As soon as they had reached the painted chamber, he commanded the female attendants, who were then in waiting, to leave the apartment; and when they had withdrawn, he touched the ground with his forehead, prostrating himself before Teaou-shin. Alarmed at these unwonted marks of respect, she fell upon her kness① and exclaimed, "Why is it that my honoured master thus abases himself before his servant?" — "Will you not," answered Wang-yun, "will you not take compassion upon the fallen state of the family of Han? will you not do your best to snatch your legitimate sovereign from destruction, and to rescue the people from oppression?" And when he had thus spoken, the tears gushed from his eyes faster than

① 编者按：kness 应为 knees。

the water bubbles from the spring.

"If you can believe the professions which I have just made to to[①] you." said the damsel, "you need say no more; only command me, and that command will I do my best to execute in the teeth of ten thousand deaths." Wang-yun, still kneeling before her, thus resumed: "The lives of the Emperor and of his faithful servants, the ministers, are as a pile of eggs, liable to be crushed at every instant; and as for the people, their misery is not less excruciating than if they were hanged up by the heels writhing under the bamboo of the executioner. It lies with you to save and deliver us: should you refuse your aid, or should you fail in your attempt to save us, the usurping minister Tung-cho will thrust himself into the throne of his sovereign; for though the faithful ministers have long perceived his traitorous intent, their wisdom can supply them with no device which looks as if it were likely to prevent it. Now hear me. Tung-cho has an adopted son, who by reason of his extraordinary strength has acquired the name of Leu as a prefix to his original name of Poo. I have discovered that Tung-cho and this[②] his adopted son Leu-poo are much given to go astray with women. Upon this weakness of theirs I have raised a scheme, in which, I trust, I shall entrap them both. My intention is, first, to promise you in marriage to Leu-poo, and then to make an offer of your person to Tung-cho. It will be for you to set the father and son at variance by every artifice that you can think of; and by working upon the jealousy of Leu-poo, to incite him to the destruction of the tyrant. If you should succeed to the full extent of my wishes, you will put an end to the tyranny under which we are now groaning; you will establish the throne in safety; and Keang-shan, the ancient and

① 编者按：此处多一 to。
② 编者按：此处多一 this。

venerable capital of the empire, will again become the seat of government. All this it lies in your power to accomplish; say, will you do it or not?"

"I have already assured you," said Teaou-shin, "that to serve your Excellency I am ready to brave ten thousand deaths. Proceed with your scheme, and rest assured that I will go through my part in it with fidelity and zeal." "If," said he, "you betray a single tittle of this matter, I and my whole family shall be utterly rooted out from the earth." "Banish such idle fears," said Teaou-shin: "if I do not do my best to requite you for your unexampled goodness to me, may I be cut into the minutest particles." Wang-yun, again prostrating himself before her, thanked her and retired.

The next day Wang-yun ordered an artizan to make a golden helmet. This helmet, which was surmounted by a ball of the same metal, and set with the richest and most brilliant of his family diamonds, he privately sent to Leu-poo. When Leu-poo beheld it, he was greatly elated at receiving so splendid a present, and immediately went to Wang-yun's palace for the purpose of offering him his thanks. Wang-yun, who expected this visit, and who had prepared an elegant repast for his reception, went forth to do the honours of his house to Leu-poo as soon as he saw him approaching; conducted him into the innermost chamber; and then pointing to the highest place at the table, requested his guest to take it.

Leu-poo, surprised though gratified by this extraordinary politeness, addressed himself to Wang-yun and said, "How is this? How can I, who am but a subordinate officer to a minister of state, how can I be entitled to such marks of distinction from one who is himself a minister?" "These attentions," answered Wang-yun, "may not perhaps be due to the rank of Leu-poo, but I think that these and even greater attentions are justly due to his unrivalled talents and courage." With this compliment Leu-poo was greatly elated.

Through the whole of the repast, Wang-yun pressed his guest to drink, and talked without intermission of the abilities of Tung-cho and Leu-poo. Leu-poo drank freely, laughing the while with pleasure at the compliments which were paid him. As soon as dinner was over, Wang-yun ordered his men servants to withdraw, and commanded his maid servants to serve them with wine. When they had drunk plentifully of wine, Wang-yun commanded that his daughter should come forth into the banqueting room; and in a few minutes Teaou-shin, elegantly attired, and attended by two female servants, made her appearance in the apartment. Leu-poo was struck with her grace and beauty and asked Wang-yun who she was? "It is my daughter Teaou-shin," said Wang-yun, "and as I look upon Leu-poo in the light of a relation, I have commanded her to come into the room and shew herself to him." He then commanded her to present Leu-poo with a cup of wine. This she did; and whilst she was in the act of presenting it to Leu-poo, their eyes met and were withdrawn together.

Wang-yun, feigning intoxication, said to Teaou-shin, "My daughter, present our honoured guest with another cup of wine. It is to him that we are indebted for the protection which we enjoy; let us not fail in the attentions which are his due." Leu-poo requested Teaou-shin to be seated; and on her making a motion as if she were about to withdraw, Wang-yun said to her, "My daughter, Leu-poo is amongst the most intimate of my friends; what should deter you from taking a seat?" She immediately seated herself by the side of Wang-yun; and Leu-poo feasted his eyes upon her, drinking the while large draughts of wine.

Wang-yun pointed with his hand at Teaou-shin, and said to Leu-poo, "There is nothing I should like so well as to have Leu-poo for my son in law. I would offer you my daughter there in marriage, but I am afraid that the proposal would not meet your wishes." Leu-poo, starting from the table and thanking

Wang-yun for his offer, said, "If you will indeed make me the husband of your daughter, neither the horse nor the dog shall surpass me in fidelity." "Then be it so," said Wang-yun: "on the very first lucky day that falls I will send her to your house." Leu-poo, drunk with joy no less than with wine, resumed his couch, and gazed upon Teaou-shin; and as Teaou-shin responded to his amorous glances, his bosom hove like the autumnal wave.

Shortly afterward the table was removed; and Wang-yun, apologizing to Leu-poo, told him, "that he wished he could pass the night there, but was afraid that Tung-chô might hear of it and be displeased." Leu-poo, bowing thrice and thanking him as often, politely took his leave and withdrew.

A few days afterward Wang-yun went to the imperial court, where he saw Tung-cho. As Leu-poo was not at the time in attendance, Wang-yun accosted the minister (first making his obeisance) and said, "Wang-yun humbly desires of your greatness that your greatness will condescend to eat of a dinner at his house, and earnestly hopes that nothing will happen to prevent you from complying with his request." With this invitation Tung-cho complied. Wang-yun took his leave, and hastened homeward to prepare for the minister's reception. The couch of the expected guest was spread out in the great hall, which was covered with a rich carpet and hung round with sumptuous curtains.

The next day, about noon, Tung-cho was seen approaching. Wang-yun went forth to receive him, and after making him the appropriate obeisance, requested him to enter the house. Tung-cho alighted from his carriage, and entered the house through a passage formed by his guards, who extended themselves in two lines as far as the door-way which led into the great hall. As soon as he had entered the hall Wang-yun again bowed himself to the ground, but Tung-cho ordered one of his attendants to raise him up, and then graciously commanded him to take his seat by his side.

During the repast Wang-yun plied the minister with compliments, assuring him "that the fame of his administration had spread itself over the whole earth, and that the ancient sages and statesmen Yen and Chow could not for a moment be compared with him." Tung-chô, elate and joyous with the compliments which he received, drank freely; and as Wang-yun was a pleasing companion, the wine retained its flavour to a late hour in the day.

After they had passed some time at table, Wang-yun requested Tung-cho to retire with him into an inner apartment. With this invitation Tung-cho complied, having first commanded his guards not to follow them. Wang-yun then presented Tung-cho with a cup of wine, and addressed him as follows: "I have studied astrology from my youth upward, and can clearly discern in the present aspect of the stars that the dynasty of Han is fast approaching to its close. Your great abilities are known and acknowledged by the whole empire. Nay, start not. If, in the olden time, Yaou was supplanted by Shun, and Shun in his turn succumbed to Yu, we may conclude that both gods and men were consenting to these changes."— "How," said Tung-cho, "how can I venture to look so high?" — "There is an ancient saying," answered Wang-yun, "that fools must give way to the wise, and the wicked yield to the virtuous. Why should this ordinary course of human affairs be interrupted in the instance before us?" — "If heaven," replied Tung-cho, "raise me to the throne, Wang-yun, the Tsze-too, may look to be promoted to the office of Yun-kewen." Wang-yun, thanking Tung-cho, commanded his female servants to light the ornamented lamps and to place wine upon the table. He also ordered music, telling Tung-cho that it was unworthy of his ear, but that he had commanded it to attend because there was an actress in waiting, who, if it pleased him, would accompany it with her voice. On Tung-cho's expressing his assent, a curtain was lowered across the room, the musicians playing in front of it, and Taou-shin[①] singing behind it.

When Teaou-shin had concluded her performance, Tung-cho requested that she might be introduced into his presence; and she accordingly came from behind the curtain and made him three low curtesies. Struck with her beauty, he asked who she was? "It is one Teaou-shin an actress," answered Wang-yun, requesting her at the same time to take the musical boards and sing them a soft air. As she sung Tung-cho was loud in her praise.

At the command of Wang-yun she presented a cup of wine to Tung-cho, who as he received it from her hands said to her, "blooming beauty! what may be your age?" "Twice eight," answered the damsel with a bewitching smile. "You are an angel among men," was the reply of the enamoured minister.

"I would fain present this woman to your greatness," said Wang-yun, "but I am not certain that the gift would be acceptable to you." "For such generosity," said Tung-cho, "how could I sufficiently requite you?" — "In waiting upon your greatness," said Wang-yun, "this damsel will be the happiest of mortals." Tung-cho thanked him thrice.

By Wang-yun's order, a carriage was got ready, and Teaou-chin[②] was conveyed to Tung-cho's palace. Shortly after, Tung-cho followed her. Wang-yun accompanied him home, and then took his leave of him.

When Wang-yun had taken his leave, he mounted his horse and rode homeward. He had hardly got half way home before he saw two rows of lanterns moving towards him. In the front of them was Leu-poo with a javelin in his hand. As soon

① 编者按：此处 Taou-Shin 应为 Teaou-Shin。

② 编著按：此处 Teaou-chin 应为 Teaou-Shin。

as he saw Wang-yun, he stopped his horse, and seizing the rider by the collar of his vest, said to him, in a rude tone, "Tszetoo, since you promised me Teaou-shin in marriage, you have presented her to his grace: are you trifling with me?" Wang-yun, hastily stopping him, said, "This is not the place to speak of that subject! I beg that you will accompany me to my house." Leu-poo accompanied him home, and went with him into the inner hall. When they had gone through the usual ceremonies, Wang-yun said, "Why were you so rude with me?" Leu-poo answered, "I am informed that you have taken coach and driven Teaou-shin to his grace's palace: why have you done so?" "It would appear," replied Wang-yun, "that you are unacquainted with the circumstances of the case. When I was at court yesterday, his grace said to me, 'I have a favor to ask of you, and you may expect me at your house to-morrow.' On receiving this intimation, I made ready for his grace's entertainment, and waited his coming.

(*To be continued.*)

材料二

THE DEATH OF THE CELEBRATED MINISTER TUNG-CHO①

(*Continued from Vol. X. page 532.*)

"WHILE we were taking wine," continued Wang-yun, "his grace said to me, 'I hear that you have a daughter named Teaou-shin, and that you have promised her in marriage to my son Fung-sëen; I am afraid that you do not mean what you have said, and am therefore come to request that it may be so; let me see

① 编者按：*The Asiatic Journal and Monthly Register for British India and its Depencies.* Vol. Ⅺ., February, 1821, London, pp. 109–114.

her. ' I could not presume to object to this command, and therefore ordered Teaou-shin to come forth to pay her respects to her father-in-law. His grace said to me, ' as this is considered a lucky day, I will take your daughter home with me, and give her in marriage to Fung-sëen. ' Consider, I pray you, that his grace paid me a visit, and that I was compelled to receive him with courtesy." Leu-poo replied, "Tsze-too, pardon me; Leu-poo sees his error, and to-morrow will bring a bundle of brambles and do penance for his fault." Wang-yun said, "my daughter has a small dowry, which is to be sent to you as soon as she goes to your house." Leu-poo thanked him, and withdrew.

The next day Leu-poo went to Tung-cho's palace for the purpose of inquiring into what had taken place. Entering the hall, he began with inquiries of the servants, who informed him that their master had brought his bride home with him the night before, and was still in bed with her. Enraged at hearing this, Leu-poo stole into Tung-cho's bedchamber, posted himself behind a screen by which the space allotted to the bed was separated from the body of the apartment; and looking over this screen, observed the motions of Teaou-shin, who having partly dressed herself, was finishing her toilet at the window. Teaou-shin, who discerned the figure of Leu-poo reflected from a fish-pond under the window, was no sooner aware of his presence than she put on the semblance of the deepest grief; knitting her eyebrows, and from time to time applying her handkerchief to her eyes, as if to wipe away her tears. Leu-poo observed her for some minutes, and then retired from the chamber with the same fancied secresy with which he had entered it. Shortly afterward he re-entered the room and accosted Tung-cho, who had dressed himself in the interim, and was then sitting in the middle of the apartment waiting for his morning repast. Tung-cho, asking him whether he had no business to attend to elsewhere, and being answered that he had none, permitted him to remain.

Whilst Tung-cho was occupied with his breakfast, Leu-poo every now and then cast an eye at the screen, and observing Teaou-shin passing and repassing behind it, was so affected that he could not altogether conceal his emotion from Tung-cho. Tung-cho conceiving some jealousy at the emotion which he betrayed, ordered him to leave the apartment; an order with which he reluctantly complied.

Tung-cho was so besotted with the love of his new concubine, that nearly a month elapsed before he could attend, as usual, to the business of his ministry; and his love was still further inflamed by the sedulous attentions which he received from her during the course of a long illness with which he was shortly afterwards attacked.

During his convalescence, Leu-poo waited upon him in his bedchamber for the purpose of making inquiries after his health. When he entered the chamber he found Tung-cho asleep, and Teaou-shin attending at the side of his bed. As soon as she was aware of Leu-poo's presence, she began to weep, laying one hand on her bosom and pointing with the other to Tung-cho. Before Leu-poo could recover from the emotion with which these demonstrations of sorrow affected him, Tung-cho awoke, rubbed his eyes, turned himself to the several quarters of the room, and observing that Teaou-shin was standing beside his bed, and Leu-poo gazing at her from behind the screen, he was so moved with jealousy and anger that he exclaimed, "Do you mean to seduce my best beloved concubine from me? Here, servants, drive this intruder from the chamber, and see that he never enter it again." Leu-poo, enraged at the harsh treatment which he had received, went homeward, and meeting Le-joo on his way, could not refrain from telling him of the indignity which he had suffered. Le-joo hastened to see Tung-cho, and addressed him thus: "How can your Lordship, with your designs upon the imperial throne, have so far forgotten your own interest as to offer an indignity to Leu-poo?

He is the ablest and most powerful of your partizans; and if he fall off from you, the high enterprise which you have in hand will never be accomplished." —"What is to be done?" said the other. "Send for him to-morrow," replied the adviser; "appease his anger with flattering words, and with costly presents of silks and gold."

In conformity with this advice, Tung-cho sent for Leu-poo on the morrow, and in a conciliatory tone addressed him thus: "The day before yesterday my mind was disturbed, and my spirits ruffled by a return of my sickness. I pray you to forget the angry words which then escaped me, and which had no deliberate meaning. As a token that my kind intentions toward you have undergone no change, I request that you will accept of these twenty pieces of rich silk and of these ten pounds of fine gold." Leu-poo received this peace-offering, thanked the giver, and with the accustomed ceremonial of respect, took his leave and withdrew.

In spite of all that had passed, Leu-poo's thoughts were still fixed upon Teaou-shin.

As soon as Tung-cho had got the better of his illness, he went, as usual, to the imperial court. Leu-poo, who attended him with his javelin in his hand, no sooner observed him in close consultation with the Emperor, than he left the imperial presence (still holding his javelin in his hand), mounted his horse, and rode with all expedition to Tung-cho's palace. On his arrival, he dismounted, fastened his horse to the gate of the palace, and made his way to the inner hall (still holding his javelin in his hand) in quest of Teaou-shin. As soon as she saw him, she said, "Go to the Fung-e's summer-house, and there await my coming." Leu-poo, with his javelin, went into the garden, and leaning against the railing of the summer-house, awaited her promised arrival. At length she made her appearance, waving in her gait, like the young and delicate branches of a tree gently moved by the wind, and looking indeed not so much like an earthly creature, as like some fair genius from the palace of the moon. Weeping, she addressed herself to Leu-poo, and said, "Although I am not Wang-yun, the Tsze-too's daughter, he always treated me as such. From the time I first saw you, Colonel, and was promised in marriage to you, the desires of my life seemed realized. Who would have thought that his Excellency cherished an impure mind, or would violate and defile my person! I detest him even unto death. Having determined on seeing you, I have endured this disgrace, and am now happy in meeting you. As my person is defiled, and I am thereby unworthy to serve the valiant of the age, my desire is to die in the presence of my lord, that he may witness my integrity." When she had thus spoken, she caught hold of the railing, and attempted to throw herself into the lily-pond. Leu-poo hastily caught hold of her, and preventing her purpose, said, with tears in his eyes, "I have known your mind for a long time, and have been grieved that we could not converse together." Teaou-shin, taking hold of Leu-poo by the hand, said, "Though I cannot now be your wife, I hope to be so in a future state of existence." Leu-poo replied, "If I do not make you my wife in this life, I am no man of valour." Teaou-shin said, "Each revolving day seems a year. I beg that you, my lord, will have pity on me and rescue me." Leu-poo said, "As I have now come by stealth, I am apprehensive that the old traitor will be suspicious; I must therefore make haste and go." Teaou-shin, seizing him by the arm, said, "If you, my husband, are thus afraid of that old traitor, I cannot live to see the light of another day." Leu-poo, stopping, said, "Wait till I have devised some practicable plan for accomplishing our purpose." When he had thus spoken, he took his javelin as if about to leave her. Teaou-shin said, "When I was in the inner apartments and heard your name, it sounded in my ears like thunder, for there is not your equal in the whole world: who do you imagine would object to receive such a man's addresses?" When she had thus spoken, the tears fell from her eyes like drops of rain. Leu-poo, laying down his javelin, blushed, and was confounded. He turned himself around, and embracing Teaou-shin, spoke to her in an affectionate manner. In a moment they were so fast locked in each other's embrace, that they found it impossible to separate.

It is further related, that shortly after Leu-poo had left the imperial presence, Tung-cho, turning himself round, and not seeing Leu-poo, immediately conceived a suspicion of what he was about; took an hasty leave of the Emperor, mounted his chariot, and rode homeward. When he arrived at his palace he beheld Leu-poo's horse fastened to the gate; and finding from his inquiries of the porter that the duke had gone into the garden, he chid the servants for their negligence, and went into the inner hall in quest of him. Unable to find him there, he then sought for Teaou-shin. She also was not to be found. He hastily interrogated the female servants; the servants replied, that Teaou-shin was in the garden looking at the flowers, Tung-cho hastily entered the garden, where he saw Leu-poo and Teaou-shin by the side of the Fung-e summer-house, conversing together, and Leu-poo's javelin placed against the wall. Tung-cho uttered an exclamation of rage. Leu-poo, seeing Tung-cho approach, and being greatly alarmed, turned himself round and endeavoured to escape. Tung-cho seized the javelin, and pursued Leu-poo; but Leu-poo running with great agility, Tung-cho was unable from his corpulency to overtake him; he therefore threw the javelin after him. Leu-poo struck the javelin to the ground. Tung-cho seized the javelin, and again pursued him. Leu-poo had got without its reach, and Tung-cho was pursuing him beyond the garden gate, when a third person hastily entered, and suddenly encountering Tung-cho laid him prostrate on the ground. This person was Le-joo. Le-joo raised Tung-cho from the ground, led him into the library, and placed him on a bench. Tung-cho said, "Why did you enter in such haste?" Le-joo replied, "When I came to your residence, I heard that you had gone out into the back garden in anger, in search of Leu-poo; therefore I hastened. When I really met Leu-poo flying, and exclaiming, 'His lordship means to murder me!' I hastened the more in order that I might appease your rage. I did not think of encountering your lordship as I have done, and I hope that you will pardon me my involuntary offence." Tung-cho said, "I cannot endure the thought of losing my beloved concubine; I swear that I will slay the seducer." — "With submission to your excellency," returned Le-joo, "I must tell you that you act unwisely. When Chwang, the monarch of Tsoo, prudently granted an amnesty to his enemies, he never thought of calling Tseay-ling to account for the seduction of his favourite concubine; and well was he rewarded for his forbearance; for when he was afterwards surrounded by his own rebellious troops, his life was preserved by a desperate effort of this same Tseay-ling. Imitate his prudence. One woman is as good as another; but the friendship of the veteran Leu-poo is beyond all price. Contend not for such an object. Let him have this Teaou-shin. He will feel your generosity, and will be ever ready to requite you by dying in your service. I implore your lordship to weigh well the faithful counsel which I give you." Tung-cho considered for a moment, and then replied, "What you say seems to be just; I will think of it." Le-joo thanked him, and withdrew.

Tung-cho went into the inner hall, and inquiring of Teaou-shin, said, "What were you doing just now with Leu-poo?" Teaou-shin, weeping, replied, "I was in the garden looking at the flowers, when Leu-poo suddenly rushed in upon me. Alarmed at his abrupt entrance, I attempted to make my escape. Leu-poo said to me, 'I am his Excellency's son, why should you leave me?' and seizing his javelin, drove me into the Fung-e summer-house. Perceiving his intentions, and fearing that he might use violence, I determined to die in the lily-pond rather than submit to dishonour; but the faithless wretch, embracing me, prevented my purpose. I was really between life and death when your excellency came to my assistance."

Tung-cho said, "What objection have you to my giving you to Leu-poo?" Teaou-shin, astonished, weeping, replied, "Hitherto I have attended on persons of rank, are you all at once determined on giving me to a slave! I had better die than disgrace myself." So saying, she snatched a sword from the wall, and attempted to plunge it into her bosom; but Tung-cho hastily caught hold of the sword, laid it aside, and embracing her, said, "I was only trifling with you." Teaou-shin fell on Tung-cho's neck, and concealing her face, wept aloud, saying, "This must be a device of Le-joo. Le-joo is the intimate friend of Leu-poo, and therefore has devised this plot; but they are wanting in respect to your excellency's person, and to my happiness. I could tear their flesh from their bones." Tung-cho said, "How could I endure to be separated from you?" Teaou-shin said, "Although I am thankful to your excellency for your kindness, love, and compassion towards me, I am apprehensive that we cannot remain here long, for Leu-poo will certainly seek our destruction." Tung-cho said, "You shall accompany me to-morrow to Metoo, where you shall be a partaker of my happiness, and where we shall have nothing to annoy us." Teaou-shin ceased weeping, and making a courtesy, thanked him.

On the following day Le-joo came to pay his respects, and said, "This is esteemed a propitious day; now, then, is the time to give Teaou-shin to Leu-poo." Tung-cho replied, "I have been thinking that Leu-poo and I are as father and son, and that it would not be right in me to give her to him. Inform him that I cannot comply with his wishes; but make the communication in a conciliatory manner." Le-joo said, "Your excellency should not be deceived by a woman." Tung-cho changed countenance, and said, "Would you give your own wife to Leu-poo? Speak no more of Teaou-shin! Another word and I cut you down." Le-joo withdrew, and lifting his eyes to heaven, said, with a sigh, "We shall all die by the hands of a woman!"

That very day Tung-cho issued orders for his return to Metoo. All the officers of state attended to take their leave of him. Teaou-shin rode in an open carriage, and saw Leu-poo at a distance, among a concourse of people, looking towards the carriage. Teaou-shin drew aside the blinds, and appeared as if she were weeping violently. When the carriage had gone to some distance, Leu-poo ascended a mound of earth, and continued gazing after the carriage till it was lost in a cloud of dust. Suddenly he was roused from his reverie by the voice of a person behind him, who said, "How is it that Leu-poo stands here lost in thought, instead of accompanying his lordship to Me-too." Turning round, he perceived Wang-yun, the Tsze-too, at his elbow. When they had interchanged the compliments of the day, Wang-yun said to him, "I have been confined to my house for several days past by sickness. To-day I have ventured abroad, though still far from well, for the purpose of taking my leave of his lordship; and I am heartily glad that this has given me the present opportunity of paying my respects to my esteemed friend Leu-poo. But how is it, I ask again, that you stand here lost in sadness, instead of attending his lordship to Metoo?" "In truth, Sir," said Leu-poo, "it is your adopted daughter that I was thinking of. I fear that she is lost to me for ever." — "How can that be," said Wang-yun, with an assumed air of astonishment; "was she not affianced to you in marriage?" — "She was," replied the other, "but the hoary traitor, Tung-cho, has nevertheless taken her from me." — "Impossible" Leu-poo informed him, point by point, of all that had occurred. Wang-yun, lifting his eyes to heaven and stamping on the ground, uttered nothing but incoherent cries of astonishment for many minutes. At length he said, "I really could not have believed that his lordship would have thus descended to the level of the brute animals; would have so far lost sight of all discrimination in his desires, as to take the affianced bride of his adopted son to his own bed. Come home with me, and we will consult on this matter."

(*To be continued.*)

材料三

THE DEATH OF THE CELEBRATED MINISTER TUNG-CHO①

(*Concluded from page 114.*)

LEU-POO followed him. On their arrival at Wang-yun's house, Wang-yun invited Leu-poo to partake of a repast which had been prepared in a private apartment. When they had finished their repast, Leu-poo recounted the particulars of the incident which had happened near the Fung-e summer house. "His Grace," said Wang-yun, as soon as he had heard the narrative, "has cheated me of my daughter and robbed you of your wife. The whole empire will laugh at our expense. As for me, I am old and infirm, and must put up with this dishonour as well as I may. But shall Leu-poo, shall the hero of our age be thus sported with, and shall he not revenge?" Leu-poo, inflamed by these suggestions, struck the table with his clenched fist and raved aloud. Wang-yun, interrupting him, said, "I ought not to have disclosed what was passing in my mind; really, you must not

① 编者按: *The Asiatic Journal and Monthly Register for British India and its Depencies*. Vol. XI., March, 1821, London, pp. 233-242.

give way to these transports of anger." "Anger!" retorted the other, "I swear by all the gods that I will wash away my dishonour in the blood of the miscreant." "Stay," said Wang-yun, stopping his mouth with his hand, "Utter not, I implore you, another word of the kind, lest you implicate me in the consequences of your rashness." "What," continued Leu-poo, "shall any man dare to dishonour me and hope to live? By heaven I will slay the tyrant. What to me are the ties that bind father and son together, wronged and humiliated as I am? And yet, if I slew him, they might call me *parricide!* my memory might be handed down to posterity loaded with execrations." "Parricide!" said Wang-yun, with an incredulous smile, "remember that you are at most but his adopted son; and where, I pray, were these tender ties when he aimed at your life with your own javelin?" "By heaven," said Leu-poo, "what you say is true: farewell remorse!"

Wang-yun, seeing him bent upon the death of the usurper, threw off all further disguise, and addressed him thus: "If you lend your powerful support to the tottering house of Han, your fidelity to your lawful sovereign will win you the respect of your contemporaries; the faithful historian will record your virtue; and your fame will descend through a hundred ages: —adhere to the cause of the usurper, and your memory will stink in the nostrils of posterity for ten thousand thousand years!" "Say no more," said Leu-poo, rising from the table and bowing to Wang-yun: "I am firmly resolved on the destruction of the tyrant, and you need not fear that I shall faulter in my purpose." "I fear it not," replied the other; "my only fear is that you may fail in the attempt, and that that abortive attempt may involve us all in one common ruin."

Leu-poo unsheathed his dagger, and piercing his arm, pledged himself to what he had uttered by a solemn vow. Wang-yun, in a transport of joy, knelt before him and addressed him thus: "Now, indeed, will the family of Han be rescued from destruction, and to Leu-poo will redound the glory of their salvation. But drop not a word of this: I will now retire and digest the plan of our conspiracy. As soon as I see my way clearly you shall hear from me." "Be it so," said Leu-poo, and taking his leave, returned home.

As soon as Leu-poo had retired, Wang-yun sent to Shun-suy, the Poo-shay-tsze, and to Whang-wan, the Sze-le-kaou-nae, requesting their attendance at his house.

These persons obeyed the call, and on their arrival fell into close consultation with Wang-yun. In the course of their deliberations, it was suggested by Shun-suy that the Emperor had lately been unwell, and during his illness had intermitted his attention to state affairs; that a message from the Emperor might therefore be sent to Tung-cho, requiring his attendance at the imperial city on business; and that on his arrival he might be put to death by soldiers, whom Leu-poo might post in ambush for that purpose in one of the antichambers of the palace. Wang-yun approved of the scheme, but asked who would undertake the proposed message? Shun-suy answered that Le-shuh, the Ke-too-nae, had been refused promotion by Tung-cho, and was on that account his secret enemy. Wang-yun exclaimed, "Excellent!" and immediately sent to Leu-poo, requesting his presence at the consultation.

A similar message was also sent to Le-shuh. On the arrival of the latter, Leu-poo, who had previously made his appearance, addressed him thus: "You know that the traitor Tung-cho aims at the destruction of the Emperor; and that from his unrelenting cruelty to the people, and his other enormous crimes, mankind and the gods abhor him. We have determined on the death of the tyrant, and expect that you will assist us in carrying our intention into effect. What we want of you is this; you must proceed immediately to Me-too, assuming the character of bearer of an imperial message, and announce to Tung-cho that his presence is required at the Emperor's palace. I in the mean time will secrete soldiers in one of the antichambers, and as soon as he makes his appearance, will give the word to them to fall on him and put him to death. Say, are you ready to bear your share in this endeavour for the salvation of the Emperor?" Le-shuh replied, "I have long desired to be rid of the tyrant. I swear immortal hatred, not only to him, but to all who hate him not as I do. Now that Leu-poo has conceived the same sentiment, I doubt not that we shall accomplish his overthrow: it is the will of heaven!" Having thus expressed himself, he took an arrow, broke it in twain, and bound himself to persist in the enterprize by a solemn vow.

"Gentlemen," said Wang-yun, "I trust that you will not be losers by your loyalty: should we succeed in our attempt to save him, be assured that the Emperor will not forget his deliverers."

The next day Le-shuh, with several companies of horsemen, proceeded to Me-too; and on entering the city, announced that he was the bearer of a letter from the Emperor. Tung-cho ordered him into his presence. Le-shuh accordingly presented himself and made his obeisance. Tung-cho asked him, "what letter have you from the Emperor?" Le shuh replied, "the Emperor has recovered from his illness, but finds himself so enfeebled by it that he has determined to abdicate the throne. He thinks that a worthier successor than Tung-cho could hardly be found amongst his subjects; and has called a meeting of the chief civil and military officers of state, in order that he may make, in their presence, a formal transfer of the empire to your excellency. This is the purport of the letter which I now present to your excellency." "Indeed!" said the minister; "But how stands Wang-yun disposed?" "Wang-yun, the Tsze-too," replied the other, "is amongst the most zealous of your excellency's well-wishers: he has issued orders for convening the intended meeting, and nothing delays it but your excellency's absence." "My dream, then, is out," exclaimed the exulting minister; "I dreamt, last night, that I was arrayed in the imperial robes; and since gods and men conspire to call me to the throne, oh! time, that will never return, I must not lose thee!" Then addressing himself to Le-shuh, he said, "As soon as I am seated on the throne you may look to be my Chih-kin-woo." Le-shuh bowed and thanked him.

He immediately ordered his favourite generals, Ko-fan, Chuy-tsee and Fan-teaou, to take the command of three thousand invincible flying troops, and keep guard in Me-too during his stay at the imperial city.

He then went into the inner apartments, to take leave of his mother. His mother, who was upwards of ninety years of age, said to him, "my son, whither are you going?" Tung-cho replied, "Going! I am going to ascend the throne of the house of Han: think of that mother; only imagine that a few days hence, you, my honoured mother, will bear the title of Tae-how!"

His mother replied, "I have of late been affected with an involuntary trembling, and my mind has been much disturbed; I fear that these symptoms are ominous of some impending disaster." "Why expect misfortune?" replied her son; "are you not to be the mother of the empire? and what more natural than that the approach of such an event should manifest itself in the symptoms which you talk of?" He then took leave of his mother, and went to bid adieu to Teaou-shin. He told her what had passed, and assured her that when he was crowned emperor she should be the honored concubine. Teaou-shin, who had already received an intimation of what was intended, made him a low curtesy, and affected the most lively joy.

Having bid adieu to his family, Tung-cho mounted his chariot and went on his way to Chang-gan; a large concourse of people preceding and following him through the whole of his journey. He had hardly gone ten miles when the axle of his chariot broke with a fearful crash. He alighted from his chariot, and mounted a led horse; but hardly had he gone three miles further, when his horse turned restive, neighed vehemently, and with a sudden jerk snapped the bit of his bridle. Tung-cho, disconcerted by these incidents, addressed himself to Le-shuh, and said, "the breaking of the axle and the snapping of the bit, what do they portend?" "As your excellency," answered Le-shuh, "is on the eve of ascending the throne, these incidents clearly indicate nothing more than that your old equipage has served its turn, and will immediately be replaced by a new; that for the chariot in which you have been riding, and for the bit which hangs at your horse's mouth, you will shortly substitute a bit made of fine gold, and a chariot studded with gems." Tung-cho, pleased with this interpretation of the omens, implicitly believed the assurances of his wily companion. The next day, as they were pursuing their journey, they were encountered by a violent gale of wind, bearing along with it clouds of dust; and on the evening of the very same day, they were suddenly enveloped in a thick and impenetrable mist. Tung-cho, abating in his confidence, again turned to Le-shuh, and said, "the wind which bore with it clouds of dust, and the mist around us which obstructs our sight, what do they portend?" "Ere many hours shall pass over our heads," was the answer of Le-shuh, "your lordship will ascend the dragon's seat: the very elements are aware of the approaching change, and shew their sense of it by these unusual manifestations of their power." Tung-cho was again satisfied with the interpretation, and resumed his former cheerfulness.

On his arrival at Chang-gan he was received in form by all the officers of state, except Le-joo, who was confined to his bed by an opportune sickness. Amongst the foremost of those who paid their respects to the minister, was Leu-poo, Tung-cho promised him that, on his accession to the throne, he should be invested with the command of all the troops in the empire. Leu-poo thanked him, but persisted notwithstanding in the resolution which he had previously formed.

That same evening, as Tung-cho was in bed, he heard the voices of children singing in the street. The wind bore the sound to the ears of the sleepless minister. This was the burthen of their song: —

"The verdant grass of a thousand le

Fades ere it attains the age of ten days. "①

The strain was melancholy; and Tung-cho was so moved by it, that he said to Le-shuh, "The song which the children are singing, does it promise me good, or is it ominous of evil?" "The song," answered Le-shuh, "has no other meaning than its obvious one; or if it foretokens any thing, it foretokens the fall of the dynasty of Han and the rise of the dynasty of Tung. "

The next day, Tung-cho proceeded in great state to the imperial palace. On his way he was encountered by one of the followers of Taou, clad in a black vest and a white turban, and holding a flag of white cloth in his hand. On two corners of the flag was inscribed the character which signifies "a mouth. "② Tung-cho turned round to Le-shuh, and asked, "What does this priest do here?" Le-shuh, replied, "he is mad;" and ordered one of the guards to remove him. Tung-cho was borne in his chair of state into the imperial palace, where all the ministers were in waiting, dressed in their court dresses. Le-shuh drew his sword, and held

---

① These lines are made up of the component parts of the characters which form Tung-cho's name. *Tung*, the first, it compounded of *grass*, *thousand* and *miles*; Cho the second, is compounded of *above day*, and *ten*. This is a specimen of the wit which the Chinese delight in.

② Of the two characters which form Leu-poo's name, the first is compounded of "*month*," repeated, with a line uniting them; the second of "*cloth*," which was implied in the flag; so that the flag was intended to apprize his Lordship to beware of Leu-poo.

by the chair as it entered. When they came to the eastern gate, Tung-cho's guards were ordered to remain without; and only the chair-bearers, with about twenty persons more, were permitted to proceed further. Tung-cho, perceiving that Wang-yun and many others of the ministers were posted at the avenue leading to the throne, each of them holding a naked sword, was somewhat disconcerted at this unusual appearance, and asked Le-shuh what it meant. Le-shuh made no answer, but urged the chair-bearers onward. At that moment, Wang-yun exclaimed, "the usurper is come: soldiers, do your duty!" Instantly, a hundred armed men rushed from the sides of the palace, and attacked Tung-cho with their spears; but as he wore a suit of mail under his vest, they were unable to pierce his body. He fell, however, with the shock; and as he was falling, cried aloud, "where is my son Fung-sëen?" Leu-poo, who was behind the chair, exclaimed in a voice of thunder, "miscreant, I have an imperial order for beheading you;" and therewith pierced his throat with a javelin. The moment after, Le-shuh severed his head from his body, and held it up in his hand; whilst Leu-poo, grasping his javelin in his left hand, and with his right drawing the imperial mandate from his bosom, called aloud to the surrounding assembly, "here is the imperial order for putting to death the usurper Tung-cho. Let no one be alarmed; he is the only person to whom it extends." The guards responded to this brief address with a loudshout, "may his majesty live for ever!"

As soon as the tyrant was dispatched, Leu-poo exclaimed, "the man who abetted Tung-cho in all his infamous projects, was Le-joo. Who will seize him?" As Le-shuh was about to obey the call, a noise was suddenly heard from without the gates. This was found, on inquiry, to proceed from Le-joo's servants, who had bound him fast, and were dragging him to the imperial palace. At the command of Wang-yun, he was taken to the market-place, and there beheaded. The head and trunk of Tung-cho were also, at the same command, taken into the street, that the people might be convinced of his death, and might behold the punishment which awaits disloyalty. Fire was placed on his navel by the guards; and as it burnt, the fat from his carcase streamed along the ground. The people vied with the soldiery in heaping indignities upon his remains; beating his head and spurning his trunk as they were dragged through the streets of the city.

The punishment due to his crimes stayed not here. Wang-foo-sung and Leu-poo were commanded by Wang-yun to march at the head of sixty thousand men to Me-too, and to root out the whole family of the traitor.

When Le-chuy, Ko-fan, Chang-tsee, and Fan-chow, heard of Tung-cho's fall, and of Leu-poo's approach at the head of an invincible army, they fled in the night to Lang-chow. On the arrival of the imperial army at Me-too, the first care of Leu-poo was to make himself master of Teaou-shin's person. Having secured his not unwilling captive, he proceeded to issue, in concert with Wang-foo-sung, the following orders: the inhabitants of Me-too were commanded to liberate all the women who had been forcibly brought to that city by the tyrannical orders of Tung-cho: they were further commanded to aid in the apprehension of Tung-cho's family; who, as soon as they were secured, were put to death, without regard to age or sex. Even the mother of Tung-cho escaped not the common fate: and, as an additional punishment, justly due to their pre-eminent treasons, the heads of Tung-yan, the usurper's brother, and of Tung-whang, his nephew, were stuck on the tops of poles, and exposed, for several days, to the view of the people. Orders were also issued for seizing the treasure which the usurper had collected in Me-too. This treasure, consisting of many hundred thousand pieces of gold, of many million pieces of silver, and of an immense quantity of silks, diamonds, precious stones, and plate, was accordingly seized and sent to Wang-yun, who divided it amongst the soldiery.

These measures having been carried into effect, a splendid banquet was prepared by Wang-yun in the hall of audience. To this banquet all the ministers of state were invited. Whilst they were feasting, news was brought to them that a certain man was lying on the ground in the market-place, weeping over the mangled remains of Tung-cho. Wang-yun, enraged at the audacity of the man, exclaimed in a loud and angry tone, "Who would have thought that any subject of the emperor, whatever his station in society, would regret the destruction of the usurper? Who is this insolent traitor that dares to lament his fall? Guards! seize him, and drag him into the hall!" In less than a minute, the guards dragged the man into the presence of Wang-yun. To the astonishment of the assembly, he proved to be no other than Fze-ying, the Se-ze-chung. Wang-yun indignantly said to him, "The carcase of the usurper is lying in the public street, and the nation is rejoicing at his fall: how is it, that you, a minister of Han, instead of sharing in the general joy, are weeping over his remains?" "Though not gifted with superior talents," was the submissive reply of Fze-ying, "I am not altogether ignorant of the leading principles of morality. Do you suppose me so unprincipled as to regret the death of an usurper? I once received an important service from this unhappy Tung-cho; and the tears which I shed over his mangled remains were not tears of regret at the fall of a tyrant, but tears wrung from me by a grateful remembrance of the service which he had rendered me. I know that even this is criminal; and shall, therefore, cheerfully submit to any punishment which you may please to impose upon me. Cut off my feet, brand my forehead; in fine, afflict me in any way short of death. I earnestly wish to live, that I may complete the annals of the house of Han, and thereby atone for the offence into which my criminal gratitude has betrayed me."

Most of the officers of state, recalling to mind the signal talents of the man, were moved to pity and sorrow; and used every effort in their power to rescue him from death. Ma-jih shen, the great historian, said aside to Wang-yun, "Fze-ying is a man of unrivalled talents; if he be permitted to finish the annals of the Han dynasty, they will be ably and faithfully written. Besides, he is universally known and respected as the most dutiful of sons; and should he be put to death at our bidding, I fear that we shall lose the confidence of the people." "Heaou-woo," answered Wang-yun, "spared the life of Sze-ma-tseën, and afterwards appointed him imperial historian. The consequence was, that Sze-ma-tseën, more mindful of his previous enmity than of the clemency which had been extended to him, belied his age; and the characters of his contemporaries have descended to our times, not as they really were, but as distorted by his malignity. The evil passions of men have been put in motion by our recent convulsions. Shall we, at such a period, commit the pencil of the historian to a man whose loyalty may be suspected? Shall we hire an enemy to vilify ourselves?"

Ma-jih-shen uttered not a word in reply; but addressing himself aside to one of the ministers, he said, "the name of Wang-yun will never descend to posterity!" Wang-yun, regardless of what Ma-jih-shen had said, ordered Fze-ying to be strangled in prison. When the officers heard these orders given, they all wept. The more recent historians and moralists are universally of opinion that it was wrong in Fze-ying to weep over Tung-cho; but that it was equally wrong in Wang-yun to put him to death for it.

It is further related, that as soon as Le-chuy, Ko-fan, Chang-tsee, and Fan-chow arrived at Shin-se, they dispatched a message to Chang-gan, imploring a pardon. "Tung-cho," said Wang-yun, on the receipt of this message, "was abetted in his crimes by these four men; and though we will extend our pardon to all the other subjects of the empire, we must not extend it to them." The messenger returned, and informed Le-chuy of Wang-yun's resolution. "Well," said Le-chuy, "as we have asked for a pardon and cannot obtain it, we must each of us do his best to escape, and save his life if he can." Hea-yun, the general's secretary, thereupon said, "General, if you disband your troops, you will infallibly be betrayed by some of them to your implacable enemy. Rouse yourselves: incite the people of Shin-se to embrace your cause, and embody as many of them as will join you with the regular army; then boldly fight your way to Chang-gan, openly proclaiming yourselves the partisans and avengers of Tung-cho. Should you be victorious, you will rule the empire; should you fail, you can run for it then as well as you can now." Le-chuy approved of his advice; convened the people of Le-lang-chow, and told them that Wang-yun had determined to extirpate them to a man. "Since nothing," he continued, "can be gained by submission, enter the ranks of my army, and join us in our resistance to him." The inhabitants, struck with a panic, embodied themselves with his army to the number of a hundred thousand men. The army, thus reinforced, was divided into four divisions, and moved forward to Chang-gan. On their route they fell in with New-poo, the son-in-law of Tung-cho, at the head of a corps of five thousand men. Le-chuy united this corps to his army, and ordered New-poo to take the command of the van; the four generals following in the rear.

When Wang-yun was informed of their advance, he hastened, in a panic, to ask the advice of Leu-poo. "Be not alarmed," said Leu-poo, "depend upon it, this horde of rats will be stopped short in their course for want of provender."

He then ordered Le-shuh to advance with an imperial army, and attack them. Le-shuh immediately advanced and attacked New-poo. After a long and bloody conflict, New-poo was obliged to retreat. On the following night, however, and during the second watch, New-poo surprised Le-shuh's camp. Le-shuh's troops were thrown into confusion by this unexpected assault, and fled to the distance of ten miles, with the loss of half their number. Le-shuh hastened to Leu-poo, and apprized him of his defeat. Leu-poo exclaimed, "Why have you stripped me of my reputation? Guards! off with his head, and fix it on a pole by the entrance to the camp."

The next day, New-poo was attacked by Leu-poo in person. After an obstinate contest, New-poo yielded to the skill and valour of Leu-poo, and fled to the main body of the rebel army.

The night after the battle New-poo opened himself to Ho-chih-urh, his confidential adviser, as follows: "This Leu-poo is resistless. There are ten thousand chances to one against our success. How much better will it be for us, unknown to Le-chuy and the other three generals, to seize the treasure which is concealed in the camp, and, in company with three or four attendants, desert the army." Ho-chih-urh consenting, they that night seized the treasure, and deserted the camp in company with three or four others. Whilst they were crossing a river in their flight, Ho-chih-urh, who had already turned over in his mind the means of getting the whole treasure to himself, murdered New-poo; and taking the head of his victim, made his way to the imperial camp, and presented it to Leu-poo. Leu-poo, inquiring into the particulars of the incident, and learning from the attendants that Ho-chih-urh had murdered New-poo, indignantly ordered Ho-chih-urh to instant execution.

Having repulsed New-poo, Leu-poo advanced upon the main body of the rebel army. In his advance he was encountered by Le-chuy, at the head of his foot and horse. Leu-poo, instead of awaiting the attack, instantly grasped his javelin, dug the spurs into his horse, and commanded his troops to follow him to the charge of the enemy. Le-chuy's troops, unable to withstand this impetuous attack, retreated to the distance of sixteen or seventeen miles from the field of battle, and entrenched themselves between two mountains. Here Le-chuy held counsel with Ko-fan, Chang-tsee and Fan-chow. He addressed them thus: "Leu-poo, though brave, is wanting in skill. Let us not be dismayed. I will daily lead out our troops to the entrance of the pass, and provoke this impetuous madman to give me battle. You, Ko-fan, as soon as he advances to attack me, will fall upon his rear; imitating the movements which were made by Poo-yul, in the battles which he fought during the war against Tsoo. You will sound the gong as you advance to the attack, and will beat the drum when you intend a retreat. In the meantime, you, Chang-tsee, and Fan-chow, will proceed by different routes to the imperial city Chang-gan. Hemmed in, in front and rear, Leu-poo will be unable to advance to the relief of Chang-gan, and it will inevitably fall into our hands." This plan was highly approved of by his colleagues.

The scheme succeeded. Leu-poo, intending an attack, led his troops to the foot of the mountain. Le-chuy advanced, as if to meet him; but no sooner did Leu-poo command his army to charge the enemy, than Le-chuy retreated and ascended the hill; from whence his troops showered down such vollies of arrows and stones, that Poo's soldiers found it impossible to proceed. At this critical moment Ko-fan's troops attacked him in the rear. Leu-poo faced to the right about, and rushed upon this fresh opponent; but as soon as he had put his troops in motion, the loud sound of the drum proclaimed that his enemy was on the retreat. Leu-poo halted. But without a moment's pause, the gong bellowed through the plain, and Le-chuy again descended from the mountain. Again Leu-poo moved forward to attack him; and again he retreated from the charge. Again, Ko-fan attacked Leu-poo in the rear; and again was the signal for retreat beat upon the drum, as soon as Leu-poo moved forward to meet the assault.

Leu-poo, whose bosom burned with rage, was thus harassed for several days. He could neither give battle to his enemy, nor repose to his own troops. Whilst thus perplexed, a messenger brought him word that Chang-tsee and Fan-chow had marched by two different routes upon Chang-gan, with large bodies of foot and horse, and that the imperial city was in imminent danger of falling into their hands. Leu-poo immediately moved towards the capital, pursued by Le-chuy and Ko-fan. Leu-poo, not venturing to give them battle, pushed onward to the relief of Chang-gan, losing a great number both of men and horses in the course of his march. On his arrival in the neighbourhood of Chang-gan, he descried the host of the enemy, numerous as the drops which fall in a shower of rain. They had surrounded the entrenchments of the city; and Leu-poo's troops, instead of moving to attack them, were so disheartened by the desperate aspect of the imperial cause, that to the grief and indignation of their leader, they deserted in great numbers and went over to the rebel army.

A few days after Le-mung and Wang-fan, two of Tung-cho's partizans, who had carried on a secret correspondence with the rebel army, threw open the city gates to them. Instantly they rushed in from every quarter. Leu-poo, at the head of a few hundred men, fled through the eastern gate; however, before his departure, he hastened to Wang-yun, and said to him, "embrace this opportunity of escape; mount this horse, and accompany me to another province: there we may devise some plan for retrieving our fortunes." Wang-yun answered, "If I could thereby uphold the commonwealth and restore tranquillity to the empire, I would do as you desire; as that cannot be, Wang-yun resigns himself to death. Could I avoid it I would not. I pray you, however, to take my last commands to the governors of the eastern provinces. Tell them to exert themselves strenuously in restoring the affairs of the nation." Leu-poo again and again exhorted him to embrace the opportunity of escape; but Wang-yun obstinately withstood his intreaties. By the time this dialogue had ended, every gate of the city was on fire. Leu-poo, in despair, threw up the game, and, in company with a few hundred men, made his way to the state Kwan, where he placed himself under the protection of Wae-shuh.

Le-chuy and Ko-fan permitted their troops to plunder the city. Chung-fuh, the Tae-chang-ying; Las-kwo, the Tae-po; Chow-ying, the Tae-kung-loo; Chuy-keih, the Ching-mun-Kaow-wae; and Wang-king, the Yue-ke-Kaou-wae, all of them perished amidst the disasters of the day.

When the enemy surrounded the palace, the throne was in imminent danger. The ministers in waiting requested his Majesty to appear in the balcony. When Le-chuy and his adherents beheld the imperial robes, they ordered the troops to stop, and shouted aloud, "may his Majesty live for ever." His imperial Majesty, leaning over the balustres, said, "Ministers, what do you ask? What is it you intend by entering Chang-gan?" Le-chuy and Ko-fan, looking up to his Majesty, answered, "Tung-cho, the Tae-tsze, was your Majesty's prime minister of state. Why did you order Wang-yun to put him to death? Our business is to revenge him. We rebel not against your Majesty; only give us up Wang-yun, and we will withdraw our troops." Wang-yun, who was standing by the side of the Emperor, addressed his Majesty thus: — "What I originally planned was for the welfare of the commonwealth, but as affairs have taken this adverse turn, your Majesty must not think of saving me at the expense of your own ruin. I request that I may be permitted to descend to the rebels." Whilst his Majesty hesitated, Wang-yun, of his own motion leapt from the balcony, and calling aloud to the rebels, said, "Wang-yun is here." Le-chuy and Ko-fan drew their swords, and cursing him, said, "Tung-cho, the Tae-tsze, why was he put to death?" Wang-yun answered, "The ineffable crimes of that monster covered the face of the earth, and stank to the very heavens; on the day that he fell, all the inhabitants of Chang-gan rejoiced, though you, ye traitors, lamented him." "But what were *our* crimes that we were not to be forgiven?" Wang-yun impatiently exclaimed, "why so many words? I am Wang-yun; if I must die to-day, so be it." The two rebels raised their hands aloft, and cut down Wang-yun below the balcony.

When the rebels had put to death Wang-yun himself, they immediately sent persons to seize his whole family, and put them to death also, without respect to youth or age. Amongst the officers of state and people at large, there were none who lamented them not.

This work mentions not the year in which Tung-cho fell. But by referring to the Standard History of China, I find, that Ling-te (of the former Han dynasty), the father of Hëen-tee, died after reigning twenty-two years, and was succeeded by his son, Tsze-p-ëen, who was then only fourteen years of age. He appointed his brother Hëe (who was only nine years of age) king of Ching-lew. During the seventh month, Ho-tsin, a nephew to the emperor, called in the assistance of Tung-cho to subdue a rebellion. During the eighth month, Tung-cho returned to the capital. During the ninth month, he dethroned the emperor, and appointed him king of Fan-nung, and raised his brother Hëe to the throne, when that emperor took the name of Hëen-te. Tung-cho appointed himself generalissimo of the troop. During the eleventh month, he became minister of state, when he appointed the whole family of Tung to the rank of duke, and gave to each a military command.

On the first month of the following year, the princes of Kwang-tung and other provinces declared war against Tung-cho. During the second month of the second year of the reign of Heen-tee, Tung-cho appointed himself prime minister of state. During the third year, and fourth month of the same reign, Wang-yun, in union with Leu-poo, put Tung-cho to death. During the ninth month, Leu-poo fled to the eastern province of Nan-yang, when Wang yun died. On his death, Le-chuy, Ko-fan, Chang-tsee, and Fan-chow, were appointed generals of the imperial troops.

中文回译

材料一

著名丞相董卓之死[①]

汤姆斯译自中文

（《亚洲杂志》编辑审阅）

编者按：《亚洲杂志》第 10 卷，1820 年 7—12 月合订本，伦敦，第 525—532 页。以下文字是汤姆斯为题目添加的注释，内容是金圣叹的《三国志序》。

本文故事摘译自《三国志》（San-kwo-che），这是一部有关中国内战的最著名的史书。这部史书得到中国人的大力推崇，不仅是因为它的文学价值，还因为它对于（中国人如此认为）其所涉及的那段时期的战争与灾难的丰富而准确的叙述。以下呈现在读者面前的是该著的序言中的部分选段，这样读者就可以借此去评价中国的读书人对于这部作品的看法了。序言出自金人瑞（Kin-jin-suy）之手，他活跃于大约 150 年前的顺治（Shun-che）统治时期。

《三国志》摘译

我曾评论过六部才子书，它们分别名之曰庄、骚、马之史记、杜之律诗、水浒和西厢。海内学人皆推许我的评价，欣然说我对于自己所评价的作者的了解，看上去不是那么的糟糕。受此鼓励，我今天贸然呈上细读《三国志》时的阅读评论。首先，这部作品不像某些伪史那样纯属臆造，而是与别的古代记录高度吻合，完全可以将之看作一部中国正史。但是，如果我们把它看作一部记录史实的信史，我们发现，其他的史书，无论怎么好，在阅读趣味与文学性方面，都远不及《三国志》。所有的中国史，自周秦而上，汉唐而下，都依史演义，或有人问，为何唯独《三国志》被人格外推崇？对此我认为，三国时期的战争，相比于所有其他的战争，无论是古代的还是现代的，都是最有趣的；而写三国之战的史学家，相比于所有其他的史学家，无论是古代的还是现代的，也是无与伦（见下页）

孙坚（Tsze-Këen）死时，董卓（Tung-cho）在长安。听说皇帝死了，卓自忖道："现在我可以不顾良心，为所欲为了。"孙坚年幼无知的儿子

（接上页）比的。异代之事，无论文武，其阅读趣味怎能与三国之事相比？一切历史著作，相比于《三国志》，岂非出自庸人之笔？

我常思考三国争霸时，各国拥有的权势，发现天道昏昧，令人费解，我几乎对上天的智慧与公正失去信心。汉献帝一死（献帝，东汉最后一位皇帝，约死于公元226年。他死时国内开始了内战），朝廷权柄就被大臣董卓篡夺，群雄纷起，国家混乱。如果上天早让刘备得到贤臣孔明，他就能先得荆襄之地，长驱河北，传檄淮南、江东、秦雍；国之乱局就能得以平定，刘备的权力声望会敌过中兴汉室的光武帝。如果上天给国事以如此转机，我就不会冒昧地质疑天道的智慧与公正了。但事实上我们真正看到的却是一片混乱：我们看到董卓为权所诱，却在篡位时被杀，而曹操则挟天子以令诸侯。尽管每年的正月，每月的朔日，野心勃勃的曹操表面上以皇帝的名义主持朝事，实际上却自己把持着朝廷大权。不能平定天下，刘备又能如何？国之南北，已为篡权者所得，并划地为疆，建立吴魏。惟独西南（the country of Se-nan）一隅，依然听命于刘备，他在那里建立了政权。事实上，当他在其领地边境东征西战时，若非得到智勇双全的孔明的帮助，汉益以及许多别的地方，早就被曹操征服了；吴国也不会独立，亦将被曹操扼制；曹操会成为另一个王莽，篡夺整个汉家江山，暴君大获全胜，后人或许会质疑天道的智慧与公正。再说曹操来到当阳（Tung-ying），由于屡战屡败，三国权侔力敌，鼎足之势遂成。我现在简要概括一下曹操这个暴君的生平，他一生恶贯满盈，神人共怒。在此我只能概而言之，在他屡遭变故的一生中有这样一段时间，在此期间王朝的每个城池都充斥着对他的声讨与反抗；在此期间他遭到辱骂与唾弃；在此期间有人公然射杀他，也有人秘密投毒或行刺。尽管屡屡被袭，数次遇险；尽管为乔装逃命而被迫割须；尽管身临绝境，有一次折断牙齿，还有一次堕下马背，蹒跚而行；尽管由于罪恶滔天，理应受到无情的追杀；但他命不该死，故逃过死劫；他为敌者众，追随者亦众。这个暴君死里逃生，究竟是否符合天意，不是由我来决定的。但有一点可以肯定，曹操的生平若非如此，始于内乱的三个敌对的国家就不会存在了。在此，姑且放下曹操这位汉室的劲敌，他像一只蠹虫，侵蚀着帝国的心脏。

上天并不满足于仅有一个成功的反叛者，遂举出另一个人周瑜，他是吴国的开创者，在智慧、勇猛和运气上，与忠心耿耿的孔明旗鼓相当。除了曹操和周瑜，上天又造就了司马懿，曹操在魏国的继任者，他也恶贯满盈、声名狼藉。似乎担心刚刚建立的三个国家中的某一个，被另一个或另两个颠覆，上天赋予三国君主同样的权能。

自古以来，篡权者时而有之，并成功自封为王。因此，有一段时期，十二个独立的国家同时并存；还有一段时期，七国并存；又有一段时期，十六国并存。此外，南北朝同时并存，东西魏同时并存。又有后梁取代前梁（编者按：毛评本此处为"前后汉"，非"前后梁"）。但是，值得注意的是，在这种情况下，政权更迭迅速。三国战争的显著不同在于，它们持续了六十年，同一时期彼此间相互抗衡，存亡与共。

我认为，这部佳作的文学特点，在于它能打动各个阶层的读者。学士读之而快；贩夫读之而快；士兵读之而快；凡夫俗子读之亦快。（编者按：此处省去一段文字，自"昔者蒯通之谏韩信"，至"人亦乌乎知其奇而信其奇哉！"）

一日访友，在友人案头看到毛子所评《三国志》草稿。初读之，发现毛子的感觉与我的一致。这促使我向同辈及后人大胆宣布，第一才子（最具文采的书）乃是一部"中国内战史"。寥寥数言，序于书首，送给毛子，以便《三国志》再版之日，弁于简端，使后人知晓，关于其文学成就，我俩持有同样的观点。

继承了王位，年方十七，这愈加助长了董卓的骄横；他认为自己的图谋无人能够阻拦，年轻的国君自会听命于他。于是，他自号“尚父”（国君的监护人或保护者）。无论何时出入宫室，都用天子仪仗。他的弟弟董旻（Tung-yan）[①] 被封为鄠侯和将军，侄子董璜（Tung-hwang）被任命为宫中的侍中，总领禁军。董氏宗族，不问长幼，皆封列侯。

董卓在距长安城二百五十里的地方建了一个新城，取名郿坞（Me-too）。为了建造这个著名的城池，他征用了二十五万人。城池被围以城墙，城墙的高度和厚度，均与京城长安（Chang-gan）的城郭不相上下。城里建有宫殿和国库，以及足以为大量人马囤积二十年辎重的粮仓。他从全国挑选了八百个标致的少女，送入新城，料理城内生活。董卓全家移居城内，又将财宝存入其中，包括不计其数的黄金、钻石、珍珠和昂贵的丝帛。

董卓统治期间，常常不得不去京城长安，或一月一回，或两周一回。每次返回，公卿大夫都把他送至京城东门外，以作饯别；临走前，还要在城门外设帐聚饮。

有一次，董卓正与宾客宴饮，几百个逃兵进来，他们来自北方诸省，根据董卓发布的一纸赦令，前来归降。董卓立即命令他们进来。但他自食其言，现场宣判，逃兵有的被砍断手足，有的被挖去眼睛，还有更残忍的是被活活扔进滚烫的大锅。可怜的归降者哀号震天，百官惊惧，以致颤抖的双手拿不住筷子[②]。董卓却镇定自若，依旧饮酒谈笑，仿佛世间什么都不曾发生过，以致糟蹋了欢宴。

另一次，董卓于城内大宴百官，酒至数巡，吕布（Leu-poo）径入宴会厅，走向董卓，耳边低言数语。百官惊惧失色，这时董卓笑道：“果真如此？速拿司空张温（Chang-wan），拖出堂去。”命令下达后不久，一个侍从

---

① 编者按：“董旻”误作“董晏”。

② 中国人用筷子把食物夹进嘴里。

进来，用一红盘托着张温的头献上。百官见此惨象，吓得魂不附体；但董卓却面带微笑，劝他们不要害怕，并告诉他们：张温交结袁术（Wae-shŭh），欲加害于他。张温写给同谋的信，暗藏不忠，错入董卓养子奉先（Fung-sëen）[①] 之手。张温的罪行一经发现，董卓即令斩其首级。各位大臣并没有参与张温的罪行，所以不必因此而惊恐。对于这一席劝言，百官唯唯作答，随即各自散去。

其中一位客人乃司徒王允（Wang-yun），回到府中，他痛心地思考着宴席上发生的事，难以入眠，拄着拐杖，借着月色步入屋后的花园，倚在荼蘼架下，望着流云，仰天垂泪。正在这时，他吃惊地听到有人在长吁短叹，那人藏在藤下。王允悄悄走过去，看是何人，惊奇地发现是貂蝉（Teaou-shin），她自幼就被收养入府，精心教以歌舞，王允待她一直像父亲那般，在他的照顾下，貂蝉已长到十六岁，而今成了一个美人，颇具魅力。听到她的叹息，王允责问她何故悲伤，又问她有何私情。“私情！”貂蝉跪下说道：“岂会有私情！我蒙大人慷慨供养，常念大人仁善，安敢有私情？”王允答道：“如无私情，为何夜深之时，在此长吁短叹？”貂蝉说：“大人可容我伸肺腑之言？”王允说：“不要隐瞒，当实告我。”貂蝉答道：“先谢大人养育之恩，尤其是令我训习歌舞。您一向待我仁善，我虽粉身碎骨，莫报万一。近见大人内心忧伤，两眉愁锁，我不敢问大人为何忧愁，但自知必是国家大事，压在大人心头。今晚又见大人行坐不安，深为大人忧之。故来此幽僻之地，暗自嗟叹，不想大人跟我至园。若能解大人之忧，有用我之处，我当万死不辞。”

王允以杖击地曰：“谁能想到！谁能想到汉家命数竟在这个孤女子的手中！随我到画阁中来。”

他们来到画阁，王允令那里的所有侍女离开；待她们退下后，王允前

① 吕布之名。

额着地，拜倒在貂蝉面前。貂蝉被这一不寻常的礼遇吓了一跳，跪倒在地，说道："大人在我面前，何故如此卑微？"王允曰："你不会不可怜汉室将倾，尽力救吾君于即亡，救百姓于苦难吧？"王允说罢，泪如泉涌。

貂蝉曰："若大人相信我方才所言，就无须多言。但有使令，万死不辞。"王允依然跪在貂蝉面前，说道："皇帝与忠臣，皆如累卵，随时会被压碎。百姓之痛，比倒悬着被刽子手鞭笞还要苦痛。这都需要你去解救。如果你拒绝帮助，或者此行失败，贼臣董卓就会篡夺王位。尽管忠臣贤士早已识其野心，却无计可施。而今我有一言，董卓有一义儿，原名布，因力量非凡而得名吕。[①] 我发现董卓及其义子吕布二人皆沉迷于女色。根据他们的这一弱点，我有一计，相信可以诱骗二人。我想先把你许配给吕布，后献与董卓。你可设法使父子二人为了你而反目成仇，令吕布心生嫉妒，以促使他杀死暴君。如果你能如我所愿，你就能结束眼下令人痛苦的暴政，建立安全的王权，并让江山（keang-shan）这一古代庄严的帝都，再次成为朝廷所在地。[②] 所有这一切都需要靠你的力量来完成，不知你意下如何？"

貂蝉说："我已向大人保证万死不辞。继续进行您的计划吧，请放心，我会忠心耿耿，热心投入的。"王允说："如果此事稍有泄露，我和整个家族就会被满门抄斩。"貂蝉说："大人勿忧。如果不尽力报答大人对我的恩情，甘愿被剁成肉酱。"王允再拜而退。

次日，王允令工匠打造了一顶金冠。金冠上有一个金球，镶嵌着王允家里的各种钻石珍宝，秘密送与吕布。吕布见到金冠，很高兴收到这么珍贵的礼物，立即前往王允宅邸致谢。王允想到吕布会来，早已备下佳肴美馔，候吕布至，王允出门迎迓，接入后堂，延之上坐，请其用餐。

吕布对此礼遇感到格外惊喜，对王允说："何故如此？我只是朝廷大臣

---

① 编者按：对原著"董卓有一义儿，姓吕，名布，骁勇异常"的错误翻译。

② 编者按：对原著"重扶社稷，再立江山"的错误翻译。

的一位下属，您贵为大臣，我哪有资格接受您如此特殊的礼遇?”王允答道：“这并非因为您的职衔，乃是因为您无与伦比的才能与勇气。”吕布闻之大喜。

饮宴期间，王允劝客饮酒，不停称赞董卓与吕布的才能。受此奉承，吕布且饮且笑。晚宴结束后，王允令男仆退下，唤来几位侍女奉酒。酒至半酣，王允唤女前来。少顷，貂蝉在两位侍女的扶持下，盛装而出。吕布惊讶于貂蝉的优雅和美貌，问王允她是何人。王允答道：“此乃吾女貂蝉，我视您如同至亲，故令貂蝉前来相见。”遂命貂蝉与吕布把盏。貂蝉吕布敬酒，两人眉来眼去。

王允假装醉酒，对貂蝉说：“孩儿再敬尊客一杯酒。我们全靠他的保护，不可怠慢。”吕布请貂蝉坐下。见貂蝉似乎想要退下，王允对她说：“孩儿，吕布乃我至友，但坐无妨。”貂蝉立即坐在王允身边，吕布边饮酒，边目不转睛地看着她。

王允手指貂蝉，对吕布说：“没有什么比您做我女婿更好的了，我想把此女许配给您，又怕这一提议不合您的心意。”吕布从桌上起身，向王允致谢，说：“若果真能成为您女儿的丈夫，我愿效犬马之劳。”王允说：“那就这样吧，我会选一良辰，把她送到您的府上。”吕布醉意绵绵，欣喜无限，回到座上，凝视着貂蝉。当貂蝉多情地回望他时，他的心中如秋波（autumnal wave）荡漾。

少顷席散，王允向吕布致歉说本想留他止宿，但怕董卓听说后心中不悦。吕布再三拜谢而去。

过了数日，王允去朝堂，见到董卓。趁吕布不在，王允搭讪（先致以敬意）说：王允恳请太师屈尊来寒舍赴宴，诚望太师不要拒绝。董卓应允了这一邀请，王允乃去，匆匆回家为接待董卓而做准备。在大厅为董卓设座，地上铺上昂贵的地毯，四周挂起华丽的帷幔。

次日晌午，董卓驾到。王允上前迎接，行过礼后，邀其入府。董卓下车，护身侍卫分列左右，簇拥入堂。董卓一入府中，王允再拜于地，董卓令一侍从将他扶起，然后和蔼地命他坐在自己身边。

席间，王允对董卓极尽恭维，称赞他盛名远播天下，即便是古代圣贤伊尹（Yen）、周公（Chow）也不能与之相比。董卓受此夸赞，格外欣喜，遂开怀痛饮。王允曲意奉承，饮酒至天晚。

他们在酒桌上畅饮一段时间后，王允请董卓入后堂。董卓应邀而来，先叱退侍从。王允遂敬上一杯酒，对董卓说："吾自幼颇习天文，现在能够清楚地看到汉朝命数将尽。您的才干威震天下。不仅如此，自古以来，舜（Shun）之代尧（Yaou），禹（Yu）之继舜，这些变局皆可说是合乎天心人意。"董卓说："安敢有此奢望？"王允道："古人云，愚者让智者，无德让有德。为何让这一人事常规在我们这里戛然而止呢？"董卓答道："如果上天果真推举我做君王，司徒王允当被提拔为元勋。"王允拜谢董卓，令侍女点上画烛，摆酒上桌。又令奏起音乐，告诉董卓，此乐不足悦耳，但仍令奏乐，原因是有一歌姬等候在外，如果董卓乐意，就让她合乐演唱。董卓应允，堂中放下帘栊，乐师奏于帘前，貂蝉唱于帘后。

貂蝉表演完后，董卓令她近前一见。貂蝉遂从帘后出来，向董卓再三施礼。董卓被其美貌震惊，问她何许人也。王允答道："这是貂蝉，乃一歌伎。"同时命貂蝉执檀板低讴一曲。貂蝉唱时，董卓大声称赞。

在王允的授意下，貂蝉为董卓把盏，董卓从貂蝉手中接过酒杯，问她："美人年方几何？"貂蝉莞尔一笑，答道："年方二八。"目眩神迷的董卓说："你真乃人间天使。"

王允说："我欲将此女献与太师，却不知太师是否肯纳。"董卓道："如此见惠，何以报德？"王允说："此女能侍奉太师，就是她的荣幸了。"董卓再三称谢。

王允命令备下车马，将貂蝉送到董卓宫中，不久，董卓随之而至。王允送董卓至家，方才离去。

王允走后，骑马回家。行不到半路，却见两行红灯向他走来。吕布持戟走在前面。一见王允，立即勒住马，一把抓住王允衣襟，厉声问道："司徒既以貂蝉许我，今又送与太师，是在愚弄我吗?"王允急忙制止他说："这不是讨论此事的地方！请随我来家。"吕布随王允至家，一起来到后堂。见过礼后，王允说："你为何对我如此无礼?"吕布答道："我听说你用车把貂蝉送入了太师府中，为何如此?"王允答道："您有所不知。昨日朝堂上，太师对我说：'我有一事请教，明日要到你家。'闻此，我备下酒宴，恭候太师前来。"

（未完待续）

材料二

著名丞相董卓之死①

（上接卷十，第 532 页）

王允继续说："饮酒期间，太师对我说：'我听说您有一女，名唤貂蝉，已许配给我的儿子奉先。我怕此言不准，故来问询，并请一见。'我不敢违令，遂命貂蝉出来拜见公公。太师对我说：'今天是一吉日，我带您的女儿回家，把她嫁给奉先。'请您想一下，太师亲自驾临，我不得不殷勤相待。"吕布回道："请司徒恕罪，吕布知错了，明日当负荆请罪。"王允说："小女略有嫁妆，她一到贵府，立即送去。"吕布拜别。

次日，吕布入相府打听发生了何事。进入堂中，侍从告诉他昨晚主人带回了他的新娘，至今未起。吕布听了大怒，潜入董卓卧房，藏身屏风后，屏风在房间里把床围挡起来。越过屏风，吕布窥见了貂蝉的举动，她尚未穿好衣服，正在窗前梳洗。貂蝉从窗外鱼塘倒影中认出了身形，知是吕布

① 编著按：《亚洲杂志》第 11 卷，1821 年 2 月，伦敦，第 109—114 页。

到来，立即装出一副无比悲痛的样子，紧蹙双眉，不时用手帕擦眼，像是拭去眼泪。吕布看了一会儿，才像进来时那样偷偷退出了卧房。少顷，吕布再次进来，向董卓问安，这时董卓已穿好衣服，坐在中堂，等候晨膳。董卓问吕布外面是否无事，得知无事后，就让他侍立一旁。

董卓忙着用膳时，吕布不时瞟一眼屏风，看到貂蝉在屏风后走来走去，吕布神魂摇荡，以致被董卓察觉。董卓见此情状，心生疑忌，命吕布离开，吕布怏怏而去。

董卓沉迷于新宠，将近一月不能像平素那般处理朝政；不久，董卓患病，貂蝉殷勤侍奉，董卓对她愈加喜爱。

董卓养病期间，吕布候在卧室，等着问安。吕布进来时，发现董卓正在睡觉，貂蝉在他床边侍候。貂蝉一见吕布，就开始哭泣，一手指心，一手指董卓。貂蝉表现的悲哀令吕布心碎，没等他回过神来，董卓醒来，揉揉眼，转过身来，发现貂蝉站在床边，而吕布正在屏风后面目不转睛地看她，董卓妒火中烧，大声喝道："你想把我的爱姬勾引走吗？来人，把他赶出去，今后不许入堂。"吕布受到如此粗暴的对待，忿然回家，路遇李儒（Le-joo），禁不住告诉了他自己遭受的羞辱。李儒急忙去见董卓，对他说道："太师欲取天下，如何忘了您自己的利益所在，而令吕布受辱？他是您最能干、最得力的助手。他若离您而去，您所从事的大业就不可能完成了。"董卓问："那该如何是好？"李儒答道："明日派人请他，好言劝慰，并赐以丝帛、黄金等贵重礼物。"

董卓依照其言，次日派人请来吕布，以安抚的语气对他说："前日我旧病复发，心思不安，精神错乱。我请求您忘记我那些顺口说出、实无深意的气话。为了表示我对您初衷未改，请您收下这二十四锦帛和十磅黄金。"吕布收下赠礼，谢过董卓，行常礼退下。

尽管一切都过去了，吕布的心思却仍然集中在貂蝉身上。

董卓病情好转，便照常上朝。吕布执戟相随，见他与皇帝密谈，便离开朝廷（仍手持画戟），上马直奔相府而去。一到相府，下得马来，将马系在宅门，便直入后堂（仍手持画戟）去寻貂蝉。貂蝉一见吕布就说："去凤仪亭（Fung-e's summer-house），在那里等我。"吕布带着画戟，奔向花园，倚在亭子栏杆上，等着貂蝉赴约。貂蝉终于来了，她步态轻摇，像纤弱的嫩枝随风摇摆，看上去确实不像凡人，仿佛月宫仙子。她哭着对吕布说："虽然我不是司徒王允的女儿，但他却一直把我当女儿看待。第一次见将军，就被许配给了您，似乎实现了我平生所愿。谁能想到太师起不良之心，强行玷污了我的身体！我至死恨他。决意见君一面，故忍辱至今，如今喜得见君，但此身已污，故不足以侍奉您这位当世英豪了，我愿死于君前，使君见我诚意。"说完，貂蝉抓住栏杆，试图跳入莲花池（lily-pond）。吕布慌忙抱住她，不让她跳，眼中含着泪说道："我很久以来就知道你的心意了，只是伤心我们不能共语。"貂蝉握住吕布的手，说："虽然我如今不能做您的妻子，希望来生能够如愿。"吕布回答："如果今生不能以你为妻，我就算不得英雄。"貂蝉说："我每天度日如年，愿君怜我救我。"吕布说："我如今偷空过来，担心老贼见疑，所以得赶紧离去。"貂蝉抓住吕布的胳膊，说道："若君如此害怕老贼，我就没有能见天日之期了。"吕布止住她说："待我谋划可行之计，以实现我俩的心愿。"说完，吕布拿起画戟，似乎想要离去。貂蝉说："我在深闺，闻君大名，如雷贯耳，因为您当世无双，无可匹敌。谁会想到您反还受制于他人？"说完，貂蝉泪如雨下。吕布放下画戟，羞惭满面，惊慌失措，回身抱住貂蝉，深情劝慰。两人紧紧相拥，难舍难分。

却说吕布离殿不久，董卓转身不见吕布，顿生疑虑，匆匆辞了皇帝，登车回府。及至相府，见吕布的马系于门前，询问门吏，得知温侯去了花园，遂斥责侍从疏忽大意，径入后堂寻找吕布。找不到吕布，遂找貂蝉，也找不到，急问侍女，侍女说貂蝉在花园赏花。董卓快步入园，看到吕布、貂蝉在凤仪亭下共语，吕布的画戟倚在墙上，董卓怒吼一声，吕布见董卓赶来，大吃一惊，转身就逃。董卓抓起画戟追赶吕布，但吕布行动敏捷，董卓肥胖，无法赶上，故将画戟投向吕布，吕布将画戟打落在地。董卓拾起画戟，接着追赶，却已追不上了。董卓追至花园门外，正逢一人急入，猛然将董卓撞倒在地。此人正是李儒。李儒将董卓从地上扶起，引入书房，让他坐在凳上。董卓问："您为何急匆匆赶来?"李儒答道："我刚入贵府，听说您生气地跑到后园去寻吕布，故急忙赶来。正遇吕布边跑边喊'太师要杀我!'我便加快步伐，赶来平息您的怒火。没想到误撞了太师，希望您能够原谅我无意的冒犯。"董卓说道："想到失去爱姬，我就无法忍受，我发誓一定要杀了吕布。"李儒回道："如果太师允许，我必须得说，您这样做并不明智。楚庄王（Chwang）谨慎地宽赦了犯人，他不曾追究蒋雄（Tseay-ling）调戏其爱姬之责，他的宽容得到了很好的回报，因为后来当他被叛军包围时，正是这个蒋雄奋不顾身地保住了他的性命，请您仿效庄王的审慎。美女可再得，但猛将吕布的情义却千金难买。切不可因此争斗。将貂蝉赐与吕布，他会感受到您的宽宏大量，日后必以死相报。恳请太师权衡我的忠告。"董卓沉吟良久，方道："所言不差，我当思之。"李儒道谢后退出。

董卓来到后堂，询问貂蝉："你与吕布刚才在做什么呢?"貂蝉哭着答道："我在花园赏花，吕布突然冲到我面前。我被他的意外闯入吓了一跳，正欲躲避。吕布却对我说：'我乃太师之子，为何相避?'他提着画戟，把我赶至凤仪亭。发现他居心不良，又怕他用力相逼，我本欲跳入莲花池，也不想失节。但这厮却抱住我，不让我跳。在这生死之际，太师前来救了我性命。"

董卓说："若把你送与吕布，如何?"貂蝉大惊，哭着说道："我已身事贵人，您却突然想把我赐给一个奴仆，我宁死也不愿受此屈辱。"貂蝉说着便取墙上宝剑，欲刺入胸膛。董卓慌忙抓住宝剑，放在一边，抱住她说："我只是在与你开玩笑。"貂蝉遂倒在董卓身上，掩面大哭，说："这必是李儒之计，他是吕布至交，故设此计。却不顾惜太师体面和我的感受。我要剥了他们的皮肉。”董卓说：“我哪里舍得与你分别?”貂蝉说：“虽然蒙受太师怜爱，但我还是担心此处不宜久留，必为吕布所害。”董卓说：“你明日跟我回郿坞，在那里与我一起享乐，不受打扰。”貂蝉才停止哭泣，行礼拜谢。

次日，李儒前来拜见，道：“今日良辰，可将貂蝉送与吕布。”董卓说：“我想吕布与我犹如父子，将貂蝉送与他恐不合礼，你转告他我不能从其所愿，但以好言相慰便是。”李儒说：“太师不可为妇人所惑!”董卓脸色突变，说：“你会把自己的妻子送与吕布吗?貂蝉之事，勿复多言；言则必斩!”李儒退下，仰天叹道：“吾等皆死于此妇人之手矣!”

董卓即日下令返回郿坞，所有朝廷官员皆去送行。貂蝉坐在车上，遥见吕布在人群中眺望其车，便把帘幕拉到一边，做痛哭状。车已远去，吕布登上土冈，继续目送马车，直到它消失在一片尘埃之中。身后一声大喝忽然把他从沉思中唤醒，那人问：“吕布为何在此沉思，却不陪太师去郿坞?”回头一看乃司徒王允站在身边，相互施礼后，王允说：“我因染微恙，几日不曾出门，今日扶病出来，只为送别太师，很高兴这让我有此机会向我最尊敬的朋友致敬。但再问一下，您为何在此神伤，却不随太师去郿坞?”吕布答道：“大人，事实上我所想的正是您的养女，我怕是永远失去她了。”“何以如此?”王允假装吃惊地问：“我不是把她许配给您了吗?”吕布答道：“是许配给我了，却被老贼董卓夺去了。”“不可能吧!”吕布将发生的一切一一道与王允。王允仰面顿足，惊得半晌不语，良久乃言：“没想到太师竟沦为禽兽，为了个人欲望，全无廉耻，把许配给养子的妻子抢到自己床上。且到寒舍，我们商量一下此事。”

（未完待续）

材料三

著名丞相董卓之死①

（上接第 114 页）

吕布随王允回家，及至府上，王允早已在密室备下酒宴，请吕布享用。宴罢，吕布将凤仪亭发生之事细述一遍。王允听罢，说道："太师骗走了我的女儿，又夺走了您的妻子。你我必被天下人耻笑。对我来说，我已年迈无能，自甘受辱，但您乃当世英雄，也该遭受这等羞辱吗？难道您不复仇吗？"吕布被此话激怒，拍案大吼。王允劝阻他说："我本不该说出心中所想，请务必息怒。""岂止愤怒！"吕布反驳说："我发誓用老贼的血来洗刷我的耻辱！""等一下！"王允用手掩住吕布的嘴，说道："恳请您勿说此言，以免因您的鲁莽而连累我！""大人何出此言！"吕布说："哪个羞辱了我的人还能活命？我要杀了这个暴君。只是我与他有父子关系，如果我杀了他，别人就会说我弑父，名声殃及子孙，遗臭万代。""弑父！"王允笑曰："记住您顶多只是他的养子，当他将您的画戟投向您时，哪有父子之情？"吕布说："大人所言甚是，我不再反悔了。"

王允见其杀贼之意已决，便直言不讳地对他说："如果您全力匡扶汉室，那么您的忠心必将得到世人的称赞，青史传名，流芳百世；如果您拥护老贼，那么您将遗臭万年！"吕布避席下拜，说："不必多言，我杀贼之意已决，大人无须担忧。"王允答道："我不担忧，只是害怕事若不成，反招大祸。"

吕布拔剑刺臂，郑重发誓。王允喜不自胜，跪谢曰："若汉室果真不被颠覆，那么您就会因救助之功而得到报偿。切勿泄露一言，我会退而再谋

① 编者按：《亚洲杂志》第 11 卷，1821 年 3 月，伦敦，第 233—242 页。

此计，想清楚了就说与您。”“悉听君命，”吕布说完，就起身回家了。

吕布走后，王允即请仆射士孙瑞（Shun-Suy）、司隶校尉黄琬（Whang-Wan）来家商议。

两人应召而来，到后遂与王允密议。协商时，孙瑞说皇帝近来抱恙，生病期间，不能料理国事。可传主上旨意与董卓，召其入宫议事，及至，则使士兵将其斩杀，士兵可由吕布埋伏于朝门之内。王允赞同此计，但问谁能前去传旨。孙瑞回答说骑都尉李肃（Le-Shuh）可担此任，董卓曾不迁其官，故私怀怨恨。王允说：“甚好！”立即派人去请吕布，邀他前来商议。

又派人去请李肃。李肃到时，吕布已至，吕布对李肃说：“老贼董卓欲杀皇帝，残害百姓，恶贯满盈，人神共愤。我等决定除掉暴君，希望您能相助。今请公速去郿坞，假扮传旨之人，宣董卓进宫。与此同时，我在宫门，埋下伏兵，董卓现身，即令伏兵诛之。我等戮力同心，欲救皇帝，尊意若何?”李肃答道：“我很久以来就想除掉此贼，不但痛恨此贼，还恨那些不像我这般恨他的人。而今您亦有此心，我不再怀疑此事不成，此乃天意！”言毕，李肃拿起一支箭，折成两段，以为盟誓。

王允道：“我相信以诸公之忠心，必能成事，若能成功救得皇帝，主上定然不会忘记封赏功臣。”

次日，李肃引数骑，前往郿坞。及入城，自称传旨之人。董卓将其召入，李肃遂得入拜。董卓问道：“你带何旨而来?”李肃答道：“主上病体新愈，但觉体弱无力，故欲让位。但思群臣中无人贤于太师，故召会文武百官，以便当面传位于太师，故发此诏。”“诚有此事！”董卓说：“然王允意下如何?”李肃答道：“司徒王允也热情拥护，他已下令召集朝会，只等太师到来。”董卓大喜，曰：“吾梦即成真矣！昨夜梦得身着皇袍，既然神人皆愿我承王位，机不可复得，我不可错失！”遂对李肃道：“我一坐上王位，即令你为执金吾。”李肃拜谢。

董卓立即命令心腹之将郭汜（Ko-fan）、张济（Chuy-tsee）、樊稠[①]（Fan-teaou），率领三千无敌飞军，在其居京期间镇守郿坞。

董卓又入后堂辞别老母，卓母已九十余岁，问道："吾儿何往？"董卓回答："儿前去接受汉室的禅让，几日之后，母亲大人即可为太后矣。"

卓母曰："我近日肉颤心惊，恐是凶兆。"儿子问："如何认为是凶兆？您不是快做国母了吗？自然会有预兆。"遂辞别其母，又去辞别貂蝉。告诉她事情缘由后，又向她承诺，他做皇帝，貂蝉当为贵妃。貂蝉虽已明知就里，仍旧拜谢，假作欢喜。

辞别家眷，董卓登车赶赴长安，途中众人跟随，前呼后拥。行不过十里，车轴断裂，董卓从车上下来，改骑一匹马。但行不到三里，那马变得桀骜不驯，咆哮嘶叫，掣断辔头。这使董卓大惊，问李肃曰："车轴裂，辔头断，是何征兆？"李肃说："太师即将登位，这些事件无非预示着弃旧换新，您现在所乘的车马，将很快代之以金勒玉辇。"董卓闻此大喜，隐然相信了李肃之言。次日，正行间，忽然狂风骤起，尘土飞扬；及至夜间，又有浓雾蔽天。董卓渐生疑虑，转问李肃："尘土飞扬、浓雾蔽天，是何征兆？"李肃答曰："时光流转，物换星移。太师即将登上龙座，自然万物知此巨变，故通过异象显示天威。"董卓闻此又喜，不复疑虑。

及至长安，朝廷百官俱出迎接，唯有李儒卧病在床。吕布于百官中最先向董卓道贺。董卓向他承诺自己登上皇位，就令他总督天下军马。吕布拜谢，但他仍然坚持此前已经做出的决定。

是夜，董卓于卧榻上，听到街上小儿的歌声，风将歌声吹来。歌曰："千里草，何青青！十日卜，不得生。"[②]

歌声悲切，董卓为之所动，问李肃曰："小儿所唱之歌，对我是吉是

---

① 编者按："郭汜"被误作"郭氾"。

② 这两句诗行中的文字取自董卓名字。第一个字"董"，由"草""千"和"里"组成；第二个字"卓"，由"上""日"和"十"组成。这是中国人热衷的文字游戏。

凶?”李肃道:“如果童谣有所预言,不过是说汉室灭亡、董氏兴起。”

次日,董卓摆列仪仗入朝。路上遇到一个道士,青袍白巾,手执一杆白旗。旗上两角各书一“口”字。[1] 董卓问李肃:“道人在此做何?”李肃答曰:“他是疯子。”遂命一卫士把他赶走了。董卓乘车进殿,群臣着朝服迎谒。李肃手持宝剑,扶车而入,及至东门,董卓的卫兵皆被挡在门外,唯有车夫二十余人得入。董卓见王允及其他大臣立于御座前,各持宝剑,不同寻常,有些不安,遂问李肃这是何意。

李肃不答,只是催促车夫前行。这时,王允大呼:“反贼在此,武士何在?”顷刻间,一百甲士自殿侧冲出,用矛刺向董卓,董卓身着铠甲,兵器无法刺穿他的身体。尽管如此,董卓惊得从车上坠下,大呼:“吾儿奉先何在?”吕布此时正在车后,厉声喊道:“老贼,我有斩你诏令!”遂以画戟刺入董卓喉咙。随后,李肃割下其头,抓在手里。这时,吕布左手持戟,右手从怀中取出诏书,大呼曰:“此乃奉诏讨伐贼臣董卓,他人不必惊慌,仅除此一人。”将士闻此皆呼:“吾皇万岁。”

除掉暴君后,吕布高呼道:“帮助董卓助纣为虐的人是李儒,谁去擒他?”李肃方要领命,忽听殿门外一声大喊,经询问方知是李儒的奴仆已将他绑缚,正拖进宫来。王允命将李儒押往市曹斩首,又命将董卓的尸首带到街衢,使百姓知道董卓已死,并目睹不忠不义遭受的下场。卫士们把火放在董卓的肚脐上,火光燃起时,尸油流溢满地。百姓与将士争相辱尸,拖着他过街,对他的尸首拳打脚踢。

董卓为其罪恶所受的惩罚还不止于此。王允命皇甫嵩(Wang-foo-sung)与吕布领兵六万赶赴郿坞,斩除了董卓全家。

李傕、郭汜、张济、樊稠听说董卓已死,吕布又领精兵将至,便连夜

① 吕布姓名的两个字,第一个字由两个“口”字组成,两字之间有一条线相连;第二个字是“布”,旗上已有暗示。所以,这面旗是为了告知太师小心吕布。

逃往凉州。吕布率兵抵达郿坞，先将貂蝉占为己有。取了貂蝉，吕布便与皇甫嵩一起下令：将奉暴君董卓之令强掳入城的所有女子，尽行释放，并协助逮捕董卓亲属，一旦捕获，无论男女老幼，立即诛戮。即便是董卓之母，也没能免于诛戮。此外，因为谋反，董卓之弟董旻、侄子董璜，其首级皆被悬于杆上，暴晒数日，以示民众。又令查缉董卓集于郿坞的珍宝，包括黄金数十万，白银数百万，以及绮罗、钻石、宝石、器皿不计其数，皆悉数收缴，送与王允，王允将之分与将士。

大事既成，王允于都堂备下盛宴，朝中群臣皆被邀来。正饮宴间，忽有报曰，一人卧于市曹，伏董卓尸首而哭。王允大怒，高声怒斥道："没想到皇帝的子民中，竟有人痛惜逆贼之死？是何狂徒，胆敢哀悼董卓？武士何在！将此人抓来，拖至堂下！"须臾，武士将此人拖至王允面前，举座皆惊，原来此人不是别人，乃是侍中蔡邕（Fze-ying）。王允叱之曰："反贼尸首弃置市曹，举国称贺，你身为汉臣，为何不为国庆，反为贼哭？"蔡邕恭顺地答道："邕虽不才，却知大义，岂敢痛惜逆贼之死？只因曾有一次受其知遇之恩。伏尸痛哭并非痛惜逆贼之死，而是感念其知遇之恩。自知此亦有罪，故您想如何惩罚，我都甘愿领受。刖足黥首均可，总之，除了死，可用任何方式折磨我。我想活下来，续成《汉书》，以赎我之罪。"

众官怜惜蔡邕之才，颇感同情，亦觉悲哀，竭力使其免于死罪。大史学家马日磾（Ma-jih shen）悄悄对王允说："蔡邕乃旷世逸才，若允许他写完《汉书》，必能尽职尽忠。此外，尽人皆知，蔡邕被奉为孝子，若我等令其死，恐将失信于天下。"王允答曰："昔孝武（Heaou-Woo）不杀司马迁（Sze-ma-tseën），后来命他著史，结果司马迁不思皇恩，反记私仇，毁谤当世，使流传下来的当时的人物，不是其本来面貌，而是被他恶意歪曲。方今世道动荡，人心汹汹。当此之际，难道我等可将史笔交付给一个不忠不信之人吗？难道我等愿意让一个仇敌来诽谤自己吗？"

马日磾无言以对，只是私下对一大臣说："王允之名将不会传之后世了。"王允不顾马日磾之言，命令将蔡邕下狱缢死。众臣闻之，尽为流涕。后世史学家和道学家普遍认为，蔡邕哭董卓固自不是，但王允因此杀之，亦自不是。

且说李傕、郭汜、张济、樊稠逃至陕西，使人送信至长安，请求赦免。王允收到信，说："董卓被这四人怂恿作恶，即使大赦天下，也不能赦免这四个人。"信使返回，将王允的决定告诉李傕，李傕说："既然得不到赦免，我等只能各自逃走，尽力保住各自性命。"但谋士贾诩（Hea-yun）说："将军，你若解散军队，必会被某些无情的仇敌所出卖。不若奋起，激励陕西民众支持君之大业，将他们并入本部军马，杀入长安，公然宣称为董卓报仇。若能取胜则统治帝国；倘若失败，再逃不迟。"李傕同意了这一提议，遂召集西凉州（Le-lang-chow）民众，告诉他们王允已决定要将他们斩尽杀绝。又说："既然投降一无所得，不若参军，随我等与之对抗。"众人大惊，从军人数多达十余万。军力遂强，分作四队，杀向长安。路上遇到董卓女婿牛辅（New-poo），领兵五千人。李傕将他的军队合并过来，令牛辅担任先锋，四将跟随在后。

王允听说他们杀来，慌忙向吕布问计。吕布曰："大人莫惊，量此鼠辈，必会因粮草短缺半途而废。"

遂令李肃带领朝廷军队前去迎战。李肃立即前去迎战牛辅。经过一场血战后，牛辅被迫撤退。但是，第二天夜间二更，牛辅突袭李肃营寨。李肃军队大乱，败走十里，损兵过半。李肃急奔吕布，言其兵败。吕布怒曰："你为何坏我名声？武士何在！斩下头来，悬于寨门！"

次日，吕布亲自带兵迎战牛辅。牛辅顽强对战，但敌不过吕布之战术与勇猛，于是逃回了叛军的主力部队。

是夜，牛辅唤来心腹胡赤儿（Ho-Chih-urh）商议，牛辅说道："吕布骁勇，万不能敌。我们不如瞒着李傕和另外三将，取军中所藏财宝，与三四随从，弃军而去。”胡赤儿应允。他们连夜取了财宝，与三四人弃营而去。奔逃途中，渡一河流，胡赤儿想把所有财宝据为己有，遂杀了牛辅。提着牛辅的头，前往朝廷营寨，献与吕布。吕布询问详请，随从告诉他胡赤儿杀了牛辅，吕布大怒，立即下令杀了胡赤儿。

击退牛辅后，吕布前去迎战叛军的主力部队。途中正遇李傕兵马。吕布不等对方进攻，立即挺戟跃马，率兵直取敌军。李傕军队挡不住这一猛烈进攻，从战场退走六七十里，在两山间下寨。李傕在此与郭汜、张济、樊稠商议道：“吕布虽勇，然无谋略，吾等不必沮丧。我每日引兵到谷口，引诱这一鲁莽之徒出战。他一出战，郭汜就攻其后方，仿效彭越（Poo-yul）攻打楚国时所用之法。你进攻时鸣锣，收兵时擂鼓。与此同时，张济与樊稠，分兵两路，径取长安，长安誓必落在我们手中。”众将纷纷赞同此计。

此计奏效。吕布引兵来到山下，准备进攻。李傕前来，似要迎战，但不等吕布领兵杀来，李傕已退至山上。山上忽然矢石如雨，吕布之兵无法前进。正在此刻，郭汜之兵攻其后方，吕布回军，迎战新敌。不等调回兵力，鼓声大震，敌军已退，吕布暂且收兵。但没过多久，锣声遍地响起，李傕再次下山，吕布再次前去迎战，李傕却又退去。郭汜也再次攻其后方，当吕布前去迎战时，却擂鼓收兵而退。

吕布胸中怒火中烧，一连几日疲于奔命。既不得与敌交战，又不能让自己的队伍休息。正困惑时，忽报张济、樊稠引大队人马，分兵两路，进犯长安，京城有落入敌手之危。吕布急忙领兵回京，李傕、郭汜追击在后。吕布无心恋战，赶着去救长安，行军途中折了大量军马。及至长安城边，望见敌兵云屯雨集，围定城池。吕布之军非但没有上前攻打，还因救援无望而倍感沮丧，大批士兵临阵倒戈，转投敌军，这令吕布格外忧愤。

数日之后，董卓余党李蒙（Le-mung）、王方（Wang-fan）暗中通敌，突然为叛军打开城门。顷刻间，叛军从四方涌入。吕布引数百人，逃出东门。离开前，急问王允道："趁此机会逃走吧，跟我上马，同往他省，别图良策。"王允答道："若能扶住社稷，恢复安宁，我愿从您所愿；若不能，我愿奉身以死。临难逃命，我不能也。但请为我传令关东诸公，让他们努力恢复朝纲。"吕布再三劝他趁机逃命，王允硬是不为所动。话刚说完，四方城门失火。吕布只得作罢，携百余人冲出关外，投奔袁术去了。

李傕、郭汜纵兵掠城。太常卿种拂（Chung-fuh）、太仆鲁馗（Las-kwo）、大鸿胪周奂（Chow-ying）、城门校尉崔烈（Chuy-keih）、越骑校尉王颀（Wang-king），皆于是日死于国难。

敌军围住宫殿，王位岌岌可危。众臣等着皇帝现身城楼。李傕等人望见龙袍，即令军队止步，高呼"吾皇万岁"。皇帝倚楼问道："卿等有何要求？径入长安，意欲何为？"李傕、郭汜仰面奏曰："太师董卓乃陛下社稷之臣。陛下何故令王允将他斩杀？我等特来为董卓报仇，并非造反。但得王允，臣便退兵。"王允当时正立于君侧，奏曰："臣本为社稷安稳计，如今形势逆转，陛下不要想着毁了自己而来救我。臣请陛下准许我下去见叛贼。"正当皇帝犹豫不定之时，王允跳下城楼，大呼道："王允在此！"李傕、郭汜拔剑叱曰："太师董卓，何故被杀？"王允答曰："董贼之罪，弥天亘地。受诛之日，长安百姓，皆相庆贺，惟有尔等反贼哀悼。""我等何罪，不肯相赦？"王允大骂："何须多言？我乃王允，如果我今天必须死，就让我死好了。"二贼手起剑落，把王允杀于楼下。

众贼杀了王允，即刻命人抓了王允全家，无论老幼，尽行杀害。举国士民，无不哀悼。

本书所叙并非董卓灭亡那年的事。根据中国正史，我发现：献帝（Hëen-tee）之父灵帝（Ling-te 汉朝先帝）统治 22 年后驾崩，其子辩（Tsze-p-nëe）继位，年仅十四岁。辩封其弟协（Hëe，年仅九岁）为陈留王。七月，皇帝的外甥[①]何进（Ho-tsin）召董卓相助平定叛乱。八月，董卓进京。九月，董卓废黜皇帝，令为弘农王，并立其弟协为帝，是为献帝。董卓又自封为军队统帅。十一月，董卓出任大臣，给全家封侯，人人担任军事首领。

次年正月，广东[②]等地诸王对董卓宣战。献帝二年二月，董卓自封为太师。三年四月，王允联合吕布诛杀董卓。及至九月，吕布逃至关东南阳，王允亦死。王允死后，李傕、郭汜、张济、樊稠皆被任命为朝廷将领。

① 编者按：非外甥，应该是国舅。

② 编者按："关东"之误。

二　德庇时与《三国志节译文》*

在《三国演义》英译史上，英国汉学家德庇时对于《三国演义》的翻译长期以来颇为扑朔迷离。直到2017年，笔者经过多方查询，找到了刊载《三国志节译文》的《汉文诗解》的三个版本，才厘清了相关问题。

正如学界所言，德庇时为《三国演义》的英译作出了很大贡献，他翻译的《三国志节译文》刊载于《汉文诗解》中，只是其译文并非咏史诗，也并非出现在《汉文诗解》正文中，而是作为“附录”刊载于1834年澳门出版的《汉文诗解》中。然而，由于这个版本印量有限，极为罕见，故此德庇时对于《三国演义》的译介长期以来以讹传讹、信息错乱。学界相关错误认识以及《汉文诗解》的三个版本情况，请参考本书“序言”部分。

简而言之，《汉文诗解》分别于1829年、1834年、1870年出版了三个版本：“首刊本”“澳门本”和“增订本”，《三国志节译文》作为附录，仅出现在1834年“澳门本”中。德庇时主要节译了两个故事：一是《造反的张氏三兄弟的命运》；一是《何进的历史与命运》。

---

* 相关研究以“19世纪英译《三国演义》资料辑佚与研究——以德庇时的《三国志节译文》为中心”为题，发表于《复旦学报》2017年第4期。

德庞时（John Francis Davis，1795—1890）

（一）黯淡的政客和耀眼的汉学家

德庇时是 19 世纪第一个全面系统地介绍中国文学的英国汉学家，在中国文学的翻译方面以涉猎广泛著称于世。在华工作 35 年间，翻译过中国小说、戏曲和诗歌等多种文类，被称为“19 世纪向英国读者引介中国文学成果卓著的硕儒大家”[①]。

① 熊文华：《英国汉学史》，学苑出版社 2007 年版，第 36 页。

德庇时又译作爹核士、戴维斯等，其父塞缪尔·戴维斯（Samuel Davis，1760—1819）曾担任东印度公司广州主管，1813 年德庇时 18 岁时来到广州，在东印度公司担任抄写员。出色的语言天赋使他很快脱颖而出，1816 年跟随阿美士德勋爵（Load William Pitt Amherst，1773—1857）带领的英国使团赴北京谒见嘉庆皇帝。在使团中，德庇时担任“中文秘书兼翻译”（Chinese Secretary and Interpreter），当时担任此职的还有 1807 年来华的第一位新教传教士、后来成为著名汉学家的马礼逊。德庇时在东印度公司度过了最美好的青春年华，学业不断精进，职位平步青云。1832 年出任东印度公司广州大班。1833 年被委任为第二任英国驻华商务总监。1844 年成为第二任香港总督兼英国驻华公使，任职四年后离开香港，返回英国。此后开始了长达 47 年的退休生活，这期间他继续从事中国研究。1852 年被任命为格洛斯特郡（Gloucestershire）副部长（Deputy Lieutenant）；1854 年被授予巴恩勋位爵士勋章（a Knight Commander of the Order of the Bath）；1876 年在牛津大学设立中国研究基金，被授予民法学博士学位（D. C. L.）；1890 年 95 岁时寿终正寝，堪称 19 世纪英国汉学家中的长寿之星。

德庇时在华期间虽然屡居要职，却备受指责。尤其是在担任香港总督期间，因人口登记和设立名目繁多的税收而受到英国商人和香港侨民的普遍反对。弗兰克·韦尔什（Frank Welsh）在《香港史》（*A Borrowed Place: The History of Hong Kong*）中说：“德庇时的个性和经历不能帮他安抚失望的殖民地侨民，他为人冷漠，难以接近，个头矮小，平庸无能，完全缺乏璞鼎查（Sir Henry Pottinger，1789—1856）那样的气派。他喜欢中国文学，还能创作水平尚可的拉丁诗歌，但这些爱好和能力都不足以使他得到极不开化的侨民的欢迎。”[①] 1848 年离开香港时，德庇时受到港英民众的故意冷落，

---

① Frank Welsh, *A Borrowed Place: The History of Hong Kong*, R. R. Donnelley & Sons Company, 1994, p. 170.

欧德理在《中国的欧洲》（*Europe in China*）一书中写到德庇时离任时没有公开的演说，没有宴会，也没有前来欢送的民众。香港的重要报纸对德庇时更是冷嘲热讽，说他“不但因为公务行为不受欢迎，而且他的个人行为和性格特点也不适合做一个殖民地的长官”。文章结尾还不忘用几句尖酸刻薄的拉丁文来向他道别，以暗讽这位总督对于拉丁文的喜爱与炫耀。[①] 德庇时遭遇的冷遇，甚至让为人宽厚的另一位著名英国汉学家理雅各感到诧异，他说：“我不知道这是怎么回事，在我们所有的总督当中，德庇时是在民众最强烈的不满中离职的。”[②]

虽然不是一位成功的外交官和政治家，但德庇时对中国文学的喜爱和译介，却使他成为19世纪英国汉学史上用力最勤、成果最丰的香港总督。不少学者认为德庇时的政治显达得益于他对中国文学的翻译和研究。张春树、骆雪伦在《中国十七世纪的危机与改革》（*Crisis and Transformation in Seventeenth-century China*）一书中说：“德庇时的翻译使他名声大噪，他被选入皇家亚洲学会，成为当时英国研究中国文学和语言的主要权威，并被委任为东印度公司广州大班，最后成为香港总督、英国驻华全权代表及商务总监。”[③] 作者显然认为德庇时的汉学成就成全了他的政治生涯。相比于政治、外交上的狼狈不堪、黯淡无光，汉学领域内的德庇时却从容自若、光彩照人，他在中国小说、戏曲和诗歌翻译方面均有力作。

① E. J. Eitel, *Europe in China*: *The History of Hongkong*, *from the beginning to the year* 1882, London: Luzac & Company; Hongkong: Kelly & Walsh, Ld. 1895, p. 249.

② “The Colony of Hong Kong”, The *China Review*, Vol. Ⅰ., Hong Kong, 1872, p. 163.

③ Chun-shu Chang and Shelley Hsueh-lun Chang, *Crisis and Transformation in Seventeenth-century China*, The University of Michigan Press, 1998, p. 19.

（二）中国小说与戏曲翻译

德庇时是李渔小说的最早英译者，这是他在文学翻译领域最突出的贡献。1815 年德庇时刚到广州两年就翻译出版了一本中国小说，该作题名《三与楼》（*San-Yu-Low: or the Three Dedicated Rooms*），出自李渔的短篇小说集《十二楼》。次年《亚洲杂志》第一卷分四次连载了《三与楼》。[①] 1822 年，德庇时又翻译了《十二楼》中的《合影楼》（*The Shadow in the Water*）和《夺锦楼》（*The Twin Sisters*），与此前翻译的《三与楼》合在一起，题名《中国小说》（*Chinese Novels, Translated from the Originals*）结集出版。年轻的德庇时对于李渔小说的译介很快引起了欧洲同行的关注。1826 年，法国著名汉学家雷慕沙（Abel Rémusat，1788—1832）在《亚洲文集》（*Mélanges Asiatiques*）中介绍了《中国小说》。[②] 翌年，雷慕沙将《中国小说》转译为法语，发表于《中国故事集》（*Contes Chinois*），在法国巴黎出版。[③] 同年，法译本《中国小说》又被转译为德译本（Chinesische Erzhlungen），在莱比锡（Liepziq）出版。从而进一步扩大了德庇时英译李渔小说在欧洲的影响。张春树、骆雪伦指出：德庇时翻译李渔小说之前英语世界仅有两部中国小说：一是 1761 年帕西（Bishop Thomas Percy，1729—1811）整理出版的《好逑传》（*Hao Kiou Choaan*）；一是 1814 年韦斯顿（Stephen Weston，1747—1830）翻译的《范希周》（*Fan-hy-cheu*）。“在英国对中国的

---

① *Asiatic Journal*, Vol. Ⅰ., January-June, 1816, pp. 37 – 41, 132 – 134, 243 – 249, 338 – 342.

② Abel Rémusat, *Mélanges Asiati ques*, Paris, 1826, Tome. Ⅱ., pp. 335 – 345.

③ Abel Rémusat, *Contes Chinois*, Paris, 1827, Tome. Ⅱ., pp. 7 – 96 (L'OMBRE DANS L'EAU); Tome Ⅲ., pp. 7 – 96 (SAN-IU-LEOU); pp. 99 – 142 (LES DEUX JUMELLES).

兴趣不断上升的时期，英译中国小说作品的缺乏使德庇时恰逢其时的翻译顷刻间获得了成功。”①

在中国小说英译方面，德庇时还是第一部英译中国小说——《好逑传》的重译者。《好逑传》是明末清初的一部才子佳人小说，写的是铁中玉与水冰心的爱情传奇，作者署名“名教中人”，鲁迅在《中国小说史略》中说该作“在外国特有名，远过于其在中国”②。据宋丽娟、孙逊统计，《好逑传》的西文译本多达26种。③《好逑传》在海外的“有名”与德庇时密切相关。目前学界通常把《好逑传》看作第一部被翻译成英文的中国长篇小说，首译者是英国东印度公司广州职员詹姆斯·威尔金森（James Wilkinson），1761年，英国德罗摩尔主教（Bishop of Dromore）帕西将英文和葡萄牙文翻译的威尔金森手稿题名 *Hau Kiou Choaan, or The Pleasing History*，在英国伦敦出版，这是《好逑传》的第一个英译本，史称“帕西译本”。德庇时认为这一译本只是对于原著内容的一个概述，不但省略了原著中的诗词韵文（without the poetical passages），而且存在大量“错译、窜改和漏译”（much was mistranslated, much interpolated, and a great deal omitted），④ 由此，他根据嘉庆丙寅年镌刻的“福文堂藏板”《好逑传》重译了该作。1829年，德庇时翻译的两卷本《好逑传》题名 *The Fortunate Union, a Romance, Translated from the Chinese Original*，在伦敦出版，这一译本可以称为“德庇时译

① Chun-shu Chang and Shelley Hsueh-lun Chang, *Crisis and Transformation in Seventeenth-century China*, The University of Michigan Press, 1998, p. 35. 作者认为韦斯顿翻译的《范希周》出自《警世通言》（*Ching-shih t'ung-yen* or *Popular Words to Admonish the World*）第12卷，这一观点目前虽在学界受到认可，但实际却不够准确。韦斯顿所译《范希周》附有中文，经笔者考察，实际出自冯梦龙的《情史》；《警世通言》第12卷确有一篇与范希周情节雷同的小说，题名《范鳅儿双镜团圆》，人物虽同是范希周，篇幅内容相比《情史》中的《范希周》却长出许多，两文不应混为一谈。

② 鲁迅：《中国小说史略》，人民文学出版社2008年版，第194页。

③ 宋丽娟、孙逊：《〈好逑传〉英译本版本研究——以帕西译本和德庇时译本为中心》，《上海师范大学学报》2009年第5期。

④ John Francis Davis, *The Fortunate Union, a Romance, Translated from the Chinese Original*, London: The Oriental Translation Fund, 1829, Preface, p. 8.

本”。帕西译本和德庇时译本是《好逑传》在欧美世界的最重要的两个译本，这两个译本不但直接推动了明末清初才子佳人小说的西译，而且为译者带来了巨大声誉。

在中国戏曲英译方面，德庇时同样功不可没，他翻译的元代杂剧作家武汉臣的《老生儿》（*Laou-Seng-Urh*，*or*，*An Heir in his Old Age*）和马致远的《汉宫秋》（*Han Koong Tsew*，*or*，*The Sorrows of Han*），打破了《赵氏孤儿》在欧洲汉学界一枝独秀的局面。1731 年，法国耶稣会士马若瑟（Joseph de Prémare，1666—1736）翻译了元代杂剧作家纪君祥的《赵氏孤儿》（*Tchao-chi-cou-eulh*，*ou L'orphelin de la Maison de Tchao*），1735 年，该作被收入杜赫德（Du Halde，1674—1743）编著的《中华帝国全志》（*Description Geographique*，*Historique*，*Chronologique*，*Politique*，*et Physique de L'empire de la Chine et de la Tartarie Chinoise*）。1755 年，伏尔泰（Francois Marie Arouet，1694—1778）将之改编为《中国孤儿》（*The Orphan of China*）搬上法国舞台。整体看来，马若瑟的译介虽影响深远，却难称完璧，因为他删除了唱词，仅保留了宾白，从而大大削弱了中国戏曲的艺术美感。相比之下，德庇时翻译的《老生儿》和《汉宫秋》则尽可能完整地翻译了曲白，更多地保留了元杂剧原本的艺术风貌，由此使西方读者第一次真正目睹了中国戏曲的体制特征，德庇时由此成为首位完整译介中国戏曲的英国人。英译《老生儿》和《汉宫秋》所据底本皆出自 *Hundred Plays of Yuen*，即明人臧懋循编著的元杂剧选集《元曲选》，又称《元人百种曲》。据此推测，他对中国戏曲的了解应该不止于这两部译作。同时，德庇时把《老生儿》与《汉宫秋》分别冠之以“中国喜剧”（a Chinese comedy）和“中国悲剧”（a Chinese Tragedy），他显然想通过这两部译作展现中国戏曲的全貌，由此推测，在译介二作之前，他对中国戏曲应该有着比较全面的认识。

事实上，《老生儿》文前附有一篇文章，题名《中国戏曲及剧场演出短评》（*A Brief View of the Chinese Drama*，*and of their Theatrical Exhibitions*），

这篇文章虽曰“短评”，篇幅却长达四十余页。作者通过系统梳理早期来华传教士、外交官及旅行家等人的所见所闻，全面介绍了中国戏曲的班社组织结构和存在状态、演员的身份地位和舞台表演、舞台的选址搭建和结构特征，这些内容对于研究清代中期的中国戏曲，以及19世纪20年代之前西方人视野中的中国戏曲，均具有重要参考价值。《短评》没有署名，1818年有评论者在《亚洲杂志》上发文指出《短评》并非德庇时所作，乃是出自英译《老生儿》编者之手，不知何据。[①] 但《短评》之前所附“导言”（Advertisement）提到这部译作“寄自广州”（sent from Canton），而《短评》之后的落款又云“广州1816”，所以笔者依然倾向于认为这篇《短评》出自德庇时之手。

此外，在德庇时1829年出版的英译《汉宫秋》的“前言”（Preface）中，他向西方读者推荐了32种中国戏曲剧目或书名，这些作品同样显示了德庇时对于当时的中国戏曲确实有着系统的把握。根据房燕的研究，这32种中国戏曲涉猎广泛。“就创作年代来讲，所列剧目自唐季始，覆盖元、明、清三代；就创作者、编者来讲，元之王实甫，明之臧懋循，清之李渔、蒋士铨、洪昇、孔尚任等在中国戏曲史上首屈一指的剧作家均在其列；就戏剧载体来讲，既有像《西厢记》《桃花扇》等戏剧单行本的存在，又有像《元人百种曲》《缀白裘》等戏剧结集的收录；就剧作内容来讲，既有表现忠义思想的《虎口余生》，又有屡遭朝廷勒令禁毁的《八美图》《碧玉狮》等剧目，内容可谓殷实丰厚。”[②] 1867年，德庇时的中国戏曲目录被附上中文，收入英国著名汉学家伟烈亚力编著的《汉籍解题》，从而进一步扩大了

---

① “Review of Books”, *The Asiatic Journal*, Vol. V., from January to June, London, 1818, pp. 33 – 37.

② 房燕：《英国汉学家德庇时与中国古典文学的早期海外传播》，硕士学位论文，中国人民大学，2012年。

其影响力。[①] 这份戏曲目录不但为此后的汉语学习者和研究者提供了资料来源，也为中国戏曲的西译打开了方便之门。

（三）《汉文诗解》与《三国志节译文》

在中国诗歌翻译方面，德庇时的《汉文诗解》为中国诗歌的英译树立了第一块丰碑，它是第一部尝试着全面、系统地介绍中国古典诗歌的专著，在欧洲流传甚广，影响颇大，堪称西方中国诗学研究的奠基之作。《汉文诗解》结构清晰，内容明朗，全书共分两个部分，分别以“part one”“part two”加以标注。第一部分探讨中国诗歌的创作技巧和形式特征，主要论及以下六方面问题：汉语的发音特点及适于韵文创作的特性；汉语的四声和平仄；中国诗歌的字数；中国诗歌的停顿；中国诗歌的押韵；中国诗歌的对仗。总的来说，他对中国诗歌艺术形式的探讨全面而深入。第二部分总结中国诗歌的题材内容和精神风貌，他将中国诗歌划分为三大类：颂歌和歌曲（Odes and Songs）；道德说教类诗歌（Moral and Didactic Pieces）；描述情感类诗歌（Descriptive and Sentimental）。

整体看来，以上三类内容的划分不但缺乏统一的分类标准，也难以含纳文中具体引述的实际诗篇。尽管上述分类方式如今看来并不科学、严谨，但德庇时却通过比较分析，凸显了中西诗歌的显著差异，他对史诗、田园诗和戏剧诗的研究尤见功力，对于《春园采茶词》等民间诗作的重视，以及对于出自中国人之手的西洋风情诗《伦敦十咏》《西洋杂咏》的青睐，均

① Alexander Wylie, *Notes on Chinese Literature*: *with Introductory Remarks on the Progressive Advancement of the Art*; *and a list of Chinese Translations from Chinese into Various European Languages*, London: Trübner & Co. 60, Paternoster Row, 1867, p. 28.

具有开创性和启发性。

1870 年版“增订本”《汉文诗解》共引用中国诗歌、韵文 100 首。这些诗歌上起秦汉，下逮明清，有出自诗坛巨擘之手的律诗、绝句，也有出自无名氏之手的里巷民谣，无论是时间跨度之长，还是诗歌类型之多，在中国诗歌英译史上都堪称绝无仅有。该作对于考察德庇时等 19 世纪初期英国人对于中国诗歌的认知和解读，以及研究中国诗歌的早期海外传播均具有重要参考价值。①

德庇时英译的《三国志节译文》即刊载于《汉文诗解》。《汉文诗解》先后出版过三个版本，简单说来，包括 1829 年伦敦出版的“首刊本”、1834 年澳门出版的“澳门本”，以及 1870 年伦敦出版的“增订本”。《三国志节译文》仅出现于“澳门本”，且作为“附录”刊载于《汉文诗解》正文之后，再加上该版本在当时印量有限，故在学界罕有人知。

尽管德庇时的三国译作湮没不闻，但其学术价值却不容低估。《三国志节译文》之前有篇“导言”（Introduction），这篇文前小序篇幅虽短，却具有重要学术价值。

首先，它为《三国演义》的海外译介提供了新的起点。在“导言”中，德庇时说：“该作已被寓居中国多年、而今担任卢卡尼亚大主教（Archbishop of Luconia）的塞吉神父（Padre Segui）全部或部分地译成了西班牙文。此外，皇家亚洲学会（The Royal Asiatic Society）还有一个以前的拉丁文译本。”② 1836 年，德庇时在《中国人：中华帝国及其居民概述》（*The Chinese: A general description of the Empire of China and its Inhabitants*）一书中又提到上述拉丁文译本，他说：“公元 184 年汉代走向衰亡时国家分裂成三

① 王燕、房燕：《〈汉文诗解〉与中国诗歌的早期海外传播》，《文艺理论研究》2012 年第 3 期。

② John Francis Davis，汉文诗解，*Poeseos Sinensis Commentarii*，*On the Poetry of the Chinese*，Macao，China：Printed at the Honorable East India Company's Press，By G. J. Steyn and Brother，1834，pp. 156 – 157.

国，这是中国历史剧和冒险故事特别钟爱的主题。其中，有一部专门用‘三国’命名的作品备受瞩目，非常流行，皇家亚洲学会图书馆里有一部某天主教传教士翻译的拉丁文译本手稿本。”① 1865 年，德庇时在整理再版自己的文集《中国杂记：随笔和评论集》（*Chinese Miscellanies*：*A Collextion of Essays and Notes*）时再次提到拉丁文译本，他说：“皇家亚洲学会保存的一本拉丁文译本，至今尚未被转译为英语。”② 德庇时提供的上述信息是探索《三国演义》早期译本的重要线索，只是后来真正著录德庇时提及的拉丁文译本和西班牙译本的资料非常罕见。1841 年 2 月，伦敦布道会传教士美魏茶在《中国丛报》上发表了一篇根据《三国演义》介绍“黄巾起义”的文章，其中称“一位西班牙著者称曹操是‘中国的波拿巴’”。他所说的这个西班牙译者也许就是塞吉神父。③ 1881 年，法国汉学家兼目录学家高第（Henri Cordier，1849—1925）在他编著的《中国书目》（*Bibliotheca Sinica*）中原文引用了德庇时在《汉文诗解》“导言”中所提供的西班牙文和拉丁文译本信息。④ 1986 年，苏尔梦（Claudine Salmon）在《文化移植》一书中说：“西方翻译这部小说（《三国演义》）的首次尝试使用的是西班牙语和拉丁语，似乎是在 19 世纪之始。”⑤ 除了类似的点滴转引，目前学界对于德庇时提及的两个译本尚无研究，这两个译本目前是否存世也不得而知。但若他的记载无误，西班牙译本当是 19 世纪初的译作，而拉丁文译本也许时间更早，或为《三国演义》西行之旅的真正起点。

---

① Sir John Francis Davis, *The Chinese*: *A General Description of the Empire of China*, *and its Inhabitants*, London: Charles knight, 22, Ludgate Street, 1836, Vol. Ⅰ, p. 176.

② Sir John Francis Davis, *Chinese Miscellanies*: *A Collection of Essays and Notes*, London: John Murray Albemarle Street, 1865, p. 66.

③ William Charles Milne, "The Rebellion of the Yellow Caps", *Chinese Repository*, Vol Ⅹ., Feb. 1841.

④ Henri Cordier, *Bibliotheca Sinica*, Paris: E. Leroux, 1881, Vol. Ⅰ., pp. 804 – 805.

⑤ Edited by Claudine Salmon, *Literary Migrations*: *Traditional Chinese Fiction in Asia* (17*th*-20*th Centuries*), Singapore: Institute of Southeast Asian Studies, 2013, p. 30.

其次，德庇时关于“演义”的讨论为我们重新审视这一文体的特殊性提供了理论依据。“导言”开篇伊始，德庇时就说：“The Historical Romance of San-kwŏ，or the Three States，commences about A. D. 170，and，for a Chinese or Oriental work，it is as little deformed by extravagancies as could be expected。”即：“《三个国家的历史传奇》讲述的内容大约开始于公元 170 年，作为一部中文作品，或者说是东方作品，其中的夸张成分比我们预想的要少得多。”值得注意的是，在此，他将《三国志演义》译作“The Historical Romance of San-kwŏ”，描述文体的核心词用的是“传奇”（romance）。在西方文学中，“传奇”指的是浪漫史或冒险故事，这是一种与“历史”迥然有别的虚构性文学作品。但在后来的《中国人：中华帝国及其居民概述》一书中，德庇时又用“历史”一词来描述这一作品的文体属性。在介绍历史上的“三国时期”（The period of the San-kuo）时，他说：“It is，however，as little stuffed with extravagancies as could be expected from an oriental history。”在此，德庇时把《三国演义》看作一部“东方历史”（an oriental history）。究竟是“传奇”还是“历史”，直到 1865 年在《中国杂记：随笔和评论集》中，德庇时才作了进一步的区分，他说：“The San-kwŏ-che，which is rather a historical novel than a history，has not been much noticed。”即：“《三国志》（The San-kwŏ-che）尚未引起太多关注，该作与其说是一部历史，不如说是一部历史小说（historical novel）。”[①] 这个迟来的判断，恰恰道出了“演义”这一文体的特殊性：它是一种介于小说与历史之间的文体，或许也是中国所特有的一种文体，故在西方文类中很难找到一个合适的对应词。

德庇时对于《三国演义》文体类别的探讨有着特殊的研究价值。在 19 世纪汉学家中，很少有人像德庇时那样对中国文学有着全面的认识，他的

---

① Sir John Francis Davis, *Chinese Miscellanies: A Collection of Essays and Notes*, London: John Murray Albemarle Street, 1865, p. 66.

翻译和研究广泛涉及中国小说、戏曲与诗歌，对于中国历史和文化也有深入探讨。虽然德庇时在“小说”与“历史”之间，将《三国演义》明确划入“小说”或“传奇”等虚构性文学作品行列，但在提及或具体运用这部作品时，德庇时却更喜欢将之纳入“历史”的门下。比如，在《中国人：中华帝国及其居民概述》中，德庇时在介绍历史上的“三国时期”时论及《三国演义》；在《中国杂记：随笔和评论集》中，德庇时也在介绍中国史书时提及《三国演义》。而在介绍中国小说时，他却只评论李渔的小说和《好逑传》，对于《三国演义》只字不提。这就使《三国演义》在“名”“实”之间处于一种尴尬的境地，明明是“小说”却被当作中国历史读本看待。在中国当然也存在这种情况，但与德庇时等西方读者不同的是，在涉及具体事件和人物时，中国读者还是会有意识地将历史真实与文学虚构区别看待，不会轻易将二者混为一谈。但在 19 世纪早期的海外汉学界，西方关于中国的整体知识相对匮乏，《三国演义》中的想象与夸张、奸诈与计谋、嗜血与屠杀，却很容易被看作中国历史上的普遍现象，这显然扭曲了中国形象，不利于中国形象的海外建构。

作为一个来自英语世界的译者，两种语言文化的碰撞自然让译者具备一种比较的视野与批评的眼光。在评论《三国演义》时，德庇时主要将《三国演义》与《荷马史诗》做了对比，其对比首先出现在《三国志节译文》的“导言”中，类似的表述在他两年后写就的《中国人：中华帝国及其居民概述》一书中也有阐发，这为我们考察中西方语境中的《三国演义》提供了可能。

第一，在语言方面，德庇时认为：《三国演义》虽然出之以“散文”，但某些特点却与用“诗歌”创作的《伊利亚特》（*The Iliad*）有些相似，尤其是在英雄们所使用的“守门人般的语言”（the porter-like language）方面。

“守门人般的语言”出自查斯特菲尔德勋爵（Lord Chesterfield，1694—1773）的《教子书》（*Letters to His Son*）。查斯特菲尔德勋爵是英国著名政治家、外交家，曾担任海牙大使、爱尔兰总督、英国国务大臣；同时，他还是一位优秀的随笔作家，成名作《教子书》至今风行于世，目前已有多个中文译本。这是一部写给儿子的书信体散文集，其中的家书不但写得款款有致，充满深情，而且被誉为“培养绅士的教科书”。作者对18世纪英国鼎盛时期的社会礼仪和行为规范有着切身体验和敏锐观察，《教子书》由此成为研习上流社会处世哲学和社会风尚的经典之作。在1750年11月写给儿子的一封信中，查斯特菲尔德勋爵叮嘱儿子说：为了成为一个博学多识的人，一定要每天坚持学习希腊文，阅读希腊书；同时强调：“我所说的并非是希腊诗人的作品，不要去读阿克那里翁（Anacreon）的感人诗篇，或者忒奥克里托斯（Theocritus）的温柔哀叹，乃至荷马（Homer）写的英雄们的‘守门人般的语言’，对于这些，所有一知半解的人都略知一二，反复引用，经常谈及。我指的是柏拉图（Plato）、亚里士多德（Aristoteles）、德摩斯梯尼（Demosthenes）和修西底德斯（Thucydides），这些人只有专家才知晓。希腊文能让你在知识界脱颖而出，仅会拉丁文是不够的。”[①] 在此，作者并没有对“守门人般的语言”多加解释，但从上下语境中不难看出他是在委婉地批评《荷马史诗》的语言过于通俗，乃至英雄人物说出的也是普通人乃至“守门人”般的粗鄙之言。

在欧美文学传统中批评《荷马史诗》用语粗俗的声音并不罕见。海伊特（Gilbert Highet，1906—1978）在《古典传统：希腊罗马对西方文学的影响》（*The Classical Tradition：Greek and Roman Influences on Western Literature*）一书中就曾指出，在古典诗歌与现代诗歌之间，有人认为“古典诗歌粗俗，因为它们描述寻常事物，使用不够庄重的言辞；他们的男女英雄性格暴躁，甚至亲手劳作。而路易十四（Louis XIV）时代的现代诗人就不写这些东西。

① Philip Dormer Stanhope Earl of Chesterfield，*The Work of Lord Chesterfield*，New York：Harper & Brothers，Cliff Street，1838，p. 361.

所以，现代诗人更为优秀。比如佩罗（Perrault）嘲笑荷马描写一个公主到河里与宫女们一起为她的兄弟们洗衣服；最有绅士风度的查斯特菲尔德勋爵也看不起荷马写的英雄们的‘守门人般的语言’；品味高雅、思想高贵的读者骇然震惊于《荷马史诗》竟然提及家畜、家用器皿等东西，用荷马率真的语言来说，就是奶牛和煮锅。在《荷马史诗》中最受指责的一段是一个著名的比喻，英雄埃阿斯（Ajax）在特洛伊人的猛烈攻击下慢慢撤退，他被比作一头误入牧场的驴，当孩子们用棍子驱赶它时，它还倔强地啃着谷物。现代诗人说，驴这个词不该被纳入英雄史诗，把一个王子比作一头蠢驴，更有着难以言喻的粗俗”。[①] 在查斯特菲尔德勋爵等人看来，奶牛和煮锅等家畜和家用器皿尚且粗俗不雅，与之相比，《三国志节译文》中出现的“猪羊狗血并秽物”就更是肮脏不堪了。

第二，德庇时虽然有意识地将《三国演义》与《荷马史诗》进行了比较，但他的比较仅三言两语，且流于表面，不够深入。他说：“《三国》英雄在力量与英勇方面均超过了所有的现代人，他们像格劳科斯（Glaucus）与狄俄墨得斯（Diomed）、埃阿斯（Ajax）与赫克托耳（Hector）那样进行交换。一个拥有一把重达 80 斤的刀，另一个则广有马匹、银两和镔铁，所谓：‘钢铁精炼，黄金灿烂。’”[②] 最后两句英文诗——And steel well-temper'd, and refulgent gold——引自英国 18 世纪伟大诗人蒲柏（Alexander Pope, 1688—1744）英译的《伊利亚特》。此处提到的两对《荷马史诗》英雄人物之间的“交换”（exchanges）是《伊利亚特》中两个广为人知的桥段。当代表两军出战的格劳科斯与狄俄墨得斯得知他们先祖之间的友情时，两人不但当即握手言和，而且交换了武器，格劳科斯用自己价值一百头牛

---

① Gilbert Highet, *The Classical Tradition: Greek and Roman Influences on Western Literature*, Oxford University Press, 1985, p. 272.

② John Francis Davis, 汉文诗解, *Poeseos Sinensis Commentarii*, *On the Poetry of the Chinese*, Macao, China: Printed at the Honorable East India Company's Press, By G. J. Steyn and Brother, 1834, p. 155.

的金甲换回了狄俄墨得斯价值九头牛的铜衣，这显示了希腊英雄对于先祖情义的尊崇。另一对希腊英雄埃阿斯与赫克托耳经过一场恶战，难分胜负，最后握手言和，交换礼物，其中透露着英雄们之间的惺惺相惜与彼此敬畏。在德庇时译介的两段译文中，并没有出现敌对的双方彼此交流、握手言欢，甚至交换兵器、以示敬重的情节。结合后面的文字："一把 80 斤重的刀，以及马匹、银两和镔铁，"这段评论更像是对《三国演义》第一回中出现的一段文字的转述："玄德请二人到庄，置酒管待，诉说欲讨贼安民之意。二客大喜，愿将良马五十匹相送，又赠金银五百两、镔铁一千斤，以资器用。玄德谢别二客，便命良匠打造双股剑；云长造青龙偃月刀，又名冷艳锯，重八十二斤；张飞造丈八点钢矛；各置全身铠甲。"[①] 对比原文，德庇时的转述显然不够准确。由此可见，虽然德庇时有一种跨文化比较的冲动与眼光，但在具体人物与情节的引用和评论上还不够谨慎，得出的结论也相对肤浅。

尽管如此，随着《三国演义》的不断译介，德庇时的观点在 19 世纪后半期也还是得到了一定关注。1876 年，英国旅行家兼摄影家约翰·汤姆森（John Thomson，1837—1921）在《中国的土地与人民》（*The Land and the People of China*）一书中引用了德庇时的观点。[②] 1877 年，威廉·斯皮尔（William Speer，1822 – 1904）在《最古老与最年轻的帝国：中国与美国》（*The Oledst and the Newest Empire*：*China and the United States*）一书中原文引述了德庇时的观点。[③] 1882 年，美国汉学家卫三畏在修订版《中国总论》（*The Middle Kingdom*）中再次提及德庇时的观点。但质疑的声音也并非没

① （明）罗贯中著，（清）毛宗岗批注：《第一才子书三国演义》，线装书局出版社 2007 年版，第 5 页。

② John Thomson，*The Land and the People of China*，London；New York：Pott，Young & Co. 1876，p. 62.

③ William Speer，*The Oldest and the Newest Empire*：*China and the United States*，Pittsburgh，PA.：Robert S. Davis & Co. 1877，p. 170.

有，1890 年，第一个全译《三国演义》的英国人邓罗就在《中国评论》上发表评论文《三国》（*The San-Kuo*），深入分析了这种平行比较的不足。[①]

（四）中文校勘与英文评议

德庇时译文最显著的特点是它第一次以中英文合璧的方式翻译并排印了《三国演义》，他对自己的这一创新颇为得意，在“导言”中说：“我们的这个译本是第一个尝试着把中英文交替排印的本子，这种设计或许有利于汉语的学习。”此前，第一位英国来华新教传教士马礼逊已对《三国演义》有所译介，甚至提倡模仿《三国演义》文白相生的语言来中译《圣经》。除了马礼逊，东印度公司的印刷工汤姆斯也翻译有《著名丞相董卓之死》。整体看来，马礼逊编辑的《华英字典》和汉语教材虽引用了《三国演义》中的个别字句，但没有完整翻译一个章节，所以，马礼逊对《三国演义》的英译可以说是仅有首倡之功而终乏译介之力；汤姆斯围绕董卓生平完整译介了“连环计”，内容主要取自《三国演义》毛评本第八回和第九回。1820—1821 年，汤译文分三次连载于《亚洲杂志》，译文虽长，但始终没有出现一个汉字。相比之下，德庇时的《三国志节译文》确实是第一次排印《三国演义》中文文字的译文，对于学习汉语的西方读者应该具有一定的参考价值，同时，中文的在场也使西方读者亲眼见证了《三国演义》的文字特点和历史风貌。

---

① Brewitt-Taylor, “The San-Kuo”, *The China Review, or Notes & Queries on the Far East*. Vol. 19, No. 3, 1890, p. 170.

考察译者采用的原著底本是研究译作的必要基础。通过对比《三国志节译文》的中文部分不难发现：在《三国演义》各版本系统中，德庇时采用的中文底本是毛评本《三国演义》。他从第二回“张翼德怒鞭督邮 何国舅谋诛宦竖”和第三回“议温明董卓叱丁原 馈金珠李肃说吕布”中摘译了两个故事：一是《造反的张氏三兄弟的命运》；一是《何进的历史与命运》。第一个故事始自“董卓当日怠慢了玄德”，止于“隽与玄德关张率三军掩杀射死韩忠”。第二个故事始自“中平六年夏四月”，止于“伏甲齐出，将何进砍为两段”。在“导言”中，德庇时说：“第一个选段讲的是张宝（Chang-paou）、张梁（Chang-leang）、张角（Chang-keo）三个造反兄弟的命运，还描述了一场攻城战。第二个选段有力地展示了何进的历史，以及在中国历史中发挥了重要作用的宦官的恶权。”① 德庇时想通过这两个故事的翻译来展现《三国演义》的全貌。他认为《三国演义》体制庞大、内容复杂，“从中摘译一部分内容非常有趣，但将之全部翻译成英文出版或许就太过卷帙浩繁了。”② 在他看来，在当时的条件下全译《三国演义》还只是一个“亟待实现的梦”③。

原著底本确定后，文字校勘是分析译者翻译策略的首要前提。德庇时虽然采用的是毛评本《三国演义》，但在排印时却删除了所有注释和评论性文字，仅保留了原作的正文部分。排版采用中文传统竖版，不加标点不分段。中文部分共 16 页，每页 12 行，每行 18 字，整体看来字迹清晰，排列整齐。尽管如此，细加阅读，不难发现，其中鲁鱼亥豕、纰漏频繁，每页

---

① John Francis Davis，汉文诗解，*Poeseos Sinensis Commentarii*，*On the Poetry of the Chinese*，Macao，China：Printed at the Honorable East India Company's Press，By G. J. Steyn and Brother，1834，pp. 156.

② John Francis Davis，*The Chinese*：*A General Description of the Empire of China*，*and its Inhabitants*，London：Charles Knight，22，Ludgate Street，1836，Vol. I.，p. 176.

③ John Francis Davis，汉文诗解，*Poeseos Sinensis Commentarii*，*On the Poetry of the Chinese*，Macao，China：Printed at the Honorable East India Company's Press，By G. J. Steyn and Brother，1834，pp. 156.

的错字、漏字、左右交换、上下颠倒少则三五处，多则七八处，错误层出不穷，校勘相当粗疏。如 158 页：“张宝遣副将高昇出马搦战，玄德使张飞击之，飞纵马挺矛与昇交战”，句中“昇”字前后出现两次，且并列排印，组成“昇”字的上下两字竟然不同，前者为上“曰”下“升”，后者为上“曰”下“弁”。又如 186 页：“张让等悔僈天帝”一句，原著为“张让等侮慢天常”，后面的四个字竟然错了三个，“侮慢”误作“悔僈”应是刻字时交换了两字的偏旁。这种一目了然的错误竟然没被检索出来，一方面说明刻工和排字工人文化水平低劣，另一方面也显示了德庇时的中文校勘能力不容高估。

英译《三国演义》之前，德庇时已翻译过大量中国文学作品，所以对于《三国演义》的翻译可谓驾轻就熟、得心应手。首先，三国人物众多，情节复杂，德庇时只是选译了其中的两个故事，这样就大大精简了人物与情节。在原著中，何进的历史主要出现在第二回，到了第三回，何进听从袁绍建议，引董卓入京，才加速了他的灭亡。为了确保故事的流畅，德庇时在中文部分就删除了第二回最后的尾评诗、第三回的回目及开头第一段，英文部分也做了相应删减，如此处理自然减少了枝蔓。其次，在英译文中，为了进一步减少复杂的人物和情节带来的阅读障碍，德庇时删除了原著中某些一闪而过的人物和地名。如，“何进引何颙、荀攸、郑泰等大臣三十余员相继而入”，英文译作：Ho-tsin assembling about thirty of the principal officers of the court，they proceeded in a body to the palace。又如，“自己却带李傕、郭汜、张济、樊稠等提兵望洛阳进发”，英文译作：He proceeded in person with his other leaders towards Lŏ-yang，the Capital。再如，“乃先伏刀斧手五十人于长乐宫嘉德门内”，英文译作：They accordingly placed fifty armed men in ambush within the palace。上述三句中出现的具体人名和地名均被删除。再者，为了避免繁杂的人名字号、官职头衔带来的困惑，译者始终采用“一人一名”的翻译方式。如袁绍出场时，中文曰：“进视之，乃司徒袁逢之子，袁隗之侄，名绍，字本初，见（现）为司隶校尉。”英文译作：Ho-tsin observed that the speaker was Yuen-shaou，the son of Yuen-foong。即：“何进发现说话的人是袁逢之子袁绍。”经过如此精心的删减，德庇时的译文整体读来简洁流畅、文理自然。

当然，明显的错误和精彩的语句交互出现也是德庇时译作的显著特点。有些译文中文部分出错，但英文部分却做了补充修订。如中文曰：“朱隽进攻张宝，（张宝）引贼众八九万屯于山后。”中文漏掉了“张宝”二字。英文译作：While Choo-tsëen threatened Chang-paou，the latter had entrenched himself with an army of eight or ninety thousand men behind a mountain。“张宝”二字如数译出。有些译文中文部分出错，英文部分也跟着译错。如中文部分误把“王美人”刻成了“玉美人”，英文部分也相应地将之错译为 Yu-mei-jin。还有些译文是中文部分正确，但英文部分却解释错误。如，中文曰：“张让等知事急，慌入告何后。”英文译作：The eunuchs，seeing themselves reduced to extremity，went altogether to the empress，the mother of Ho-tsin。“何后”乃“何进之妹”，译者却解释为“何进之母”。

除了这些显而易见的错误，不可否认，德庇时英译文中也有许多精彩的语句。如，中文曰：“袁绍（若）曰，不斩草除根，必为丧身之本。”英文译作：To this Yuen-shaou observed，that if they did not effectually remove the weeds，their remaining roots might become a source of danger。在此，“斩草除根”这一成语翻译得相当传神。又如，中文曰：“扬汤止沸，不如去薪；溃痈虽痛，胜于养毒。”英文译作：but the best mode of stopping the ebullition of the cauldron is to withdraw the fuel；and though to get rid of the peccant humor（编者按：humor 应为 tumor）be painful，it is better than letting the poison continue。这两句英译文虽不如中文读起来铿锵有力，但其中隐含的逻辑关系却被充分地揭示了出来。类似的点睛之笔穿插在平实的叙述中，自然增加了译文的可读性。

（五）《三国志节译文》的影响与接受

《三国志节译文》附录于1834 年“澳门本”《汉文诗解》之后，这种出版方式使这一译作本身就很容易被学界忽略，而且这一版本印量有限，所以很难说德庇时英译的《三国演义》在当时产生过广泛影响。造成这种情况的原因主要有两方面。

首先，德庇时本人对《三国志节译文》这部译作的刊印不够重视。德庇时翻译的小说、戏曲和诗歌，多数首先在杂志上发表，然后再出单行本。即便是像《汉宫秋》那样篇幅不足 40 页的短剧，也印有单行本。单行本出版后，德庇时还常在其他杂志或著作中反复引用，多次论及。而《三国志节译文》却被当作附录出版，不但没有单行本，而且此后他也没再强调过自己的这篇译作。由此可见，德庇时对于《三国志节译文》的刊印确实不够积极，个中缘由或许与另一位《三国演义》的译者汤姆斯有关。

1830 年《亚洲杂志》发表了一篇题为《中国诗歌翻译评论》（*On Translation of Chinese Poetry*）的文章，作者自称是一位“中国文学的爱好者与研究者”（an admirer and a student of Chinese Literature），该文站在汤姆斯的立场上批评德庇时英译的《好逑传》（*The Fortunate Union*）译笔拙劣。[①] 开篇伊始，作者指出：有英国评论员声称德庇时是“唯一有能力翻译中国诗歌的人”，这种横扫一切的评论是想故意贬低另一部英译中国诗

① “On Translation of Chinese Poetry”, *The Asiatic Journal*, London: Parbury, Allen, And Co., Vol. Ⅱ., New Series. May-August. 1830, pp. 32 – 37.

歌——汤姆斯翻译的《花笺记》（*The Chinese Courtship*）。在《中国诗歌翻译评论》的作者看来，虽然德庇时具有长期学习汉语的优越条件，又有中国本土生活经验以及当地人的帮助，但从《好逑传》英译诗歌的翻译质量来看，德庇时其实不具有翻译中国诗歌的能力。文章同时透露，德庇时对于汤姆斯的翻译颇不以为然，他在《好逑传》的“序言”（Preface）中曾暗讽汤姆斯在他英译的《花笺记》和《宋金郎团圆破毡笠》中用“夫人”“小姐”等称呼中国的女性或婢女，德庇时认为这种译法不但荒唐可笑，而且有违于原著。

由此可见，德庇时与汤姆斯虽然都是19世纪二三十年代在中国小说翻译领域用力颇勤、成就显著的业余汉学家，但两人的关系却非常微妙。《中国诗歌翻译评论》的作者明显回护汤姆斯而批判德庇时，由此推测，作者如果不是汤姆斯本人，也该是非常熟悉或支持汤姆斯译作的英国人。鉴于当时有能力翻译和评论中国诗歌并在《亚洲杂志》上发表中国译作的英国人实在屈指可数，笔者倾向于认为这篇文章的作者就是汤姆斯本人。文章的最后，汤姆斯对德庇时再译《好逑传》这样一部已经被英译过的作品深表遗憾。同时希望德庇时的下一部译作是《诗经》（*She-king*），他说如果德庇时果真承担起翻译《诗经》的重担，那他的汉学成就或许可以达到斯当东爵士（Sir George Staunton）的水平。斯当东在当时因翻译《大清律例》而享有盛誉。但对于德庇时来说，汤姆斯的这种建议却充满揶揄和讥讽。更何况，汤姆斯早在1820年就翻译了《三国演义》中的两个章节，并在《亚洲杂志》上公开发表，德庇时步其后尘，十年后才开始着手翻译《三国演义》，作为一位有身份的贵族学者，他或许不愿意再被汤姆斯这样一位名不见经传的“印刷工”公开批评，所以宁愿把《三国志节译文》附录在《汉文诗解》之后。

其次，当时的英国人对中国文学和中国历史了解有限，整体文化氛围不利于《三国演义》这样的长篇小说广泛传播，这应该是《三国志节译文》

不被重视的重要原因。

在中国文学英译方面，不妨从《汉文诗解》的初版来看当时英国人对中国诗歌的接受。德庇时在 1870 年“增订本”《汉文诗解》的“导言”（Introduction）中曾提到该作最初发表时遇到的某些尴尬，他说：“当这本专著第一次在四开本的《皇家亚洲学会会刊》上用中国带来的字模排印出版时（距今已有四十多年了），上面的中国字在英国鲜为人知，乃至一贯幽默的帕默斯顿勋爵（Lord Palmerston）说他‘乍一看竟把它当成了一本昆虫学著作。’”在汉字尚且陌生的年代，很难想象当时的英国人会对中国文学抱有热情。美国汉学家哈特（Henry H. Hart）在《百姓诗》（*Poems of the Hundred Names*）中也曾指出：鸦片战争之前，英国远离中国，对中国所知甚少，在当时，不必说普通民众，“对于那时的英国评论家来说，中国以及中国的诗歌都是古怪、乏味而难以理解的。”[①] 由此可见，《汉文诗解》及《三国演义》在鸦片战争之前几乎不可能拥有一个广阔的阅读市场。

在中国历史英译方面，鸦片战争前夕的英国汉学界同样乏善可陈。1865 年，德庇时在《中国杂记：随笔和评论集》中说：“耶稣会士冯秉正（the Jesuit Mailla）早在 1770 年就在北京翻译了《通鉴纲目》（*Tung-kien-kang-mo*），巴黎出版，四开本，12 卷；但这部书的收益却抵不上付出，该作虽然多年来被大量参考，可是除了汉学家（sinologues），它几乎无人知晓。《三国志》尚未引起太多关注，它与其说是一部历史，不如说是一部历史小说。皇家亚洲学会保存的一本拉丁文译本，至今尚未被转译为英语。因此，它所使用的定然是时至今日依然有别于世界上其他国家的一种内部的编年史。”[②] 由此可见，在当时，《通鉴纲目》这样的历史著作尚且仅有少数汉学

① Henry H. Hart, *Poems of the Hundred Names*, Stanford, California: Stanford University Press, 1954, p. 2.

② Sir John Francis Davis, *Chinese Miscellanies: A Collection of Essays and Notes*, London: John Murray Albemarle Street, 1865, p. 66.

家知道，《三国演义》这样的“演义”之作，自然也不可能引起“太多关注”。在这种情况下，很难想象《三国志节译文》在当时能产生广泛影响。

尽管从接受史的角度来看，《三国志节译文》影响有限，但作为中英文合璧刊印《三国演义》的第一次尝试，德庇时的译文依然有着重要的学术价值：作为《三国演义》英译史上的重要一环，它在研究该作的早期海外传播上不可或缺，在研究维多利亚时代来临前夕的英国对于中国文化的理解与接受方面，也是一个难得的个案，它以自身独特的存在言说着那时中国文学在西方的真实处境和步履维艰。

附：英文原文

志國三①

TRANSLATED EXTRACTS FROM THE HISTORY OF THE THREE STATES

INTRODUCTION

The Historical Romance of San-kwŏ, or the Three States, commences about A. D. 170, and, for a Chinese or Oriental work, it is as little deformed by extravagancies as could be expected. It bears some resemblance, in what Lord Chesterfield calls "the porter-like language" of its heroes, to the Iliad. These heroes, in like manner, surpass all moderns in strength and prowess, and make exchanges after the fashion of Glaucus and Diomed, Ajax and Hector. One possesses a sword weighing 80 kin, another shews his liberality in horses, silver, a *weight of iron*,

① John Francis Davis, 汉文诗解, *Poeseos Sinensis Commentarii*, *On the Poetry of the Chinese*, Macao, China: Printed at the Honorable East India Company's Press, By G. J. Steyn and Brother, 1834, pp. 153 – 191.

"And steel well-temper'd, and refulgent gold."

Society seems to have been in much the same state, as it was split into something like feudal principalities, hanging loosely together under the questionable authority of one head. That great step in civilization, the important invention of printing, had not yet taken place,① and even the manufacture of paper had only just been introduced.

The reigns of the last Emperors of the Han Dynasty, Ling-te and Hëen-te, were disturbed by their wars with the revolted Hwong-kin, or 'yellow caps', and by the machinations of the eunuchs of the palace. At this time, so little was left of the sovereign authority, that the Emperors are frequently styled by historians only Choo, or Lord. Tung-chŏ, who bears a very bad character in the San-kwŏ, being the general of the last sovereign of Han contrived to murder his master, and usurp the throne, but was soon afterwards put to death.

The first extract here given, with the original text, relates the fate of the three rebel brothers, Chang-paou, Chang-leang, and Chang-keo, and describes a siege. The second strongly displays, in the history of Ho-tsin, the mischievous power of the eunuchs, a remarkable feature in Chinese history. 'The yellow caps' were in time destroyed by Tsaou-tsaou, who in his turn usurped the Empire, but was finally exiled. Lew-pei of the imperial race, who makes a great figure in this history, finally became the founder of the How-Han, or Han restored, under the name of Chaou-leih, A. D. 226.

The two specimens now printed may serve to shew how far an English translation of the whole work, which is pretty voluminous, might be considered as a desideratum. It has been translated into Spanish, the whole or in part, by Padre-

① Chinese annals place it in the 10th century of our era.

Segui, many years resident in China, and now Archbishop of Luconia. There is, besides, an old Latin translation belong to the Royal Asiatic Society. Our's is the first attempt to print Chinese and English in alternate pages, a plan which might be found useful in studying the language.

中文回译

《三国志节译文》[①]

导　言

《三个国家的历史传奇》（*The Historical Romance of San-kwŏ*）讲述的内容大约开始于公元170年，作为一部中文作品，或者说是东方作品，其中的夸张成分比我们预想的要少得多。该作与《伊利亚特》（Iliad）有某些相似之处，查斯特菲尔德勋爵（Lord Chesterfield）就说其英雄人物说的是“守门人般的语言”（the porter-like language）。其英雄在力量与英勇方面均超过了所有的现代人，他们像格劳科斯（Glaucus）与狄俄墨得斯（Diomed）、埃阿斯（Ajax）与赫克托耳（Hector）那样进行交换。一个拥有一把重达80斤的刀，另一个则广有马匹、银两和镔铁，所谓：“钢铁精炼，黄金灿烂。”

社会似乎停滞不前，被分裂成几个有点像封建领地的邦国，一起松散地挂靠在一个有问题的政权之下。那时尚没有文明的伟大进步和印刷的重大发明，[②] 就连纸张的生产也才刚刚起步。

---

① 编者按：德庇时：《汉文诗解》，澳门出版，1834年，第153—191页。

② 中国史书记载，印刷术出现在公元10世纪。

汉朝的最后两个皇帝——灵帝、献帝（Ling-te and Hëen-te）——统治时期，朝廷与反叛的黄巾军之间的战争，以及宫中宦官的阴谋，造成一片混乱。就在这时，皇帝的权威所剩无几，以致史学家们经常用“主”（Choo，or Load）来称呼皇帝。董卓（Tung-chŏ）在《三国》中性情暴虐，作为汉朝最后一个皇帝的将军，他想方设法杀了主子，篡夺王位，但不久以后他也被杀了。

这里的摘译附有中文原文，第一个选段讲的是张宝（Chang-paou）、张梁（Chang-leang）、张角（Chang-keo）三个造反兄弟的命运，还描述了一场攻城战。第二个选段有力地展示了何进的历史，以及在中国历史中发挥了重要作用的宦官的恶权。“黄巾”军被曹操及时地摧毁了，他接着篡夺了君权，但最后却被放逐了。皇室后裔刘备在这部史书中格外引人注意，最终，他在公元 226 年，以“昭烈”（Chaou-leih）的名义，成了后汉（How-Han）或曰复辟的汉朝的创建者。

目前发表的这两个选段，可以用来展示该作的英文全译本会是什么样，那会相当卷帙浩繁，或许是个亟待实现的梦。《三国志》已被寓居中国多年、而今担任卢卡尼亚大主教（Archbishop of Luconia）的塞吉神父（Padre Segui）全部或部分地译成了西班牙文。此外，皇家亚洲学会（The Royal Asiatic Society）还有一个以前的拉丁文译本。我们的这个译本是第一个尝试着把中英文交替排印的本子，这种设计或许有利于汉语的学习。

文献图片

《三国志节译文》中文部分影印图片选自《汉文诗解》（1834 年版）第158—191 页。原书中文在左页，英文在右页，以便中英文左右对照阅读。

材料一 《造反的张氏三兄弟的命运》(*Fate of the Three Rebel Brothers Chang*)

158 ***History of the Three States.***

董卓當日怠慢了玄德張飛性發便欲殺之玄德與關公急止之曰他是朝廷命官豈可擅殺飛曰若不殺這厮反要在他部下聽令其實不甘二兄要便住在此我自投別處去也玄德曰我三人義同生死豈可相離不若都投別處去便了飛曰如此稍解吾恨於是三人連夜引軍來投朱儁儁待之甚厚合兵一處進討張寶是時曹操自跟皇甫嵩討張梁大戰于曲陽這裏朱儁進攻張寶引賊衆八九萬屯於山後儁令玄德爲其先鋒與賊對敵張寶遣副將高昇出馬搦戰玄德使張飛擊之飛縱馬挺矛與昇交戰不數合刺昇落馬玄德麾軍直衝過去張寶

EXTRACTS,

&c.

FATE OF THE THREE REBEL BROTHERS CHANG.——MAGIC ARTS, AND A SIEGE DESCRIBED.

Tung-chŏ having treated slightly Lew-pei, the anger of Chang-fei was roused, and he would have slain the aggressor. —Lew-pei with Kwan-koong, however, anxiously restrained him, saying, 'You must let him alone,—he is an especial appointment of the Emperor." "But, said the other, if this fellow goes free, it is very hard upon us to be subject to his insolent sway — Friends, you may remain with him if you chuse: I shall withdraw myself elsewhere!"—" We three, replied Lew-pei, have agreed to live and die in company, and must never separate—let us therefore all retire together." "This, observed Chang-fei, will satisfy my resentment effectually." The three chiefs, accordingly, on the following night withdrew their troops and went over to Choo-tsëen, who received them very honorably, and, joining his forces with theirs, went in pursuit of Chang-paou; meanwhile Tsaou-tsaou himself followed Hwong-foo-soong in search of Chang-leang, giving him battle at Keo-yang. While Choo-tsëen threatened Chang-paou, the latter had entrenched himself with an army of eighty or ninety thousand men behind a mountain, and

就馬上披髮仗劍作起妖法只見風雷大作一股黑氣從天而降黑氣中似有無限人馬殺來玄德連忙回軍軍中大亂敗陣而歸與朱雋計議雋曰彼用妖術我來日可宰猪羊狗血令軍士伏于山頭候賊趕來從高坡上潑之其法可解玄德聽令撥關公張飛各引軍一千伏于山後高崗之上盛猪羊狗血并穢物準備次日張寶搖旗擂鼓引軍搦戰玄德出迎交鋒之際張寶作法風雷大作飛砂走石黑氣漫天滾滾人馬自天而下玄德撥馬便走張寶驅兵趕來將過山頭關張伏兵放起號砲穢物齊潑但見空中紙人草馬紛紛墜地風雷頓息砂石不飛張

Choo-tsëen sent Lew-pei to dislodge him. Chang-paou having deputed his lieutenant Kaou-shing to meet this force, Lew-pei sent Chang-fei to encounter him; and this leader, giving his horse the rein, charged with his spear Kaou-shing, who presently fell dead from his horse. Lew-pei took advantage of this to steal upon Chang-paou with his whole force, to baffle which, the latter mounted his horse, and with dishevelled hair and waving sword betook himself to magic arts. The wind arose, with loud peals of thunder, and there descended from on high a black cloud, in which appeared innumerable men and horses as if engaged.

Lew-pei instantly drew off his troops in confusion, and giving up the contest retreated to consult with Choo-tsëen. The latter observed, 'Let him have recourse again to magic—I will prepare the blood of swine, sheep, and dogs, and placing a party on the heights in ambush, wait until the enemy approaches, when his magic will be all dispersed by projecting the same upon him. Lew-pei assented to this, and directed Kwon-koong and Chang-fei each with a thousand men to ascend the highest part of the mountain, supplied with the blood of swine, sheep, and dogs, with other impure things.

On the following day, Chang-paou with flags displayed and drums beating came forth to offer battle, and Lew-pei proceeded to meet him; but scarcely had they joined, before Chang-paou put his magic in exercise, the wind and thunder arose, and a storm of sand and stones commenced. A

賓見解了法急欲退軍左關公右張飛兩軍都
出背後玄德朱儁一齊趕上賊兵大敗玄德望
見地公將軍旗號飛馬趕來張寶落荒而走玄
德發箭中其左臂張寶帶箭逃脫走入陽城堅
守不出朱儁引兵圍住陽城攻打一面差人打
探曰皇甫嵩消息探子回報且說皇甫嵩大獲
勝捷朝廷以董卓屢敗命嵩代之嵩到時張角
已死張梁統其衆與我軍相拒被皇甫嵩連勝七
陣斬張梁於曲陽發張角之棺戮尸梟首送往
京師餘衆俱降朝廷加皇甫嵩爲車騎將軍
領冀州牧皇甫嵩又表奏盧植有功無罪朝廷
復盧植原官曹操亦以有功除濟南相卽日將

dark cloud obscured the sky, and troops of horsemen seemed to descend. Lew-pei upon this made a shew of retreating, when Chang-paou followed him: but scarcely had they turned the hill when the ambushed troops started up, and lanced upon the enemy their impure stores.—The air seemed immediately filled with paper men, and horses of straw, which fell to the earth in confusion; while the winds and thunder at once ceased, and the sand and stones no longer flew about. When Chang-paou saw his magic thus baffled, he would have quickly retreated, but Kwon-koong on one side, and Chang-fei on the other, made their appearance; while Lew-pei and Choo-tsëen pursued in the rear. The rebels were defeated with great slaughter.

Lew-pei seeing the flag inscribed "Lord of Earth," ran full speed on his horse towards Chang-paou, who took to flight, and in his retreat was wounded in the left arm with an arrow discharged at him by Lew-pei. He entered the city Yang-ching, which he strongly fortified, and Choo-tsëen, bringing up his army, laid siege to it. He at the same time sent a messenger to obtain intelligence of Hwong-foo-soong, who on his return related that the said general having obtained a great victory over the rebels, the Emperor had appointed him to supersede Tung-chŏ. Hwong-foo-soong had not arrived at his command before Chang-keŏ (one of the rebel brothers) was dead, and Chang-leang opposing his troops to the imperial general, was repeatedly worsted by

班師赴任朱儁聽說催促軍馬悉力功打陽城
賊勢危急賊將嚴政刺殺張寶獻首投降朱儁
遂平數郡上表獻捷時又黃巾餘黨三人趙宏
韓忠孫仲聚衆數萬望風燒刦與張角報仇
朝廷命朱儁即以得勝之師討之儁奉詔率軍
前進時賊據宛城儁引兵攻之趙宏遣韓忠出
戰儁遣玄德關張攻城西南角韓忠盡率精銳
之衆來西南角抵敵朱儁自縱鐵騎二千逕取
東北角賊恐失城急棄西南而回玄德從背後
掩殺賊衆大敗奔入宛城朱儁分兵四面圍定
城中斷糧韓忠使人出城投降儁不許玄德曰
昔高祖之得天下蓋爲能招降納順公何拒韓

him in seven battles, and at length lost his head. The coffin of Chang-keŏ was likewise despoiled of its contents, his body exposed, and his head sent to the Capital. The rebels all surrendered, and Hwong-foo-soong was raised to a higher dignity, and made governor of Ke-chow. He immediately reported to the Emperor the innocence and merits of Lew-chĕ, who was accordingly restored to office, and Tsaou-tsaou, the partner of his successes, was likewise promoted.

Choo-tsëen, on the receipt of this intelligence, pressed the siege, and, when the rebels were reduced to extremity, one of their leaders Yen-ching murdered Chang-paou, and presenting his head to the conqueror gave up the place. When Choo-tsëen had reduced some other districts he presented an address to the Emperor concerning his successes: but soon afterwards, some remnants of the yellow-capped rebels, viz. Shaou-hoong, Han-choong, and Sun-choong, collecting together myriads of disaffected persons, spread fire and devastation around, declaring themselves the avengers of Chang-keŏ. The Emperor commanded Choo-tsëen to attack them with his victorious troops, and, as the rebels had gained possession of the city Won-ching, he led his army to invest it. Shaou hoong sent Han-choong to meet him; upon which Choo-tsëen despatched Lew-pei to attack the south-west side of the city, which Han-choong perceiving, hastened to meet him: but Choo-tsëen himself, leading two thousand heavy-armed, at the same time attacked the north-east corner. The rebels, being afraid

忠耶儁曰彼一時此一時也昔秦項之際天下
大亂民無定主故招降賞附以以勸來耳今海
內一統惟黃巾造反若容其降無以勸善使賊
得利恣意刦掠失利便投降此長寇之志非良
德玄策也曰不容寇降是也今四面圍如鐵桶
賊乞降不得必然死戰萬人一心尚不可當況
城中有數萬死命之人乎不若撤去東南獨攻
西北賊必棄城而走無心戀戰可即擒也韓然
之隨撤東西二面軍馬一齊攻打西北韓忠果
引軍棄城而奔儁與玄德關張率三軍掩殺射
死韓忠

of losing the city, quickly abandoned the south-western part and returned towards the other, upon which Lew-pei made his attack successfully, and the rebels retreated into their strong hold. Choo-tsëen then proceeded to invest the four sides of the city, and cut off all supplies of grain: and when Han-choong sent persons to propose submission, he would not accept it. Upon this Lew-pei observed, "When Kaou-tsoo formerly obtained the sovereignty, it was chiefly by accepting submission, and thus inducing obedience—Why do you reject their offer?"—Choo-tsëen replied, "The occasions are very different. At that time the Empire was in great confusion, and the people without a fixed head:—it was therefore right to invite allegiance, and reward submission, as an inducement to join. But at present there are no rebels within the whole compass of the seas, expect these yellow-caps. It they are allowed to submit without punishment, they will continue their courses while successful, and, whenever unsuccessful, obtain an easy immunity by submission. This, therefore, would not suit our case."—"It is right not to allow them to escape punishment, replied Lew-pei,—but hemmed in, as they now are, on every side, if they cannot obtain some terms, they will be desperate, and all die with one heart, which might make them dangerous; besides which, in this city there are several myriads of persons careless of life or death. It will, therefore, be best to abandon the south-east side, and attack the north-west, which will certainly induce the enemy to leave the city and fly. When they are retreating in disorder they may be routed.—Choo-tsëen assented to this, and leaving the south-east side attacked with his whole force the north-west, upon which Han-choong, according to their expectations, abandoned the city, and took to flight with his army. Choo-tsëen, with his three generals at the head of three divisions, followed them with great slaughter, and Han-choong was slain.

材料二：《何进的历史与命运》（*History and Fate of Ho-tsin*）

中平六年夏四月靈帝病篤召大將軍何進入宮商議後事那何進起身屠家因妹入宮爲貴人生皇子辨遂立爲皇后進由是得權重任帝又寵幸王美人生皇子協何后妒嫉鴆殺王美人皇子協養于董太后宮中董太后乃靈帝之母解瀆亭侯萇之妻也初因桓帝無子迎立解瀆亭侯之子是爲靈帝靈帝入繼大統遂迎養母氏于宮中尊爲太后董太后嘗勸帝立皇子協爲太子帝亦偏愛協欲立之當時病篤中常侍蹇碩奏曰若欲立協必先誅何進以絕後患帝然其說因宣進入宮進至宮門司馬潘隱謂進曰不可入宮蹇碩欲謀殺公進大驚急歸私

History and fate of Ho-tsin——Intrigues of the eunuchs.

In the 4th. moon of the 6th. year of his reign, the Emperor *Ling-te*, being seized with a mortal sickness, sent for the general Ho-tsin, stating that he desired to consult with him regarding the succession. This person was sprung from a very low family, his father having been a butcher; but when his younger sister had been admitted into the Emperor's palace, and borne him a son, who was named Pëen, she become soon elevated to the rank of empress, and Ho-tsin in consequence was raised to high offices. The Emperor had also been very fond of another mistress whom he had taken, named Yu-mei-jin, and who had likewise produced him a son, named Hëë: but the sister of Ho-tsin having poisoned the mother through jealousy, the son was brought up by the Emperor's own mother, Tung-tae-how. She had been the wife of the minister Lew-chang, but as the Emperor then reigning had no offspring, he chose the son of his minister to succeed him, which was Ling-te; and when Ling-te obtained the Empire, he raised his mother to the rank of empress. She constantly urged her son to select *Hëë* as his successor; a measure which the Emperor was already inclined to, as he had a partiality for the youth. Being at the point of death, the eunuch *Këen-shë* advised him thus—"If your majesty wishes to

宅召諸大臣欲盡誅宦官座上一人挺身出日
宦官之勢起自冲質之時朝廷滋蔓極廣安能
盡誅倘機不密必有滅族之禍請細詳之進視
之乃典軍校尉曹操也進叱日汝小輩安知朝
廷大事正躊躇間潘隱至言帝已崩今蹇碩與
十常侍商議秘不發喪矯詔宣何國舅入宮欲
絕後患冊立皇子協爲帝說未了使命至宣進
速入以定後事操日今日之計先宜正君位然
後圖賊進日誰敢與吾正君討賊一人挺身出
曰願借精兵五千斬關入內冊立新君盡誅閹
豎掃清朝廷以安天下進視之乃司徒袁逢之
子袁隗之姪名紹字本初見爲司隷校尉何進

nominate *Hëë*, you must first cut off *Ho-tsin*, in order to prevent after troubles." The Emperor assented to this counsel, and sent for Ho-tsin to the palace. Scarcely, however, had the latter reached the palace gate, when P'wan-yin advised him by no means to enter, as the eunuch intended to murder him. Ho-tsin in great consternation retired to his private dwelling, and, having summoned all the great officers of the court, proposed to them the extermination of the eunuchs. Upon this one of the assembly rose up and said, "They have been so long established, and have become so numerous and powerful, that it will be a difficult matter to exterminate them entirely. Unless our measures are taken with prudence, we may suffer in the destruction of our own families. Let us then deliberate with care."—Ho-tsin looked at the speaker, and, seeing that it was Tsaou-tsaou, observed with an exclamation of contempt, "How should you be acquainted with what relates to Imperial matters?"—But in the midst of the debate entered Pwan-yin, to report that the Emperor was just dead, and that the eunuchs were all deliberating whether they should not defer his burial, and drawing all their enemies within the palace, put them to death, in order to raise the young *Hëë* to the throne. This notice was scarcely received, before a message came to *Ho-tsin* inviting him to enter the palace quickly, in order to settle the succession. Tsaou-tsaou observed, "Our business at present is to establish the new Emperor, after which we may

大喜遂點御林軍五千總全身披掛何進引何顒荀攸鄭泰等大臣三十餘員相繼而入就靈帝柩前扶立太子辯即皇帝位百官呼拜已畢袁紹入宮收蹇碩碩慌走入御園花陰下爲中常侍郭勝所殺碩所領禁軍盡皆投順紹謂何進曰中官結黨今日可乘勢盡誅之張讓等知事急慌入告何后曰始初設謀陷害大將軍者正蹇碩一人並不干臣等事今大將軍聽袁紹之言欲盡誅臣等乞娘娘憐憫何太后曰汝勿憂我當保汝傳旨宣何進入太后密謂曰我與汝出身寒微非張讓等焉能享此富貴今蹇碩不仁既已伏誅汝何聽信人言欲盡誅宦官耶

punish the traitors."—Ho-tsin upon this exclaimed, "Who will assist me to punish them?"—Somebody rose up and said, "With 5,000 chosen troops I will engage to establish the new Emperor in the palace, and to restore peace to the Empire by exterminating the eunuchs." Ho-tsin observed that the speaker was Yuen-shaou, the son of Yuen-foong, and gladly provided him with five thousand troops; upon which he prepared himself, and Ho-tsin assembling about thirty of the principal officers of the court, they proceeded in a body to the palace. There, before the bier of the late Emperor, they placed his son, and, having done homage to him, Yuen-shaou proceeded in search of the eunuch *Kēen-shĕ*, who, seized with terror, sought concealment in the imperial gardens, and was there slain by one of his brother eunuchs Kwo-shing. The soldiers that had been in the service of Kēen-shĕ all submitted to Ho-tsin, and Yuen-shaou then advised that, as the whole number of eunuchs were together in one body, the opportunity should be seized for exterminating them. The eunuchs, seeing themselves reduced to extremity, went altogether to the empress, the mother of Ho-tsin, declaring that the plot laid against his life was entirely the work of Kēen-shĕ, and that they had no concern in it whatever; that Ho-tsin, being now ready to believe the allegations made by Yuen-shaou, was prepared to exterminate them, and they accordingly entreated the empress to take compassion on their body. She dismissed them with an assurance of protection, and sending for her

何進聽罷出謂衆官曰蹇碩設謀害我可族滅其家其餘不必妄加殘害袁紹若曰不斬草除根必爲喪身之本進曰吾意已決汝勿多言衆官皆退次日太后命何進參錄尚書事其餘皆封官職董太后宣張讓等入宮商議曰何進之妹始初我擡舉他今日他孩兒即皇帝位內外臣僚皆其心腹威權太重我將如何讓奏曰娘娘可臨朝垂簾聽政封皇子協爲降加國舅董重大官掌握權軍重用臣等大事可圖矣董太后大喜次日設朝董太后降旨封皇子協爲陳后王董重爲驃騎將軍張讓等共預朝政何太后見董太后專權于宮中設一宴請董太后赴

brother said to him privately, "We both of us rose from a very low origin, and, had it not been for Chang-yang and the other eunuchs, could never have enjoyed our present situations. The guilty Këen-shě being already put to death, why need you listen to people's suggestions, or desire to exterminate the whole body of eunuchs?"*—Ho-tsin assented to this advice, and going forth to the other ministers said to them. "Këen-shě having laid a plot against my life, the extirpation of his own family and relatives will be sufficient—there is no need to extend the persecution to the rest."—To this Yuen-shaou observed, that if they did not effectually remove the weeds, their remaining roots might become a source of danger. "My mind, replied Ho-tsin, is already made up; there is no need of farther words." The ministers then all retired, and on the following day Ho-tsin, at his sister the empress's request, appointed all the new officers, which when the empress-mother heard, she sent for Chang-yang and the other eunuchs to consult with them, saying,—"The sister of Ho-tsin owed her first elevation to myself; but, her son being now Emperor, the ministers all side with her, and her weight and authority are great—what then am I to do?"—The chief eunuch advised her to hold a council, to declare the prince Hëě successor to the throne, to appoint her relative *Tung-choong*, to the command of the army, and restore the

* The Chinese commentator here quotes an old maxim, that "Women are the promoters of trouble—the ruin of public business."

席酒至中酣何太后起謝掩杯再拜曰我等皆婦人也參預朝政非其所宜昔呂后因握重權宗族千口皆被戮今我等宜深居九重朝廷大事任太臣元老自行商議今國家之幸也願垂聽焉董后大怒曰汝酖死王美人設心嫉妒今倚汝子為君與汝兄何進之勢輒敢亂言吾敕驃騎斷汝兄首如反掌耳何后亦怒曰吾以好言相勸何反怒耶董后曰汝家屠沽小輩有何見識兩宮互相爭張讓等各勸歸宮何后連夜召何進入宮告以前事何進出召三公共議來早設朝使廷臣奏董太后原係藩妃不宜久居宮中合仍遷于河間安置限目下即出國門一

eunuchs to their power. She received this counsel with the utmost satisfaction, and holding a court on the following day followed the eunuch's advice in every particular. But when the sister of Ho-tsin observed this encroachment on her authority, she prepared an entertainment, and invited the empress, mother of the late Emperor, to join it. When they had made some progress in the feast, the young empress rose, and saluting her guest with a cup of wine, observed, "We are both of us women, and to intermeddle in state affairs does not become us. The former empress *Leu-how*, who ventured to exercise the chief authority, was at last sacrificed with a thousand of her kindred—let us then take warning by her example, and dwell in befitting retirement, leaving the business of government to the ministers of the Empire; a measure which will be so much for the public benefit, that I trust you will not object to it."—Incensed at this, the other replied, "Shall a treacherous upstart creature like yourself, with a heart full of malignity, relying on your relationship to your son, and on the power of your brother, dare to address me in this way? —I can order you brother's head to be taken off, as easily as I can turn my hand."—The other princess now became angry in her turn, and said, "My friendly advice little deserved this furious return."— "What pretensions, rejoined the old empress, has the family of a mean butcher to offer any advice at all?"—The dispute thus continued, until Chang-yang and the eunuchs interfered

面遣人起送董后一面黜禁軍圍驃騎將軍董
重府宅追索印授董重知事急自刎于後堂家
人舉哀軍士方散張讓段圭見董后一枝已廢
遂皆以金珠玩好結搆何進弟何苗并其母舞
陽君令早晚入何太后處善言遮蔽因此十常
侍又得近幸六月何進暗使人酖殺董后于河
間驛庭舉柩回京葬于文陵進托病不出司隸
校尉袁紹入見進曰張讓段圭等流言于外言
公酖殺董后欲謀大事乘此時不誅閹宦後必
有大禍昔竇武欲誅內豎機謀不密反受其殃
今公兄弟部曲將吏皆英俊之士若使盡力事
在掌握此天贊之時不可失也進曰且容商議

and advised them to retire: but the younger empress that very night sent for her brother Ho-tsin, and informed him of what had occurred, upon which he immediately appointed a council to meet on the following morning, and a memorial to be presented, stating that the old empress, being no longer the wife or consort of the reigning Emperor, should not remain in the palace, but be immediately transferred to a distant residence. Persons were accordingly sent at once to convey away the princess; while, at the same time, a force surrounded the dwelling of Tung-choong, her relative, and reducing him to extremity, caused him to cut his throat; after which all his retainers and followers dispersed.—Chang-yang and the other eunuchs, seeing they could no longer derive support from that quarter, set themselves to work with gold and jewels to bribe Ho-meaou, the young brother of Ho-tsin, and his mother, causing them to repair constantly to the empress, Ho-tsin's sister, and solicit her favor on their behalf; by which means they became restored to safety. In the following summer, Ho-tsin caused the old empress to be secretly poisoned in her place of exile, and when the body was taken to the capital to be interred in state, he counterfeited sickness, and would not go to meet it.—Yuen-shaou came to Ho-tsin soon after, and told him that Chang-yang and the rest were spreading abroad rumours of his having poisoned the old empress, and of his meditating ambitious projects for himself.

"If, said he, you do not seize this occasion to exter-

左右報張讓讓等轉告何苗又多送賄賂苗入
奏何后云大將軍輔佐新君不行仁慈專務殺
伐今無端又欲殺十常侍此取亂之道也后納
其言少頃何進入白后欲誅中涓何后曰中官
統領禁省漢家故事先帝新棄天下爾殺誅殺
舊臣非重宗廟也進本是沒決斷之人聽太后
言唯唯而出袁紹迎問曰大事若何進曰太后
不允如之奈何紹曰可召四方英雄之士勒兵
來京盡誅閹豎此時事急不容太后不從進曰
此計大妙便發檄至各鎮召赴京師主簿陳琳
曰不可俗云掩目而捕燕雀是自欺也微物尚
不可欺以得志況國家大事乎今將軍仗皇威

minate these eunuchs, you will hereafter have certain cause to regret it. When *Tŏ-woo* formerly desired to rid himself of that tribe, he allowed his plans to transpire, and became consequently involved in ruin. Your family and friends are now in full power: if you exert yourself prudently, the thing is in your own hands, and the opportunity is so manifestly afforded be heaven, that it should not be lost."—Ho-tsin replied, that "There was time enough to consider about it,"—and this at length being reported secretly to Chang-yang, he applied to Ho-meaou, and induced him by bribes to go to the empress, saying, "My brother has committed great cruelties in upholding the new Emperor, and extinguished several families; in addition to which, he is determined, with equal injustice, to exterminate the eunuchs, which is a certain way to produce disorder,"—She agreed with him, and Ho-tsin soon after coming in, made the proposition, but the empress replied, "The eunuchs possessed the chief officers under the Han dynasty, and were you, so soon after the late Emperor's decease, to put the former officers to death, it would be a slight upon the imperial temple of ancestors."—Ho-tsin, being a man of no decision, listened to his sister's words, and assented to what she said; but being met by Yuen-shaou as he went out, the latter asked how matters stood?—"The empress is averse from the plan, replied Ho-tsin—there is nothing to be done."—"But, observed the other, you may collect together a sufficient number of leaders with their troops

掌兵要龍驤虎步高下在心若欲誅宦官如鼓烘爐燎毛髮耳但當速發雷霆行權立斷則天人順之却反外檄大臣臨犯京闕英雄聚會各懷一心所謂倒持干戈授人以柄功必不成反生亂矣何進笑曰此懦夫之見也傍邊一人鼓掌大笑曰此事易如反掌何必多議視之乃曹操也

董卓先為破黃巾無功朝議將治其罪因賄賂十常待幸免後又結托朝貴遂任顯官統西州大軍二十萬常有不臣之心是時得詔大喜點起軍馬陸續便行使其壻中郎將牛輔守任陝西自己却帶李傕郭汜張濟樊稠等提兵望洛

to put an end to these eunuchs—the occasion is urgent, and it is needless to attend to the empress's wish."—"Your proposition is a good one," said he,—"I will presently send to the different districts to collect troops." One of the council endeavoured to dissuade him from this, observing that it was a common maxim not to shut one's eyes, or deceive oneself as to consequences, in the pursuit of any object whatever—and how much rather in the affairs of the Empire. "Being now invested, said he, with the supreme authority, you can act with irresistible power, and at once proceed to exterminate the eunuchs, in such a way as to strike awe into the Empire. But should you collect together at the capital all the leaders from the provinces, they will feel their strength, and may produce a revolution." Ho-tsin laughed at this, as the opinion of a mere man of letters; but *Tsaou-tsaou*, who stood by, clapped his hands together and exclaimed, "It might be done with the utmost ease: why make so much of it!"

* * * * * * *

Tung-chŏ, having been formerly unsuccessful against the yellow-capped rebels, was condemned to punishment, but had contrived, by means of bribes to the eunuchs, to escape it. In consequence, too, of his connections and intrigues with those at court, he became appointed to the command of Se-chow, with 20 myriads of men. Being always inclined to treachery and rebellion, he received the invitation of Ho-tsin with great joy, and gradually collecting his forces left New-

陽進發卓壻謀士李儒曰今雖奉詔中間多有暗昧何不差人上表名正言順大事可圖卓大喜遂上表其畧曰竊聞天下所以亂逆不止者皆由黃門常侍張讓等悔慢天帝之故臣聞揚湯止沸不如去薪潰癰雖痛勝於養毒臣敢鳴鐘鼓入洛陽請除讓等社稷幸甚天下幸甚何進得表出示大臣侍御史鄭泰諫曰董卓乃豺狼也引入京城必食人矣進曰汝多疑不足謀大事盧植亦諫曰植素知董卓為人面善心狼一入禁庭必生禍患不如止之勿來免致生亂進不聽鄭泰盧植皆棄官而去朝廷大臣去者大半進使人迎董卓于澠池卓按兵不動張

foo in charge of Shen-se, while he proceeded in person with his other leaders towards *Lŏ-yang*, the Capital.—Tung-chŏ's counsellor, Le-yu, said to him, "We have certainly received a summons on the occasion, but it is a very doubtful and obscure one—Why, then, should we not send forward an address, worded in such terms as may suit our views."—Tung-chŏ followed this advice very gladly, and despatched a paper which ran as follows.

"I understand that the continued disorder of the Empire "arises from the treasonable conduct of Chang-yang and the "eunuchs: but the best mode of stopping the ebullition of "the cauldron is to withdraw the fuel; and though to get "rid of the peccant humor be painful, it is better than "letting the poison continue. I therefore venture to sound "the alarm, and enter *Lŏ-yang*, recommending that the traitors "be exterminated, to the joy of the empire and its guardian "deities."

When Ho-tsin received this, he made it known to all the chief ministers, upon which one of them, Ching-tae, observed, 'Tung-chŏ is a wild beast, and, if he enters the capital, will devour many.'—Ho-tsin replied to this by saying, "You are too suspicious, and do not understand state matters."—Leu-chĭh, however, confirmed the other's opinion by observing, "I have long known Tung-chŏ to be a man of a plausible face, but a wolfish heart; if he once enters our precincts, he will cause us sorrow; better, then, prevent his coming, and

讓等知外兵到共議曰此何進之謀也我等不先下手皆滅族矣乃先伏刀斧手五十人於長樂宮嘉德門內入告何太后曰今大將軍矯詔召外兵至京師欲滅臣等望娘娘垂憐賜救太后曰汝等可詣大將軍府謝罪讓曰若到相府骨肉虀粉矣望娘娘宣大將軍入宮諭止之如其不從臣等只就娘娘前請死太后乃降詔宣進進得詔便行主簿陳琳諫曰太后此詔必是十常侍之謀切不可去去必有禍進曰太后詔我有何禍事袁紹曰今謀已泄事已露將軍尚欲入宮耶曹操曰先召十常侍出然後可入進笑曰此小兒之見也吾掌天下之權十常侍敢

obviate the confusion which must ensue." As Ho-tsin would not listen to either of these counsellors, they resigned their offices and retired; and about one half of the ministers likewise took their departure. Ho-tsin sent a deputation to meet Tung-chŏ at Ying-che, where he stopped and encamped with his army.

Chang-yang and the eunuchs, when they heard of the approach of the distant troops, consulted together. "This is a scheme of Ho-tsin, said they—if we do not anticipate him, we shall all be destroyed." They accordingly placed fifty armed men in ambush within the palace, and going to the Empress complained, that the general, her brother, had sent for the distant troops purposely to exterminate their body, and entreated her to have compassion on them, and interfere for their safety. "But you may proceed at once to him, replied she, and solicit his pardon."—"Were we to go, exclaimed Chang-yang, we should be chopped into small pieces!—Let us hope that your majesty will send for your brother and give him your instructions. Should he not listen to you, we can but die before you majesty's face." The Empress in consequence sent a message, desiring to see Ho-tsin, who made haste to comply, but was entreated by Chin-lin to refrain, on the ground that this invitation was a scheme of the eunuchs for his destruction." "What danger can there be, he exclaimed, when the empress sends for me?"—"Will you still resolve on going, said Yuen-shaou, when these plots are all apparent?"—Tsaou-tsaou advised that the eunuchs

待如何紹曰公必欲去我等引甲士護從以防不測于是袁紹曹操各選精兵五百命袁紹之弟袁術領之袁術全身披掛引兵布列青鎖門外紹與操帶劍護送何進至長樂宮前黃門傳懿旨云太后特宣大將軍餘人不許輒入將袁紹曹操等都阻住宮門外何進昂然直入至嘉德殿門張讓段珪迎出左右圍住進大驚讓厲聲責進曰董后何罪妄以酖死國母喪葬托疾不出汝本屠沽小輩我等薦之天子以致榮貴不思報効欲相謀害汝言我等甚濁其清者是誰進急欲尋出路宮門盡閉伏甲齊出將何進砍爲兩段

should be drawn out before he entered; but Ho-tsin ridiculed the idea as childish—"With the supreme authority vested in my person, said he, how shall they presume to maltreat me?"—"If your highness is resolved on going, said Yuen-shaou, we will take an armed guard as a precaution against the worst." With this they selected some hundreds of picked troops, and gave them in charge to the younger brother of Yuen-shaou, who, arming himself, led them to the gate of the palace; while the others, taking their swords with them, escorted Ho-tsin to the Empress's gate. An order, however, was communicated, as from the Empress, that none but Ho-tsin might enter to the audience, and his companions being thus stopped, he went in alone. When he had arrived at an inner gate, Chang-yang and the others met and surrounded him, upon which Ho-tsin was alarmed; while Chang-yang began in a harsh tone to upbraid him, saying, "What was the offence of the late queen, that you should have poisoned her; or, when carried to her tomb, that you should have neglected to attend under plea of sickness? You originated in a butcher's paltry tribe, and it was our interest with the Emperor that made you what you are; for which, however, in lieu of gratitude, you have sought our destruction. If you say that we are stained with guilt, prove that yourself are purer?"—Ho-tsin, seized with consternation, would gladly have retired, but the gates were all shut, and the armed men, issuing from their ambush, took him and divided him in twain.

第四部分

汉语教材文献研究

一　卫三畏与《三国演义》在美国的译介

卫三畏被称为美国“汉学之父”，在中美外交史上举足轻重。他 1833 年来华，1876 年返美，在华四十余年之久，从一名普通的印刷工，做到美国驻华使团的秘书和翻译。1878 年受聘耶鲁大学，成为美国历史上第一位汉学教授。

在《三国演义》英译史上，卫三畏功不可没。他是第一位将《三国演义》翻译到英语世界的美国人，时间上虽不及马礼逊、德庇时等英国人早，但就笔者调查，他至少三次集中译介过该作，对于这部中国小说的重视程度绝不亚于此前的译介者。只是他的译介文零散地刊印在汉语教材、英文报刊等出版物中，搜集起来相当困难，故此学界至今没有相关的研究成果出现。

1842 年，卫三畏独自编撰的汉语教材《拾级大成》出版，其中的汉语语料大量采用《三国演义》中的字词、语句和故事片段，这是他首次关注《三国演义》。1848 年，卫三畏出版了成就其汉学声望的专著《中国总论》，其中翻译了“王允设计诱吕布”（Scheme of Wóng Wan to inveigle Lü Pò）这一故事片段。1849 年，卫三畏在著名英文报刊《中国丛报》上翻译了“桃园结义”这一故事情节。以上三次译介，开启了美国人翻译与研究《三国演义》的历程。

本部分内容在广泛搜集第一手英文资料的基础上，结合相关出版媒介和译文文本，细致分析了卫三畏所译《三国演义》的具体内容、翻译理念，以及其翻译特色和学术影响。这不仅是研究《三国演义》美国之行的逻辑起点，也是探讨其英译历程的重要一环。

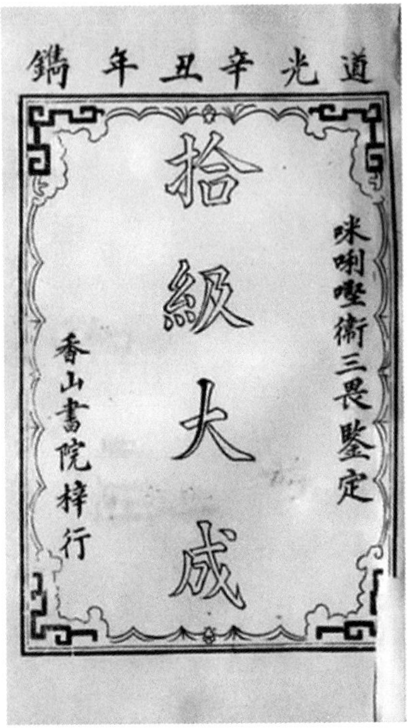

《拾级大成》中文封面

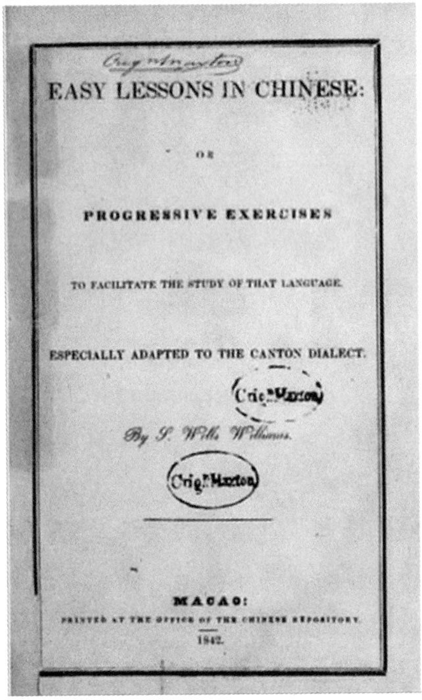

《拾级大成》英文封面

（一）《拾级大成》与《三国演义》

《拾级大成》是卫三畏编写的汉语教材，1842 年在澳门出版。英文书名题作 *Easy lessons in Chinese*，*or Progressive Exercises to Facilitate the Study of that Language*，*especially adapted to the Canton dialect*。顾名思义，这是为英语世

界的读者编写的汉语学习材料，尤其适合于粤语方言的学习。在“序言”中，编者交代这部教材的读者对象主要是“初学汉语的人”，其中不仅包括寓居中国的外国人，也包括尚在本国的外国人，以及正在赶赴中国的外国人；此外，由于这部教材使用中英文合著，所以对于学习英语的中国青少年（Chinese lads）来说也大有裨益。

卫三畏将中文书名题作《拾级大成》，隐含着读者若拾级而上将终有所成之意，在编辑体例上遵循着由易到难、循序渐进的原则。全书共有十章，分别是：第一章“部首”（Of the Radicals）；第二章“字根”（Of the Primitives）；第三章“汉语的读写”（Of Reading and Writing）；第四章“阅读练习”（Lesson in Reading）；第五章“对话练习”（Exercises in Conversation）；第六章“阅读文选”（Selections for Reading）；第七章“量词”（The Classifiers）；第八章“汉译英练习”（Exercises in Translating）；第九章“英译汉练习”（Exercises in Translating into Chinese）；第十章“阅读和翻译练习”（Lessons in Reading and Translating）。十章内容的编排，由字到词，由句到篇，确实遵循着《礼记·曲礼》所谓“拾级聚足，连步而上”之意。

在汉语材料的选用上，《拾级大成》具有以下四方面特点。

一是基础性。如第一章讲授汉字的偏旁部首，编者逐一介绍了《康熙字典》（*The Imperial Dictionary of Kánghí*）中重要的214个偏旁部首的读音、意义。第二章讲授字根，编者将汉字字根分为五种类型，并以“可”“龙”“丁”等偏旁或字根为例，介绍了汉字的基本构成。第三章讲授汉语的读写，编者不仅介绍了平、上、去、入四种声调，而且通过王右军（Wóng Yaukwan）的“笔阵图”，以“永”字为例，介绍了汉字书写的八种基本笔画。以上三章内容涉及的汉字的偏旁、结构、读音和书写等，都是汉语学习的入门知识，体现了《拾级大成》的基础性特点。

二是实用性。如第五章的对话练习，编者设计了三个对话场景，分别是来华西士与老师、买办、仆人之间的对话。鸦片战争前后，来华传教士、外交官、商人等避居广东一隅，因此，三个对话场景采用的语言均是粤语；对话的内容，也是来华西士日常生活与工作中常见的应答。又如，在第十章阅读和翻译练习中，编者采用了 18 篇应用文。其中前 10 篇为父子、夫妻和朋友之间的往来书信；后 8 篇为道光年间的朝廷公函，这些公函大多涉及中英、中美之间的外交事务，有道光二十一年（1841）4 月 29 日皇帝回复奕山的上谕，也有道光十九年（1839）2 月林则徐、邓廷桢等人写给英国女王的照会。私人书信和朝廷公函均是来华西士日常生活和工作中交流感情、处理公务的工具，具有很强的实用性。

三是教化性。《拾级大成》毕竟是一部教材，所以在材料的选用上格外重视其思想性。这主要体现在以下两个方面：一方面，《拾级大成》虽然出自西方人之手，但对于某些中国传统思想却颇为认可。比如，在第四章阅读练习中，编者选用的 11 篇短文中有 7 篇来自《鹿洲女学》。该书出自清代康熙、雍正年间的学者蓝鼎元（1680—1732）之手。蓝鼎元字玉霖，号鹿洲，著有《鹿洲全集》，《女学》是其中之一。[①] 在《女学序》中，作者自云该书：“采辑经史诸子百家，及《列女传》《女诫》诸书，依《周礼》妇学之法，开章总括其要，后以妇德、妇言、妇容、妇功，分为四篇。”[②] 实际收录历代女性故事 300 余篇，《拾级大成》所选 7 篇主要取自“妇德”，在内容上以彰显女性的忠孝节义为主。如冯昭仪为保护汉元帝而表现出的忠勇，张氏女遇恶婆而表现出的温顺，以及李景让之母的教子严明、秋胡子之妻的深明大义等。另一方面，身为传教士，卫三畏在选材上也格外重视基督教思想的渗透。比如，在第十章阅读和翻译练习的选文中，有不少内容出自《劝世良言》《新遗诏书选》等布道手册。这些材料均具有明显的教化色彩。

---

① 卫三畏曾在《中国丛报》(*Chinese Repository*) 1840 年第 8 卷介绍蓝鼎元的《鹿洲女学》。

② 沈云龙主编:《近代中国史料丛刊续编》第四十一辑《女学》，文海出版社有限公司，1977 年 4 月影印版。

四是趣味性。《拾级大成》大量选用小说中的文字片段，仅从《聊斋志异》一书中就选用了17个故事，其中第四章阅读练习选用了《种梨》《曹操冢》《骂鸭》3个故事；第八章汉译英练习选用了《鸟语》《红毛毡》《妾击贼》《义犬》《地震》5个故事；第十章阅读和翻译练习选用了《鸲鹆》《黑兽》《牛飞》《橘树》《义鼠》《象》《赵城虎》《鸿》《牧竖》9个故事。这些故事多以动物设喻，短小精悍，意蕴隽永，形制颇似西方人熟悉的《伊索寓言》。此外，《拾级大成》还从《三国演义》《玉娇梨》《子不语》中选择了大量文字片段，从而大大提高了这部早期海外汉语教材的文学性和可读性。

值得注意的是，《拾级大成》是目前所知英语世界最早译介《聊斋志异》的汉语教材。1842年4月，德国第一位来华新教传教士郭实腊在《中国丛报》上发表了《来自聊斋的非凡传奇》（*Extraordinary Legends from Liáu Chái*）一文，粗陈梗概地译介了9篇聊斋故事，笔者认为这是《聊斋志异》在英语世界的最早译介。[①] 对此，顾钧先生提出异议，他认为同年出版的《拾级大成》译介了17篇聊斋故事，所以卫三畏才是最早接触《聊斋志异》的西方人士。[②] 虽然就翻译数量和质量而言，郭实腊对于《聊斋志异》的译介远远逊色于卫三畏的翻译，但在出版时间上却难以查实《拾级大成》早于《来自聊斋的非凡传奇》，故此，郭实腊与卫三畏谁更早接触《聊斋志异》尚难确定。

从传播媒体来看，郭实腊的译文刊载于《中国丛报》，而卫三畏的译文则刊载在自己编辑的汉语教材中，《中国丛报》堪称鸦片战争前后传播中国资讯最著名的英文期刊，所以郭译在当时的影响力应该更为广泛。只是两人的译介风格相去甚远。郭译重在聊斋故事的转述与介绍，泛泛而论，态

---

① 王燕：《试论〈聊斋志异〉在西方的最早译介》，《明清小说研究》2008年第2期。
② 顾钧：《也说〈聊斋志异〉在西方的最早译介》，《明清小说研究》2012年第3期。

度草率；而卫译重在文本翻译，字斟句酌，下笔谨慎。而且，郭实腊此后在《聊斋志异》的译介方面再无建树，而卫三畏不仅在1848年出版的专著《中国总论》中重译了《种梨》与《骂鸭》，还在翌年8月出版的《中国丛报》上发表了他翻译的第18篇聊斋故事《商三官》。整体来看，在《聊斋志异》的英译和传播方面，卫三畏的贡献远远超过郭实腊。

除了《聊斋志异》，《三国演义》是《拾级大成》在中国小说译介方面的另一重要作品。在《拾级大成》译介的四种小说中，《三国演义》所占篇幅最大，总计有三十多页，大约相当于《拾级大成》全书八分之一的篇幅。除了直接译自《三国演义》的文字，《拾级大成》还有三个三国故事。一是来自《聊斋志异》的《曹操冢》；另外两个来自《漉洲女学》，其一是皇甫规之妻拒绝董卓强聘而被其杖杀的故事，其二是吴夫人教导孙策优贤礼士的故事。在近五百篇聊斋故事中，《曹操冢》罕为人知；在300多篇女学故事中，皇甫规之妻与吴夫人的故事也算不得上乘佳作，这些故事之所以得到卫三畏的青睐，或许因为其中的人物都出自三国时期。

《拾级大成》直接选自《三国演义》的文字集中分布在五个章节。第一次出现在第三章第五节，卫三畏在介绍汉字排版及中国标点符号的使用时，引用了《三国演义》中的一句话："登曰：'儿亦有计了。'乃入见吕布，曰：'徐州四面受敌，操必力攻'。"卫三畏解释说："地名旁加画双线，人名旁加画单线，这两种情况均可见于这一句子，该句出自《三国志》（*Sám Kwók Chí*）。"[①] 卫三畏此处所提《三国志》即《三国演义》，这是他在《拾级大成》中第一次提及该作。

第二次出现在第四章阅读练习中。该章从《三国演义》《玉娇梨》《聊斋志异》中引用了91个句子，其中有68个句子出自《三国演义》。这些句

① S. Wells Williams，拾级大成，*Easy Lessons in Chinese: or Progressive Exercises to Facilitate the Study of that Language*，Macao：Printed at the Office of the Chinese Repository，1842，p. 56.

子先给出汉语文字，汉字下逐一标出读音，读音下逐一提供英文字意，在页下脚注中，再将这一句子翻译为符合英语表达习惯的流畅的英文。卫三畏提醒学生要充分利用这种编排方式来学习汉语，他说："如果遮住汉字，就根据读音写出汉字；如果遮住读音，就流畅地读出汉字；如果露出英文字意，就能立即想起中文汉字与读音。"① 如此反复练习，就能有效地学习汉语。

第四章开篇伊始，卫三畏就明确提出两种英译方式：一是直译（the literal translation）；二是意译（the free idiomatic translation）。直译主要是为每个汉字提供一个准确的英文注释；意译主要是为整个句子提供一个符合英语表达习惯的翻译。整体看来，卫三畏的注释和翻译大都准确精当，但也存在个别错误。比如，第62页第3句："吾与奉先无隙，何故引兵至此?"在《三国演义》原文中，这句话本是刘备质问吕布（奉先）手下大将高顺为何引兵前来。卫三畏却错误地理解为：I have no dispute with Fungsín，and why therefore should I lead troops here? 回译为中文，意思是："我与奉先并无隔阂，那么我为何引兵来此呢?"这里的"我"（I）显然应改为"你"（you）。又如，第69页第50句："左慈掷杯空中，化成一白鸠，绕殿而飞。"在解释字意时，卫三畏把"白鸠"注释为"百鸽"（one hundred pigeons），翻译句子时重复了这一错误。再如，第75页第77句："操问曰：'何故见赐?'承曰：'因念某旧日西都救驾之功，故有此赐。'"在解释字意时，卫三畏把"操问曰"三个字分别注释为"Ts'ò asking said"；在翻译句子时，同样使用了这三个单词，如此翻译显然不对，"问曰"二字是同义复词，英译时理当合并处理，故"操问曰"最好译作"Ts'ò asked"。

第三次出现在第八章汉译英练习中，该章从《三国演义》中选用了两个故事：第一个出自第十一回，题名"孔融之智"（Cleverness of Hung

① S. Wells Williams，拾级大成，*Easy Lessons in Chinese：or Progressive Exercises to Facilitate the Study of that Language*，Macao：Printed at the Office of the Chinese Repository，1842，p. 62.

Yung)，始于“北海孔融，字文举，鲁国曲阜人也”，止于“座上客常满，罇中酒不空，吾之愿也”，大约 200 字。第二个出自第八回，题名“王允设计诱吕布”（Scheme of Wóng Wan to inveigle Lü Pò），始于“董卓一日大会百官”，止于“布再三拜谢而去”，大约 1000 字。

第八章是为学生准备的汉译英材料，与第四章相比，本章只提供中文原文、汉字读音和英文注释，要求学生将中文故事翻译成流畅的英文。在此，卫三畏提出了自己的翻译理念。他说：“在将中文翻译成英文时，需要格外注意避免因为恪守汉语表达习惯而使语言风格颠倒错乱，那样不但无助于表达的明晰，也常使译文变得过于生硬。在汉语作品中，复合词或双音节词随处可见，固定搭配也很少分开使用，但它们却只有一个意思，有时可以用一个词来翻译。仅仅知道汉字的意思不足以使一个人成为一个好的译者，他还得注意词语或短语在原文的前后关联中的含义，以便挑选一种恰当的表达来翻译它。同时还得注意那些原文中的特殊短语，如果值得翻译，不要死板地忠实于原文，否则就会造成译文的不雅或无趣。”①

结合上述翻译理念，通过考察卫三畏对于两个故事的逐字对译，可以进一步分析其翻译特点。第一，卫三畏对于中国传统文化有着比较深入的了解，所以能够恰当地翻译出某些具有浓郁的中国文化特点的词汇。比如，他将“秋波”译作“ogling-glances”，“肺腑”译作“inmost”等，都能准确地传达词语隐含的文化意蕴。第二，卫三畏的翻译灵活多变，针对汉语“一词多义”的现象进行了“一词多译”。比如，根据上下文语境的不同，分别将“曰”字译作 say、remark、reply、rejoin 等；将“妾”字译作 I、handmaid、concubine 等。第三，汉语是典型的孤立语（isolating language），没有语态、时态的变化；而英语属于屈折语（inflecting language），有语态、

① S. Wells Williams，拾级大成，*Easy Lessons in Chinese*：*or Progressive Exercises to Facilitate the Study of that Language*，Macao：Printed at the Office of the Chinese Repository，1842，p. 149.

时态的变化。为了区分二者，卫三畏在翻译汉语动词时，适当地添加了时态变化。比如，将“我观二人皆好色之徒”中的“观”字译作“have-observed”，用了现在完成时，表示这是王允对于董卓、吕布的既有认识。第四，两个故事的中英文中均存在少量错误，其中汉语错误集中出现在排印上，比如将“荼蘼”误作“荼薇”；“目不转睛的看”误作“目不转睛的省”。英译错误主要出现在汉语虚词的翻译上。比如，“孔子曾问礼于老子”中的介词“于”，卫三畏将之译作“of”显然不如译作“from”更为合适；“是夜”中的代词“是”不应译作“in”，而应译作“this”。还有个别错误当是理解方面有误，比如，“恐太师见疑”，其中的“太师”指的是吕布的义父董卓，而卫三畏却将之错译为“you”，误作吕布。整体看来，类似的错误屈指可数，这从另一角度显示了卫三畏汉语水平的精湛。

《拾级大成》最后两次集中引用《三国演义》的文字，分别出现在第九章英译汉练习和第十章阅读和翻译练习，前一章提供英语句子，后一章提供汉语答案，相关内容恰好对照阅读。

《拾级大成》第九章共分四节，卫三畏编译了大量英文短句作为练习素材，要求学生回译为中文，第二、四节中都有选自《三国演义》的句子。其中第二节共有 29 个句子，全部出自《三国演义》第二回“张翼德怒鞭督邮　何国舅谋诛宦竖”；第四节共有 73 个句子，其中 44 句出自《三国演义》，原句散见于原著第二回至第五十四回。[①] 这些英文句子意思完整，长短不一，为了方便学生回译为中文，译者在括号里为某些专有名词提供了汉字。

第九章第二、四节编译的英文句子的汉语答案，分别见于第十章第二部分（Without an English Version）第一节“此数句见《三国志》”（Miscel-

---

① 第 25 句至第 67 句均出自《三国演义》，其中，第 57 句尚难确定是否出自《三国演义》。英文“If you plunder the blackhaired race，azure heaven will not protect you.”中文“劫掠黎民，苍天不祐。”这 44 个句子过于分散，故本著没有提供文献图片。

laneous extracts from the History of the Three States）和第三节“杂句”（Short Sentences）。[①] 第十章第二部分没有英文，只有汉语。汉语竖排，从左向右阅读，每页 12 行，每行 21 字。每两句之间用占据一个汉字的空心圆隔开。每句中有标点断句，标点主要是黑点和句号两种，置于汉字右下角。人名右侧用单线标出，地名右侧用双线标出。整体看来文字清晰，排列整齐。

根据相关中英文信息，可以推测卫三畏编辑《拾级大成》时所采用的《三国演义》的中文底本。第九章第二节开篇，编者直接用中文说明：“此数句选《三国志》卷一第二回第十一板之后”。接着，又用英文指出：“以下数句要求回译为中文，在句子的最后可以找到原文出处。所用汉语底本为十二开本，每页 22 行，从右侧第一行数起。”[②] 后面列了 29 个句子。第一句如下：

1.“On the day, he having been disrespectful to Üntak（玄德）, Chéung Fí（張飛）of a hasty temperament, straightway wished to kill him.”—（15 characters.）section 2d, leaf 11, last column.

第十章第二部分第一节提供的相关汉语答案为：“当日怠慢了玄德．张飞性发便欲杀之。”对比现存《三国演义》不同版本的相关部分，卫三畏选文的文字内容、字数与《四大奇书第一种》完全相同，但页码和行列存在明显差异。尽管没有在现存版本中找到直接对应的版本，但至少可以由此推断，卫三畏依据的底本，当是当时较为常见的毛评本。

第九章的英译句子完全符合英语表达习惯，在翻译方式上主要采用的是直译，这种翻译方式可以最大限度地保留汉语的语言特点。为了说明这点，不妨以第九章第二节第 12 句为例，将卫三畏的翻译与英国汉学家德庇时在《三国志节译文》中的相关翻译做一对比。

---

① 第 59 句至第 63 句英文句子排序与相应的汉语答案排序略有错乱。

② S. Wells Williams，拾级大成，*Easy Lessons in Chinese*: *or Progressive Exercises to Facilitate the Study of that Language*, Macao: Printed at the Office of the Chinese Repository, 1842, p. 200.

中文原文：

玄德曰：不容寇降是也，今四面围如铁桶，贼乞降不得，必然死战。

德庇时译作：

It is right not to allow them to escape punishment, replied Lew-pei, —but hemmed in, as they now are, on every side, if they cannot obtain some terms, they will be desperate. ①

卫三畏译作：

Üntak said, Not to permit the rebels to submit is correct. Now they are hemmed in on all sides like an iron tube, and the rebels beg to submit; if they cannot, they will assuredly fight to the last. ②

两相对比，德庇时的翻译不但调整了语序，而且省略了个别字眼，“铁桶”二字就没有译出；而卫三畏的翻译却严格遵循中文语序，努力做到中英文丝丝入扣。如此亦步亦趋地紧贴中文，确实可以使某些词语的翻译更为精准。比如，根据《汉语大词典》，“落荒而走”的意思是“向荒野逃去”，德庇时将之译作“took to flight”；卫三畏将之译作“entered the wilds and fled”，相较之下，卫三畏的翻译明显更为准确。但某些时候，直译又确实显得比较生硬，不如意译来得自然流畅。比如，卫三畏将“身无寸功”译作“their body has not one inch of merit”；将“长江一带，如横素练”译作“the whole length of the river was like a band of clear white”。

① John Francis Davis，汉文诗解，*Poeseos Sinensis Commentarii*，*On the Poetry of the Chinese*，Macao，China：Printed at the Honorable East India Company's Press，By G. J. Steyn and Brother，1834，p. 167.

② S. Wells Williams，拾级大成，*Easy Lessons in Chinese*：*or Progressive Exercises to Facilitate the Study of that Language*，Macao：Printed at the Office of the Chinese Repository，1842，p. 201.

由此可见，为了服从汉语教学的需要，卫三畏翻译的《三国演义》句子，大多采用了直译的方式。《三国演义》在《拾级大成》中只是汉语学习的语言材料，编者几乎没有论及该作自身的文体属性和艺术特征。

（二）《中国总论》与《三国演义》

1847 年，回到美国耶鲁大学担任汉学教授的卫三畏发现，中英战争以来，中国被迫开放，当时的美国人对于鸦片战争极为关注，对于中美之间的贸易和交往更是充满兴趣。作为在广州和澳门生活了 12 年的美国人，卫三畏对于中国的方方面面都有着毋庸置疑的发言权。为了解答人们的疑问，卫三畏赴尤蒂卡（Utica）、克利夫兰（Cleveland）、布法罗（Buffalo）、纽约（New York）等城市作了一系列演讲。在此基础上，于 1848 年整理成书出版了《中国总论》。

《中国总论》（1848 年版第 1 卷）封面

《中国总论》（1848 年版第 2 卷）封面

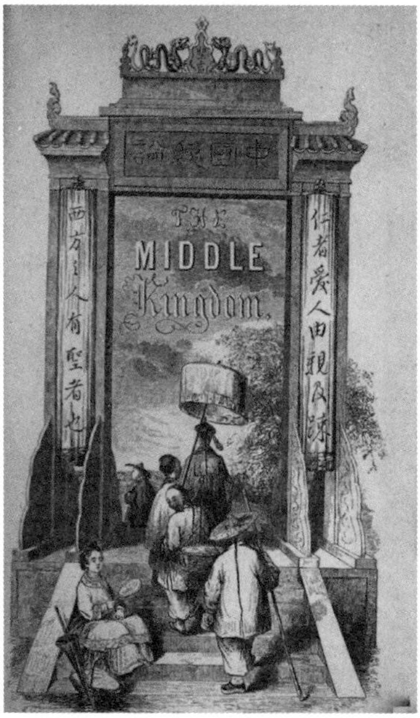

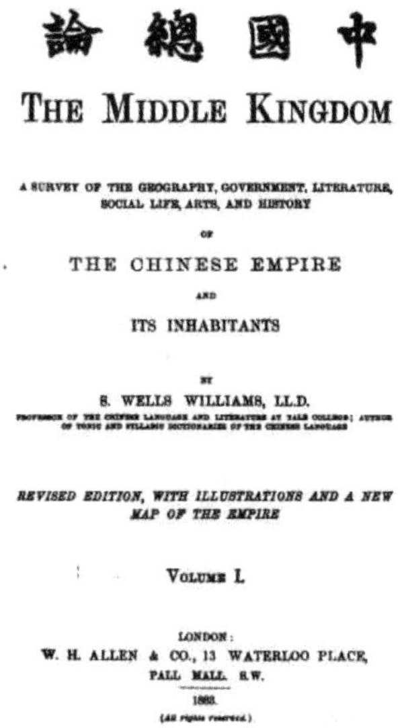

論總國中

THE MIDDLE KINGDOM

A SURVEY OF THE GEOGRAPHY, GOVERNMENT, LITERATURE, SOCIAL LIFE, ARTS, AND HISTORY

OF

THE CHINESE EMPIRE

AND

ITS INHABITANTS

BY

S. WELLS WILLIAMS, LL.D.

PROFESSOR OF THE CHINESE LANGUAGE AND LITERATURE AT YALE COLLEGE; AUTHOR OF TONIC AND SYLLABIC DICTIONARIES OF THE CHINESE LANGUAGE

REVISED EDITION, WITH ILLUSTRATIONS AND A NEW MAP OF THE EMPIRE

VOLUME I.

LONDON:
W. H. ALLEN & CO., 13 WATERLOO PLACE, PALL MALL. S.W.
1883.
(*All rights reserved.*)

《中国总论》（1848 年版第 1 卷）扉页　　《中国总论》（1883 年版第 1 卷）扉页

《中国总论》的装帧设计显示着卫三畏作为“中国通”的骄矜自恃。《中国总论》的封面插图是一位身着清朝官服的西方人的半身像，左上侧写着“诗书结静缘”五个汉字，透露出卫三畏的在华生活颇为自适。扉页插图是一位官员在三四位仆人的簇拥下步入一座中式牌坊，头顶的华盖和高大的背影，以及台阶上蹲坐的中国妇人和负箕、拽杖的中国仆人，无不在反衬着这位官员的尊贵与显达。联系封面画像，不难猜测这位官员当是卫三畏的自况。牌坊匾额上写着“中国总论”四个汉字，左右所挂对联“西方之人有圣者也”“仁者爱人由亲及疎”。由此可见，卫三畏对于自己的中国文化颇为自得，他的步入中式牌坊颇有几分“学造渊源，道升堂奥”之意。

《中国总论》是一部系统介绍中国知识的百科全书。19 世纪中叶，这类综合性图书备受青睐，不少早期来华西士都出版过类似作品。比如，第一位来华新教传教士马礼逊著有《中国一览》（*A view of China*），第二任香港总督德庇时著有《中国人：中华帝国及其居民概述》等。卫三畏对于后者极为赞赏，只是认为该作虽然包罗万象，但出版于 1836 年，内容不免陈旧，不能满足西方人对于中国近况的追问，于是萌生了出版《中国总论》的念头。该作 1848 年初版时共有 23 章，涉及中国的地理、人口、自然、法律、教育、语言、文学、建筑、工艺、科学、历史、宗教、商业、战争等各个方面。之后不断再版，广受欢迎，1883 年推出了修订本，内容由原来的 23 章扩充至 26 章，文字总量增加了三分之一，插图更是增加了一倍，该作至今依然是研究 19 世纪中国文化的重要文献。

《中国总论》大约有四页篇幅涉及《三国演义》，具体内容出现在卫三畏对于“中国文献”的介绍中。他根据中国图书分类模式，在第十一章“中国经典文献”（Classical Literature of the Chinese）和第十二章“中国的雅文学”（Polite Literature of the Chinese）中依次介绍了中国的经、史、子、集（Classical，Historical，and Professional writings，and Belles-lettres）。

在向美国读者系统介绍“中国文献”时，卫三畏格外倚重于《四库全书总目》。《中国总论》1848 年初版时即提到该作，1883 年修订版进一步补充说：“在浏览中国文献时，《四库全书总目》（*The Sz' Ku Tsiuen Shu Tsung-muh*，or *Catalogue of all Books in the Four Libraries*）是最好的入门书，因为它涵盖了中国文献的全部，对于最好的中文书籍提供了一个完整而简明的概览。该书有 112 卷，八开本，本身就很有价值，对于外国人来说更是如此。中国的全部书籍被分为四个部分，即：经、史、子、集。《总目》囊括了大约 3440 部书，共有 78000 多卷；此外还有 6764 部书，共有 93242 卷，记录在其他皇家藏书目录中。这些目录包括了中国文献的大部分，但没有涵盖小说、佛经译作和最近的出版物。”①

① S. Wells Williams，中国总论，*The Middle Kingdom*，London：W. H. Allen & Co.，13 Waterloo Place，Pall Mall. S. W. Vol. Ⅰ.，1883，pp. 626 –627.

值得注意的是，作为禁毁小说，《三国演义》绝不可能出现在乾隆年间官修的《四库全书总目》中，那么，为何根据《总目》介绍中国文献的《中国总论》却有大量篇幅言及《三国演义》呢？原来在《中国总论》初版中，卫三畏把史书《三国志》与演义《三国演义》混为一谈，所以在介绍陈寿的《三国志》时，实际论说与引用的材料却是《三国演义》。他说：

> 在中国文学作品中，没有几部作品比陈寿（Chin Shau）的历史小说《三国志》（The *San Kwoh Chí*，or History of the Three States）更为著名，该作创作于公元350年左右。小说的场景被设置在中国北部，时间阶段是公元170年至317年之间。那时有几个野心勃勃的首领，联合起来反对曾经称雄一时的汉代的愚笨君王。汉代被推翻之后，他们之间互相争斗，直到晋代重新统一了全国。由于这部作品具有双重属性，时间跨度又长，所以必然缺少一部小说应有的整体性。对于中国人来说，作品的魅力在于栩栩如生地描写了阴谋与反阴谋、战斗、围攻和撤退中的各种关系，还有书中描绘的人物的优秀品格，以及妙趣横生的情节中交织的人物行动。①

这段文字出自《中国总论》第十二章“中国的雅文学”。卫三畏在介绍中国的“史”部图书时，主要论及三部作品：司马迁的《史记》、司马光的《资治通鉴》和陈寿的《三国志》，但所用笔墨却相差悬殊，介绍前两部史书的内容加起来也不及《三国志》的一半，只是他所讲的《三国志》实际上是《三国演义》。在1883年修订版的相关陈述中，卫三畏沿袭了这一错误，继续将《三国志》与《三国演义》混为一谈，这一错误论断后来遭到

---

① S. Wells Williams, *The Middle Kingdom*, New York & London: Wiley and Putnam, Vol. Ⅰ., 1848, pp. 544 - 545.

了英国著名汉学家梅辉立的批评。[①]

令人困惑的是，卫三畏明知《三国演义》是一部“历史小说”（a historical novel），却还执着地将之置于正史的行列。1848 年，《中国总论》初版第十七章“中国的历史与纪年”（History and Chronology of China）在介绍汉代历史时，卫三畏另有一段文字涉及《三国演义》的文体特征，他专门强调了该作的小说属性。他说：“从公元 190 年汉代被推翻，到公元 317 年东晋建立，是中国历史上最有趣的阶段之一，这一时期的时代混乱造就了各色人物。《三国志》（*The History of the Three States*）描述了这一时期的混乱，但这部有趣的作品，充其量不过是一部历史小说（historical novel）。”[②] 在 1883 年的修订版中，卫三畏进一步补充说：“尽管如此，《三国志》就像司各特的故事（Scott's stories）那样，把当时的事件和人物植入了人们的头脑，比任何一部中国史书都更受欢迎。”[③] 对于一向治学严谨的卫三畏来说，误把《三国演义》当成《三国志》固然是一个不可原谅的错误，但这也从另一方面显示了《三国演义》的影响所及远远超过了《三国志》，以致西方学者博学如卫三畏者，竟也难辨个中究竟，以致犯下这样一个常识性错误。

在具体内容上，《中国总论》对于《三国演义》的介绍主要是翻译了一个片段。这个片段与《拾级大成》第八章所译第二个故事——“王允设计诱吕布”完全一致，这是他对于自己既有汉语研究成果的继续沿用，同时也显示了卫三畏对于“连环计”这一故事的特别喜爱。六年后再译“连环计”，《中国总论》较之《拾级大成》做了三点调整：第一，在《拾级大成》第八章中，卫三畏只提供了这段小说的中文原文、汉字读音和英文注释，要求学生

① W. F. Mayers, “Ⅱ. Historical Romances”, *Notes and Queries on China and Japan*, Edited by N. B. Dennys, Volume Ⅰ., January to December, Hongkong: Charles A. Saint. 1867, p. 103.

② S. Wells Williams, *The Middle Kingdom*, New York & London: Wiley and Putnam, Vol. Ⅱ., 1848, p. 214.

③ S. Wells Williams, 中国总论, *The Middle Kingdom*, London: W. H. Allen & Co., 13 Waterloo Place, Pall Mall. S. W. Vol. Ⅱ., 1883, p. 164.

将中文故事翻译成流畅的英文；而这恰恰是《中国总论》提供的内容。所以，《中国总论》无异于为《拾级大成》的读者提供了一份“汉译英练习”的标准答案。第二，在英译方面，《中国总论》的句子翻译多数情况下紧紧追随《拾级大成》的英文注释，由此而使个别句子翻译得相当生硬。比如，在《拾级大成》中，卫三畏为“布当效犬马之报”一句提供的逐字英文注释为 I will emulate dogs horse's requital；在《中国总论》中此句译作：I would emulate the requital dogs and horses give for the care taken of them。译者只是补充了个别连词，由此而使整个句子勉强贯通，直译的色彩相当明显。第三，由于《拾级大成》的预设读者主要是身处广州的来华西士，所以在人名的音译上具有明显的粤语发音特点；在《中国总论》中，卫三畏有意识地重译了相关人名，使之更符合北方官话的发音特点。比如，在《拾级大成》中，董卓、王允、貂蝉、吕布分别被音译为 Tung Ch'éuk、Wóng Wan、Tiú Shín、Lü Pò；在《中国总论》中则分别改为 Tung Choh、Wang Yun、Tiau Chen、Lü Pu。后一种翻译方法在 19 世纪英译三国人名中显然更为常见。

1883 年，卫三畏在修订版《中国总论》的“序言”中说他对语言和文学两章做了大量改动。但经笔者仔细比对，发现前后两版言及《三国演义》的文字改动却极为有限。明显的变化主要有两个方面：一是通过在句子中添加括号，补充了个别信息。比如，“汉室”在时间上是“147 年至 184 年”；“吕布”乃“董卓之义子”。二是修改了某些表达不够精确的地方。比如，“汉王的帝国被分成了魏、蜀、吴三国”这句（divided the empire of the Han princes into the three states of Wu，Shuh，and Wei），被修改为“帝国被分成了魏、蜀、吴三国”（divided the empire into the three states of Wu，Shuh，and Wei）。又如，“德庇时因为《三国志》的总体布局和英雄人物的狂暴性格而将其非常恰当地比作是《伊利亚特》”，1883 年再版时删除了“非常恰当”（very appositely）两个词。这或许是因为当时有论者指出卫三畏把《三国演义》比作《伊利亚特》不够恰当，他显然吸收了这一意见，故在修订版中做了措辞上的微妙改动。

整体看来，卫三畏在《中国总论》中大量论及《三国演义》不是一个偶然，这与他此前在《拾级大成》中大量引用《三国演义》的字句密切相关，同时也显示了他对这部作品的一贯重视。

（三）《中国丛报》与《三合会会员的誓言及其来源》

卫三畏在《中国总论》初版“序言”中说，该著的资料来源主要有两个方面：一是他在中国的所见所闻和对于中国典籍的研究引用；二是裨治文（E. C. Bridgman，1801—1861）创办与编辑的《中国丛报》。实际上，卫三畏对该刊的贡献绝不亚于裨治文。

卫三畏之所以来华与《中国丛报》密切相关。《中国丛报》于 1832 年 5 月创刊于广州，在美国商人奥立芬（D. W. C. Olyphant，1789—1851）的赞助下建起了印刷所（The office of the Chinese Repository），当时急需一名熟练的印刷工来华帮助印刷《中国丛报》，裨治文遂向“美部会”提出请求。1833 年 10 月，卫三畏在父亲的推荐下来到广州，这时他已大学毕业，并在父亲的印刷所学习了半年印刷业务。此后，他就肩负起了管理印刷所的重任，直到 1851 年《中国丛报》停刊。即便是在 1844 年 11 月至 1848 年 9 月返美期间，他也不忘为印刷所购置印刷设备。《中国丛报》前后出版 20 年，卫三畏负责印刷管理工作长达 14 年之久。

除了是《中国丛报》的印刷业务管理者，卫三畏还是《中国丛报》的重要撰稿人。1834 年 2 月，抵达广州后四个月，《中国丛报》第 2 卷第 10 期“杂录”栏目就刊登了卫三畏的两篇文章：一是《中国的度量衡制度》（*Chinese Weights and Measure*）；二是《广州的进出口货物》（*Imports and Exports of Canton*）。此后，他笔耕不辍，成为《中国丛报》的第二大撰稿人。

根据《中国丛报总索引》统计，该刊20年间共发表各类文章1378篇，其中有114篇出自卫三畏之手，约占《中国丛报》用稿总量的十分之一，在数量上仅次于该刊的创办者裨治文。①

1848年年底从美国归来后，《中国丛报》的编辑出版日趋困难，卫三畏临危受命，继裨治文及其堂弟詹姆斯·裨治文（James Granger Bridgman，1820—1850）之后，出任该刊第三任主编，全面承担起编辑、印刷、出版、营销业务。但是，随着五口通商和传教人员的离散，“该报的许多支持者都迁居别的沿海城市或者去了欧洲，它的发行量大大减少了，并且开始资不抵债。除了极少数文章是由以前的支持者们撰写的之外，大部分稿件都出自卫三畏之手。甚至有一期从头到尾都是卫三畏的手笔。”② 1851年12月，《中国丛报》在发布了赞助商奥立芬和撰稿人郭实腊去世的消息后宣告停刊，卫三畏几乎亲历并见证了这个刊物的整个生命历程。

1849年6月，《中国丛报》第18卷第6期刊载了一篇关于“三合会”的文章，题名《三合会会员的誓言及其来源》（*Oath taken by members of the Triad Society*, *and notices of its origin*）。文中介绍“三合会”成员的誓言时，提及“桃园结义”（pledged each other in the Peach garden）。作者说：“此处提及的誓言在中国广为人知，立誓的三人所发的誓言，或对三合会会员有所启发，表面看来都是本着爱国的目的。《三国志》（*The Sán Kwoh Chí*）是这样描写三人以及他们的桃园结义（the oath they took in the Peach garden）的。”接着，作者在注释中翻译了《三国演义》第一回“宴桃园豪杰三结义 斩黄巾英雄首立功”中的相关文字。起于“那人不甚好读书，性宽和，寡言语，喜怒不形于色”；止于“祭罢天地，复宰牛设酒，聚乡中勇士，得三百余人，就桃园中痛饮一醉”。

---

① 数据统计参考了仇华飞《裨治文与〈中国丛报〉》，《历史档案》2006年第3期，第49页。

② ［美］卫斐列：《卫三畏生平及书信》，顾钧等译，广西师范大学出版社2004年版，第95页。

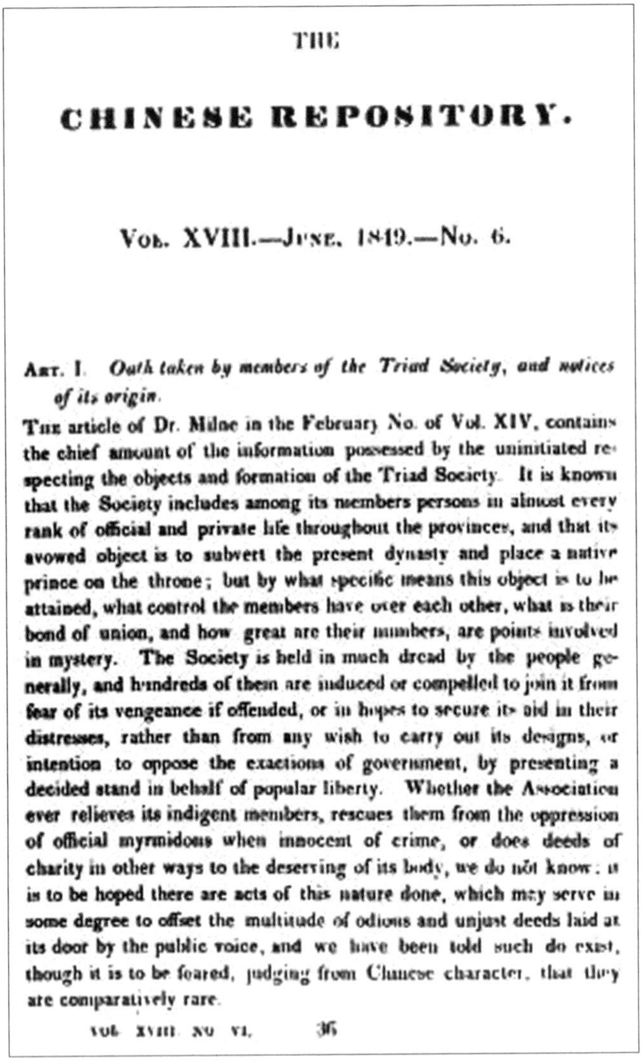

THE

CHINESE REPOSITORY.

VOL. XVIII.—JUNE, 1849.—NO. 6.

ART. I. *Oath taken by members of the Triad Society, and notices of its origin.*

THE article of Dr. Milne in the February No. of Vol. XIV, contains the chief amount of the information possessed by the uninitiated respecting the objects and formation of the Triad Society. It is known that the Society includes among its members persons in almost every rank of official and private life throughout the provinces, and that its avowed object is to subvert the present dynasty and place a native prince on the throne; but by what specific means this object is to be attained, what control the members have over each other, what is their bond of union, and how great are their numbers, are points involved in mystery. The Society is held in much dread by the people generally, and hundreds of them are induced or compelled to join it from fear of its vengeance if offended, or in hopes to secure its aid in their distresses, rather than from any wish to carry out its designs, or intention to oppose the exactions of government, by presenting a decided stand in behalf of popular liberty. Whether the Association ever relieves its indigent members, rescues them from the oppression of official myrmidons when innocent of crime, or does deeds of charity in other ways to the deserving of its body, we do not know: it is to be hoped there are acts of this nature done, which may serve in some degree to offset the multitude of odious and unjust deeds laid at its door by the public voice, and we have been told such do exist, though it is to be feared, judging from Chinese character, that they are comparatively rare.

VOL. XVIII. NO. VI. 36

《三合会会员的誓言及其来源》

这篇文章最初发表时没有署名，查找作者成为第一要务。1851 年《中国丛报》停刊后出版的《总索引》将该刊发表的重要文章进行了分类编目，对于出自裨治文、卫三畏等重要撰稿人之手的文章，做了作者标注。在第二类“中国政府与政治”（Chinese Government and Politics）中，涉及“三合会”的文章被重新题作《三合会誓言译文及其组织结构介绍》（*Translation of the oath of the Triad Society, and account of its formation*），作者标注为 S. W. W.，由此推测，这篇匿名发表的“三合会”文章当出自卫三畏之手。或许也只有酷爱《三国演义》的卫三畏，才会在一个注释中不失时机地塞入一个三国故事；倘若不是对这部演义格外熟稔，很难想象其他作者会有这样的热情和耐心。

卫三畏在《拾级大成》和《中国总论》中翻译三国故事时，大致采用“直译”的方式，中英文严格对译，尽可能保留中文语序与字意。与之相比，“桃园结义”的翻译也以恪守原著为主要特色，但其翻译较为灵活，某些句子不再紧贴原著亦步亦趋。比如，刘备出场时，原著写作：“那人不甚好读书；性宽和，寡言语，喜怒不形于色；素有大志，专好结交天下豪杰。”[①] 英文译作：This man did not love study very much; he was a man of few words, liberal and kind disposition, not showing his feelings in his countenance, and keeping to his purpose of uniting all the heroes in the country。其中，“性宽和”与“寡言语”颠倒了顺序。

虽然都是“直译”，但在翻译描述人物外貌的文字时，“桃园结义”的译文出现了明显改动。比如，对于张飞的外貌，原著写作：“玄德回视其人：身长八尺，豹头环眼，燕颔虎须；声若巨雷，势如奔马。玄德见他形貌异常，问其姓名。”卫三畏译作：Hiuentch turned, and seeing a man about eight cubits high, with a round head and goggle eyes, a bull neck, tiger's whiskers, a voice like thunder, and the strength of a wild horse, altogether a strange object, inquired his name. 其中的“豹头”被译作“圆头”；“燕颔”被译作“牛颈”。又如，对于关羽的外貌，原著写作：“玄德看其人：身长九尺，髯长二尺；面如重枣，唇若涂脂；丹凤眼，卧蚕眉；相貌堂

① 本部分所引原著文字参考《第一才子书三国演义》，线装书局2007年版，第4—5页，此后不再一一注释。

堂，威风凛凛。”卫三畏译作：He was nine *chih* high，his beard two *chih* long，dark complexion，red lips，narrow eyes，and his whole appearance dignified and imposing. 其中，“面如重枣，唇若涂脂；丹凤眼，卧蚕眉”被转译为“黑脸，红唇，细眼”。

之所以改动，显然是因为“豹头”“燕颔”“重枣”“涂脂”“丹凤眼”“卧蚕眉”等字眼对于卫三畏等英语读者来说过于陌生，译者不得不用浅显易懂、明白晓畅的词语加以替换。但是，经过这种词语转译后，张飞的粗犷之气或无大碍，关羽的英武之气却消失殆尽。比如，“面如重枣”言关羽面色呈深红色，而译者却译作“黑脸”，完全改变了中国民间流传的“红脸关公”的典型形象。“丹凤眼”是一种眼角上翘的眼型；“卧蚕眉”指形如卧蚕的浓眉。美髯、红脸、丹凤眼、卧蚕眉无不在在体现着关公的威严、庄重，但转译为“黑脸、红唇、细眼”后，就无所谓“相貌堂堂，威风凛凛”了。

实际上，哪怕遵照原著恰当直译，英译文依然难以完成不同文化间审美情趣的自然转换。比如，《三国演义》原著在描写刘备外貌时写道：“生得身长七尺五寸，两耳垂肩，双手过膝，目能自顾其耳，面如冠玉，唇若涂脂。”卫三畏译作：He was eight *chih* tall，had pendent ears which he could see himself，his hands hung below his knees，his face was pale and lips red. 其中，除了“面如冠玉”被误作“面色苍白”，别的地方翻译得基本准确。即便如此，西方读者也很难从中捕获文字背后隐含的文化信息，即刘备的形象在中国传统文化中颇有“王者之相”。古代帝王“奉天承运”，出生时多有瑞兆，相貌也异于常人。东汉王充在《论衡·骨相》中记载：“黄帝龙颜，颛顼戴干，帝喾骈齿，尧眉八采，舜目重瞳，禹耳三漏，汤臂再肘，文王四乳，武王望阳，周公背偻，皋陶马口，孔子反羽。”[①] 由此，刘备的

① 王充著，北京大学历史系《论衡》注释小组注释：《论衡注释》，中华书局 1979 年版，第 158 页。

“两耳垂肩，双手过膝，目能自顾其耳”也是一种“王者之相”。但对于19世纪西方读者来说，这种样貌的怪异不言而喻，其中隐含的“王者之相”却未必能够体会得到。这在译文中时有流露，比如，在翻译张飞“形貌异常”时，卫三畏没有使用abnormal appearance等常用词语，而是说张飞“全然一个怪物”（altogether a strange object）。这种表述直接将一雄壮威猛的“英雄”贬低为莫名其妙的“怪物”，与中国读者初识张飞时的阅读感受大异其趣。

除了人物外貌描写的翻译与原著相比存在较大改动，卫三畏的译文还有三点值得注意。

其一，译者删减了原著中与“桃园结义”故事情节关系不是很紧密的个别句子。如原著在介绍刘备家世时提供了详细信息：“昔刘胜之子刘贞，汉武时封涿鹿亭侯，后坐酎金失侯，因此遗这一枝在涿县。玄德祖刘雄，父刘弘。弘曾举孝廉，亦尝作吏，早丧。”卫三畏将这几句浓缩为一句“父刘弘早丧”。此外，在“年十五岁，母使游学”后，删除了“尝师事郑玄、卢植，与公孙瓒等为友”。这些被删除的信息，多是历史人名，如果没有相关文化知识，即便音译为英文，读者亦不知所云，故在翻译时删除这些信息更有利于阅读的顺畅。

其二，“逐字直译”的翻译方式紧扣原文，使某些常见词语的隐含意义得以彰显。如，卫三畏将“黎庶”翻译为“黑发百姓”（the blackhaired people），此前，在《拾级大成》中也出现过the blackhaired race。“黎”有“黑色”之意，“黎庶”即“黎民”，在古代确实可以理解为“黑发百姓”之意，如朱熹在解释《尚书·尧典》“黎民于变时雍”一句时说：“黎，黑也。民首皆黑，故曰黎民。”只是近现代以来，“黎庶”通常直接解释为黎民百姓，“黎”字本身的含义反被忽略不计。①

其三，虽然存在个别漏译、错译，但不少词句翻译得非常准确、巧妙。

① （宋）朱熹：《朱子全书》，上海古籍出版社2002年版，第3155页。

如，“皇天后土”在中文典籍中是对“天神”“地祇”的尊称。“皇”与“后”均有赞美之意，用来修饰“天”与“土”。汉代许慎《五经异义·天号》引古《尚书》说：“天有五号，各用所宜称之。尊而君之则曰皇天。”①《左传·僖公十五年》：“君履后土而戴皇天。”② 卫三畏将“皇天后土”翻译为：O Imperial Heaven！O Queenly Earth！准确把握了“皇”与“后”对“天”与“土”的修饰功能。

“桃园结义”是卫三畏为介绍“三合会”的文章而添加的一个注释，很难说这段译文对《三国演义》的海外传播产生了怎样深远的影响。只是作为一个注释，“桃园结义”几乎可以独立成文，在篇幅上远远超过一般的注释，这从一个侧面反映了卫三畏对《三国演义》的熟稔和喜爱。

（四）《东周列国志》与《三国演义》

从影响研究的角度来看，卫三畏对于《三国演义》的译介深化了他对中国历史小说的认识，推动了他对《东周列国志》的译介。

卫三畏是第一个将《东周列国志》译成英文的西方人。根据卫三畏之子卫斐列（Frederick Wells Williams）整理的《卫三畏生平及书信》（*The Life and Letters of Samuel Wells Williams*）记载，1853 年 6 月至 1854 年 7 月出使日本期间，卫三畏把主要精力都花在了《东周列国志》的翻译上。“这本书共有 19 章，密密麻麻地印在四开本大小的纸上，有将近 330 页。卫三畏要将它全部译成英文，这是他一生中投入较长时间和较多精力的工作之一，

---

① （清）陈寿祺撰：《五经异义疏证》，（清）皮锡瑞撰：《驳五经异义疏证》，王丰先整理，中华书局 2014 年版，第 14 页。

② 杨伯峻编著：《春秋左传注》，中华书局 2016 年版，第 391 页。

也是他唯一一次不带任何目的做的一项纯文学性的工作。”① 只是翻译完后，卫三畏没有急于将之付之梨枣，直到 1880 年，《新英格兰人》（*The New Englander*）第 1 期才发表了他翻译的前两章译文，题名《一部中国历史小说》（*A Chinese Historical Novel*），副标题是《列国志，或封建王国的记录；第一、二章译文》（*Lieh Kwoh Chi*, or *The Records of the Feudal Kingdoms*; with a translation of Chapters Ⅰ. and Ⅱ.）。

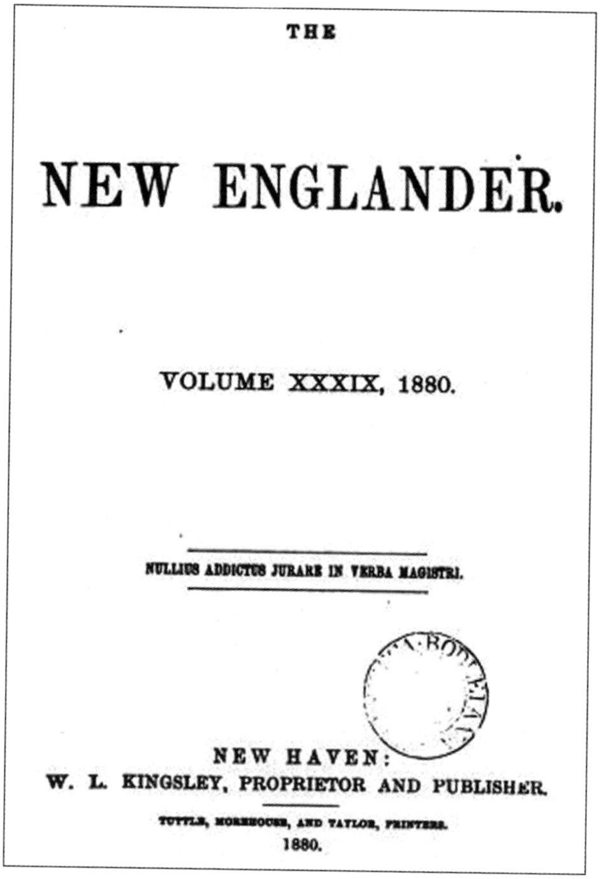
THE

NEW ENGLANDER.

VOLUME XXXIX, 1880.

NULLIUS ADDICTUS JURARE IN VERBA MAGISTRI.

NEW HAVEN:
W. L. KINGSLEY, PROPRIETOR AND PUBLISHER.

TUTTLE, MOREHOUSE, AND TAYLOR, PRINTERS.
1880.

《新英格兰人》杂志封面

① ［美］卫斐列：《卫三畏生平及书信》，顾钧等译，广西师范大学出版社 2004 年版，第 142 页。

ARTICLE II.—A CHINESE HISTORICAL NOVEL.

Lieh Kwoh Chi, or *The Records of the Feudal Kingdoms;* with a translation of Chapters I. and II.

AMONG the fields of literary research still unexplored, and almost unknown to Western scholars, the annals of China present one of the most promising. The rulers of that empire have distinguished themselves for their munificent and personal patronage of letters, and the efforts they have made to preserve the records of their dynasties. The digested histories of the successive families which have occupied the throne of the *Hwangti*, are divided into twenty-four separate works, and contain in all 3264 books or chapters. The number of their authors is twenty, of whom Sz'ma Tsien, the earliest, B. C. 163–85, has been aptly styled the Herodotus of China to indicate his lively narrative as well as his priority in date. We do not intend to describe or analyze them at all, but to merely show somewhat of the extent of this untrodden field. A critical synopsis of the historians then extant was made in the XIIth century by the famous philosopher Chu Hi, in fifty-nine chapters, under the title of *The Mirror of History;* the French translation of which, by Père Mailla, makes eleven quarto volumes, including, however, the annals of the succeeding three dynasties down to A. D. 1780.

In addition to the various kinds of historical writings in Chinese literature, such as dynastic histories, annals, complete records, separate histories, or *mémoires pour servir*, local or biographical histories, and official or documentary records or rolls, there are hundreds of authors whose works have exerted much more influence in diffusing a knowledge of their national life and prominent actors among the people. They answer very nearly to our historical novels, but it is not easy to decide, from present knowledge, in which of them fact, and in which of them fiction most prevails. The literati regard them all with much the same feeling as we might suppose Gibbon would have reviewed Old Mortality or Rienzi; and yet the insight

《一部中国历史小说》

在众多的中国文学作品中，卫三畏之所以选译《东周列国志》，与他对《三国演义》的熟悉与推崇密切相关，这从《一部中国历史小说》的“序言”中即可见出。卫三畏说：

> 到目前为止，大约有20部富于想象力的（中国）文学作品被翻译成了其他语言，包括戏曲、小说和诗歌的选段，只是除了《正德皇游江南》（*Rambles of Chingtih in Kiangnan*），还没有其他任何规模的历史小说得到译介。1845年，西奥多·帕维（Theo. Pavié）出版了一个《三国志》（*The San Kwoh Chi*, *or Records of the Three Kingdoms*）法译本，大约44章，相当于原著三分之一的篇幅，该作是中国历史小说中流传最广的一部作品。这是一部真正天才的作品，在普及历史知识方面发挥了重要作用，其中的人物和事件也成了民歌、故事和戏曲的常见题材。其中描绘的一位英雄，现在已被神化为战神（the God of War），他名叫关帝（Kuan-ti），是万神殿中最伟大的神灵之一。他的图像被精心地描画在竹片、纸张和丝帛之上，这样的场景屡见不鲜。在广州一个被称为“打醮”（Ta Tsiao）的秋节上，有个类似“万灵节”（All Souls Day）上的仪式，那时街上挤满了用各色丝绸花边装饰的帐篷，它们被上百个玻璃吊灯和彩色灯笼照耀着。每当这时，我都能看到许多相关的历史场景展台（historic tableaux），它们被安放在三四英尺长的木板上，恰好悬吊在人们的头顶上，当拥挤的人群簇拥而过时，就吸引着人们的注意力，激发起他们的好奇心——这很像落入保尔丁（Paulding）及其同伴们之手的安德烈（André），或者史密斯船长（Captain Smith）和波卡洪塔斯公主（Pocahontas），他们同样也会引起美国人的兴趣。
>
> 在中国知识分子看来，本文标题涉及的这部作品，与《三国志》相比更接近于历史真实，但作为一部优秀之作，却较之逊色。该作全

称是《东周列国志》，或《东周封建王国的记录》（*Tung Chau Lieh Kwoh Chi*，or *the Records of the Feudal Kingdoms during the Easter Chau Dynasty*）。①

文中提到的《三国志》，即《三国演义》。由上述文字可以看出：英译中国历史小说的阙如、法译《三国演义》的问世、《三国演义》的盛行不衰及历史价值，以及三国人物和历史场景在民间的普及与影响，都是卫三畏关注该作的原因。与之相比，《东周列国志》虽然整体成就不及《三国演义》，但在历史真实性方面却略胜一筹，这是卫三畏翻译《东周列国志》的理由。但根本上，他之所以译介《东周列国志》，主要还是由于《三国演义》的广泛传播与影响，以及他对这类历史小说的重视与熟稔。

卫三畏译文发表后，陆续出现了几篇《东周列国志》译作。有趣的是，后期译者在提及《东周列国志》时，也像卫三畏那样将之与《三国演义》进行对比，其中的某些言辞，显然受了卫三畏的影响。比如，1893 年，以翻译“四书五经”著称于世的英国汉学家理雅各在《皇家亚洲学会学报》上发表了他翻译的《姗姗来迟的中国传奇与小说：伟大的弓箭手养由基的历史》（*The Late Appearance of Romances and Novels in the Literature of China*：*With the History of the Great Archer*，*Yang Yû-chî*），其中译介的养由基的故事，实际出自《东周列国志》。文中，理雅各指出：

> 在中国传奇与小说中，《三国演义》独树一帜，然而，另有一部作品虽不在“十才子”之列，却很接近《三国演义》，这就是《东周列国志》（*Tung Châu Lieh Kwo Chih*，*or History of the various States or Kingdoms during the time of the Eastern Châu*）。伟烈亚力先生（Mr. Wylie）

① Prof. S. Wells Williams，M. D.，“A Chinese Historical Novel”，*The New Englander*，Volume XXXIX.，No. 1.，New Haven，1880，p. 30.

> 说："该作写作时虽然采用了小说的形式，但相比于其他作品，却与真实的历史差别不大。"某些中国作家认为，《东周列国志》的真实性使它明显区别于其他传奇。该作虽然写得不像《三国志》（*The History of the Three Kingdoms*）那般辉煌，其叙事却饶有趣味。这两部作品使我想到了司各特爵士（Sir Walter Scott）伟大的历史小说《祖父的故事》（*Tales of a Grandfather*）。前者有着丰富的骑士画卷和战争描写；后者虽然比较安静，却也更为柔和，同样给人留下了深刻印象。①

在此，理雅各强调《东周列国志》的历史真实性，又把这部作品比之于司各特的作品，这两点均是卫三畏论及《东周列国志》或《三国演义》时的创见。不仅如此，理雅各在文章的开篇，还区别了《三国演义》和《三国志》，继梅辉立之后进一步纠正了卫三畏在这方面所犯的错误。他说："《三国志演义》（*San Kwo Chih Yen Î*）即'三国历史的扩展叙事'（The Expanded Narrative of the History of the Three Kingdoms）。该作生动、浪漫地讲述了汉朝末期的历史事件，涉及的时期不足一个世纪，从公元198年，直至265年晋朝建立。外国学者普遍认为这是一部史书，而非一部历史传奇。即便是像卫三畏博士这样著名的学者，也将其归于公元4世纪作家陈寿的名下。陈寿写的是那个朝代的历史《三国志》（*The Three Kingdoms*），该作在史书中并非一部坏书，但也绝不比另外的几部史书更为优秀。"② 虽然是批评性文字，但从另一侧面反映了当时的学者对卫三畏研究的关注，由此看出卫三畏英译《三国演义》的深远影响。

① Professor Legge, "The Late Appearance of Romances and Novels in the Literature of China: With the History of the Great Archer, Yang Yû-chí", *The Journal of the Royal Asiatic Society of Great Britian and Ireland*, October, 1893, p. 806.

② Ibid., p. 803.

（五）卫三畏译文的整体特点

整体看来，卫三畏对于《三国演义》的译介主要有以下三个特点。

第一，根据在中国的生活阅历与社会观察，卫三畏认为《三国演义》是“一部真正天才的作品，在普及历史知识方面发挥了重要作用”，这是他反复译介该作的根本原因。作为一部历史小说，该作生动形象地展示了历史人物与战争画面，具有一定的艺术性；但是，根据西方古典戏剧艺术法则，尤其是“三一律”（three unities）创作思想，“由于这部作品具有双重属性，时间跨度又长，所以必然缺少一部小说应有的整体性（unity）。”① 由此看来，卫三畏对于《三国演义》的文学性评价不高，认识有限。

第二，卫三畏的译介文刊发于综合性中国学读物，从而为《三国演义》的海外传播拓展了道路。比如，《拾级大成》是面向来华西士的汉语教材，《中国总论》是介绍中国文化的综合性图书，《中国丛报》是研究中国资讯的学术性刊物。在 19 世纪来华西士中，这些读物在传播中国知识方面追求基础性、全面性、系统性，相对而言内容杂、受众广、传播快，在一定程度上推动了《三国演义》的广泛传播。

第三，卫三畏对于《三国演义》的译介始终抱持实用主义观念。比如，他在《拾级大成》中用《三国演义》的字词、语句作为汉语学习语料；在《中国总论》中借三国故事解说中国历史；在《中国丛报》中用

① S. Wells Williams，中国总论，*The Middle Kingdom*，London：W. H. Allen & Co.，13 Waterloo Place，Pall Mall，S. W. Vol. Ⅰ.，1883，p. 677.

“桃园结义”注解“三合会”的誓言与章程。这种实用主义观念，使《三国演义》从古代而至近代，由中文而入英文，径直介入了19世纪来华西士的语言学习与日常沟通，从而以一种极具亲和力的方式走入了他们的中国认知与学术视野，由此而为这部历史演义的美国之旅开辟了一条独特的路径。

附：文献图片

《拾级大成》(*Easy Lessons in Chinese*)①

《拾级大成》引用《三国演义》材料统计表

章节序号	英文章节	中文章节	教材内容	所在页码
第三章	Reading and Writing	阅读与书写	1个句子	56
第四章	Lesson in Reading	阅读练习	68个句子	62-75
第八章	Exercises in Translating	汉译英练习	故事片断：孔融之智	149-150
第八章	Exercises in Translating	汉译英练习	故事片段：王允设计诱吕布	151-157
第九章	Exercises in Translating into Chinese	英译汉练习	29个句子	200-203
第十章	Lessons in Reading and Translating	阅读和翻译	29个句子	249-252

① 编者按：S. Wells Williams, *Easy Lesions in Chinese*, Macao: Printed at the Office of the Chinese Repository, 1842.

carefully punctuated. According to this work, "a complete proposition, where the sense also is complete, makes a period (*kü* 句), and is indicated by a small round mark placed at the side of the word [where it terminates]. A complete proposition, where the sense is not complete, makes a clause (*tau* 讀), and is indicated by a small round mark placed between the words." The former of these answers to the period in English, the latter to the comma; the first is frequently met with in common books, but the last is more seldom used.

Paragraphs are indicated by a large circle ○ placed between two sentences in the column, and called *tái hün*, but neither is this mark much used. There is a mode of emphasizing certain passages, analogous to the use of italics and capitals in English, frequently employed, which consists in marking a row of points or circles down the column, one or more opposite each character. This plan has been refined upon by the compilers of the *Kóng Kám*, who have, by a row of white open circles given praise to the subject matter of the passage, and by a row of black circles, passed censure upon it. Names of places are sometimes designated by double lines drawn down the side of the characters, while names of persons are marked by a single line drawn in the same manner—both of which are shown in the following sentence, taken from the *Sám Kwók Chí*. Names of books are, in Kánghí, in the *Pún Tsò*, and in some other works, quoted by being inclosed in lines drawn around them.

登曰兒亦有計了乃入見呂布曰徐州四面受敵操必力攻

"Tang said, '*I also have a plan;*' then entering and seeing Lüpò he said, 'Chüchow will be attacked on all sides, and Tsò will strenuously fight.'"

There is another way of marking respect, somewhat analagous to capitalizing or spacing a word in English, common in public documents, prefaces, &c., which is done by placing the word or name at the top of a new column. The rule appears to be to place the name of the reigning emperor's father or ancestors four characters above the other columns; the name or titles of the emperor himself, three

Chapter Fourth.

LESSONS IN READING.

The following sentences are all selected from good Chinese writings, such as the *Sám Kwŏk Chì*, *Liu Chái*, &c. Each one of them forms a complete period, and is read from left to right for convenience in printing the sound, and the signification underneath. The literal translation of each word is placed underneath its sound, and the free idiomatic translation at the foot of the page. To derive all the benefit possible from the lessons, the sound and sense of every character as it here stands should be committed to memory; so that if the Chinese line be covered, every character can be written by seeing its sound; if the sounds be covered, the line of Chinese can be read off fluently; or if the line of English be exposed, the Chinese characters and sound will immediately recur to the mind.

1 呂布無義之人不可信也
'Lü Pò' ˌmò i' ˏchí ˌyan, pat˒ 'hó sun' 'yá.
Lü Pò no principle 's man, not can believe truly.

2 屈身守分以待天時不可與命
Wat˒ ˏshan 'shau fan' 'i toi' ˏt'in ˌshì, pat˒ 'hó 'ü ming'
Succumb myself keeping place by waiting heaven's time, not can with fate

爭也
ˏchang 'yá.
quarrel.

3 吾與奉先無隙何故引兵至此
'Ng 'ü Fung' ˏsin ˌmò kwik˒, ˌhó kú' 'yan ˏping chí' 'tsz'.
I with Fungsin without altercation, what reason lead troops to this-place?

4 公等皆讀書之人何不達理
ˏKung 'tang ˏkái tuk˒ ˏshü ˏchi ˌyan; ˌhó pat˒ tát˒ 'li?
Sirs all read books 's men; how not understand reason?

---

1. Lu Pò, a man of no principle, cannot be trusted.
2. By succumbing and keeping my place, I shall await heaven's time; I cannot contend with fate.
3. I have no dispute with Fungsin, and why therefore should I lead troops here?
4. You, gentlemen, are all scholars; how is it then that you do not understand what is right?

5 你年尙輕未可爲大將
'Ní ˏnin shéung' ˏhing, mi^{2} 'hó ˏwai tái^{2} tséung'.
Your years still few, not-yet able to be great captain.

6 可惜當日火不大不曾燒死你這國賊
'Hó sik,! ˏtóng yat, 'fó pat, tái^{2}, pat, ˏts'ang 'shíú 'sz' 'ní ché' kwók, ts'ak,.
How sad! that day fire not powerful, not yet burned dead you that state rebel.

7 宮曰汝心術不正吾故棄汝
ˏKung üt,, 'ü ˏsam shut, pat, ching' ˏ'ng kú' hí' 'ü.
Kung said, 'Your heart's designs not upright, I therefore discarded you.'

8 廟堂之上何太無禮
Míú^{2} ˏt'óng ˏchí shéung^{2}, ˏhó t'ái' ˏmò 'lai?
Ancestral court 's within, how greatly destitute of propriety?

9 欺君罔上乃爲無禮
ˏHí ˏkwan 'móng shéung^{2}, 'nái ˏwai ˏmò 'lai.
Deceiving prince, despising superiors, is to be destitute-of propriety.

10 先生此去天各一方未知相會却於何日
ˏSín ˏshang 'ts'z' hü', ˏt'ín kók, yat, ˏfóng, mi^{2} ˏchí ˏséung üí^{2} k'éuk, ˏü ˏhó yat,.
Sir this departure, heaven each one place, not know mutual meeting will-be in what day.

11 其人身長七尺面黃睛赤形容古怪
ˏK'í ˏyan ˏshan 'ch'éung ts'at, ch'ik, mín^{2} ˏwóng, ˏtsing ch'ik, ˏying 'yung 'kú kwái'.
This man's body length seven cubits, face yellow, pupil reddish, form appearance odd wild.

---

5. You, still young in years, are not able to act as a high general.

6. How sad, that on that day the fire was not powerful enough to have burned you to death,—you that rebel against the state!

7. Kung said, 'your designs were not upright, and I therefore cast you off.'

8. In the court of ancestors, how can you be so utterly devoid of propriety?

9. He, who deceives his prince and despises his superiors, is one who is without propriety.

10. After this departure, sir, each of us will have his own sky; we know not the day when we shall meet again.

11. This man was seven cubits tall, his face yellow, his pupil reddish, and his whole appearance very remarkable.

12 兄 長 不可去 呂布必有異 心
ˌHing ʻchéung pat, ʻhó hüʼ, ʻLü Pòʼ pit, ʻyau iʼ ˌsam.
Elder brother not can go, Lü Pò certainly has specious intentions.

13 卓 擎 杯 問 曰 青 春 幾何
Chʻéuk, ˌkʻing ˌpúi manʼ üt, ˌtsʻing ˌchʻun ʻkí ˌhó?
Chʻéuk, raising glass, asked, saying, 'Green springs many how?'

14 適 間 所 囑 不 可 有 悞
Shik, ˌkán ʻshó chuk, pat, ʻhó ʻyau ʼngʼ.
Just while what ordered, not can be unfulfilled.

15 此 計 速 行 不可 遲 悞
ʻTsʻzʼ kaiʼ chʻuk, ˌhang, pat, ʻhó ˌchʻi ʼngʼ.
This plan quickly accomplished, not can tardily miss.

16 既 子 敬 相 請 我 明 日 便 來 赴 宴
ˌKí ʻTszʼ kingʼ ˌséung ʻtsʻing, ʻngó ˌming yat, pínʼ ˌloi fúʼ ínʼ.
Already Tszʼking has invited, I to-morrow then come to feast.

17 不 必 多 言 來 日 到 府 下 公 議
Pat, pit, ˌtó ˌín, ˌloi yat, tòʼ ʻfú háʼ ˌkung ʻí.
Not needed much talking, coming day come-to office down publicly consult.

18 見 一 人 綸 巾 道 服 坐 在 船 頭 乃
Kinʼ yat, ˌyan ˌkwán ˌkan Tòʼ fuk, tsóʼ tsoiʼ ˌshün ˌtʻau, ʻnái
Saw a man, silken cap, Taou dress, sitting on vessel's head, it-was

孔 明 也
ʻHung ˌming ʻyá.
Hungming indeed.

19 向 慕 先 生 才 德 未 得 拜 晤 今 幸
Héungʼ mòʼ ˌsín ˌshang ˌtsʻoi tak, míʼ tak, páiʼ ʼngʼ, ˌkam hangʼ
Long esteemed your talents virtue, not-yet obtained respect meet, now happy

相 遇
ˌséung üʼ.
mutual meeting.

---

12. My brother must not go, for Lü Pò certainly has some specious designs.
13. Chʻéuk raising his glass, asked, 'How old are you?'
14. That which I have just ordered you to do, must not fail to be fulfilled.
15. This scheme must be quickly acted upon and not lost by delay.
16. Tszʼking has already invited me, and to-morrow I shall come to the feast.
17. We do not want so much talking; to-morrow come down to the office for a public consultation.
18. He saw a man sitting on the vessel's bow, dressed in a silken cap, and garb of the Taou sect, who was Hungming.
19. For a long time, I have admired your talents and virtues, but

20 見張飛怒目橫矛立馬于橋上
Kín' ˌChéung ˌFi, nò² muk₂ ˌwâng ˌmau, lap₂ ʻmá ˌü ˌkʻíú shéung².
Saw Chéung Fi, menacing eyes, rested spear, standing horse on bridge top.

21 孔明安在願求一見
ʻHung ˌming ˌón tsoi²? ün² ˌkʻau yat₂ kín'.
Hungming where is? I wish to seek an interview.

22 賢弟見過吳侯却來敘話
ˌI'n tai² kín' kwò' ˌ'Ng ˌhau, kʻéuk₂ ˌloi tsü² wá².
Worthy brother seen have 'Ng's prince, then coming converse words.

23 何事在心寢食俱廢
ˌHó sz'² tsoi² ˌsam, ʻtsʻam shik₂ ˌkʻü fai'?
What affair in heart, sleeping eating both gone?

24 兩國相爭不斬來使
ʻLéung kwók₂ ˌséung ˌchang, pat₂ ʻchám ˌloi sz'².
Two states together contending, not kill coming messenger.

25 子敬休問來日便見
ʻTsz' king' ˌyau man², ˌloi yat₂ pín² kín'.
Tsz'king cease asking, coming day then see.

26 瑜日軍中無戲言
ˌU üt₂ ˌkwan ˌchung ˌmò hí' ˌín.
U said, army midst have-no idle words.

27 曹操馬步水軍約有一百五十餘萬
ˌTsʻò ˌTsʻò ʻmá pò² ʻshui ˌkwan yéuk₂ ʻyau yat₂ pák₂ ʻng shap₂ ˌü mán².
Ts'ò Ts'ò's cavalry, infantry, marine troops, about were one hundred fifty more myriads.

---

hitherto have had no opportunity of paying my respects; now I have the pleasure of meeting you.

20. He saw Chéung Fi, with menacing eyes and rested spear, standing his horse on the bridge.

21. Where is Hungming? I wish to seek an interview.

22. When you, worthy sir, have seen the prince of 'Ng, then return to me to talk over the matter.

23. What is there on your mind that your sleep and appetite have both failed?

24. When two states are at war, public messengers are not killed.

25. Tsz'king cease to ask, for to-morrow you will know about it.

26. U said, 'we have no idle talk in the army.'

27. Ts'o Ts'ò's cavalry, infantry, and marines, were in all about one million five hundred thousand.

66 LESSONS IN READING.

28 瑜 大 驚 流 汗 滿 臂
˛U táí² ˓king˛ ˛lau hón² ˋmún pí².
U much alarmed, flowed perspiration filled arms.

29 丞 相 勿 言 恐 有 泄 漏
˛Shing séung² mat˛ ˛ín, ˋhung ˋyau sít˛ lau².
Your excellency, do not speak, lest there be leak ooze.

30 連 日 不 晤 君 顏 何 期 貴 体 不 安
˛Lín yat˛ pat˛ ˋng² ˓kwan ˛ngán, ˛hó ˓k'i kwai² ˋt'ai pat˛ ˓ón!
Successive days not seen your face, why now your body not well?

31 大 霧 迷 漫 百 步 之 外 人 亦 不 見
Táí² mò² ˛mai mán˛ pák˛ pò² ˓chí ngoi², ˛yan yik˛ pat˛ kín².
Thick fog concealed covered hundred step 's beyond, man even not visible.

32 遙 望 山 清 水 秀 景 致 異 常
˛I'ú móng² ˓shán ˓ts'ing ˋshui sau², ˋking chí² í² ˛shéung.
Distant seeing hills distinct, water picturesque, prospect fine unlike usual.

33 吾 自 幼 熟 讀 兵 書 深 知 奸
˛'Ng tsz'² yau² shuk˛ tuk˛ ˓ping ˓shü, ˓sham ˓chí ˓kán
I from youth thoroughly read military works, fully know deception

僞 之 道
ngai² ˓chí t'ò².
strategy 's rules.

34 其 船 拽 起 滿 帆 乘 順 風 去 了
˛K'i ˛shün yai² ˋhí ˋmún ˛fán ˛shing shun² ˓fung hü² ˋliú.
His vessel hoisted raised full sail, improved favorable wind went away.

35 孤 意 已 决 先 生 勿 疑
˓Kú í² ˋí k'üt˛ ˓sín ˓shang mat˛ ˛í.
Our determination already fixed, sir do not doubt.

---

28. U was so much alarmed that the flowing perspiration covered his arms.

29. Let not your excellency (i. e. the prime minister) speak about it, lest the affair become divulged.

30. For several days I have not seen you; why now are you so ill?

31. The thick fog concealed things, so that at the distance of more than a hundred paces even a man was not visible.

32. Looking at a distance the hills were distinct, and the water picturesque,—the prospect was unusually fine.

33. From my youth, I have thoroughly read military authors, and fully know the rules of deception and strategy.

34. The sails being hoisted to their full extent, he took advantage of the fair wind, and departed.

35. My royal determination is already fixed, and you sir, need not doubt.

36 得 功 者 賞 何 計 貴 賤 乎
Tak, ˏkung ‘ché ‘shéung, ˏhó kai’ kwai’ tsín’ ˏú?
Obtaining meritorious persons reward, why reckon honorable mean eh?

37 詩 詞 歌 賦 妙 冠 當 時
ˏShí ˏts‘z’ ˏkó fú’ miú’ kún’ ˏtóng ˏshí.
Poetry, songs, ballads, lays, excellent preëminent that day.

38 曹 子 建 詩 成 七 步 世 罕 其 儔
ˏTs‘ò ‘Tsz’ kín’ ˏshí ˏshing ts‘at, pò’, shai’ ‘hón ˏk‘i ˏch‘au.
Ts‘ò Tsz‘kín stanza completed seven paces, age rare his class.

39 道 士 出 一 葫 盧 拔 其 塞 無
Tò’ sz’ ch‘ut, yat, ˏú ˏlú, pát, ˏk‘i sak, ˏmò
Taou priest brought-out a gourd, drew its stopper, without

限 兵 馬 殺 出
han’ ˏping ‘má shat, ch‘ut,.
limit war horses furiously issued.

40 廟 堂 重 地 禁 止 喧 嘩
Miú’ ˏt‘óng chung’ tí’, kam’ ‘chí ˏhün ˏwá.
Temple hall important place, prohibit stop boisterous talk.

41 孔 明 亦 人 耳 臣 何 畏 彼 哉
‘Hung ˏming yik, ˏyan ‘i, ˏshan ˏhó wai’ ‘pí ˏtsoi?
Hungming but man indeed, I why fear him eh?

42 街 上 大 多 光 棍 須 要 小 心
ˏKái shéung, tái’ ˏtó ˏkwóng kwan’, ˏsü iú’ ‘siú ˏsam.
Street in great many sharpers, must need careful attention.

43 匪 徒 太 多 隄 防 剪 綹
‘Fí ˏt‘ò t‘ái’ ˏtó, ˏt‘ai ˏfóng ‘tsin nau’.
Vagabonds great many, take care cut purses.

---

36. In rewarding the meritorious, why bring into account their honorable or low rank?

37. For poetry, songs, ballads, and lays, he was preëminent in his time.

38. Ts‘ò Tsz‘kín could complete a stanza while taking seven paces; the age had few such men.

39. The Taou priest, producing a gourd, drew the stopper, when innumerable war horses furiously issued.

40. In the temple's venerated spot, all boisterous talk is strictly prohibited.

41. Hungming is nothing but a man, why I should dread him?

42. In the streets are numerous sharpers, it is necessary to take great care.

43. The vagabonds are very numerous, take care lest your purse be cut.

44 兄 今 番 出 征 何 故 如 此 忙 速
Hing kam fán ch'ut, ching, hó kú' ü 'ts'z' fóng chuk,.
Brother this occasion go-out rectify, what reason such this bustling haste?

45 將 在 外 君 命 有 所 不 受
Tséung tsoi' ngoi' kwan ming' 'yau 'shó pat, shau'.
General is abroad, prince commands are what not obey.

46 鄭 康 成 好 學 多 才 侍 婢 俱
Ching' Hóng shing hò' hók, tó ts'oi shi' 'pi k'ü
Ching Hóngshing loved study esteemed talents, waiting maids all

通 毛 詩
t'ung mò shí.
thorough-in Ode poetry.

47 僧 繇 善 畫 嘗 畫 一 鷹 于 壁
Sang Yau shin' wák, shéung wák, yat, ying ü pik,,
Sang Yau expert drawer; had drawn one hawk on wall,

雀 鴿 不 敢 近
tséuk, kóp, pat, 'kóm kan'.
sparrows doves not dare approach.

48 李 思 訓 善 畫 山 水 極 窮 其
'Lí Sz' fan' shin' wák, shán 'shui, kik, k'ung k'í
Lí Sz'fan expert drawing land water, extremely like their

態 恍 聞 水 聲
tái', 'fóng man 'shui shing.
form, almost hear water dash.

49 後 主 有 畫 牛 一 軸 晝 則 嚙
Hau' 'chü 'yau wá' ngau yat, chau'; chau' tsak, it,
Hauchü had painted ox one sheet; day then ate

草 欄 外 夜 則 歸 卧 欄 中
'ts'ò lán ngoi', yé' tsak, kwai ngó' lán chung.
grass fence beyond, night then returned sleep fence within.

---

44. Why, sir, on this occasion of going out to restore order is there such bustle?

45. When a general is abroad there are at times orders from the prince which he does not receive.

46. Ching Hóngshing so loved study and esteemed talents that his waiting-maids were all well versed in the Book of Odes.

47. Sang Yau was skillful at drawing; he once drew a hawk on the wall, which the sparrows and doves did not dare to approach.

48. Lí Sz'fan cleverly drew landscapes, so extremely like their appearance, that one could almost hear the dashing of the water.

49. Hauchü had a painting of an ox, which by day cropped grass beyond the fence, and by night returned to sleep within it.

50 左 慈 擲 盃 空 中 化 成 一 白
꜂Tsó ꜁Ts‘z' chak꜇ ꜀púi ꜀hung ꜀chung fá꜄ ꜁shing yat꜆ pák꜇
Tsó Ts‘z' tossed cup sky in metamorphosed into one hundred

鳩 遶 殿 而 飛
꜀kau, ꜃ü t‘in꜅ ꜁i ꜀fi.
pigeons, encircled palace and flew.

51 久 不 相 見 今 居 何 處
꜂Kau pat꜆ ꜀séung kín꜄, ꜀kam ꜀kü ꜁hó ch‘ü꜄?
Long not each-other seen, now live what place?

52 孟 德 此 行 將 欲 何 往
Mang꜅ tak꜆ ꜂ts‘z ꜁hang ꜀tséung yuk꜇ ꜁hó ꜃wóng꜅?
Mangtak this walk about wishing where go?

53 某 今 興 兵 討 賊 正 爲 國 家
꜃Mau ꜀kam ꜀hing ꜀ping ꜂t‘ò ts‘ak꜇ ching꜄ wai꜅ kwók꜆, ꜀ká
I now raise troops destroy rebel, truly for country's house

除 害 耳
꜁ch‘ü hoi꜅ ꜃i.
drive-off trouble.

54 至 夜 深 月 明 允 策 杖 步 入 後 園
Chí꜄ yé꜅ ꜀sham üt꜇ ꜁ming, ꜃Wan ch‘ák꜆ chéung꜅ pò꜅ yap꜇ hau꜅ ꜁ün.
At night late moon light, Wan taking cane walking entered rear garden.

55 此 等 碌 碌 小 人 何 足 挂 齒
꜂Ts‘z' ꜂tang luk꜆ luk꜆ ꜂siú ꜁yan, ꜁hó tsuk꜆ kwá꜄ ꜂ch‘i?
This sort so so small men, what worth hang-on teeth?

56 轉 盼 間 狐 忽 化 一 美 人
꜂Chün p‘án꜄ ꜀kán, ꜁ú fat꜆ fá꜄ yat꜆ ꜃mí ꜁yan,
Turning gazing whilst, fox suddenly metamorphosed a beautiful person,

光 艷 奪 目
꜀kwóng ím꜅ tüt꜇ muk꜇.
bright lustrous fixed eyes.

---

50. Tsó Ts‘z', tossing the cup into the air, it was metamorphosed into a hundred pigeons, which flew around the palace.

51. We have not seen each other for a long time, where do you now live?

52. Where does Mangtak intend going in this walk?

53. I am now raising troops to destroy this rebel, simply for the purpose of averting harm from the imperial family.

54. Late at night, when it was moonlight, Wan, taking a cane, walked into the rear garden.

55. Why longer speak about such a contemptible set of fellows?

56. In the twinkling of an eye, the fox was metamorphosed into a beautiful person—her bright splendor fixed the gaze.

57 汝 無 端 獻 讒 欲 害 好 人 耶
ˢU ˌmò ˌtün hin' ˌts'án yuk, hoi' 'hò ˌyan ˌyé.
You without cause offer accusations wishing injure good man eh!

58 慈 曰 我 數 十 年 不 食 亦 不
ˌTs'z' üt, 'ngó shò' shap, ˌnín pat, shik, yik, pat,
Ts'z' said, I several tens years not eat and not

防 日 食 千 羊 亦 能 盡
ˌfóng; yat, shik, ˌts'ín ˌyéung yik, ˌnang tsun'.
matter; day eat thousand sheep and can finish.

59 車 已 去 遠 布 緩 轡 于 土 岡
ˌKü ˢi hü' ˢün, Pò' ún' pí' ˌü 'tò ˌkóng
Carriage already gone far, Pò slacked bridle on earthy hillock

之 上 眼 望 車 塵 嘆 惜 痛 恨
ˌchí shéung', 'ngán móng' ˌkü ˌch'an t'án' sik, t'ung' han'.
's top, eyes beheld carriage's dust, sighing grieved pained exceedingly.

60 布 曰 吾 欲 殺 此 老 賊 奈 是
Pò' üt, ˌ'ng yuk, shat, 'ts'z' ˢlò ts'ak, noi' shí'
Pò said, I wish kill this old rebel, only is

父 子 之 情 恐 惹 後 人 議 論
fú' 'tsz' ˌchí ˌts'ing, 'hung ˢyé hau' ˌyan ˢi lun'.
father son 's relations, fear induce after men reflect remark.

61 布 拔 帶 刀 刺 臂 出 血 爲 誓
Pò' pat, tái' ˌtò ts'z' pí' ch'ut, hüt, ˌwai shai'.
Pò drew belt sword pricked arm drew blood for oath.

62 卓 大 喜 曰 吾 夜 夢 一 龍 罩
Ch'éuk, tái' 'hí üt, ˌ'ng yé' mung' yat, ˌlung cháu'
Ch'éuk much pleased said, I night dreamed one dragon covered

身 今 日 果 得 此 喜 信
ˌshan, ˌkam yat, 'kwò tak, 'ts'z' 'hí sun'.
me, to day truly obtained the joyful verity.

---

57. Do you thus needlessly bring in accusations, desiring to injure a good man!

58. Ts'z' replied, 'If I should not eat for several tens of years it would be of no consequence, while, in one day, I could consume a thousand sheep.'

59. The carriage was already distant, when Pò, slacking his bridle on the top of a hillock, and following with his eyes the dust, sighed most deeply.

60. Pò said, 'I wish to kill this old rascal, but, on account of our relation of [adopted] father and son, I fear lest it will induce the criticism of future ages.

61. Pò, drawing his belt sword, pricked blood from his arm to declare his oath.

62. Ch'éuk, much pleased, said, 'In the night, I dreamed that a

63 卓 出 塢 上 車 前 遮 後 擁 望
Ch'éuk, ch'ut, 'Ü' 'shéung ,kü; ,ts'ín ,ché hau' 'yung, móng'
Ch'éuk leaving Ü' ascended chariot; before guarded behind protected towards

長 安 來 行 不 到 三 十 里 所
,Ch'éung ,ón ,loi; ,hang pat, tò' ,sám shap, 'lí 'shó
Ch'éungón went; gone not to thirty lí that

乘 之 車 忽 折 一 輪
,shing ,chí ,kü fat, chít, yat, ,lun.
rode-in 's carriage suddenly broke a wheel.

64 卓 問 肅 曰 車 折 輪 馬 斷 轡
Ch'éuk, man' Suk, üt, ,kü chít, ,lun, 'má 'tün pí',
Ch'éuk asking Suk said, chariot broke wheel, horse split bridle,

其 兆 若 何
,k'i chiú' yéuk, ,hó?
these omens how what?

65 肅 曰 乃 太 師 應 詔 漢 禪 棄
Suk, üt, 'nái t'ái' ,sz' ying' chiú' Hón' ,shím, hí'
Suk replied, are great officer responding call Hán throne, discard

舊 換 新 將 乘 玉 輦 金 鞍 之 兆 也
kau' ún' ,san, ,tséung ,shing yuk, 'lín ,kam ,ón ,chí chiú' 'yá.
old change new, about mounting gemmeous chariot golden saddle 's omens indeed.

66 王 允 大 呼 曰 反 賊 至 此 武
,Wóng 'Wan tái' ,fú üt, 'fán ts'ak, chí' 'ts'z', 'mò
Wóng Wan loud calling said, lawless rebel to this, military

士 何 在 兩 旁 轉 出 百 餘 人
sz'' ,hó tsoi'? 'Léung ,p'óng 'chün ch'ut, pák, ,ü ,yan
officers where are? Both sides sallied out hundred more men

---

dragon covered me, and to-day, behold, I obtain the joyful verification.'

63. Ch'éuk, going out of Ü', got into his carriage, guarded in front and protected in rear; setting his face towards Ch'éungón, he had not proceeded thirty *lí*, when a wheel of the carriage in which he rode suddenly broke.

64. Ch'éuk, asking Suk, said, 'What do the omens of breaking the carriage wheel, and snapping the horse's bridle, prognosticate?'

65. Suk replied, 'They foreshow that a great statesman is responding to the call from the throne of Hán, who, discarding the old and changing it for new, will shortly occupy the imperial chariot and royal saddle.'

66. Wóng Wan exclaimed aloud, 'The rebellious outlaw has come, where are the officers?' From both sides, armed with halberds and maces, more than a hundred men rushed out and attacked him;

持戟挺槊刺之卓裹甲不
ch'í kik, 'ting shók, ts'z' chi; Ch'éuk, 'kwó káp, pat,
grasping halberds holding maces wounded him; Ch'éuk's inner armor, not

入傷臂墮車
yap, shéung pí chúi ku.
pierce wounded arm fell-out chariot.

67 吾匣中寶劍新磨汝試言
'Ng háp, chung, 'pò kím' san mó, 'ü shí' ín
My armory in valuable sword newly ground, you try speak

之其言不通便請試劍
chi, k'i ín pat, t'ung pín' 'ts'ing shí' kím'.
it, your words not intelligible then request try sword.

68 某雖不才願去萬軍中取
'Mau sui pat, ts'oi ün' hü' mán' kwan chung, 'ts'ü
I although not clever wish go myriad troops among get

其首級來獻丞相
k'i 'shau k'ap, loi hín' shing séung'.
his head skull bring present prime minister.

69 融諫操曰楊公四世清
Yung kán' Ts'ò üt,, Yéung kung sz' shai' ts'ing
Yung remonstrating Ts'ò, said, Yéung lord four generations unsullied

德豈可因袁氏而罪之乎
tak,, 'hí 'hó yan Un shí' í tsúi' chi ú?
virtue, how can because Un family also criminate him eh?

70 謀士程昱說操曰今明公威
Mau sz' Ch'ing Yuk, shui' Ts'ò üt,, kam ming kung wai
Counselor Ch'ing Yuk addressing Ts'ò said, now distinguished lord's awful

名日盛何不乘此時行王霸之事
ming yat, shing', hó pat, shing 'ts'z' shí hang wóng pá' chí sz'?
reputation daily increases, why not improve this time to do ruler tyrant 's affair?

Ch'éuk's hauberk could not be pierced, but wounded in the arms, he fell from his carriage.

67. In my armory is a valuable sword just sharpened; you can try to speak about it (the business), but if your words are not straightforward then I shall beg to use the sword.

68. Although I am not clever, yet I wish to go into the midst of the multitude of troops, and get his head to present to your excellency.

69. Yung, remonstrating with Ts'ò, said, lord Yéung is a man whose family for four generations has maintained an unsullied virtue; why do you criminate him on account of the Messrs. Un?

70. Counselor Ching Yuk, speaking to Ts'ò, said, Your honor's reputation is now daily increasing in dignity; why do you not take advantage of this opportunity to become the ruling prince!

71 帝日朕今欲看皇叔射獵
Tai' üt, cham' ,kam yuk, hón' ,wóng shuk, shé' lip,.
Emperor said, we now wish see imperial uncle shoot archer-like.

玄德領命上馬忽草中趕起
,Un tak, 'ling ming' 'shéung 'má, fat, 'ts'ò ,chung 'kón 'hí
Untak obeying order mounted horse, suddenly grass midst drove up

一兎玄德射之一箭正中那兎
yat, t'ò'; ,Un tak, shé' ,chi yat, tsin' ching' chung' 'ná t'ò'.
one hare; Untak shooting it one shot directly hit the hare.

72 建寧二年四月望日帝御温德
Kin' ,ning, í' ,nín, sz' üt, móng' yat, tai' ü' ,Wan Tak,
Kinning, 2d year, 4th month, 15th day, emperor visiting Mild Virtue

殿方陞座殿角狂風驟起只見
tin', ,fóng ,shing tsó', tin' kók, ,kwóng ,fung cháu' 'hí, chat, kin'
palace, just ascended throne palace corner furious blast suddenly arose, only saw

一條大青蛇從梁上飛將下來
yat, ,t'iú tái' ,ts'ing ,shé ,ts'ung ,léung shéung' ,fí ,tséung há' ,loi
one single great green serpent from ridge above glided directly down coming

蟠于椅上帝驚倒左右急救
,pún ,ü 'í shéung'; tai' ,king 'tò, 'tsó yau' kap, kau'
wound about throne on; emperor affrighted fell, left right quickly caught-up

入宮百官俱奔避須臾蛇不見
yap, ,kung; pák, ,kún ,k'ü ,pan pí'. ,Sü ,ü ,shé pat, kin'
entered apartment; the officers all hastily fled. Instantly serpent not observ-

了忽然大雷大雨加以冰雹落
'liú fat, ,in tái' ,lui tái' 'ü ,ká 'í ,ping puk, lók,
ed, suddenly loud thunder great rain, added to which icy hail fell

到半夜方止壞却房屋無數
tò' pún' yé' ,fóng 'chi, wái' k'éuk, ,fóng uk, ,mò shò'.
till mid night then stopped, ruin ed buildings dwellings without number.

---

71. The emperor said, 'We now wish to see our uncle draw the bow in an archer-like manner.' Untak obeyed the order, and mounted his horse, when suddenly from among the grass a hare was started up, which was directly shot through with an arrow thrown by him.

72. In the 15th day of the 4th month, 2d year of Kinning's reign, the emperor was visiting the palace of Mild Virtue, and had just ascended the throne, when at the corner of the house a furious blast suddenly arose, and a large green serpent was seen gliding down from the ridge, which wound itself around the throne; the affrighted emperor fell to the ground, and his attendants instantly taking him up carried him into his apartment, and all the officers fled in terror. In a moment, the serpent vanished, and suddenly there was loud thunder

73 於 是 揀 選 良 馬 名 鷹 俊 犬
U shí kán sún léung má ming ying tsun hün
There upon selected chose gentle horses famous falcons apt dogs

弓 矢 俱 備 先 聚 兵 城 外 操
kung ch'i; k'ü pí, sín tsü ping shing ngoi, Ts'ò
bows arrows; all prepared, first collecting troops city without, Ts'ò

入 請 天 子 畋 獵
yap ts'ing t'in tsz t'in lip.
entering invited heaven's son field hunt.

74 便 縱 馬 接 戰 典 韋 畧 戰 數 合
Pín tsung má ts'íp, chín; Tín Wai léuk chín shò hóp
Then giving-reins horse joined fight; Tín Wai briefly fought several times,

便 回 馬 走 壯 士 只 顧 望 前 赶 來
pín úi má tsau, chóng sz chat kú móng ts'ín kón loi,
then turning horse fled, brave man only intently looking before pursuing after,

不 隄 防 連 人 帶 馬 都 落 于 陷 坑 之 內
pat t'ai fóng lín yan tái má tò lók ü hám háng chí noi.
not caring guarding both man and horse all fell into trap pit 's within.

75 操 忙 下 帳 叱 退 軍 士 親 解
Ts'ò móng há chéung ch'ik, t'úi kwan sz, ts'an kái
Ts'ò hastily descending-from tent, hooted retire army officers, himself loosed

其 縛 急 取 衣 衣 之 命 坐 問 其 鄉
k'i fók, kap, ts'ü i í chí, ming tsó man k'i héung
his bonds quickly taking clothes clothed him, ordering sit asked his village

貫 姓 名
kún sing ming.
native surname name.

---

and heavy rain, together with hail, which, falling till midnight, stopped, having ruined innumerable dwellings.

73. He thereupon selected gentle horses, famous falcons, and excellent dogs, with bows and arrows; when all things were in readiness, Ts'ò, having first marshaled his troops without the city-walls, entered and invited his majesty to take a hunt.

74. Then giving reins to his horse, he joined in battle, but Tín Wai, after engaging in a few rencontres, turned his horse and fled; the brave man, only looking straight before him, pursued after him, but not heeding his steps, both he and his horse tumbled into a pit.

75. Ts'ò, hastily coming out of his tent, shouted to the officers of the army to retire, and, unloosing his bonds with his own hands, quickly disrobed himself and clothed him, bidding him to be seated, and asking his native village, his surname and name.

76 賊驅牛至塢外 牛皆奔走 回還 被
Ts'ak₂ ‚k'ü ‚ngau chí' 'U' ngoi², ‚ngau ‚kái ‚pan 'tsau ‚úi ‚wán, pí²
Robbers drove oxen to U' without, oxen all quickly ran turn back, by

我雙手掣二牛尾倒行 百餘步
'ngó ‚shéung 'shau chai' í² ‚ngau 'mí, 'tò ‚hang pák₂ ‚ü pò².
my two hands grasped two oxen tails backwards dragged hundred more paces.

77 操問曰何故見賜 承曰 因 念
‚Ts'ò man² üt₂ ‚hò kú' kín' ts'z'? ‚Shing üt₂, ‚yan ním²
Ts'ò asking said, what cause has conferred? Shing replied, because remembering

某舊日西都救駕之功故 有此賜
'mau kau² yat₂ ‚Sai ‚tò kau' ká' ‚chi ‚kung, kú' 'yau 'ts'z' ts'z'.
my former day Saitò saved car 's merit, therefore have this reward.

78 他爲人沉靜寡欲不貪 名利
‚T'á ‚wai ‚yan ‚ch'am tsing² 'kwá yuk₂ pat₂ ‚t'ám ‚ming lí²,
He was man very quiet few desires not coveting reputation profit,

懶于逢迎但以詩酒自娛
'lán ‚ü ‚fung ‚ying, tán² 'í ‚shí 'tsau tsz'² ‚ü.
heedless in meeting receiving, but for poetry wine self delighted.

79 這白太常官又高家又富才
Ché' Pák₂ t'ái' ‚shéung ‚kún yau² ‚kò, ‚ká yau² fú', ‚ts'oi
This Pák superior constant office also high, family also rich, talent

學政 望又大有聲名
hók₂ ching' móng², yau² tái² 'yau ‚shing ‚ming.
learning government conspicuous, besides great has fame reputation.

80 尊寓在何處尙未曾到拜候
‚Tsün ü² tsoi² ‚hó ch'ü'? shéung² mí² ‚ts'ang tò' pái' hau².
Sir live in what place? still not yet come respect wait-on.

---

76. The robbers had driven the oxen to the outskirts of U', when they all turned to run back, but with my two hands grasping two of them by their tails, I dragged them backwards more than a hundred paces.

77. Ts'ò asking said, 'Why has he conferred them upon you?' Shing replied, 'Because, remembering my meritorious action on a former day when I saved his majesty at Saitò, he in consequence has bestowed this.'

78. He was a man very fond of quiet, with few desires, not coveting reputation or gain, and careless about the etiquette of society, but delighting in poetry and wine.

79. This president (of the Sacrificial Court) Pák fills a high office, his family is rich, his talents and learning are conspicuous in the government, and besides his reputation is also very high.

80. Where, sir, do you reside? I have not yet called to pay my respects,

Chapter Eighth.

EXERCISES IN TRANSLATING.

The literal version and sounds of the characters of the lessons contained in this chapter are only given, as the student is expected by this time to have learned enough of the idiom of the language to be able to translate them into good English without much if any assistance. In translating from Chinese into English, great care ought to be taken to avoid inversions of style from following too closely the Chinese idiom, which will often render the style of the version stiff, without adding to its perspicuity. Compound or dissyllabic terms are common in Chinese writing, and stereotyped phrases that are seldom if ever separated, but which contain only one idea; these are in some cases properly translated by a single word. Knowledge of the meaning of the characters merely is not sufficient to make a person a good translator; he must attend also to the force of the word or phrase in its connection in the original so as to select an apt expression by which to render it. Some attention should be paid to such peculiar phrases in the original as are deserving of being transfused into the version, while too close a fidelity will make it inelegant or vapid. Good taste will prove the best guide in the choice of words, and teach when to express a native phrase in its literal dress, and when to render it by an equivalent; so that while the reader is not offended by barbarisms and harsh epithets, he will feel that he is possessed of whatever in the original is witty in thought, and elegant in expression.

No. 1.—Cleverness of Hung Yung.

(見三國志 卷之六 第十一回)

北海孔 融字文 舉魯 國 曲 阜人也
Pak, 'hoi, 'Hung ,Yung, tsz'² ,Man 'kü, 'Lú kwok,, Huk, fau' ,yan 'yá
Pakhoi, Hung Yung, styled Mankü, [was a] Lú state, Hukfau man

孔 子 二 十 世 孫 泰 山 都 尉
'Hung 'tsz' í' shap, shai' ,sün. T'ái' ,shán ,tò wai',
Confucius twentieth generation's descendant. T'áishán general soother,

孔 宙 之 子 自 少 聰 明 年 十 歲
'Hung Chau' ,chí 'tsz'. Tsz'² shiú' ,ts'ung ,ming; ,nín shap, sui'
Hung Chau 's son. From youth clever intelligent; aged ten years

時 往 謁 河 南 尹 李 膺 閽 人 難 之
,shí, 'wóng it, ,Hó ,nám 'wan, 'Lí ,Ying; ,fan ,yan ,nán ,chí.
time, went visit Hónám officer, Lí Ying; door porter hindered him.

融 曰 我 係 李 相 通 家 及 入 見
ˏYung üt,, ʻNgó hai² ʻLí séung² ˏtʻung ˏká; kʻap, yap, kín².
Yung said, I am Lí minister allied family; and entering saw.

膺 問 曰 汝 祖 與 吾 祖 何 親
ˏYing man² üt,, ʻü ʻtsò ʻü ˏʻng ʻtsò, ˏhó ˏtsʻan?
Ying asked saying, Your ancestor and my ancestor, what connection?

融 曰 昔 孔 子 曾 問 禮 于 老 子
ˏYung üt,, Sik, ʻHung ʻtsz ˏtsʻang man² ʻlai ˏü ʻLò ʻtsz;
Yung replied, Anciently Confucius already asked propriety of Laoutsze:

融 與 君 豈 非 累 世 通 家 膺 大
ˏYung ʻü ˏkwan: ʻhí ˏfí ʻlui shai², ˏtʻung ˏká! ˏYing tái²
Yung with Lí: how not bound generation, allied family! Ying much

奇 之
ˏkʻí ˏchí.
surprised-at him.

少 頃 大 中 大 夫 陳 煒 至 膺 指
ʻShiú ʻkʻing tái² ˏchung tái² ˏfú ˏChʻan ʻWai chí², ˏYing ʻchí
Short space, principal inner great lord Chʻan Wai coming, Ying pointed-to

融 曰 此 奇 童 也 煒 曰 少 時 聰
ˏYung üt,, ʻTsʻz ˏkʻí ˏtʻung ʻyá. ʻWai üt,, Shiú² ˏshí ˏtsʻung
Yung said, This remarkable lad. Wai replied, Young time clever

明 大 時 未 必 聰 明 融 即
ˏming, tái² ˏshí mí² pit, ˏtsʻung ˏming. ˏYung tsik,
intelligent, old time not certainly clever intelligent. Yung immediately

應 聲 曰 如 君 所 言 幼 時 必
ying² ˏshing üt,, ˏü ˏkwan ʻshó ˏin, yau² ˏshí pit,
echoing tone said, According-to honor what says, young time must

聰 明 者 煒 等 皆 笑 曰 此 子 長 成
ˏtsʻung ˏming ʻché. ʻWai ʻtang ˏkái siú² üt,, ʻTsʻz ʻtsz ʻchéung ˏshing,
intelligent person. Wai others all laughing said, This child older become,

必 當 代 之 偉 器 也 自 此 得 名
pit, ˏtóng toi² ˏchí ʻwai hí² ʻyá. Tsz² ʻtsʻz tak, ˏming.
certainly present age 's renowned individual. From this got reputation.

後 爲 北 海 太 守 極 好 賓 客
Hau² ˏwai Pak, ʻhoi tʻái² shau², kik, hò² ˏpan hák,;
Afterwards was Pakhoi head defender, exceedingly loved entertain guests;

常 曰 座 上 客 常 滿 罇 中 酒
ˏshéung üt,, Tsó² shéung² hák, ˏshéung ʻmún, ˏtsun ˏchung ʻtsau
usually remarking, Hall in guests always full, bottle in wine

不 空 吾 之 願 也
pat, ˏhung, ˏʻng ˏchí ün² ʻyá.
never empty, my 's wish.

No. II.—Scheme of Wóng Wan to inveigle Lü Pò.

(見三國志 卷之四 第八回)

董 卓 一 日 大 會 百 官 酒 至
'Tung Ch'éuk, yat, yat, tái' úi' pák, ,kún; 'tsau chí'
Tung Ch'éuk one day greatly entertained all officers; wine reached

數 巡 呂 布 向 卓 耳 邊 語 卓
shò' ,ts'un, 'Lü Pò' héung' Ch'éuk, 'í ,pin 'ü. Ch'éuk,
several bouts, Lü Pò turning-to Ch'éuk's ear side spoke. Ch'éuk

命 于 筵 上 揪 張 溫 下 堂 不 多
ming' ,ü ,in shéung' ,tsau ,Chéung ,Wan há' ,t'óng. Pat, ,tó
ordered from feast above carry Chéung Wan below hall. Not much

時 侍 從 將 紅 盤 托 張 溫 頭
,shí shí' ,ts'ung, ,tséung ,hung ,p'ún t'ók, ,Chéung ,Wan ,t'au,
time, waiting follower, taking red waiter bearing Chéung Wan's head,

入 獻 百 官 魂 不 附 體 卓 笑
yap, hin'. Pák, ,kún ,wan pat, fú' 't'ai. Ch'éuk, siú'
entered handed-up. All officers' souls not left-in body. Ch'éuk laughing

曰 諸 公 勿 驚 張 溫 結 連 袁 術 欲
üt, ,Chü ,kung mat, ,king; ,Chéung ,Wan kít, ,lin ,Un Shut, yuk,
said, All sirs no fear; Chéung Wan leagued joined Un Shut, about

圖 害 我 因 使 人 寄 書 來 錯
,t'ò hoi' 'ngó; ,yan 'sz' ,yan kí' ,shü ,loi, ts'ók,
scheming to-injure me; because messenger brought letter here, inadvertently

下 在 吾 兒 奉 先 處 故 斬 之 公 等
há' tsoi' ,'ng ,í Fung' ,sin ch'ü', kú' 'chám ,chí: ,kung 'tang
delivered in my son Fungsin's place, therefore behead him: Sirs all

無 故 不 必 驚 畏 衆 官 唯 唯 而 散
,mò kú', pat, pit, ,king wai'. Chung' ,kún 'wai! 'wai! ,í sán'.
is-no cause, not need fear dread. All officers [said] Yes! Yes! and separated.

司 徒 王 允 歸 到 府 中 尋 思 今
,Sz' ,t'ò ,Wóng 'Wan ,kwai tò' 'fú ,chung ,ts'am ,sz': ,Kam
Chancellor Wóng Wan returning to house in deeply thought: This

日 席 間 之 事 坐 不 安 席 至 夜 深
yat, tsik, ,kán ,chí sz'', tsó' pat, ,ón tsik,. Chí' yé' ,sham,
day feast during 's acts, sitting not easy seat. At night deep,

月 明 策 杖 步 入 後 園 立 於
üt, ,ming ch'ák, chéung', pò' yap, hau' ,ün, lap, ,ü
moon bright, taking cane, walked into rear garden, standing at

荼 薇 架 側 仰 天 垂 淚 忽 聞 有
,t'ò ,mi ká' chak,, 'yéung ,t'in ,shui lui', fat, ,man 'yau
small - rose frame side, looking-up heaven falling tears, suddenly heard was

人 在 牡 丹 亭 畔 長 吁 短 嘆 允
ˌyan tsoi2 ʻmau ˌtán ˌtʻing pún2, ˌchʻéung ˌhü ʻtün tʻán2. ʻWan
person in peony arbor's side, long sighs short groans. Wan

潜 步 窺 之 乃 府 中 歌 妓 貂 蟬 也
ˌtsʻim pò2 ˌkwʻai ˌchí, ʻnai ʻfú ˌchung ˌkó kí2 ˌTíú ˌShín ʻyá.
carefully stepping watched person, was house in singing girl Tíú Shín.

其 女 自 幼 選 入 府 中 教 以 歌
ˌKʻí ʻnü tsz2 yau2 ʻsün yap2 ʻfú ˌchung, káu2 ʻí ˌkó
This girl from youth brought into house within, taught to sing

舞 年 方 二 八 色 伎 俱 佳 允
ʻmò; ˌnín ˌfóng í2 pát, shik, kí2 ˌkʻü ˌkai. ʻWan
dance; age just twice eight, beauty accomplishments both superior. Wan

以 親 女 待 之 是 夜 允 聽 良 久
ʻí ˌtsʻan ʻnü toi2 ˌchí. Shí2 yé2, ʻWan tʻing2 ˌléung ʻkau
as if own daughter behaved her. In night, Wan listening good while

喝 曰 賤 人 將 有 私 情 耶 貂 蟬
hót, üt, Tsin2 ˌyan ˌtséung ʻyau ˌsz' ˌtsʻing ʻyé? ˌTíú ˌShín
exclaiming, said, Low person about having underhand designs eh? Tíú Shín

驚 跪 答 曰 賤 妾 安 敢 有 私
ˌking kwai2, táp, üt, Tsin2 tsʻíp, ˌón ʻkóm ʻyau ˌsz'?
alarmed kneeled replied saying, Poor handmaid how dare have treachery?

允 曰 汝 無 所 私 何 夜 深 於 此 長
ʻWan üt, ʻü ˌmò ʻshó ˌsz', ˌhó yé2 ˌshʻm ˌü ʻtsʻz' ˌchʻéung
Wan said, You nothing which-is secret, why night's depth in here long

嘆 蟬 曰 容 妾 伸 肺 腑 之 言 允 曰
tʻán'? ˌShín üt, ˌYung tsʻíp, ˌshan fai2 ʻfú ˌchí ˌín. ʻWan üt,
sighs? Shín replied, Permit handmaid express inmost 's words. Wan said,

汝 勿 隱 匿 當 實 告 我 蟬 曰 妾 蒙
ʻü mat, ʻyan nik, ˌtóng shat, kò2 ʻngó. ˌShín üt, Tsʻíp, ˌmung
You not hide conceal, must truly tell me. Shín replied, I grateful

大 人 恩 養 訓 習 歌 舞 優
tái2 ˌyan ˌyan ʻyéung, fan2 tsáp, ˌkó ʻmò, ˌyau
your honor's kindness care, teaching practice singing dancing, utmost

禮 相 待 妾 雖 粉 骨 碎 身 莫 報
ʻlai ˌséung toi2; tsʻíp ˌsui ʻfan kwat, súi2 ˌshan, mók, pò2
propriety towards behave; I, if powder bones crush body, not recompense

萬 一 近 見 大 人 兩 眉 愁 鎖 必
mán2 yat,. Kan2 kín2 tái2 ˌyan ʻléung ˌmí ˌshau ʻsó, pít,
myriad one. Lately seen your honor's two eyebrows anxiety knit, must

有 國 家 大 事 又 不 敢 問 今 晚 又
ʻyau kwók, ˌká tái2 sz'2; yau2 pat, ʻkóm man2; ˌkam ʻmán yau2
have state family great affairs; still not presume ask; this evening also

見 行 坐 不安 因此 長 嘆 不 想
kin' ‚hang tsó' pat‚ ‚ón. ‚Yan 'ts'z', ‚ch'éung t'án'; pat‚ 'séung
saw moving sitting not easy. Because this, long sighing; not thinking

爲 大 人 窺 見 倘 有 用 妾 之 處
‚wai tái' ‚yan ‚kw'ai kín'. 'T'óng 'yau yung' ts'ip‚ ‚chi ch'ü',
was your honor furtively observing. If have use my 's place,

萬 死 不 辭
mán' 'sz' pat‚ ‚ts'z'.
myriad deaths not decline.

允 以 杖 擊 地 曰 誰 想 漢 天 下
'Wan 'i chéung' kik‚ ti', üt‚, ‚Shui 'séung Hón' ‚t'in há',
Wan with cane striking earth, said, Who thought Hón's dominion,

却 在 汝 手 中 耶 隨 我 到 畫 閣 中
k'éuk‚ tsoi' 'ü 'shau ‚chung ‚yé? ‚Ts'ui 'ngó tò' wá' kók‚ ‚chung
really in your hands' within eh? Follow me to picture gallery in

來 貂 蟬 跟 允 到 閣 中 允 盡 叱
‚loi. ‚Tíú ‚Shin ‚kan 'Wan tò' kók‚ ‚chung. 'Wan tsun' ch'ik‚
come. Tíú Shin followed Wan to gallery in. Wan entirely ordering

出 婦 妾 納 貂 蟬 於 坐 回 頭 便 拜
ch'ut‚ 'fú ts'ip‚, náp‚ ‚Tíú ‚Shin ‚ü tsó', ‚úi ‚t'au pin' pái'.
out wives concubines, instated Tíú Shín in chair, turning head then bowed.

貂 蟬 驚 伏 于 地 曰 大 人 何 故
‚Tíú ‚Shin ‚king, fuk‚ ‚ü tí', üt‚, Tái' ‚yan ‚hó kú'
Tíú Shín alarmed, prostrate on ground, said, Your honor what reason

如 此 允 曰 汝 可 憐 漢 天 下 生
‚ü 'ts'z'? 'Wan üt‚, 'ü 'hó ‚lín Hón' ‚t'in há' ‚shang
as this? Wan replied, You able compassionate Hón's empire's living

靈 言 訖 淚 如 泉 湧
‚ling. ‚Yn kat‚, lui' ‚ü ‚ts'ün 'yung.
souls. Words finished, tears like fountain's bubbling.

貂 蟬 曰 適 問 賤 妾 曾 言 但 有
‚Tíú ‚Shin üt‚, Shik‚ ‚kán tsin' ts'ip‚ ‚ts'ang ‚in, tán' 'yau
Tíú Shín rejoined, Just now humble handmaid already said, only have

使 令 萬 死 不 辭 允 跪 而 言
'sz' ling', mán' 'sz' pat‚ ‚ts'z'. 'Wan kwai' ‚i ‚in,
employ command, myriad deaths not decline. Wan kneeling and speaking,

曰 百 姓 有 倒 懸 之 危 君 臣 有 纍
üt‚, Pák‚ sing' 'yau 'tò ‚ün ‚chi ‚ngai, ‚kwan ‚shan 'yau 'lui
said, The-people are-in topsy-turvy 's danger, prince lords are-in piled

卵 之 急 非 汝 不 能 救 也 賊 臣
'lun ‚chí kap‚; ‚fí 'ü pat‚ ‚nang kau' 'yá. Ts'ak‚ ‚shan
eggs 's hazard; without you not able save. Treacherous minister

董卓將欲篡位朝中文武
'Tung Ch'éuk, ꜀tséung yuk, 'shán wai', ꜁ch'iú ꜀chung ꜁man 'mò
Tung Ch'éuk presently wishes supplant throne, court among civil military

無計可施董卓有一義兒
꜁mò kai' 'hó ꜀shí. 'Tung Ch'éuk, 'yau yat, í' ꜁í,
have-no plans available. Tung Ch'éuk has an adopted son,

姓呂名布驍勇異常我
sing' 'Lü, ꜁ming Pò', ꜀hiú 'yung, í' ꜁shéung. 'Ngó
surnamed Lü, named Pò, daring brave, unlike usual. I

覩二人皆好色之徒今欲
꜀kún í' ꜁yan ꜀kái hò' shik, ꜀chi ꜁t'ò. ꜀Kam yuk,
have-observed two men both lustful beauty 's slaves. Now wish

用連環計先將汝許嫁呂布後
yung' ꜁lin ꜁wán kai'; ꜀sin ꜀tséung 'ü, 'hü ká' 'Lü Pò', hau'
employ inveigling scheme; first taking you, promise to-wed Lü Pò, then

獻與董卓汝于中取便諜間
hin' 'ü 'Tung Ch'éuk: 'ü ꜀ü ꜀chung 'ts'ü pín' tip, kán'
offer to Tung Ch'éuk: you in betwixt seize opportunity slander sever

他父子分顏令布殺卓以
꜀t'á fú' 'tsz' ꜀fan ꜁ngán ling' Pò' shát, Ch'éuk, 'í
this father son sunder-faces [disagree], cause Pò kill Ch'éuk, in-order-to

絕大惡重扶社稷再立江山
tsüt, tái' ók, ꜁ch'ung ꜁fú 'shé tsik, tsoi' lap, ꜀kóng ꜀shán:
terminate great evil, again uphold country's - gods, re - establish government:

皆汝之力也不知汝意若何
꜀kái 'ü ꜀chi lik, 'yá. Pat, ꜀chi 'ü í' yéuk, ꜁hó.
all your 's courage. Not aware your notions as how.

貂蟬曰妾許大人萬死不辭
꜀Tiú ꜁Shin üt, Ts'ip, 'hü tái' ꜁yan, mán' 'sz' pat, ꜁ts'z'.
Tiú Shin replied, I promised your honor, myriad deaths not decline.

望即獻妾與彼妾自有道理允
Móng' tsik, hin' ts'ip, 'ü 'pí, ts'ip, tsz', 'yau tò' 'lí. 'Wan
Trust when offered me to them, I myself have proper plans. Wan

曰事若洩漏我滅門矣貂蟬
üt, Sz', yéuk, sit, lau', 'ngó mit, ꜁mún 'í. ꜀Tiú ꜁Shin
said, Affair if leaks out, us exterminate house truly. Tiú Shin

曰大人勿憂妾若不報大
üt, Tái' ꜁yan mat, ꜀yau; ts'ip, yéuk, pat, pò' tái'
rejoined, Your honor need-not be-anxious; I if not requite great

義死于萬刃之下允拜謝
í', 'sz' ꜀ü mán' yan' ꜀chi há'. 'Wan pái' tsé'.
liberality, kill in myriad sword s' under. Wan bowing thanked.

次日便將家藏明珠數顆
Tsz' yat, pín' tséung ká ts'óng ming chü shò' 'fó,
Next day, then taking family preserved brilliant pearls several ones,

令良匠嵌造金冠一頂使人
ling' léung tséung' 'kám ts'ò' kam kún yat, 'ting; 'sz' yan
ordered skillful workman inlay make golden crown one piece; sent man

密送呂布布大喜親到王允
mat, sung' 'Lü Pò'. Pò' tái' 'hi, ts'an tò' Wóng 'Wan
secretly gave Lü Pò. Pò much pleased, himself went-to Wóng Wan's

宅致謝允預備嘉殽美饌
chák, chí' tsé'. 'Wan ü' pí' ká ngáu 'mi chán'
house render thanks. Wan had-prepared excellent meats delicious viands.

候呂布至允出門迎迓接入後
hau' 'Lü Pò' chí'. 'Wan ch'ut, mún ying ngá', tsip, yap, hau'
waited Lü Pò's arrival. Wan went out to meet waited into rear

堂延之上坐布曰呂布乃相府
t'óng, in chí shéung' tsó'. Pò' üt, 'Lü Pò' 'nái séung' 'fú
hall, invited him at-top sit. Pò said, I am premier's office

一將司徒是朝廷大臣何
yat, tséung'; sz' t'ò shí' ch'iú t'ing tái' shan: hó
a general: your excellency is imperial court high minister: what

故錯敬允曰方今天下別
kú' ts'ók, king'? 'Wan üt, Fóng kam t'in há' pít,
cause mistaken respect? Wan replied, Just now empire besides

無英雄惟有將軍耳允非敬
mò ying hung, wai 'yau tséung kwan 'í. 'Wan fí king'
without hero, only is you, sir. I do-not reverence

將軍之職敬將軍之才也
tséung kwan chí chik, king' tséung kwan chí ts'oi 'yá.
your honor 's rank, reverence your honor 's talents.

布大喜允慇懃敬酒口稱
Pò' tái' 'hi. 'Wan yan k'an king' 'tsau, 'hau ch'ing
Pò excessively pleased. Wan diligent-attentive urged wine, mouth praised

董太師並布之德不絕布大
'Tung t'ái' sz' ping' Pò' chí tak, pat, tsüt,. Pò' tái'
Tung high statesman and Pò 's virtues un-ceasingly. Pò loud

笑暢飲允叱退左右只留
siú' ch'éung' 'yam. 'Wan ch'ik, t'úi' 'tsó yau', 'chí lau
laughter hilariously drank. Wan ordered retire attendants, only detained

侍妾數人勸酒酒至半酣
shí' ts'ip, shò' yan hün' 'tsau. 'Tsau chí' pún' hóm,
waiting maids several persons serve wine. Drank till half merry,

允 曰 喚 孩 兒 來 少 頃 二 青 衣
'Wan üt, Fún' ,hoi ,i ,loi. 'Shiú 'k'ing, i' ,ts'ing 'i
Wan said, Call young child come. Little while, two green-dresses

引 貂 蟬 艷 粧 而 出 布 驚 問
'yan ,Tiú ,Shin im' ,chóng ,i ch'ut,. Pò' ,king man'
led Tiú Shín gorgeously dressed and came-out. Pò surprised asked,

何 人 允 曰 小 女 貂 蟬 也 允 蒙
,Hó ,yan? 'Wan üt, 'Siú 'nü ,Tiú ,Shin 'yá. 'Wan ,mung
What person? Wan replied, Little daughter Tiú Shín. I grateful for

將 軍 錯 愛 不 異 至 親 故 命
,tséung ,kwan ts'ok, oi', pat, i' chi' ,ts'an, kú' ling'
your honor's mistaken kindness, not unlike nearest relatives, therefore ordered

其 與 將 軍 相 見 便 命 貂 蟬 與 呂
,k'i 'ü ,tséung ,kwan ,séung kin'. Pin' ming' ,Tiú ,Shín 'ü 'Lü
her with your honor interview. Then bid Tiú Shín to Lü

布 把 盞 貂 蟬 送 酒 與 布 兩 下
Pò' 'pá 'chán. ,Tiú ,Shin sung' 'tsau 'ü Pò', 'léung ha'
Pò hand goblet. She presenting wine to Pò, both parties

眉 來 眼 去 允 佯 醉 曰 孩 兒
,mi ,loi 'ngán hü'. 'Wan ,yéung tsui' üt, ,Hoi ,i
eyebrows coming eyes going. Wan feigning drunkenness said, The child

央 及 將 軍 痛 飲 幾 盃 吾 一
,yéung k'ap, ,tséung ,kwan t'ung' 'yam 'ki ,púi; ,'ng yat,
requests to your honor strongly to-drink several cups; my single

家 全 靠 着 將 軍 哩 布 請 貂 蟬 坐
,ká ,tsün k'áu' chéuk, ,tséung ,kwan ,lé. Pò' 'ts'ing ,Tiú ,Shin tsó'.
family entirely depend upon your honor. Pò requested Tiú Shín to sit.

貂 蟬 假 意 欲 入 允 曰 將 軍
,Tiú ,Shin 'ká i' yuk, yap,. 'Wan üt, ,Tséung ,kwan
She feigning wish about to-retire, Wan observed, The general

吾 之 至 友 孩 兒 便 坐 何 妨 貂
,'ng ,chi chi' 'yau, ,hoi ,i pin' tsó': ,hó ,fóng? ,Tiú
my 's intimate friend, my child then be-seated: what apprehension? Tiú

蟬 便 坐 于 允 側 呂 布 目 不 轉 睛
,Shin pin' tsó' ,ü 'Wan chak,. 'Lü Pò' muk, pat, 'chün ,ts'ing
Shín then sat at Wan's side. Lü Pò's eyes not strayed pupil

的 看 又 飲 數 盃
tik, hón'; yau' 'yam shò' ,púi.
's gaze; also drinking many cups.

允 指 蟬 謂 布 曰 吾 欲 將 此 女 送
'Wan 'chi ,Shin wai' Pò', üt, ,'Ng yuk, ,tséung 'ts'z' 'nü sung'
Wan pointing-to Shin spoke-to Pò, saying, I wish taking this girl give

與將軍爲妾還肯納否布
ˊü ˏtseung ˏkwan ˏwai tsʻip, ˏwán ˊhang náp ˊfau? Pòˋ
to your honor to-be concubine, but willing receive or-not? Pò

出席謝曰若得如此布當效
chʻut, tsik, tsé ˊüt, Yéuk, tak, ˏü ˊtsʻz', Pòˋ ˏtóng háu
leaving table thanked saying, If obtain as this, I will emulate

犬馬之報允曰早晚選一
ˊhün ˊmá ˏchí pòˋ. ˊWan üt, ˊTsò ˊmán ˊsün yat,
dogs horse 's requital. Wan replied, Immediately selecting a

良辰送至府中布欣喜無
ˏleung ˏshan sungˋ chiˋ ˊfú ˏchung. Pòˋ ˏyan ˊhí ˏmò
fortunate day send-her to house in. Pò pleased delighted im-

限頻以目視貂蟬貂蟬亦以
hán, ˏpʻan ˊi muk, shí ˏTiú ˏShin. ˏTiú ˏShin yik, ˊi
measurably, continually with eyes observed Tiú Shin. She also with

秋波送情少頃席散允曰
ˏtsʻau ˏpó sungˋ ˏtsʻing. ˊShiú ˊkʻing, tsik, sánˋ. ˊWan üt,
ogling - glances exhibited passion. Little while, feast broke-up. Wan said,

本欲留將軍止宿恐太師見
ˊPún yuk, ˏlau ˏtseung ˏkwan ˊchí suk, ˊhung tʻáiˋ ˏsz' kínˋ
I would detain your honor stop sleep, fear you may-be

疑布再三拜謝而去
ˏi. Pòˋ tsoiˋ ˏsám páiˋ tsé ˏi hüˋ.
apprehensive. Pò again thrice bowing thanked and departed.

No. III.—Prescience of the Birds.*

(見聊齋 卷之十 第六十八篇)

中州境有道士募食鄉村
ˏChung ˏchau ˊking ˊyau Tòˋ szˋ mòˋ shik, ˏheung ˏtsʻün.
[In] Chungchau borders, was Taou priest begging food country village.

食已聞鸝鳴因告主人使
Shik, ˊi, ˏman ˏli ˏming, ˏyan kòˋ ˊchü ˏyan ˊsz'
Eaten having, heard parrot sing, therefore told head man to-order

---

* *Liú Chái* 聊齋 or Pastimes of the Study, is a collection of stories usually printed in sixteen duodecimo volumes. It was written by Pò Tsʻungling 蒲松齡 a distinguished scholar of Shántung province, who flourished in the reign of Kánghí; his preface is dated in 1679. It is regarded as a highly finished production, and is written in excellent style and pure Chinese.

SELECTIONS

FROM THE HISTORY OF THE THREE STATES.

(此數句選三國志卷一第二回第十一板之後)

These are successive extracts to be retranslated into Chinese, and the reference to the original is given at the end of each sentence, by which the place can be found. The edition is the common duodecimo one, having twenty-two columns on a leaf; they are num bered from the first column on the right side.

---

1. "On that day, he having been disrespectful to Üntak (玄德), Chéung Fí (張飛) of a hasty temperament, straightway wished to kill him."—(15 *characters.*)—section 2d, leaf 11, last column.

2. "Fí said, If I do not kill that fellow, then it will be necessary, being in his clan, to obey his commands: this, indeed, would not be pleasant."—(19 *char.*)—*Ibid.*, leaf 12, column 1st.

3. "Thereupon, the three men by night and day, led their troops to Chü Tsun (朱雋); Tsun acted towards them very friendly."—(17 *char.*)—*Ibid.*, col. 4th.

4. "Chéung Pò (張寶) ordered colonel Kò Shing (副將高昇) to sally out on horseback, and provoke a combat."—(11 *char.*)—*Ibid.*, col. 7th.

5. "Üntak sent Chéung Fí to fight him; Fí giving reins to his horse and grasping his spear, joined battle with Shing; after a few onsets he pierced Shing, who fell off his horse."—(23 *char.*)—*Ibid.*, col. 8th.

6. "Chéung Pò, then on horseback, disheveling his hair and brandishing his sword, performed his magical arts; there was only to be seen a great wind and thunder, and a mass of black vapor descending from the sky; within this black vapor what resembled innumerable horsemen furiously sallied forth."—(38 *char.*)—*Ibid.*, col. 9th.

7. "Üntak, hearing the orders, directed Lord Kwán (關公) and Chéung Fí each to lead a detachment of a thousand, and hide behind the hills on a high eminence."—(22 *char.*)—*Ibid.*, col. 13th.

8. "Chéung Pò, seeing his arts all fail, hastily endeavored to withdraw his troops; but on the left Lord Kwán, on the right Chéung Fí, both detachments sallied out, and in the rear Üntak and Chü Tsun simultaneously coming up, the rebel soldiers were completely routed."—(34 *char.*)—*Ibid.*, col. 19th.

9. "Üntak, seeing afar the banner of general Lord of Earth (地公將軍) wite flying horse pursued after; Chéung Pò entered the wilds and fled, and Üntak, letting fly an arrow, hit his left arm."—(28 *char.*)—*Ibid.*, col. 20th.

10. "Opening Chéung Kok's (張角) coffin, he cut his corpse in pieces, cut off his head, and sent it to the capital; the rest of the troop all submitted."—(17 *char.*)—*Ibid.*, leaf 13th, col. 14th.

11. "Üntak, following in the rear assaulted and killed them; the robbers were routed and fled into the citadel of Ün. (完) (15 *char.*) *Ibid.*, col. 14th.

12. "Üntak said, Anciently, Kòtsò's (高祖) obtaining of the empire was because he was able to invite submissions and receive their fealty;—why do you, sir, repel Hòn Chung? (韓忠)—(20 *char.*)—*Ibid.*, col. 16th.

13. "Üntak said, Not to permit the rebels to submit is correct. Now they are hemmed in on all sides like an iron tube, and the rebels beg to submit; if they cannot, they will assuredly fight to the last."—(25 *char.*)—*Ibid.*, col. 20th.

14. "Kín (堅) speaking to his father said, 'These robbers should be seized.' Then, rousing his energy and grasping his sword, he ascended the bank, lifting up a loud voice, calling and pointing to the east and west as if ordering men; the robbers, supposing them to be soldiers of government coming, all left the property and hastily fled. Kín rushing forward killed one robber."—(46 *char.*)—*Ibid.*, leaf 14th, col. 7th.

15. "After he had occupied his office, he ate at the same table and slept in the same bed, with Kwán and Chéung; whenever Üntak sat in the midst of a crowd of people, Kwán and Chéung stood behind him the whole day without being fatigued."—(31 *char.*)—*Ibid.*, leaf 15th, col. 9th.

16. "The clerk said, Tuk Yau (督郵) is acting pompously; it is nothing he wants but a douceur."—(12 *char.*)—*Ibid.*, col. 19th.

17. "Üntak replied, I have not committed the least illegality with the people; where shall I get a bonus to give him?"—(16 *char.*)—*Ibid.*, col. 19th.

18. "Chéung Fí, in great anger, rolling his eyes and grinding his teeth firmly, vaulted down from his horse, and straight entered the post-house, thrust aside the door-keeper, who there was opposing his way, and rushed directly into the back hall, where he saw Tuk Yau just sitting up in the hall, while the district clerk was lying bound on the ground. Fí cried out, 'Villainous oppressor of the people! Do you know who I am?' Tuk Yau did not have time to say a word, before his hair was firmly grasped by Chéung Fí, and he dragged out of the post-house straight to a horse-post before the magistrate's, and fast tied up to it."—(84 *char.*)—*Ibid.*, leaf 16th, col. 2d.

19. "Pulling down a branch of a willow, upon Tuk Yau's two thighs, with all his strength, he whipped him. Each time he struck, he snapped ten and more twigs of the willow."—(23 *char.*)—*Ibid.*, col. 6th.

20. "Fí said, Such a rascally oppressor of the people, for what shall I wait before beating him to death? Tuk Yau calling said, Lord Üntak save my life."—(23 *char.*)—*Ibid.*, col. 10th.

21. "Tò (陶) said, On all sides, thieves and robbers simultaneously rise up, devastating and robbing the country; these evils all spring from the ten eunuchs selling offices and oppressing the people; they despise their prince and contemn their superiors, and all upright men have left the court; evil is before your eyes."—(38 *char.*)—*Ibid.*, leaf 17th, col. 4th.

22. "The ten eunuchs all took off their caps, and knelt prostrate before the emperor, saying, 'The high minister not agreeing with us, we cannot live; we wish to beg our lives, return to our fields and villages, and employ all our possessions to aid the expenses of the army.' Their words ended, they wept bitterly."—(42 *char.*)—*Ibid.*, col. 6th.

23. "Lau Tò (劉陶) cried out, My death is unimportant: how sad that the house and empire of Hòn, [enduring] four hundred years and more to this time, as in one night, should be extinct."—(24 *char.*)—*Ibid.*, col. 9th.

24. "Tám (耽) said, The people of the empire wish to eat the flesh of the ten eunuchs; your majesty respects them like a father and mother; their body has not one inch of merit, and all have been created noble earls."—(28 *char.*)—*Ibid.*, col. 12th.

25. "Lau Ü (劉虞) privately memorializing regarding Lau Pí's (劉備) great merit, the court pardoned his offense in whipping Tuk Yau."—(12 *char.*)—*Ibid.*, col. 22d.

26. "The emperor Ling (靈) being dangerously sick, called the high general Hó Tsun (何進) into the inner palace to consult upon subsequent business."—(16 *char.*)—*Ibid.*, leaf 18th, col. 3d.

27. "Now, the high general hearing Ün Shíú's (袁紹) words, wishes to exterminate all the ministers; we beg your ladyship to pity us."—(19 *char.*)—*Ibid.*, leaf 19th, col. 6th.

28. "Ün Shíú said, If you do not cut off the plant and extirpate the root, it certainly will become a tree to kill us."—(15 *char.*)—*Ibid.*, col. 11th.

29. "The empress Tung (董) summoning Chéung Yéung (張讓) and the others into the inner palace to consult, said, Hó Tsun's sister, from the first I have promoted her; now her son sits on the

throne as emperor, and all the ministers within and without are her bosom friends, her dignity and power is very great: what shall I do?" —(47 *char.*)—*Ibid.*, col. 13th.

SELECTIONS FROM THE YUK-KIÚ LÍ.

(此數句選玉嬌梨 第一回之後)

1. "Within this village, although there were a thousand and more dwellings of the residents, if you should number the rich and honorable families, you would select that of the councillor Pák (白太常) as the first."—(25 *char.*)—Chapter 1st, leaf 1, col. 16th.

2. "He only regretted that he was past forty, and still without a son and heir."—(11 *char.*)—*Ibid.*, col. 18th.

3. "Mr. Pák (白公) sighed, and regarding it as his fate, did not thereafter again buy concubines."—(15 *char.*)—*Ibid.*, col. 20th.

4. "On the day that she was born, Mr. Pák dreamed that a divine personage bestowed upon him a single beautiful gem, the color ruddy as the sun; therefore in choosing her milk name he called her *Red-gem.*"—(30 *char.*)—*Ibid.*, col. 22d.

5. "By eight or nine years, she had learned female work and needlework, in every branch surpassing ordinary people."—(15 *char.*) —*Ibid.*, leaf 2, col. 3d.

6. "By the time she was fourteen or fifteen, she was acquainted with authors and could compose, till at last she became an accomplished female scholar."—(19 *char.*)—*Ibid.*, col. 7th.

7. "He only wished to choose a proper son-in-law, talented and handsome, to match her."—(15 *char.*)—*Ibid.*, col. 11th.

8. "He supposed that in this single village and town the men of talents were limited."—(10 *char.*)—*Ibid.*, col. 17th.

9. "Every day, when public business was over, he did nothing but quaff wine and compose verses."—(13 *char.*)—*Ibid.*, leaf 3, col. 3d.

10. "Mr. Pák, seeing that one of his clerks had given him twelve jars of chrysanthemums, arranged them at the foot of the library stairs."—(19 *char.*)—*Ibid.*, col. 5th.

11. Whenever, in the leisure from governmental duties, you are seeking for me, then I also am inquiring for you."—(17 *char.*)—*Ibid.*, col. 13th.

12. "Yesterday, I was indeed coming to visit [the flowers], but unexpectedly, just as I got out of the door, I ran against old Yéung (楊) (the loathed thing) holding a longevity address, whch he wished me to stop and correct that he might give it to general Shik (石

此數句見三國志

俱降。○玄德從背後掩殺。賊衆大敗。奔入宛城。○玄德
箭中其左臂。○發張角之棺。戮尸梟首。送往京師。餘衆
望見地公將軍旗號。飛馬趕來。張寶落荒而走。玄德發
兩軍都出背後。玄德朱儁一齊趕上。賊兵大敗。○玄德
高崗之上。○張寶見解了法。急欲退軍。左關公右張飛
殺來。○玄德聽令。撥關公張飛各引軍一千。伏于山後
風雷大作。一股黑氣從天而降。黑氣中似有無限人馬
合刺昇落馬。○張寶就馬上披髮仗劍。作起妖法。只見
廝戰。○玄德使張飛擊之。飛縱馬挺矛與昇交戰。不數
引軍來投朱儁。儁待之甚厚。○張寶遣副將高昇出馬
這廝。反要在他部下聽令。其實不甘。○於是三人連夜
當日怠慢了玄德。張飛性發便欲殺之。○飛曰。若不殺

此數句見三國志

驛，直到縣前，馬椽上縛住，○攀下柳條，去督郵兩腿上
認得我麼，督郵未及開言，早被張飛揪住頭髮，扯出館
堂，見督郵正坐廳上，將縣吏綁倒在地，飛大喝，害民賊
牙，滚鞍下馬，逕入館驛，把門人那裏阻擋得住，直奔後
毫無犯，那得財物與他。○張飛大怒，睜圓環眼，咬碎鋼
○吏曰，督郵作威，無非要賄賂耳。○玄德曰，我與民秋
桌，寢則同牀，如玄德在稠人廣坐，關張侍立，終日不倦
財物奔走。堅起上，殺一賊。○到任之後，與關張食則同
岸，揚聲大叫，東西指揮，如喚人狀，賊以爲官兵至，盡棄
得必然死戰。○堅謂父曰，此賊可擒也。遂奮力提刀上
○玄德曰。不容寇降，是也，今四面圍如鐵桶，賊乞降不
日昔高祖之得天下，蓋爲能招降納順，公何拒韓忠耶。

此數句見三國志

曰。若不斬草除根。必爲喪身之本。○董太后宣張讓等
大將軍聽袁紹之言。欲盡誅臣等。乞娘娘憐憫。○袁紹
之罪。○靈帝病篤。召大將軍何進入宮商議後事。○今
功皆封列侯。○劉虞表奏劉備大功。朝廷赦免鞭督郵
天下人民欲食十常侍之肉。陛下敬之如父母。身無寸
不惜。可憐漢室天下四百餘年。到此一旦休矣。○躭曰。
田里盡將家產以助軍資。言罷痛哭。○劉陶大呼。臣死
伏於帝前曰。大臣不相容。臣等不能活矣。願乞性命歸
問上。朝廷正人皆去。禍在目前矣。○十常侍皆免冠跪
盜賊並起。侵掠州郡。其禍皆由十常侍賣官害民。欺君
不打死等甚。督郵告曰。玄德公救我性命。○陶曰。四方
着力鞭打。一連打折柳條十數枝。○飛曰。此等害民賊

此數句見玉嬌梨

盆菊花。擺在書房堦下。○每每于政事之暇。不是你哥
事完了。便只是飲酒賦詩。○白公因一門人送了十二
貌的佳壻配他。○料此一鄉一邑。人才有限。○每日公
書能文。竟已成一個女學士。○只要選擇一個有才有
歲。便學得女工針指。件件過人。○到得十四五時。便知
玉一塊。顏色紅赤如日。因取乳名叫做紅玉。○到八九
以爲有命。以後遂不復買妾。○白公夢一神人。賜他美
常爲第一。○但只恨年過四十。却無子嗣。○白公嘆息。
這村中。雖有千餘戶居民。若要數富貴人家。當推白太

由此而下四篇見玉嬌梨。

皇帝位。內外臣僚皆其心腹。威權太重。我將如何。
入宮商議曰。何進之妹。始初我擡擧他。今日他孩兒即

英文原文

材料一

The Middle Kingdom①

Chapter Ⅻ. Polite Literature of the Chinese.

Few works in Chinese literature are more famous than a historical novel by Chin Shau, about A. D. 350, called the *San Kwoh Chí*, or History of the Three States; its scenes are laid in the northern parts of China, and include the period between A. D. 170 to 317, when several ambitious chieftains conspired against the imbecile princes of the once famous Han dynasty, and after that was overthrown, fought among themselves, until the empire was again reconsolidated under the Tsin dynasty. This performance, from its double character, and the long period over which it extends, necessarily lacks that unity which a novel should have. Its charms, to a Chinese, consist in the animated descriptions of plots and counter-plots, in the relations of battles, sieges, and retreats, and the admirable manner

① 编者按：S. Wells Williams, *The Middle Kingdom*, Vol. Ⅰ., New York & London: Wiley and Putnam, 1848, pp. 544 – 548。

in which the characters are delineated, and their acts intermixed with entertaining episodes. The work opens with describing the distracted state of the empire under the misrule of Ling tí and Hiuen tí, the last two monarchs of the house of Han, who were entirely swayed by eunuchs, and left the administration of government to reckless oppressors, until ambitious men, taking advantage of the general discontent, raised the standard of rebellion. The leaders ordered their partisans to wear yellow headdresses, whence the rebellion was called that of the Yellow Caps, and was suppressed only after several years of hard struggle by a few distinguished generals who upheld the throne. Among these was Tung Choh, who, gradually drawing to himself all the power in the state, thereby arrayed against himself others equally as ambitious and unscrupulous. Disorganization had not yet proceeded so far that all hope of supporting the rightful throne had left the minds of its adherents, among whom was Wang Yun, a chancellor of the empire, who, seeing the danger of the state, devised a scheme to inveigle Tung Choh to his ruin, which is thus narrated:

> "One day, Tung Choh gave a great entertainment to the officers of government. When the wine had circulated several times, Lü Pu (his adopted son) whispered something in his ear, whereupon he ordered the attendants to take Chang Wăn from the table into the hall below, and presently one of them returned, handing up his head in a charger. The spirits of all present left their bodies, but Tung, laughing, said, 'Pray, sirs, do not be alarmed. Chang Wăn has been leaguing with Yuen Shuh how to destroy me; a messenger just now brought a letter for him, and inadvertently gave it to my son; for which he has lost his life. You, gentlemen, have no cause for dread.' All the officers replied, 'Yes! yes!' and immediately separated.
>
> "Chancellor Wang Yun returned home in deep thought: 'The proceedings of this day's

feast are enough to make my seat an uneasy one;' and taking his cane late at night he walked out in the moonlight into his rear garden, when standing near a rose arbor and weeping as he looked up, he heard a person sighing and groaning within the peony pavilion. Carefully stepping and watching, he saw it was Tiau Chen, a singing-girl belonging to the house, who had been taken into his family in early youth and taught to sing and dance; she was now sixteen, and both beautiful and accomplished, and Wang treated her as if she had been his own daughter.

"Listening some time, he spoke out, 'What underhand plot are you at now, insignificant menial?' Tiau Chen, much alarmed, kneeling, said, 'What treachery can your slave dare to devise?' — 'If you have nothing secret, why then are you here late at night sighing in this manner?' Tiau replied, 'Permit your handmaid to declare her inmost thoughts. I am very grateful for your excellency's kind nurture, for teaching me singing and dancing, and for the treatment I have received. If my body should be crushed to powder [in your service], I could not requite a myriad to one [for these favors]. But lately I have seen your eyebrows anxiously knit, doubtless from some state affairs, though I presumed not to ask; this evening, too, I saw you restless in your seat. On this account I sighed, not imagining your honor was overlooking me. If I can be of the least use, I would not decline the sacrifice of a thousand lives.' Wang, striking his cane on the ground, exclaimed, 'Who would have thought the rule of Han was lodged in your hands! Come with me into the picture-gallery.' Tiau Chen following in, he ordered his females all to retire, and placing her in a seat, turned himself around and did her obeisance. She, much surprised, prostrated herself before him, and asked the reason of such conduct, to which he replied, 'You are able to compassionate all the people in the dominions of Han.' His words ended, the tears gushed like a fountain. She added, 'I just now said, if I can be of any service I will not decline, though I should lose my life.'

"Wang, kneeling, rejoined, 'The people are in most imminent danger, and the nobility in a hazard like that of eggs piled up; neither can be rescued without your assistance. The traitor Tung Choh wishes soon to seize the throne, and none of the civil or military officers have any practicable means of defence. He has an adopted son, Lü Pu, a remarkably daring and brave man, who, like himself, is the slave of lust. Now I wish to contrive a scheme to inveigle them both, by first promising to wed you to Lü, and then offering you to Tung, while you must seize the opportunity to raise suspicions in them, and slander one to the other so as to sever them, and cause Lü to kill Tung, whereby the present great evils will be terminated, the throne upheld, and the government re-established. All this is in your power, but I do not know how the plan strikes you.' Tiau answered, 'I have promised your excellency my utmost service, and you may trust me that I will devise some good scheme when I am offered to them.'

"'You must be aware that if this design leaks out, we shall all be utterly exterminatd.'—'Your excellency need not be anxious, and if I do not aid in accomplishing your patriotic designs, let me die a thousand deaths.'

"Wang, bowing, thanked her. The next day, taking several of the brilliant pearls preserved in the family, he ordered a skilful workman to inlay them into a golden coronet, which he secretly sent as a present to Lü Pu. Highly gratified, Lü himself went to Wang's house to thank him, where a well prepared feast of viands and wine awaited his arrival. Wang went out to meet him, and waiting upon him into the rear hall, invited him to sit at the top of the table, but Lü objected; 'I am only a general in the prime minister's department, while your excellency is a high minister in his majesty's court; why this mistaken respect?'

"Wang rejoined, 'There is no hero in the country now besides you; I do not pay this honor to your office, but to your talents.' Lü was excessively pleased. Wang ceased not in engaging him to drink, the while speaking of Tung Choh's high qualities, and praising his guest's virtues, who, on his side, wildly laughed for joy. Most of the attendants were ordered to retire, a few waiting maids stopping to serve out wine, when, being half drunk, he ordered them to tell the young child to come in. Shorly after, two pages led in Tiau Chen gorgeously dressed, and Lü, much astonished, asked, 'Who is this?'

" 'It is my little daughter, Tiau Chen, whom I have ordered to come in and see you, for I am very grateful for your honor's misapplied kindness to me, which has been like that to near relatives.' He then bade her present a goblet of wine to him, and as she did so, their eyes glanced to and from each other.

"Wang, feigning to be drunk, said, 'The child strongly requests your honor to drink many cups; my house entirely depends upon your excellency.' Lü requested her to be seated, but she acting as if about to retire, Wang remarked, 'The general is my intimate friend; be seated, my child; what are you afraid of?' She then sat down at his side, while Lü's eyes never strayed from their gaze upon her, drinking and looking.

"Wang, pointing to Tiau, said to Lü, 'I wish to give this girl to you as a concubine, but know not whether you will receive her?' Lü, leaving the table to thank him, said, 'If I could obtain such a girl as this, I would emulate the requital dogs and horses give for the care taken of them.'

"Wang rejoined, 'I will immediately select a lucky day, and send her to your house.' Lü was delighted beyond measure, and never took his eyes off her, while Tiau herself, with ogling glances, intimated her passion. The feast shortly after broke up, and Lü departed."

The scheme here devised was successful, and Tung Choh was assassinated by his son, when he was on his way to depose the monarch, although many evil omens were granted to deter him from his unlawful course. His death, however, brought no peace to the country, and three chieftains, Tsau Tsau, Liu Pí, and Sun Kiuen, soon distinguished themselves in their struggles for power, and afterwards divided the empire of the Han princes into the three states of Wu, Shuh, and Wei, from which the work derives its name. Many of the personages who figure in this work have since been deified, among whom are Liu Pí's sworn brother

Kwan Yü, who is now the Mars, and Hwa To, since made the Esculapius, of Chinese mythology. Its scenes and characters have all been fruitful subjects for the pencil and the pen of artists and poetasters, while all classes delight to dwell upon and recount the exploits of its heroes. One commentator has thrown his remarks between the text itself in the shape of such expressions as "Wonderful speech! What rhodomontade! This man was a fool before, and shows himself one now!" Davis very appositely likens this work to the Iliad for its general arrangement and blustering character of the heroes; and like that work, it was composed when the scenes described and their leading actors existed chiefly in personal recollection, and the remembrances of both were fading away in the twilight of popular legends.

材料二

Oath Taken by Members of the Triad Society, and notices of its origin. ①

The engagement here referred to is well known among the Chinese, and the covenant of these three men may have suggested the oath taken by members of the Triad Society, ostensibly for a similar patriotic purpose. The Sán Kwoh Chí thus describes the persons, and the oath they took in the Peach garden.

"This man did not love study very much; he was a man of few words, liberal and kind disposition, not showing his feelings in his countenance, and keeping to his purpose of uniting all the heroes in the country. He was eight *chih* tall, had pendent ears which he could see himself, his hands hung below his knees, his face was pale and lips red. His name was Liú Pí, and his title Hiuenteh

---

① 编者按：*The Chinese Repository*, Vol. XVIII., No. 6, June 1849, pp. 282 – 283。

(i. e. Dark Virtue); his father Liú Hung died when he was young, and he dutifully served his mother, living near a mulberry grove, the trees of which were over fifty feet in height, and their tops hung down like a canopy. A geomancer looking at the situation said, This family will certainly produce an honorable man; and Hiuenteh himself was once playing with his mates under the trees, when he said, When I am emperor, I'll ride this canopy. His uncle marked these sayings, and because the family was poor, often gave them money, so that his mother sent him off to school when he was fifteen years old, where he made many friends.

"When 28 years old he one day read a proclamation of Liú Yen inviting recruits for the army, and groaned aloud. A man behind him cried out, Why do you groan, great Sir, and not go to the help of the country? Hiuenteh turned, and seeing a man about eight cubits high, with a round head and goggle eyes, a bull neck, tiger's whiskers, a voice like thunder, and the strength of a wild horse, altogether a strange object, inquired his name. I am Cháng Fí, styled Yihteh (i. e. Winged Virtue); I live in Tioh-kiun, where I have a farmhouse, and sell spirits and pork; my great desire is to band all our heroes together, and seeing you, Sir, look at the proclamation and groan, I wished to know the reason, Hiuenteh told him he was a relative of the emperor's, and desired to put down the Yellow Cap rebels, and restore peace to the state, but sighed because his strength was unequal to the task; upon which Cháng Fí proposed they should unite their fortunes and call some retainers to their standard for the purpose of assisting the emperor against his enemies. Hiuenteh agreed, and they went into a pot-house to talk it over.

"While drinking there, they saw a man push a cart up to the door, and stop it, to come in and rest; he hastily called for a cup, saying he was going into the city to join the army. He was nine *chih* high, his beard two *chih* long, dark complexion, red lips, narrow eyes, and his whole appearance dignified and imposing. Hiuenteh invited him to join them, and learned that his name was Kwán Yü, and his title Yuncháng; that five or six years before he had unluckily killed a braggart for insulting a man, and left his home in consequence; and that, hearing of the proclamation for recruits, he had now come to join the army. The two friends were pleased to hear his account, and told him their plans, when the three repaired to the farmhouse. Cháng Fí said 'I have a peach-garden back of my house now in full bloom; let us all meet there to-morrow, and sacrifice to heaven and earth, when we three will adopt each other as brothers with all our heart and strength; after this ceremony, we will plan our arrangements.' They agreed to the proposal, and a black ox, a white horse, and other sacrificial things, were duly made ready. On the morrow, the three men worshiped and burned incense there, and took an oath saying, 'We, Liú, Kwán and Cháng, although our surnames are unlike, do adopt each other as brothers, that with united heart and strength we may save our country from its dangers, and raise it from its distress, at once requiting his majesty and restoring peace to the blackhaired people. We were not born on the same day, but we wish to die together. O Imperial Heaven! O Queenly Earth! Look down into our hearts! If we abjure right and forget kindness, may heaven and men destroy us!' The oath having been taken, Hiuenteh was acknowledged as the elder brother, Kwán Yü as next to him, and Cháng Fí as the youngest; and after the sacrifices to heaven and earth were finished, they killed oxen and spread out a feast in the peach-garden, to which they invited the literary and ablebodied men of the village to the number of three hundred men, who drank themselves quite tipsy."

中文回译

材料一

《中国总论》[①]

第十二章　中国的雅文学

在中国文学作品中，没有几部作品比陈寿（*Chin Shau*）的历史小说《三国志》（The *San Kwoh Chí*, or *History of the Three States*）更为著名，该作创作于公元 350 年左右。小说的场景被设置在中国北部，时间阶段是公元 170 年至 317 年之间。那时有几个野心勃勃的首领，联合起来反对曾经称雄一时的汉代的愚笨君王。汉代被推翻之后，他们之间互相争斗，直到晋代重新统一了全国。由于这部作品具有双重属性，时间跨度又长，所以必然缺少一部小说应有的整体性。对于中国人来说，作品的魅力在于栩栩如生地描写了阴谋与反阴谋、战斗、围攻和撤退中的各种关系，还有书中描绘的人物的优秀品格，以及妙趣横生的情节中交织的人物行动。作品开头描写了灵帝（Ling tí）、桓帝（Hiuen tí）统治时期的一片混乱，汉室最后的这两位皇帝完全受制于宦官的摆布，朝政由此落在了不计后果的压迫者的手中。野心勃勃的首领煽动群

① 编者按：卫三畏：《中国总论》第 1 卷，纽约、伦敦出版，1848 年，第 544—548 页。

情，伺机而起，举起反叛的大旗。他们命令追随者头戴黄巾，这次叛乱因此号称“黄巾起义”。经过几年艰苦战斗，“黄巾起义”才被几个支持王权的著名将领镇压下去。其中一位名叫董卓（Tung Choh）的将领，逐渐攫取了国家大权，由此引起了同样野心勃勃而又肆无忌惮的首领们的一致反对。政权尚未瓦解，王权支持者们的所有希望却已破灭，其中有个叫王允（Wang Yun）的朝廷大臣，看到国家危难，设下一计诱使董卓走向灭亡，书中是这样讲述的：

> 董卓一日大会百官。酒至数巡，吕布向卓耳边语，卓命于筵上揪张温下堂。不多时，侍从将红盘托张温头入献。百官魂不附体。卓笑曰：“诸公勿惊。张温结连袁术，欲图害我，因使人寄书来，错下在吾儿奉无处。故斩之。公等无故，不必惊畏。”众官唯唯而散。
>
> 司徒王允归到府中，寻思今日席间之事，坐不安席。至夜深月明，策杖步入后园，立于荼蘼架侧，仰天垂泪。忽闻有人在牡丹亭畔，长吁短叹。允潜步窥之，乃府中歌妓貂蝉也。其女自幼选入府中，教以歌舞，年方二八，色伎俱佳，允以亲女待之。
>
> 允听良久，喝曰：“贱人将有私情耶？”貂蝉惊跪答曰：“贱妾安敢有私！”允曰：“汝无所私，何夜深于此长叹？”蝉曰：“容妾伸肺腑之言。妾蒙大人恩养，训习歌舞，优礼相待，妾虽粉骨碎身，莫报万一。近见大人两眉愁锁，必有国家大事，又不敢问。今晚又见行坐不安，因此长叹。不想为大人窥见。倘有用妾之处，万死不辞！”允以杖击地曰：“谁想汉天下却在汝手中耶！随我到画阁中来。”貂蝉跟允到阁中，允尽叱出妇妾，纳貂蝉于坐，回头便拜。貂蝉惊伏于地，曰：“大人何故如此？”允曰：“汝可怜汉天下生灵！”言讫，泪如泉涌。貂蝉曰：“适间贱妾曾言：但有使令，万死不辞。”
>
> 允跪而言曰：“百姓有倒悬之危，君臣有累卵之急，非汝不能救也。贼臣董卓，将欲篡位；朝中文武，无计可施。董卓有一义儿，姓

吕名布，骁勇异常。我观二人皆好色之徒，今欲用连环计，先将汝许嫁吕布，后献与董卓；汝于中取便，谍间他父子反颜，令布杀卓，以绝大恶。重扶社稷，再立江山，皆汝之力也。不知汝意若何？”貂蝉曰：“妾许大人万死不辞，望即献妾与彼。妾自有道理。”

允曰：“事若泄漏，我灭门矣。”貂蝉曰：“大人勿忧。妾若不报大义，死于万刃之下！”

允拜谢。次日便将家藏明珠数颗，令良匠嵌造金冠一顶，使人密送吕布。布大喜，亲到王允宅致谢。允预备嘉肴美馔；候吕布至，允出门迎迓，接入后堂，延之上坐。布曰：“吕布乃相府一将，司徒是朝廷大臣，何故错敬？”

允曰：“方今天下别无英雄，惟有将军耳。允非敬将军之职，敬将军之才也。”布大喜。允殷勤敬酒，口称董太师并布之德不绝。布大笑畅饮。允叱退左右，只留侍妾数人劝酒。酒至半酣，允曰：“唤孩儿来。”少顷，二青衣引貂蝉艳妆而出。布惊问何人。

允曰：“小女貂蝉也。允蒙将军错爱，不异至亲，故令其与将军相见。”便命貂蝉与吕布把盏。貂蝉送酒与布。两下眉来眼去。

允佯醉曰：“孩儿央及将军痛饮几杯。吾一家全靠着将军哩。”布请貂蝉坐，貂蝉假意欲入。允曰：“将军吾之至友，孩儿便坐何妨。”貂蝉便坐于允侧。吕布目不转睛的看，又饮数杯。

允指蝉谓布曰：“吾欲将此女送与将军为妾，还肯纳否？”布出席谢曰：“若得如此，布当效犬马之报！”

允曰：“早晚选一良辰，送至府中。”布欣喜无限，频以目视貂蝉。貂蝉亦以秋波送情。少顷席散，吕布离去。①

① 编者按：本文回译主要依据《拾级大成》所载中文文字，第151—157页。修改了《拾级大成》中的三个明显错误：一是将“荼薇”改为“荼蘼”；二是将“分颜”改为“反颜”；三是将“目不转睛的省”改为“目不转睛的看”。

这个计谋成功了，在董卓前去废黜皇帝的路上，尽管出现了许多恶兆阻止他去篡权，但他还是被他的儿子刺杀了。然而，他的死并没有给国家带来和平，有三个首领——曹操（Tsau Tsau）、刘备（Liu Pí）和孙权（Sun Kiuen），很快从权力斗争中脱颖而出，其后，汉王的帝国分裂为魏、蜀、吴三国，这就是《三国志》得名的由来。书中所写的许多人物此后被神化，其中就有刘备的结拜兄弟关羽（Kwan Yü），他是现在的战神；还有华佗（Hwa To），此后成了中国神话中的阿斯克勒庇俄斯（Esculapius）。相关场面和人物全都成了艺术家和蹩脚诗人们笔下的丰富话题，所有阶层全都高兴地回味或讲述英雄们的丰功伟绩。有个评论者在作品中甚至用这样的语言评论道："妙语！狂言！此人前作愚人，而今露出本色！"[①]《三国志》的总体布局和英雄人物的狂暴性格，使德庇时将其恰当地比作《伊利亚特》；像《伊利亚特》一样，书中描写的场景和主要角色主要靠作家的个人回忆完成，这些内容正逐渐消失在流行传说的薄暮中。

材料二

《三合会会员的誓言及其来源》[②]

此处提及的誓言在中国广为人知，立誓的三人所发的誓言，或对三合会会员有所启发，表面看来都是本着爱国的目的。《三国志》是这样描写三人以及他们的桃园三结义的：[③]

那人不甚好读书，寡言语，性宽和，喜怒不形于色，结交天下英

---

① 编者按：《三国演义》第 34 回毛宗岗评刘备："前于曹操面前，假作愚人身分；今在刘表面前，却露出英雄本色"。

② 编者按：《中国总论》，第 18 卷，第 6 期，1849 年 6 月，第 282—283 页。

③ 编著按：以下回译参考了《第一才子书三国演义》，罗贯中著，毛宗岗批注，线装书局 2007 年版，第 4—5 页。

雄，素有大志。他身长八尺，两耳下垂，目能自顾其耳，双手过膝，面色苍白，唇色红润。名曰刘备，字玄德（即黑暗之德）。父刘弘早丧，玄德事母至孝，家住桑园边，园中桑树高五丈余，树冠垂若车盖。相者观其势，云："此家必出贵人。"玄德曾与伙伴戏于树下，曰："我为天子，当乘此车盖。"叔父奇其言，因见玄德家贫，常资给之，年十五岁，母使游学，广交朋友。

年二十八，一日，读刘焉招募新兵榜文，慨然长叹。背后一人厉声说道："大丈夫不与国家出力，何故长叹？"玄德回视，见其人身长八尺，圆头环眼，牛颈虎须，声若巨雷，势如奔马，全然一个怪物，遂问其姓名。"某乃张飞，字翼德（即有翼之德）。家住涿郡，有一农舍，沽酒卖肉，渴望结交天下豪杰。恰才见公看榜而叹，故此相问。"玄德道，他本皇帝宗亲，欲破黄巾贼，以安社稷，恨力不能，故长叹耳。张飞提议两人联合起来，招募乡勇，协助主上抗击逆贼。玄德应允，两人遂入村店饮酒。

正饮间，两人见一大汉推一车子来到店门前歇了，入店坐下，便匆忙索酒来吃，并说他要赶入城去投军。他身长九尺，髯长二尺；黑脸，红唇，细眼；相貌堂堂，威风凛凛。玄德就邀他同坐，得知其名关羽，字云长。五六年前，因一势豪倚势凌人，不幸被他杀了，因此逃出家园。今闻此处招军，特来应募。两人闻之甚喜，述其大计，三人来到庄上。张飞曰："吾庄后有一桃园，花开正盛；明日当于园中祭告天地，我三人结为兄弟，协力同心，可图大事。"两人应允，及时备下乌牛、白马、祭礼等物。次日，三人焚香再拜，誓曰："念刘关张，虽不同姓，既结为兄弟，则同心协力，救困扶危，上报皇帝，下安黎庶。虽非同日生，但愿同日死。皇天后土，实鉴此心，背义忘恩，天人共戮！"誓毕，拜玄德为兄，关羽次之，张飞为弟。祭罢天地，复宰牛设酒，聚乡中勇士，得三百余人，就桃园中痛饮一醉。

二　艾约瑟与海外佚书《汉语会话》*

19 世纪英国著名传教士汉学家艾约瑟对于《三国演义》的译介，学界至今无人关注，究其原因，主要是他的译文出现在《汉语会话》（*Chinese Conversation*）中，该作在国内未见藏本。

《汉语会话》1852 年由上海墨海书馆（The Mission Press）出版发行，封面未署作者，只道：translated from native authors，即“译自中国作家的作品”。故此，考证作者是研究该作的第一步。结合英国传教士汉学家兼目录学家伟烈亚力的相关著述，这个问题不难解决。

1867 年伟烈亚力出版了两本著作，均将《汉语会话》放在艾约瑟的名下。第一本著作是《来华新教传教士回忆录》，伟烈亚力编写此作时，艾约瑟已来华近 20 年之久，他在该作中简单介绍了艾约瑟的生平与著述，列举了他的 19 种著作和若干文章，其中包括 12 种中文著作和 7 种英文著作，而

* 相关研究以“艾约瑟《汉语会话》与《三国演义》的英译”为题，发表于《明清小说研究》2017 年第 2 期。此外，关于艾约瑟，笔者还撰写过另外一篇文章，题名《19 世纪西方人眼中的“淫书”〈红楼梦〉——以艾约瑟〈红楼梦〉书评为中心》，发表于《红楼梦学刊》2016 年第 4 期。文章刊出后不久，笔者发现 1892 年《中国评论》（*The China Review*）第 20 卷第 1 期所载《红楼梦书评》（*Hung-lau-meng; or the Dream of the Red Chamber. A Chinese Novel. Book Ⅰ.*），作者署名 E. J. E.，实际是 19 世纪德国来华新教传教士欧德理（Ernest Johann Eitel，1838—1908）之名的缩写，并非艾约瑟英文名（E. J.）的缩写。笔者误把二人混为一谈，特此向学界道歉，并予以更正。

《汉语会话》在英文著作中位列第一，格外醒目。[①] 第二本著作是伟烈亚力根据《四库全书总目提要》编写的目录学专著《汉籍解题》（*Notes on Chinese Literature*），在介绍"欧译中国作品"（*Translations of Chinese Works into European Languages*）时，伟烈亚力辑录的第139种作品是中国戏曲《借靴》，而《借靴》的最早英译者便是艾约瑟，伟烈亚力说："《借靴》（*TSEAY-HEUE*，*The Borrowed Boots*）选自《缀白裘》（*Chuy pih K'ew*）第206页，由艾约瑟（Rev. J. Edkins）翻译并收于1852年上海印行的《汉语会话》第1至56页。"[②] 由上述两条著述不难得出结论：《汉语会话》出自艾约瑟之手。

伟烈亚力与艾约瑟相互熟知，他的著述应该可信。两人同是英国伦敦会传教士，1852年艾约瑟编写《汉语会话》时，两人正一起供职于墨海书馆，此后还一起成立了上海文理学会（Shanghai Literary and Scientific Society）、创办了中文期刊《六合丛谈》等。1897年伟烈亚力去世十年后，艾约瑟为其纪念文集《中国研究》（*Chinese Research*）撰写了序言《伟烈亚力先生的中国研究之价值》（*The Value of Mr. Wylie's Chinese Researches*），开篇伊始，艾约瑟就说："我和伟烈亚力先生是多年的好友，我们初次相识于1848年，自那以后，直到他1887年去世，我都可以证明他是远东地区最博学多识的苏格兰人之一。"艾约瑟认为，在对中国文化的了解方面，伟烈亚力堪与理雅各比肩而立，只不过"理雅各对中国典籍的了解最多；伟烈亚力对中国文学的了解最广"[③]。艾约瑟既与伟烈亚力互为好友，伟烈亚力又以著录中国书目、精通各类书籍著称于世，那么他对艾约瑟著作的记录应不会有误，何况《来华新教传教士回忆录》和《汉籍解题》出版时艾约瑟尚健

---

① Alexander Wylie, *Memorials of Protestant Missionaries to the Chinese*, Shanghae: American Presbyterian Mission Press, 1867, pp. 187 - 191.

② Alexander Wylie, *Notes on Chinese Literature*, Shanghai: American Presbyterian Mission Press, 1867, p. XXVII.

③ Alexander Wylie, *Chinese Research*, Shanghai, 1897, p. 1.

在，如果有误，势必会被及时发现。

从伟烈亚力所列艾约瑟作品来看，《汉语会话》位列艾约瑟英文著作之首。作为一种汉语教材，它显然是艾约瑟学习和研究汉语的试笔之作，这或许是他没有署名的主要原因。

艾约瑟（Joseph Edkins，1823—1905）

（一）生平著述及汉学成就

艾约瑟 1823 年 12 月 19 日出生在英格兰格洛斯特郡的奈斯沃斯（Nailsworth，Gloucestershire），1843 年获得伦敦大学（University of London）学士学位，之后进入科沃德学院（Coward College）接受神学训练，24 岁时接受神职，1847 年 12 月被伦敦布道会派往中国传教，次年 7 月 2 日抵达香港，9 月 2 日到达上海，最初供职于著名传教士麦都思、美魏茶、慕维廉（William Muirhead，1822—1900）等人创办的伦敦布道会出版社（The London Missionary Society Press）——墨海书馆。该书馆是当时中国唯一一家有铅印设备的出版机构，艾约瑟不凡的语言能力和学术素养很快在此显露出来。此期间，他与李善兰、王韬等人合作翻译了大量西方科学著作。同时，作为皇家亚洲学会会员，他还参与了《圣经》的中译。从 1852 年到 1858 年，他编辑出版了《华洋和合通书》（*Chinese and Foreign Concord Almanac*），即后来的《中西通书》（*The Chinese and Western Almanac*）。1858 年返回英国休假一年，1859 年回到上海，1860 年到芝罘（烟台）传教，翌年到天津，两年后又到北京，此后长期留在北京。1872 年，与丁韪良合作创办了北京近代第一份综合性科技期刊《中西闻见录》（*The Peking Magazine*），该杂志刊行 3 年，出版 36 期。这时的艾约瑟已享誉欧洲，1875 年被授予爱丁堡大学荣誉神学博士学位，1880 年辞去伦敦布道会教职，加入大清海关（The Chinese Imperial Maritime Customs）担任翻译，主持翻译了一系列介绍西方科技的著作。1903 年，80 岁高龄的艾约瑟染上了伤寒，但仍笔耕不辍，直到 1905 年复活节病逝于上海，享年 82 岁。

艾约瑟一生在中国居留 57 年之久，供职于多个部门，身份复杂，角色多元，他是一位传教士、语言学家、翻译家。他的著述丰富，不但涉及宗教、语言、西学等多个领域，而且在每个领域都有重要著作，在 19 世纪来华传教士中堪称博学多才的汉学家。

作为一名传教士，宗教研究是艾约瑟终生的兴趣，他不仅用中文撰写了大量向中国读者宣传基督教的著作，还用西文撰写了大量向西方读者介绍中国宗教的著作，在中西宗教交流史上扮演了重要角色。前者如《孝事天父论》《三德论》《福音选篇》《颂主圣诗》《新约官话》《圣经斤两考》等；后者如《道家的发展阶段》（*Phases in the Development of Tauism*）（1855）、《早期的道家法术》（*On Early Tauist Alchemy*）（1857）、《中国的宗教状况：中国人信仰基督教前景之评论》（*The Religious Condition of the Chinese*：*with Observations on the Prospects of Christian Conversion amongst that People*）（1859）、《中国的宗教：中国三大宗教简介》（*Religion in China*；*Containing Brief Account of the Three Religions of the Chinese*）（1878）、《中国的佛教：概况、历史、叙述与批评》（*Chinese Buddhism*：*a Volume of Sketches*，*Historical*，*Descriptive*，*and Critical*）（1880）、《远东地区宗教思想的早期传播》（*The Early Spread of Religious Ideas especially in the Far East*）（1893）等。

在西学东渐方面，艾约瑟的成就尤其显著。无论是在墨海书馆工作期间还是在大清海关工作期间，艾约瑟都致力于西学的翻译与出版。代表作如《西学启蒙十六种》，李鸿章、曾纪泽为其作序。其中，第一种《西学略述》相当于这套书的“弁言”，乃艾约瑟自撰的著作，仅“格致”一卷就介绍了天文、质学、地学、动物学、金石学、电学、化学、天气学、光学、重学、流质重学、气质重学、身体学、较动物学、身理学、植物学、医学、几何医本学、算子、代数学、历学、稽古学、风俗学 23 个学科的基本概况。另外的十五种启蒙著作同样涉及多个学科，分别为：《格致总学启蒙》《地志启蒙》《地理质学启蒙》《地学启蒙》《植物学启蒙》《身理启蒙》《动物学启蒙》《化学启蒙》《格致质学启蒙》《天文启蒙》《富国养民策》《辨学启蒙》《希腊志略》《罗马志略》《欧洲史略》。此外，他还与王韬、李善兰等人合译了《格致新学提纲》《重学》《圆锥曲线说》《光学图说》《西国天学源流》《代数学》《代微积拾级》等科学著作。不少著作在当时具有开风气之先的重要价值，如艾约瑟与李善兰合译的《重学》是晚清第一部较为系统地介绍牛顿力学的译著。

在中国语言研究方面，艾约瑟可谓硕果累累。先后编纂的重要著作包括：《上海方言口语语法》（*A Grammar of Colloquial Chinese*：*as Exhibited in the Shanghai Dialect*）（1853）、《汉语官话口语语法》（*A Grammar of the Chinese Colloquial Language*，*Commonly Called the Mandarin Dialect*）（1857）、

《汉语口语进阶》（*Progressive Lessons in the Chinese Spoken Language*）（1862）、《上海方言字汇》（*A Vocabulary of the Shanghai Dialect*）（1869）、《中国在语文学上的地位：证明欧亚语言同源的一个尝试》（*China's Place in Philology*：*an Attempt to Show that the Language of Europe and Asia Have a Common Origin*）（1871）、《汉字学习入门》（*Introduction to the Study of the Chinese Characters*）（1876）、《汉语的演化：人类语言起源和生长的例证》（*The Evolution of the Chinese Language*：*as Exemplifying the Origin and Growth of Human Speech*）（1888）等。这些语言学著作涉及汉语的方言与官话、汉字与音韵、语法及结构、来源及生成等各个方面，出版以来备受瞩目。尤其是最早出版的两本有关上海方言和汉语官话的著作更是汉语研究的翘楚之作。伟烈亚力曾评论二作说："艾约瑟先生居中国九年，于音韵之学穷流溯源，辨之甚精。凡士自各省来者，无不延接讨论……观此二书，知艾君于中国声音之理，博考而详，探讨于古书者久，故得自立一说。"① 目前，这两本著作已有了中译本，并在语言学研究领域受到重视。

艾约瑟写作了大量有关中国经济、社会、文化等方面的著作。比如，他对中国的经济颇有研究，先后出版的相关著作包括：《中国的货币》（*Chinese Currency*）（1901）、《中华帝国的税收》（*The Revenue and Taxation of the Chinese Empire*）（1903）、《中国的银行和物价》（*Banking and Prices in China*）（1905）等。此外，艾约瑟还写作了大量有关中国社会与文化的书，涉及中国社会生活的方方面面，著名的如《福州苗族》（*The Miau-tsi Tribes*, *Foochow*）（1870）、《鸦片：历史记载或中国的罂粟》（*Opium*：*Historical Note or the Poppy in China*）（1898）等。除了专著，他还是《六合丛谈》《中西闻见录》《万国公报》《北华捷报》等报纸杂志的创办者或撰稿人，

① 伟烈亚力：《新出书籍》，《六合丛谈》第1卷第10号，咸丰丁巳年九月朔日（1857年）江苏松江上海墨海书馆印，第11页。

为这些刊物撰写了数百篇文章，是 19 世纪传教士中屈指可数的高产作家，也是中西方公认的“中国通”。

TABLE OF CONTENTS.

	Page
The Borrowed Boots, 借靴	1
From the Pe-pa Ke, 琵琶記	
	Page
Living on Chaff. 吃糠	57
Drawing Likenesses, 描容	76
Farewell to the Grave, 別墳	89
The Portrait left behind in the Temple. 寺中遺像	118
The Meeting of the Two Wives, 兩賢相遘	130
The Library, 書館	145
History of the Three Kingdoms. Extract from Chap. 29. 三國志第二十九囘	
	Page
Death of Yü Keih the Magician.	158

《汉语会话》的目录

（二）《汉语会话》的语料来源

《汉语会话》的“序言”（Preface）为研究该作的内容选材提供了重要信息。艾约瑟说：“这部作品的翻译是为了帮助那些想要开始学习汉语口语的外国人。书中绝大部分选文的出处与马礼逊《对话》中的选文来源一样。马若瑟在其博学而又珍贵的著作《汉语札记》（*The Notitia Linguae Sinicae*）中也曾说过，该作第一部分例文所用素材，来自中国的戏曲和小说。”① 由

① Joseph Edkins, *Chinese Conversations*, *Translated from Native Authors*, Shanghai: The Mission Press, preface. 本部分引自《汉语会话》一书的内容，一律同此，后文不再一一注释。

此可见，在内容选材上，《汉语会话》主要模仿了马礼逊和马若瑟的相关著作。

马礼逊是1807年来华的第一位英国新教传教士。艾约瑟所说的《对话》即马礼逊编写的 *Dialogues and Detached Sentences in the Chinese Language*，该作中文书名通常被回译为《中文会话及凡例》或《中文对话与单句》，1816年在澳门出版，封面上印着“为学习汉语的学生设计的入门之作”（designed as an initiatory work for the use of students of Chinese）。全书主要由31段对话组成。对话涉及的话题大都与日常生活密切相关，有主仆、师生、商客之间的对话，也有关于中国礼节拜访、宗教习俗的讨论。书末还附有甲子纪年图表，以及书信、请柬的写作模板。由此可见，这是一部实用性很强的汉语教材。有趣的是，在语料来源上，作者引用了大量小说、戏曲中的材料。笔者曾发表《作为海外汉语教材的〈红楼梦〉》一文，在哈佛大学韩南（Patrick Hanan）教授的启发下，首次披露《对话》是西方汉学界最早在正式出版物中提及《红楼梦》的作品。实际上，除了《红楼梦》，《对话》中还有引自《荆钗记》《说唐前传》《笑林广记》《英云梦传》《西厢记》等小说、戏曲中的对话。这种利用小说、戏曲来学习汉语的方法，是马礼逊汉语教材的一大特色，也是他一贯的主张。比如在次年出版的《中国一览》（*A View of China*）的“结语”（Conclusion）中，马礼逊就说：“对一个欧洲人来说，没有中国人帮助，要想学好中文几乎是不可能的。掌握中文最好的途径是从阅读一本小说开始。”①

法国耶稣会士马若瑟是另一位主张利用小说、戏曲等通俗文学作品学习汉语的著名传教士。他1698年来华，在华居住30多年，是18世纪欧洲最杰出的汉语语法学家，被誉为法国早期三大汉学家之一。马若瑟一生著

① Rev. R. Morrison, *A View of China*, Macao: Printed at the Honorable East India Company's Press, 1817, p. 120.

述颇多，在中国语言、文学方面，以《汉语札记》一书影响最为深远，该作被看作西方人编写的第一部汉语教材。《汉语札记》写成于 1728 年，但直到 1831 年才得以付梓出版，1847 年被翻译成英文。全书分为口语和书面语两个部分。马若瑟说："汉语，无论是古籍保存的，还是日常应用的，都有其恰当而独特的美，传教士们在很大程度上还没有充分意识到这点。"为了传达"汉语的特殊风貌和固有之美"，马若瑟选取了一些中国文学作品作为素材，他认为最重要的是"喜剧和小说"。他说："第一个要提到的是《元人百种》（*Yuen jin Peh chung*），这一合集包括一百种喜剧，最早出版于元代；戏剧场景均在四五场之内。第二个是《水浒传》（*Shwui-hú Chuen*）；为了欣赏这部作品内在的优点，须得选择富有独创性的金圣叹评点的本子，在书中，他第一次揭示了该书作者令人钦佩的技巧。这部传奇（legend）篇幅很长，有 15 卷。另外还有些篇幅较短的作品，如《画图缘》（*Hwá-tú Yuen*）、《醒风流》（*Sing-fung liú*）、《好求传》（*Háu-kiú Chuen*）、《玉娇梨》（*Yoh-kiáu Lí*）等。此外，这种'小说'每部都有四五卷，包括十六到二十回。"① 在具体讲习汉语时，《汉语札记》确实大量引用了《元人百种》和《水浒传》中的文字与短句。后来他还将《元人百种曲》中的《赵氏孤儿》译成法语，介绍到欧洲。

受马礼逊、马若瑟的启发，艾约瑟的《汉语会话》在内容取材上选择了两人都很重视的小说和戏曲；与之相比，艾约瑟对中国小说和戏曲的重视更为强烈，也更为纯粹。实际上，《汉语会话》整部作品就是《借靴》《琵琶记》和《三国演义》三种作品的英译合集，除此之外再没掺杂任何其他中文语料。

---

① Joseph de Premare, Translated into English by J. G. Bridgrnan, *Notitia Lingae Sinicae*, Canton: Printed at the office of the Chinese Repository, 1847, p. 26. 编者按：英译本《汉语札记》把《好逑传》错写成《好求传》。

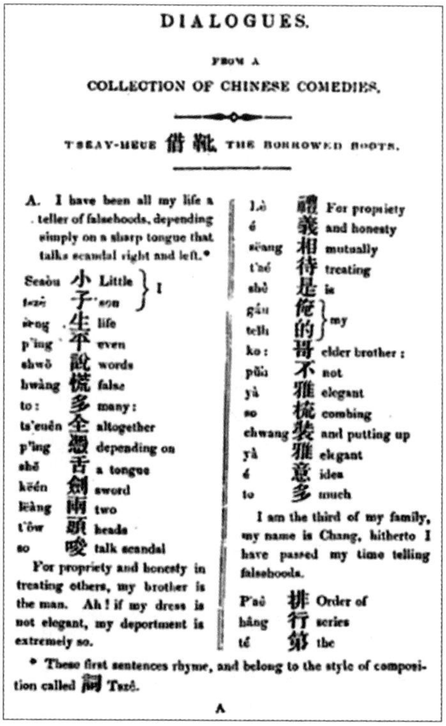
DIALOGUES.

FROM A

COLLECTION OF CHINESE COMEDIES.

TSEAY-HEUE 借靴 THE BORROWED BOOTS.

A. I have been all my life a teller of falsehoods, depending simply on a sharp tongue that talks scandal right and left.*

Seaòu 小 Little
tsze 子 son } I
săng 生 life
p'ing 平 even
shwŏ 說 words
hwàng 慌 false
to: 多 many:
ts'euên 全 altogether
p'ing 憑 depending on
shĕ 舌 a tongue
këen 劍 sword
lëàng 兩 two
t'ôw 頭 heads
so 唆 talk scandal

For propriety and honesty in treating others, my brother is the man. Ah! if my dress is not elegant, my deportment is extremely so.

Lè 禮 For propriety
é 義 and honesty
sëang 相 mutually
t'aé 待 treating
shè 是 is
gàu 俺 } my
teïh 的
ko: 哥 elder brother:
pŭh 不 not
yà 雅 elegant
so 梳 combing
chwang 裝 and putting up
yà 雅 elegant
é 意 idea
to 多 much

I am the third of my family, my name is Chang, hitherto I have passed my time telling falsehoods.

P'aê 排 Order of
hâng 行 series
tè 第 the

* These first sentences rhyme, and belong to the style of composition called 詞 Tszê.

A

《汉语会话》中的《借靴》

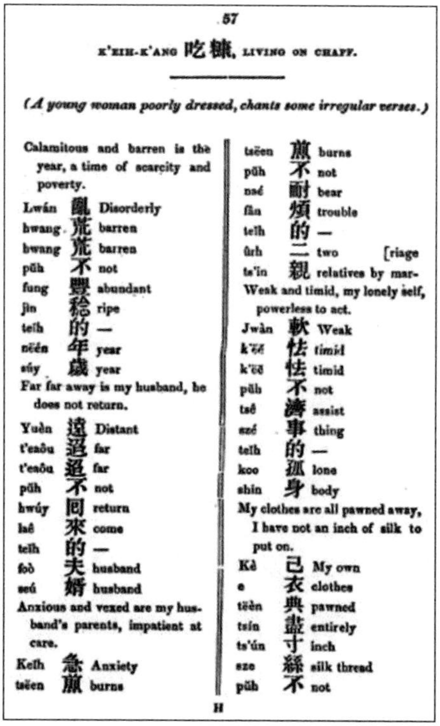
57

K'EIH-K'ANG 吃糠, LIVING ON CHAFF.

(A young woman poorly dressed, chants some irregular verses.)

Calamitous and barren is the year, a time of scarcity and poverty.

Lwán 亂 Disorderly
hwang 荒 barren
hwang 荒 barren
pŭh 不 not
fung 豐 abundant
jin 稔 ripe
teïh 的 —
nëën 年 year
súy 歲 year

Far far away is my husband, he does not return.

Yuên 遠 Distant
t'eaôu 迢 far
t'eaôu 迢 far
pŭh 不 not
hwúy 囘 return
laê 來 come
teïh 的 —
foô 夫 husband
seú 婿 husband

Anxious and vexed are my husband's parents, impatient at care.

Keïh 急 Anxiety
tsëen 煎 burns

tsëen 煎 burns
pŭh 不 not
naé 耐 bear
fân 煩 trouble
teïh 的 —
ûrh 二 two [riage
ts'in 親 relatives by mar-

Weak and timid, my lonely self, powerless to act.

Jwàn 軟 Weak
k'ëë 怯 timid
k'ëë 怯 timid
pŭh 不 not
tsê 濟 assist
szé 事 thing
teïh 的 —
koo 孤 lone
shin 身 body

My clothes are all pawned away, I have not an inch of silk to put on.

Kè 己 My own
e 衣 clothes
tëèn 典 pawned
tsin 盡 entirely
ts'ún 寸 inch
sze 絲 silk thread
pŭh 不 not

H

《汉语会话》中的《琵琶记》折子戏

（三）《借靴》与《琵琶记》

《汉语会话》分为两个部分，第一部分为“对话”（dialogue），主要内容取自《借靴》和《琵琶记》两部戏曲，是中英文合璧的本子。

艾约瑟翻译的《借靴》是该作最早的英译文，共 56 页。在《汉语会话》的目录中，《借靴》下标注“From *the Pe-pa Ke*，琵琶记”，由此使不少读者误认为《借靴》出自《琵琶记》。比如，1874 年《中国评论》第二卷刊载的费理雅（L. M. Fay，1804—1878）翻译的《借靴》，即云该作“译自

《琵琶记》”①。事实上，《借靴》选自清代戏曲选集《缀白裘》第 11 集，列为高腔，隶属花部乱弹，作者不详。写一个市井无赖张三因赴宴缺少一双靴子，遂向老友刘二求借。刘二生性悭吝，百般刁难，不肯出借，最终抵不住张三的纠缠，忍痛借靴。张三赶到宴席，早已酒阑人散，懊恼之余，倦卧街头。刘二惦记靴子，一路寻来索回。这是一出讽刺闹剧，通过张三与刘二的讨价还价，刻画了前者的刁诈和后者的吝啬。这出短剧幽默诙谐，几乎全用活泼生动的对话构成。只是作为戏剧语言，《借靴》中的对话与日常用语存在较大差异，但是对于外国人来说，这种语际内部的差异相比于中英文之间的差异可谓微乎其微，何况结合人物形象和具体情境，语言的学习也变得饶有趣味。由于《借靴》本身篇幅有限，是个短小精悍的折子戏，所以艾约瑟全文英译了该剧。

《琵琶记》是元代南戏中的佼佼者，被尊为“南曲之首”“传奇之祖”，作者高明，字则诚。目前所见通行本为汲古阁所刻《六十种曲》本《琵琶记》，全剧共 42 出。《汉语会话》节译的《琵琶记》长达 101 页，共 6 出，在 3 种英译作品中所占篇幅最多，但其内容却并非直接取自通行本《琵琶记》，而是根据《琵琶记》改编的 6 出折子戏：“吃糠”“描容”“别坟”“寺中遗像”“两贤相遘”和“书馆”。对比通行本《琵琶记》，这 6 出戏不但对应着第 21 出以后的后半部分故事情节，而且相对完整地讲述了赵五娘上京寻夫的整个过程，所以应该是艾约瑟精心挑选的 6 出折子戏。既然《借靴》出自清代戏曲选集《缀白裘》，所以有必要首先核查《缀白裘》中所收的 26 出《琵琶记》折子戏。结果发现前 3 出与《缀白裘》中的内容基本相同，“寺中遗像”“两贤相遘”不见于《缀白裘》，“书馆”与《缀白裘》中的“书馆”所用底本不同。笔者又尝试着从其他明清戏曲选集中寻

① L. M. Fay, “The Borrowed Boots”, *The China Review, or Notes and Queries on Far East*, Vol. 2, No. 6, 1874.

找后3出所用底本，根据韩国学者金英淑的研究，明清时期的戏曲选集所收《琵琶记》折子戏总计29种，《汉语会话》中的“寺中遗像”“两贤相遘”和“书馆”与这29种均有较大差异，由此推测，《汉语会话》中保存的3出《琵琶记》折子戏应该是新发现的版本，这对于研究《琵琶记》折子戏而言当有一定价值。

据王尔敏的《中国文献西译书目》记载：1840年《亚洲杂志》上刊载了一首摘自《琵琶记》的诗歌，这是目前所知的最早的《琵琶记》英译资料。① 1841年，法国著名汉学家巴赞（Par M. Bazin Aine，1799—1863）全文翻译了《琵琶记》。② 关于这个法译本，艾约瑟在《汉语会话》“序言”中表示自己尚未看过。所以，其英译文直接译自中文，艾约瑟由此成为第一个英译《琵琶记》折子戏的西方汉学家。

《借靴》与《琵琶记》编辑体例一致，都以句为单位，先用流畅的英文将整句话译成英文，再将中文竖排在下，中文左右分别标以相应的汉语拼音和英文单词。这样，读者既可以明白整句话的意思，又方便学习单个字词的读音和意义。这种编排方式，确实有利于汉语的学习。

在体制结构上，戏曲一般有场次和幕数，人物分生旦净末等具体角色，文本分唱词、宾白和科介三个部分，在保留这些体制特点方面，《汉语会话》可谓乏善可陈。比如，在角色上，中文部分省略了角色名称，英文部分也只用A、B、C、D等字母进行简单的人物区分。在唱词上，中英文均省略了曲牌名，曲白不分。舞台动作和音响效果等科介也仅在英文部分做简单介绍。这些简化和省略显然不利于中国戏曲体制特点的传达。尽管如此，艾约瑟对于戏曲的文体结构却有着敏锐的观察，尤其从语音的角度关注其韵律。比如，《借靴》开篇两句云：“小子生平说谎多，全凭舌

① “Chinese Poetry: extracts from the Pe Pa Ke”, *Asiatic Journal*, No. 1, 1840.

② Par M. Bazin Aine, *Le Pi-Pa-Ki ou l'histoire du Luth*, Paris: Imprime Par Autorisation Du Roi A. L'imprimerie Royale, 1841.

剑两头唆。”译者为此所作的注释云：“开篇两句押韵，所用文体被称为词。”又如，在“别坟”一出中，“此去孤坟望公公看着。”艾约瑟将“着”注音为 chǒ，在拼音后添加注释曰：“后面有十五六个句子重复使用本字韵脚，由此而形成一种不规则的韵律，有助于诵唱。”为了显示相应的韵脚，他用 ǒ 将之逐一标出，如：索（sǒ）、落（lǒ）、略（lëǒ）、约（yǒ）、乐（lǒ）等。这些地方都显示了艾约瑟对于中国戏曲唱词韵律节奏的重视。

就翻译策略而言，艾约瑟主要采用“直译法”（literal translation），力求字句对应、文化传真，以最大限度地贴近汉语语境。如，《借靴》有云：“又只见喳喳的，又只见喳喳的喜鹊在枝头上戏”，英译文为：and nothing was heard but chatter chatter，nothing but chatter chatter，from a fortunate magpie，sitting on a tree amusing himself。艾约瑟不但将拟声词一一译出，为了保留汉语的表达习惯，甚至没有根据英语读者的需要调整语序，这种翻译方式，显然是以汉语为中心构建译文，以尽可能全面地译介汉语的文化信息。比如，“喜鹊”这一意象在英语世界略带贬义，可以引申为聒噪、饶舌的人，但在中国文化中却被奉为报喜鸟。如，《西京杂记》卷三云：“乾鹊噪而行人至，蜘蛛集而百事嘉。”[①] 艾约瑟将喜鹊翻译为 a fortunate magpie，即“一只吉祥的喜鹊”，恰当地传达出了“喜鹊”的汉语引申义。其实，即便译者并不知晓这层含义，仅仅遵循既定原则忠实地译解文本，相信他也不会漏掉这一文化信息。

在翻译某些文化专有词时，艾约瑟相当用心，这使他的译文从字句对译、信息保真的角度来看具有较高的准确性。比如，在文字释义时，他将“丹青”二字分别解释为“红色”和“蓝色”，然后又将两字括在一起解释

① （汉）刘歆撰，（晋）葛洪集，向新阳、刘克任校注：《西京杂记校注》，上海古籍出版社 1991 年版，第 151 页。

为“绘画”。遇到难解的字句，他就添加注释，这些注释有的旨在说明文字出处，如在“人而无信，不知其可也。大车无輗，小车无軏”后添加注释：“此句出自孔子的《论语》。”有的旨在说明人物来源，如在“柳盗跖”后添加注释：“柳盗跖是周朝的一个著名的盗贼。”还有的是解释字词意思转换的缘由。如艾约瑟将“金风”译作“西风”，相关注释曰：“‘金’字面意思是金属，此元素指代西方。”这些注释虽然数量有限、文字简短，却体现了艾约瑟对于中国文化的了解相当广博。如在“正是青龙共白虎同行”一句下，艾约瑟分别为“青龙”和“白虎”添加注释“幸运星宿”和“晦气星宿”。同时，这些注释也体现了艾约瑟在翻译时的字斟句酌、小心谨慎，如，他为“忽梦神人自称当山土地，带领阴兵与奴助力”添加注释：“神人（genius）这个词被阿拉伯或波斯故事的译者用来表示那些具有某种能力的生灵，他们有时为了因果报应而出现在人类面前。对这段中文来说，用这个词来翻译或许最为合适。”

当然，艾约瑟的翻译也存在一些明显的错误。如将“长生殿”误作“长王殿”；将“老面皮的杀才”误作“老面皮的没才”。这种错误多数情况下首先是中文出错，由此相应的注音和释义也跟着出错，严重时个别文字的错误还会引起整句话翻译的错误。如在“吃糠”一出戏中，艾约瑟将“苏卿犹健”误作“苏卿九健”，这句话被他错译为：The noble Kew-këen of the Soo family，即“苏家高贵的九健”。有时中文虽然没错，但理解出现了偏差，也会造成整句话翻译的错误。同样是在“吃糠”一出戏中，赵五娘说“非不欲买些鲑菜”，“鲑菜”指的是鱼类菜肴，如杜甫《王竟携酒》诗云：“自愧无鲑菜，空烦卸马鞍。”[①] 艾约瑟译文中的“鲑”字虽然没错，但他却将之误当成了“蛙”，拼音写作 wa，释义为 frogs，整句话也被错译为：And as to buying a few frogs and vegetables, it was not that I did not wish it,

① （唐）杜甫撰，（清）仇兆鳌注：《杜诗详注》，中华书局 1979 年版，第 864 页。

如此翻译不免令人啼笑皆非，似乎五娘欲给公婆买青蛙来吃。除了文字方面的错误，句读有时也有个别地方出错。如《借靴》中原为“非是我舍不得穿，似我这般人儿常常有，那无福之人难消受”，译者误作：“非是我舍不得穿似我这般人儿，常常有那无福之人难消受。”断句出错，相应的翻译自然也跟着出错。

总体来看，在戏曲翻译方面，艾约瑟不仅是《借靴》的最早英译者，也是第一个将《琵琶记》折子戏大量翻译到英语世界的西方汉学家。他对中国戏曲，尤其是《琵琶记》有着很高的评价，在《汉语会话》“序言”中，艾约瑟说：“《琵琶记》（*Pe pa ké*, *Tale of a Guitar*）为本书提供了大部分语料。这部作品在中国一直非常流行。它描述了当地人性格中的某些优秀品质，故事本身也非常有趣。”五年后，艾约瑟在《汉语官话口语语法》一书中再次提及《琵琶记》，他说：“巴赞先生在其著作《元朝》（*Siecle des Youen*）中已经对最优秀的小说《水浒传》（*Shui-hu-chwen*）和最优秀的戏曲《西厢记》（*Si-siang-ki*）做了大量节译。在同一本著作中，他还详细介绍了一百种元代剧作家的戏曲。他单独拿出一卷篇幅大量翻译《琵琶记》。对《琵琶记》的优美动人，读者自然毫无异议地表示赞同，但有趣的是，在翻译的过程中，巴赞先生从原著的序言中敏锐地判断出了这部作品在中国人心目中的地位。中国人视之为二流作品，但是巴赞先生却认为，因其不相上下之作《西厢记》在情节上存在缺陷，所以外国人的判断或许会扭转中国人对于《琵琶记》的看法。”① 由此可见，早期的西方汉学家在中国经典的建构方面并不仅仅满足于做一个翻译者和旁观者，他们还想做一个组织者和评判者；他们不仅积极构建西方文化谱系中的中国经典，还力图改变中国人心目中的经典。在这一过程中，《琵琶记》就是巴赞、艾约瑟格

① Joseph Edkins, *A Grammar of the Chinese Colloquial Language, Commonly called the Mandarin Dialect*, Shanghai: Presbyterian Mission Press, 1864, pp. 270 – 271.

外青睐的作品，在介绍“曲子”的文体风格时，艾约瑟又翻译了《琵琶记》中的两支曲子作为例证，由此可见他对《琵琶记》的赞赏，这种态度势必影响读者及周围的来华西士，从而有利于推动以《琵琶记》为代表的中国戏曲的英译。

（四）“神仙于吉之死”的英译

《汉语会话》的第二部分内容取自《三国志》（*San-kwo-che*，*History of the Three Kingdoms*）第 29 回“小霸王怒斩于吉 碧眼儿坐领江东”。中文部分只有回数，没有回目名称；英文部分不仅说明“摘自第 29 章”，还将摘译内容题名为“神仙于吉之死”（*The Death of Yu Keih the Magician*）。实际上，艾约瑟并没有将第 29 回完整地翻译过来，而是围绕于吉、孙策之死节译了中间部分，始于“正话间，忽报袁绍遣使陈震至”；止于“言讫，瞑目而逝，年止二十六岁”。

在排版上，小说部分相比于戏曲部分出现了明显改动：中英文左右分开，英文在左页，中文在右页，以方便读者对照阅读。中文部分保留了传统竖排版式；英文部分汉语拼音与英文单词上下对应，拼音在上，英文在下。如此排版，自然也是为了满足汉语学习的需要。

考察中文底本是研究译作的前提。经过版本比对不难发现，艾约瑟所用底本为清代康熙年间毛纶、毛宗岗父子评点本。与原著不同的是，中文正文部分删除了所有评语，部分评语被翻译成英文，附在右页中文下边，总计 20 条。此前出版的附有中文原文的《三国演义》英译文有《三国志节译文》，该文作为附录出现在第二任香港总督德庇时于 1834 年出版的《汉文诗解》中，与之相比，艾约瑟的中文排印质量有了明显提高，一是两千余汉字几乎没有错漏。二是为了方便阅读，不但增加了句读，部分人名旁还用竖线作了标识。

在英译方面，艾约瑟继续采用逐字逐句翻译的“直译法”。这种翻译方法突出优势主要有两点。一是通过中英文逐字对译，可以最大限度地保留原著的文化信息。比如，艾约瑟将“枷锁”译作“wooden collar and locks”，“枷”是套在脖子上的木枷，“锁”是手铐或脚镣，比后来邓罗在《孙策之死》(*The Death of Sun Tse*)① 中译作“fetters”更为精确。又如，将“印绶”译为“the seal and ribbon of government”，这一翻译不仅突出了“印绶”本身由“印章”和“绶带”两部分组成，后面附加的“government”进一步强调了“印绶”是权力的象征，由此使西方读者迅速获悉，孙策临终前将“印绶”转交给孙权，实际是将权力移交给他。二是成语、俗语因具有浓郁的民族特色，很难通过字面意思翻译转换，故此一般采用“意译”的方式；但若能恰当地“直译”，有时也会收到意想不到的效果。如艾约瑟把“杀人如麻”译作“killing men as if they were raveled hemp”，即“把人当成纠缠在一起的乱麻来砍杀”。这句直译转换得非常巧妙，哪怕不懂中文的西方人也能通过这种画面感很强的表达很快知晓孙策的言下之意是说自己杀过很多人。又如，于吉被孙策擒来后，辩解自己“惟务代天宣化，普救万人，未曾取人毫厘之物”，艾约瑟将“毫厘之物”译作“a hair's breadth of recompense”，即“头发丝般大小的报偿”，此处“毫厘”的直译就相当传神。

直译的方法也有天然缺陷。第一，有些逐字逐句的对译显得过于生硬。比如，艾约瑟将“晴雨乃天地之定数”译作“Fine weather and rain come by the fixed arrangements of heaven and earth”。在此，“天地”被对译

---

① C. H. Brewitt-Taylor, “The Death of Sun Tse (孙策)”, *The China Review, or notes & queries on the Far East*, Vol. 18, No. 3, 1889, pp. 147 - 151.

为“heaven and earth”，不但不能传达出中国的“天地”所特有的宗教意味，也不如转译为“nature”更近自然。第二，直译带来的最大问题是文字表达的冗长。如“众将俱曰：‘主公玉体违和，未可轻动。且待平愈，出兵未迟’”一句，邓罗在《孙策之死》中译作“But the officers objected as their chief was not yet recovered and urged him to wait till his wound was well”。艾约瑟译作：The generals all said，“Your highness is in poor health，and must not lightly undertake a journey. If you wait for a time till you are well，and then lead out the army，it will not be too late.”两相对比，邓罗的“意译”虽然不如艾约瑟的“直译”精准，但就语言的简洁而言，邓罗的“意译”则略胜一筹。

虽然都是“直译”，但相比于《借靴》与《琵琶记》，艾约瑟对《三国演义》的翻译整体看来更为灵活自如。究其原因，这或许与两部分内容的排版有一定关系。《借靴》与《琵琶记》以“句”为单位排印，在翻译时往往逐字对译，不容改换；而《三国演义》却以“篇”为单位整体排印，在翻译时可以前后照应，灵活调整。

最典型的一个例子莫过于艾约瑟对于“妖人”这一词汇的翻译，该词前后出现8次，贯穿选文始末。孙策对道士于吉深恶痛绝，不杀之不足以解其恨，故每每提及必称“妖人”。在于吉登台祈雨之前，艾约瑟将“妖人”一律译作“wizard”；等到于吉登台施法之时，天空只见阴云，不见甘雨，孙策骂道：“正是妖人。”对于孙策而言，如果此前的“妖人”只是出于义愤做出的臆断，这里的“妖人”则是经过亲自验证之后得出的论断，由此，艾约瑟将之译作“a false pretender to magical arts”，强调了于吉不过是个“假装会施展法术的冒牌货”，此后，孙策在与母亲的辩论中，又两次使用“a false sorcerer”（虚假的术士）来翻译“妖人”，与其母吴太夫人始终用“神仙”（a wonderful magician）一词来称呼于吉形成了鲜明对照。同一名词的译介，根据情节的转换，译者先后使用了三种译法。

类似的例子还有很多，比如同一段文字中出现了三次“狱吏”，为了避免重复，译者先后使用了“prison attendants”“prison keepers”“jailors”。词语的灵活转换和运用，使得艾约瑟的翻译不但用词准确，而且表述多样，在他的努力下，不少句子译得相当精妙，如“倘内事不决，可问张昭；外事不决，可问周瑜”，艾约瑟译作：If internal matters cannot be arranged，you may appeal to Chang Chaou. If external affairs are hard to control，you can appeal to Chow Yü。这句译文不但辞采丰富，而且句式整饬，由此大大提高了译作的文学性与可读性。

尽管艾约瑟博闻强记、学贯中西，但他的英译还是出现了一些问题。

第一，相比于德庇时翻译的《三国志节译文》，以及美国传教士汉学家卫三畏在其汉语教材《拾级大成》中对《三国演义》的引用和翻译，艾约瑟的错译明显减少，显而易见的错译仅有一两处，比如，把“掣宝剑”译作“During his sword”，“掣”字的动词属性完全被忽略；把“登坛求雨”译作“ascent the terrace and pray for rain”，此处用“terrace”来翻译“坛”字显然不如“altar”更能体现其宗教意味。

第二，多数错译、误译出现在成语或习语中，虽然这类词语本身难度未必很大，但因为蕴含着丰富的信息，所以很难被译者准确把握。比如，“鼓瑟焚香”是鼓瑟、焚香两事并举，而译者却翻译为“burnt incense with drums and harps”，即“带着鼓和琴焚香”。“鼓瑟”即“弹瑟”，“鼓”在此作动词用，而艾约瑟却错当成了名词。又如，孙策临终前，叮嘱母亲朝夕训导弟弟孙权不要轻视“父兄旧人”，这里的“父兄旧人”当指一直追随孙坚和孙策的部从，而艾约瑟却将其中的“从属关系”理解成了“并列关系”，将此句误译作“And he may be careful not to dispise his father and brother，and the officers grown old in their service”，即“他（孙权）当小心谨慎，不要轻视他的父亲和兄弟，以及那些服侍他们的年迈的官员”。实际上，如果了解孙策去世时其父孙坚早已去世这一历史常识，艾约瑟或许可以避免这一错误。

第三，还有个别错译涉及中国语言中的“一词多义”，这对于外邦译者而言提出了双重挑战：译者不仅要了解词语的多种用法，还要从中选出恰当的用法。比如，“策命将其尸号令于市，以正妖妄之罪”，艾约瑟将这句译作：Sün Ts'ïh gave orders to take the dead body，and proclaim in the market place，that it was correcting the crime of sorcery and imposture。“号令”一词被译作“proclaim”，即宣告、公布、声明之意，但这种翻译明显不通。究其原因，乃是因为艾约瑟对于“号令”的理解有误。在古汉语中，“号令”除了号召、命令或发布号召与命令等常见用法，还有另外一种不太常见的用法，即“将犯人行刑以示众”。如《元典章·工部二·船只》：“如有违犯之人，捉拿到官，取问是实，定将犯人对众号令，严行断罪。”① 这种用法在明清小说中比较常见，如《水浒传》第 116 回：“宋江令讨放砲火种，吹起灯来看时，上面写道：‘宋江早晚也号令在此处！’”②《东周列国志》第 59 回：“厉公重赏甲士，将三郤尸首，号令朝门，三日，方听改葬。”③ 由此，“策命将其尸号令于市”中的“号令”，本应理解为“斩首示众”，英文最好译作 behead 或 cut off his head in public。

第四，某些错译源于译者对于中国典籍的了解不够全面，这也从一个侧面显示了译事之难。比如，“母谓策曰：‘圣人云，鬼神之为德，其盛矣乎！又云，祷尔于上下神祇。’”于吉被孙策斩杀后，吴太夫人为了让儿子拜祷谢罪，专门引用了两句古语进行劝慰。前一句出自《中庸》第十六章：“子曰：鬼神之为德，其盛矣乎！视之而弗见，听之而弗闻，体物而不可遗。”④ 显然，此话出自孔子之口，言鬼神的德行之盛。后一句出自《论

① 陈高华、张帆、刘晓、党宝海点校：《元典章》（四），天津古籍出版社 2011 年版，第 1981 页。
② 施耐庵、罗贯中：《水浒传》，人民文学出版社 2014 年版，第 1245 页。
③ （明）冯梦龙著，蔡元放编：《东周列国志》，人民文学出版社 1986 年版，第 560 页。
④ 王国轩译注：《大学·中庸》，中华书局 2007 年版，第 81 页。

语·述而》："子疾病，子路请祷。子曰：'有诸?'子路对曰：'有之。《诔》曰：祷尔于上下神祇。'子曰：'丘之祷久矣。'"杨伯峻注曰："诔，本应作讄，祈祷文，和哀悼死者的诔不同。"[1] 由此可见，"祷尔于上下神祇"乃上古讄文，并非出自孔子之口。而艾约瑟却将吴太夫人的话译作：She then addressed him as follows，"The wise man says，'The works of the superior and inferior spirits how vast and various are they！' And again he says，'Pray ye to the spirits above and the spirits beneath.'"两句引文本身翻译得都很精当，尤其是译者结合后一句引文中的"上下神祇"（the spirits above and the spirits beneath）来理解前一句引文中的"鬼神"，他没有简单地将"鬼神"直译为ghosts and gods，而是译作the superior and inferior spirits，从而巧妙地传达出了鬼神的无所不在和无所不能，由此将后面的"其盛矣乎"译作"how vast and various"也就顺理成章了。唯一的遗憾是两句引文之间的"又云"被译作"and again he says"，这种翻译使人误以为前后两句引文出自同一"圣人"（the wise man）之口。显然，由于中国典籍知识储备不足，艾约瑟在此确实犯了错。但若就此谴责译者，未免过于苛求，因为恐怕没有哪个译者能够了解中国典籍的全部。即便是中国读者，如不借助古籍资料，也很难发现这一问题。当然，除了知识储备的不足，艾约瑟犯错的真正原因或许是对中国古文表达习惯的不够精通。实际上，"又云""又曰"等省略了主语的表述在中国古文中极为常见，这种前置引语的主要作用是引出下文，其前后所引内容却未必来源一致。由此可见，译者需要掌握的知识可谓汗牛充栋，翻译绝非易事，它不单单是两种文字的转换与对接，更是两种语言与文化的交流与对话。

艾约瑟所译《三国演义》的一个突出特点是保留了毛评本《三国演义》的部分评论。他对这些评论相当重视，在《汉语会话》"序言"中就

---

① 杨伯峻译注：《论语译注》，中华书局2006年版，第87页。

说："最后一部分附录的评论可以用来举例说明中国批评的精神和方式。"这些评论在中文正文中没有出现，它们被直接译成英文，作为注释附在中文正文的下边，总共20条。其中有的评论写作技巧，如，"看他一时写出风、云、烟、火、雷、电、雨、日，令读者惊心悦目"。有的评论世风民情，如"今之信佛信仙者，偏会引孔孟之言为证，不独一吴太夫人也"。数量最多的还是对孙策和于吉两个人物的评论。前者有："孙策明理，毕竟英雄。""孙策事母至孝，岂有神仙而害孝子者?""曰'金疮迸裂'，则孙策仍死于许贡之客，非死于吉也。""孙策可谓孝于父母，友于兄弟。""此是孙策当死，切勿认作于吉有灵。"后者有："能于既死之后摄去其尸，何不先于未死之前遁去其身乎?""既往东北，何又来东南?""人之将死而鬼神侮之，非真于吉之能为祸也。""种种兴妖作怪，神仙必不为此。此时何不更求甘雨以灭火耶?""披发而来，一发像鬼，不像神仙也。"①

总体看来，毛氏父子肯定孙策而否定于吉，这与《三国演义》作者罗贯中对两人的态度截然不同。在《三国演义》第29回中，于吉被刻画成一个普救万民、受人爱戴、呼风唤雨、精魂不死的活神仙；孙策虽称霸江南、为人至孝，却性情暴躁、固执己见，因此在怒杀于吉后，被其阴魂索命、伤重而亡。毛氏父子对孙策大加赞扬，对于吉却充满狐疑，这尤其体现在第二十九回的一则总评中，毛氏父子云："孙策不信于神仙，是孙策英雄处。英明如汉武，犹且惑神仙、好方士，而孙策不然。此其识见，诚有大过人者。其死也，亦运数当绝，适逢其会耳，非于吉之能杀之也。世人不察，以为孙策死于于吉。"毛氏父子认为孙策英明而有识见，不信鬼神就是其英雄本色的集中体现。叱责异教、反对鬼神等迷信思想是艾约瑟等西方

① （明）罗贯中，（清）毛宗岗批注：《第一才子书三国演义》，线装书局2007年版，第256—259页。其中"偏为引孔、孟之言为证"一句，根据其他毛评本更正为"偏会引孔、孟之言为证"。

传教士一贯的立场，毛氏父子的评论恰恰契合了他的这一宗教立场，这或许是艾约瑟翻译这 20 条评论的根本原因。

（五）艾约瑟的中国小说观

《汉语会话》的出版，使艾约瑟成为第一个翻译清代戏曲高腔《借靴》的译者，第一个大量翻译《琵琶记》折子戏的译者，同时也是相对完整地翻译《三国演义》第 29 回的译者。这些译文对于研究中国戏曲、小说的早期英译，都有一定参考价值。《汉语会话》因藏本有限，目前国内学者罕有人知，但在当时却有一定影响。比如，1854 年 12 月 26 日，英国驻华总税务司赫德（Robert Hart，1835—1911）在日记中提到过这本教材，这是《赫德日记》（*Entering China's Service*，*Robert Hart's Journals*，*1854—1863*）在《圣谕广训》《麦都思汉英字典》之外提及的少数汉语学习用书之一。[①] 此外，当时的不少书目，也将这部汉语教材看作汉语学习的重要工具，比如《中国海关书目辑存》（*Catalogue of the Chinese Imperial Maritime Customs Collection*）等。

《汉语会话》对于中国戏曲、小说的重视，是艾约瑟译介中国文化的一大特点。1857 年，他在《汉语官话口语语法》一书中说："无论是小说，还是戏剧，都不见于皇家目录。这些作品在中国人看来仅仅是娱乐型的，不值得学者去研究。但是对于外国人来说，它们却饶有趣味，体现了东方人的想象力，就像我们的戏剧和小说体现了西方人的想象力一样。同

---

① E. Katherine F. Bruner，John K. Fairbank，Richard J. Smith，*Entering China's Service*，*Robert Hart's Journals*，*1854 - 1863*，Cambridge（Massachusetts）and London：The Council on East Asian Studies，Hardvard University，1986，p. 43.

时，这些作品也能让外国人快捷地了解这个国家的历史、习俗和语言。”①1890 年，他在《中国人的小说观》（*Chinese Views on Novels*）一文中再次指出：“尽管中国读者轻视小说、中国官方禁毁小说，但是阅读中国小说的外国读者却不必不分青红皂白地对之妄加指责，因为部分中国小说展现了美好的男女形象，其人物也有着许多高尚的道德品质。”② 艾约瑟对于中国戏曲、小说的正面评论，显然有利于这类通俗文学作品的早期海外传播。

---

① Joseph Edkins, *A Grammar of the Chinese Colloquial Language*, *Commonly called the Mandarin Dialect*, Shanghai: Presbyterian Mission Press, 1864, pp. 270 – 271.

② Joseph Edkins, *Chinese Views on Novels*, *The North-China Herald and Supreme Court & Consular Gazette*, Shanghai, Aug 1, 1890.

附：文献图片

三國志 SAN-KWO-CHE

HISTORY OF THE THREE KINGDOMS.

Extract from Chapter 29.

THE DEATH OF YU KEIH THE MAGICIAN.

Chéng hwá këen, hwŭh paóu Yuên Shaóu
Just as he was speaking, it was suddenly announced, that an envoy sent
k'ëen shè Ch'in-chín ché. Ts'ih hwáh
by Yuên Shaóu, named Ch'ên-chin had arrived. Sün Ts'ih calling him
jŭh, wún ĉhe; Ch'ên keu yên Yuên
to enter, made inquiries of him; Ch'ên-chin fully narrated how Yuen
Shaóu yŭh këë Tung Woô wei
Shaou wished to form a league with the Woo country in the East as
waé yíng, kúng kung Ts'aoû T'saoû.
his ally, that they might carry on war together against Ts'aou Ts'aou.
Ts'ih tá hè, tseih jih hwúy choo
Sün Ts'ih greatly delighted, on the same day assembled all his
tsëáng yû ch'ing lôw sháng, shë yên k'wàn taé Ch'in
generals in the city tower, and prepared a feast to entertain Ch'in
Chín. Yin tsèw che këen, hwŭh këen choo tsëáng
Chin. While at their wine, all the generals were suddenly seen to be
hoó sëang, ngòw yù fun fun hëá
talking together, and then in hurry and confusion, they descended
lôw. Ts'ih kwaé wún hô koó. Tsò
from the tower. Sün Ts'ih wondering, inquired the reason. His
yéw yuĕ, yèw Yü shin sëen chày, kin ts'ûng
servants said, that Yü one of the genii, was now passing by
lôw hëá kwó, choo tsëáng yŭh wàng paé che ŭrh.
beneath the tower, and the generals wished to go and bow to him.
Ts'ih k'è shin p'ing lân kwan che. Këén
Sün Ts'ih rose and leaning over the balcony looked for him. He saw
yĭh Taóu jin shin p'e hŏ ch'àng
a follower of Taou wrapped in a cloak of stork feathers, and holding in
shòw hé Lè ch'ang. leih yû tang loó.
his hand a Le-tree staff. He was standing in the middle of the road,
Pih síng keu fûn hëang, fŭh taóu ûrh
and the people were all burning incense, lying down on the pathway and
paé. Ts'ih noó yuĕ, "shé hó yabu
worshipping him. Sün Ts'ih was angry and said, "What wizard is

三國志第二十九回

正話間，忽報袁紹遣使陳震至，策喚入問之，震具言袁紹欲結東吳爲外應，共攻曹操，策大喜，即日會諸將於城樓上，設宴欵待陳震，飲酒之間，忽見諸將互相偶語，紛紛下樓，策怪問何故，左右曰，有于神仙者今從樓下過，諸將欲往拜之耳，策起身凭欄觀之，見一道人身披鶴氅，手携藜杖，立於當道，百姓俱焚香，伏道而拜，策怒曰，是何妖

jin ! k'waé yù wò k'in che." Tsò yéw kaóu yuĕ,—" T'szè
this? catch him for me quickly." His servants informed him,—" This
jin síng Yû ming Keĭh, yù keu
man's surname is Yū and his name Keĭh, he is now residing
tung fang, wáng laê Woô hwúy,
in the eastern region, and goes about in the Woo country, every-
p'oò she foô shwùy kéw jin wán píng, woô
where distributing charmed water to cure men of all diseases. Never
yĭh pŭh yén. Tang shé hoó wei shin sëen.
failing of success, the whole world call him one of the genii.
We k'ŏ k'ing tŭh." Ts'ĭh yù noó, hŏ
He cannot be lightly insulted." Sūn Ts'ĭh still more angry, shouted
líng, sŭh sŭh k'in laê :— weí chày
a command, that on the moment he should be seized ;—should any
chàn. Tsò yéw pŭh tĭh ò,
disobey, their heads were to be cut off. The servants unable to avoid it,
chà tĭh heá lôw yùng Yû Keĭh ché lôw sháng.
could do nothing but descend and take Yū Keĭh up upon the tower.
Ts'ĭh ch'ĭh yuĕ, " K'wâng Taóu tséng kàn shèn hwŏ
Sūn Ts'ĭh chiding him said, " Mad priest, how dare you deceive
jin sin "? Yû Keĭh yuĕ, " P'in Taóu naè
men's minds "? Yu Keĭh replied, " I a poor follower of Taou am a
Lâng-yà kung Taou szé. Shún Té shĭ ts'ëng
priest of the Lang-ya temple. In the reign of Shūn Te, having gone
jŭh shan ts'aè yŏ, tĭh shin shoo yu
to the mountains to pluck medicinal herbs, I found a mysterious book at
K'eŭh-yâng ts'euàn shwùy sháng haóu yuĕ, *T'aé p'ing ts'ing*
the K'eŭh-yang fountain, named T'AE P'ING TS'ING
ling taóu.
LING TAOU. (THE WAY TO PEACE AND PURITY POINTED OUT.)
Fân pĭh yù keuén, kene
In all there were more than a hundred chapters, containing methods
che jin tseĭh píng fang shŭh. P'in taóu tĭh che, wŏ
for curing the diseases of mankind. When I had obtained it, I gave
woó taé t'ëen seuen hwá, p'oò
myself on behalf of heaven to propagate the knowledge of it, every-
kéw wán jin ; wé ts'ĕng ts'eù jin haôu lê che
where healing mankind ; and have never received a hair's breadth of
wŭh ; ngan tĭh shén hwŏ jin sin ?" Ts'ĭh yuĕ,
recompense ; how should I deceive men's minds ?" Sūn Ts'ĭh replied,
"joô haôu pŭh ts'eù jin e fŭh
" If you have not taken a hair's value from any one of raiment and

161

人、快與我擒之、左右告曰、此人姓于名吉、寓居東方、往來吳會、普施符水救人萬病、無有不驗、當世呼爲神仙、未可輕瀆、策愈怒、喝令速速擒來、違者斬、左右不得已、只得下樓、擁于吉至樓上、策叱曰、狂道怎敢煽惑人心、于吉曰、貧道乃瑯琊宮道士、順帝時曾入山採藥、得神書於曲陽泉水上、號曰太平青領道、凡百餘卷、皆治人病疾方術、貧道得之、惟務代天宣化、普救萬人、未曾取人毫釐之物、安得煽惑人心、策曰、汝毫不取人衣服

U

yin shĭh, ts'ûng hô ûrh tĭh ?" Joò tseĭh
food, from whence did you obtain them ?"—You are surely one of the
Hwâng kin Chang-kĕŏ che lêw ; kin jó pŭh choo,
Yellow turban band, an associate of Chang-kĕŏ ; If you are not killed
peĭh wei hów hwán. Ch'ĭh
now, there will certainly be mischief coming of it. He then com-
tsò yéw chàn che. Chang Chaóu kéén
manded his servants to kill him. Chang Chaou urging him to refrain
yuĕ, " Yü Taóu jin tsaé Kĕang Tung soó shĭh
said, " Yü the priest of Taou has been for many years in the region of
nëën, píng woô kwó fán ; pŭh k'ò shă haé."
Kĕang Tung, and committed no crime ; he must not be put to death."
Ts'ĭh yuĕ, " Ts'zè tèng yaou jin woô shă che, hô é
Sün Ts'ĭh replied, " A wizard like this, if I kill him, what is it more
t'oò choo kòw ?" Chúng kwan keae
than killing a swine or a dog ?" The assembled mandarins all
k'oò kéén ; Ch'ìn Chín yĭh k'euén ; Ts'ĭh
earnestly entreated him ; Ch'in Chin also urged him ; but Sün Ts'ĭh
noó wé seĭh, míng ts'cày ts'ĕw
still not desisting from his anger, commanded him to be placed for a
yù yŏ chung. Chúng kwan keu sán, Ch'ìn Chín
while in prison. The mandarins then all separated, Ch'in Chin
tszé kwei kwàn yĭh gnan hĭh, Sün Ts'ĭh kwei foò.
returned to his lodging to rest, and Sün Ts'ĭh to his residence. The
Tsaòu yèw núy shè ch'uên shwŏ ts'zè szé, yú Ts'ĭh moò
servants within soon related this matter to the mother of Sün Ts'ĭh,
Woô T'aé foo jin che taóu. Foo jin hwán Sun Ts'ĭh
the Dowager lady Woo, for her information. She called Sün Ts'ĭh
jŭh hów t'âng weí yuĕ, " Wò wûn joô tsëang
into the back hall and addressing him said, " I hear that you have
Yü shin sëen, hëá yû lûy sëĕ.
taken Yü the wonderful magician, and placed him in confinement.
Ts'zè jin to ts'êng e jin tseĭh píng. Keun míng
This man has healed many persons of diseases. All the people
kíng nëáng. Pŭh k'ò këa haé." Ts'ĭh
reverence and look up to him. He must not be injured." Sün Ts'ĭh
yuĕ, " Ts'zè naé yaou jin nêng ê yaou shŭh hwŏ cháng ;
replied, " He is a wizard who deceives the multitude by magical arts ;
pŭh k'ò pŭh ch'oô." Foo jin tsaé san
he cannot be allowed to live." The lady a second and a third time
k'euén keaè ; Ts'ĭh yué, " Moò ts'in wŭh t'ing
entreated him to yield ; but Ts'ĭh replied, " Mother do not listen to

163

飲食、從何而得。汝即黃巾張角之流。今若不誅、必爲後患。叱左右斬之。張昭諫曰、于道人在江東數十年、並無過犯、不可殺害。策曰、此等妖人、吾殺之、何異屠猪狗。衆官皆苦諫、陳震亦勸。策怒未息、命且囚於獄中。衆官俱散。陳震自歸館驛安歇。孫策歸府。早有內侍傳說此事與策母吳太夫人知道。夫人喚孫策入後堂間曰、我聞汝將于神仙下於縲絏。此人多曾醫人疾病、軍民敬仰、不可加害。策曰、此乃妖人、能以妖術惑衆、不可不除。夫人再三勸解、策曰、母親勿聽

waé jin wáng yên, ûrh tszé yèw k'eu ch'oo."
other persons' idle talk, your son has a fixed resolution that he can-
Naè ch'ùh hwán yŏ lé
not forego." He then went out, and called to the prison attendants
ts'eù Yü Keih laê wún. Yuên laê yŏ lé
to bring in Yü Keih for examination. Now the prison keepers had
keae kíng sín Yü Keih.
all of them from the first reverenced and believed in Yü Keih.
Keih tsaé yŏ chung shê, tsín k'eú k'ê këa
While he was in the prison, they had entirely removed the wooden
soò, keih Ts'ih hwán
collar and locks from him, until Sün Ts'ih called for him to be
ts'eù, fang taé këa soò úrh ch'ŭh. Ts'ih
brought. He then came wearing the collar and locks. Sün Ts'ih
fâng che tá noó, t'úng
finding by inquiry how it had been, was very angry and severely
tsih yŏ lé, jíng tsëang Yü Keih heae hé
rebuked the jailors, who as before took Yü Keih chained him, and
hëá yŏ. Chang Chaou têng, soó
placed him in the prison. Chang Chaou, and those with him, to the
shih jin, lëên ming tsŏ
number of several tens, subscribed their names in succession to a
chwáng, paé k'âw Sün Ts'ih, k'eih
memorial respectfully addressing Sün Ts'ih, and entreating him to
paòu Yü shin sëen. Ts'ih yuĕ, "Kung têng
protect Yü the wonderful magician. Sün Ts'ih replied, "Gentlemen,
keae tŭh shoo jin, hô pŭh tă lè?
you are all educated men, why do you not understand reason? For-
Seih Keaou Chow ts'zé shè Chang Tsin, t'ing sín
merly the prefect of Keaou Chow named Chang Tsin, believing in a
sëây keaóu, koò sih fûn hëang,
depraved superstition, burnt incense with drums and harps, and
ch'âng è hûng p'ŏ koò t'ôw. Tszé ch'ing
always wore on his head a red silk turban. He gave out that he
k'ŏ tsoó ch'ŭh keun che wei.
should thus aid the advancing army by imparting to it an air of
Hôw kíng wei teih keun sò shă. Ts'zè
grandeur. But in sooth he was killed by the enemy's army. This
têng szé shín woò yih, choo keun tszé wé woó ŭrh.
sort of thing is quite useless, yet you chiefs do not perceive it.
Yŭh shă Yü Keih, chíng sze kín sëây
In wishing to kill Yü Keih, I only desire to check depraved supersti-

外人妄言、兒自有區處、乃出喚獄吏、取于吉來問、原、來、獄吏、皆、敬、信、于吉、吉、在、獄、中、時、盡、去、其、枷、鎖、及、策、喚、取、方、帶、枷、鎖、而、出、策、訪、知、大、怒、痛、責、獄、吏、仍、將、于吉、械、繫、下、獄、張昭、等、數、十、人、連名作狀、拜求孫策、乞保于神仙、策曰、公等皆讀書人、何不達理、昔交州、刺、史、張津、聽信邪教、鼓瑟焚香、常、以、紅、帕、裹、頭、自、稱、可、助、出、軍、之、威、後、竟、爲、敵、軍、所、殺、此等事、甚無益、諸君自未悟耳、吾欲殺于吉正思禁邪

kĕŏ mê yày." Leù Fán yuĕ. "Meù soó
tion and awaken the deluded." Leu Fan replied, "I have always
che Yü Taóu jin, nêng k'ê. fung taòu yù.
understood that Yü the disciple of Taou, could bring wind and rain
Fang kin t'ëen hàn; hô
in answer to his prayers. Just now the weather is dry; why should
pŭh líng k'ê, k'ê yù è shŭh taúy?"
you not command him to pray for rain, as a ransom for his crime?"
Ts'ïh yuĕ, "Woŏ ts'ëay k'án ts'zè yaou jin
Sün Ts'ïh then said, "I will then for the time see what this wizard
jŏ hô." Súy míng yù yŏ chung ts'eù
can do." Immediately he sent orders to the prison, that Yü Keïh
ch'ŭh Yû Keïh, k'ae k'ê kĕa sò,
should be brought, and after the wooden collar and locks were re-
líng teng t'ân k'ĕw yù.
moved, he was ordered to ascend the terrace and pray for rain. Yü
Keïh ling míng, tseïh mŭh yŭh keng
Keïh having received the command, bathed his body, and changed his
e; ts'eù shing tszé fŏ yü lëĕ jïh che chung.
dress; then taking a cord he bound himself in the hot sun. The
Pïh síng kwan chày t'ëën keae sïh hëáng. Yû Keïh weí
people looking on, filled up the streets and lanes. Yü Keïh addressed
chúng jin yuĕ, "Woŏ k'ĕw san ch'ïh kan lin, è
the multitude saying, "I pray for three feet depth of good rain, to
kéw wán min, jên wò chung
save the ten thousands of the people, but as for myself I must
pŭh mëën yïh szè." Chùng jin yuĕ, "Jŏ yèw ling
inevitably die." The people answered him, "If your prayer be
yén, choò kung peïh jên kíng
heard, our lord governor will surely regard you with reverence and
fŭh." Yü Keïh yuĕ, "K'é soó ché ts'zè
submission." Yü Keïh said, "My life's numbers having reached thus
k'ùng pŭh nêng t'aoû." Shaòu k'íng Sün Ts'ïh
far, I fear there can be no escape." After a short time, Sün Ts'ïh
ts'in ché t'ân chung, hëá líng jŏ woó shê woŏ
himself ascended the terrace, and commanded that if by noon no
yù, tseïh fân szè Yü Keïh. Sëen
rain fell, Yü Keïh should be burnt to death. He also beforehand
líng jin tuy tseïh kan ch'aê szé hów.
directed his attendants to pile up dry firewood, and be in readiness.
Tsëang keïh woó shê, kwáng fung tseu k'è.
Just as the hour of noon drew near, a strong wind sprung up violently.

167

覺迷也、呂範曰、某素知于道人、能祈風禱雨、方今天旱、何不令其祈雨以贖罪、策曰、吾且看此妖人、若何、遂命於獄中取出于吉、開其枷鎖、令登壇求雨、吉領命、即沐浴更衣、取繩自、縛於烈日之中、百姓觀者、塡街塞巷、于吉謂衆人曰、吾求三尺甘霖、以救萬民、然我終不免一死、衆人曰、若有靈驗、主公必然敬服、于吉曰、氣數至此、恐不能逃、少頃、孫策親至壇中下令、若午時無雨、即焚死于吉、先令人堆積乾柴伺候、將及午時、狂風驟起、

168

Fung kwó ch'oó szé hëá yin yûn tsëén hŏ.
As the wind passed by, all around dark clouds gradually collected.
Ts'ïh yuĕ, "Shê è kin woó k'ung yèw
Sün Ts'ïh then said, "It is nearly noon, it is nothing that there are
yin yûn úrh woô kan yù. Chíng shé yaou jin."
dark clouds, while there is no good rain. He is just a false pretender
Ch'ïh tsó yèw tsëang Yü Keïh, kang
to magical arts." He then bade his servants take Yü Keïh, carry
sháng ch'aê tuy, szé hëá keù hò.
him up the pile of faggots, and set them on fire all round. The
Yén sûy fung k'é. Hwŭh këén hïh yen
flames followed where the wind blew. Suddenly was seen a stream
yïh taŏu ch'ung sháng k'ung chung, yïh shing hëàng
of black smoke rising into the air above, and a sound was heard loud
lëáng. Lûy tëén ts'ê fă,
and clear. Thunder and lightning together rolled and flashed.
tá yù joô choó, k'íng k'ïh che këen, keae szé ch'ïng hô,
Heavy rain fell in floods, and in a moment the streets were a river, the
k'e këén keae mwàn, tsŭh yèw san ch'ïh kan
water-courses were all filled, and there were quite three feet of good
yù. Yü Keïh nëàng gnó yû ch'aê tuy che sháng,
rain. Yü Keïh as he lay on his back upon the faggot pile, uttered
tá hŏ yïh shing. Yûn show yù choó, fŭh këén
a loud cry. The clouds then withdrew, the rain ceased, and the sun
t'aé yâng. Yú shé chúng kwan keïh pïh síng kúng
was again seen. On this the mandarins with the people together
tsëang Yü Keïh foô hëá ch'aê tuy. Keaè
took Yü Keïh and supported him down from the pile. They then
k'eú shing sŏ, tsaé paé ch'ing sëáy.
loosened the cords and bowing down to him as before, expressed their
Sün Ts'ïh këén kwan mîn
thanks and admiration. Sün Ts'ïh seeing the mandarins and people
keú lô paé yù shwùy chung,
all prostrating themselves in regular order in the midst of the water,
pŭh koó e fŭh, naè pŭh jên tá noó ch'ïh yuĕ,
regardless of their dress, was violently angry and chiding them said,
"Ts'ing yù naè t'ëen té che tíng soó.
"Fine weather and rain come by the fixed arrangements of heaven
Yaou jîn ngòw shíng k'ê pëén; ùrh
and earth. A wizard happening to fall on a seasonable time, why
tèng hô tïh joô ts'zé hwŏ lwán?" Ché
do you all suffer yourselves to be deluded in this way?" During

風過處四下。陰雲漸合。策曰。時已近午。空有陰雲。而無甘雨。正是妖人。叱左右。將于吉扛上柴堆。四下舉火。燄隨風起。忽見黑烟一道冲上。空中一聲響亮。雷電齊發。大雨如注。頃刻之間。街市成河。溪澗滿皆。足有三尺。甘雨。于吉仰臥於柴堆之上。大喝一聲。雲收。雨住。復見太陽。*於是衆官及百姓。共將于吉扶下柴堆。解去繩索。再拜稱謝。孫策見官民。俱羅拜於水中。不顧衣服。乃勃然大怒。叱曰。晴雨乃天地之定數。妖人偶乘其便。爾等何得如此惑亂。擊

* *Note of the commentator.* When we see him describing in one breath, wind, rain, smoke and fire, thunder, lightning, rain and sunshine, the reader's heart thrills and his eyes sparkle with pleasure.

paòu këén, líng tsò yéw sŭh chàn Yŭ Keĭh.
his sword, he then commanded his servants quickly to kill Yŭ Keĭh.
Chúng kwan leĭh këén, Ts'ĭh noó yuĕ, "Urh
The mandarins urged him to desist, but Sŭn Ts'ĭh said angrily, "Do
tèng keae yŭh ts'ûng Yŭ Keĭh tsaóu făn yày ?" Chúng kwan
you all wish to follow Yŭ Keĭh into rebellion?" The mandarins
naè pŭh kàn fŭh yên. Ts'ĭh ch'ĭh woò szè, tsëang
dared not reply, and at the command of Sŭn Ts'ĭh, the soldiers took
Yŭ Keĭh yĭh taou chàn t'ôw lŏ té. Chè
Yŭ Keĭh and severing his head at a blow, it fell to the earth. There
këén yĭh taóu ts'ing k'é, t'ôw
was nothing seen but a stream of azure vapour, which floating to the
tung pĭh k'eú leaòu. Ts'ĭh míng tsëang k'è she,
north-eastward, disappeared. Sŭn Ts'ĭh gave orders to take the dead
haóu líng yŭ shé, è chíng
body, and proclaim in the market place, that it was correcting the
yaou wâng che tsúy. Shé yáy fung yù keaou
crime of sorcery and imposture. On that night there were both wind
tsŏ, keĭh heaòu pŭh këén leaòu Yŭ Keĭh she shòw.
and rain, and at daybreak the body and head of Yŭ Keĭh could not
Shòw she keun szé, paóu che
be seen. The soldiers who were set to watch the body, reported this
Sŭn Ts'ĭh, Ts'ĭh noó yŭh shă shòw
to Sŭn Ts'ĭh, who in his fury was going to put to death the soldiers
she keun szé, hwŭh këén yĭh jin, ts'ûng t'âng
who kept guard, when suddenly he noticed a man in front of the
ts'ëën seû poó ûrh laê. Shè che
hall, at a slow pace approaching. He looked at him more closely, and
k'ëŏ shé Yŭ Keĭh. Ts'ĭh tá noó, chíng yŭh
it was certainly Yŭ Keĭh. Sŭn Ts'ĭh in great anger, was just going
pă këén k'àn che, hwŭh jân hwun
to draw his sword and cut him through, when he suddenly fainted
taòu yù té. Tsò yéw keĭh kéw
and fell to the ground. The attendants came in haste to help him
jŭh gnó núy Pwán hëàng fang
to enter the inner apartment and sleep. When after some time he re-
soo; Woô T'aé foo jin laê shé tseĭh, weí Ts'ĭh
vived, the Dowager lady Woo came to see how he was, and addressing
yuĕ, "Woô ûrh, ke'ŭh shă shìn
him said, "My son, you have done wrong in killing a wonderful
sëen, koó chaou ts'zè hó."
magician, and therefore have brought on yourself this calamity."

寶劍令左右速斬于吉衆官力諫策怒曰爾等皆欲從于吉造反耶衆官乃不敢復言策叱武士將于吉一刀斬頭落地只見一道青氣投東北去了策命將其屍號令於市以正妖妄之罪是夜風雨交作及曉不見了于吉屍*首守屍軍士報知孫策策怒欲殺守屍軍士忽見一人從堂前徐步而來視之却是于吉†策大怒正欲拔劍砍之忽然昏倒於地左右急救入臥內半晌方甦吳太夫人來視疾謂策曰吾兒屈殺神仙故招此禍

* *Note of the commentator.* Since he could carry away his corpse when he was dead, why could he not escape while alive?

† *Do.* Since he had already gone to the north-east, why should he come back to the south-west?

Ts'ïh seaóu yuĕ, "Urh tszé yéw sûy
Ts'ïh laughing said, "I your son, from my youth have followed my
foó ch'ŭh ching, shă jin joô mâ,
father, and gone out fighting, killing men as if they were ravelled
hô ts'êng yèw wei hó che lè. Kin shă
hemp; and without causing any calamity to myself. Now in killing
yaou jin chíng tseuĕ tá hó, an ŭh
a false sorcerer I put an end to a great calamity, and how should it
făn weî wò hó?" Foo jin yuĕ,
cause on the other hand calamity to me?" The lady replied, "It is
"yin joô pŭh sín, è ché joô
because you do not believe in such things, that you have come to this
ts'zè. Kin k'ò tsŏ haòu
condition. It would be well for you now to perform some virtuous
szé è jâng che." Ts'ïh yuĕ, "Wò míng tsaé
action to propitiate him." "My life," said Sün Ts'ïh, "is controlled
t'ëen. Yaou jin keuĕ pŭh nêng wei hó.
by Heaven; a false sorcerer most certainly cannot cause me calamity.
Hô peïh jâng yày?" Foo jin leaòu k'euén
Why should I try to propitiate him?" His mother conceiving that
pŭh sín, naè tszé líng
he would not mind her exhortations, herself gave orders to the
tsò yéw, ngán sew shén szé jâng
attendants to perform secretly some religious acts, as a propitiatory
keaó. Shé yáy úrh keng, Ts'ïh
offering. On that night during the second watch, as Sün Ts'ïh was
gnó yu núy tsïh, hwŭh jên yin fung tséw k'è, teng
lying in the inner apartment, suddenly a cold wind rushing in, blew
meïh; úrh fŭh ming. Teng ying che hëá,
out the lamp; again it burnt brightly, and in the shadow of the lamp,
këén Yü Keïh leïh yu ch'wâng ts'ëên. Ts'ïh tá hŏ
he saw Yü Keïh standing before the bed. Sün Ts'ïh calling to him
yuĕ, "Wò p'íng seng shé
loudly said, "I have sworn to make it the business of my life to
choô yaou wáng. è tsíng t'ëen hëá. Joò
extirpate sorcery and delusion, and give rest to the world. Why do
ké weî yin kwei, hò kàn kín wò?"
you, already a demon of darkness, dare to approach me?" Then
ts'eù ch'wâng t'ów këén chïh che, hwŭh jên
seizing the sword at the bed's head, he threw it at him, but in an
pŭh këén. Woô t'aé foo jin wûn che,
instant he had disappeared. The Dowager lady Woo hearing him,

策笑曰、兒自幼隨父出征、殺人如麻、何曾有爲禍之理、今殺妖人、正絶大禍、安得反爲我禍*、夫人曰、因汝不信、以致如此、今可作好事以禳之†、策曰、吾命在天、妖人决不能爲禍、何必禳耶、夫人料勸不信、乃自令左右暗修善事禳解‡、是夜二更、策臥於內宅、忽然陰風驟起、燈滅而復明、燈影之下、見于吉、立於床前§、策大喝曰、吾平生誓誅妖妄、以靖天下、汝既爲陰鬼、何敢近我、取床頭劍擲之、忽然不見、吳太夫人聞之、

* *Note of the commentator*. Sün Ts'ih knew how to distinguish truth and falsehood;—he was a true hero.

† *Do*. These are without doubt the words of a woman. At the present time in Këang-nan such customs are still more prevalent.

‡ *Do*. The superstition of a credulous woman, and the love of an affectionate mother combined.

§ *Do*. A ghost may appear and insult a dying man, but certainly it was not from Yü Keih that any harm could come.

174

chuèn seng yew mún Ts'ïh naè foô píng k'ëâng
fell into the deepest grief. Sün Ts'ïh although sick, constrained
hìng, è k'wan moò sin. Moò weí
himself to walk, in order to ease his mother's mind. She then addres-
Ts'ïh yuĕ, "Shíng jìn yûn, kwei shin che
sed him as follows, "The wise man says, 'The works of the superior
wei tïh k'ê shíng é hoó!' Yéw
and inferior spirits how vast and various are they!' And again he
yûn, 'Taòu ùrh yü sháng hëá shin k'â.'
says, 'Pray ye to the spirits above and the spirits beneath.' In these
Kwei shin che szé pŭh k'ò pŭh sín, Joô k'euĕ
superior beings you may not disbelieve. You having wrongfully
shă Yü sëen seng, k'ò woô paóu yíng? Wò
killed the teacher Yü, how should there not be retribution? I have
è líng jin shă tscaóu yù
therefore already directed, that a service should be performed in the
keún che yŭh ts'ing kwan núy. Joô k'ò
chief temple of this department, the Pearl-pure temple. You yourself
ts'in wàng paé taòu, tszé jên gan
must go to worship and pray; then you will certainly obtain entire
t'ó." Ts'ïh pŭh kàn wei moò míng,
tranquillity." Sün Ts'ïh dared not disobey his mother's command;
chè tïh mëen k'ëàng ch'ëng keaóu,
he could only, though much against his will, takeh is seat in his sedan,
ché yŭh ts'ing kwan. Taóu szé tsëë
and proceed to the Pearl-pure temple. The priests of Taou came to
jŭh, ts'ing Ts'ïh fûn hëang,
meet him and lead him in, and when they invited him to burn
Ts'ïh fûn hëang ûrh pŭh sëáy. Hwŭh jên
incense, he did so but declined acknowledging his error. Suddenly
loó chung yen k'ê pŭh sán
the smoke that rose from the incense urn, instead of dispersing was
këë ch'ëng yïh tsó hwâ kaé. Sháng mëén
seen to collect, and form into an elegantly-shaped canopy. Upon it,
twan tsó chŏ Yü Keïh. Ts'ïh noó t'ó
in an attitude of dignity, sat Yü Keïh. Sün Ts'ïh in anger spitting
má che, tsòw lé tëén yù.
at him and reproaching him, took his departure from the temple, but
yéw këén Yü Keïh leïh yù tëén mûn shòw, noó mŭh shé
again saw him standing at the doorway, with angry eyes gazing at
Ts'ïh. Ts'ïh koó tsò yéw yuĕ, "Joô tèng këén
himself. Sün Ts'ïh turning to his attendants asked, "Do you see

轉生憂悶。策乃扶病。强行以寬*母心。母謂策曰。聖人云。鬼。神。之。爲。德。其盛。矣。乎。又云。禱爾於上下神祇。鬼。神。之。事。不。可。不。†信。汝屈殺于先生。豈無報應吾已令人。設醮於郡之玉清觀‡內。汝可親往拜禱。自然安妥。策不敢違母命。只。得。勉。强。乘。轎。至。玉。清。§觀。道士接入。請策焚香。策焚。香。而。不。謝。忽然爐中。煙起不散。結。成。一。座。華。蓋。上。面。端。坐。着。‖于吉策怒唾罵之。走離殿宇。又。見。于吉立。於。殿。門。首。怒。目。視。策。策顧左右曰。汝等見

* *Note of the commentator.* Sün Ts'ih being so filial, how could any magician or genius do him an injury ?

† *Do.* Those who believing in Buddha and the genii, draw their weapons of defence from the armory of Confucius and Mencius, are not limited to the Dowager lady Woo.

‡ *Do.* The getting ready of a religious service before the temple, saying nothing about it till now, and then ascribing it entirely to the Dowager lady Woo, was well conceived by the author.

§ *Do.* Sün Ts'ih obeyed his mother's commands because he was obliged, and is not to be confounded with those moderns, who in compliance with feminine entreaties, worship the genii and Buddhas.

‖ *Do.* The whole of this is magic and necromancy.

yaou kwei fow ?" Tsò yéw keac yûn, "Wé
this demon sorcerer or not ?" The attendants all replied, "We do
këén." Ts'ih yù noó pă peí këén
not see him." Sün Ts'ih more enraged, drew the sword that hung
wáng Yü Keih chih k'eú. Yih jin chúng këén
at his side, and aiming at Yü Keih, threw it. A man was struck by it
ûrh taòu. Chúng shé che naè
and fell. The people looking at him, saw that it was the very soldier
ts'ëën jih túng show shă Yü Keih che seaòu tsüh.
who the day before, had with his own hand, killed Yü Keih. The
Peí këén k'àn jüh naòu taé, ts'eih k'eaóu
sword had pierced his scull, and blood flowing from eyes, ears, nose
lêw heuĕ ûrh szè. Ts'ih míng kang
and mouth, he died. Sün Ts'ih after giving orders that he should be
ch'ŭh tsáng che, pè keih ch'ŭh kwan yéw këén Yü
carried out and buried, when just leaving the temple, again saw Yü
Keih tsòw jüh kwan mûn laê. Ts'ih yuĕ, "Ts'zè kwan yih
Keih entering the temple gates. He then said, "This temple is a
ts'âng yaou che sò yày." Sûy tsó yù kwan ts'ëën,
refuge for followers of the black art ;" and sitting down before it,
míng woò szé woò pih jin ch'ih hwùy che.
commanded his soldiers, in all five hundred men, to pull it down.
Woò szé fang sháng ŭh k'eih
The soldiers accordingly had ascended the roof, and were tearing
wà, k'ëŏ këén Yü Keih leih yù ŭh
away the tiles, when lŏ ! he saw Yü Keih standing on the top of the
sháng, fei wà chih té. Ts'ih tá
building, dashing the tiles down to the ground. Sün Ts'ih violently
noò, ch'uên líng chĕh ch'ŭh pùn kwan taóu
angry, delivered orders to drive out the Taouist priests from their
szé, fáng hò shaou hwùy tëén yù.
temple, set the building on fire, and burn it to the ground. Where
Hò k'è ch'oó, yéw këén Yü Keih leih yü hò kwang
the fire was raging, he again saw Yü Keih standing in the midst of
che chung. Ts'ih noó kwei foò, yéw
the flames. Sün Ts'ih angry, returned to his residence, but again
këén Yü Keih leih yu foò mûn ts'ëén. Ts'ih naè pŭh jüh foò;
saw Yü Keih standing before the gates. Sün Ts'ih would not enter,
sûy tëén k'è san keun ch'ŭh ch'êng waé hëá chaé.
but counted his army, went outside the city, and formed an encamp-
Ch'uên hwán chúng tseáng shang é,
ment. He then gave orders for the generals to assemble for

妖鬼否、左右皆云、未見、策愈怒拔佩劍、望于吉擲去、一人中劍而倒、衆視之乃、前、日、動、手、殺、于吉之、小、卒、被劍斫入腦袋、七竅流血而死、策命扛出葬之、比及出觀又、見、于吉走入觀門來、策曰、此、觀亦、藏妖、之、所、也、遂坐於觀前、命武士五百人、拆、毀之、武士方上屋揭瓦、却見于吉立於屋上、飛、瓦、擲、*地、策大怒、傳令逐出本觀道士、放火燒燬殿宇、火起處、又見于吉立於火光之†中、策怒、歸、府、又、見、于吉立、於、府、門、前、策乃不入府、隨點起三軍出城外下寨、傳、喚、衆、將、商、議、

* *Note of the commentator.* He could not prevent his destroying the temple, all he could do was to assist in the work of demolition. This was in truth a sorcerer's act.

† *Do.* All this was sorcery and witchcraft. (興妖作怪) This was not the work of good and noble genii (神仙). Why did he not, just at this time when it was wanted, pray for rain to extinguish the fire ?

yŭh ch'ŭh ping tsoó Yuén Shaóu keă kung Ts'aôu
deliberation, on an expedition to aid Yuen Shaou and attack Ts'aou
Ts'aóu. Chúng tsëáng keú yuĕ, "Choò kung
Ts'aou on two opposite sides. The generals all said, "Your highness
yŭh t'è wê hô, wé k'ò k'ing túng.
is in poor health, and must not lightly undertake a journey.
Ts'ëày taé p'ing yù, ch'ŭh ping
If you wait for a time till you are well, and then lead out the army,
wé ch'ê." Shé yày Sŭn Ts'ĭh sŭh yü chaé núy,
it will not be too late." Sün Ts'ïh passed that night in the camp,
yéw këén Yü Keĭh p'e fă ûrh laê. Ts'ĭh
and again saw Yü Keĭh with hair dishevelled approaching. Sün Ts'ĭh
yü cháng chung, ch'ĭh hŏ pŭh tseuĕ. Ts'zé
on his bed, called and shouted without intermission. On the next
jĭh Woô T'aé foo jin, ch'uên míng chaóu Ts'ĭh hwûy
day, the lady Woo gave directions to call Sün Ts'ĭh to return to his
foò. Ts'ĭh naè kwei këén k'ê moò foo jin
palace. Sün Ts'ĭh then returned and saw his mother, who when she
këén Ts'ĭh hing yûng ts'eaôu sùy k'eĭh yuĕ, "Urh shĭh
saw his emaciated features, weeping said, "My son, your visage
hing è." Ts'ĭh tseĭh yin kíng
is changed." Sün Ts'ĭh then took a mirror and looking at his
tszé chaóu, kwò këén hing yûng shĭh fun sów
reflected image, saw that in truth his features were very much ema-
sùn. Pŭh k'ëŏ shĭh king koó tsò yéw
ciated. Involuntarily shuddering, he turned to his attendants and
yuĕ, "Wô naè hŏ ts'eaôu sûy ché ts'zè yày?"
said, "How have I come to be so emaciated as this?" Before he
Yên wé è, hwŭh këén Yü Keĭh leĭh yu
had done saying this, he suddenly saw Yü Keĭh standing in the
kíng chung. Ts'ĭh p'ĭh kíng tá keaóu yĭh shing,
mirror. Sün Tsĭh struck the mirror and uttering a loud cry, the
kin ch'wang ping lëĕ,
spear-wound (that he had previously received) burst open, and he
hwun tseuĕ yü té. Foo jin líng
fell fainting and senseless on the ground. His mother directed that
foô jŭh ngó núy. Seu ûrh
he should be supported into his sleeping chamber. In a short time
soo sùy tszé t'án yuĕ, "Wò pŭh nêng fŭh seng é."
he revived and sighing said, "I cannot return to life again." He
Sûy chaóu Chang Chaou tèng choo jin, keĭh
then called for Chang Chaou and the rest (of the officers), with his

欲出兵助袁紹夾攻曹操衆將俱曰主公玉體微和未可輕動且待平愈出兵未遲是夜孫策宿於寨內又見于吉*披髮而來策於帳中叱喝不絕次日吳太夫人傳命召策回府策乃歸見其母夫人見策形容憔悴泣曰兒失形矣策即引鏡自照果見形容十分瘦損不覺失驚顧左右曰吾奈何憔悴至此耶言未已忽見于吉立於鏡†中策拍鏡大叫一聲金瘡迸裂昏絕于‡地夫人令扶入臥內須臾甦醒自嘆曰吾不能復生矣隨召張昭等諸人及

* *Note of the commentator.* That he should come with his hair scattered abroad is still more like the act of a demon, and quite unlike the immortal genii (神仙).

† *Do.* I have heard that the immortal genii can transform animals with a magical mirror. But I did not think that any common man could have a mirror that would shew him the genii.

‡ *Do.* It was by the wound received before from the sword of Heu-kung, that he died, and not through Yü Keih.

té Sün K'euên ché ngó t'ă ts'ëên. Chŭh foó
brother Sün K'euen, to come to his bedside. Then giving them his
yuĕ, "T'ëen hëá fang lwán, è
instructions he said, "The empire is now in disorder, but with the
Woô Yuĕ che chúng,
collected force of the Woo and Yuĕ kingdoms, and the strength of
san Këang che koó,
the three Këang districts, (Sung-këang, Chĕ-këang and Yang-tsze-
tá k'ò yèw wei. Tszè Poó tèng, hing
këang) much may be done. Tsze Poo and the rest of you, be good
shén sëáng wò té." Naè ts'eù yín shów,
and faithful in assisting my brother." Then taking his seal, he gave
yù Sün K'euên, yuĕ, "Jŏ keù Këang-
it to Sün K'euen, and said, "If you merely take the force of Këang-
tung che chúng, keuĕ ke yü lëàng ch'ín che këen, yù t'ëen
tung, lay plots between the two hostile armies, and oppose the
hëá tseng ch'úng; k'ing pŭh joô wò. Keù hëên
whole empire; you will not equal me. But if you raise men
jín, nêng shè kŏ tsín leïh,
of ability to power, and cause them each to exert themselves to the
è paòu Këaou-tung; wò pŭh joô k'ing.
utmost, to protect Këaou-tung; I shall not have been so good as you.
K'ing ê nëên foó heung ch'wáng
Be sure you remember the difficulties encountered by your father
nëĕ che këen nân. Shén tszé t'oô
and brother in establishing their cause. Let your plans be formed
che." "Keuên tá k'ŭh, paé
wisely and well." Sün K'euen wept aloud, and bowing to the ground,
shów yín shów. Ts'ïh kaóu
received the seal and ribbon of office. Sün Ts'ïh then said to his
moò yué, "Urh t'ëen nëên è tsín. Pŭh
mother, "The days of your son's lifetime are numbered. I can-
nêng fúng ts'zê moò. Kin
not return by filial service my mother's affection. Now that I have
tsëang yín shów foó té, wáng
entrusted the seal and ribbon of government to my brother, I look to
moò chaou seïh heún che, foó heung
you day and night to instruct him, that he may be careful not to dis-
kéw jin shin wŭh k'ing taé."
pise his father and brother, and the officers grown old in their service."
Moò k'ŭh yuĕ, k'ùng joô té nëên yéw,
His mother weeping said, "I fear that your brother being so young,

弟孫權、至臥榻前、囑咐曰、天下方亂、以吳越之衆、三江之固、大可有爲。子布等、幸善相吾弟。乃取印綬、與孫權曰、若舉江東之衆、决機於兩陣之間、與天下爭衡、卿不如我。舉賢任能、使各盡力、以保江東、我不如卿。卿宜念父兄創業之艱難、善自圖之。權大哭、拜受印綬。策告母曰、兒天年已盡、不能奉慈母、今將印綬付弟、*望母朝夕訓之。父兄舊人、愼勿輕怠。母哭曰、恐汝弟年幼、

* *Note of the commentator.* Sün Ts'ih may be truly said to have been a filial son, and affectionate brother.

182

pŭh nêng jín tá szé; táng
he will be unable to undertake so great a service; what should be
fŭh joŏ hô?" Ts'ĭh yuĕ, "Té ts'aâ
done in this case?" Sŭn Ts'ĭh replied, "My brother's abilities are
shíng ûrh shĭh p'eî. Tsŭh tang tá jín.
ten times superior to mine. He is quite capable of a great undertaking.
T'àng núy szé pŭh keuĕ, k'ŏ wún Chang
If internal matters cannot be arranged, you may appeal to Chang
Chaou. Waé szé pŭh skeuĕ, k'ŏ wún Chow
Chaou. If external affairs are hard to control, you can appeal to Chow
Yû. Hún Chow Yû pŭh tsaé ts'zè, pŭh tĭh mēén
Yü. Unhappily Chow Yü is not now here, and I cannot myself tell
chŭh che yày." Yéw hwán choo té
him my wishes." After this he again called for all his brothers, and
chŭh yuĕ, "Wŏ szè che hów,
addressed them in the following terms, "'After my death, what I
joŏ tèng píng foŏ Chúng Mŏw,
entreat of you is, together to assist Chung Mow, and should there be
tsung tsŭh chung kăn yèw seng é
any one in our common family, who should dare to differ from the
sin chày, chúng kúng choo che. Kŭh jŭh
rest in action, let them all put him to death. Among our kindred
weî neih " pŭh tĭh jŭh
should any one oppose the family cause, he cannot be permitted to lie
tsoŏ fŭn an tsáng." Choo té k'ŭh shów
in the ancestral tomb." His brothers all weeping received his last
míng. Yéw hwán ts'e K'eaóu foo jîn,
commands. He then called for his wife, a lady of the K'eaou family,
weí yuĕ, "Wŏ yù joŏ pŭh híng
and addressing her said, "You and I are unhappily called to separate
chung t'oŏ sēang fun. Joŏ seu heaóu yàng
in the midst of our life's journey. It will be your duty to be filial
tsŭn koo. Tsaou wàn
and attentive to your husband's parents. And morning and evening
joŏ meí jŭh kēén, k'ŏ chŭh k'ê chuèn
when your sister comes to see you, you can instruct her to tell her
che Chow lâng tsín sin foo tsoó wŏ té; hew fów
husband Chow Yü to do all he can to assist my brother; and by no
wŏ p'ìng jĭh sēang che che
means should he forget the intimacy of our friendship when I was
yà." Yèn ke'ĭh, míng
living." When he had finished saying these words, he closed his
mŭh ûrh shé. Nēēn chè úrh shĭh lŭh súy.
eyes and died. His age was only twenty six years.

不能任大事。當復如何。策曰。弟才勝兄十倍。足當大任。倘內事。不决。可問張昭。外事。不决。可問周瑜。恨周瑜不在此。不得面。囑之也。又喚諸弟囑曰。吾死之後。汝等並輔仲謀。宗族中。敢有生異心者。衆共誅之。骨肉爲逆。不得入祖墳安葬。諸弟泣受命。又喚妻喬夫人謂曰。吾與汝不幸中途相分。汝須孝養尊姑。早晚汝妹入見。可囑其轉致周郎。盡心輔佐吾弟。休負我平日相知之雅。* 言訖。瞑目而逝。年止二十六歲。†

* *Note of the commentator*. The addition of this sentence has an excellent effect.

† *Do*. Thus it is seen that Sün Ts'ïh died when he ought. It is not by any means to be supposed that his death was caused by Yü Keïh.

参考文献

外文文献

The Chinese Repository, 1832 – 1851.

The China Review, or notes & queries on the Far East, 1872 – 1901.

The Chinese Recorder and Missionary Journal, 1868 – 1941.

The Asiatic Journal and Monthly Register for British and Foreign India, 1840 – 1854.

Notes and Queries on China and Japan, 1867 – 1868.

The Far East, illustrated with photographs, 1870 – 1878.

Alexander Wylie, *Memorials of Protestant Missionaries to the Chinese*, Shanghae: American Presbyterian Mission Press, 1867.

Alexander Wylie, *Notes on Chinese Literature*, Shanghae: American Presbyterian Mission Press; London: Trübner & Co. 60, Paternoster Row, 1867.

Alexander Wylie, *Chinese Research*, Shanghai, 1897.

Henri Cordier, *Bibliotheca Sinica*, Paris: E. Leroux, 1881.

Robert Morrison, *Horae Sinicae: translations from the popular literature of the Chinese*, London, 1812.

Robert Morrison, *A Dictionary of the Chinese Language*, Macao: Printed at the Honorable East India Company's Press, by P. P. Thoms, 1815 – 23.

Robert Morrison, *A Grammar of the Chinese Language*, 通用汉语之法, Serampore: Printed at the Mission Press, 1815.

Robert Morrison , *Dialogues and Detached Sentences in the Chinese Language*, Macao: Printed at the Honorable East India Company's Press, by P. P. Thoms, 1816.

Rev. R. Morrison, *A View of China*, Macao: Printed at the Honorable East India Company's Press, By P. P. Thoms, 1817.

Robert Morrison, *Chinese Miscellany*, London: Printed by S. Mcdowall, Leadenhall Street, for the London Missionary Society, 1825.

Eilza Morrison, *Memoirs of the Life and Labours of Robert Morrison*, London: Longman, Orme, Brown, Green, and Longmans, 1839.

William Milne, *A Retrospect of the First Ten Years of the Protestant Mission to China*, Malacca: Printed at the Anglo-Chinese Press, 1820.

William C. Milne, *Life in China*, London: G. Routledge & Co. Farringdon Street; New York: 18, Beekman Street, 1857.

Peter Perring Thoms, *The Affectionate Pair*, *or the history of Sung-Kin*, London: Printed for Black, Kingsbury, Parbury, and Allen, Leadenhall Street, 1820.

Peter Perring Thoms, 花笺, *Chinese Courtship*, London: Published by Parbury, Allen, and Kingsbury, Leadenhall Street, Sold by John Murray, Albemale Street; and by Thomas Blanshard, 14, City Road; Macao, China: Printed at the Honorable East India Company's Press, 1824.

Charles Gutzlaff, *Journal of Three Voyages along the Coast of China*, *in 1831*, *1832*, *&. 1833*, *with notices of Slam*, *Corea*, *and the Loo-choo Islands*, London: Frederick Westley and A. H. Davis, Stationers' Hall Court, 1834.

Charles Gutzlaff, *A Sketch of Chinese History*, *Ancient and Modern*, London: Smith, Elder and Co. , Cornhill, Booksellers to their majesties, 1834.

Charles Gutzlaff, *China Opened; or A Display of the Topography, History, Customs, Manners, Arts, Manufactures, Commerce, Literature, Religion, Jurisprudence, etc. of the Chinese Empire*, London: Smith, Elder and Co. 65, Cornhill, 1838.

George Carter Stent, *A Chinese and English Vocabulary in the Pekinese Dialect*, Shanghai, 1871.

Mun Mooy Seen-Shang, *Esop's Fables Written in Chinese*, Printed at the Canton Press office, 1840.

Thomas Thornton, *A History of China*, London: Wm. H. Allen and Co. , 7, Leadenhall Street, 1844.

E. J. Eitel, *Europe in China: the History of Hongkong, from the beginning to the year 1882*, London: Luzac & Company; Hongkong: Kelly & Walsh, Ld. , 1895.

Abel Rémusat, *Mélanges Asiatiques, ou choix de morceaux de critique et de mémoires*, Paris, 1826.

Abel Rémusat, *Des Contes Chinois*, Paris: Chez Moutardier, Rue Cit-le-Coeur, No 4, 1827.

Joseph de Premare, *Notitia Lingae Sinicae*, Canton: Printed at the office of the Chinese Repository, 1847.

Par M. Bazin Ainé, *Le Pi-Pa-Ki ou l' histoire du luth*, Paris: Imprime par Autorisation Du Roi a L'imprimerie Royale, 1841.

John Francis Davis, *Laou-Seng-Urh or an Heir in his old Age*, London: John Murray, Albemarle Street, 1817.

John Francis Davis, *Chinese Novels, translated from the Originals*, London: John Murray, Albemarle Street, 1822.

John Francis Davis, *Hān Koong Tsew, or the Sorrows of Hān, a Chinese Tragedy, Translated from the Original, with Notes*, London: Printed for the Original Translation Fund, by A. J. Valpy, Red Lion Court, Fleet Street, 1829.

John Francis Davis, *The Fortunate Union, a Romance, Translated from the Chinese Original*, London: The Oriental Translation Fund, 1829.

John Francis Davis, 汉文诗解, *Poeseos Sinensis Commentarii, On the Poetry of the Chinese*, Macao, China: Printed at the Honorable East India Company's Press, By G. J. Steyn and Brother, 1834.

Sir John Francis Davis, *The Chinese: a general description of the empire of China, and its inhabitants*, London: Charles Knight, 22, Ludgate Street, 1836.

Sir John Francis Davis, *Chinese Miscellanies: A Collection of Essays and Notes*, London: John Murray Albemarle Street, 1865.

Philip Dormer Stanhope Earl of Chesterfield, *The Work of Lord Chesterfield*, New York: Harper & Brothers, Cliff Street, 1838.

John Thomson, *The Land and the People of China*, London; New York: Pott, Young & Co., 1876.

William Speer, *The Oldest and the Newest Empire: China and the United States*, Pittsburgh, PA.: Robert S. Davis & Co., 1877.

S. Wells Williams, 拾级大成, *Easy Lessons in Chinese, or Progressive Exercises to Facilitate the Study of that Language*, Macao: Printed at the Office of the Chinese Repository, 1842.

S. Wells Williams, *The Middle Kingdom*, New York & London: Wiley and Putnam, 1848.

S. Wells Williams, 中国总论, *The Middle Kingdom*, London: W. H. Allen & Co., 13 Waterloo Place, Pall Mall. S. W., 1883.

Joseph Edkins, *Chinese Conversations: translated from native authors*, Shanghai: The Mission Press, 1852.

Joseph Edkins, *A Grammar of Colloquial Chinese, as exhibited in the Shanghai Dialect*, Shanghai, 1853.

Joseph Edkins, *The Religious Condition of the Chinese*, London: Routledge, Warnes, & Routledge, Farringdon Street; New York: 56, Walker Street, 1859.

Joseph Edkins, *A Grammar of the Chinese Colloquial Language, Commonly called the Mandarin Dialect*, Shanghai: Presbyterian Mission Press, 1864.

Joseph Edkins, *A Catalogue of Chinese Works in the Bodleian Library*, Oxford: at the Alarendon Press, 1876.

Joseph Edkins, *Modern China: Thirty-one Short Essays on Subjects which Illustrate the Present Condition of the Country*, Shanghai: Sold by Kelly & Walsh, Ld., and by W. Brewer; London: Sold by Trübner & Co., Ludgate Street, 1891.

Henry H. Hart, *Poems of the Hundred Names*, Stanford, California: Stanford University Press, 1954.

Edited by Kwang-ching Liu, *American Missionaries in China*, Published by the East Asian Research Center, Harvard University, 1970.

Gilbert Highet, *The Classical Tradition: Greek and Roman Influences on Western Literature*, Oxford University Press, 1985.

E Katherine F. Bruner, John K. Fairbank, Richard J. Smith, *Entering China's Service, Robert Hart's Journals*, 1854 – 1863, Cambridge (Massachusetts) and London: The Council on East Asian Studies, Hardvard University, 1986.

Frank Welsh, *A Borrowed Place: The History of Hong Kong*, R. R. Donnelley & Sons Company, 1994.

Chun-shu Chang and Shelley Hsueh-lun Chang, *Crisis and Transformation in Seventeenth-century China*, the University of Michigan Press, 1998.

Edited by Claudine Salmon, *Literary Migrations: Traditional Chinese Fiction in Asia (17th-20th Centuries)*, *Singapore: Institute of Southeast Asian Studies*, 2013.

中文文献

永瑢、纪昀等编:《四库全书总目提要》,商务印书馆 1931 年版。

鲁迅:《中国小说史略》,上海古籍出版社 2011 年版。

胡适:《中国章回小说考证》,北京师范大学出版社 2013 年版。

郑振铎:《中国文学研究》,人民文学出版社 2000 年版。

孙楷第:《中国通俗小说书目》,作家出版社 1957 年版。

柳存仁:《伦敦所见中国小说书目提要》,书目文献出版社 1982 年版。

王丽娜:《中国古典小说戏曲名著在国外》,学林出版社 1988 年版。

王尔敏:《中国文献西译书目》,台湾商务印书馆发行 1975 年版。

萧相恺、欧阳健等编:《中国通俗小说总目提要》,中国文联出版社 1990 年版。

傅璇琮、谢灼华主编:《中国藏书通史》,宁波出版社 2001 年版。

张秀民、韩琦:《中国活字印刷史》,中国书籍出版社 1998 年版。

陈洪:《"四大奇书"话题》,江苏人民出版社 2015 年版。

石昌渝:《中国小说源流论》,生活·读书·新知三联书店 1994 年版。

刘世德:《刘世德话三国》,中华书局 2007 年版。

沈伯俊:《罗贯中和三国演义》,春风文艺出版社 1999 年版。

杨义:《中国古典小说史论》,中国社会科学出版社 2004 年版。

陈平原:《陈平原小说史论集》,河北人民出版社 1997 年版。

[美] 浦安迪:《中国叙事学》,北京大学出版社 1996 年版。

［美］浦安迪：《明代小说四大奇书》，沈亨寿译，生活·读书·新知三联书店 2006 年版。

［英］魏安：《三国演义版本考》，上海古籍出版社 1996 年版。

莫东寅：《汉学发达史》，上海书店 1989 年版。

马祖毅、任荣珍：《汉籍外译史》，湖北教育出版社 2003 年版。

方豪：《中国天主教史人物传》，中华书局 1988 年版。

何寅、许光华主编：《国外汉学史》，上海外语教育出版社 2002 年版。

韩琦、米盖拉编：《中国和欧洲》，商务印书馆 2008 年版。

徐宗泽编著：《明清间耶稣会士译著提要》，中华书局 1989 年版。

李志刚：《基督教早期在华传教史》，台湾商务印书馆 1998 年版。

张国刚：《明清传教士与欧洲汉学》，中国社会科学出版社 2001 年版。

严建强：《18 世纪中国文化在西欧的传播及其反映》，中国美术学院出版社 2002 年版。

孙越生、王祖望主编：《欧洲中国学》，社会科学文献出版社 2005 年版。

范存忠：《中国文化在启蒙时期的英国》，上海外语教育出版社 1991 年版。

许明龙：《欧洲 18 世纪中国热》，山西教育出版社 1999 年版。

钱林森：《中国文学在法国》，花城出版社 1990 年版。

熊文华：《英国汉学史》，学苑出版社 2007 年版。

张弘：《中国文学在英国》，花城出版社 1992 年版。

陈铨：《中德文学研究》，商务印书馆 1936 年版。

陈铨：《中国纯文学对德国文学的影响》，台湾学生书局 1971 年版。

曹卫东：《中国文学在德国》，花城出版社 2002 年版。

段怀清、周俐玲：《〈中国评论〉与晚清中英文学交流》，广东人民出版社 2006 年版。

张西平：《传教士汉学研究》，大象出版社 2005 年版。

苏精：《马礼逊与中文印刷出版》，台湾学生书局2000年版。

顾长声：《从马礼逊到司徒雷登——来华新教传教士评传》，上海书店出版社2005年版。

葛桂录：《中英文学关系编年史》，生活·读书·新知三联书店2004年版。

王镛：《移植与变异》，中国人民大学出版社2005年版。

丁伟志、陈崧：《中西体用之间——晚清中西文化观述论》，中国社会科学出版社1995年版。

朱学勤、王丽娜：《中国与欧洲文化交流志》，上海人民出版社1998年版。

刘登阁、周云芳：《西学东渐与东学西渐》，中国社会科学出版社2000年版。

石云涛：《早期中西交通与交流史稿》，学苑出版社2003年版。

朱谦之：《中国哲学对于欧洲的影响》，上海世纪出版社2006年版。

阎宗临：《中西交通史》，广西师范大学出版社2007年版。

何绍斌：《越界与想象——晚清新教传教士译介史论》，生活·读书·新知三联书店2008年版。

林庆彰等主编：《晚清四部丛刊》第7编《万国史论》，文听阁图书有限公司2012年版。

沈云龙主编：《近代中国史料丛刊续编》第41辑《女学》，文海出版社1977年版。

周宁：《天朝遥远——西方的中国形象研究》，北京大学出版社2006年版。

孟华主编：《比较文学形象学》，北京大学出版社2001年版。

[美] 卫斐列：《卫三畏生平及书信》，顾钧等译，广西师范大学出版社2004年版。

［英］汤森：《马礼逊——在华传教士的先驱》，王振华译，大象出版社 2002 年版。

［西］门多萨：《中华大帝国史》，何高济译，中华书局 1998 年版。

［葡］曾德昭：《大中国志》，何高济译，上海古籍出版社 1998 年版。

［美］萨姆瓦等：《跨文化传通》，陈南等译，生活·读书·新知三联书店 1998 年版。

［法］维吉尔·毕诺：《中国对法国哲学思想形成的影响》，耿昇译，商务印书馆 2000 年版。

［德］歌德：《歌德谈话录》，朱光潜译，人民文学出版社 1981 年版。

陈寿：《裴松之注三国志》，天津古籍出版社 2009 年版。

司马光：《资治通鉴》，中华书局 2007 年版。

罗贯中：《三国演义》，上海古籍出版社 2015 年版。

（明）罗贯中著，（清）毛宗岗批注：《第一才子书三国演义》，线装书局 2007 年版。

钟宇辑、李贽、毛宗岗、鲁迅等评：《三国演义名家汇评本》，北京图书馆出版社 2007 年版。

施耐庵、罗贯中：《水浒传》，人民文学出版社 1957 年版。

名教中人：《好逑传》，中华书局 2004 年版。

梁培炽辑校：《花笺记》，暨南大学出版社 1998 年版。

抱瓮老人：《今古奇观》，人民文学出版社 1957 年版。

李渔：《十二楼》，人民文学出版社 1986 年版。

冯梦龙著，蔡元放编：《东周列国志》，人民文学出版社 1955 年版。